TWO

TWO SISTERS

TWO SISTERS

Nancy Livingston

LITTLE, BROWN AND COMPANY

A *Little, Brown* Book

First published in Great Britain in 1992 by
Little, Brown & Company

Copyright © Nancy Livingston 1992

The right of Nancy Livingston to be identified as author
of this work has been asserted by her in accordance
with the Copyright, Designs and Patents Act 1988.

A CIP catalogue record for this book is
available from the British Library.

ISBN 0 356 20662 9

Typeset by Leaper & Gard Ltd, Bristol
Printed and bound in Great Britain by
Clays Ltd, St Ives plc

Little, Brown & Company (UK) Limited
165 Great Dover Street
London SE1 4YA

Dedication

This book is dedicated to my mother, Nancy Hewitt, who remembers how it all began.

Acknowledgement

I wish to acknowledge with gratitude the help and assistance given to me by Miss Jenny Parker, Senior Assistant Librarian at Middlesbrough Library, County Cleveland.

Apology

To the citizens of the Northern Territories in Australia, for building a *depot* where none exists.

Chapter One

Mr Right, 1920

It was a dank November afternoon. In the chilly, rented parlour, two sisters in formal black dresses sat beside an inadequate coal fire waiting for their visitor, who was overdue.

The shabby room was above a shop. A smaller room behind was where they both slept. There was a landing between with a stove, a geyser and, hidden behind a folding screen, an old enamel tub. The arrangements were far from ideal, the elder sister, Gertie, complained endlessly. For Rose it was adequate and cheap; a refuge where they could afford to stay until they'd decided what to do.

This afternoon she was uneasy. Harold Brigg was Gertie's visitor and preparations had been lavish. On the folding card-table a starched tablecloth had been laid with the remains of their bone china tea service. One of the cups was cracked and had been carefully positioned; on no account must it be handed to today's guest. As Gertie proudly pointed out, Harold was particular, he had 'standards'.

The tiered cake-stand contained dainty triangular sandwiches, scones and sliced seed cake. Everything had a breathless precision, even the supply of coal. A much larger piece lay in the tongs ready to enliven the fire the instant the doorbell rang.

The north-east wind rattled the window and blew smoke back down the chimney. Rose shivered and coughed. 'I shall have to find a shawl. This frock's too thin – I'm chilled right through.'

'Sssh!' Gertie's eyes shone behind her spectacles; she made

1

as if to rise, 'Wasn't that . . . Didn't I hear . . .?'

'No, you didn't. It was next door's clock striking the half, not the bell.'

Gertie stiffened. 'There's no need to be rude. Anyway, you haven't a shawl that's suitable. You can't let me down this afternoon, Rose. I want everything to be – nice.'

It was Gertie's favourite word. She'd even used it when describing their parents' funeral arrangements. Relphs, the undertakers, had been 'helpful', the coffins had been 'best quality', but the funerals had been, 'very nice'.

Rose had found the experience macabre. After surviving the loss of their brother, for both parents to die of rheumatic fever within two years of the Armistice, seemed cruel. As for the way Gertie had squandered money on the burials, that had been ludicrous.

Their father's modest income had died with him; their mother had had no money of her own. After bills had been paid, the girls' sole inheritance amounted to a few hundred pounds and Gertie had insisted on lilies and freesias out of season!

It was Rose who made the decisions after that. She had found these rooms while Gertie wailed to any who would listen that they could never hold their heads up again.

'What will people *say* when they discover we no longer live in Clairville Road?'

'Does it matter?' Rose demanded wearily. 'We had to leave, we couldn't afford the rent, Gertie. Rooms are so much cheaper in Fleetham Street.'

It was the word 'street' which hurt; in Middlesbrough it meant those hastily erected terraces, marching obediently towards the sources of employment in the ironmasters' district, cradled in the curve of the Tees.

Fleetham Street was livelier than most. Morning and evening a noisy population hurried past on their way to the school but Gertie complained the children gave her a head-ache. In her opinion, living here was no better than dwelling among the working class. She yearned to be in Linthorpe or, better still, Albert Park. If only Rose weren't so obsessed with their need to economize!

'Fleetham Street is so convenient,' Rose had pleaded, 'we'll be near the centre of town … closer to whatever jobs we choose.' Gertie pretended to be deaf. If her sister wanted to soil her hands that was up to her, she had no intention of seeking employment. Her future was assured, it had been foretold and was part of the mystical daydream into which she retreated at the least sign of unpleasantness.

It had begun one hot midsummer at the church Fête. Their mother had paid her twopence to the 'gipsy' outside the fortune-teller's tent. Rose had spoiled it. She had recognized the woman and demanded to know, 'Why are you wearing that hanky with gold coins on your head, Mrs Birtles? Why is your face painted brown?'

Gertie refused to listen. Even though the 'fortune-teller' looked suspiciously like the woman who worked at Coopers the butcher's, Gertie, like her mother, wanted to believe in magic.

The butcher's assistant, recalling this customer usually ordered best steak, had conjured up generous visions. Untold wealth was to be Gertie's portion. For her, 'Mister Right', as plain as a pikestaff, was there in the crystal, waiting at the altar. All Gertie had to do was bide her time.

Gertie left school the very next day. Her elder daughter would remain at home from now on and learn to be a good wife, the credulous mother explained to her husband. When Mr Bossom protested, he was informed there was no need for Gertie to addle her brains.

Mercifully, Rose was permitted to addle hers. She had scowled at the butcher's assistant; her prospects had, in consequence, been far less promising.

Thanks to her brother's encouragement, Rose progressed at her studies until the outbreak of war. Now, six years later, like so many of their generation, she and Gertie were having to make the best of a world turned upside down.

She couldn't understand why Gertie fussed so over this

3

wretched tea today – surely she didn't still believe in that crystal ball nonsense? They had kept up the pretence while their mother was alive but the time had come to be realistic; under no circumstances could Harold Brigg be described as Mr Right.

Sadly, Gertie with her plain looks had never attracted the menfolk. Her mother discouraged the use of powder and scent: nice girls had no need of artifice according to Mrs Bossom, which was strange considering she used cosmetics herself. Hair brushed straight, wearing youthful frocks, Gertie was paraded at tennis parties and whist drives where male eyes drifted automatically to Rose. She seldom noticed, being preoccupied with thoughts of a career once she left school.

During the war years both sisters poured endless cups of tea for convalescent soldiers. Rose, never Gertie, received many requests to 'be my girl'. Jealous for her favourite daughter, their mother did not permit Rose to accept these invitations. Girls had to be properly introduced and then only to officers, Mrs Bossom announced: other ranks should be ignored.

How circumstances had changed and in such a short time. Several of their friends were employed either in offices or the more select Middlesbrough shops nowadays. One brave soul, a receptionist in a garage, risked rubbing shoulders with mechanics but she continued to survive. Such young women introduced their new friends to their parents, not the other way round as formerly.

Life was so much freer but not for Rose and Gertie. They had to find a way to earn their living and quickly, but what could Gertie do? Whenever Rose tried to discuss it, she refused to listen. Surely Harold Brigg wasn't the answer?

With a spurt of anger she said, 'If I can't afford a suitable shawl today it's because we daren't waste any more money. The sooner Harold Brigg knows how poor we are, the better, Gertie.'

He made her uneasy with his constant references to money. She gestured at the table. 'It's not as if we normally eat this sort of tea.' When Gertie ignored her, Rose tried another tack.

4

'Suppose he doesn't come? It wasn't a *definite* arrangement, was it?'

'Oh, yes. I made a point of repeating the date and time so that he couldn't be mistaken.'

She was throwing herself at him, thought Rose with dismay.

'I really don't think you should—' she began but Gertie grasped her wrist.

'Don't say anything, Rose,' she begged as if guessing what was in her mind. 'Harold is a decent man; just remember that.'

There were too many hopeful, single young women now-adays and far too many brothers who lay forever beside their own dear Cecil in the Flanders' mud.

Harold Brigg had not been involved in the conflict. A widower of thirty-three, tall, balding, with a mouth overfull of teeth, and a supreme conviction as to his own self-importance, he was neither a fool nor an educated man. He was evasive, however, successfully concealing facts he didn't wish the Misses Bossom to know. Rose considered him a slippery character.

How Gertie had met him was still a mystery. He wasn't one of Cecil's friends, he'd never been invited to those long-ago tennis parties – the very idea made her giggle; Harold certainly wasn't 'their sort'. Gertie refused to acknowledge this; she'd even kept his existence a secret during their parents' lifetime, finally confessing only because she'd been forced into it.

A week after their mother's funeral when she'd announced, 'I shall be visiting the lending library this evening ...' Rose had interrupted.

'There's no need. I'm going there myself, I can take your books.'

To her surprise Gertie had burst out, 'I forbid you to!'

'What?'

'You have no right,' the thin voice had trembled. 'You must *not* visit the library tonight.'

5

'Why on earth ...'

The hot muddled jumble had been half defiant, half imploring: Gertie had 'a follower', a 'gentleman friend' with whom she had an assignation that evening in the upstairs gallery which housed the local history section, 'where it's quiet.'

The affair progressed in fits and starts. Having met the gentleman, Rose thought she understood why: it was Gertie who was eager, Harold Brigg was merely using her sister for companionship when it suited him.

This concerned her deeply. Gertie was in such emotional thrall that should the widower throw her over the consequences would be dreadful. Rose ventured a warning now. 'You know, we may be misinterpreting the *strength* of Mr Brigg's affections, Gertie.'

'How can you say such a thing!'

If Rose had been alert to the tension in the voice, she might have held her tongue.

'It wouldn't be the end of the world if he didn't come; at least we two should have a splendid tea!' she teased. 'You aren't going to tell me *he* was the figure in the crystal – you can't pretend you actually *like* the man?'

'Rose—'

'He's so much older—'

'I forbid you to criticize—'

'I'm not criticizing, dear, but he's very sly.' Memories of dear departed friends fuelled her indignation. 'Remember how he boasted of fibbing to avoid even the chance of the call-up? I thought that was shameful.'

'Harold is as brave as the next man!'

'He must thank heaven he never had to prove it.' She'd gone too far. Gertie was oblivious to everything except achieving her objective, matrimony.

'How dare you!'

'What?' Both were so upset, neither heard the downstairs bell.

'This afternoon, Harold will propose, I'm certain of it. You are to remain here beside me for appearance's sake. I shall accept, naturally. Our engagement will be kept short. No one bothers about mourning nowadays. Once we are united, you will have to find somewhere else to live. I cannot share a roof with anyone who *despises* my future fiancé!'

Despite her shock, Rose saw the irony. After all the fuss about Fleetham Street Gertie intended to go on living here. But what if Harold didn't propose? That could be equally disastrous.

'Gertie, please don't be precipitate. I know you're anxious and your happiness matters to me, truly it does. You're far too sensible to believe that fortune-teller business,' she begged. 'Reflect for a moment. We need to know much more about Harold Brigg before you even think of ...' She caught sight of Gertie's obstinate expression and burst out, 'I refuse to believe you actually care for him!'

Tight-lipped, Gertie refused to answer.

'If you don't,' Rose persisted, 'just imagine what marriage to him will be like. Waking every morning to find that dreadful leery face on the pillow beside you—'

'Mr Harold Brigg, miss ...' Both women whipped round.

The maid stood in the doorway, clutching Harold's hat. 'I tried to cough, but neither of you was listening ...'

'Thank you, Queenie.' Rose was the first to recover. 'Good afternoon, Mr Brigg.'

'Harold, Miss Rose.'

'Harold, then.' He advanced ponderously and took Gertie's hand.

'Miss Bossom, I trust I find you well?'

'Oh, yes ... quite. Do sit down. It's all right, you can bring tea, Queenie.' Gertie was flustered; her nerves in a jangle, her nice arrangements threatened, all because of Rose.

Harold had turned to her sister. 'I trust I find you in similar good health, Miss Rose?' She inclined her head and moved nearer the window to recover.

He took possession of the hearthrug and stood feet apart, his coat-tails raised to expose his posterior to the fire. 'Inclement weather, Miss Bossom, for the time of year.' It was

7

said pointedly and Gertie realized her sin of omission.

'Oh, dear!' She snatched at the tongs.

'Allow me.'

Rose watched the stout shiny bottom as he bent to add the coal to the fire. Pompous and fat. He was wearing new spats; did that mean he intended to propose? The idea made her quake with both suppressed laughter and despair. Oh, Gertie, don't! It was no use, her sister wouldn't change her mind. As soon as she decently could Rose would make an excuse and escape. Harold's voice broke through her reverie.

'As I disrobed in the hallway, I couldn't help overhearing part of your conversation.'

Oh, Lord!

He had grasped his lapels. 'You appeared to be discoursing on the benefits or otherwise –' his glance at Gertie was almost coy '– of matrimony. Ah ...'

Queenie had appeared in the doorway with the teapot, a jug of hot water and hot buttered teacakes.

If Harold realized his lateness for tea, he saw no reason to apologize. In his eyes, it was perfectly proper for women to dance attendance on a man. He watched as Gertie and Rose lifted the tea-table to a more convenient position.

'The cup that cheers, eh?' Seizing a chair he waited with ill-concealed impatience for them to be seated so that he could do likewise.

He was full of purpose for he had indeed come to propose. Rose's presence was no impediment. She could learn the advantages the second Mrs Brigg would enjoy. Afterwards, she and her sister would no doubt marvel over Gertrude's good fortune.

He was confident Miss Bossom would accept but intended she should have the opportunity to show gratitude first. She wasn't his first choice; he had tried to find a female more to his liking. Indeed, on first meeting Rose he'd felt aggrieved; she was so much more attractive, so womanly. He cursed fate that had led him to bump into Gertrude rather than her sister at the bus terminus.

There was, however, a coolness in Rose's manner, a disdainful smile when listening to his carefully prepared witticisms, which he found most annoying. At least Gertrude understood when to laugh; given time, she could be moulded into a suitable wife.

Harold preferred not to make a move until he had discovered the precise extent of Miss Bossom's fortune but that information proved elusive. Frustrated by her secretiveness, he'd been at the point of ending their acquaintance when a letter arrived from a certain Miss Ruby Winnot of Haverton Hill which changed the situation dramatically.

Harold had known Ruby briefly a month or two ago. She referred to these occasions and the consequence which had ensued. As well as describing the wrath of her large, coalminer brothers, her final sentence contained a threat: Miss Winnot wanted a wedding ring; she was not prepared to wait.

Harold abhorred blackmail. The need for a wife was obviously much more urgent but she would be of *his* choosing. Wives gave protection. In the eyes of the Miss Winnots of this world, they were permanent, immovable objects.

He hadn't mentioned Ruby's existence to Gertrude Bossom. There was no necessity. The two young women were unlikely to meet; indeed, he intended to ensure they never did.

Unattractive though Gertrude was, she was eminently suitable. Her respectability was beyond reproach. Even more important, from various hints dropped by her, he truly believed she had money.

On the death of his first wife, her entire dowry had reverted to a family trust. He had learned the sad fact at her funeral and had vowed he wouldn't be deprived a second time. Until the arrival of Miss Winnot's letter he had been doing his utmost to discover the circumstances governing Gertrude's wealth. It was most annoying to be forced to proceed before his researches were complete.

He'd questioned her many times but, to his chagrin, he'd learned precisely nothing. Miss Bossom could, when she chose, be extremely obstinate. As to why she and Rose had left the family home, Fleetham Street was, she assured him airily, a temporary measure; Rose was nervous of overspending.

'I had to agree, Harold. Rose is only twenty – she's the only family I have. If living here convinces her we are being sensible, so be it.' He wasn't entirely convinced but a frugal outlook was to be encouraged, especially in a female.

Faced with the need to act, he'd seriously considered switching to Rose. He'd done sums on scraps of paper but, being the younger daughter, she was unlikely to have inherited much of the fortune. Reluctantly, he'd tossed the scraps onto the fire: sacrifices had to be made; Gertrude was the only rational choice.

Her eagerness to be married had daunted him before but today that was forgiven. Thank heaven for such keenness! With luck, he could place the announcement in Monday's *Gazette*, then let Miss Winnot and her brothers do their worst!

He caught sight of the skinny body and spectacles and his mind was filled with enticing images of Ruby. He banished them sternly, he must concentrate on the business in hand. Once Gertrude's promise was obtained, only then would he be safe. But even if he had to forgo the pleasure of Ruby's charms, at least his attractive sister-in-law would be within reach. It was sufficient consolation for him to bestow a smile on the object of his affections.

Gertie tried to still the beating of her heart and preside as a proper hostess should.

'Thank you, Queenie.' When the door closed behind the maid, she asked genteelly, 'With milk and sugar, Harold?'

He raised exaggerated eyebrows. 'Does the maid not remain to wait at table?'

'Er, no.' They weren't entitled to Queenie's services but Gertie kept silent.

It was Rose who explained. 'Queenie is Mrs Potter's servant and kindly agreed to make tea for us this afternoon but we do not pay her wages. We are lodgers and cannot make demands on her.'

Harold sipped, cocking his little finger skywards. 'In my opinion it is most important, after the upheavals we have endured since the war, to maintain *proper standards*, especially in the home. I would expect it in any establishment of mine.'

'Cucumber sandwich?' offered Gertie.

Rose put down her cup. 'I don't think I understand,' she said slowly. 'We certainly live much more simply since Father and Mother died but our *standards* haven't changed, only our circumstances.'

'Circumstances. Quite,' Harold said vaguely. 'No doubt a large house ... two young females ...'

'And a complete lack of resources. We must both seek employment as there's so little money left—'

'Rose, please!' Gertie said hastily, 'Harold doesn't want to hear about that.'

'What I wanted to explain, Gertie, is that even if we cannot afford servants, standards which are important to us, such as our self-respect, those haven't changed at all.'

An alarm bell had rung for Harold Brigg. 'Only a little – money?' he echoed, his nose twitching.

'Very little,' Rose was emphatic. Gertie managed to keep her voice steady.

'My sister means – very little – compared to what we had when Father was alive. We have been brought up not to – to be *profligate*.'

'Ah ...'

Rose was astonished; that sounded like deception.

'But I agree with my sister,' Gertie continued quickly, 'neither of us finds it demeaning to practise life's little economies. Dear me, no!' She laughed affectedly. 'Of course, things were very different when we lived in Clairville Road. What a pity you never met Father, Harold.'

He dabbed at his mouth. 'A great pity.'

Rose was silent. In her opinion, Harold wouldn't have been invited; neither Cecil nor her father tolerated fools.

'To return to the present,' Harold was heavily coy, 'and what I believe I overheard ... hmm?' He looked at Rose. Her cheeks began to redden. 'Were you not trying to *dissuade* your sister, Miss Rose? I understand your reasons, indeed I do. Your delicate sensibility – particularly after the loss of your parents – must assume that I am come to rob you of your dearest possession. Let me assuage that fear.'

He stuffed the rest of the sandwich in his mouth and reached for a scone. Rose watched fascinated as morsels of bread and cucumber poked between the crowded, champing teeth.

'It was always my intention ... to offer not only my hand and heart to you, Miss Bossom ... but shelter beneath our roof to you, Miss Rose.'

Gertie made an noise somewhat between a gasp and a squeak. Was this her proposal at last? If so, why wasn't Harold addressing *her*?

Harold waited for Rose to exhibit delight. He even debated whether or not to help himself to seed cake but decided he'd better bring matters to a conclusion first.

'Gertrude has already told me of your intentions to seek employment. Let me dissuade you from that. Your place is here, beside your sister.'

Rose was astonished. 'Doing – what?' she asked.

'I'm not sure I understand?'

'How am I to occupy my time, Mr Brigg?'

'Harold, please.' She inclined her head.

'Harold, then. I cannot sit twiddling my thumbs. I need employment, both to occupy my mind as well as to earn a living. Gertie and I cannot continue using up our capital ... whatever she may decide to do about – matrimony,' Rose finished lamely.

There, she thought, at least I've provided Gertie with a way to escape. Her sister refused to meet her eye. As for Harold, this was another disturbing phrase: 'Using up capital'? What did the girl mean? It couldn't cost more than a few shillings a week to live here.

He pressed on. 'As to how you would occupy yourself, Miss Rose, surely that is obvious? You will assist your sister with housewifely duties. In return for a home, without the worry of earning a living, no doubt you would wish to express your gratitude in many helpful little ways?'

I'm to be a replacement for Queenie, Rose realized. He wants Gertie to have a servant – the cheek of it! He'll be ordering me to warm his slippers next.

Harold waited confidently. Gertie stared hard at the table. The pause grew painful. Harold, unwisely, began to expound.

'I am accustomed to females practising such courtesies about the house. At home with my late, dear mother; throughout married life with the first Mrs Brigg, I never so much as reached for the teapot because there was always someone, ready and willing ...'

'Another cup?' asked Gertie, hastily.

'Thank you.' As she began to pour he said, 'Tea first, Miss Bossom. It is the *correct* way, after all,' and Gertie's hand shook. She had failed; the first social occasion with Harold and she had performed incorrectly!

The sight of those golden droplets spilling into the saucer ignited Rose. 'What exactly *is* your background, Harold? We know very little about you. Were you born in Middlesbrough?' He was uncharacteristically silent. Having been born in Smeaton Street, a fact he normally managed to gloss over, as who would not, he was surprised by Rose's bald approach. Frustrated by the lack of response, she went on sarcastically, 'Gertie has obviously told you a great deal about us.'

'Rose!' begged Gertie.

'No doubt she also told you of the servants we had when Father was alive. There was cook, our old nurse and a girl who came in to do the rough twice a week. Then Father took ill and without his salary to support them, they all had to go. Now Gertie and I see to everything.'

'Do be quiet!' her sister whispered urgently.

'Heavens, why shouldn't we tell him? We're capable and healthy, we don't need anyone else to wait on us. However ...' Rose looked at Harold pointedly. 'While we might be content to wait on *each other*, I fail to understand why I should become

13

your servant simply because Gertie *might* choose to marry you.'

'Rose!' Gertie quivered with apprehension.

'I thought I had made that sufficiently plain,' Harold floundered, 'as the protector, the *male* of the household – the superior being . . .'

Don't say anything. Don't be tempted, Gertie's look implored; above all, don't spoil my chances! Rose was filled with contempt. Beneath the tablecloth, her nails bit into her palms.

'What an interesting theory.' A superior being? 'Well, that may be so but I'm afraid I cannot, under any circumstances, accept your offer, Mr Brigg. It is against my nature to stay at home doing nothing but "housewifely duties".'

Harold breathed deeply and gazed into his teacup. 'And you, Miss Bossom? Do you prefer to earn your living?'

'I . . . I . . .' Gertie was appalled. Behind the spectacles, her eyes began to lose hope. Was her only prospect about to escape? 'No . . . I . . .'

Rose's anger had evaporated; she needed to stiffen Gertie's resolve. 'Please don't concern yourself about us. I hope to earn sufficient to learn shorthand and type-writing at Miss Wade's next spring. After that, I shall be in a position to support both of us.' It was reckless but she had to give Gertie courage.

'Indeed?'

'I begin working at Miss Lawson's refreshment rooms on Monday. I intend to save all my tips!'

Harold Brigg flung down his napkin. 'That is out of the question.'

'I beg your pardon?'

'No relative of mine will be permitted to wait on members of the public. I have made you an excellent offer, Miss Rose. What could be more proper, in return for board and lodging, to care for your sister – and future brother-in-law?'

She was staring at him. 'You – forbid me!' She turned on her sister. 'Gertie, if you're fool enough to accept this man, on your own head be it but he's not telling me how to run my life.

14

Not he, nor any other man – not ever!'

Rose was on her feet, out of the room. Grabbing her coat and hat she rattled down the stairs to the street door. Queenie stood open-mouthed.

As Miss Potter came out of her shop below, Gertie called down, 'Rose, you can't go out.' She lowered her voice. 'You mustn't *leave* me, it wouldn't be proper.'

Rose stared up at her. 'Do you intend changing your mind?'

'No!'

Rose pulled on her hat.

'Where are you going?'

'Out. I shall be late back.' The front door slammed. Harold Brigg felt relieved. Then he remembered he was about to become related to that termagant!

Despite the rain, Rose kept on walking, fuelled by alternate bursts of temper and fear. It only Gertie would change her mind! She wouldn't, though. She saw Harold as her only chance.

Rose recollected Harold's expression and shivered. He'd looked at *her* the way a man should look at his wife.

'He doesn't care for Gertie one little bit.' Why on earth was he so intent on marrying her sister? Misery made her thoughts incoherent. She couldn't stay on in Fleetham Street, she would have to find other lodgings. What a mess and a muddle it all was!

Surely Harold had a house of his own? Did Gertie object to occupying her predecessor's bed? When did the first Mrs Brigg die? They knew so little! Gertie was behaving like a besotted schoolgirl instead of a prudent woman of twenty-four.

'I wish there was someone I could ask!'

'Pardon?'

'Oh!'

Without realizing it, Rose had reached the outskirts of Albert Park. In the gloom, a stranger had turned at the sound of her voice.

'Sorry if I startled you – were you speaking to me?' The working-class accent made her answer off-handedly.

'I was speaking aloud.' She spun on her heel but the rain had transformed fallen leaves into a slimy carpet. Rose slipped, turning her ankle and fell heavily on to her hands and knees.

'Ouch!'

'Are you all right? Are you hurt?'

His face was in shadow from the brim of his cap but the voice was concerned, not threatening. 'Let me help you up, miss. There's a bench over there – d'you see. If we can get you that far, you could rest for a bit.'

Finding she could scarcely hobble, the stranger put his shoulder under her arm and half carried her. Pain made Rose gasp as he lowered her on to the wet seat.

'You'd better stretch out your leg. Have you a hanky – or a scarf, mebbe?' He took the scarf she offered and began to bind her ankle. 'I've got a hanky at home but I keep it smart. For interviews, that sort of thing. Can't afford not to look smart these days, can you?' He wanted to distract her, he'd learned to do that during the war. Divert the attention of a wounded man from what you were about to do.

Rose held out her own hanky. She'd never been out at night alone before, her mother hadn't permitted it. Before the war Cecil or Father always accompanied her and here she was at the mercy of a strange man. She watched nervously as he soaked it in rainwater.

'Here, I think you grazed your knee when you fell. Roll down your stocking – it's all right, I shan't look. Clean it as much as you can.' He distanced himself but when she moaned, called out, 'Swear all you want, miss. I don't suppose there'll be any words I haven't heard.' He listened for the rustle that signified she'd adjusted her skirts. 'Would you like me to find you a cab?'

'Thanks, I'll manage.' Rose tried to stand upright. He watched her grab at the bench for support.

'It's a sprain, I reckon.'

16

'It can't be!' In the darkness, she sounded distraught. 'I'm due to start work Monday at Miss Lawson's. I shall be on my feet all day.'

He laughed, not unkindly. 'You caught a blighty one when you slipped, miss. You won't be going anywhere on Monday. Let's just try and get you home. Can you manage as far as the tram?'

Miss Lawson's meant the tea rooms in Albert Road. This young woman wasn't what he'd first assumed. For all her nice manners, she must be an ordinary working girl.

'Where d'you live?'

'Fleetham Street.' That confirmed it. She'd fooled him properly. From her voice, he'd imagined she was a nob.

'That's not too far.' He didn't have to be so respectful, she wasn't a lady. 'We should manage that. Give us your arm.'

But once inside the brightly lit tram, Ned Harrison knew he'd been mistaken a second time. Despite the fall, her dark gold hair was tidy and her hat on straight. In his street women were always too busy with children to bother with things like that.

Was she married? He judged her to be about twenty. His neighbours had had three or four children by then. Why did she have to work? Had her husband lost his job, perhaps? That was the likely explanation, could happen to anybody, that.

She had no ring on her ungloved finger. Not married, then. Perhaps her family could no longer afford to support her. The more he thought about it, the more of an enigma she became. One thing was clear though, she was a real good-looker.

She began to ease off her shoe and he leaned across to tell her she must leave it on. By the look of the swelling foot, he'd have to help her all the way home.

'Fares, please.'

'Here.' The girl held out a sixpence before he could reach into his pocket. Thank God for that. If he'd had to pay, he'd have been skint. It made him ashamed.

He muttered, 'I'm sorry.'

17

'Whatever for? It was my stupid fault. And thanks for helping – Mr . . .?'

'Ned. Ned Harrison.'

'Rose Bossom. I couldn't have managed on my own.'

'No.'

The tram jerked and rumbled, rain hissed and electricity flashed between the pole and cable. Each livid burst showed another detail: Rose Bossom's pale skin, her soft mouth now closed tight against the pain and the wide-apart, dark blue eyes. These closed too, as the tram jolted over a crossing.

Ned felt increasingly awkward. What was this young woman doing out alone? He'd probably let himself in for trouble – it was bucketing down. He'd get soaked a second time, walking back. Not much chance of drying his clothes at home, either. Blast, damn and hell! Without money for coal it was like the ruddy trenches all over again.

She'd noticed the scowl. 'Is this taking you out of your way . . .'

Ned indicated her ankle. 'Can you move it?' She tried and winced. 'You daren't risk putting any weight on it.' He was right, of course. Would he be offended if she offered the return fare? He whispered suddenly, 'Cheer up!'

She smiled and Ned cursed again. Why was it the good-lookers were always the wrong class! Maybe it was because they could afford dentists and didn't lose their teeth.

Tea was finished, Queenie had cleared away. Harold resumed his former position on the hearthrug and began to speak.

Gertie was attentive. Somehow it wasn't quite as she'd pictured it. The fortune-teller had not been specific, she hadn't seen any physical details *clearly*. Even so, Gertie had been surprised to find Harold so much older than the man in her dreams.

With a shock, she realized she hadn't been listening. She must! The most important occasion of her life, she had to treasure every blissful moment.

But he continued to ramble. Rose's behaviour had been unacceptable, he informed her. He began to describe at length how he'd often had to reprimand or crush subordinates at work. The minutiae of daily toil that he valued so highly, he poured into Gertie's ear. If Rose grumbled they knew very little before, Harold was now making good the deficiency in certain self-important areas.

He dwelt briefly on his personal circumstances. He'd had to give up his house – the reasons were vague – he was in lodgings but he would find a more suitable abode. There were so many decent properties to choose from nowadays.

As Harold droned on, Gertie began to furnish the house, room by room with those items she so admired in the windows of Dickson & Benson.

He'd switched back to his work. Miss Bossom would doubtless be amused to hear of a colleague in the office who had failed to address him correctly. Harold had rebuked the man's lack of 'standards'. Gertie found herself giving the word an automatic, dutiful nod. Despite her passion, she swallowed a yawn which threatened to expose her boredom.

He'd stopped. She jerked awake. He was looking expectant? Had he Popped The Question? Gertie gazed at him wildly. Had she missed what she'd been waiting for all these years?

'Well?' He sounded impatient.

'Yes,' she said quickly. Whatever else, this wasn't the occasion to say no. Harold Brigg smiled. He reached down to caress one of her hands.

'My dear Miss Bossom. Gertrude ...' He kissed her hand and returned it to her lap.

Was it over then? She hadn't the slightest recollection of how it had happened. Desperately, Gertie cast about for some way to make him say it again. To see him kneel at her feet. She'd been waiting so long! Surely Harold wouldn't mind repeating himself just this once?

The street door opened below, there was the chatter of hushed voices. She heard Mrs Potter's nervous, 'Who's that? Is that you, Miss Rose?'

Her sister called out, 'It's all right, Mrs Potter. I've

damaged my foot ... these gentlemen are helping me.'

Gertie stared at Harold in alarm. He raised a hand. 'Don't excite yourself, Gertrude. I will ascertain ...' But she followed him on to the landing.

She found herself staring down at Rose's hat. Her sister was hopping awkwardly upstairs, one hand grasping the banister, the other – round the shoulder of a man! A stranger!! Behind them was another, rough-looking fellow who called out, 'You can manage?'

'Aye, thanks,' replied Ned.

'I'll say goodnight.' The rough fellow glanced at the two on the landing. 'She'll be all right now,' and backed out, pulling the street door shut behind him.

'Rose! What's happened?' Gertie hurried down.

'Don't fuss, Gertie, please.' Pain made her sharp.

Ned Harrison touched his cap apologetically, 'It's her ankle, miss. That chap helped me get her this far. Can you take her other arm?'

The two of them hauled Rose upwards. As they reached the top, Ned demanded, 'Where shall I take her?'

'In here.' Gertie pushed open the parlour door. Ned half carried Rose to the sofa where she sank down with a groan.

'A bowl of cold water – and something I can use as a compress.'

Harold Brigg realized he was being addressed. 'I beg your pardon?'

'The colder the better,' Ned said briefly, 'but she'll need a warm drink afterwards, to stop the shivering. Now, miss,' he'd turned to Gertie, 'that shoe'll have to come off. We'll use this to give a bit of support.' He began easing a stool under the injured leg when he noticed Harold still standing there. 'Be quick. It'll hurt like blazes till we get a compress on it.'

Harold drew himself up.

'Do you realise to whom you are speaking?'

Oh, give over! he thought irritably.

'Look, she's injured and needs attention. Will you see to her or will I?'

'I?' Harold could already see several inches of Rose's white limb. Gertrude had exposed it in front of this stranger. Disgraceful behaviour! 'I cannot possibly—'

'Fine. Then fetch the water and let me do it.'

Ned wanted to be off home but he couldn't leave the girl in this state. She looked faint, was she about to be sick? He cut through Harold's, 'We don't even *know* this person, Gertrude—'

'Bring a pail or a large bowl. She's looking – poorly.'

Rose whispered, 'This is Mr Harrison, Gertie. He's been ... very kind ... Ah!' Ned had wrenched off the shoe.

'Be quick,' he ordered Harold. He'd only the one pair of trousers; he couldn't afford to have Rose spew over them.

Harold continued to wring his hands while Gertie fetched the bowl, renewed the compress and mixed a headache powder. Realizing this stranger was attracting too much of his fiancée's attention, Harold forced his way back into the conversation.

'No doubt you acquired your medical expertise while on, ah, military service, Mr ...'

'Harrison. Aye, in France. We got a lot of practice over there. Where were you stationed?'

Gertie said quickly, 'Our brother was killed at Ypres. Our parents never recovered, they died six months ago.'

Ned nodded sympathetically; things were falling into place. 'My mum and dad went for the same reason. When my elder brother didn't come back, they caught pneumonia and lost heart.' He was conscious of his own damp clothes. 'I think we'd best get you to bed, miss,' he told Rose.

Her foot was a tight, hot balloon. She tried to rise.

'Stay put, we'll make a chair.' Ned held out crossed arms. Harold saw he was expected to do the same and clasping each other's wrists they stooped to take her weight.

In the bedroom Gertie took charge, murmuring, 'If you wouldn't mind waiting, Mr Harrison,' and closed the door.

Back in the parlour Harold began his interrogation. 'You and Miss Rose Bossom were not formerly acquainted?'

21

'No.'

'Merely an – accidental encounter?'

'Yes.'

'I – see.' He managed to inject a wealth of meaning. 'Miss Bossom and I are – affianced. This evening, she did me the honour of accepting my proposal. I now consider myself Miss Rose's mentor – and friend.'

Ned said bluntly, 'You've no need to worry. As soon as I've bid Miss Bossom good night, I'm off.'

Having achieved his objective, Harold was gracious, 'I was not imputing any *dishonourable* motive, Harrison.'

Ned looked him firmly in the eye. 'Just as well because there was nothing dishonourable about it.'

'Oh, quite, quite ...'

'And if you are looking after her interests, I think a doctor ought to see that ankle. Miss Rose told me she didn't want one but it seemed to me she was trying to avoid the expense.'

Harold was offended. 'Oh, no. Dear me, no. It must have been the lateness of the hour rather than any other consideration ...' All the same, the suggestion fretted him. He really must pin Gertrude down about the money before he left. 'How fortunate you were there and knew what to do.'

'Aye, we learned fast during the war.'

'I was unable to volunteer because of my late wife's ill health,' Harold said glibly. 'Sadly, despite our best efforts, she passed away.'

He makes it sound like it was her fault, thought Ned. Aloud, he murmured, 'My condolences,' but Harold recalled his newly engaged state.

'Now, of course, a whole new future beckons, with Miss Bossom.'

'Look, I'd better be off. Perhaps you'd be good enough to explain?' But before Harold could agree, Gertie had returned.

'I'm sorry to keep you, Mr Harrison. I'll see you out. No, you stay here, Harold. I need to make sure the sneck is down, Mrs Potter is always so anxious.'

She led the way downstairs, lowering her voice, 'We don't

want you to be out of pocket. Please don't be offended.'

Ned felt the hard shape of a sixpence; he could ride home after all. 'That's very good of you ... I hope your sister won't be tempted to put weight on that foot too soon.' When Gertie frowned, he explained, 'She mentioned a position as a waitress?'

Her brow cleared. 'Oh, that!' What a relief; Rose couldn't work there now even if she wanted to. 'It doesn't matter – Harold was very much against it.' She opened the door.

'All good wishes, miss.'

For a moment Gertie stared, then remembered. 'Oh, yes. Thank you. Goodnight.'

As he took his leave, Harold said, 'Monday's *Gazette*, if you've no objection?'

'Er, no. None at all.'

'We can settle the date of the wedding tomorrow. Shall I call about ten forty-five?'

'I doubt if I shall go to church, Harold. It depends on Rose.' He was annoyed. Gertrude's presence at his side would have helped spread the news quickly, possibly as far as Haverton Hill.

'I shall pray that her recovery is speedy.'

'I must do what I think best,' she told him firmly. He had been intending to kiss her but remembered the most pressing business of all: her fortune? He opened his mouth to ask but Gertie Bossom had had enough.

'Goodnight, Harold.' She shut the door before he could utter another word.

Rose stared at the moon while Gertie undressed. Nothing had been said. Her sister slipped into bed beside her.

'Did Harold propose?'

'Yes. We're to be married very soon.'

'I hope you'll be very happy.'

'Thank you, dear.' But there was a new awkwardness that hadn't existed before.

23

'When is it to be?'

'We haven't decided. We might have discussed dates had you and Mr Harrison not arrived.'

'I'm sorry,' Rose sighed. 'I've just about ruined your day, first criticizing, then losing my temper like that.'

'You must learn to love Harold just as I do.'

'I'll try ... I promise. If you care for him, he must be a good man. Your "Mr Right" at last, Gertie!' But her sister didn't reply.

They lay side by side, immersed in their own thoughts. Eventually Gertie asked, 'Is your foot more comfortable?'

'It's easing all the time. I'm sure it'll be better by Monday.'

'No, Rose. Harold doesn't wish you to work – at least, not as a waitress.'

'But I'm not qualified to do anything else. How are we to pay the rent? I know these rooms are cheap but we can't continue using what's in the bank. You don't intend asking Harold for money, I hope?'

'Goodness, no.' Gertie guessed it would be futile. 'I expect we'll manage,' she offered feebly.

'Have you discovered anything more about him?'

'He's an under-manager at Hill's rolling mill,' she answered promptly. 'He's highly thought of, he's been there since before the war.'

Rose couldn't hide her astonishment. 'I thought he worked in an office?'

'He does. It's attached to the mill. His responsibilities are very heavy. They *rely* on Harold.' Rose didn't comment. After a pause, her sister's voice came trembling out of the darkness. 'Rose ...'

'Yes?'

'Mother always promised, once I'd found my Mr Right, I should have a dozen of everything in my trousseau.'

'You know that's not possible.' But it was one daydream too many for Gertie to lose today. Tears began to flow.

'This should have been ... the happiest day of my life ... apart from my wedding day.'

'Don't cry, dear. I'll do what I can.' With a sinking heart, Rose continued, 'If I work as a waitress, you can have a share of my wages.'

'Oh, Rose – you are a brick!'

'We could sell Mother's dressing-table set. It's silver, it should fetch quite a bit.'

'No!'

'But you and I don't have any use for such things any more.'

Gertie sobbed louder than ever, 'I'm sure, if she'd lived, Mother would have wanted me to have that set, now that I'm engaged.'

Oh, dear ... and how many other treasures would Mother have wanted you to have, wondered Rose; the lot, probably. Would there be anything left when her turn came?

'Gertie ...'

'What?'

'Can I have the tea service? I've always liked it and you never did, you said it was garish.' For Rose, the cornflowers and poppies twining round the rim were a constant reminder of summer.

'I suppose so. Provided I can keep what's left of the bone china.'

'Thank you, that's very generous.'

'Go to sleep.'

Despite the painfully swollen ankle, Rose did manage to fall asleep. As for Gertie, she wondered why, after years of anticipation, she should feel so flat.

It was Rose's fault. If she hadn't come home with that rough workman, if only she hadn't been so clumsy. 'I'd planned this afternoon so carefully ... it should have been nice ...' Even securing the silver dressing-table set wasn't much consolation.

Ned Harrison slipped inside the terraced house and padded through to the scullery. Clothes hung thickly round the still-warm stove. His sister Muriel must have found money from

25

somewhere, she hadn't had any coal when he'd gone out this evening. He tore up a newspaper and began to stuff it in the toes of his boots.

'Where have you been all this time?' Mu was barefoot in her nightgown, a shawl round her shoulders.

'You gave me a fright! A woman sprained her ankle near the park. She couldn't walk. I had to take her home.'

'Wasn't someone with her?' Nice women didn't walk alone at night, especially near the park.

'She'd been bothered by something at home. She'd taken herself out then slipped in the wet.'

'Here ...' She made a place for the boots on the stove. 'Give us your things. Hey, these are soaked right through! I hope they're dry enough by morning.' Jacket and trousers were draped over the clothes-horse.

'Where did you get money for the coal?'

'Lionel got an extra shift. Have you had your supper?'

'It doesn't matter.'

'Sit down.' She began to stir the pan on the hob and one hand went to ease her back in a familiar way.

'Here, you haven't fallen again?'

'God, I hope not!' Muriel's face was expressionless as she did a swift calculation. 'No ... I'm not due for another four days.' The nightdress outlined her sagging belly and tired breasts.

'Three's enough, Mu.'

'Don't I know it. Get this down.' Ned spooned hot stew ravenously.

'Lionel's working then?'

'Yes. You found anything yet?' He didn't bother to look up. 'Summat'll turn up, you'll see.' She rose. 'I'm for bed. There's hot water in the kettle for your wash.'

'Thanks, Mu.'

She bent to kiss the top of his head. He could feel her warmth, the milky smell. They'd lived in this crowded terrace all their lives. As children they'd shared the same bed. Ned knew the shape of Muriel's body as well as he did his own.

She'd been bonny and slim before he and George went away. When he returned alone, their parents were already dead, she and Lionel were married and expecting their second child; the lithe figure had disappeared for ever.

'Night, Ned.'

'Night, pet.'

He refilled the kettle and put it back on the hob. It would have the chill off it by the time Lionel returned.

There were only two bedrooms. Ned had offered to share with the children but Mu wouldn't hear of it. Instead, after his wash, he took his bedding through to the front parlour and spread a blanket over the ice-cold linoleum.

The battered furniture had belonged to their parents. These scarred wooden legs he'd once used to pull himself upright. Living here was a temporary arrangement which had already lasted far too long. Neither Mu nor Lionel made him feel unwelcome but if only he could find a job, then he could have a place of his own.

Ned huddled under his army greatcoat. Come to think of it, Miss Rose Bossom didn't have much better quarters. He remembered her despair at being unfit for work followed by Gertie's relief when she'd learned of it. 'I reckon Rose Bossom is the practical one in that house.' As for becoming engaged to Harold Brigg ... Ned yawned. Miss Bossom needed her head examined.

Before falling asleep he offered up his one and only prayer: Dear Lord, please send me work.

Harold debated over his announcement for the *Gazette*. Too few lines and Miss Winnot might not notice, too many and the cost would be excessive.

Brigg – Bossom
The engagement is announced between Harold, son of the late Mr and Mrs Arnold Brigg of North Ormesby ...
[which was the best possible way to describe Smeaton Street]

and Gertrude Ada, elder daughter of the late . . .

Harold frowned as he tried to recall Mr Bossom's name. No matter.

. . . of the late Mr and Mrs Bossom of Clairville Road.

He counted. Seven lines. He deleted the last three words and inserted a full stop after Bossom: six lines. It would do.

The two surnames would be in heavy type for the benefit of those who might be scanning the column.

A happy coincidence struck him: both surnames began with B. If there was any household linen remaining, Gertrude was undoubtedly entitled to it.

Rose was too young to think of matrimony, anyway. She would need his advice before making her choice. Harold didn't think it likely she would find anyone suitable before she was thirty. A woman's looks often began to fade at that age. Until then she would be a part of *his* household. Perhaps she would warm his slippers?

Linen sheets . . . and warm slippers. How much *had* Gertrude got tucked away? He'd been about to ask when Rose had arrived with that fellow.

Gertrude should have been more forthcoming, he thought sternly, he shouldn't have to press so hard. She'd also behaved very strangely when he suggested she might like the first Mrs Bossom's engagement ring. She'd had her chance. He would trade the diamond against a less costly stone.

The candle guttered and died. He felt his way across to his bed. Only a few more weeks on this uncomfortable mattress. If there was a mahogany bed among the Bossoms' furniture – Harold had always fancied mahogany, preferably a half-tester – so much the better. He would ask Gertrude for a complete list of what was in store tomorrow.

Chapter Two

Little White Lies, 1920

Gertie had hardly slept, she'd tossed and turned so much. Her conscience had begun to nag in earnest. Up to now she'd ignored it but reality was upon her. If only she could continue with pretence; better still, if only Harold would cease being so inquisitive! It was vulgar to press her about money. He made it sound as though she were going to support him rather than the other way round, which was nonsense. All the same . . .

Harold Brigg, my fiancé. Once she'd imagined those words would have her bounding out of bed. On this, the first morning of her new life, all she wanted to do was hide beneath the eiderdown. Was it really time to get up? Perhaps five more minutes . . . it was Sunday after all. Gertie looked at the clock. Bother!

Rose normally made the tea but Rose was temporarily an invalid. She would, however, provide protection from Harold. Gertie could count on a respite of at least a week. If he suggested visiting during the next seven days, she would plead Rose's indisposition. Surely he wouldn't want to upset her in front of her sister by asking about their inheritance?

Supposing he did though? Rose with her blunt manner was bound to tell him the truth – the last thing Gertie intended he should learn – until they were married, of course, and then only if absolutely necessary. Wide awake now, Gertie faced the fact that her sister and fiancé must be kept apart.

It had been true romance between her and Harold at the beginning. If only it could have continued like that! A casual encounter at a bus stop, a gallant hand helping with her umbrella after the wind had turned it inside out. Gertie had kept their meetings a secret, never dropping a hint at home. Harold 'wasn't quite', not like Cecil's friends. But he was her own dear *boy*, someone she could dream about – wasn't that enough?

There had been small deceptions to begin with, on both sides. It was a fortnight before she realized he was prematurely bald. He removed his hat for the first time and she found herself inhaling the pomade that kept the strands in place. It didn't matter, Gertie told herself bravely, for Harold's was such a fine manly figure. He was tall, which accounted for his booming voice and his feet, which were large.

He'd sought her sympathy. His late wife's family had treated him disgracefully; they'd taken back her dowry. He'd been ordered to vacate her fine house as well. Gertie found herself wondering what he had contributed to the marriage? When she began asking a few tentative questions, he'd changed the subject.

Egged on by his little fibs, Gertie began to enhance her own circumstances, which was a mistake. She might view *his* exaggerations tolerantly but Harold wanted to believe her every word.

It had been a game at the beginning, foiling his attempts. All those hints about probate and whether their solicitor was reliable. Harold had even offered to supervise the legal work himself but Gertie had told him firmly there was no need, he mustn't concern himself.

The temptation to enlarge the glories of Clairville Road had been too great, however. She'd even promoted her father from head clerk to general manager of his insurance company. The trouble was Harold had such high expectations. He expected his second wife to be as well endowed as his first.

'What does it matter,' Gertie demanded of the empty chilly kitchen, 'if I don't have a dowry; at least I shall have a trousseau now that Rose has promised to help.' Alas, she knew dowries were far more important in the eyes of her fiancé.

Yet her mother had assured her Mr Right would provide. 'All he will expect is a sweet-natured, accomplished girl, Gertie.' She had worked so diligently, embroidering countless traycloths. Her bottom drawer contained linen sheets and no one could crochet as finely as Gertie Bossom.

Waiting for the kettle to boil, Gertie put aside worries about Harold and began to calculate the yards of crêpe de Chine and lawn she would need for chemises and camiknickers. She planned to vary the trimmings: picot, crochet, lace and scallop, using pink and apricot silks. If only she could afford a silver fox fur! It was the height of Gertie's ambition. What ecstacy to have a fox fur to complete her going-away outfit!

The whistle of the kettle woke Rose. That and her throbbing ankle. She tried wiggling her toes. Ah, careful! It still hurt. She persevered, cautiously this time. Yes, it was definitely less painful. Thank goodness. Tomorrow she could begin at Miss Lawson's as planned. She heard the chink of cups. Dear, kind Gertie, she did so dislike the mornings. It was like seeing a small animal emerge from its burrow, watching her come to life and grope for her spectacles.

Fine work had made those necessary. Rose fingered the drawn threadwork on her nightgown – a surprise last Christmas. And now Gertie would want to sew all sorts of things for her wedding. Rose sighed. Gertie seemed to think that while there was money in the bank all you had to do was withdraw it and by tomorrow the account would automatically be replenished. Their solicitor, exasperated, had demanded, 'Can you not make your sister understand? She must not squander one more penny on fripperies! This is all the capital you young ladies have left.'

Rose had done her best. She kept the bank book – it was too risky to let Gertie have it. She would share her wages. These didn't add up to much: a pound a week plus tips. After paying the rent of five shillings, allowing another five shillings for food, if they halved the remaining ten shillings, Gertie could have five shillings a week towards new clothes. Rose sighed again. No doubt Gertie would grumble but she'd have to manage.

31

Rose suddenly remembered: once her sister was married, *her* troubles would be over. Harold would provide, he was an under-manager at Hill's – what a relief! She really must try harder to like him. No doubt he could support one or two little extravagances. Provided Gertie didn't go wild, her future would be secure. It was enough to make her joyful as Gertie came in with the tea.

'Congratulations, dearest! How does it feel to be the future Mrs Brigg this morning?'

Gertie was too preoccupied to respond in kind. 'Rose, I need to have a serious talk,' she hurried to finish before she lost her nerve. 'I realize Harold doesn't mean to be inquisitive but he has been asking rather a lot of questions.'

'Naturally.' Rose was baffled. 'He wants to know everything there is to know about you, as you do of him. I was wondering, we know so little about him, do we have any friends in common?'

'I'm not aware of any. The trouble is ... I know you'll think it silly – Harold believes you and I have inherited a fortune.'

Rose gave a shocked laugh. 'Goodness! You dispelled that notion, I hope? We must be the most poverty-stricken pair that ever emerged from Clairville Road.' When Gertie didn't reply, she said, 'You have told him the truth? Once or twice it seemed as if he ... Oh, Gertie, you haven't been telling fibs?'

'No!'

'Then it's perfectly simple. All you have to say is, "Dearest Harold, neither Rose nor I have a bean. However, we – that is to say Rose – will earn our crust and not be a burden to you, which is just as it should be."' Rose beamed, 'Speaking of which, you'll be glad to hear my ankle's much better so I *can* earn my crust after all.'

'It's just ... I think Harold may have misunderstood ...'

'What?' The glow had gone. Clutching her tea, Rose looked at her steadily. 'Why should he unless you've misled him?'

'I haven't, not – intentionally.'

Rose smiled. 'I'll tell him for you, shall I? I can explain our position exactly, nothing could be easier.' She flung back the

bedcovers. 'You dislike figures, Gertie, but at least I understand them. It's the sort of conversation a chap would expect
to have with poor dear Father, but no doubt Harold will make
allowances. Is he taking you to church this morning?'

'I don't think I— '

'No, no, you must go. I can manage perfectly well. And you
certainly wouldn't want me with you today!' Rose hobbled
round the bed to give her a hug. 'Enjoy yourself, dearest.
You're making your first official appearance as Harold's
fiancée. Everyone will want to congratulate you and I insist on
being the first!'

Gertie found little comfort in the warm embrace. Now she
was faced with two problems instead of one. Why on earth
had she told Rose? Her sister only ever saw things in terms of
black or white. She must prevent Rose and Harold having a
tête-à-tête. Nothing could stop her then from telling Harold
the truth!

She dealt with the problem over breakfast. Rose, wrapped
in blankets, was on the sofa, her ankle propped on a cushion, a
tray on her knee. 'If Harold should come back here today . . .'

Rose put down her spoon. 'I hope he does. Please tell him I
would like to see him. Yesterday I was extremely rude and I'm
sorry. The more I see of him, the sooner I shall come to love
him, just as you do.'

'I'd rather you didn't say anything about money.'

Rose frowned. 'Why ever not? The sooner he knows exactly
how we're placed —'

'No!' Gertie was emphatic. 'That's where you're wrong.
The less he knows the better. Promise me you won't bring up
the subject or answer his questions.'

'Gertie!'

'To tell you the truth . . . he's not been completely honest.'
She was bright red, every word was costing her dear. 'He's
unwilling to tell me anything concerning his first wife. It's not
sorrow – he claims he wasn't particularly fond of her – he just
refuses to discuss it. Not only that, I don't really know
anything about him. He hasn't a home to offer, I've no idea if

33

he has any savings ... Why should *we* tell him anything?'

'But Gertie ...' Rose was stunned. 'That's nonsense! We must have it out. This is the man you're going to marry!'

'Yes!' It was so raw, it was painful. 'Of course I'm going to marry Harold. What other choice have I? I've never attracted anyone. You make it plain I'm not capable of earning a living.' As Rose tried to protest, she said grudgingly, 'All right, you don't mean to be unkind but it's true. I am pretty helpless, thanks to Mother, so what else is there? I shall make Harold a good wife and in return he will look after me.'

It was worse than Rose imagined. She didn't want to believe it, she refused to. 'Gertie!'

'No ...!' she was in danger of breaking down. 'Listen to me, Rose, for I never want to talk of this again. Harold may not be the man of my dreams – I don't think such a phenomenon exists. He's what I need. He represents security and the chance of a home. Please God, we shall have a family and then I shall have someone to love.' Rose gasped.

'You're different,' Gertie was remorseless. 'I can't pick and choose, I don't attract the menfolk as you do.' As Rose tried to speak she said fiercely, 'It didn't matter what fine clothes Mother bought, no one noticed me if you were there.'

If that were true, thought Rose in dismay, how she must have suffered. Here am I, heart-free, looking forward to whatever the day may bring. Instinctively, she reached out a hand. Gertie backed away.

'I don't want – pity!' Rose blinked as though she'd been slapped.

'Then what *do* you want of me?'

'I've told you. I realize you know about money but I don't want the subject discussed. Harold has this bee in his bonnet about a dowry. I don't know why as he's an under-manager, it must be some quirk of character. Once we're married, I shall just have to prove to him money isn't everything.' Her voice cracked with the effort to sound optimistic. 'In a year or two you and I will probably wonder why we were so worried.'

I hope so, thought Rose. The most important person in

your life and you can't risk telling him the truth? What a way to begin. She heard her own voice saying, 'I will keep silent but I refuse to tell a lie. If Harold is curious you'd better make sure he doesn't come back today. From tomorrow, I shall be at work during the week so you'll be safe.'

'Thank you.' Gertie took the cup from her. 'Would you like more tea?'

'No thanks.' As her sister left the room, Rose shuddered. What would come of it? How could those two find happiness together?

As for Gertie, the truth had been so horrendously painful she vowed she would avoid it in future.

Ned Harrison got up as soon as he woke. If he lingered, the cold from the linoleum seemed to lap under his greatcoat, reaching for tender, warm skin.

He pulled on his shirt and went in search of his trousers. Muriel was pressing them with the old flat iron. She threw across another pair.

'Here, Lionel won't be needing them till tonight. As for these,' She held them up to the light, 'you've got to be more careful. They're your only pair and the knees were filthy.'

'It was helping that girl last night.'

'So you said.' He wondered why she sounded cool.

'Will I get the kids' breakfast?'

'That'd be a help.' Her face was bright once more. 'I want to finish this ironing and there's a pile of mending in the basket.'

It might be the Lord's day of rest but in this terrace the women weren't so lucky.

It was brisk this morning. Ned set off as he did most days, to get out of Muriel's way. The rest of the week there was a regular routine in search of work but Sundays were different, although the day still had its own pattern. Mu's three children had to be taken to Lionel's parents for Sunday dinner – one less meal for Mu to provide – after that, the day was his own.

35

Ned spent twopence on Woodbines; recompense to Lionel for the loan of his trousers. His stride lengthened. It was a fair step down Marton Road and the wind held a promise of more rain.

As always, as he approached Grove Hill allotments, the old wrought-iron gate stood out boldly. It was no true barrier; there were no hinges, it was fastened to two uprights with bits of wire and rope with neither fence nor hedge on either side. Painted bright blue, the only colour Hayden had managed to cadge, it was a beacon amid decaying sprouts and yellowing potato tops and marked the entrance to his kingdom. Pass, friend, it indicated: the rest of you, stop here.

Ned went through the ceremony of untying and refastening the rope, aware he was being watched. 'Anyone home?' The response from the ramshackle shed was grudging.

'Might be.' But as soon as the gate was back in position, excited barking began. 'Quiet, you stupid bitch!'

Ned tapped on the lintel. 'Morning, Boadicea ... permission to enter?'

'Away in, ye daft bugger, and shut the door, there's a draught.' The mongrel terrier tumbled about in a slavering, eager welcome. As was his custom, Hayden had given her a regal name. Over the years, Ned could remember a Victoria, Elizabeth and Matilda. 'Give over,' Hayden grumbled, 'let him be, you'll mucky him.'

'Down, girl, down.' Fawning, still occasionally leaping up to give him a lick, Boadicea subsided as Ned eased the warped door shut.

Hayden's hut had evolved, there had never been any overall plan. The first piece of salvage dictated the length, the cast-off door, the height. This could, with difficulty, be locked, but the hut remained open to the elements. The window lacked glass and was supported on an old pew, sufficient wood not having been found to complete the fourth wall.

It could still be made snug. There were shutters and bits of corrugated iron which were fastened across at dusk. The roof might rattle ominously but the walls were lined with layers of

36

sacking and cardboard, there was even a cast-off piece of carpet. One old armchair, another fashioned out of boxes, shelves for seedlings, tools, a tilley lamp, a kettle, a tin for tobacco and a box lined with straw for Boadicea in a space roughly ten foot by six. Hayden had spent every day of his life there since being laid off.

He'd once earned a living as a riveter. He'd taught Ned during his apprenticeship but riveters were no longer needed, especially older ones.

Ned put his bait alongside the other man's. They would measure out the day carefully. It was Sunday, therefore only idle work would be done; an odd bit of tidying or sprouts to be picked. Hayden sold them door to door to earn a bit extra.

Sunday was the day he gathered flowers, grown round the edge of his allotment, to take home for his mother and aunt. The three of them loathed one another but none could exist alone; without this refuge, Hayden swore he'd have killed the two biddies long since. The flowers were to calm him during the many occasions his mother whined and nagged.

He puffed at his pipe. 'Nothing yet?' Ned shook his head. 'Heard there was jobs going at Ayresome's?'

'Two. Over three hundred applied for them.'

Hayden's eyebrows shot up. 'Three hundred *qualified* men?'

'Course not. Desperate enough to swear they could do the work, though.'

'But you could've. Why didn't they pick you?'

Ned shrugged. 'I was too far down the line. They'd chosen who they wanted by then. How's things?'

Hayden's expression changed. 'Me aunt had the doctor, Wednesday.'

Ned was astonished. 'Where did she get the money for that? Is she ill?'

'Number one: out of the tin she keeps under the bed. Number two: no, blast it. And *he* says to *her*... "My word, Mrs Bennet, we have got a strong constitution, haven't we? We'll live to be a hundred yet." So *I* says to *him*... "You can live as long as you like but do the rest of us a favour and see she doesn't." '

Ned grinned. 'What'd he say to that?'

Hayden struggled with his emotions. 'Stupid bugger ... threatened to report me. I told him. If I'd wanted to, I could've done her in years ago. Everyone knows how I feel but I've got no bloody choice. Do you think I like seeing to the washing and feeding of two smelly old women? You should try it, I says; I'm stuck with it. I can't afford no one to help. It's only kind neighbours who let me have time off during the day.'

'Never mind, you've got this place,' said Ned soothingly. 'Look at that view.'

Hayden chuckled. 'Aye, straight across to the asylum. Please God one or other of 'em gets took there soon. Or put in a box. It won't mean complete starvation if they do, thanks to Lloyd George. Anyhow ...' He eyed Ned shrewdly. 'Summat's happened. You look like Boadicea does when she's slipped the leash and found old Charlie's whippet.'

Ned was embarrassed. 'Nothing as romantic as that.'

Hayden growled, 'Who's talking of romance?'

'All it was ... I was out walking last night near Albert Park. A young woman fell and hurt herself. I saw her home, that's all.'

'What sort of young woman.'

'Pretty.'

'The worst sort.'

'Oh, give over. Shall I put the kettle on?'

'What for? It's too soon.' They sat, staring through the empty window frame. 'So you took her home ... what's her family like?'

'She's only got a sister. They're living above a shop in Fleetham Street. The sister had just got engaged.' He described what happened, finishing, 'I hope Rose Bossom doesn't try and walk on that foot too soon. It looked bad to me.'

'How much money've you got?'

Ned was surprised. 'A penny.'

Hayden reached into various pockets until he found another. 'There y'are. You'll need twopence.'

'What for?'

'Cuppa tea at the refreshment rooms. To ask if her foot's better. Now, let's have one here, only I won't ask you for nothing, I'm generous. I'll put it on the slate instead.'

He busied himself with the kettle going out to fill it at the allotment tap. When he returned, he pumped up the pressure in the tilley. 'There was summat I heard this week. About a job, like. It's not much. I mean, not for a qualified chap ...'

'What is it? I'd scrub floors if it meant I could pay Mu for me keep.'

'Happen you'll have to, if you apply,' Hayden said grimly. 'They need a caretaker for that school off Normanby Road. It's not full time – I think they meant for a woman to tek it on.'

'How much, any idea?'

Hayden shook his head. 'Women's wages. Nowt and a half per hour, shouldn't wonder.'

Harold was miffed; he'd been told firmly, he wasn't welcome in Fleetham Street after the service. He and Gertie battled with the wind on their way to church, managing only snatches of conversation. 'Rose needs peace and quiet ... healing nicely ... in a day or two.'

'I particularly wanted ... Tomorrow night?'

'Tomorrow night,' Gertie agreed, 'in the library.'

'I would much prefer ...'

'Not until Rose is better.'

He grew more peeved; a sprained ankle was such a trivial thing. There were so many private matters to discuss, the library was far too public.

'You're being over-cautious—' At that moment the wind snatched away his bowler. Gertie watched as he ran after it, observing sadly that nothing made a man look more foolish than chasing after his hat.

The wind had no idea it was dealing with someone of

importance; it grew impudent. The gap between Harold and his headgear increased. He was fraught, he yelled. Once or twice he even cursed. Catching sight of an urchin, he bawled and began to point. Gertie was too far away to hear. From the gestures, the fact the boy refused to move, she guessed negotiations were in progress.

The wind tossed the bowler as if it were a gull's feather. Harold increased his offer rather than lose it. Galvanized, the boy chased until he managed to catch it.

Approaching, he stopped out of reach and demanded to see what the outstretched hand contained. Immediately his face turned sullen. He ran towards a puddle obviously intending to fling the bowler in rather than return it. Only when Harold's hand went once more to his pocket was his property restored. His expression as he rejoined Gertie was thunderous.

'Bare-faced robbery!'

'What a shame.' Seeing his face, she amended quickly, 'And how – *annoying.*' Harold wasn't entirely mollified but then he hadn't seen it from her point of view.

Properly clad, they entered the church porch. Gertie was shaking hands with the churchwarden when Harold murmured in her ear, 'Tomorrow's *Gazette*, six lines. I couldn't recall the name of your esteemed parent.' He broke off to bow to a couple walking past. 'Perfectly satisfactory, I trust?' Confused, Gertie nodded. She'd never dream of disagreeing in public, whatever Harold said. It would offend against his standards.

During the reading from the Old Testament, Harold fretted again over her refusal to invite him back. He had planned to reprimand Rose about her attitude, then he realized he could still do so later in the week. He began to savour the prospect; Rose listening dutifully as he listed the defects in her behaviour. He came to with a start: Gertie was finding his place in the hymn book.

'Three hundred and twenty-seven. "Fight the good fight".'

'Thank you, my dear.' It was the first time he'd used the endearment. She smiled. For a moment she looked almost attractive.

'I shall have to take care of you, Harold, I can see that.' He was touched. The slender hand in black suede rested lightly on his arm as, with the rest of the congregation, they rose and drew breath.

'Fight the good fight wi-ith all thy might.'

I hope someone from Haverton Hill sees us, he thought absently; the sooner that disgraceful young woman knows I am betrothed, the better. And surely with Gertrude beside him, he had all the protection he needed?

'God is thy strength and God thy ri-ight.'

It was nearly two months before Ned managed to fit in a visit to Miss Lawson's refreshment rooms. In his new job he was at the beck and call of an autocratic headmistress who exercised her dislike of all mankind on her new cleaner. Even on Saturdays she could be relied on to find jobs needing urgent attention.

Ned stuck it out, he had to; to be sacked would be worse. All the same, he was eager for a Sunday when he could let off steam to Hayden. Within the safety of the shed, they would sit and curse the female species. Except for one or two of its members.

Ned had kept the twopence in anticipation of his treat. Whenever the coins chinked, he thought about the tea rooms.

Maybe Rose Bossom was no longer there? But he recalled her determination to save for typewriting lessons and dismissed that idea. He took a seat there one Friday evening and began to study the menu. When Rose didn't appear, he began to worry. Had the ankle cost her the job after all?

The proprietress came with his tea and buttered toast.

'Does Miss Rose Bossom work here?'

'She's having time off, just this afternoon and tomorrow morning. For her sister's wedding.'

'Ah, yes ... to Mr Harold Brigg.'

'Are you a friend?'

'I met Miss Rose the night she sprained her ankle.'

'Ah.' She assessed him briefly. When she passed his table

41

again, she said, 'If you're in no hurry, Rose ought to be back later to help me clear up.'

Ned decided to wait.

That afternoon, Rose and Gertie had visited the bank to divide their inheritance.

'It's fair and means we shall have a bank book each. You must keep yours safe, Gertie. Whatever you do, don't withdraw anything without consulting Harold.' Rose hesitated, remembering the awkward interrogation she'd endured. 'Or me, if you'd rather.'

He'd begun his attack as soon as he'd been permitted to visit. He'd sent Gertie on an errand and talked at first of 'my former abode' where, Rose was assured, everything had been of the 'best possible quality'.

Behind the remark was the desire to know whether Gertrude could match her predecessor in worldly goods. This Rose didn't understand but she listened to talk of damask and silver and in a pause, asked innocently, 'Did you have to give back the contents as well as the house?'

'I do not wish to discuss the past,' Harold said abruptly. 'Suffice it to say the terms of my late wife's trust were unjust.'

Rose was confused. 'You mean you still have *some* of the furniture?'

'Everything had to be returned.' Did that mean the undermanager had no possessions at all?

'You mean – there's nothing?' He was annoyed: as he'd planned it, she would answer his questions, not the other way round.

'Everything belonging to Agnes reverted on her death to the family.' He'd said more than he intended; Rose's level gaze unnerved him.

'What a disappointment for you, ' she said gravely, 'but since her sad demise, did you not consider setting up house once more? We'd appreciate some reassurance, Harold. Are you able to offer my sister a comfortable home?'

He fumed. 'What is your sister able to offer me?' he

42

demanded, hotly. 'That is what you and I must discuss first. I assume she is the principal beneficiary of your parents' estate?'

Rose was nervous. She'd given her word not to speak of this. 'You can see for yourself how simply we live,' she gestured.

'Yes, yes. It's obvious you have no room for possessions here. But the furniture in store from Clairville Road? The silver and crystal? You must have a list?' She was speechless, bound by her promise, but what on earth had Gertie been saying?

'You must speak to my sister about that.'

The fibs Gertie must have told! Their home had been rented furnished with a few small additional pieces and these they now had in Fleetham Street. As for silver, there was only the dressing-table set.

Should she point out the small mahogany side table and dinner wagon? Better not. Stick to what she'd said: it was up to Gertie to sort things out. And though he continued to press her, Rose remained silent.

Gertie returned and Rose retired, thankful to leave the lovers alone, resolutely shutting her ears to sounds of re-crimination. When the front door banged and Gertie crept into the bedroom, she commented, 'Harold really has the most extraordinary ideas—'

'Do be quiet!'

This exasperated her. 'That's not good enough. You have to be honest, it's becoming ridiculous – and dangerous.'

'I absolutely refuse.' Gertie was resolute. 'If Harold decides to tell *me* the truth about his circumstances, then I shall do the same. He must be a miser living in lodgings when he could perfectly well afford a house.'

'Has he offered you a proper home?'

'He's offered nothing,' Gertie was forced to admit. 'If only Father was alive to speak to him ... it's very difficult.'

It was on the tip of Rose's tongue to suggest the engagement be broken off. Instead she asked, 'What do you intend to do?'

'Wait for Harold to come to his senses. I've no intention of answering any more of his absurd questions.'

That night Harold was very angry indeed. He would have evidence of her fortune or by God, he wouldn't permit the banns to be announced. He'd present Gertrude with that ultimatum tomorrow. But before he set out for Fleetham Street the following evening, fate took a hand: Harold received an unexpected visit from Haverton Hill.

His landlady's opinion wasn't favourable. 'They said their name's Winnot. I've left them in the front parlour but I want them off my premises as soon as possible, Mr Brigg. Those two are not the sort I'd normally allow over my threshold, far too rough. It was only because they were asking for you.'

With an attempt at bravado Harold closed the parlour door and demanded to know what this was about. Ruby's brothers eyed him coolly. Harold began to insist they'd no business to come pestering him when one silenced him by grabbing his lapels. He clamped his hand over Harold's mouth.

'You know why we're here. We knew where to find you because you were daft enough to tell our Ruby where you worked.'

Which must mean they had visited the rolling mill! Who had they spoken to? What had they said? Harold's eyes bulged.

The second brother spoke. 'Are you going to do right by our Ruby?' The hand was released to enable him to reply.

'I cannot. I am betrothed—'

'She wrote you that letter, *then* you announced you was engaged. Whichever way you look at it, Ruby's got first claim over you, Brigg.'

'I tell you, I cannot! I've given my word!'

'You gave it to Ruby an' all—'

'I did not! I categorically deny—'

'All right, all right. She can tell a tale if she wants, I'll grant you, but the bairn's yours, you cannot deny that.'

'What my brother means, Brigg, is you may be marrying Miss Gertrude Bossom but you're still the father of Ruby's child. What are you going to do about it?'

'I – I . . .' He hadn't planned to do anything but these men were so muscular!

'You weren't thinking of *avoiding* your responsibilities were you?'

Harold tried to prevent his inmost thoughts illuminating his countenance.

'You've been telling everyone at the mill you're about to make a good marriage, there's plenty of gossip about it.'

Harold made a noise, half supplicatory, half in disgust with himself; why couldn't he have been more discreet!

'Which means you can afford to pay for your past mistakes. And we mean to see that you do, don't we, Alf?'

'We do. Every week.'

'We'll be in touch. We'll let ourselves out.'

Harold's first reaction was panic but common-sense intervened. He sat in the dusk and considered his situation. Last night, when he'd demanded that Gertrude tell him her circumstances, she'd shrieked that she'd had enough and he must leave. At the time, he'd been glad. He didn't love her, he'd threatened to cancel the banns and leave it to her as to whether the marriage would go ahead.

Now he was terrified. Supposing Gertrude called his bluff and *she* broke the engagement? Without a fiancée to protect him, those hefty brothers could demand he marry Ruby, they could expose him to his superiors at the mill! His position there, greatly exaggerated to Gertrude, couldn't withstand that – he'd be dismissed. As his wife, Ruby Winnot would drag him down to the level of Smeaton Street. All his efforts to improve his status would be trampled into the slime. Facing up to the truth made him groan.

He'd misjudged Gertrude. It hadn't occurred to him that beneath the compliant exterior was a woman of spirit. Rose could be difficult but for Gertrude to behave in similar fashion was unnerving. He dared not provoke her further. If she was

45

unwilling to answer his questions he would have to be patient until they were married. Then of course, he would have a right to know.

In the days that followed, therefore, Harold exerted himself with a return to his gallant ways, urging only that the banns be announced as soon as possible. With that, Gertie was willing to comply.

It was now the afternoon before the happy day and to be wandering among the smart shops of Linthorpe Road was pure nostalgia.

'Do you remember, Rose. Mama bought me the sweetest little bonnet here, with a plait of blue ribbons.' Window-shopping made Gertie light-headed. Her favourite occupation! She had prepared a list of essential items without which no trousseau would be complete but it was awfully long! She hadn't dared show Rose.

At the bank she'd been content to let her sister do the talking and now both of them had brand new bank books.

'Divided down to the last penny,' said Rose, showing her. 'Our precious capital which is increasing at two and a half per cent per annum. You won't be tempted to spend too much today, will you?'

'No.' It was what Rose wanted to hear; Gertie could see she was pleased.

'This is for you.' It was a new five-pound note. 'My personal wedding present.'

'Oh, Rose ...' She knew how little Rose earned, this must have been withdrawn from the sacred account.

'Keep it safe.'

'Oh, I will! Thank you so much.'

'You might need it for sheets and blankets as we're still not sure what Harold will be providing.'

It was ludicrous, in Rose's opinion, on the day before the wedding, not to know anything beyond the honeymoon destination. Whenever she asked, Gertie became secretive and told her not to worry.

46

It was trespassing on Miss Lawson's kindness to stay out too long but she didn't intend to let Gertie shop alone. Finally, when Rose had cut the list of essentials by half and the purchases were made, they decided to give themselves one last treat: tea at Hintons. She went ahead to order it. There was just one more item Gertie needed to purchase, she would be along directly.

To be waited upon was sheer luxury. Rose was storing up the details to describe to Mrs Lawson when Gertie reappeared, carrying an expensive-looking box. Immediately Rose remembered the bank book.

'Gertie ...?' Her sister sat composedly and began drawing off her gloves.

'Shall we order a fresh pot?'

'Gertie!'

'Don't scold, Rose.'

'What have you been up to?' Gertie debated how best to describe it.

'I've been buying myself a little consolation.'

When Rose returned to Miss Lawson's that evening she didn't notice Ned at first. The proprietress indicated his table and she hurried across, full of apologies,.

'I'm so sorry, I gather you've been waiting to see me.' She might be dressed in a waitress's apron and cap but she was still very much the lady. He felt awkward.

'I just came to see how you were.'

'It's very good of you.' Rose put aside her worries and smiled, 'I'm afraid I can't stop to talk now, I must help with the customers.'

'Well ...' He didn't want to spend more money but was too embarrassed to explain.

She murmured persuasively, 'I can sit after everyone's gone.'

Hang the expense. 'Better bring me another cup.'

'Compliments of the management,' she whispered as she set it down.

He looked his fill while the tea room slowly emptied. Rose walked easily, the black dress swinging from her hips, emphasizing her shapeliness. She hadn't cut her hair as so many women did nowadays; it was in a thick braid pinned up under her cap. Her eyes were dark blue, the hair browny-gold, but hers wasn't a chocolate-box prettiness. There was a vivacity about Rose Bossom. When she laughed, most turned to share the enjoyment. Not that she did that often tonight.

As she rejoined him she said, 'My ankle healed swiftly, thanks to your treatment. I only needed a stick for about a week. Miss Lawson was very understanding. I wanted to write and thank you but didn't know where to send the letter.'

'You'd have upset my sister,' Ned grinned. 'The only time our postman calls is with a bill. She might have torn it up before I could open it.'

'In that case, I'm even more pleased you came.'

He indicated the proprietress. 'She mentioned you were out with your sister today.'

Rose drew a deep breath and expelled it, staring at her hands. 'Tomorrow is her wedding day.'

'I hope the sun shines for you both.'

'Yes ...' It was obvious the weather was the least of her problems.

Ned probed delicately. 'Mr Harold Brigg ... he's well I trust?'

'Oh, yes ...'

She continued to fiddle with the sugar spoon so he asked bluntly, 'Is something wrong, miss?'

Rose gave an embarrassed laugh. 'Gertie was rather impulsive today, she bought herself a silver fox fur. I was wondering how Harold will react.'

'My word.'

'She's always wanted one, you see.'

'Maybe Mr Brigg will treat her to it?' Rose's eyebrows went up. Ned said cheerfully. 'I wouldn't know the difference between fox fur or tom cat.'

48

She replied drily, 'One costs thirty guineas,' which stunned him.

'Deary me!' It was almost an accusation.

Rose said quickly, 'She was using her own money. I oughtn't to criticize.'

'I expect Mr Brigg will understand. Has your sister known him long?' It was verging on impertinence but Rose had been too shy to confide in former friends so that it came as a relief to be able to talk to a stranger.

'About six months. He and Gertie collided, literally, at a bus stop. That's how they met.'

'There's no harm in that, miss. Times have changed. You don't need a chaperone nowadays. I presume Mr Brigg has a good job?'

'He's an under-manager at Hill's rolling mill.' Ned wondered why she sounded so worried.

'Then you must be very pleased for your sister. Will you be staying on in Fleetham Street?'

It was less personal and she answered readily, 'We give up the rooms there next weekend, when Gertie and Harold return from honeymoon, but I've had a stroke of luck. A customer – a widow – has invited me to be her lodger.'

'Splendid.'

'Provided Harold agrees, of course.'

'Goodness, why shouldn't he?'

Rose said reservedly, 'He sees it as my duty to move in with him and Gertie.'

The devil he does, thought Ned.

'Wouldn't your sister prefer to begin her new life alone with her husband?' Privately, Rose thought it was probably the last thing Gertie wanted.

'Harold is a very protective person ...' From her expression Ned knew this was dangerous ground, and changed the subject.

'May I ask how your plan to learn shorthand and type-writing is progressing?'

Rose relaxed. 'Oh, very well indeed. I hope to begin lessons soon. People have been extremely generous with their tips.'

'I'm not surprised, miss.' She blushed.

The proprietress coughed discreetly. Ned stood and held out his hand. 'I've stayed too long. Please excuse me if I spoke out of turn.'

'Not at all,' she said formally, then smiled. 'You've done me good, coming here tonight. It was just what Cecil might have done, to scold me from worrying too much over Gertie. I'm truly grateful.'

Alas, it was not brotherly feelings which had directed Ned's footsteps. He placed an additional penny on top of the bill.

'Towards those lessons.' He saw her about to refuse. 'I can afford it, I've found myself a job.'

Her face lit up. 'I'm so glad ... I've worried that you might still be ...'

'Standing in the rain near the park? No, I've better things to do now.' This wasn't the moment to describe his new occupation however. 'May I call on you again?'

She said pertly, 'We're open from Monday to Saturday. Please come any time you feel the need of refreshments.'

'I will. Good night, miss.' Buoyed up with happy thoughts of those dark expressive eyes, Ned recalled Rose's reserve over Harold Brigg. There was a neighbour who worked at Hill's, he would know. It would give Ned an excuse for repeating his visit to the tea rooms if he could give a reassuring report on her brother-in-law. Anything to make Rose Bossom smile. When she did that, she was the best-looking girl in Middlesbrough.

The trousseau was spread out on the bed: delicately embroidered underwear, two new blouses, the made-over skirt, a new hat and, rising like grey foam from a sea of tissue, the silver fox fur. On a hanger was the second-hand wedding dress and veil. Gertie gazed at these disparagingly.

'It's old-fashioned.'

'Gertie!' The dress represented earnings she could ill afford. 'Anyway, "something borrowed" ...'

'It's not borrowed, only the veil. We bought it second-hand.

50

If Mother knew I was to be married in a second-hand wedding dress she'd turn in her grave.'

'What else could we have done?' demanded Rose.

'I'm sorry. I was remembering all the beautiful things she said I should have.'

'Mother was a romantic,' Rose said curtly. 'I doubt if Father's income could have supported much more of her extravagance. The solicitor was surprised there was so little left, remember.' But Gertie didn't want to be reminded of unpleasant things.

'Pearls,' she sighed. 'Mother insisted no bride should be without a single strand of pearls.'

'You might suggest it to Harold for a present. I should leave it for a while, as he's been kind enough to arrange the wedding.' Gertie was gazing at her engagement ring. 'It's very charming,' Rose said encouragingly.

'It's half the size of the one that belonged to his first wife. And it's a ruby. I told Harold I'd prefer an emerald. Red doesn't suit me.' The chip was so tiny, Rose thought it scarcely mattered.

'How long will you be away, have you decided?' The honeymoon was to be spent at Redcar.

'Until Wednesday. I still don't know where we'll be staying.'

'Harold obviously wants it to be a surprise. Has it been decided where you'll live?' The happy couple had been viewing furnished properties. 'You won't forget we're due to vacate these rooms by Saturday.'

Gertie said unhappily, 'I told Harold which house I preferred. He kept repeating the amount of rent as if *I* would be the one to be paying it.'

Unease resurfaced in Rose. 'You did make it plain, Gertie? You didn't leave him under any illusion this time?'

Her sister was emphatic. 'I said all you and I could afford was to live in Fleetham Street. Then I asked which of the houses *he* preferred and he replied again that it was up to me. You know, Rose, there are times when I don't think Harold listens to a word I'm saying.'

51

*

The bridegroom was in sombre mood. Another skirmish had left him badly shaken. On his way home after buying his reluctant best man a celebratory drink, he'd turned the corner and bumped into Ruby Winnot.

'Sprig of heather for your buttonhole?'

'What the devil ...!'

She tilted her head provocatively. 'It's for luck, Harold. I reckon you're going to need some of that.'

Lamplight gave her skin a bluish pallor but couldn't detract from her kittenish allure. Beneath the cape, he could see her thickening body.

'Why do you and your brothers keep pestering me? I've given my word, I'll not renege.'

She slipped the sprig into his buttonhole. 'This is a reminder, seeing as you're getting married tomorrow and need to plan your housekeeping, you and your good lady.'

'Get away from me!'

'Five bob a week, to begin with. Soon as it's born one of my brothers will be round. Friday nights. Don't try and make some excuse or Alf might be tempted to tell your wife. Either that or we'll bring the bairn to show her.'

'You wouldn't dare!'

'Don't be stupid.' The kitten had become a cat, spitting her contempt. 'It's your fault, I warned you to be careful. How am I supposed to support myself with a kid hanging about? You'll pay up because your new wife can afford it – you've been telling people what a good marriage you're making. Well, fair's fair, Harold Brigg. Just be thankful I didn't ruin everything by suing you for breach of promise.'

'Oh, my God ...' She walked away, leaving him stranded.

In the privacy of his room, Harold brooded. On the bed lay his suitcase packed with his worldly possessions. His trousers were beneath the mattress, his jacket on the back of the chair. Clad only in his nether-garments, with his coat over his knees, he tried to calculate a way out of his dilemma.

Five shillings out of a weekly wage of £3 6s 6d, left him with

52

inadequate funds for saving towards his great purpose in life, the secret ambition he'd been cherishing. Soon, very soon indeed perhaps, his name would go forward for admission to The Brotherhood!

Of those furnished houses he and Gertrude had been viewing, the least expensive cost twenty-five shillings per week. She'd already dropped hints they should engage a maid – say, 7/6d, maybe even eight shillings, as wages had risen since the war. Well, Gertrude must pay for the maid but as for food, he would have to contribute towards that. He doubted whether his new wife would prove to be economical – if only Rose would agree to live with them. She could curb Gertie's excesses and do away with the need for a maid. Not only that, life would be so much more *agreeable* if she were there.

As Rose insisted on moving in with the widow, Gertie would be able to go shopping unchecked. Say ten shillings a week to allow for extravagance. As for coal, gas and electricity, a three-bedroomed house could cost a fortune to run; Gertie must certainly contribute towards that.

How much income did she have? He had a nasty suspicion she might not have more than a few thousand invested. It was his own weakness that having boasted of a wealthy bride he had done nothing to eradicate the impression.

Five shillings a week with more demands to come. Between them the Winnots could bleed him dry! When was the child due? Another three months – if only he could escape! On their return from honeymoon, he and Gertrude would have to live economically until he'd worked out a way of paying off the Winnots. It might mean his wife couldn't have any 'at homes' for a while; explanations would be difficult but he'd think of an excuse, he always did.

Hailstones rattled against the window pane; the wind was increasing, too. His second wedding day looked like being as unseasonable as his first.

Chapter Three

Playing the Game, February 1921

It was a blustery, bright morning with air sharp enough to redden noses. Rose moved about quietly on the other side of the partition. Hearing her, Gertie gave up further pretence at sleep. She'd been dozing for ages, wondering, shivering with nervous excitement. Was it really going to be all right? Harold had been so much *nicer* lately, almost fulfilling her hopes; he'd even stopped bothering her about money. But tonight in Redcar, would he remember to be *kind*?

Her feelings were a mixture of bewilderment and fear; The Day had finally arrived. In the end it had crept up surreptitiously and taken her by surprise. Did she really want to get married? Shocked by that thought, she sat bolt upright.

Thin spring sunlight shone on the second-hand wedding dress, but Gertie was too worried to notice. For years her mother's ambition had been to see her daughter as a bride. Now apprehension made Gertie feel sick. According to Mother, each day would be perfect once Gertie was the object of a man's desire. Perhaps she didn't love Harold enough because it hadn't turned out to be like her mother's predictions.

She recalled her first impressions: a pounding of the heart, breathlessness whenever Harold approached. Once or twice she'd nearly swooned, overcome by his stature and manliness. The trouble was, that had been several months ago and the effect hadn't lasted.

Love had been Mother's favourite topic. She dwelt on it endlessly. The closer two people grew together, the more love

54

flourished, or so she claimed. Gertie recognized that for her, love – if that's what it had been – had dwindled. She wasn't overwhelmed any longer, instead she had began to notice Harold's irritating habits. The way he snorted into his handkerchief for instance. The manner in which he cleared his throat when about to speak, the monotony of his conversation, always on the subject of 'standards' or yet another criticism of Rose.

The last time he'd done that Gertie announced Rose was an independent person and could choose what she said or did. Thank goodness she would not be living with them, considering how much Harold disapproved, Gertie told him. Harold harrumphed and examined the hairs on the back of his hands. That was another irritation, his way of demonstrating displeasure.

'I must try and love him again,' she whispered, frightened. 'It's not impossible, I did once. How can I go ahead and marry him unless I do?'

Rose hadn't helped. 'Being a bride is all very well, Gertie, it's being a *wife* that matters.' It was typical that her sister should make her face the one fact Gertie had been avoiding: she would be Harold's wife for the rest of her life. She might come to enjoy it in time – certainly the security Harold represented would be more than welcome but as for certain other aspects ...?

Gertie was unsure how she was expected to behave on her wedding night. Mother had avoided all discussion of marital bliss. Was she supposed to lie inert and permit Harold to *do things*? That didn't appeal in the least but there was no one to ask. Rose couldn't possibly know and Gertie had no close women friends. She was far too shy to enquire of her fiancé. It wasn't a suitable subject for a *nice* girl to discuss.

There were other questions which worried her. Rose would be living elsewhere so she would have to do all the household shopping and cooking. At Clairville Road, Mother had simply discussed menus with cook, complained if the butcher's bill was too large and grumbled if the picture rails hadn't been

55

dusted. These tasks, Gertie realized unhappily, might now become hers. Not the *cleaning*, of course, Harold wouldn't expect her to do that, but he was adamant about not engaging a cook.

'Are you aware that women's wages have risen?'

'No.'

'Well, they have, to ridiculous levels. A cook is an impossibility unless *you* are willing to pay for both her and the maid.'

She was shocked. 'How could I possibly do that?' But he hadn't enlightened her.

Later, when she'd tried to bring up the subject again, he'd refused to discuss it saying only, 'You must take your share of our joint responsibilities, Gertrude.'

Would he remember to behave like a *gentleman* tonight?

Mother had outlined in vague terms, what was to be expected. 'Provided your Mr Right is a gentleman, you'll never need to worry, my darling.' Gertie had mumbled a question. Mrs Bossom had replied archly, 'That's something my innocent girl doesn't need to be told, not yet,' but added ambiguously, 'sometimes men need to be that extra bit *loving*. We have to be nice about it and that makes them very happy. It's usually a good time to ask for any little extras you might want, afterwards, when they're feeling content.'

Gertie Bossom had no immediate requests with which to bombard Harold; she'd be relieved if the night passed off without complaint.

'Breakfast in bed!' Rose pushed open the door. On her laden tray were the poppy and cornflower cups which Gertie considered vulgar. 'How's the bride this morning?'

'I think I have a cold coming.'

'Oh, Gertie!' Rose was full of concern, 'Would an aspirin help?'

'No, thank you.' The sight of the lace-panelled wedding dress made her mood even more sombre.

'It's no use, Rose, I can't wear it, I've never been happy about it.'

Rose experienced a stab of impatience. Gertie had insisted on a white dress even though they couldn't afford it. They had pored over advertisements until they'd found the right one and she had made endless enquiries to find a dressmaker to do the alterations.

'Gertie, dearest, if I could wave a wand and conjure up a new one, I would. No one will know it's second-hand. It fits you beautifully and you can borrow my woollen chemise to wear underneath, that'll help keep the jitters at bay.'

'I don't think I'm well enough to get up ...' Gertie looked at her imploringly. 'Can you go round and tell Harold?'

Rose stared. 'Tell him – what precisely?'

'I don't think I want to marry him ... at least, I'm not sure ... I don't believe he loves me.' This was terrible. Rose thought quickly: sympathy wasn't much use. She must try and shock Gertie into being sensible.

'Very well.' She whipped away the lovingly prepared tray. 'Up you get. I'll run you a bath. You can go and tell him and I'll let the vicar know. Come on, there's no time to lose ...'

Gertie was agitated.

'I can't possibly go round ... Besides, it's unlucky.'

'Not if you're *not* going to marry him. That is what you've decided, isn't it?'

'You're so hard!' wailed Gertie. 'You're an absolute bully!'

'Please don't cry, dear, it'll make your eyes all red.'

'You see!' Gertie smacked the eiderdown in frustration, 'You're cruel not to try understand how I feel. If only Mother were here ...'

'I wish she were, too. I'm afraid it's beyond me.' Rose said in bewilderment. 'When I tried to dissuade you before, you told me I was mistaken. Now *you* want to call it off. What am I to make of that? I doubt if Mother could have helped any more than I can. Just what *do* you want, Gertie?'

'I want to get married!'

'Yes, well ...' she shrugged, 'that could be difficult if you no longer care for Harold.'

'Does he care for me, that's the real question?' Gertie

57

leaned forward. 'You don't like him, do you? You've never liked him.'

'Gertie, I'm not about to marry him. You told me you loved Harold enough to want to spend the rest of your life with him.'

'I never said that,' she muttered sulkily.

'But that's what it means, becoming someone's wife. It's not just for the day. Now, come along. You must decide, and quickly.' Rose picked up the despised tray. 'And you must have something to eat. Shall I leave you tea and a piece of toast?'

'Not in one of those beastly cups.'

Wisely, Rose held her tongue and disappeared. Moments later the bed creaked and Gertie emerged, clutching her wrapper.

'I suppose I might as well have my bath.'

'I've put out the last of the crystals, help yourself.'

The geyser exploded into life. Behind the screen, water gushed. 'Thank heaven I shall never have to sit in this horrid cracked bathtub again.'

Does that mean she actually intends to marry him? Rose wondered in amazement. I think it must. She would have been appalled to learn the reason: Gertie finally decided to go ahead because of the shame over what the neighbours might say if she withdrew.

About the time his fiancée was having doubts, Harold awoke and remembered in a panic those things he'd left undone which he ought to have done. He dressed extremely quickly.

Rash promises had been made during his period of gallant appeasement when Gertie had confessed her ignorance of wedding procedure. What arrangements had to be made before man and woman could be joined together? Harold became authoritative. Assuring her he would take care of everything, he'd booked the church and the vicar and forgotten everything else. With fewer than three hours left there was much to accomplish.

His landlady had planned a leisurely farewell breakfast.

This was abandoned and she was pressed into service. He'd forgotten to order the flowers. Gertie had chattered on and on about the composition of her bouquet but he hadn't bothered to listen.

'Her wedding flowers? Oh, Mr Brigg!'

'Just an attractive bunch of whatever you think suitable, Mrs Benson. Plus a nosegay for Rose – oh, and photographs. Can you think of anyone who would take a few snapshots? As for luncheon, perhaps your neighbour's child could nip down to The Clifton and book a table, what d'you think?'

'For your wedding breakfast?' The Clifton was an hotel near the station where commercial gentlemen stayed. Indignation reduced her to a squawk. '*I* wouldn't want to be taken there.'

'All right, all right. Where then?'

'I don't know ...' It was Saturday, the town would be full. 'You'll be wanting somewhere special.'

'Not too ...' Harold caught sight of her face. 'That is, it should be *quiet*. Refined, and quiet. Yes, that is what we would prefer.'

'It's such short notice. Maybe they could take a booking at The Star and Garter?' It was expensive. 'Or the King's Head.' Even more so. Harold pretended to consider.

'I wonder which would be best?' His landlady grew impatient.

'You could always take her and Miss Rose to the Winter Gardens. It only costs a penny to get in and they do a nice bath bun.' That settled it.

'The Star and Garter.' They would have the set menu.

'What about a taxicab?'

'I shall walk, Mrs Benson. A fine morning like this? Shanks's pony—'

'Not *you*. Her. You don't expect Miss Bossom to traipse through the streets in her veil, do you?'

So many things to organize! At his first wedding, his wife's family had taken charge; all Harold had had to do was turn up at the church, which was why he'd assured Gertie there was nothing to it.

59

'Who's giving Miss Bossom away?'

'Er, Mr Robinson, one of the churchwardens. He knew the late Mr Bossom, apparently.'

His landlady folded her arms across her bosom. 'That's settles it. Your fiancée can't arrive at St Hilda's in anything less than a proper motorcar with a chauffeur. I'll send Eric to Crooks in Zetland Road. And I'll do what I can about a bouquet.'

The suggestion that a small spray would be sufficient was stillborn. Harold faced up to inevitability: he would have to visit the bank.

After her bath, Gertie appeared resigned. She made no demur as Rose offered to help her dress and sat impassive while her sister wielded the curling tongs. Today, Rose insisted the mass of fine mousy hair would not have a centre parting and be brushed straight back, it would be crimped and softly waved. When this was done, the Juliet cap was pinned in place and Rose began to adjust the veil.

She didn't dare ask what Gertie had decided, she simply carried on as if nothing had been said. When it was finished she surveyed her handiwork.

'There, what do you think?'

They stood in front of the full-length mirror. Rose, in her old blue crêpe-de-chine teagown, now with a small cape in honour of the day. Gertie, frail and very pale, the lace 'handkerchief' skirt panels drooping from slender hips, revealing flesh-coloured silk stockings.

'I look ill.'

'You look very sweet and not the least bit ill,' Rose said quickly. She searched the dressing-table drawer. 'Here, this'll help. Shall I do it?' Rouge was applied gently then a dab of powder. 'Is that better?'

Gertie considered her image dispassionately. 'It's the lace. It's so dull and thick, it isn't becoming to my skin. Mother said years ago I should wear slipper satin.'

It was true, the fabric didn't enhance Gertie's delicate

features. Rose had urged her to choose a dress in a pastel shade but Gertie had refused; now there was nothing they could do.

'I think I hear the bell. It could be your bouquet.'

They waited, listening to the murmurs downstairs.

'Providing it's large enough, it'll help conceal the worst of the dress.' Gertie indicated where the bodice hung slackly over her childlike bosom and dipped below her waist. Anticipation cheered her a little. 'I told Harold exactly what I wanted; creamy roses mixed with lily of the valley, with a trail of ivy entwined with orange blossom. If it's pretty enough, people will notice the flowers, not my dress.' As it was February, Rose thought there might be modifications to the order; neither was prepared for the landlady's choice.

'Narcissi! With – freesias!'

There had been freesias at both their parents' funerals. For Gertie and Rose the sweet, sickly perfume would always be associated with death.

'And this is for you, miss.' Rose accepted the small corsage silently, numbed by Gertie's disappointment.

'Harold wasn't to know about the wreaths . . .' she faltered but Gertie's tragic face galvanized her. 'Queenie, there's obviously been a mistake. D'you think you could run to the florists for us . . .' The doorbell rang once more.

'I'll have to answer that first, miss.' As Queenie went downstairs, Gertie pointed with a trembling finger at the clock.

'There isn't *time* to buy more flowers. And I told him exactly what I wanted. That's Mr Robinson arriving. I can hear his voice,' her voice was choked with disappointment. Rose straightened her shoulders and took charge.

'Don't be upset, dear. What I suggest we do about the flowers is this . . .'

St Hilda's could accommodate nine hundred souls. Gertie Bossom advanced up its empty vastness on Mr Robinson's arm. An anxious Rose followed. There was no music; Harold hadn't thought to book the organist. A thousand miles away, or so it seemed, a few friends from Clairville Road plus one or two acquaintances of their parents occupied the front rows of pews. On the right, stood the groom; beside him, the best man. He was Harold's head of department but Rose had already forgotten his name despite being reminded many times, and of the deference due to him.

Drat the man and damn Harold! She didn't normally swear, especially in church, but those narcissi had been the last straw: irrefutable evidence of Harold's indifference. Concern for Gertie consumed her so that she never even noticed Ned Harrison in a side pew.

Watching her sister so intently, Rose wasn't following the service. She reacted with a start as Gertie handed her the prayer book with the corsage pinned to it. There was a flicker of a smile between them as they both remembered the narcissi now adorning the shop in Fleetham Street.

In his pew, Ned wondered what he ought to do. The conversation with the neighbour who worked at the rolling mill had been revealing. Despite the late hour, Ned had debated whether to send a note. In the end he decided against it. It was too late now to interfere, the vicar was pronouncing the couple man and wife. From where he stood, Rose's expression seemed full of sadness.

The wedding group disappeared into the vestry, the silence became oppressive. There was a whispered consultation. A member of the congregation rose and lifted the lid of the harmonium. Schumann's 'Träumerei' flowed over them. It was an improvement. Up to now, in Ned's opinion, a stranger might think he'd stumbled in on a funeral.

Rose signed the register and gave silent thanks for Gertie's calmness. From the moment Mr Robinson had arrived in Fleetham Street there had been an end to hysterics.

Harold screwed the cap back on the pen and offered his arm to Gertie. The best man did the same to Rose, saying, 'I can hear music. Has someone stepped into the breach, Brigg?'

Pent-up anger exploded in Rose. Despite good intentions, she said loudly, 'Harold obviously forgot the organist. Poor Gertie's bouquet wasn't right, either. Thank goodness there was no mistake over the ring.'

She was a charming-looking girl, this must be some kind of joke. The best man laughed and laughed. It bounced infectiously among the empty choir stalls. In the front pews, people reminded one another this was a happy occasion and what a pity Mr and Mrs Bossom weren't here to see it.

Gertie could feel the tension beneath Harold's sleeve. He obviously believed the laughter was directed at him. Sympathy welled up. She guessed it wasn't easy to organize a wedding. Harold had probably done his best, she wanted to show her appreciation. She squeezed his arm. 'Never mind,' she whispered. 'It doesn't matter about the freesias.' Harold didn't know what she was talking about.

They processed down the aisle. A breeze filled the porch, sending Gertie's veil skywards.

Rose asked, 'Is there to be a photographer, Harold?'

The mumbled reply was followed by the best man's, 'Pity you didn't ask me, old man. I could have brought my Zeiss. I say, has anyone here got a camera? The photographer hasn't been booked.' Rose swallowed more anger.

The congregation crowded round them anxious to shake hands with the happy couple. Rose watched anxiously. It hadn't been much of a wedding, it must be an effort for Gertie not to let her feelings show. The large black car drew up and someone flung rice. It was enough to make Harold urge his bride forward. Rose and the best man followed. All those years, listening to Mother describe the glories of a wedding day. What a fiasco!

The sight of starched tablecloths, of waiters keen to be of service, helped restore the new Mrs Brigg's shattered confidence. She still wasn't sure whether or not she loved Harold; it was impossible now to analyse her feelings. Perhaps in time, love would develop; if not she would have to do without. Until she had a child, of course. A child would gaze with innocent eyes and say, 'I love you, Mummy,' and Gertie would reach into her own bottomless well of affection and smother him.

Harold shot his cuffs and seized the menu. 'What d'you say? Shall we stick to the table d'hôte and not worry about the rest?'

One of the waiters, too attentive by half, hovered at the bride's elbow. 'Wine for you, madam?'

Dreaming of the child, she smiled radiantly, 'Do you have champagne?'

'Oh, I don't think—' but Harold was overruled.

'Bravo!' cried the best man, 'that's the spirit.'

Harold capitulated reluctantly. 'If you think so, certainly, certainly. Er, have you any half-bottles?' He was out of luck. Not only that, Rose declared she was thirsty and didn't want a glass of water, not today.

When the champagne arrived, the best man gave a toast.

'To the happy couple, and to you, Miss Rose. The prettiest bridesmaid in Middlesbrough. I say, what about a spot of dancing?'

'Dancing?'

'What say we toddle out to Ormsby Bungalow and shake a leg?'

'Oh, I don't think, do you, Gertrude?' Harold was already consulting his watch. 'We have a train to catch.'

'There's bound to be another.' The best man wasn't to be denied the chance to cuddle Rose. 'We can dance for a bit and get you back in time for a later one.' Which meant, as Harold quickly calculated, retaining the car and chauffeur for the rest of the day.

'I hardly think ... do you, Gertrude?' She failed in her first duty as a married woman.

'I'd love to dance with you, Harold.'

They ordered à la carte. Harold extolled the virtues of plaice and potatoes but neither wife nor sister-in-law wanted fish and chips. 'Not today, thank you, Harold.'

Rose kept her expression pleasant and detached the hand

that groped beneath the table for her garter. The best man certainly wasn't a gentleman. But then, neither was Harold.

She surprised herself by thinking that. Did it matter nowadays? It had been their mother's constant cry. 'A perfect gentleman, such lovely manners ...' She remembered a long-ago conversation between mother and Gertie.

'Provided Mr Right is a gentleman ...'

'Yes, Mother.'

'You'll never need to worry.'

'No, Mother.'

And Rose had thought at the time what tommy-rot it all sounded. But wasn't it now the reason she found Harold repulsive? Oh my Lord, what a hypocrite I am, she sighed.

The best man's sweaty hand was once more nearing her thigh. Rose fixed him with an enigmatic eye. 'I think not ... if you don't mind.' Her tone was icy.

He flushed. 'Don't know what you mean,' but the errant member remained where Rose could see it for the rest of the meal. Definitely not a gentleman – there was no other way to describe it.

The meal over, they gave their destination to the chauffeur.

'The Ormsby Bungalow? That's only open on Wednesday afternoons, sir.'

Harold tried to sound sincere. 'Better luck next time, old man.'

The best man was insistent, 'There must be a *Thé Dansant* somewhere?'

'It's too early in the year, sir. There are one or two theatre matinees, though.'

Harold consulted his bride. 'Does a visit to the theatre interest you, my dear?'

'No, thank you.' Gertie had no intention of exhibiting herself in the hated lace dress.

'Well, that settles it. Back to change our togs, then Redcar.'

The best man leered, 'Redcar, playground of the North-East.'

*

65

In Fleetham Street, the new costume gave Gertie confidence and the pretty blouse flattered her complexion. Rose had eclipsed her in church. Now Rose was back in her working clothes and by contrast Gertie looked elegant. The dusky-pink felt hat was tipped saucily over an eyebrow. Deep, soft grey fur encircling her shoulders made an ideal frame for her dainty face. Mother's best suede bag and gloves completed the ensemble. Without a smidgen of jealousy, Rose said happily, 'You look wonderful.'

'I feel better. The lace was a mistake.' Silently, Rose agreed.

'Never mind, that outfit suits you perfectly. Let's go and dazzle the chaps.'

'Rose ...'

'Yes, dear?'

Gertie was tweaking a suede glove. 'Whatever Mr Simmonds suggests, you will be careful?' Mr Simmonds was the best man. 'In the restaurant, he and Harold were discussing ...' she reddened. 'I was rather surprised. Harold seemed to think ...'

'What?'

'Oh, never mind.' Rose could look after herself. 'But remember Harold's prospects, won't you.'

'I don't understand?'

'He *is* Harold's head of department.'

Rose's brow cleared; she knew there must be a reason such an obnoxious person had been given the honour of being best man.

Gertie's appearance impressed her bridegroom. The best man began to smile excessively at Rose. They trooped downstairs and entered the limosine for the last time. On the station platform, the sisters clung to one another.

'Oh, Rose ... d'you realize this is the first occasion we've been parted?'

'Redcar's scarcely the end of the world, dearest!'

'I shall send you a postcard.' Rose saw Harold advancing to claim a farewell kiss. She couldn't bear the thought.

'All aboard,' she said hastily. 'In you get, Gertie. Help her up the step, Harold.' He allowed himself to be hustled on to the train.

Gertie leaned out of the window. 'Rose ...'

'Yes?' The guard was blowing his whistle, she strained to hear.

'It won't make any difference, my being married.' Gertie was flushed, 'We will still look after one another?'

'Yes ... of course.' Gertie looked relived, Rose was baffled. They waved to one another until the train disappeared from view. The best man attempted to whisper in her ear.

'I beg your pardon?'

'I asked where shall you and I have our spot of dinner, Miss Rose? There's a charming little restaurant out Marten way.'

She became excessively polite. 'How kind, but I'm afraid I can't accept your invitation.'

His expression hardened. 'Don't play the coy maiden with me. Brigg assured me I could count on your company this evening.'

Had he indeed? Was that what Gertie had been hinting? Had Rose been dangled as bait in exchange for the services of a best man? Despite her indignation Rose behaved charmingly; never let it be said *she* had prejudiced Harold's prospects.

'I fear Harold is not entitled to make promises on my behalf. Also he must have forgotten my promise to my employer – I have to be back at work this afternoon and I'm late already. *So* sorry, Mr Simmonds.' Ignoring his protests, feeling shaken, she hurried away to catch her tram.

If only Cecil were alive to protect her, she thought, brimming with anger, then, quickly recovering her sense of humour, wondered: would he have challenged the dreadful Simmonds to a duel? Water pistols at dawn perhaps? But how could Harold suggest such a thing! 'Oh, I do hope he makes Gertie happy!'

The tea room closed late on a Saturday. It was nearly eight o'clock when Rose arrived back at Fleetham Stret. There was an envelope on the mat. Inside was Ned's note.

Dear Miss Rose,

I trust you will not find this letter an impertinence.

Yesterday I happened to meet a neighbour who works at Hill's. Mr Harold Brigg works there as a progress clerk. That is, he chases orders for customers. He is one of six similarly employed in the Sales department. I understand it is considered responsible work.

Yours faithfully,
Ned Harrison.

Ned had omitted his neighbour's opinion, that Harold Brigg was much disliked.

''E's an arrogant bastard an' a snob. Sucks up to the bosses, promises everything the day before yesterday, then bawls them out in the mill if they can't keep up. Friend of yours, is he?'

'Someone wanted to know about him.'

'I'll tell you this for nowt, Brigg is unpopular. 'E needs to watch 'is step.'

Ned's note lay on the table. How could she break this news to Gertie: '... a progress clerk, one of six.' By no stretch of the imagination an under-manager.

'She would marry him ...' she whispered. Did it matter if he had an ordinary job so long as he and Gertie loved one another? It could still be a good marriage, Rose told herself valiantly.

All the same, it wasn't playing the game.

And if Harold had told fibs, so had her sister. Her thoughts see-sawed: if he and Gertie were happy, none of it would matter. But was that likely on a basis of lies? The kettle began to sing. She reached for the teapot. She couldn't tell Gertie to her face; she'd follow Ned's example and write.

If Harold hadn't warned her they were booked into an hotel, Gertie would have described the place as a boarding house. It was in a side street, not on the front; a natural precaution according to her husband. Whenever the wind blew, sand penetrated every nook and cranny of those rooms with an uninterrupted view of the North Sea, whereas here ...

The building was three-storied, of dull red brick. If anything, the wind was stronger here, channelled between the rows of houses. Gertie hurried up the steps into the small, dark hall.

Their room was, as the proprietor promised, quiet because it was at the back and faced a wall. 'We could have one overlooking the street,' Harold told her, 'for half a crown extra.'

Gertie knew what she was expected to say, but inside, something rebelled. 'I'd prefer to be nearer the bathroom.'

'Ah, yes ...' He hesitated. 'It will mean speaking to the land ... er – the manageress.' Of course it would, it would mean asking for another room. 'I don't know whether this is a good time to disturb her.' Good heavens, was he nervous of the woman?

'Shall I do it?'

'No, no. Unless you'd like to accompany me ...?'

'No, thank you. I'll wait. Oh, and Harold ...'

'Yes?'

'A room with a fire, please. It's such a cold time of year.'

'I'll see what I can do.'

He paid the extra half-crown.

They would eat out in celebration of their wedding day. Along the front they battled through an equinoctial gale. Behind plate glass and velvet curtains there was warmth and comfort. Gertie burrowed deep into the silver fox while Harold wondered aloud which restaurant they should patronize. Eventually she could stand it no longer and made a dash for a doorway. 'This one looks nice, let's eat here.'

To his dismay, he saw she was already inside. Tomorrow he would indicate firmly that a wife's first duty was to abide by her husband's judgement.

There was a blazing fire. Gertie spread her fingers to the

warmth. 'I'm so cold, may I have a brandy?' He reminded himself it was wedding nerves and ordered two glasses.

They dined. Outside, breakers crashed over the sea wall. Gertie flatly refused to walk back. Finally, he ordered a cab. Back in their room, he watched glumly as she fed the gas meter with pennies.

'There's no need ... we're only here til Wednesday.' Gertie ignored him. 'I said—'

'Harold, it's so bitterly cold.' He reminded himself he must be patient.

'Would you prefer that I retire while you – disrobe?'

'Yes, please.'

Harold wandered along empty landings and staircases. His first honeymoon had been at a luxurious establishment in Bournemouth (paid for by his wife), and Agnes, being ten years older, had been grateful and compliant. This time promised to be different.

When he returned, the gas fire was still full on and Gertie was in bed. As he went to turn it off, she said, 'Leave it, please.'

'Pardon?'

'This bed feels damp.'

'This hotel was recommended. Simmonds and his wife stayed here.'

'I don't value his opinion. Did you see the way he behaved toward Rose – and now you tell me he's married!'

'Gertrude, he is my head of department—'

'So you've said, many times.' It popped out before she could stop herself; the clammy sheets were making her short-tempered.

In injured silence, Harold proceeded to remove jacket, waistcoat, trousers, tie, shirt, socks and shoes. Clad only in his union suit, the all-in-one garment with sleeves which covered him from neck to ankle, he began to search for his pyjamas.

By the light of the fire, Gertie pretended not to look. She'd never seen her father or Cecil other than fully dressed or in their dressing-gowns. Soiled garments went in the laundry basket and were dealt with by the maid or Nanny Dawson. What men wore beneath their clothes came as a complete revelation.

As Harold bent to search in his suitcase, she saw the two-buttoned flap which gave access to his behind. And at the front ...? Gertie screwed her eyes tightly shut.

Harold scratched his stomach absent-mindedly. 'I could've sworn I packed them.' He hadn't. He remembered in the haste of last minute arrangements, he'd left them folded on his pillow. 'Blast!'

'Harold!'

'I beg your pardon, my dear. I shall have to remain as I am.' The bed lurched. His body shuddered as he came into contact with the sheets.

Beside him a small voice said, 'I did warn you it was damp.'

'Yes, yes.' Did she have to keep harping on it!

'Could we have a hot-water bottle tomorrow?'

He attempted a little joke. 'If you feel it's necessary?'

Gertie didn't even smile. 'Yes.'

'Gertrude, would you like to remove your nightgown?'

'No!' He reminded himself she was younger than Agnes and far less experienced than Ruby Winnot. If only she *were* Ruby – he clenched his fists against wicked thoughts.

'Harrumph! Gertrude ...'

'Yes?'

'Did your late mother ever describe to you – The Act?'

'What act, Harold?'

'Between men and women, dearest. Once they were married. The sacred act – of love.'

'No.'

'Ah ... Then I will explain.' She wasn't much wiser when he'd finished, being distracted by hands which searched beneath her nightgown for parts of her body, hitherto alto-gether private. Hands covered in hair, she remembered.

'Aah!'

'What's the matter?'

'You're so cold!' It was tiresome but he blew and rubbed

71

them together with great vigour.

'How's that?'

'Better.' Harold had omitted to explain the purpose of these exploratory moves and Gertie held herself tight as a bowstring.

After a moment or two, he asked again, 'Would you like to remove your nightgown now?'

'I don't think so, thank you.'

'Perhaps if I turned that fire off ...' Darkness was always a help. 'You will find the ambient temperature quite comfortable—'

'No, Harold. Leave it on.' She'd no intention of being in the dark with him.

Harold breathed deeply. 'I will, nevertheless, divest myself ...' The bed heaved, the eiderdown slithered away as Harold stood and unbuttoned the back flap and wriggled out of his jaegar carapace. She peeped. To her horror she saw that hair was thickly matted on both his chest and back. Eyes closed, she clung to the blankets as he climbed back into bed. 'There, that's better. Come over to my side, my dear.' She slid an inch or two towards the middle. Harold enveloped her in a hirsute embrace.

I loved him once, Gertie told herself in a panic, and I will again. I must!

'Dear little Gertrude, light of my life ... Let big bear make you happy.'

Should she tell him she had no inheritance? Now, before it was too late?

'Harold—'

'Hush!'

He pushed himself inside her and she, tense, fought to prevent it. It hurt so much, Gertie screamed.

'Be quiet, woman! D'you want everyone to hear?' She didn't care, she had to get away from him but Harold bore down, faster and faster, smothering her with his need. She was crying, struggling, begging him to stop but he took no notice. Finally, with a groan he collapsed and rolled over to his side of the bed.

She was wet between her legs. Surely it wasn't the time of the month? It couldn't be – Harold must have torn her flesh. Something had obviously ruptured inside when Harold had ... and why had he been so hateful, forcing himself on her even though she implored him to stop; that was surely *not* how gentlemen behaved? How embarrassing to have to wash the sheets in the morning! How awful for him to see the stain ... A snore interrupted Gertie's agony. Her lover was asleep.

Rose watched the moon whiten the curtains and window pane. She'd had several attempts at a letter but it could wait; it would have to because until the promised postcard arrived she didn't know the honeymoon address. There was no urgency with this unhappy news.

Perhaps Gertie wouldn't care that Harold was only a clerk? But Rose recalled how she had boasted to their friends at church. There was no avoiding it, Gertie would be humiliated.

Her mind wandered over the events of the day ... the appalling Mr Simmonds. ... What a wedding! 'If I ever marry, I hope it won't be like that!' It occurred to her, reluctantly, that Gertie and Harold were two of a kind and neither had played the game. Then she remembered Gertie's face as she leaned out of the carriage, the anxiety.

'I can't be hard on her, or desert her. She obviously doesn't believe Harold will prove *reliable.*' Rose shifted, uncomfortably. If only Gertie had been less determined to find Mr Right, none of this would have happened. '*I* shan't,' Rose yawned. 'I'd rather be a spinster than end up with a Harold Brigg.'

Gertie lay awake. That was it, then, The Act. It was over but where, oh where was the romance? All those years listening to Mother's rapture about ecstacy – Gertie hadn't experienced any such thing.

She'd done her duty. Even though it had hurt so much, she'd lain as still as she could while Harold performed. Afterwards, when he asked if she was all right, she'd said yes. What other reply was possible? He'd complained she was making too much of a fuss.

That dreadful sensation as he pushed his way into her body! Gertie felt her gorge tighten, was she going to be sick? The way he'd licked her breasts and poked inside down below with his fingers ... Her whole body felt dirty! She pulled down her nightdress, wrapping it tightly round her feet like a shroud. That was what was so awful about The Act, having to permit Harold access to her body. Perhaps it would have been better in the dark, then she wouldn't have had his face looming over her. Tense, wide awake, she listened as he came to with a snort.

'You awake?'

'Yes, Harold.'

'Turn off the gas, would you.' She slipped out of bed and back again, keeping well over to her side.

'Goodnight, Gertrude.'

'Goodnight.'

Should she say her prayers? Was there any point in asking God to help her love her husband? Tears fell unchecked. She tried to think of something to alleviate her wretchedness. Harold had sworn to endow her with all his worldly goods so at least her future was secure. That must have been what Mother meant: one had to put up with the rest of it in order to obtain security. Another thought cheered her. They'd performed The Act long enough to make a baby so he wouldn't need to trouble her again for ages.

Why hadn't she thought of that before? 'We might decide not to have a second child.' Now that she must be pregnant with the first, there would be no further demands. Oh, the relief!

Moonlight silvered the soft grey of her fur on the arm of the chair. Compared to everything else that had happened it was a great comfort to own it and know that no one could take it from her. Calm at last, Gertie slept.

Chapter Four

Revelations

The following morning, Harold Brigg concluded he had to make the best of a bad job. Such a situation was not unknown; by his standards yesterday had not gone too badly. He felt the same sense of relief as he did when deliveries went awry at the rolling mill and he escaped criticism.

He was not a man of intellectual resource, he veered between melancholy and optimism. His ambition was simple: to climb the social ladder. He had promised his mother he would in that mean street where he'd been born. He would have made the same vow to his father had the man stayed to be told.

Harold was unable to recognize that deficiencies in his own character had been his principal impediment. He'd been lazy at school. If his examination results were poor, why then, the teachers were to blame. He was a natural bully, which made him unpopular with his contemporaries but he didn't care. His chief – his *only* concern – were those who he believed might influence his future prospects; he was, in consequence, ever eager to impress.

The servile attitude became more transparent as he grew to manhood. It was the reason he advanced so slowly at the rolling mill, from mailing room boy to progress clerk where he had remained, consistently passed over in favour of younger men. Harold was mystified. He had a suspicion too, that people poked fun at him behind his back; he couldn't understand it and resorted to his old habit of hectoring subordinates, which left him friendless. Once again, he didn't particularly care. It was the managers and the Brethren whose approbation he sought.

He had not been tempted to seek a mate until his middle twenties. His doting mother had been extremely protective. At home, after his father had disappeared, there was unstinting warmth, love and admiration. Mrs Brigg had devoted herself to her large, ungainly son. There was little money, she had had to go out cleaning but this wasn't mentioned. If pressed, Harold would describe his mother as having been 'a companion'.

Big Wesley had been Harold's outlet, not from religious conviction but because it offered treats and picnics. Later, following his mother's death, it had also provided him with Agnes.

He'd felt affronted when she and her property were taken from him; it was a serious social set-back. Following his loud complaints over the injustice of the trust, a coolness developed among the congregation. Harold saw the light; he must transfer his allegiance to a more advantageous and fashionable God, at St Hilda's.

His most deeply held conviction was the need to enter the Brotherhood. Those bonds written in blood, promising life-long fellowship and support! Once he was an entered apprentice on the greatest social ladder of all that would be a glorious achievement!

Harold reviewed the events of yesterday. In his opinion, those last-minute efforts had succeeded, the wedding had passed off without complaint. He was angry that Rose should be so sarcastic about the bouquet, what was wrong with a bunch of narcissi? He wondered uneasily how she had behaved in the evening, he couldn't afford to have Simmonds upset. Simmonds would have given her a good time, he told himself, drowning his conscience. No doubt she enjoyed herself dancing. Yesterday was past and apart from Gertrude's frigidity, it had been a complete successs.

He brooded as to why Gertrude had proved so uncoopera-

76

tive in bed. Agnes hadn't been particularly exciting either. Neither behaved like Ruby, with her it was always a delicious frolic. Why couldn't Gertrude be the same?

He cast an eye over his sleeping spouse: what an odd creature, curled up in a ball, arms wrapped around her chest. She must arise and inhale the life-giving sea breezes. If it stayed fine, they might be able to walk as far as Marske this morning. His affectionate whisper thundered in her ear, 'Up you get, bunnykins!'

'Aah!' Terrified, Gertie fended off the fuzzy monster.

'Don't do that, Gertrude. It is I, Harold.'

'Oh, yes ...' Trembling hands found her spectacles and put them on. 'I was fast asleep ...'

'It is seven o'clock. High time we were up and dressed.'

'Is it?' Gertie showed an extreme reluctance to stir.

Harold flung back the bedclothes and strode to the window, the flap of his union suit dangling like a lamb's tail.

'Look here,' he yanked the curtains apart, 'see what a fine day it is.' Salt spray caked on the outside of the glass sparkled in brilliant winter sunlight. He breathed in and out and thumped his chest. 'Will you go through the bathroom first or shall I?'

There was a mumble from beneath the bedclothes.

'You won't fall asleep again, will you, Gertrude? We don't want to miss our cooked breakfast. Hours are strict here, I recall Simmonds mentioning it.'

He stepped into his trousers, heaved up his braces, found his shaving kit and came to nuzzle Gertie's cheek.

'Why doesn't my sweet little bunnykins try and find her bear a cup of tea, hmm?' His beard scratched her skin. 'Big bear is thirsty, precious.'

There was a warning note. Gertie struggled upright. 'Did you remember to order any?'

'Well, no ... But there's no harm in you nipping into the kitchen. Who knows, our land – manageress might have another cuppa to spare in her pot.'

'Harold ...' She adjusted her glasses and stared severely.

'One doesn't "nip" into a hotel kitchen, it just isn't done. If you want tea – and I would like some, too – one of us must order it.'

But that meant an extra sixpence on the bill.

'See what you can manage, precious. Big bear won't be long.'

His large feet flapped along the passage. Gertie nipped out of bed, examined the sheets and turned on the gasfire. There were only a few drops of blood, thank goodness. Back under the eiderdown, she began to sort out her thoughts.

She was married and must learn to bear her cross. She didn't mind being kissed but surely it wasn't necessary for Harold to behave so *boisterously* in bed? His feet were sweaty, he'd been quite smelly at the finish. As for all that nonsense about being a bear, it was sheer embarrassment. Grown men shouldn't behave childishly.

She would have to have a word, be gentle but firm and explain how much *nicer* it would be if ever he needed to perform The Act again, to behave as a gentleman and not act the fool.

There were more urgent problems to be dealt with, however. They had to decide where they were to live. Their departure from Fleetham Street couldn't be delayed – she must begin to pack the minute they returned – but they had to settle which rented property was to be their new 'abode'.

The room was a little warmer now. Reluctantly she pushed back the blankets. The bed still felt damp. She draped the sheets and elderdown over a chair in front of the fire. There was probably another bathroom on the floor above. In her jap silk kimono and slippers, she hurried away up the stairs.

When Harold returned, Gertie was almost dressed. She'd found the chambermaid and a tray of tea and digestive biscuits lay on the bedside table. He was sullen as she filled both cups.

'There was no need to go to any expense.' Gertie recognized a phrase that might become a theme of their married life. She would deal with that too, but not this morning. She offered him the biscuits. He hadn't yet used the pomade and strands of overlong hair dangled over his ear.

'We'd better hurry, Harold. They stop serving breakfast in half an hour.'

His earlier sunny mood had begun to evaporate but Gertie's was improving as they took their places in the dining room. She enjoyed being waited upon – the proprietress addressed her as Mrs Brigg – she had status at last! She gave her husband a demure wifely smile.

Due to the time of year, there were only two other couples; one decrepit pair sharing an ear trumpet and the other, too far gone in matrimony to converse.

Gertie and Harold kept their conversation to a murmur, as was proper. They admired the heavy flocked wallpaper and brown lincrusta, telling one another how tasteful these were. Conversation lapsed. Gertie searched for another topic. There must be so much they could talk about – Heavens, they'd only been married twenty-four hours.

The porridge arrived. Relieved, she picked up her spoon and began, 'We ought to decide where we are to live, Harold. We could write and confirm to the agents this afternoon.'

'Hush!' His finger was on his lips, '*Pas devant les domestiques*, Gertrude.' She looked about, astonished. The proprietress, who also waited at table, had disappeared through the baize door.

'There are no *domestiques*, Harold. She's gone.' Annoyed, he looked pointedly at the other couples. Gertie lowered her voice still further. 'I don't think either of them can hear.'

'It is a private matter,' he reproved. 'We will wait until we have complete privacy, if you please.'

Before making a decision, Harold needed to discover precisely how much Gertrude could afford. Since his first estimate of their outgoings, it had occurred to him – why not make Gertrude responsible for the rent as well as the servants? It would mean a careful scrutiny of her income first. He was looking forward to that. At long last, he would know how he was placed, financially. He attacked his porridge with gusto,

79

humming in between sips of his tea. Another habit Gertie realized she disliked.

If his wife turned out to be wealthier than he had first thought, Harold knew precisely which rented house he preferred. If not, there were several others. Optimism triumphed as usual.

They crunched through eddies of sand blown inland by the gale. Gertie bought her postcard and struggled to keep up with his strides. When a light drizzle began, at his suggestion they headed for a shelter.

He waited as she pencilled a few lines to Rose. They were alone. The tide was receding, showing ribs of bare scarred rock. Far away a man was exercising his dog but here, in the empty shelter, was the privacy Harold required.

'Gertrude, the time has come to be completely frank with me. You've been avoiding my questions for some considerable time but now that we are married ...' He hadn't intended to sound threatening. He tried again, reaching for her hand. 'All I want is for bunnykins to tell her big bear how much money she has.'

Gertie was cornered. Her bag lay on the bench between them. She saw him gazing at it.

'I'm not entirely sure ...' Harold's eyebrows went up. 'Not to a penny, that is. Rose would know. She manages to remember figures wonderfully well.'

'Tell me what you can,' he urged with a smile. What a silly bunnykins it was, what did pennies matter! Gertie fished out the brand new bank book. He examined the front page. 'This account was only opened a couple of days ago ...' He frowned as he looked at the columns because the amount was so insignificant. 'Is this your pocket money, my dear?'

'It's my bank book. Rose and I have one each now. The manager explained I would have to call again and register my new signature,' she explained proudly, 'in my married name.'

'But, Gertrude, there was only one hundred and ninety seven pounds when you opened this account—'

80

'We split the total, half for me, half for Rose—'

'—and you have already withdrawn thirty-one pounds and three shillings?'

'Thirty guineas. For my silver fox.'

'*How much?*' Harold didn't know it was possible to spend that amount on a dead animal.

'It's very good quality,' she assured him. 'I shall probably never need another as long as I live.'

Incredulity made speech difficult. He began the familiar gesture of flapping his hands, waving the bank book at her, 'But ... this cannot be the account to which I refer. This is your own money—'

'Yes,' Gertie said quickly, 'yes, it is. The bank manager said so.'

'— for you to spend – some would say fritter – as you please.'

'Yes.' This scolding wasn't proving as bad as she'd feared although Harold's colour was high.

'Gertrude, I am referring to that other settlement, no doubt invested in government stocks and securities, made by your dear father and mother. Their bequests to you and Rose, following their sad demise.' His voice tightened as a sudden fear enveloped him. 'Perhaps you do not remember the exact figure?' If only his sister-in-law were here with her grasp of financial detail! He tried to be explicit. 'Can you remember in approximate terms what the solicitor told you at the time of reading the wills? If you've forgotten, I can apply to him on our return. Or we might even catch a train and visit him tomorrow?'

Gertie didn't speak at first. She took back her bank book and tucked it inside her bag. It was, after all, her own money.

'That's all there was, Harold. After the bills had been paid, the funerals, the hospital bills and suchlike. Rose saw to that. We knew there wouldn't be much left. The solicitor warned us not to waste it. Rose and I went to the bank the day before yesterday so that the manager could halve what was left plus the interest. That's when he gave us each a new book. It was the only fair way.'

81

Disbelief threatened to choke him. 'All?'

'Yes.'

'It cannot be *all*! What about the property in Clairville Road? The contents – the furniture?' Gertie quailed. Her husband was intimidating when he was angry, she was glad there was no one to hear him shout.

'We rented the villa. I did mention that before, Harold.'

'But the furniture? What is there in store, Gertrude? I demand to know!'

'Not in store, in Fleetham Street.'

'What!' He was on his feet, fists clamped to his sides.

'Our house was rented *furnished*. I'm sure I mentioned that as well. The remaining pieces, the little odds and ends belonging to Mother and Father, we brought with us. I haven't discussed it but I'm sure Rose won't object if we have the small mahogany table. And the dinner wagon, she won't have any need of that. We've already agreed on the dressing-table set and the bone china dinner service.' Gertie's smile, in the face of his obvious anger, was tremulous. 'Aren't you going to ask about my bottom drawer, dearest? I've been wanting to tell you about that.'

Harold sat, clasping his hands tightly and leaned towards her. 'Gertrude – don't play games with me.'

'I'm not.' she was hurt. 'I must say you're behaving very strangely, Harold. I wanted to tell you but whenever I've spoken of my bottom drawer, you've stopped listening. It means a great deal to me.'

'Yes, yes. What does it contain?' Perhaps this was her odd way of referring to securities? He could scarcely bear the suspense.

Gertie sat back happily. 'Well, to begin with, there are at least two dozen traycloths, embroidered in various styles, mostly edged with crochet work and each with a matching apron. I've only kept the best. The others went in various sales of work during the war.

'There's one large linen tablecloth with twelve matching napkins – creamy Irish linen, Harold. Such good quality.

82

With a drawn threadwork motif that took me nearly a year to finish. And there's another smaller damask tablecloth with a rolled hem. As for sheets, Mother always encouraged me to embroider those as well – I've three pair of Egyptian cotton, two of flannelette for winter and some ordinary poplin ones. And masses and masses of pillowcases, some with handmade lace inserts.' Gertrude was truly proud. 'Whatever happens, we'll never be short of pillowcases. I must have nearly three dozen tucked away.'

She waited, confident of approbation. Harold's voice was hoarse.

'What of ... silver? Carpets and curtains ... crystal?'

'I told you, Mother's silver dressing-table set. The furnishings came with the house, we left those behind. I suppose there must be five of the Waterford tumblers – those are crystal, of course. And one or two wine glasses. Rose and I haven't discussed how we're going to divide those ...' His expression wasn't encouraging; her confidence ebbed.

'What else, Gertrude? What are you keeping from me?' When was she going to tell him about war bonds or a deposit account?

'There is nothing more. Nothing at all.' Nervousness was replaced by indignation. 'I don't know why you keep on, Harold. I've given you a complete list – it took me years and years to do the sewing – but you haven't begun to tell me about *your* bits and pieces. You must have something left from your first home?'

He was a man in a trance; the enormity of his position reached his understanding slowly. Truth so cruel could only be faced a little at a time. A few pathetic items of furniture ... no carpets or curtains ... derisory items of silver and glass. And she expected praise for embroidered aprons! The weight of emotion made him stammer.

'I told you from the beginning, Gertrude, I *needed* a wife with a dowry.'

Her hand went to her neck to seek comfort from the fur.

'I have a dowry, Harold. I just showed it to you in my bank

book. It may not be much but it will pay for my clothes. You won't have to make me an allowance for years.' His expression annoyed her now. 'I don't think you realize how practised I am at sewing. I make all my own underwear and blouses.'

How could he begin to make her understand?

'The dressing-table set will have to be sold.'

'No!' Anger made her pink. 'That does not belong to you but to me. Rose agreed I should have it and I don't wish to sell.' It was oppressive being with him in the shelter. 'Harold, I don't wish to continue this discussion. I've answered all your questions, there's nothing more I can tell you and as this rain seems set in for the day, can we now find somewhere for coffee and then return to the hotel?'

He was still in a daze. He walked, unaware of his surroundings. Gertrude took his arm to guide him into the café. There was a fire. She made him sit in the chair nearest to it and ordered hot buttered scones. After a moment or two, he roused himself.

'And Rose ... does she have the same amount?' Had he married the wrong sister after all?

'Oh, no!' Gertrude was smug. '*Her* needlework is shocking. She has practically nothing worth speaking of in her bottom drawer. Apart from one pretty tablecloth worked in daisy chain.'

It took an effort for Harold even to speak. 'Just – daisy chain? Well, well ...'

That same Sunday, Hayden was more agitated than usual. He called out as soon as he saw Ned approaching, 'Come on, come on. Don't waste time admiring the view.' He was even harsh with Boadicea. 'Get down, you stupid bitch, leave him alone.' The dog gave a last apologetic lick to Ned's hand and slunk to her box.

'What's the matter?'

'Nowt as I know of. Haven't seen you for so long I thought you must've fallen down a hole.'

'It's the job. She keeps finding me so much work on

84

Saturdays – I've got to give Mu and Lionel a hand with the kids on Sundays—'

'Yes, yes. Just see that door's shut fast. Don't want the whole world peering in.'

Ned grinned, this was more like it. He eased the warped wood tight against the jamb.

'That do you?'

'Suppose so. Got any baccy?'

It was raining hard. Hayden had rigged a canvas strip as an awning to deflect the worst of it. They sat for a moment or two, listening to the drumming of the rain, content to let smoke rise from their pipes.

'Well, now that you've finally got here ... I've got summat to show you. I've been keeping it safe.' Hayden indicated the biscuit tin in which he kept personal documents. 'On the top.'

Ned took out the torn piece of newspaper.

'Where did this come from?'

'Library reading room. I waited till someone had a fit of coughing, then I ripped it out.'

The article, dated four weeks previously, was headed: STOCKTON MAN MAKES A SUCCESS OF IT! Underneath was a smudged photograph of a stranger.

'His family moved to Middlesbrough from Stockton,' Hayden explained. 'He used to work at Victoria Iron Foundry ... I knew his mam.'

'Oh, aye.' Ned went through the article slowly.

'Looks like what they say in there is right,' Hayden challenged. 'Sounds as if he has done well for himself, out in Australia.'

'Aye.' Ned's thoughts were racing. He stared out at the rain rather than look at his friend. 'Why did you want me to see it?'

Hayden, likewise excited, puffed rapidly to conceal his feelings. 'Seemed to me ... young chap like you ... ought to think about the future. Unless you want to make a career of scrubbing floors?'

'It says here ...' Ned found the phrase, '"Mr Fryer already had a position arranged in New South Wales."'

'Position! They mean he was fixed up wi' a job. There was people wrote to the paper the week after, asking how he managed it. And last week ...' Hayden produced it from his pocket with a flourish, 'there was this.'

Ned smoothed out the newsprint. 'You never nicked the entire paper?'

'As a matter of fact I *bought* a copy, specially for you. After I'd read it in the library.' Ned took so long this time, Hayden grew impatient.

'Well?'

'Well what?'

'What d'you think? They give the address.'

'I can read.'

'Well, don't just sit there. I've had that burning a hole in my pocket for six whole days. You'll find pen and ink on the shelf. An' I got a stamp. Stuck it on the envelope, all ready.'

The sheet of paper and envelope, when produced, were pale green. The stamped envelope was much thumbed.

'I will admit I pinched these,' Hayden confessed. 'Me aunt gave me mother the writing paper and envelopes for Christmas but she never sends letters. She'll never miss 'em.'

He set off for the allotment tap while Ned attempted to compose his first draft. He was hunched up over the newspaper. Hayden wasn't a fool, he knew what this might mean. If Ned were successful, they might never see one another again.

Boadicea was watching him steadily. It wasn't a day when he carried a handkerchief. He dashed his sleeve across his eyes and picked up the pen. He'd made so many previous applications words flowed automatically. By the time tea was ready, the envelope was sealed. Hayden handed him his mug.

'Spit on it for luck, that's what they say.'

'It looks as if that's happened too many times already.'

'They'll think the postman's got mucky habits,' Hayden said comfortably. As it was an important occasion, he made a concession to the bitch. 'Here, Boadicea, ruin your appetite, go on.' They stared at her rather than each other as the biscuit

86

disappeared in two swift gulps. Hayden sought to distract him. 'So, has the headmistress been behaving herself?'

Ned responded, as he was expected to do, with a list of complaints. They had a second cup; neither felt like drinking it. Ned tackled the painful subject. 'Have you thought what it could mean?'

'You're counting your chickens,' Hayden jeered.

'You must want to get rid of me.'

'Don't be stupid!' He turned on the silent Boadicea, 'An' you shut up an' all ...' When he was calmer, he went on, 'If you must know, I've been thinking of nowt else ever since I read that first article. But it was put there for me to find, I'm convinced of it, so's I could show you.'

'There'll be hundreds of other blokes thinking the same thing,' Ned reminded gently, 'all those who wrote and asked.'

'This time I want you up in the front of the queue, not down the back.'

Ned re-read the article slowly, pointing out possible ambiguities.

Hayden discussed them seriously. 'When I first read it, I lay awake wondering if it weren't a bit – you know – exaggerated. The way newspapers can be when they want you excited. But after a bit I thought what it was really saying was if a chap's prepared to take a chance, an' work hard, he won't be any worse off there than here. And ...' Hayden stared at him, 'he'll be a damn sight more likely to make a go of it out there. That's what I think it means.'

His friend had never delivered himself of such sentiments before. Ned was quiet. Eventually he said, 'I might never get back.'

'Why should you? What is there for you here?'

'I belong, that's what.'

'You might do but there's nowt for you. You're young enough to put down new roots. Provided you don't hang about.'

Ned laughed abruptly. 'You'd have me down the docks and on a boat tonight if you could.'

'Why not?' Hayden looked at him steadily. 'Best way, sometimes. A clean break.'

'What about Mu and Lionel—'

'Ha'way.' He was impatient. 'You're under their feet, always will be in that house. She'll be glad to see the back of you.'

'She was glad to see me come home after the war.'

'Aye ... that was different. We were all glad ... there was so bloody few of you. The war's over, lad. Time for a fresh start. Look here, you don't want to end up in a rotten hut staring at rows of rotten sprouts, do you?'

The ache in Ned's throat made speech difficult.

'Who's counting chickens now? I might not get the job. I might not even be given an interview.'

'You better bloody had! What's the matter – didn't you write a decent letter? That stamp cost money, you know.'

Later, when they were tidying up, Hayden asked casually, 'What about the pretty waitress, have you seen her lately?'

'She's not really a waitress. It's only temporary until she learns type-writing. Her sister got married yesterday. I went to the church.' Ned remembered his note. 'She's got a bit of a shock coming,' and described what he'd learned.

'Bit of a difference, a clerk instead of under-manger. Fancy telling her a great big whopper like that – she'll find out soon as she sees his wage packet—'

'*If* she sees it. He didn't strike me as the sort that would show it to anyone.'

'So you reckon she still doesn't know?'

'That's why I sent the note to her sister.'

'Pity they didn't have a father to ask the right questions. Or a brother.'

'They had both before the war.'

'Poor lasses.'

They set off, departing through the blue gate and then in single file along the trodden path. Under a thin moon the shadows were deep. Boadicea stayed close.

'When will you be seeing your waitress again?'

'Her name's Rose. Miss Rose Bossom, and she's not mine.'
Nor ever likely to be, Ned thought sadly. 'I'll leave it for a bit because of the note.'

They had reached Bishopton Road. Hayden said, 'You won't forget to post that envelope?'

'All right, all right.'

During the remaining three days of her honeymoon, Mrs Harold Brigg learned more of the facts of life and few were to her taste. Making babies, for instance, was not the main purpose of The Act; never mind what it said in the book of Common Prayer, it was for man's pleasure. Man, the superior being, man the provid— At this point, Harold usually remembered to stop.

Gertie put up a spirited defence: why was it solely for *man*'s pleasure? Why should woman have to put up with it when it was so unpleasant? And, no thank you, she didn't want to play bunnies and bears during the afternoon. Frustrated, clumsy in his love-making, Harold went into a sulk. He resorted to his grievance.

'You deceived me, Gertrude. You led me to believe you had a dowry.'

Gertie's lips were compressed. The sum might have been smaller than he'd hoped but that was his misfortune, it wasn't a real fib. 'Harold, I haven't complained, despite the fact my bouquet was not as I wished, nor was there a photographer to record my wedding day. I think you should bear your disappointment with equal fortitude.'

At this, his eyes bulged. 'You refer to – to trivia!'

'I refer to the most important day in a girl's life, according to my mother,' she said tartly. 'Sadly, for me, it was not.'

That afternoon, they went on an outing. They had been married three days and were as far apart in understanding as two people could be. Side by side, they gazed down at the rollers buffeting the foot of Huntcliff. They had joined the morose couple from their hotel for the occasion. The other husband, hand clutching his hat, struggled across to where they stood.

89

'The site is clearly marked, where they found the bodies of the Roman soldiers. If you're interested.' They followed him across the close-cropped grass past sheep who gazed at them curiously. The morose wife stared at the pile of stones while her husband read from the guide book.

'"At this Roman signalling station, fourteen guards were caught unaware by a raiding party who, after murdering them, threw their bodies down the well ... About AD390."'

'It makes you think,' said his wife.

'It does indeed.' Harold was hearty. 'Caught them napping, eh! On guard duty, too? They got what they deserved, that's all I can say.'

Those poor young men, thought Gertie miserably. In this lonely spot at the edge of the known world, and then to be killed like that. Was there no happiness anywhere? Tears spilled down her cheeks, the first she'd shed since her wedding night.

'There, there,' Harold said in alarm.

'My dear Mrs Brigg, it was a long time ago.' The morose couple were animated with concern. Gertie blew her nose.

'I was remembering Cecil ... in the trenches.'

'Her brother,' mouthed Harold. The other two nodded sagely and moved a discreet distance away. He gathered her in his arms. 'Dear little Gertie ... My precious. Don't cry.'

She felt smothered. 'Don't, Harold – supposing somebody sees us!' He was touched. Almost alone on one of England's highest cliffs, his dear little wife was worried about appearances.

'I'll protect you.' From sheep, wind, sea, sky and ghosts but not when it came to bills. 'Try not to upset yourself, Gertrude.'

'The thing that still worries me most of all—'

'Yes?'

'We haven't yet decided where we're going to live.'

The widow who had offered Rose a home was in her early thirties but with such a grave disposition, she appeared older.

She stood in her hallway as the cab driver struggled with Rose's possessions.

'That box is very precious ... it contains a tea service and must go that way up. Thank you so much.' Rose smiled gratefully. 'How much do I owe you?' she paid him and apologized to her landlady, 'I'd no idea I had so much baggage!'

For Mrs Porteous, who owned the six-bedroomed house, it appeared very little. 'Is that all?'

'There may be a small mahogany table. I'll have to wait until Gertie returns from honeymoon. It's silly – there was so much to arrange we never discussed who should have that.' Mrs Porteous pictured the countless small tables scattered throughout her mansion.

'No doubt we shall find room for it.'

'Apart from that, just one small grip. Is it convenient for me to move in tomorrow night, once Gertie and Harold have returned?'

'Of course.' Mrs Porteous's gravity disappeared. 'I am looking forward to your company, Rose. Let me show you your room.'

The house was grander than Rose had assumed. She followed Mrs Porteous up the wide staircase, past snarling heads of beasts. 'My late husband's father was a keen sportsman.'

'Yes ...' It was a pity he had had to kill so many.

'This is my room, with the dressing-room beyond ... my maid Eloise is next door. Then the bathroom. And this will be your room. I thought you might prefer to look out over the garden.'

'Oh, my!' After the rich furnishings downstairs, this was a delight. A faded yellow paper with a pattern of blue birds, a comfortable armchair, a bed with a white counterpane. Rose beamed with delight. 'This is wonderful!'

'It's very old-fashioned. We thought of redecorating. Had there been a child ... In the end, there was no reason to ...'

'I'm fond of old-fashioned things.' Rose wondered if that

91

sounded tactless. 'At home, although the house was new, the furniture was old. This is beautiful ...' She ran a hand over the brass inlay in the walnut tallboy, 'Is this room really to be mine?'

Mrs Porteous retreated behind her reserve.

'For as long as we both suit one another. Since my husband failed to return ... the winter evenings can be tedious.' Rose nodded sympathetically. 'Let me show you round. Hoskins will see to your things.'

Goodness, thought Rose. She followed her new landlady downstairs.

'Where did you say you and your sister have rooms?'

'In Fleetham Street. We had to find somewhere quickly that we could afford.'

To move from Fleetham Street to Albert Road was to be in a different world. I must be honest, thought Rose, even if there was a risk of Mrs Porteous changing her mind. Please, dear Lord, don't let this glorious bubble burst!

'It's a fearfully shabby place, above a shop.'

'It must have been very frightening for you, both so young,' the widow said simply. 'Under similar circumstances, I should have been terrified. This is the dining-room ...' There were eight chairs round the circular table. 'Through here, the sitting-room.' It was small by comparison, with easy chairs in front of a bright fire. 'This is where I spend most of my time,' she admitted. 'But there is also the main reception room.'

She led the way across the hall and opened the door on a large formal drawing-room. The air was cold. 'Now that I am alone ...' Rose nodded silently that she'd understood: this was kept for grand occasions. They returned to the sitting-room. A manservant was already removing her bags from the hall.

'Is anything wrong, Rose?'

'No, no, indeed ...' How to explain? The lonely woman who came so regularly to the tea rooms – Rose had had no idea she would live in such a house as this. 'I feel ... slightly overwhelmed.' It was difficult not to gush. 'I hope I shall succeed in providing the company you seek,' she said formally.

'I daresay there will be evenings when each of us would prefer our privacy.'

Rose nodded. In this house, there was plenty of space for that. On an impulse, she said, 'Mrs Porteous, I'm the luckiest girl in the world. I only hope I can afford the rent!' She'd raised a smile at last.

'I discussed the matter with my solicitor; he suggested half of whatever you and your sister pay at present. In other words, the same amount for you.'

'Oh, I pay all of it. Gertie didn't have a situation, you see, but I have my wages. Five shillings – that doesn't include coal. I couldn't possibly pay you any less, Mrs Porteous. I should feel *riddled* with guilt.' Her landlady smothered what could have been a giggle.

'We cannot have that. Five shillings will be ample but this time that will include breakfast and supper.'

'Thank you very much indeed!' At this rate she would soon have enough for the lessons. Rose felt guilty when she glanced at the clock. 'Would you excuse me? Gertie and Harold are returning tomorrow and I want the place to be spick and span. Queenie's offered to help.' Mrs Porteous tried to imagine working alongside her parlourmaid, and failed.

'I shall expect you tomorrow evening. Shall you have dined?'

'Yes, thank you.' Rose planned to cook Finnan haddock for the homecoming; in Fleetham Street that counted as a treat but not here perhaps. She didn't mention it to Mrs Porteous.

Gertie now knew her future abode. It made her so angry she could scarcely think of anything else. She refused to accept it was necessary but needed Rose to back her up. Arguing with Harold was exhausting, she hadn't the stamina. She would wait until they were back in Middlesbrough.

Slightly worried by her temper, her husband had become conciliatory. He'd ceased to complain of her lack of dowry, hinting instead at his own straightened circumstances. She didn't believe him: why could an under-manager not provide a decent home for his wife? It didn't occur to Gertie that Harold might not be telling the truth concerning his position at the rolling mill.

'In time, my dear, I hope to lead you over the threshold of a semi-detached. You shall choose it yourself. But until then, as you are unable to contribute to our expenditure ...'

'Surely you realized that from the beginning, Harold?' He maintained a lofty silence, Her conscience failed to remind her how evasive she'd been. Contribute? How was she expected to do that?

Over breakfast that Wednesday morning, they were as silent as the long-married pair. They spent the day walking because they weren't expected back early. In the train, they watched the dusk soften the outline of ironworks and foundries and when they climbed the stairs at Fleetham Street, they were so quiet, they startled Rose.

'I didn't hear the door. Gertie, how are you, dearest?' She embraced her sister enthusiastically and held out her hand to Harold. 'How was Redcar?'

'Splendid, splendid. See how well your sister looks, Rose, positively blooming.' Rose considered Gertie looked pale but didn't say so.

'It rained much of the time,' Gertie said, listlessly.

'Oh, dear! Never mind, supper is nearly ready. Would you like to take off your hat?' She followed Gertie into the bedroom. 'I've made up the bed. I assume you and Harold will want to stay on until Saturday morning.'

Alone with Rose, Gertie broke the dreadful news. 'Harold and I won't be moving out.'

'What?' There was an odd sound from the partition. Gertie lowered her voice. 'That's him gargling. He does it three times a day.' She saw the silver dressing-table set spread out beneath the mirror. 'You've removed your things?'

'Most of them, yes. I'm off to Albert Road tonight. Gertie, what do you mean, you won't be moving out?'

'Our future abode is to be right here in Fleetham Street. Harold assures me it's only temporary ...' Her eyes were overfull with unshed tears. 'I want you to help me persuade him otherwise. I can't do that on my own, Rose, he's too strong. It must be some kind of punishment, making me stay on here. Ever since he looked at my bank book, Harold's been acting strangely. He refused to offer any explanation.'

'Oh.' Rose sat abruptly. Gertie must realize how disappointed Harold would have been over the bank book? Unfortunately she was about to receive a worse shock. The moment Rose had been dreading had arrived. There was nothing else for it; she handed her sister Ned's note.

'I had intended to write to you ... your postcard only arrived yesterday. Ned Harrison came to the tea rooms. I happened to mention Harold was an under-manager at Hill's. He knew of someone who works there. After speaking to him, he sent this. Stay and read it. I shall tell Harold you're unpacking.'

She closed the door behind her. Harold was in the parlour, examining the small mahogany table. He straightened abruptly.

'Ah, Rose.'

'Gertie will be with us shortly, Harold. She's – she's just changing out of her things. Would you help me with the table?'

'Isn't Queenie about?'

'Queenie doesn't wait on us. And this table needs two pairs of hands.' He helped reluctantly then watched as she shook out the tablecloth. 'I shall be leaving after supper.'

'Ah, yes. You're off to Albert Road.'

She said brightly, 'Gertie tells me you plan to stay on here for a while.'

'Er – yes, that is so. As a – temporary measure.'

'Have you told Mrs Potter? She's already advertised, there has been at least one applicant.'

'Perhaps, after supper, if Gertrude were to go down ...'

'I think you should go and see her now, Harold. To avoid any misunderstanding.'

And to give Gertie time to recover. Rose waited until he'd

gone, checked the simmering pan and knocked on the bedroom door.

Gertie had thrust the note into the dressing-table drawer. The first effect of it had been to make her hate her sister. Throughout their lives, Rose had been the one to make her face reality. Tonight, thanks to Rose, the last illusion had been swept away: Gertie wasn't married to an under-manager at all, she was the wife of a clerk!

Their father had been a clerk, that was why they had so few possessions. Their mother's extravagances, the villa in Clairville Road plus a cook as well as a maid, meant his salary had been stretched to the uttermost.

But at least Father had been the *head* clerk: Harold was only one of six! Staring in the mirror, Gertie saw Rose's anxious face appear behind her.

'I am sorry to give you such news the instant you returned.'

'You shouldn't have discussed it with – that person.' Gertie spoke mechanically. 'It was disloyal to me, Rose.'

It was unkind to refer to Ned like that but Rose wasn't going to scold, not now.

'I thought you ought to know straight away.'

'It's probably nothing but gossip. There may not be a word of truth in it!'

Rose said cautiously, 'I believe we can rely on it. Ned's neighbour wouldn't have any reason to lie. But it doesn't really matter, it won't make the slightest difference to your feelings for Harold.'

Gertie swung round. 'You think not?'

Rose's heart sank. 'It will mean less money, of course. It's bound to, until Harold is promoted.'

'And when will that be, d'you think? He's still telling fibs. He told me he was twenty-nine. On the marriage certificate it states quite clearly he is thirty-three.'

'Oh, well ... I shouldn't let that worry you, dear.' Rose was dismayed. Gertie sounded so fractious, not at all as a happy bride should. 'He must have felt self-conscious, being that little bit older than you. I must go and see to the supper. Try not to brood.'

96

The little kitchen was full of steam. Rose opened the window. She felt stifled. Thank goodness she would be out of here by tonight.

The sight of the geyser reminded her of Gertie's plight. How her sister would hate having to use that cracked old tub again. And for how long? If this was all Harold could afford, he must be on a very low salary indeed? The fish-slice hovered above the pan.

Surely a modest furnished house wasn't beyond his means? Or was Gertie right, was Harold punishing her for being comparatively penniless?

I mustn't become involved, Rose told herself, it does no good. Gertie had been very angry over the note. Rose couldn't tell her or Harold about that delightful room waiting for her in Albert Road. Such comfort and luxury there, whereas here . . .

She took the plate of sliced bread and butter through to the parlour. Harold must have returned, she could hear his rumble from the bedroom.

'Supper's ready,' she called. When she returned with the fish, he was already at the table.

'A summons to dinner, Rose, should not be a *shout*. A tap on the bedroom door, a polite request is what is required. One must keep up *standards* of behaviour.' He began to eat. Rose waited for Gertie.

Her grip was packed; all that remained was to fold her apron and change her shoes. She felt like a prisoner at the point of release.

Gertie slipped in quietly and took her place. Rose made an attempt at conversation. 'Was it a pleasant hotel?'

'Excellent, excellent,' Harold said loudly. 'Recommended by Simmonds, of course.' He hesitated with a slight feeling of unease but Rose said nothing. 'I shall be able to thank him for his kindness on both counts tomorrow, for consenting to be my best man and for suggesting an excellent hotel.'

I shall never like Harold, thought Rose, however hard I try. His teeth champed away as he continued to speak.

'On the subject of Simmonds . . .'

97

'Yes?'

He gave a heavily coy wink. 'Did you and he succeed in "shaking a leg" last Saturday?'

'I've no idea what happened to him, Harold. I returned to the tea rooms.'

'I trust he didn't feel let down?'

Gertie said warningly, 'Harold!'

Rose's cheeks were flushed. 'I must ask you not to promise me as a partner again. You put me in a very awkward position.'

Harold brushed this aside. 'Don't be such a goose.'

'I prefer to choose my own friends.'

'You are too young to know who is suitable,' he announced loftily.

Rose couldn't contain herself, 'Suitable? A person who reaches for my garter under the table? I am not some chattel to be dangled in front of your fellow employees, Harold!'

'Hoity-toity! Simmonds wanted a bit of fun, that's all.'

Gertie said icily, 'Do you consider a married man a suitable partner for my sister?'

'Married!' Rose was fiery, 'Oh, no – you must be mistaken, Gertie?' She stared at Harold and knew it to be true. His gaze faltered before her fierce stare.

'Dear me, what a fuss about nothing,' he blustered. 'I don't understand you, Gertrude. Simmonds *is* married, it's true, but his wife does not choose to go dancing.'

'It's abominable of you! How could you attempt to compromise me like that?' Rose was extremely agitated. 'Gertie, I'm sorry, I can't stand to be here another minute. Let me explain what I've done before I go. There's bacon, eggs, butter and the rest of the loaf in the meat-safe. I've taken the poppy tea service, also the single sheets as you and Harold won't be needing those and three small towels. You can keep the rest.'

'That's very generous.'

'Harold was examining the little table just now – no doubt he wants you to have that. You might as well have the dinner wagon but I'll take Mother's and Father's photograph if you don't object?'

'Of course I don't.'

'Am I to be included in this discussion?' Two pairs of eyes turned on him.

'I think, better not,' Gertie said coldly. 'Rose and I can arrange this between ourselves.' Rose remembered Gertie's appeal for support.

'Harold, I do think Gertie deserves a proper home. These rooms were nothing but a temporary measure and extremely cramped. I don't wish to appear rude but can you not afford something better?'

His eyes began to bulge in a familiar way. Rose knew it was useless ... She brushed her sister's cheek, murmuring, 'I'm sorry. If I've forgotten anything, leave it with Mrs Potter. I'll collect it when I can.'

Back in the bedroom she thrust her apron and shoes into her grip. She wouldn't wait to change, she would walk to Albert Road in her slippers. Shaking fingers found coat buttons difficult. The beret was on, the scarf tucked under her collar.

Harold was poised at the top of the stair, demanding an apology. 'Your attitude to Gertrude and myself, this running off into the night, is nothing short of hysteria.'

Rose spoke to Gertie through the open parlour door. 'I've left my address on the mantelpiece, Gertie.'

'You will beg your sister's pardon—'

'Goodbye, dear.' Gertie raised a hand in a silent farewell.

'Rose, I haven't finished.' But she had squeezed past him and hurried down the stairs. Husband and wife were alone.

Gertie collected their plates. To and fro she went, removing the fish and replacing it with slices of apple pie. She indicated he should rejoin her. Still grumbling, Harold returned to his chair.

'Your attitude baffles me, Gertrude.'

'Does it, Harold? So does yours.'

'That you should— What did you say?'

It was easier not to look at him.

'That you should treat my sister's reputation so lightly. Do you imagine when our parents were alive, Rose or I ever partnered a married man?' Harold's mouth opened then closed again. 'Had Cecil been alive, he would have demanded an explanation.'

'Gertrude, I will not permit you to criticize. For heaven's sake, why keep carping about such a trivial matter?'

'Is it also trivial to claim to be under-manager at Hill's?' A wiser woman might have chosen a better moment but Gertie's emotions were too frayed. This time, the colour drained away leaving Harold's face mottled.

'How dare you! Of course I'm under-manager—'

'That is not my understanding. I have been told that you are a progress clerk, one of six.'

Trapped, he flung down his spoon.

'That bitch of a sister – how dare she!' Shocked by his language, Gertie watched the thin trickle of syrup spread across the beautiful delicate embroidery. It was her favourite tablecloth; no doubt Rose had chosen it specially.

'Damn it, I will not be accused by my wife, or anyone else for that matter!' It was obviously true. Gertie's heart felt leaden.

'Was it said to impress me?' she asked, meaning to be kind.

'If I lied, so did you,' he countered thickly.

It had been a game, to begin with; he had been her own special *boy*.

'Will you answer one question truthfully, Harold?'

'How dare—'

'Is it really necessary to continue living here? You know how much I have in the bank, can we not use some of that towards a proper home?'

'Gertrude, I don't think you understand: that is all we have in the world!' He certainly wasn't plundering his little nest-egg, saved toward membership of the Brotherhood. Besides, there were those damned payments due to the Winnots in a month or two. His bluster had paid off: Gertie assumed she'd been told the truth. Harold must be on the lowest clerical salary of all.

'I see.'

She washed up the dishes and put the tablecloth in to soak. When she returned to the parlour Harold spoke as if nothing untoward had occurred.

'Gertrude, I visited Mrs Potter to let her know we would be staying on. She appeared not to understand. Perhaps you would go down and explain.'

Gertie's heart sank even further. 'Did you upset her? Did you try and insist that Queenie—'

'I did nothing of the sort. It's not my fault if the woman is deficient in her faculties.'

'Harold, if you have offended her we could be out on the street by Saturday!' Without Rose to protect her, Gertie felt defenceless. Harold's chin went up. He refused to accept the blame.

'Rose insisted I go down. It would have been much better had you done it.'

It was too late to go down now. Gertie would have that worry to face in the morning. To soothe her nerves, she fetched a piece of tapestry and settled beside the fire.

'I trust you don't intend to sulk, Gertrude. It's not encouraging for a man to see his wife behave like that.'

'I'm tired, Harold. This helps quiet my thoughts. Have you not a book you could read?'

Harold didn't enjoy reading. 'In my opinion, people fritter away too much of their lives on books and newspapers. I daresay, if one had a mathematical turn of mind, one could make an interesting study. Ten minutes here, three hours there, all wasted on reading. Who is to say how much more one might have achieved, had that same amount of time been devoted to – an object?'

'What object?'

'Hmm?'

'What did you have in mind?'

'I? Nothing. I was demonstrating a valid point. Illustrating

101

the common misapprehension as to the value of time spent in reading.'

The needle flashed in and out. I won't listen, she thought grimly. I'll do what he does and pretend not to hear. Tomorrow, I shall *beg* Mrs Potter to let us stay, at least until I've persuaded Harold to move. We must be able to afford something better than this!

The parlour maid answered the door in Albert Road. 'Madam is expecting you, miss. She's in the little sitting-room.'

All Rose wanted to do was hide away in her room. Instead she replied feebly, 'I'll just take my things upstairs. I shall be down shortly.'

The water in the jug on the washstand was tepid. Rose splashed it over her burning cheeks. She'd gone over and over the conversation with Harold. How could she have been any more polite? It was monstrous that he should offer her among his married colleagues as if she were a – a . . .

Rose couldn't bring herself even to think the word, it was too degrading! 'I never want to see him again.' But she had to, she couldn't let Gertrude down; her sister depended on her.

Rose gave herself a shake. Pull yourself together, she scolded. Here in this charming old-fashioned room she was safe. Even the furniture gave solace. She ran a hand over the scuffs made by previous generations, now polished and mellow.

It was a new beginning. Such a stroke of luck! Her hostess – she couldn't think of Mrs Porteous as a landlady – was expecting her. It weighed a little heavily to know that she couldn't have the privacy she'd been promised whenever she wanted it. Companionship in lieu of rent, was it? Well, it would be churlish to try and avoid it.

Tidying her hair, Rose hurried past the snarling silent beasts on the stairs. I must be cheerful at all times, she thought, and tapped on the sitting-room door. She nearly giggled: how Harold would envy her all this. 'Here I am at last,' she cried happily.

Mrs Porteous flung aside her book. 'I thought you were never going to arrive.' Her voice had a plaintive note Rose had never noticed before. She shivered involuntarily. Mrs Porteous noticed immediately.

'You're cold. Have you eaten? Would you like cocoa or hot milk?'

'Cocoa would be delicious. Shall I go and make it?'

'Sit down.' She tugged the bell-pull. 'Goodness, what are servants for?'

Am I not a servant, wondered Rose? I wait on customers in the tea rooms. She watched as the order was given and the parlour-maid left the room.

Mrs Porteous patted the sofa. 'Come and sit beside me. I want to hear what happened to amuse you today. You always make me smile, Rose, even on the dullest days.'

Oh, Lord! thought Rose, there's poor Gertie, as unhappy as sin and now I'm expected to be jolly. Mrs Porteous was looking expectant. For five bob a week, she sighed, I must sing for my supper, but I wonder how long before I can decently slip away to bed? She took a deep breath.

'Dear old Mrs Ballin came in the tea rooms today. She wears the oddest clothes, they probably belonged to her grandmother. She always carries her little dog in her basket. Have you ever noticed her?'

Mrs Porteous shook her head. 'I visit the tea rooms far less often. I lead such a busy life, you know.'

Another pitfall; illusions had to be maintained, obviously. Rose's eyelids were heavy. She craved nothing but her bed. She hoped the cocoa would be good and hot.

'Well, Mrs Ballin always sits at the corner table with her back to the wall and pushes her basket underneath – where she thinks we can't see her little dog ...'

It was midnight before her hostess declared it was time to retire. As Rose climbed the silent stairs, Mrs Porteous's words were ominous. 'I trust you won't be late home tomorrow night, Rose. I depend on you to keep me amused from now on.'

Sing for her supper *every* night? No time to herself at all? Rose almost laughed in her despair. Gertie dependent on her, now this? In her bedroom, she whispered to the faded birds on the wallpaper, 'I'm trapped in a beautiful gilded cage, just like you.' But they'd been pinioned to the wall for years!

Chapter Five

An Offer, 1921

The interviews were to take place in Newcastle and Ned was told to present himself at 11.00 a.m. He broke the news to the headmistress who declared flatly he couldn't go.

'You're not entitled to time off!'

'With luck, it'll only be half a day, Miss Renfrew. I shall make up the time afterwards.'

'I forbid it. I shall have you sacked if you do.'

'Why deny me the chance to make a new life for myself? I don't plan to spend the rest of my time scrubbing floors, you know. If I'd claimed to be sick, you'd have been none the wiser but I prefer to be honest.'

'There's plenty who would be glad of your position.'

'Poor beggars.'

'Harrison!'

'I have a trade, Miss Renfrew. I'm a riveter, not a cleaner. I gave two and a half years of my life defending my country – now I'm reduced to this. I've got the right to a chance.' He hadn't intended to be threatening but he saw her shrink away. In a more even tone he said, 'I shall take the time off and make it up when I get back. If after that you still want to sack me, that's up to you. Goodnight.'

Mu had done her best with his old shirt. Lionel had loaned him a tie. As he looked down on the Tyne from the train, Ned felt his guts tighten the way they had before every 'big push'.

I survived a lot; maybe this time I'll be even more lucky. Which reminded him, he still owed Hayden for the stamp. My last will and testament, he thought sourly. I give and bequeath to Hayden Cooke enough for a stamp, an envelope and a sheet of paper. If there's anything left, it can be spent on biscuits for Boadicea.

In the old drill hall, he stood to attention in front of the two men seated at a trestle table. The questions came quickly but Ned answered openly and promptly. The pace slowed, he began to relax. His war record was examined, his ability with machinery investigated. Ned admitted he hadn't learned to drive but he had 'given a hand' on many occasions.

'If something didn't work we'd all pitch in. I had a friend who'd been a blacksmith. He showed me how an engine worked.' Remembering the comrade who hadn't come back brought him up short. He recovered and said quietly, 'Not many stood on ceremony in the trenches.'

One of the questioners nodded. Ned realized the man had probably served in the Australian Army. When the final question came, 'Why do you want to go to Australia, Harrison?' he directed his answer to him.

'It wasn't my idea, to be honest.'

'What?'

Ned reddened. Had he been a fool?

'It was a pal who knew the difficulties I'd had trying to find work. He kept those newspaper articles. It seemed to be the chance I'd been waiting for. Since then, I've read every book in the library about Australia.'

'Did any of them describe the heat and the flies?'

'Yes, sir. And the struggle those first chaps had, trying to find that inland sea.'

'Life in the outback is still very tough. Isolated, too. Reckon you could stand it?'

'Certain of it, sir.'

The other chimed in, 'What about your wife, Harrison?'

'Wife?' Ned tried to hide his disappointment.

The ex-army man said sympathetically, 'Although the article didn't make it plain, we need married men with wives who are prepared to work. Wives who understand what a rugged life can mean. All those we've interviewed already are either engaged or married. We assumed you were as well.'

Ned swallowed. 'Sorry, sir, afraid not.'

The sympathetic man leaned forward. 'We're planning to ship those whom we select in two boatloads. The second departure is scheduled for June. If we make an offer, would that give you enough time?'

To find a wife? Ned was stunned.

'It might,' he ventured.

The other grinned. 'That's the spirit. As for travel, it won't be luxurious but your fares will be subsidized. We're asking twenty pounds per head as a token of goodwill, plus you'll have to sign a contract guaranteeing to work for the company for at least three years.'

That settled it; twenty pounds was impossible, but Ned immediately thought of Mu and Lionel. Such an opportunity might be attractive to them.

'What would the women be expected to do?'

'Cooking, washing, cleaning. Nothing they haven't done before. It's the climate that makes it tough. And the lack of female company. There wouldn't be many other women around for a gossip or to help out if things got rough. You'd have to make that plain. Think about it. We'll be in touch.'

Ned wondered again about Mu as he walked back to the station. His whole being was longing to go but if he couldn't, his sister and the children should have their chance; he'd discuss it with Lionel this evening.

After he'd gone the two interviewers considered his application. 'Will he manage it?'

'Looked pretty resourceful to me. He should go on the list.'

The other added a note. 'Spouse's Christian name to be advised.'

The following Sunday morning Ned went through the blue gate on leaden feet, even Boadicea couldn't rouse him. Hayden was impatient. 'Well?'

'They've offered me a place.'

'That's grand, lad!'

107

'No, it's not. They only want married men with wives who'll pitch in and help. I tried to persuade Lionel to apply. Mu was keen but he wasn't, more's the pity.'

Hayden nodded thoughtfully, 'I can see the sense in it. If there's not many females to choose from, it could lead to trouble – a lot of fellows squabbling. And they'd need the right sort, there'd be no place for dainty, finicky females in Australia.'

'You've missed the point,' Ned said harshly, 'I can't go because I haven't a wife, dainty or otherwise.'

'Ha'way, of course you can. Fine upstanding lad like you.'

'Who'd have me? What have I got to offer, eh? Would *you* consider marrying a stranger with no money and no guarantee of a future except hard work? Away from all your loved ones.'

'The right girl would.'

'Oh, aye. Take a miracle to find her, though.'

'How long have you got?'

'Till June. And there's twenty quid each to raise towards the fare as well. As a token of goodwill.'

'Anything else?'

'A promise to stay three years before striking out on my own.'

'Not too bad, then,' Hayden's eyes narrowed, he stared unseeing at Boadicea in her basket. 'Forty pounds. That's a bit of a facer.'

'Hayden ...' Ned stared at him. 'Never mind the cash, how'm I going to find a wife?'

'I should have thought that was obvious – Miss Rose Bossom?'

Ned scoffed, 'Oh, yes? A proper *lady*? I told you, she's got to be prepared to work.'

'Isn't she doing that already at the tea room?'

'They're not talking about cucumber sandwiches ... Listen.' Ned tried to make him understand. 'I scarely know her. Just because I helped when she'd turned her ankle doesn't give me any rights—'

'I'm not talking about *your* rights, Ned. I'm talking about opportunities. What chance has that young woman got, eh? She may be a lady but she's on her own. There's no wealthy parents backing her now. You say she plans to learn type-writing – she's obviously an independent sort. She could be just the one for you. I don't suppose her heart's set on being in an office. I'm not saying it'll be easy but there's no harm in asking her.'

Ned reddened. 'Can you imagine her reaction if I told her my parents were born in Dacre Street? Like I said, I scarcely know her.'

'Best way,' growled Hayden. 'You'll be so busy finding out about one another, you won't have time to quarrel. As for Dacre Street ...' He was pensive. 'That sort of thing *used* to matter once, still does for those who cling to being middle class. You're not like that. You came out of that bloody war into a different world – so forget the past. Go and find out if that girl has got the same sort of pluck. If she has, she won't care where your parents came from.'

Ned remembered Gertie's wedding.

'Her sister wouldn't agree with you but you could be right about Rose.'

'You're fond enough of her, aren't you?' It was abrupt and embarrassed him.

'I used to kick myself for even thinking about her.'

'Aye, well, that sounds like affection to me. Enough for a beginning. You'll have to keep your fingers crossed about the rest.'

'It's too much to ask of any girl!' Ned burst out.

'There's only one way to find out. And you'd better not dilly-dally. She might not be starry-eyed, dreaming of satin and orange blossom but she's still a female. She might need coaxing. Have you got any money?'

'No!' It had taken all his spare cash for the fare to Newcastle.

'Hang on a bit ...' Hayden pulled aside the orange box that did duty for a table and folded back the rug. Beneath, under the loose-laid boards there were layers of newspaper and under these, an old cash box.

109

'Tek this.' It was a gold half sovereign. 'It'll not cover a lot of courting but you haven't got much time anyway. Be romantic for a change. Sweep her off her feet with a slap-up pork pie then ask her if she'd like to go with you to Australia.'

Gertie had taken to 'dropping in' at the tea rooms after doing her shopping. Rose dreaded the visits. First because Gertie was disinclined to pay, and secondly because she expected Rose to sort out the disastrous results of her house-keeping.

It was Wednesday and the café was particularly busy. Rose paused at her table. 'I can't stop and talk, dear. Tea or coffee?'

'Coffee and ginger cake.'

'That'll be sevenpence. Can you afford it?'

Her sister pouted. 'Don't be silly!' As this meant she couldn't, Rose brought tea and bread and butter. Gertie scowled. 'You are mean!'

'I'm still trying to save, Gertie.'

'You must have tons now you pay so little rent, *and* you have breakfast and supper provided.'

'Not supper, dear. Breakfast, yes, but I pay for supper here before I go. Mrs Porteous treats me to cocoa at bedtime, that's all.'

It had been a mistake to describe any aspect of life at Albert Road. Staying on at Fleetham Street had been the worst privation of all for Gertie – and so far Harold showed no sign of agreeing to rent a decent home.

Rose sped between the kitchen and three other tables before pausing beside Gertie again. Her sister was in a mood.

'I think it's beastly of you not to bring me even a little piece of cake.'

'I have to pay if you don't. I can't afford to keep treating you.'

'I bet you've still got oodles in your bank book.'

Rose's forehead creased. 'Oh, Gertie, you haven't been withdrawing any more?'

'Harold doesn't give me enough.'

'You know you have to learn to manage. They showed you

how to plan a budget at housewifery classes. Why don't you make a list and stick to it when you go shopping?'

Gertie touched the comforting fur at her neck. 'Those classes suggested such dull menus, Rose. Stodgy old milk puddings – you know I can't bear sago. Anyway, it wasn't food which made me overspend today, it was the sweetest little matinee jacket threaded with blue ribbon. I simply had to have it.'

Rose stared. 'Gertie – are you . . .?'

'No, I'm not.' The pale eyes were filled with self-pity. 'I let Harold do what he wants, as often as he wants – you know how much I dislike it – but I'm still not pregnant. It's so unfair!'

Rose glanced nervously at the tables on either side. 'Finish your tea. I'll join you once this rush is over.'

She served the orders with efficiency and an absent-minded smile. So many customers were regulars, she often knew their preferences without having to ask, leaving her mind free to consider Gertie's dilemma.

Her sister was as single-minded in her desire for a baby as she had once been for 'Mr Right'. Yet how would it help if Gertie did become pregnant? She couldn't manage to spin out her house-keeping now with just two mouths to feed. Nor could they bring up a child in that poky accommodation. Harold had referred mysteriously to 'stealing away to another abode, ere long', but Gertie didn't know what this meant. Rose believed privately it was his way of preventing her from grumbling too much.

Poor Gertie, marriage hadn't been much fun. With her fastidious feminine ways, Fleetham Street must be anathema: so difficult to keep clean and with no privacy for either of them.

'I do wish she wouldn't keep bringing her problems here,' but Rose immediately scolded herself. Gertie had no one else to turn to. 'The sooner I begin those classes the better. She might try to manage if I wasn't so easily available.'

Rose had problems of her own. She'd let fall a hint about

111

the type-writing and Mrs Porteous had been censorious. The late Captain Porteous disapproved of women going out to business: a woman's place was in the home.

'That is certainly true for a wife and mother,' Rose agreed politely, 'but for a single person such as myself who has to earn her living ... My present occupation isn't particularly *satisfying*, I'm afraid.' Mrs Porteous frowned. Rose must be patient. A suitable young man would present himself, sooner or later.

'But I'm not prepared to wait for "Mr Right". I might end up with someone as abominable as Harold!' Rose muttered in the privacy of her room. All the same, it was a worry. She'd never find other digs as inexpensive or as pleasant as Albert Road.

The tips weren't so generous nowadays. She'd become a fixture and regulars didn't see the necessity. There was also additional expenditure on new shoes, aprons and caps, and, finally, Mrs Porteous had suggested Rose might like to wear a more suitable dress in the evenings.

'Now the days are drawing out, friends of mine are bound to come to visit. You wouldn't want to be seen in that black dress, would you, Rose?' Her old blue tea-gown was past its best. Rose resigned herself, called at the bank and found a demure dark red frock in Wilson's.

Mrs Porteous's callers were few but at least she was presentable. She had the suspicion her hostess wanted to exhibit her as she might some new pet. Rose was expected to say something *amusing* and once this was done to Mrs Porteous's satisfaction, she was encouraged to withdraw. It was a subservient role, neither servant nor paid companion, and Rose chafed against it.

The lunch-time rush was over, the proprietress suggested Rose might like a break with her sister before the tea trade began. Gertie was bursting with news as soon as Rose sat down.

'I haven't told you the real reason why I'm here today;

Harold says we may be moving.'

'That's wonderful!' How encouraging to see Gertie happy for once.

'You remember he was always saying we might 'steal away' one day? Well, last night, two men called. I don't know what it was about, they didn't give their names. I showed them into the parlour and as soon as he saw them Harold said I should wait in the bedroom, he would let me know once they'd gone. It wasn't a long visit but afterwards, Harold said we should "steal away" very soon.'

' "To a new abode" you mean?' They giggled but Gertie stopped herself quickly; it wasn't *nice* to make fun of one's husband.

'It's Harold's way of describing it, certainly. He refused to say where – I think he wants to keep that a secret.'

Gertie assumed a tolerant, wifely expression. 'He's such a dear boy sometimes, with his surprises. But I shall make quite sure he knows exactly which house I'd prefer.'

'Perhaps the two men were from the Masons?' It still surprised Rose that Harold should be so open in discussing a secret society but he did so, constantly.

'He didn't appear particularly *pleased* by their visit. He certainly didn't want to talk about it afterwards.'

'How odd.'

Gertie took a deep breath and revealed her next proposal in a rush. 'Rose, as we are about to move, would you reconsider? If you paid a share of the rent, it would mean we could afford a much *nicer* place.'

'Please, Gertie, we've been through this before. You know my reasons. They haven't changed.' The sullen look had returned. 'Try and see it from my point of view,' Rose pleaded. 'It would only cause friction. Harold disapproves of me in so many ways – he can't seem to stop himself criticizing. We should come to blows, I know we should. Look how he dislikes me working here.'

'But you wouldn't need to any more,' Gertie said eagerly. 'You could stay at home and help me manage instead.'

113

Rose looked at her sternly. 'You're as bad as he is. Gertie, I'm not a substitute for Queenie. And how could I pay rent if I'm not earning?' She saw a familiar expression on her sister's face and raised a hand. 'No, don't say it. Once and for all I am not withdrawing money from my bank book. What would happen when it's all been used up? We could hardly expect Harold to support both of us.'

'You'd find someone. A nice boy of your own. Harold knows lots of people. We could have pleasant little dinner parties ...'

'And invite people like Mr Simmonds? No, Gertie. You must let me live my life as I think best. I shall stay in Albert Road for as long as it suits Mrs Porteous.'

'You're so unkind.' Gertie pulled on her gloves and ignored the folded bill in the saucer. 'You know how I *depend* on you, Rose.'

'And I shall continue to help whenever I can, provided that doesn't mean living with you and Harold.'

She put her sister's cup, plate and bill on her tray. Gertie repeated a familiar complaint. 'You still haven't invited us to see your room. Harold is most upset about it.'

Rose swallowed her annoyance. This happened every visit. 'As I've explained before, I'm a guest, not a lodger – that's how Mrs Porteous sees it and she is a very private person. Unless she changes her mind, I am not entitled to invite anyone.'

Her hostess had been adamant: relatives and friends were not permitted to call. Her solicitor had not thought it advisable.

'Harold says you've become a snob.'

Rose grimaced. Harold would, she thought. He must be *aching* to see inside such a grand house. Gertie had already mentioned naïvely how often her husband 'chanced' to walk past. 'It's circumstances that have changed, not I. One day, when I'm earning sufficient to afford a place of my own, then you and Harold shall come. In Albert Road, it just isn't possible.' To divert her she asked, 'Where will you look for a house? Shall you move back nearer Clairville Road?'

'How should I know,' Gertie said shortly. 'You should realize by now Harold never consults me about anything.'

Rose wasn't inclined to hurry home. The privacy she craved was here, after the tea rooms were closed and the blinds drawn. She stayed behind helping to clean and tidy and afterwards, for a precious half-hour or so, sat alone in the empty quietness.

She must make a decision. If she really wanted a career, she must take the plunge and use her money to pay for those lessons. Trying to save more would take too long. Without her tiny wage she would have to use capital to support herself as well as rent for new digs. And how much should she allow for food?

She sat, totting up figures. The course would take six months – how long after that before she found a position? There would be postage for applications. She would need smart business clothes too, before she could attend an interview. What a pity she wasn't as clever as Gertie when it came to sewing. Perhaps she could offer to pay Gertie to make new clothes? Provided Harold didn't consider it demeaning ... Rose was considering this and didn't hear the tap on the glass. When it was repeated, she called out, 'We're closed.'

'It's me, miss. Ned Harrison.'

She tugged at the blind. It shot up, revealing him on the pavement, clutching his cap.

'I can't let you in ... we really are closed.'

'It's important,' Ned mouthed back.

Not another problem, she thought, I've had my fill today. But his eyes implored and she called, 'I'll get my coat and hat. We can talk outside.' He looked relieved. She pulled on her beret, wrapped her scarf tightly and fastened the door behind her.

'I'm sorry to arrive unexpectedly. Can we walk for a bit?'

Rose looked pointedly at the leaden sky. 'It's going to rain.' He was dismayed. He hadn't seen her tired and out of sorts before.

115

'It's very important. Would you – could I take you for a drink?'

'In a public house!' Her shock would have made him laugh had he not been so desperate.

'Look, can we not take the risk and walk? It might not rain for a while.'

Rose was doubtful. 'Where do you suggest? The park will be shut by now.'

Ned had a flash of inspiration. 'No, not there. Somewhere completely different. Let me show you a part of Middlesbrough you won't have seen before.'

The idea put a spring in his step. They took a tram but the route was unfamiliar. It was almost dark. Regular street lights gave way to meaner, narrower, darker streets as they neared the works area. Here furnace chimneys spilled hot redness and smoke into the night. She knew they must be close to the Transporter bridge when Ned indicated they'd reached their destination. She followed him. It was colder so close to the river, with a brisk wind whipping the Tees into wavelets.

Ned knew his way around. He led confidently and she stayed close, uncertain why they'd come so far. Once he held a broken fence apart so that she could climb through. He spoke briefly, 'Have you ever seen it when they pour the steel?'

'No.'

'It's a sight you'll never forget.'

Rose was fairly certain they had no business to be here yet she didn't question it because Ned strode with such purpose.

At the end of a roadway was a building, as high as a cathedral. He took her through a small side door, picking his way past cables and obstacles. Rose clutched his sleeve, afraid of getting lost. Ahead of them under the arched dome of the building, men scurried like ants. They took no notice as she and Ned stayed in the shadows close to the wall.

This was a different world. Here in a steelworks lay the reason for the town's existence, but it was a man's world; a woman had no place in it. Nervous, Rose moved closer to Ned.

116

'I'm known to one or two,' he murmured. 'Provided we stay quiet, we won't be challenged.'

She became absorbed in what was happening. Bells rang. Men shouted to one another the length of this vast hall. Ned pointed to the huge metal door of the converter.

'Keep your eyes on that.'

There was a high-pitched grinding noise, more shouting and the door opened slowly. Flame belched and writhed inside; it was yellow-white heat, blistering to the eyeballs and hotter than hell. Even at this distance, Rose could feel the intensity of the furnace. She watched in amazement as men approached, apparently careless of their safety.

The vast container began to tilt and a molten yellow stream poured steadily. The power of the heat was beyond anything in her experience; she felt her breath being sucked out, drawn towards the maw of the furnace.

Men moved steadily, walking between the flames and the liquid heat. Rose was so afraid for them, she held her body stiffly, fighting against the terror of what might happen should any of them stumble. How could they stand it, tending this monster night after night?

Ned noted each new detail since his last visit, eager to learn the processes. He became aware of Rose's tension, the moist sweat on her face, the way her hands were clenched. 'Don't be afraid, they know what they're doing,' but she couldn't hear above the roar of flames.

The converter door began to close, he nudged her: time to move on. He hadn't finished his tour. Outside, the shifts were changing. Men swept past, ignoring them. The hard day was finished and they were eager to be gone.

The two of them walked on beyond the works, out through another gap in a railing, across a road and up a steep piece of waste land. With Ned's hand under her elbow, they climbed to a vantage point from where they could look across at the high steel web of the Transporter bridge.

'I used to come here when they were building it. There were some top-class riveters working on that, I can tell you.'

He gazed at the engineering masterpiece. 'There's so much I haven't been able to show you. I'd like to take you to the docks where they built ships but so many are idle now, there's nothing but rust and ghosts.'

Rose was exhausted. 'I don't think I can take much more.'

'Are you tired? Will I find you somewhere to sit?' She could hear the concern even if she couldn't see his face clearly.

'I never knew what it was like. I've heard people speak of "a steel foundry", "a rolling mill" – it was impossible to imagine any of that.'

Ned nodded. 'That's why I wanted to show you, so as you could understand. That was my life, you see. This is my town as well as yours. When I got back from France, I wanted to spend the rest of my time here. Get a decent job, have a family, that's all most of us want. We'd had a bellyful of war, we wanted nothing more but to live in peace and put down roots. We used to tell God that's all we wanted, back in the trenches. Seemingly, there's no place for me here, though. I have to move on.'

The darkness provided concealment for many things. For the ugly gauntness of the works, the chimneys covering the landscape with smoke. It hid the emotion in Ned's eyes but she could hear it in his voice.

'You mean – you're leaving?' Her energy was spent. Rose made no attempt to disguise her disappointment. 'Leaving Middlesbrough?'

'I have to if I'm to make anything of my life.'

'When?'

'Very soon.'

'I'm sorry. I shall miss your visits.'

'Will you? Does this town mean the same to you?' Rose felt disembodied, in a waste land, away from familiar landmarks.

'I'm beginning to think I never knew the place properly. To me it's been streets, houses, shops ... not the works, which is the heart.'

'You've friends here.'

'A few. Fewer than when our parents were alive.' The war

118

had swept away more than just the social round. 'Once we left Clairville Road there weren't as many invitations. But Gertie and I have always been close. We didn't really miss the parties.' No mention of Harold, he noticed. 'I suppose she's my reason for staying in Middlesbrough, as much as I am hers.'

'Aye.' He sounded despondent. 'I guessed you might feel like that.' Rose tried to gather her wits. It felt so strange to be alone in the darkness with this man. She watched the illuminated cabin beneath the Transporter slide across the river and come to a halt on the opposite bank. The human cargo and cars dispersed into the night.

Ned spoke carefully. 'Those type-writing lessons ...? Have you decided when you'll begin?'

'I was trying to do that this evening. It's a bit risky, using capital in order to start at Easter instead of saving a little longer. The trouble is, Gertie so often has problems ...' Rose stopped but Ned had already guessed.

'She can't make ends meet so you help out.'

'Sometimes,' Rose admitted.

'Isn't she – leaning on you too much?' It was presumptuous but she wasn't offended.

'She can't help it, she's always been the same.' Rose hesitated, 'Her marriage hasn't been quite ...' He waited. 'Your note was a bit of a blow.'

'I'm sorry.'

'It wasn't your fault, it was better that we knew.'

They watched in silence as the suspended cage began the return journey. It was late, the wind was much keener. Ned took his courage in both hands.

'I asked you to come out tonight for a reason. It's taken a couple of days to summon up the courage, to be honest.' She didn't speak and it came tumbling out. 'Last week, I was offered a job. It'll mean hard work. For three years I shall be doing labouring work but after that I can strike out on my own. And I shall succeed. There's space enough out there. A chap can make a place for himself.' He waited.

119

In the darkness, her reply was scarcely more than a whisper.

'Out – where?'

'Australia.' She was very still. He couldn't think of any fine words, so said plainly, 'There's a condition attached to the job: it's for a married man. And his wife will have to work alongside. Not type-writing, tea rooms or anything genteel like that, but cooking and cleaning for a whole bunch of chaps on a cattle station. That's a kind of farm, miles from anywhere. It'll be hot, dusty, no proper company. None of the comforts you're accustomed to ...' Rose didn't utter a sound.

The rain that had threatened before began to fall steadily. Ned had never felt so hopeless in his life. 'I'm sorry,' he said abruptly, 'let's get you home before you're soaked.'

She stared, trying to catch one glimpse of his face in the dark. 'I don't understand ... are you ...?'

'Asking if you'd come with me? Yes. Become a labourer's wife, that's what I'm offering.' He couldn't prevent the sneer at his own presumption. 'I could make promises – make the future sound wonderful but there's no guarantee of anything. None whatsoever. We could begin and end our lives out there as nothing better than I am now. In other words, I could drag you down. Come, let's get back. I'm sorry I brought you here.' He reached for her arm to help her down to the road.

'But why me?' She sounded so bewildered it added to his pain. This girl had obviously never given him a second's thought.

'Because I love you, Rose Bossom. I love the ground you tread on and I've wanted to marry you ever since that first evening ... It's stupid. I've nothing to offer. I'm twenty-four and I've nowt. I don't even know how we'd get to Australia. The firm are charging twenty pounds each towards the fare and all I've got is half a sovereign – even that's a loan. So now you know. Ned Harrison, the biggest idiot in Middlesbrough, has brought you all this way on a fool's errand. Come on. I'll put you on that tram and there's an end of it. You'll probably catch pneumonia, you'll be so wet when you get back.'

She followed obediently. The pent-up furious shape walked on ahead, leading her through a maze of paths towards where the street lights began. Once there, Ned kept his cap pulled well down so that she could not see his face.

On the tram, rain trickled off her sodden beret, making fresh water tears on her cheeks. Rose, normally volatile and impulsive, was utterly silent.

Australia.

This man loved her.

But why should love make him so *angry*? She caught one glimpse of his face but there was so much hurt there, she couldn't bear it.

Back in the town centre, he helped her descend and began to walk beside her down Albert Road. There was space between them. Neither took the other's hand or arm. He spoke once, to ask the number of the house. Rose indicated the wrought-iron gates.

As they drew near she murmured, 'When do you ... when are you leaving?' His heartbeat quickened but he saw she didn't look at him. It was curiosity, nothing more.

Keeping his tone brusque, he said, 'June. As there's no possibility of my going I shall try and persuade my sister and her husband to take my place.'

'You said you had work, here in Middlesbrough?'

'I'm a cleaner at a school. Part-time. It was a job intended for a woman but I managed to get it. I doubt I shall be there much longer. The headmistress wants to sack me for taking time off for the interview.'

When Rose spoke, her voice was so quiet, he had to incline his head to hear. 'Had you not been offered the situation in Australia ... would your feelings have been the same ... towards me?'

His rage evaporated for the first time since leaving the waste land. He faced her squarely, speaking from the heart. 'I've told you no lies, Rose. I have felt for you the way a man does for a woman ever since that first evening. There's never been anyone before nor will there be again. Nor shall I ever feel differently towards you. But nothing can come of it so I won't be bothering you again. It wouldn't be fair. Whoever does take your heart, though – he's the luckiest chap on earth.' Tears were close, he could say no more. 'God bless you.'

Replacing the sodden cap, he walked away. Still in a daze, clinging to the rail for support, Rose climbed the steps and rang the bell.

Mrs Proteous was displeased. She found it disagreeable to have her plans disrupted and didn't notice the pool of rainwater on the cold tiled floor of the hall. Rose's face reflected the strain of the past couple of hours, the blue eyes so dark with fatigue the pupils were almost black, but this wasn't immediately apparent to her hostess.

'Rose, I fear I must express my disappointment. My friends waited over an hour and still you didn't come. In future, kindly let me know if there is a possibility you might be late.' When Rose didn't reply, she frowned, 'What is the matter – are you ill?'

'No.'

She peered more closely. 'You're frightfully wet. Where on earth have you been?'

'To see the Transporter.'

'In the rain!' Had the girl gone mad? 'You must take those things off. Give your shoes and coat to Eloise, she can deal with them. Come down as soon as you're changed.'

'I would prefer to stay in my room, Mrs Porteous ... I'm very tired.' Her hostess looked at her reproachfully.

'Now that you're back we can at least play a few hands of Bezique.'

Eloise insisted she change her stockings as well as her dress, murmuring, 'It was a sudden whim madam had this evening, to invite the Colonel and his wife. She'll get over it. Try not to be sad, you can cheer her up if you try.'

But for once Rose's concentration was lacking and her play, dispirited. Mrs Porteous declared the game had better be

122

abandoned. She rang for cocoa and gazed at the apathetic girl.

'What has come over you, Rose? You've usually so much *sparkle*. I'm beginning to think it was a mercy Colonel and Mrs Bowaters left early. You wouldn't have contributed to their enjoyment.'

Rose sipped the warm sweetness and felt her courage and energy begin to return. After tonight, nothing would be the same again. She felt extremely vulnerable and needed security. What, for instance, was her precise status in this house? 'Mrs Porteous . . .'

'Yes.'

'Forgive me but is it necessary for me to be available every night?'

The mood in the sitting-room changed from cool to frosty.

'I don't think I can have understood?'

'What happened this evening was completely unexpected. A – friend called at the tea rooms and we went for a walk. I should like to think I could accept such an invitation, should it occur again, without first consulting you.' This probably sounded impolite; she added tiredly, 'I mean no discourtesy, Mrs Porteous.'

'Who was this friend?' No reply. 'I trust it was someone known to your sister and her husband? A *family* acquaintance?' Still no answer. 'I shouldn't like to think you accepted invitations on a casual basis, Rose, from any – passer-by.'

This time Rose's voice had an undercurrent of anger. 'He is known to my sister, as it happens, but I don't consider that a necessary qualification. We each have our own friends.' Mrs Porteous's expression changed to self-righteous disapproval.

'Rose, you are very young. How can you judge who is suitable? And this – person – was a man? It is highly improper for you to be out late at night, unchaperoned. I'm sure your sister would agree with me.'

Rose's weary mind churned with rebellion and turmoil. We've had the war to end all wars, she thought; men have given their lives as Cecil did. Freedom isn't *dangerous* provided one is sensible – I know the difference between right and

123

wrong! And those men who came back should be able to take their place in society. Stand tall. Cleaning floors isn't proper work for any of them.

Why should Ned have to do that?

Harold didn't even serve and he has a secure position.

Why shouldn't I at least go out with Ned Harrison?

I'm not making any sense at all, she thought abruptly, and I can't afford to be put out on the street, not tonight. Draining her cup she set it down on the tray.

'I'm truly sorry your evening was spoiled, Mrs Porteous. I will try and give notice in future, before accepting further invitations.'

You won't receive one from Ned, whispered a voice inside, you've said no and he won't come back! The thought weighed so heavily, she could scarcely drag herself to the door.

As she reached it, Mrs Porteous called, 'Before you go, would you ring for the maid to take away the tray.'

In her bedroom there were unexpected signs of kindness from Eloise. A small stove stood in the fireplace to warm the room, her nightgown was wrapped around a hot-water bottle. Hanging in the wardrobe her old black dress had been freshly pressed. Rose brushed away tears. In the old days, before Gertie met Harold, they used to do such acts for one another but this was new.

I wish I could talk to Eloise, Rose thought wistfully, but she would be bound to tell her mistress. She couldn't discuss it with Gertie either. These days, Harold's attitude had rubbed off sufficiently to make her sister an unsympathetic listener.

Hugging the bottle, Rose tried to quiet her mind. She considered Ned dispassionately. He was so unlike anyone she'd met before. Perhaps among those half-forgotten convalescent soldiers there had been similar men but she'd never been alone with any of them.

Ned wouldn't have been invited to Clairville Road, he wasn't part of that pre-war world. Mother and Father would have judged him totally unsuitable and she wouldn't have

124

argued with that. However much it hurt she had to be honest: I'd have been 'kind but firm' she thought wryly, just as Mother would have expected.

Yet Ned was as kind and sensitive as anyone she'd ever met – it had caused him such pain to confess his love! It shook her to recall the look on his face. Such naked emotion – such love!

Australia?

How could she possibly marry a stranger and live in a foreign land? She tried to remember what she'd learned. An arid country where convicts were sent, that's all. In her shattered, dazed state, her body felt as weak as her mind, even the warmth of the bottle didn't dissolve her fear.

To be the object of a man's love was a terrifying thing.

How could she abandon Gertie?

Work among labouring men, in the hope of a prosperous future? You'd have to love a man heart, mind, body and soul to risk that.

Had she the courage?

Do I love him at all?

Into her weary brain came the image of him as he'd whispered, God bless you.

'God bless you too, Ned Harrison,' she whispered into the darkness. It was a beginning.

Chapter Six

Spring Fever

It was impossible for Rose to remain still. She woke with a temperature but couldn't be sure if the cause was emotion or leaky shoes. Fresh air would cure it, she decided. Besides, in her febrile state she couldn't bear to be cooped up: the cage had become a prison.

She slipped out of the house earlier than usual. At the tea rooms she asked if she could discuss a private matter and told the proprietress of her intention to leave at Easter.

'I'm sorry to give notice after all your kindness but if I don't begin those lessons soon . . .'

'I understand, my dear,' she soothed. 'Our customers will miss you but it's for the best, I'm sure.' She noticed Rose's restlessness and high colour. 'Are you well enough to work today?'

'Oh, yes. I was caught in the rain last night, that's all.'

But by midday, she was flushed and giddy. Miss Lawson wasn't taking any risks.

'You're to go back home to bed. Mrs Porteous will see you're looked after. Don't try and struggle in tomorrow. We can manage without you for the rest of the week.'

Strangely, Mrs Porteous reacted magnanimously. She withdrew into her shell after issuing her orders but these were that Eloise was to nurse the invalid and cook must prepare plenty of broth and steamed fish. She uttered no criticism.

She sees it as a punishment, thought Rose, light-headed. I was out unchaperoned with a strange man, now I must suffer for it. Until I'm purged, I shan't be fit company.

126

But she drank the hot drinks and accepted having her pillows plumped and a shawl put round her shoulders. 'It's ridiculous ... I'm never ill,' she said drowsily.

'Of course you're not,' Eloise agreed but privately she told Mrs Porteous it was a mild attack of fever. Hoskins was sent round to Fleetham Street with a note.

Her sister was indisposed but not seriously so, Gertie was informed. Should it be necessary a doctor would be sent for but at present Rose appeared to be making a good recovery. However, should Mrs Brigg wish to reassure herself, the maid would admit her between two and three on Saturday afternoon. Mrs Porteous regretted that she herself would not be at home and therefore unable to receive Mrs Brigg.

'It is a deliberate snub,' declared Harold wrathfully, 'the woman is treating us with contempt.'

'Why should you think that, Harold? She's obviously concerned that I shouldn't be worried.'

'But what about *me*? Why am I not included in either the letter – which is addressed exclusively to you – or the invitation?'

'You could hardly visit Rose in her bedroom,' Gertie pointed out, 'it wouldn't be proper. And why risk infection? What good would that do?'

'You would go to the bedroom, Gertrude, as any caring sister should. I should proceed to the drawing-room where Mrs Porteous would receive me.'

'But the woman makes it perfectly plain she will be out.'

'Which makes it even more of a snub!' he cried pettishly. 'Besides, it's high time we saw for ourselves whether Rose is properly accommodated. It might not be a suitable establishment for your sister.'

What you're after is to see inside that fine house, thought Gertie. But she'd been married long enough to know when to hold her tongue.

According to Harold, he and Gertie had by now 'shaken down' together. Gertie thought of it differently. In the small, cramped rooms she felt swamped. The mean-sized double bed was purgatory, too; she couldn't avoid him even by pressing up against the wall.

The awkward arrangement with the screen shielding the little bath from the kitchen area was hazardous. Harold demanded it be abolished, exposing the occupant of the tub to every passing draught. Gertie refused.

Then there was the laundry. Sheets and pillowcases still went to the bagwash as did Harold's shirts but he insisted his union suits be done by a gentler hand. Gertie squeezed the solid locknit, and cursed. She and Rose washed out their delicate underwear overnight. Harold's garments retained their moisture. There was no outside line. The shapes, redolent of their owner, dangled over the wooden clothes-horse for days.

Rose had always managed the money. Now Gertie was handed a sum every Friday and told to make it last. After the first acrimonious week, she discovered this was not simply for food but for coal and any personal expenditure as well. In high dudgeon, she hurried round to the tea rooms. Rose listened patiently; even by her frugal standards, Gertie was being pushed too far.

A tactful approach would be best, she suggested. A loving wife, a carefully prepared supper and a quiet discussion in front of the fire but Gertie preferred to be dramatic. There was no food on the table, steaming washing concealed the fire and Rose's calculations were brandished as soon as Harold walked in through the door. Turning the screw, Gertie began her attack by reminding him of his past deceptions.

'Why did you not tell me you were only a clerk? Why ask me to marry you if you could not afford to support me?' Her voice was shrill, her hair clung in damp tendrils around her face. She hadn't bothered to change out of her morning overall. It was all part of the demonstration as to how low she'd sunk.

Harold refused to be impressed. He addressed her coldly. Had she not been equally wicked? Where was the dowry that would have saved them from this humiliation? He had made his position plain enough. And look how she squandered her resources: a woman who wasted over thirty pounds on an animal skin could not complain afterwards of poverty.

He snatched up the list and began to cross out certain items. It might be unseasonably cold but they could do without more coal; Gertie must move about to keep warm. And why buy flowers? That was a stupid waste of money.

'Harold, we have to have a fire to dry your wretched underwear. As for the daffodils, they only cost a penny. The market was nearly over, they were clearing what was left from the stalls.'

'Nevertheless. . . .' But he could not think of many uses for a copper.

It was, of course, his own secret saving towards membership of the Brotherhood which was causing the problem. He and Gertie could have managed resonably well, could even have afforded an hour or two of help from Queenie, had it not been for that obsession. But he had to be ready! When the call came, Harold knew he would be expected to make donations to charity. No matter what privations his wife might suffer, he intended to be as lavish as fellow brethren once that happened.

He'd never told Gertrude how much he earned; to Harold's mind that was not a wife's concern. All she needed to know was what she might expect on Friday nights. He saw it as a bestowal rather than a right and expected gratitude in return. Tonight he was faced with outright mutiny.

'We cannot continue like this, Harold. If you want me to pay for fuel as well as food you'll have to give me more. There just isn't enough. Rose has done the sums, you can see for yourself.'

'Damn Rose!'

'Harold!'

He was savage. He wanted to throw her out, order her home to her mother – but Gertrude no longer had a mother, her home was here. He was the one who would have to go. He couldn't leave her penniless, nor could he afford to support two separate households. And what would happen once word out out? It wouldn't enhance his prospects of becoming an entered apprentice.

'How much do you earn, Harold?'

'Mind your own business!'

He was disturbed by the way she refused to be cowed. When she next spoke, directly and honestly, it had even more impact.

'If they don't pay you enough, can you not ask for more? Are you due for promotion? What about Mr Simmonds, could you not approach him? You're always telling me how much he admires your conscientiousness.'

'Good Heavens, Gertrude, you don't know what you're saying!' He pretended to deliberate and calculated furiously. 'Look here, supposing I managed to let you have an additional ten shillings. That should be more than sufficient. You would have to promise, though. No more pleading poverty, Gertrude. No more wasting money on flowers.'

It would mean cutting back on his savings and those damned payments were due to begin any day. Far from grateful, Gertie was adamant.

'Twelve and sixpence, Harold. Rose says that is the minimum extra I need.'

Damn, damn, damn!

'All right. Twelve and sixpence. God knows how I am to afford it.'

'She suggests you and I should make a proper budget. Here, you see. She has drawn up one column labelled "Income" – under that you enter your wages. Opposite under "Expenditure", she has listed all those items due each week . . .'

He'd had enough. He put up a newspaper in front of his face and became as deaf as the proverbial post.

Mrs Porteous's invitation had been specific. At two o'clock the following Saturday Gertie was led directly upstairs without a moment to linger in the hall.

130

'This way, madam. Your sister is expecting you.'

In Rose's room a fire was burning! Gertie recalled her own chilly bedroom and loosened the silver fox.

'My word, this is nice. What a charming room.'

'Gertie – how lovely to see you!'

Remembering the reason for her visit, Gertie moved over to the bed. 'How are you feeling?'

'Much, much better. Everyone has been so very kind.'

She looked at Rose critically. 'You're all eyes and far too thin. Have you been eating properly?'

'They've been spoiling me dreadfully. Eggs coddled in milk, beef broth – how could I not get well? Sit down, dearest. How nice you look – that pretty scarf is very flattering. Tell me all the news. How is Harold?'

Gertie examined the upholstery. This armchair was better quality then those at Clairville Road.

'I can see why you kept quiet about this place.'

Rose sank back against the pillows. 'Please, Gertie, that's unkind. And it's not true.' Not entirely, anyway. Her sister fingered the cushions.

'You never mentioned you were living in *luxury*.' Rose was silent. Gertie shrugged. 'There's nothing much to tell. Harold has said nothing further about our moving even though I've asked several times. Those two strange men called again last night – I still don't know what it's about. Oh, and the spring hats have arrived at Dickson and Benson.'

'Describe them to me.' Rose wasn't particularly interested but she could doze without Gertie noticing. Talk of a sweet little yellow-green felt cloche with white pom-poms flowed on and on until it was interrupted by the parlour-maid arriving with the tea-tray.

'Well?' Gertie demanded.

'Well what, dear? I'm afraid I wasn't paying attention. Thank you, Susan, my sister will pour.' Gertie waited until the maid had attended to the fire and closed the door.

'I was asking what you'd like for your Twenty-first? It's only ten days away.'

'Nothing expensive,' Rose said hasily. 'In fact, I did have one idea. I was wondering if I could ask you to make me a blouse. Two, in fact. Ready for when I begin secretarial work.'

Gertie looked up from the selection of biscuits.

'Is that likely to be soon?'

'Yes,' Rose said decisively, 'I've told them at the tea rooms I shall leave at Easter. I haven't saved as much as I'd hoped ... I shall have to use money from the bank book. Unfortunately, it may mean moving away from here.'

'Why?' Gertie was astonished. 'This is an absolutely splendid room. You're perfectly comfortable.' She looked around indignantly, 'Much more than we are.'

Rose tried to explain but Gertie wasn't convinced.

'You can't be sure Mrs Porteous will object to the lessons. If I were you I'd withdraw my notice rather than risk losing this place.'

'I can't go on being a waitress. I don't like the work and I earn only a pound a week.'

Gertie shrugged. 'Oh, pooh. You'll meet someone, you'll get married.' To her surprise, Rose blushed. 'Goodness, have you found a boy already?'

'No!'

Gertie knew a fib when she heard it from Rose. 'You secretive thing! Who is he, anyone I know?'

'Gertie, stop it. I haven't met anyone. I'm not going to be married, I'm planning a career.' Rose drank her tea to calm herself. For some reason, her heart was beating unsteadily. When she'd recovered, she asked, 'Will you make the blouses? I'll pay for the material.'

'Not if it's for your birthday,' Gertie said firmly. 'Harold can pay, then it'll be from both of us. I saw just the colour to suit you yesterday. A printed chiffon in shades of turquoise.'

'Gertie – no! It's for business wear. What I need are two shirt-waists with high-fastening collars.'

Gertie's face fell. 'How boring. You must have been telling the truth after all. You wouldn't wear a blouse like that to go out with a boy.'

132

'No, I wouldn't. So stop quizzing me about it. Did you see any sensible poplin in the shops? Cream or pale grey, I think. Nothing showy.'

'Urgh!' Gertie brushed away the crumbs and licked the tips of her fingers delicately. 'That was a delicious tea. Harold will be even more furious when I tell him. When d'you expect to be up and about?'

'I shall be back at work on Monday,' Rose said firmly. 'Thank you for coming.'

'I wouldn't have missed seeing this place for anything,' Gertie said frankly. 'Do you think I can have a peek in the downstairs rooms before I go?'

'No!' Rose was adamant. 'Sorry, Gertie, but I'm here on sufferance at present. Mrs Porteous disapproves of the very idea of those lessons. She might put me out on the street if you upset her.'

'As you might have to find another room, anyway,' Gertie said slowly, 'shall I ask Mrs Potter if she knows of one?'

Living near to Harold didn't appeal but an idea began to take shape. 'If Harold really does intend renting a house, perhaps I could move back to Fleetham Street? It would be respectable enough and I could afford it.'

Gertie was immediately cheerful.

'That's a splendid idea. I shall tell him we must be out by Easter so that you can be sure of a roof. Good. That's settled.' She embraced Rose and produced a small tissue-wrapped packet from her bag. 'Here, one of my crocheted hankies to help you feel better.'

'Dear, dear Gertie,' Rose hugged her, 'you are a kind soul.' A small voice inside whispered, 'And I've managed to divert you from asking questions about Ned.'

The following Monday, Rose was welcomed back to the tea rooms with a piece of news. 'A person came enquiring about you. Not one of our regulars. I explained you were ill and he said he'd call again.'

Rose had gone scarlet. 'What sort of person? Was he young?'

133

'No, in his sixties. Not very *presentable*, I fear. In fact, I debated asking whether he had any money before I served him.'

Her spirits plummeted then rose. Did Ned have an uncle? Had he come to plead on his nephew's behalf? Was there a chance she might discover where Ned lived?

'Are you fully recovered?' asked the proprietress.

'Oh, yes, thank you!' Rose found herself smiling idiotically. 'And I'm so glad to be back at work.'

'Is there any chance you might reconsider? You know how pleased we'd be if you stayed.' The girl's cheeks flushed a second time and Miss Lawson began to wonder seriously if she hadn't returned too soon.

'I'm afraid not.... At least, I don't know. Can I take a few more days to decide?'

'Of course. Now, if you're sure you're fit, you can make a start with the tables.'

Harold was finding life unfair. It began with Gertrude's demand for extra money and grew worse when the Winnot brothers turned up at his home to inform him Ruby had been delivered of a son. His son. Despite fierce protests at such an intrusion into his privacy, conducted in whispers for fear Gertrude might hear, he had to agree to make good his promise.

'Why come here? You could have told me outside the mill!'

'Want to tell the world, do you, Brigg? Want all those colleagues of yours to see us standing there and guess what you'd been up to?'

That was the last thing. Harold had to contain his fury and pray that Gertrude didn't become inquisitive. He had been half inclined to deny the child was his but his nerve gave way. For the first time in his life he was being bullied and found it most unpleasant.

'Five shillings a week,' he hissed, 'that was what was arranged, not a penny more.'

'There were things needed for the bairn, Briggs. Ruby had

it at home and there was the midwife to pay. The child was sickly so there was medicine as well. Ruby can't earn for a bit. We've had our wages cut so you'll have to fork out. We've made a list of what had to be bought. Two pounds will cover the lot.'

'Two pounds!'

'Let us have what you can now,' George Winnot suggested. 'We'll collect the rest next Friday when I come for the week's five bob.'

'I can't afford—'

'Of course you can!' Alf's fists tightened menacingly. 'Listen, Brigg, we're not prepared to waste time. That little bastard's yours. He even looks like you. Ruby's a good mother but she's got nothing put by and we've families of our own. My wife's given her all our cast-off baby clothes, we're not being unreasonable.'

They stood, solid as two great oaks, waiting for him to find his purse. Harold tried to pretend it was nearly empty, which was a mistake. Alf reached out a large hand and took it from Harold's limp fingers.

'There's two ten shilling notes ... as well as half a sovereign.' Alf finished shaking the contents onto the table. 'We'll leave you the coppers and silver.'

Harold was savage. 'How am I going to manage?'

'Ask your wife for a handout,' George was contemptuous. He looked about. 'This the best you could do for her? She looked a dainty thing, she deserves better.'

'Get out!'

'We're going. One of us'll be back, come Friday.' At the door, Alf asked softly, 'Don't you want to know what she's called him?'

Harold looked at him in horror. 'Not ... not—'

'No. He's Valentine, poor little tyke. She said he was a lovechild so he might as well know it. He's been baptized. The midwife did it because he was sickly. He's a grand little lad now, though. Flourishing.'

Valentine Winnot. Fruit of his loins. Would to God he'd never survived the birth!

135

'We'll let ourselves out.'

Harold's mind did a sudden volte-face.

Suppose this was to be his *only* son?

Gertrude showed no sign of becoming pregnant. He'd had some vague idea that if she had, he might have grounds for refusing to pay Ruby Winnot but suppose Ruby's child were to be his only posterity?

He was not quick-witted; he gasped as the idea slowly took hold. The sound halted Alf Winnot. Harold had a sudden, urgent desire to see the boy. He looked at Alf and made as if to speak. Alf waited. Harold's mouth opened and closed; he couldn't, finally, humble himself enough to make the request.

Alf grinned. 'We'll be back on Friday,' he promised and disappeared.

Gertie heard footsteps descending and ventured out of the bedroom. 'Have they gone?' When Harold didn't answer she peered round the parlour door. 'Have you finished your business meeting? It's freezing in there.'

He was bemused. 'What did you say?'

Gertie spread her hands to the fire. 'Were they from a Masonic Lodge?'

'No!' It was so violent, she rocked back on her heels.

'There's no need to shout, Harold.'

'I – beg your pardon.'

'If those men are coming again, we shall have to make other arrangements. It may be spring but it's far too *cold* to wait in the bedroom.' She looked at him impatiently, his eyes were dull. As usual he hadn't listened to a word.

It was ten days before the unknown customer returned to the tea rooms. When he was pointed out, Rose could understand the proprietress's doubts. He was clean enough, but his clothes were rough; she asked politely if he was ready to order.

'Excuse me asking, are you Miss Rose Bossom?'

'Yes.'

'May I enquire if you're better?'

'Yes, thank you.'

136

'I'd like a pot of tea, a cheese sandwich and a chat. Take your time, I'm in no rush. The name's Cooke, by the way. Hayden Cooke.'

Not Harrison? Rose was puzzled. She served other tables and Hayden had plenty of time to observe her from behind his old copy of the *Gazette*.

She was comely, which pleased him. He belonged to an age when women were proud of their figures, not like nowadays. Hayden approved of a girl with proper hips and a bosom that was not flattened to resemble a boy's. She was still very pale, except when she blushed. He liked that as well. Today's hussies, smoked in the street with skirts above the knee, they'd forgotten how to blush. Such bold faces, all rouged and coloured, it made a man feel queer to see it.

Rose's skirts reached mid-calf and she had decent black stockings. She was bonny, too, she didn't need paint. Plenty of dark gold hair and a searching pair of eyes. Ned could pick a winner all right.

There was no doubt she was a lady. Hayden sighed. Her manner, the correct way of speaking, everything was as different from Ned as could be. Did it matter? He'd spoken out confidently but faced with the reality of Rose, Hayden was unsure.

She came with his sandwich.

'Can you not sit down, lass? I'll not bite.'

'We're not supposed to be familiar with customers.'

'I'm not a customer,' Hayden said bluntly, 'I'm here because of Ned Harrison – not that he knows anything about it.' She'd turned a fiery shade. He was worried he'd frighten her off. 'Listen, Miss Bossom, it's embarrassing for you but please hear me out. I've no family I care about. Ned's been more of a son to me. He served his apprenticeship with me. He was good, still is. A really intelligent chap. If it hadn't been for the war, he might have gone far in the ship-building business. Become an engineer, made something of hisself. Then again, if it hadn't been for that war, you wouldn't have ended up a waitress?'

She gave a brief shake of the head.

'It's set the world topsy-turvy but we've got to make the best of it.' Rose's eyes were downcast. 'It's impertinent of me but are you set on being a lady type-writing assistant? Ned told me about it, d'you see.' When she didn't answer, he said, 'The lad's plain spoken. He's got this one chance. After he helped you that night, he was so struck he planned to work hard, save a bit, then come courting in a proper way. But he hasn't a hope, the job he's got now. He'd be an old man before he'd got enough put by.

'After he'd shown you the furnaces and everything, I've never known him so dejected. He told me about seeing you back to that grand house . . . He could think nothing but that you were a proper lady and he was nowt but a labourer. That's how it is at present but with you beside him, Miss Bossom, Ned will prove himself, I'm sure of it. He needs a comrade, one that'll stick by him. That's the encouragement that boy needs.'

He'd exhausted himself. He sat back and waited. When her murmur came it was so low, he could only catch part of it.

'Only seen him . . . times . . . my life.'

Hayden nodded helplessly, 'I know. You're practically strangers, the pair of you – it's a terrible risk. But then again, I don't suppose you realize how strong his feelings are?'

When he saw her face suffuse with colour, Hayden shook his head. 'Shocking,' he said suddenly, 'that lad's feeling worse than my Boadicea. My bi— dog,' he explained. 'I've got her shut up because of Charlie's whippet. She's already gnawed her way through two boxes an' a plank . . .'

You great fool! he told himself, talking this way to a lady.

'I'd better go . . .' He cleared his throat, 'You wouldn't have an old paper bag . . . this sandwich – it's very good, I'm sure, but I'm not hungry just now . . . it would mebbe take Boadicea's mind off . . . off the whippet.'

Rose's eyebrows went up and up; the expression in her dark eyes was unfathomable. Hayden felt extremely hot.

'Look, I'm sorry.' He fumbled in his pockets. 'I've no

business talking to you like that. I've got my money ready ... here.' He popped it into the saucer and Rose took it with his bill to the desk. When she returned, she had in addition to his change a bulging paper bag plus an empty one.

'These scraps are for your dog. The sandwich,' she whisked it into the empty bag, 'is for you. You may feel hungry later on. If you happen to see Ned,' her voice threatened to wobble, 'please tell him I think we should at least discuss his – proposition – calmly and *carefully*.' She touched her cheek, it felt as if it were burning. 'He doesn't need to spend any money. I will meet him outside the park. We can go for a walk. Two o'clock. Sunday.'

Hayden's face shone like the sun. He seized her hand and wrung it thoroughly. 'I'll tell him. I'll see the stupid bug— lad's on time.'

'There's no *commitment* on either side,' Rose said hastily.

'A'course not. How could there be? And thanks for ...' he waved the bag of bits, 'it could tek Boadicea's mind off it, you never know.'

Spring, which had been so reluctant to show itself, put forth coy feelers that week, even in Middlesbrough. By Sunday, the temperature was almost pleasant. Rose hadn't specified which particular entrance to the park; it was a challenge which Ned solved easily. He was already waiting by the railings, at the exact spot where she had first turned her ankle, at five to two precisely.

The passers-by were savouring the sun like deprived drunk-ards in sight of their first glass of ale. On the opposite side of the pavement Rose nodded to him as she waited for perambu-lators and children to go past. Her heart was thumping despite her best intentions.

Ned managed to keep his face resolutely free of emotion ... almost. Seeing it, Rose began to relax. There would be no embarrassing declarations today. Indeed, his conversation was so stilted and formal to begin with, it made her want to giggle. Hayden Cooke must have been drilling him rigorously.

After enquiring politely of one another's health, Rose asked, 'How's Boadicea? Is she more – comfortable?' He was stunned.

'Did Hayden tell you ...?'

'About the whippet? Yes.'

'Well ...' He didn't know how to proceed. 'She's quieter, like. He keeps her on a lead whenever they go out.' It had broken the ice. He didn't pursue the topic, remaining silent until they'd shuffled through the entrance gates with the rest of the crowd.

They wandered along municipal paths that wound through shrubberies. Ned described without rancour his week spent cleaning the classrooms with the headmistress constantly finding fault. For her part, Rose made him laugh over the antics of her customers.

By and by he asked after Gertie. She mentioned her worry that her sister was not managing her household budget.

'I'm partly to blame. When Gertie and I were together, I looked after things.'

Ned tried to estimate what a clerk might earn. 'The rent can't be that much.'

'It isn't and I daresay Harold earns a reasonable salary. Unfortunately he hasn't taken Gertie into his confidence.'

Ned said bluntly, 'I earn three pounds a month.'

'Is that all?' She was shocked. 'I'm sorry, I didn't mean to ... to criticize.'

'It's supposed to be part-time but I never finish before five or six in the evening. There's no overtime paid. Still, I can give my sister a bit, which means a lot to me. She and Lionel have been very generous.'

'But how do you ...' Her voice trailed away. Live, was what she'd nearly said. He guessed.

'Aye. Not much for a man of twenty-four. "Could do better", as they say. How, is the problem.' She was beginning to understand why Australia appeared so attractive a proposition.

Out of the wind and with the benefit of bright sunshine,

140

Rose introduced the difficult topic tentatively. She told him she knew very little about the country.

Ned began to describe what he'd learned so far. He didn't attempt to hide the drawbacks, the desert conditions inland, the cattle and sheep stations 'up country', miles from anywhere in the middle of hot, dusty scrub. The lack of water, of female company and the abundance of snakes, insects and flies.

Growing bolder, he began to sketch out a possible future once he'd served his time. 'Lionel suggested it must've been the same for the first convicts,' Ned said cheerfully. 'When their sentence was complete they were given a chance to stake a claim. A new beginning, which is how it should be.'

Rose asked cautiously, 'Is that how you see it?'

'I'm not sure,' he admitted. 'I'm not committing myself until I've got the *feel* out there. Maybe I will try for a small freehold, maybe something more ambitious. The two representatives of the company were encouraging, they might help me get started.' He sighed. 'It's all pie in the sky, even though Hayden wants to lend me the money.'

She remembered the twenty pounds. 'Because of the fare?'

'Aye. He can't afford it. And how would I pay him back? I might take years – he could be needing the cash long before then. I reckon I'll have to turn the offer down.' The conversation was veering towards forbidden ground.

'When do you have to let them know?'

'In a week or two. D'you fancy walking a bit further?'

At the lakeside they watched the first inexpert rowers of the year while the sun sank and the air turned colder. Ned talked of parakeets and emu, kangaroos and wombats, of the first explorers and their tragic fate.

Rose listened, thinking what a mass of information he'd managed to accumulate in so short a time. When she told him so, Ned grinned.

'Must be the library's best customer, me. My father took me there many years ago. We stood in the hall and he pointed to all the signs: history, geography, science, engineering, then he said, "If there's anything you want to know, don't ask a fool, come here and find out from the experts." Mind you, they haven't got a *big* selection on Australia.'

'But you've read the lot?'

He laughed aloud, 'Twice over.'

'Would you accept my invitation,' she said carefully, 'to a cup of tea? I normally have one about now. I wish I could entertain you to one at Albert Road but my hostess won't agree to *any* visitors, not even family. Gertie was allowed to visit when I was ill, that was all.'

'Not even Mr Brigg?'

'No.' She chuckled. 'He did try, though. He rang the bell at three o'clock on the pretext of collecting Gertie but Hoskins left him waiting on the step. Harold was dreadfully put out but Mrs Porteous had made it clear in her note.'

'Dear me!'

Rose flushed. 'She's a very *private* person. Visitors have to be of her choosing.' She shivered.

Ned said immediately, 'Rose, I accept your kind offer. Let's find a café.'

Inside he asked, 'Do you intend staying on at Albert Road?'

'When I begin the lessons I think Mrs Porteous will ask me to leave. Her late husband disapproved of women having a career.'

'How are they supposed to support themselves?'

She replied lightly, 'They are intended to wait at home for "Mr Right".'

'Suppose he gets held up?' When she laughed he added, 'No, I'm serious. Those women who knew their men were lost to them for ever after the war, what happens to them?'

Rose said sadly, 'They have to do the same as I do, battle on. Convince our loved ones that virtue isn't endangered by going out to work.'

'Bravo,' he encouraged.

She sighed. 'I'm subject to all manner of inducements. Yesterday Mrs Porteous invited me to become her permanent companion.'

He frowned, 'You're not going to accept?' He withdrew the remark quickly. 'I mean – you'd lose all your independence that way.'

'I also pointed out that I would be a very *dull* person, without the stimulus of the tea rooms. It's that which keeps her friends amused.' Rose described her appearances in front of visitors.

Ned's face darkened. 'She's treating you like a pet monkey—' Oh God! he swore silently, why can't I *think* before I speak.

Rose answered after a pause. 'I fear you could be right. What are you doing?' He was signalling to the waitress.

'I can afford two more teas.' They were both silent until the steaming liquid appeared.

'I've a suggestion to make,' he said shyly, 'an outing. Have you ever been to Roseberry Topping?'

She smiled. 'Father once took all of us there on a picnic. We travelled in a charabanc.'

'It'll be different this time. I have the loan of – an alternative form of transport.'

'What, exactly?'

'Wait and see! Would next Sunday suit you?' Rose nodded, eyes full of delight. 'Can you meet me about ten o'clock?' It would mean missing church, Gertie might start asking questions.

'Where?'

'Say, the corner of Princess Road and Diamond Road?'

'All right.'

'If it's pouring with rain, we won't go.'

'No.' But she'd pray every night that it didn't.

'Have you a stout pair of shoes? It can get muddy, this time of year.'

'I've galoshes.'

'And a scarf. The wind gets fierce on the top.'

'You've been there before?'

'Once or twice with Hayden. Before the war with Mu, my sister.' She'd been bonny and single then, he remembered,

143

without a care in the world. 'I think it's time I walked you home. We don't want Mrs Porteous to start worrying.'

'I told her I was going for a walk in the park,' Rose said, primly, 'That is all that need concern her.' But there would be repercussions if the widow discovered the truth!

A few yards short of the handsome wrought-iron gates, Ned raised his cap. 'I'll leave you here, Rose.'

'Thank you,' She held our her hand. 'I've enjoyed my afternoon immensely Ned. It's been so – *interesting*.'

But he'd only nine more days before he had to let the company know! Don't think about that, Hayden had insisted, don't let it enter your head. Ned managed to say equally calmly, 'I've enjoyed every minute, too. Until next Sunday then.' When she smiled like that, his heart turned over. 'Au revoir,' and stayed turning!

One of the customers for whom Harold was responsible had cause for complaint. Bobbins of wire had arrived in too bruised a condition to be usable. On the floor of the rolling mill, Jack Wilson, the newly appointed works manager, was angry.

'Please don't come complaining to me, Mr Brigg. I warned you that order should be specially inspected at every stage. It also required a waterproof wrapping but you refused to listen. You kept insisting it was a rush job. Now Hunters are upset.'

'I'd promised them they should have it by last Wednesday.'

'It's my understanding there was no need for such haste—'

'Don't you try and teach me!' flared Harold.

'If you had come to me first and asked whether it was *possible*,' Wilson said earnestly, 'or even *advisable*, I could have explained . . .'

'It is not for you to tell me—'

'Mr Brigg, that's part of the reason I'm employed here.' He was seven years younger than Harold, better paid, in a more responsible position. Harold knew the man was being impertinent. He couldn't put his finger on it, he just knew! It took all his self-control to curb his temper. At the back of his mind was

144

the thought that tomorrow was Friday and one of those damn Winnots would be round for another five shillings.

The younger man stood his ground, refusing to be intimidated. After more acrimony, it was agreed the unusable wire would have to be remade.

But by the time Harold returned to the crowded sales office, as was his habit he had reworked the scene, ending with him supremely in charge of the situation, in the right, ordering a humbled works manager about his business. Smugly, he sat at his desk. Simmonds appeared in the doorway.

'Mr Brigg, I'd like a word.'

'Yes, Mr Simmonds. Of course. Immediately.' Harold swept past colleagues with an eager smirk. To be singled out was rare. There was also the possibility it could be to do with the Brethren. Harold was fairly confident his boss was 'on the square'. Inside the office, he stood in the secret, approved position which unfortunately gave him the appearance of a penguin.

If Simmonds understood; he ignored it, saying instead, 'Close the door.' When this was done, he eyed Harold coolly. 'I've had this from Hunters.' With one finger, he pushed the letter across the desk.

It was a statement, blaming Harold Brigg for unnecessarily rushing through an order which had then turned out to be unsatisfactory.

'But – that's outrageous!'

'I'm glad you realize that.'

It had never got as far as this before with any of his customers; he'd always been able to smooth things over. The size of the order meant it was serious; Harold started to panic.

Simmonds began, 'Hunters will be returning the rest of the bobbins—'

'I shall make it my business to be there when they arrive, Mr Simmonds,' Harold interrupted importantly. 'I shall reprimand the works manager and see to it that he chastises whoever is responsible.'

Simmonds leaned across, stabbing the letter.

'Are you blind? The name of the culprit is there, Brigg. You alone are responsible. Hunters state very plainly that they wanted to allow sufficient time for the order to be made properly and that it required special packaging. Jack Wilson assures me he pointed that out. You were the one who countermanded—'

'Wilson had no right to tell tales ...' Harold stopped himself; this was the wrong approach. 'I'll put the remake in hand straight away, Mr Simmonds.'

'I've already done so. If you'd kindly let me finish ... When this came, I went straight down to the floor. Jack Wilson told me what had happened.'

The sneak! thought Harold wildly. Simmonds was still very annoyed.

'I waited until the first of the bobbins arrived, to see for myself. Hunter's claim is just, the wire is completely useless. Wilson is now in charge of the remake. *He* will tell *you* when to let Hunters know it's ready. Is that procedure clearly understood? Meanwhile, you will write to their purchasing manager and apologize for this extremely regrettable lapse. I want to see that letter before it's posted. Is that also understood?'

Harold was beside himself. 'Jack Wilson had *no* business ... a mere five years working in this firm—'

'Five years *learning* every aspect of the rolling mill, Briggs. Studying at night, in his own time. A bright young chap, able and keen. He deserves to succeed, don't you agree?'

Harold allowed himself to be tempted. 'Since you ask my opinion, Mr Simmonds, no, I do not. Wilson is not a man worthy of praise. He has no background – the fellow's an upstart.'

Simmonds leaned back in his chair. Tapping his teeth with a pencil, he appeared to consider Harold. After a while he said, 'It's not very sensible, making promises you cannot fulfil.' Harold didn't know what he was talking about. Simmonds went on, 'But then that's a habit of yours, isn't it, Brigg? I seem to remember at your wedding, I was promised a dancing partner. How is she, by the way?'

The change of subject baffled Harold. 'Rose is in excellent health.'

'Still working as a waitress?'

'Yes. Regarding Hunters. I—'

'Perhaps I'll look her up. We live in difficult times, Harold ... Firms cannot get orders. Those who manufacture are often kept waiting for payment. *We* may have to tighten our belts, who can tell? Not *averse* to dancing, is she?'

It took Harold another moment to catch up. 'Er, no, indeed not. I understand Rose is a very good dancer.'

'Perhaps I will look her up. All right, Brigg, you can go. Send Mardell in, would you?'

Mardell? he wondered feverishly. There was a vacancy pending for deputy head clerk. The position was Harold's by right, he'd been waiting for promotion far too long. Mardell hadn't enough seniority ... What did Simmonds mean about Rose?

Harold tried to work it out. Dancing, that was it. Simmonds said he wanted her to be his dancing partner. But what if Rose refused again ...? She couldn't!

Suddenly it was obvious. Simmonds was hinting there'd be dismissals at the rolling mill! He'd sent for Mardell simply as a warning to Harold – a warning! Rose must agree to 'shake a leg'. Heavens, it was a small thing to ask. The girl must stop being prudish for the sake of Harold's future. He would speak to Gertrude tonight.

And tomorrow evening one of those dreadful Winnots would be back for another five shillings. He must arrange another venue; Gertrude might begin to guess. He would arrange to meet the man in some dark alleyway.

Really, fate was damnably unkind sometimes.

With the coming of spring, Gertie had tired of her cloistered state and was determined to begin paying calls. She'd had three dozen cards printed, in anticipation:

Mrs Gertrude Brigg
At Home
Tuesdays and Thursdays
2 p.m. – 4 p.m.

That was before Harold decided they should continue living in Fleetham Street. She'd no intention of writing *that* address on the small square of pasteboard, she would wait until they'd moved somewhere socially acceptable. Harold had so very *nearly* agreed they should.

Spring revived so many urges. The desire to buy clothes was strong but shopping was forbidden. She hadn't enough to treat herself at the tea rooms today so the only alternative was to go visiting where refreshments would be free! After lunch therefore, her hat at a jaunty angle, she set off for Clairville Road.

Spring had stimulated many people. There was a collective wish to be out of doors and to throw off the lethargy of winter. At the first two houses, the mistresses had gone for a walk but at the third, Gertie was lucky. Not only was this particular friend indoors, she was throwing an At Home on behalf of the London Missionary Society. The house was overflowing with ladies eager to do good works. Remembering all those beautiful traycloths, anticipating she might be about to donate another, the hostess greeted Gertie with rapture.

She apologized shame-facedly, she'd come empty-handed, she'd had no idea! Ladies cooed and sympathized; what did it matter? The missionaries would benefit another time. Mrs Brigg must come and sit down, loosen her fur – 'How exquisite, is it a silver fox?' and tell them her news.

How was hubby?

Was this a special occasion ...? Could it be that Mrs Brigg had come here today to tell them of an impending Special Event? Beady eyes examined her waist line. Colour mantled Gertie's cheeks.

'Not yet.'

'Not yet.'

'Ah ...' The sigh was borne on a discreet breath around the assembled company.

'And where are you living now?' asked one.

'We're still in rooms,' Gertie had rehearsed her reply. Harold simply could not make up his mind when we were first married. Shall we go here ... shall we go there, you know how it is. Then we thought – why not leave it until the fine weather? Moving can be so trying; at least in the spring it would be so much *nicer*.'

'Oh, how true!' Heads nodded wisely.

'So ...' she looked at them brightly, 'any day now, we shall decide. As soon as we have a "permanent abode", I shall send cards.' Satisfaction was universal.

Conversation had swung round to the perpetual worry of the servant problem, when one of their number piped up, 'And how is Rose?'

'Very well. She was indisposed a week or two ago but is now fully recovered.'

'Still working as a waitress?' There was tinkling laughter at Rose's strange behaviour.

'She is.' Gertie tipped her head to one side and confided, 'Do you know, I believe she actually enjoys it.'

'No!'

'She does. She keeps Harold and me in stitches of laughter, describing the oddities among her customers.' There was laughter again until they remembered they too had visited the tea rooms. Silence fell.

A former, elderly neighbour broke it. 'And does Rose still intend to take up a career? She was always such a *clever* girl.'

Gertie pouted. 'I'm afraid so. Her heart is set on typewriting. Harold is very much against it but Rose was – is – obstinate. I simply don't know how we are to dissuade her. If only she could meet her "Mr Right", as I have done.' She simpered slightly; murmurs of agreement were muted. The next comment came from a young woman nursing her infant.

'Your sister already has an admirer, hasn't she?'

Gertie's mouth dropped open. 'Pardon?'

149

'I understand Miss Bossom was seen out with him last Sunday, in the park.'

'Good Heavens!' It was obvious this was a surprise to Mrs Brigg. One or two tried tactfully to turn the conversation to the increase in the price of butter but Gertie couldn't contain her curiosity. 'Who was it?' she demanded. 'Did you recognize the boy?'

'It wasn't I who saw her,' the young matron replied. 'I'm simply repeating what I heard, that Miss Rose Bossom was seen last week, standing by the lake, with a – person.'

A *person*? There was a quiver at that. Conversation dried up. All eyes were riveted on Gertie and her informant. Too late, Gertie regretted her impulsive questioning. Was this why Rose had been so secretive at Albert Road?

'A person,' she repeated woodenly.

'So I understand.'

In the silence, her hostess came to her rescue. 'Another cup of tea, Mrs Brigg? Or an almond biscuit – though I say so myself, they really are delicious.'

'Thank you, no.' Gertie rose, adjusted her fur. 'Goodness, is that the time? I've stayed far longer than I intended.' The words, like the smile, were automatic. 'Goodbye.' She began the round of farewells, shaking hands, promising effusively to notify everyone of her new address. Only when she'd finally disappeared did attention revert to the young matron now trying to quell her fractious child.

'Are you *sure* it was Rose Bossom?' asked the elderly neighbour. 'Dear me, I hope she's not being foolish. She's still very young, with no mother to advise her.'

'Rose must be ... almost twenty-one,' another calculated. 'As for advice, Rose Bossom had more common-sense than her mother and Gertie put together.' There were nods as they gave each other examples of the late Mrs Bossom's excesses.

The elderly neighbour was still far from satisfied. 'A *person* though. I blame the war, it's made so many young people *unstable*.' She, too, declined her hostess's offer of a biscuit, shaking her head absently. 'I hope nothing comes of it, for Rose's sake.'

'Who told you about it?'

The young matron nuzzled her infant who was struggling to throw a tantrum.

'A neighbour of mine. Her son goes to the school where this fellow works.'

'As a teacher?'

'A cleaner. Apparently, he begged for the situation.'

'Ooh!'

Ladies stared at one another: cleaning? It was hardly fit work for a *man*!

'He won't be there much longer either, apparently. According to May, my neighbour, the headmistress says he's unreliable and takes time off.'

'You would think,' the self-righteous voice came from their midst, 'with all this unemployment, when a man does find work he'd do it and be grateful.' Sanctimonious sighs almost drowned the howling of the child.

'I can remember when every member of the tennis club wanted to be Rose Bossom's beau. Not Gertie's, of course; she was always far too eager.'

The young matron had one more titbit.

'According to May, the person Rose was with, his family came from Dacre Street.'

'Never!'

'I don't believe it. What *is* Rose thinking of?'

'I hope Gertie's hubby puts a stop to it.' They gazed at one another avidly.

'Before it's too late, you mean?'

Gertie's first intention had been to tell Harold but commonsense intervened. What if it was just gossip? Her sister might have gone for an innocent walk and *happened* to meet a customer from the café. That was it. Gertie straightened her shoulders thankfully. She would warn Rose against speaking to casual acquaintances in public, a girl's reputation was too tender.

She could invite her sister to Fleetham Street next Sunday

on the pretext of fitting the two blouses. Gertie had found a pretty shade of blue poplin and had fashioned one with a sailor collar that tied loosely in front, much more flattering than a shirt-waist. She planned to trim it with blue and white checked piping.

Her sunny mood evaporated when one of the two strange men called before Harold had returned from the rolling mill. She showed George Winnot into the parlour where he stood, declining her invitation to sit.

'Nay, missus. I'll not mucky your chairs. Will Mr Brigg be long?'

'I really couldn't say. Would you prefer to leave a message?'

George shook his head. 'It'll not tek but a minute.'

'Please excuse me. I must see to the supper.'

He sniffed appreciatively, 'Smells nice.'

This was impertinent; she gave him a frosty look and withdrew. It was too bad of Harold. This wasn't the sort of person she wanted in her parlour. Once they moved, she would insist neither man be invited to the new house.

Harold was late because he'd been walking the streets to rid himself of his fear and rage. Gertie met him at the top of the stairs.

'One of those men is here. He's been waiting ages.'

'He didn't—' Harold checked himself; of course Winnot hadn't told her.

'You won't let him stay long, will you? Supper's nearly ready.'

Not a second longer than necessary, thought Harold. He closed the door and faced his tormentor. 'These visits must cease. I am not refusing to pay but I will not allow my wife to be incommoded in this way. We must meet elsewhere, Winnot.'

'I'm not hanging about outside if it's wet.'

'There is a small entrance not far from Hill's main gate.' Harold described the location. 'In future we will meet there.'

'I shall turn up here if you're late, wife or no wife.' Winnot was impatient; smells from the cooking made him hungry.

'Hand it over then and I'll be off.'

Harold jingled the coins, hating to be a suppliant. 'I have a request. I want to see the child.'

'Whatever for?'

Harold could feel temper building up again. 'That's my business. Dammit, I'm paying for his upkeep.'

'An' Ruby's doing the caring. Up half the night she's been sometimes. He's not been so well and there's a lot of pneumonia in Haverton Hill.'

Harold said quickly, 'If that child is exposed to danger ...'

George's hands formed fists. 'You've been told before, our Ruby has turned out a grand little mother. It hasn't been easy but she's coped. Val's doing well enough. As for seeing him, I'll give you her answer next week. Now, let's have that five bob and be done wi' it.'

Over supper, husband and wife were each wrapped in their own thoughts. When Gertie eventually enquired, Harold admitted things had not gone smoothly today. How to introduce the subject of Rose? Fortunately, Gertrude did it for him.

'Those blouses I'm making for Rose's birthday ... I thought I'd ask her to come for a fitting after church.'

'Good idea.' He seized the opportunity. 'I was having a chinwag with Simmonds today.'

'Oh, yes?'

'Man to man, you know the kind of thing. Patently, she didn't. 'He was saying how he wished his wife could go dancing ... poor thing's an invalid – have I told you?'

'Yes, Harold, you did. More than once.'

'Ah ... He's a terribly decent type, Simmonds. Between you and me, I've often wondered whether or not he was the Worshipful Master. You know ...' Harold tapped the side of his nose to indicate the secret nature of the remark. 'Yes, he's on a high rung of *that* particular ladder, take my word for it.' Still Gertrude waited. 'He was asking after Rose. I told him she was *blooming*!' This was one of his regular jokes. Harold

153

laughed loudly. Thinking he'd reached the end, Gertie began to clear away. 'No, wait a moment, Gertrude. The thing is, Simmonds told me he's still on the lookout for a dancing partner.'

'No.' It was adamant.

'When she comes round on Sunday you could tell Rose what a decent chap Simmonds is.'

'Harold, Mr Simmonds is married. We do not know his wife, there's never been an invitation to their home. Were he a *very* old friend of the family, known to my parents perhaps, and his wife attended the same social functions as we do, then and *only* then, could my sister dance with him without injuring her reputation.'

'Gertrude, you don't understand. Rose *has* to agree to dance with Simmonds. My whole future might depend on it!'

She stared. 'Don't be ridiculous.'

Harold began to wring his hands. 'Look, I haven't been quite open with you. When I said things hadn't gone too well today, that wasn't the half of it. There was a ridiculous misunderstanding. A young fellow, extremely uppity, doesn't know his place ...'

She'd heard these excuses before. 'What went wrong?'

He retreated. 'You wouldn't understand.'

Gertie folded her hands in front of her. 'Harold, if you are in trouble, it is your *duty* to explain so that I *do* understand.' He loathed her for taking that tone.

'An order turned out to be unsatisfactory and I am being blamed. It's ridiculous, of course.' She didn't bother to ask whether he was responsible.

'And how does Rose come into this?'

'Simmonds wants to take her dancing. He actually asked after Rose's health – I'm sure there's nothing dishonourable, she might even enjoy herself.'

Gertie's eye blazed. 'A man like that? Have you forgotten how he behaved at our wedding breakfast? Don't you ever mention the word "standards" to me again.'

'Gertrude!'

'My sister is not a commodity to be offered in the market place to compensate for your failures at work.'

She was implacable. However much Harold might seethe, he knew she wouldn't budge.

They sat in silence till bedtime. Gertie sewed and wondered again whether there was any truth in the gossip about Rose. Harold pretended to read the *Gazette*. He had done nothing to prevent Simmonds going out with her. The girl was available. All Simmonds had to do was go to the café and ask.

And be turned down. He knew what the outcome would be. Rose was even more of a stickler over behaviour than his wife. So annoying, with that womanly figure at variance with her prudishness. He had tried to manoeuvre Rose into a corner once when Gertrude had been busy elsewhere, for a cuddle and squeeze. The girl had been unreasonable, calling him a cad and threatening to tell her sister.

He crackled the newspaper angrily. It only needed Mardell to be appointed as deputy head clerk to complete a rotten day. And what if Simmonds were to make good his threat? 'Tightening belts' was a euphemism for the sack. To be unemployed in Middlesbrough at present, where hungry men stood six deep on street corners, was a terrifying prospect.

Chapter Seven

Secrets

Rose waited on the corner of Diamond Street hoping she didn't took too ridiculous. The sun shone. Everyone else wore new spring hats and pale-coloured gloves, yet here she stood in her old winter beret, scarf and galoshes.

Would Gertie have ever turned out for 'Mr Right' dressed like this? Rose chuckled. Ned saw the smile as he guided his borrowed motor-cycle combination to a careful halt. He tried to quiet the beating of his heart. Rose's expression changed to astonishment as she peered beneath the leather helmet and goggles.

'Is that really you?'

'It is. And this is Lionel's cousin Fred's pride and joy.'

'Goodness!'

'Ours for the day. Would madam care to climb aboard?' He folded back the sidecar cover and opened the small door. Inside, his one and only blanket had been tucked round a cushion to make a more comfortable seat.

Rose was enchanted. 'I say, that does look snug.'

'You've come properly dressed,' he said approvingly.

'I feel idiotic, it's so warm.'

'You'll be glad of that scarf when we get up there.' She lowered herself onto the seat and slid her legs forward. She felt ridiculously excited; she'd never been in anything half as dashing as this.

'Are we really going all the way to Roseberry Topping?'

'We can ride to Newton under Roseberry. We do the rest on foot.' He fastened the door and checked the buckles on the

156

cover. 'Is madam comfortable?'

'Extraordinarily comfortable, thanks. Pray, let go the horses, my man!' Ned advanced the magneto lever a notch, kicked the starter and let the engine roar. Rose squealed. Satisfied, he eased back the throttle and checked the air control to the carburettor, a weakness on this model.

Rose called, 'I didn't realize you knew how to drive one of these things.'

'Fred showed me. I've been out with him twice.' He'd not been any distance to speak of, this was more of an adventure than Ned cared to admit.

'What's this by my feet?'

'Spare can of petrol. I've no idea whether any garages will be open on a Sunday. Ready?'

'Ready!'

It was more a slither than a start, over the cobbles. Rose clung tightly to the small brass handrail. 'I say ...' They bumped forward towards Southfield Road. She had to shout above the engine, 'Which way are we going?' On the pavement, passers-by stopped to watch them chug past.

'Out through Nunthorpe,' Ned shouted back. 'On to Great Ayton. All right?'

'Marvellous!' And then on to Roseberry, wonderful!

They left the town behind. An empty country road led past pasture with birds busy in the hedgerows. At her level, Rose gazed at cowslips and primroses, she craned to see skylarks hovering above and shouted gleefully when startled rabbits leapt out of their way. Ned kept up a steady twenty miles per hour which seemed to her a perfect speed.

They rested the engine at a roadside brook. Rose produced her offering of scones and biscuits which they washed down with water from the spring. In Great Ayton they stopped again so that Ned could adjust the timing mechanism and top up the fuel tank.

Rose leaned against a grey stone wall in the sunshine, listening to church bells and watching the worshippers returning to their homes. She rubbed her back and shoulders

157

catlike against the stones, murmuring lazily, 'No doubt Gertie will be round tomorrow, asking questions, wondering why wasn't I at church.'

'What will you tell her?'

'The truth, of course.'

He was kneeling close to the machine and asked casually, 'Won't there be a fuss?'

'You mean Harold?' She sighed, 'You're probably right but I don't see why. He still insists he should choose my friends but as from next Friday, he won't be entitled to any longer. I shall be twenty-one – *properly* independent. I shall tell Harold to mind his own business!'

'Perhaps you should try and stall any questions until next Friday? It might make it easier for you.'

'Oh, I couldn't deceive Gertie.' Rose shook her head vigorously, 'We've never had secrets from one another.'

Beyond the village, the triangular cone of Roseberry Topping showed up clearly against the sharp blue sky. They were close enough now to see every detail; the fields on the lower slopes, the path through the belt of trees and the hard rocky outline of the peak.

Ned searched ahead for the farm where the farmer's wife was reputed to welcome travellers who would pay for a bite to eat. He spotted it, tucked into a fold of the land; a low stone building with a lichen-covered roof. He hoped the remains of Hayden's half-sovereign would be sufficient.

'That's where I intend to leave the machine.'

The cart track jolted every bone in Rose's body. She clung to the rail trying not to mind the sheep dog who bounded beside her, barking hysterically. They finally skidded to a halt on farmyard mud.

The farmer's wife had seen them approach. She waited in the doorway as Ned helped Rose climb out and straighten her stiff limbs.

'Will you be eating now or when you come back down, m'dears?' There was no question where they might be headed. Rose looked at Ned.

'Afterwards—?' Would he be offended if she offered to pay her share?

'That would be fine,' he agreed. The woman pointed to a folded tarpaulin.

'Cover your machine up, otherwise the hens will be using it as a roost.' She looked at the sky. 'You've picked a good day for it. There'll be ham and eggs waiting. I'll be watching out for you.'

They walked back down the track, crossed the road and took the path along the edge of the field that led to the base of the hill. Following the contours, they began the climb, past gorse and gnarled clumps of hawthorn to the first belt of trees. Rose could hear skylarks clearly now. In the empty silence, the birdsong was deafening. She stopped to listen, crushed sappy flowers beneath her feet sending up a scent to make her senses reel. They were already high enough to look down on the railway track that linked Middlesbrough with Kildale and Danby.

'We'll stop when we get to the top.' Ned didn't want to waste any time. 'The view's best up there.'

So was the wind. It stung their ears and whipped hair into their eyes. Rose wrapped her scarf over her face. Her top lip was frozen, she couldn't speak.

Ned mouthed at her, 'A little further, can you manage it?' She nodded gamely. A few more steps, a few more, a final haul and suddenly she was being buffeted on the roof of the world.

Standing on huge, flat, brown rocks she gazed across the vast river plain. In the distance hung the pall of smoke and grime that was Middlesbrough. This vicious wind didn't reach that far, it would surely scour the town clean if it did. Rose turned east, shielding her eyes. Ned bellowed, 'Must be Runswick Bay over there. Can you see the sea?'

Eyes half closed, she tried to distinguish it. The blue of the sky and the bay merged into one. Between here and the coast were the moors of Commondale and Leaholm with small farms and villages widely spaced. South was Glaisdale.

159

Further off in the haze nestled Farndale, renowned for daffodils at this time of year. They were spoken of in wonder, thousand upon thousand carpeting the entire dale.

Wherever she looked the moors were covered with the fresh green of new heather, dotted with yellow gorse and snow-white sheep. She could hear the rill close by, the beginning of a stream. Every sense was catered for. It was so beautiful, Rose felt her heart bursting with the joy of it. She looked at Ned to share it. With a shock she saw he looked bleak. She seized his hand.

'What is it? What's wrong?' She held back the strands of hair that were making her eyes water. It must be something dreadful to make him so desolate. 'Can you not tell me?'

'Rose – why have I got to leave all this behind? This is where I belong.' The passion was as strong as she'd seen on the night he took her to the steelworks. 'You feel it too, don't you? This is ours. The mucky old town back there, all this beauty in compensation. I don't want to go. I can't!' He strode away from her, nearer the edge.

She crouched by high stones, needing their protection now she was alone. She was frightened for him. Please God, don't let him be careless in his turmoil.

There was no one else nearby. In the distance there were one or two groups of walkers, too far away to hear. The wind was so strong Ned had to bend his body forward against the force of it. He was hunched up, staring out over the plain but she guessed he wasn't even seeing it. He was wrestling with the conflict in his mind.

He'd not talked of the war, except obliquely, but she knew the desire to return home had been the force that kept him going. He'd held the picture of Mu in his mind, the warm family fireside; those images had conquered the stench and fear of the trenches.

He'd only spoken of one pal who didn't come back, a man who'd taught Ned all he knew about engines. She knew Ned was haunted by the memory of seeing that particular friend die.

160

Rose moved further along the rocks until she found a niche. Out of the wind, the sun was warm. She tugged off her hat, closed her eyes and let the heat ease her taut muscles. She had no wise words to comfort Ned. He had to fight the longing within himself and decide.

It was up to her, too. It wasn't fair to deny him any longer, she knew she had to give him her answer today. He might say it didn't matter but the time must be near when the company had to be told.

'A comrade who'll stick by him,' Hayden had said. He believed she didn't know the strength of Ned's feelings but those had been revealed to her twice.

He loved her with the same degree of passion as he felt for his roots; the thought was almost oppressive. He had put no pressure on her as he'd promised but Rose understood. Ned would try no further persuasion. He had declared himself, now it was up to her. He had been totally honest, she must be the same.

Before the war the two of them would have passed without a second glance, she and Gertie would have found husbands among those dear, dead ghosts whose faces they now found difficult to recall. But again Hayden was right, they had to make the best of what was left. Gertie might pretend the world hadn't changed but it just wasn't true.

Did she care for Ned enough? Could she endure the life in Australia – he hadn't disguised how hard it would be, especially for her. Could she leave behind all that was familiar? How could she bear to be parted from Gertie!

Something blotted out the sun. She knew it must Ned. He would have made his choice. When she opened her eyes she would see what it was. When he looked into hers, he must have her answer.

She saw immediately that he was leaving the north-east. There was sorrow but there was fierce intent. His desire for her was obvious yet he made no attempt to come any closer. 'Rose ...?'

She reached out, pressing her hands against his chest. He

was scarcely an inch taller. They faced one another as equals. She could feel sinew and bone beneath his coat. She knew her love wasn't as great as his. She would give what she had and pray the rest would come one day.

'I'll go with you, Ned.'

The farmer's wife was worried. She threw more wood on the roaring fire in the stove. Normally when young folks came back they were full of it, couldn't stop telling her about the marvellous views but these two were silent. The girl was very pale. The woman needed to find out if something was wrong.

'Most come back with ever such a good complexion,' she said amiably, 'the wind blows away the cobwebs, gives them an appetite. I like to see my plates clean, mind. Them eggs is so fresh I reckon they was laid while you was up there on the top. See the sea, did you, like Captain Cook?'

'We did.' Ned had found his voice. 'We're headed in the same direction ourselves.'

'What – to Australia?'

'Seemingly,' He looked at Rose. The pale skin suddenly took on a glow. The farmer's wife marvelled at the change.

'Well I never! Well I never did. Here . . . Father!' They were in the kitchen and she bawled through the half-open door to her unseen husband in the yard, 'Father, come here quick. Come and see – these youngsters are off to Australia! Here . . .' She waddled back to the table, 'You'll need feeding up if you're going that far. Have some more ham and fried bread, young man.'

Ned said awkwardly, 'I've only got six shillings and seven-pence—'

'Don't be silly.' She was severe, Three shillings for the two of you is what I charge. Eat up. There's scones and fruit cake to come. If either of you wants the privy, it's back behind the barn. I'll just make the tea.'

Conversation wasn't easy above the noise of the engine but on the way back, in Great Ayton, where Ned had stopped to

162

make adjustments, Rose asked tentatively, 'You're not saying much. Is anything wrong?'

He stood and faced her. 'I may have won you with a falsehood. I boasted we were Australia-bound but I've still no idea how I will earn the fare. If I beg the headmistress to let me stay on, there's no chance of saving forty pounds in a couple of months – I cannot borrow again from Hayden—'

'Hush ...' Rose pressed the tips of her fingers against his lips. 'I have enough for both of us. We'll use that.'

He was shocked. 'Those are your savings. If I fail, you may need every penny—'

'Hush!' This time she was mock severe. 'Ned Harrison, I trust you are not going to be a *tiresome* husband?'

'What?'

'You and I are not going to have *disagreements* as Harold and Gertie do, I hope.'

'No, we are not!'

'Good. You will let me know when the money is to be handed over and I shall withdraw it from the bank. There.' She pretended to dust the matter off her hands, 'The subject is closed.'

'Rose ... dear, darling girl, how am I ever going to repay you?'

'We're comrades as Hayden would say. No debts can exist between those.'

About a hundred yards from the wrought-iron gates he turned off the ignition. The engine spluttered and died. Ned eased off the borrowed helmet.

'Have you decided what you'll tell Mrs Porteous or your sister?'

'I've been wondering about it all the way home. I shall *try* to keep it a secret after all.' Rose sighed. 'It's so difficult avoiding questions but I shall do my best, at least until my birthday is past. After that, there's nothing anyone can do – even Harold can't interfere!'

Ned wasn't so sure but he nodded. 'I don't think we should marry until nearer the departure date. We can discuss it once

163

I've written to the company. It's not what I want …' In the dusk she could hear rather than see his embarrassment. 'I can't offer you a home. Oh, Rose, I've won your heart but I bring you *nothing*.'

'Let's be practical,' she said cheerfully. 'We both need to save all we can so it's common-sense to continue as we are. A few more weeks and then we shall be together for the rest of our lives. It's better for us to live quietly and be discreet at present.'

'I'll write to the company tonight and come to the tea rooms once I have their answer.'

'And I shall tuck the memory of today away and take it out when I'm alone. It'll warm my heart!'

'Rose!' Despite their intention to behave like strangers, they clung to one another. When Rose broke away, she wondered breathlessly if she were more in love than she thought?

'Goodnight, dearest Ned.'

He stood until she'd disappeared, then pushed his cumbersome machine a little further off before kicking the starter. It was essential to be discreet in every possible way.

Full of good intentions, Rose fell at the first hurdle. She murmured as the butler opened the door, 'Has Mrs Porteous gone to bed, Hoskins?'

'Madam is in the small sitting-room, miss. She particularly wanted to see you.'

Heart sinking, Rose walked across the hall and tapped on the door. 'I'm home, Mrs Porteous.'

Her hostess looked at her coolly. 'What a very long day out, Rose.'

'Yes, Mrs Porteous.' The colour was coming and going in her cheeks.

'Did you go far?'

'Up Roseberry Topping.'

'Indeed. Was it an excursion?'

'No.' Mrs Porteous waited. Rose remained stubbornly silent.

'What is that you are carrying?' Relief was at hand.

'Galoshes!' She tried not to sound eager. 'They're terribly muddy, I'll take them straight to the kitchen if I may. Then I think I'd rather go to bed ... so much fresh air ...'

But Mrs Porteous hadn't done with her. 'Take your galoshes by all means, and order the cocoa. And Rose ...'

'Yes, Mrs Porteous?'

'Come back afterwards. I wish to know all that happened.'

Full of rebellion, Rose withdrew.

I shan't tell her about Ned, I simply can't, she thought.

But her open honest face had already been enough for Mrs Porteous. She decided it was high time she sent another note to Mrs Brigg.

Gertie began her attack in the tea rooms the following morning. 'You weren't at church yesterday?'

'No, dear. Would you like a coffee?' Gertie waited impatiently. Despite Harold's protests, she'd prevented him calling at Albert Road after the service but although she didn't mind him not knowing what had happened she was determined to satisfy herself. She'd been debating whether or not to tell her sister the Clairville Road gossip. Better wait.

Rose set down the cup. 'That'll be threepence. You must pay, Gertie, I need my wages now.' Slightly miffed, Gertie produced the coppers from her purse.

'What happened to you?'

'I went out with a friend. You might as well know the whole of it because Mrs Porteous bullied me until I told her and then threatened to write to you.' Threatened?

'What d'you mean?'

'Ned Harrison asked if I'd like a day out in the country. He had the loan of a motor-cycle and sidecar. We went to Roseberry Topping and back.'

'You lucky thing!' Ned Harrison? Wasn't that the man who ... Suddenly, the gossip slid into place. 'Rose – have you been out with him before,' she cried, 'in Albert Park?' Rose's face betrayed her. 'You were seen.' And Gertie told her the rest.

To give herself a breathing space, Rose took her sister's bill

165

to the cash desk. When she returned, she said, 'I don't mind you knowing I've been out with Ned. As for those women, they don't concern me for I no longer meet them but I'd rather you didn't tell Harold.'

'He may discover by accident as I did.' Gertie sniffed. 'I'm sure he'll be furious – it's absolutely dreadful behaviour. What can you be thinking of?'

What will her reaction be when I tell her I'm marrying Ned? Rose wondered wryly. I won't think of that now, if I do I shall betray myself; one step at a time.

'Gertie, I have to find other lodgings. Mrs Porteous has given me notice.'

'Oh, Rose! You are still going to take those lessons?' Suddenly Gertie was anxious Rose should learn to type-write: anything was preferable to Ned Harrison. Once established in some superior office, Rose would no longer want to see him. To encourage her Gertie said, 'It's certainly better than working here.'

Rose replied evasively, 'I'm glad you agree but as we are rather busy ...'

'Come round this evening. I need a fitting for your blouses. Mrs Potter may know of somewhere. You can move back to Fleetham Street the instant Harold makes up his mind but he still won't say when we're to leave.'

'About eight o'clock?' If would mean escape from further interrogation at Albert Road. 'And Gertie, you won't tell Harold?'

'Not a word.'

Sadly, Rose's troubles weren't over. At five to seven, as they were clearing the tables, a customer arrived. She was too preoccupied to notice until she'd arrived at the table.

'Evening, Miss Bossom, and how are you?'

She was blank for a moment, then, 'Mr Simmonds!'

'Thought I'd see how you were getting on,' he said easily. She was more charming than he remembered.

Inside Rose's breast anger stirred: was this Harold's doing?

Watching her closely, Simmonds continued, 'Seen anything of your brother-in-law?'

'Not for a few days.'

'Ah. Thought it was your custom to spend part of Sunday with your sister?'

Why was he questioning her like this? 'Not always, no. I'm afraid I can't offer to take your order. We're about to close.'

'I didn't come to give an order.' He fingered the small vase of flowers. 'So Brigg hasn't spoken to you?'

'Concerning what, Mr Simmonds?'

'Why so formal, Rose? Conerning dancing, of course. I suggested that you and I might slip over to Marton on Wednesday. The season's begun, you know. Brigg saw no objection, positively encouraged me, in fact. Told me you were sadly in need of exercise.'

Oh, did he! Anger exploded. Despite her tiredness, Rose lost her temper. 'Harold had no business ... Kindly leave at once. I don't wish to discuss the subject.'

The proprietress came hurrying across. 'Is something wrong?'

'Now, look here—'

Rose cut across his protest. In two sentences she had explained. The proprietress was appalled; a married man importuning one of her girls!

'These premises are used by respectable people. I must ask you to leave.'

Simmonds stared balefully at Rose. 'You may have done your sister a very bad turn.'

She marched across and held open the door, saying, 'Understand once and for all I don't wish to go dancing or see you ever again.'

He replaced his hat. 'I understand. I doubt whether *you* do.'

On the way to Fleetham Street that evening, Rose argued with herself: Harold wouldn't have *encouraged* Mr Simmonds? He knew her views perfectly well. But what did the man mean by his threat – and how could it possibly affect Gertie?

167

She wouldn't mention his visit, not yet. Too much had happened during the last twenty-four hours; Rose needed to think things out.

First she had to let Ned know she'd be leaving Albert Road by Saturday but she wasn't sure of his sister's address. Suddenly she remembered Hayden. Ned had described his hut. She'd go to the allotments next Sunday and explain – she might even meet Ned there!

Much more cheerful, she nodded to Mrs Potter and climbed the stairs. Harold had finished his supper and was sitting beside the fire. He appeared disconcerted at seeing her. 'Your sister has taken her sewing things through to the bedroom.'

'Thank you, Harold.'

The blouses were on the bed but Gertie had important matters to discuss. She held out the note.

'This has arrived from Mrs Porteous. Harold doesn't know about it yet.'

As she read it, Rose said angrily, 'That's both beastly and unfair. She wanted me to become her companion instead of taking the lessons and when I refused, that's when she told me I couldn't stay. Now she's using Ned as the excuse.'

To Gertie, being a companion spelled security. Ned she brushed aside. 'Rose, you really must be sensible. You must accept, it's a very good offer. Look, she says she's quite willing to reconsider.'

'She may be, Gertie. I am not. If I stayed at Albert Road, I'd be worse than a servant. They can give notice. I should be trapped.'

'But – that house, your lovely room, you wouldn't wish for anything better,' Seeing her expression, Gertie picked up the first blouse. 'We'd better do this while we discuss it otherwise Harold will feel neglected. Try this one first ... Stand still while I pin the sleeve. All Mrs Porteous *says* is that your choice of friends is not suitable and I agree with her. If you assure her you won't see that person again, she'll relent.'

'I don't want to stay, don't you understand? Mrs Porteous is trying to dictate the course of my life!' Rose added more quietly, 'Miss Lawson is trying to find me a room.'

'I asked Mrs Potter to put a card in her window. If you're set on going, one of them should come up with something. Do you like the style?'

Rose put troubles aside and gazed at her reflection. 'It's delightful, Gertie. Very neatly done.'

'I *can* sew.' Gertie was offended, 'I may not be clever but I can design a blouse.'

'This room so much prettier, too.' Rose wanted to make amends. She admired the scarf over the ugly lampshade, the patchwork cushions on the counterpane.

'When we move, that's when I shall really be able to let myself go. Oh, Rose, I am looking forward to it! This place does get me down.'

'Poor Gertie!'

'Try this one. It's a different style because of the stripes.'

'It's so elegant! Sort of Edwardian but up to date at the same time.' Rose was delighted. 'You're a clever old thing!'

Pleased, Gertie said, 'It's no use giving you a modern style because, let's face it, you're not flat-chested.'

'No, I'm not.'

'Kindly note the high neck and long sleeves, as per your instructions.'

'Thank you very much!'

'Careful, the tacks will give way. Ease it off gently ... that's it. Come round on Friday and have a birthday supper. They'll both be ready by then.'

'I may be moving out on Friday.'

'You have to eat! You can move on Saturday instead. Mrs Porteous can't dump you on the street, dearest. Think what the neighbours would say.'

They were giggling as they returned to the parlour. Harold was irritated. 'I've been waiting for my cup of tea, Gertrude.'

'I'll make it now. You'll stay for one, Rose?'

'Thank you.' When her sister disappeared, Rose was

169

uneasy. Harold was gazing at her in a way she didn't like.

'Rose, I wonder if you realize how anxious Gertrude is nowadays?'

'About moving house? Oh no, Harold, she's looking forward to it enormously—'

'Damn moving house! We shan't be moving, there's not the slightest possibility ...' He saw her face and tried to retract. 'That is to say, we shall move once my position is secure, not before. Unfortunately, nowadays with so few orders, many firms are slimming down. Tightening their belts ... A man had to think of his position.' She obviously didn't understand. He gave up being subtle.

'Simmonds was asking after you. He's still very keen to go dancing. There's no harm, Rose. He's an honourable chap, take my word for it.'

She sat straighter in her chair. 'I prefer to stay in during the evenings, Harold.'

'But Simmonds particularly—'

'I would *never* accept an invitation from a married man. Please stop. It's demeaning for both of us. I must insist you do not mention the subject again.'

Faced with such obstinacy, he was non-plussed. 'Get out, do you?' he asked vaguely. 'Fresh air, that kind of thing?'

'Yes, thank you.'

'You missed church yesterday. Gertrude was most distressed.'

'I shall be there next week.'

And I shall be twenty-one! That would put an end to interference. Rose hugged the knowledge like a talisman.

He'd done his best. If Rose refused to go dancing there was nothing more he could do. He would explain to Simmonds when the opportunity arose.

But the following day at the rolling mill Simmonds took no notice of him. Harold twisted the whole business around. The cause of the trouble was undoubtedly Jack Wilson; if *he* hadn't slipped up over the special attention and packing needed ...

170

Oh, yes. By now Harold was confident *he* had issued the relevant instructions and that Jack Wilson hadn't carried them out. Whenever he could he remarked loudly that Wilson had come too far, too fast, oblivious that his words were rebounding against him.

A colleague dropped a hint: it was unwise, Jack Wilson was proving extremely competent. Harold was deaf. He ignored the jitters over the thin order books. He became obsessed with the need to impress Simmonds as to Wilson's unreliability. He even failed to be disturbed by the rejection of his letter to Hunters.

It had gone to Simmons for approval. It came back screwed into a ball. Harold smoothed it out. 'Pompous and inaccurate' was scrawled across it.

Harold breathed deeply; this was grossly unfair. He'd given a truthful account: Wilson was to blame. Harold hadn't apologized but then as he wasn't the culprit, why should he?

He had other matters on his mind: would Ruby agree to him seeing the child? He'd have to think of an excuse for the visit, not that Gertrude was inquisitive, she scarcely bothered to enquire if he was late. She seldom remembered to ask if he'd had a bad day. Harold drifted off into a reverie.

'Any letters, Mr Brigg?' He came to with a rush. Good heavens. He glanced at the office clock: almost time to go home and he hadn't even begun the first one.

'Bring the stamps. I'll put these in the post myself.'

The boy replied hesitantly, 'That's against the rules, Mr Brigg.'

'I said, bring me six stamps. This correspondence is too important to be rushed.'

Simmonds saw the exchange from behind his window. He called as the boy passed, 'What has Brigg asked you to do?' and when told, nodded the boy should obey. Later, when Harold had gone, Simmonds checked his mail tray. The urgent correspondence was still lying there, unanswered.

On Thursday, the announcement of the appointment of the new deputy head-clerk, Mr J.T. Mardell, was posted on the

171

notice board. Harold didn't join in the congratulations. It was another insult. He also failed to hear any instruction passed to him by the new appointee.

He couldn't tear his thoughts away from Ruby and whether she would grant permission tomorrow. 'She can't refuse. I have a right ...' He was oblivious of the urgent correspondence, brusque with colleagues, cherishing past imaginary hurts until they festered, but all the time his thoughts kept reverting to Ruby.

'A woman like that who gives herself to men, she shouldn't be allowed to bring up a child. Not *my* child.'

Fellow clerks asked one another whether Brigg was bent on being dismissed and when Harold seized his hat five minutes ahead of time on Friday night, older hands shook their heads; with Simmonds still there in his office, it was sheer madness.

Alf Winnot came to the rendezvous, a less flexible man than his brother. He and Ruby had worked out their terms.

'You can see the bairn for ten minutes, provided one of us is there, an' it'll cost an extra ten bob.'

'How dare ...'

'Suit yourself. I'll tek the five bob now anyhow.'

'But I want to see *my* son.'

'Not yours, hers.' Alf poked his finger into Harold's chest. His voice was loud and emphatic.

At the far end of the alleyway, a figure stopped in the shadows to listen.

'Our Ruby's kiddie, Brigg, not yours, always will be. You planted it in her, and granted it's costing five shillings per week for its upkeep, but she's the one who's suffered. You could've wed her, you knew about it soon enough but you went for that rich woman instead.'

'Rich ...' The irony of it left Harold speechless.

'Hand over the five bob, don't keep me waiting.'

'I want to see the boy. What's to stop me turning up in Haverton Hill?'

Alf laughed. 'I wouldn't do that if I were you. You're not

172

the most popular bloke in our street. Accidents can happen, if you tek my meaning.'

The man at the end of the alley heard the chink of coins, followed by Harold's pleading, 'I must see the boy, just once.'

'I've told you—'

'All right. I'll pay. When can it be arranged?'

'Say, this time next week?'

'Not before?'

'No,' he was decisive, 'Ruby doesn't want you at her place unless I'm there to protect her.'

'Don't be ridiculous! All I want is to see the child.'

'Next Friday.'

Alf Winnot strode heavily away. Harold went in a different direction while the watcher resumed his journey to the Hare and Hounds. In the public bar was the young works manager, Jack Wilson. After the first pint, the watcher said judiciously, 'Heard summat might interest you, Mr Wilson.'

'Oh, yes?'

'Concerning a certain person ... Turns out he's not all he pretends to be.'

Jack Wilson was guarded. 'Oh?'

The watcher gazed into his empty glass. 'The certain person who rams down our throats every time he comes down to the floor, as how none of us has "standards".'

Jack Wilson grinned tiredly. 'Oh, him. What's he been up to now?'

'Got a by-blow, seemingly.'

'What!'

'By a girl in Haverton Hill.' Jack Wilson signalled for two more pints. The watcher reciprocated with a packet of Woodbine.

Wilson lit up, inhaled and asked, 'So how do you know?'

'I saw Brigg hand over cash to a bloke. He was after asking if he could see the bairn. The bloke said it would cost him ten bob.'

'Ha'way! Then what?'

'Brigg agreed. He's seeing the child next Friday.'

'Well . . . well, well.'

'The girl was expecting before Brigg got married. I got the impression he hasn't told his wife. He's keeping it a secret.' They raised glasses.

'I wouldn't tell too many people,' suggested Jack Wilson guilelessly. 'It's not something that ought to get about.'

'Why, no. That wouldn't do at all.'

That same evening Rose arrived slightly breathless at Fleetham Street. Harold wasn't back. She and Gertie began to exchange news swiftly, listening out for his foot on the stair.

'Many, many happy returns!'

'Thanks, dearest. The best possible present – Miss Lawson's heard of a room, bless her. I'm off to see it tomorrow after we close.'

'Have you told Mrs Porteous?'

'I'll wait until I know if it's suitable.'

'Oh, Rose . . . Will it be convenient for when you begin your typewriting lessons?'

Rose found it difficult to keep up the pretence that she had applied for the course. 'I think so. May I open my parcels?'

'Of course.'

First there was a card, a delicate water-colour sea-scape painted by Gertie. Wrapped in silvery paper were the blouses. The striped Edwardian shirt-waist now had a ribbon rose fastening the high collar, the sailor blouse sported the checked blue and white piping.

Rose sighed with gratitude. 'They're so exquisite. How can I bear to wear them? They must be hung on the wall like tapestries.'

'Don't be silly!' Gertie was pleased. No one had praised her sewing since their mother died. 'I couldn't help remembering *my* twenty-first . . . strawberries and cream in the garden, then when Cecil arrived unexpectedly, it was the perfect end to the day . . . Yours has been so ordinary.'

'I've enjoyed it,' Rose protested, 'the customers made a fuss when they found out, it's been fun. And you've been so generous.'

174

'We'll wrap these up ready for you to take home. Come and talk while I finish the supper. It's pigeon pie tonight.'

'It's so heavenly to be spoiled, Gertie!' Rose managed to put from her mind all thought of their forthcoming separation. She and Gertie who'd been so close before! I must make her happy tonight, she thought fiercely, she's done so much for me.

When Harold finally arrived home Gertie reminded him tactfully of the date. He congratulated his sister-in-law and, as they sat down at the table, announced he would 'say a few words'.

These turned out to be a homily on Rose's deficiencies of character. For Gertie's sake, Rose continued to eat in silence. Plates were cleared, the rice pudding was brought in. Harold began once more, this time praising her for finding such an elegant, suitable 'abode' in Albert Road.

Gertie said carelessly, 'Rose is moving from there, Harold.'

'Oh? Why?'

Rose struggled to stick to part of the truth, 'Mrs Porteous objects to my type-writing lessons. She offered me the post of companion but I prefer to be independent.'

'My dear Rose ...' Harold was appalled. 'When such a genteel person, the widow of an officer and gentleman ... You must change your plans, I insist.'

Rose put down her spoon. 'No, Harold, I shall not.'

'I beg your pardon!'

'The time has come for you to cease giving me advice, unless I ask for it, of course. After all, I have reached the age of discretion.'

'But not – of wisdom.' Harold puffed out his chest. 'I shall speak to Mrs Porteous myself.'

'Harold!'

'I shall explain that you were mistaken, that you humbly beg her pardon for being so obstinate and are most grateful for her very handsome offer. In short, that you accept the post of companion to – a lady.'

'I forbid you – you have absolutely no right – No, Gertie,

175

don't interrupt. Your husband must learn to hold his tongue!'

Harold's mouth gaped wide. This was insolence! 'How dare you speak to me like that – *me*!'

Rose was on her feet looking for her bag. 'I'm sorry, Gertie, I cannot stay. I'll get my coat.' Gertie followed her out to the bedroom. 'Gertie, dearest, don't show Harold Mrs Porteous's letter. There's no need for him to know about my excursion, it will only inflame matters. Let me at least find somewhere else to live first.'

'Rose, you should listen to Harold for once. I agree with him over this.'

'You don't know what it's like, living there. If the room Miss Lawson knows of is suitable I shall move there immediately.'

'Rose, promise me you won't allow – that person – to call on you again?'

Rose tucked the parcel under her arm. 'Thank you for my lovely blouses. I've never had such beautiful garments before.' She went to kiss Gertie's cheek but her sister turned away. 'I'm sorry, I don't mean to offend you or Harold but he really mustn't interfere and I'd prefer it if you didn't criticize my friends.'

All the way home, the thought pounded in time with her footsteps: how am I going to tell Gertie Ned and I are to be married? How can I possibly tell her about Australia!

It was a small, grubby, back bedroom that overlooked a yard with the outdoor privy. Once Rose would have found it difficult to imagine such a place. The slovenly landlady pointed out the amenities. 'There's a bolt on your door for when you're in at night.'

'Why should I need that?'

'My husband drinks ... He doesn't mean to be violent, it's his little weakness.'

'Oh.'

'Four shillin'. You supply your own sheets. Sixpence extra for washing 'em.' Rose wondered if the mattress was clean.

'The rent's too high.' She saw the woman's shoulders sag. 'I'm sorry but I don't earn very much, I am trying to save.'

The landlady played her trump card. 'You won't find many willing to let to a woman. Round here they only take men.' It was true.

Rose said bravely, 'Three and six. I'll use the bagwash. Threepence for the loan of your iron.'

The woman shrugged. 'All right.'

'Have you a key for my door when I go out?'

'There's one somewhere.'

'I should like to move in after church tomorrow.'

It would only be for a few weeks, until they sailed. She wasn't strong enough to endure this for very long.

Lights and laughter streamed from the sitting-room when she returned to Albert Road. Mrs Porteous was entertaining her friends to a soirée. Hoskins confirmed as much when he let her in.

'I shall not be joining them this evening, Hoskins. I need to pack.' He remained imperturbable. 'I shall be leaving tomorrow morning.'

He bowed. She felt weary and frightened. Her new room was such a mean, bare little place compared to all this.

'My instructions were to invite you to join the company in the sitting-room, miss. After you had changed.'

'Please present my apologies. I will see Mrs Porteous in the morning.'

'Certainly, miss.'

It didn't take long to fill her small trunk and grip. The pretty tea service was back in its cardboard box and Rose sat at the open window, clutching Ned's birthday card. Mrs Porteous's expensive gilt-edged offering stood on the mantelpiece. She would leave that and take only Ned's simple picture of a crimson rose. On the back he'd written, 'I cannot give you jewels, only my heart. You have that, always.'

Outside birds chirruped to their fledglings in the spring dusk. 'They're free ... I shall be too. I'm leaving the caged ones behind.'

177

To give up this luxury in exchange for a drunken landlord, Harold would judge it madness. Yet how else could Ned and she meet? If Mrs Porteous learned they were to marry, life would become intolerable.

'At least where I'm going, if I pay the rent in advance, no one will bother me.'

Harold wouldn't come calling, nor Gertie, just Ned. Her heart somersaulted at the thought she might see him tomorrow. She settled herself to sleep oblivious to the gaiety below.

Rose had to endure much that Sunday. First there was Harold's temper after church, shouting that she was an obstinate fool to leave Albert Road. Then, on her return, Mrs Porteous refused to see her to bid farewell. Eloise tried to console her as Hoskins and the cab driver loaded the luggage.

'Madam refuses to believe you're leaving. She'll be down to pester you at the tea rooms.'

'It's no use, I shan't change my mind.'

'I know. Good luck, Rose. Here . . .' She thrust a parcel into her hand. 'I meant to give this to you yesterday. It's two chemises and a petticoat.' She lowered her voice, 'The ones Madam ordered a size too small. She told me to send them to a jumble sale but they're *silk*.' Eloise's shoulders lifted expressively, 'Far too good for that.'

'Bless you,' Rose hugged her, 'a little touch of luxury will be more than welcome.' These would be her trousseau, plus the new blouses. Flagging spirits revived, she ran down the steps to the cab. 'Derby Street, driver.'

'What, near the gasometer?'

'The very same.' With that towering above the roofs and the railway line bordering the end of the street, no wonder the rents were low.

'Bit of a change from this.'

'It has its merits,' Rose told him.

At the allotment, she let herself through the blue gate, retying the knots carefully; Ned had explained the procedure. Please let Ned be there! But it was only Hayden who came to greet her, with a fawning small dog leaping down the path.

'Down, Boadicea! Keep your paws to yourself. Afternoon, lass, what brings you here?'

'Is Ned . . .' She could see that he wasn't.

'He's helping Fred strip out the carburettor of his bike, in return for borrowing it, like. Come on in. I was just about to brew up.'

He let her feed broken biscuits to the dog with only the mildest of protests.

'She'll lose her figure. She'll be as fat as my auntie before she's through. Sit down.' He spread the newspaper over the chair. 'There you are. D'you take sugar?'

'No thank you.'

He waited until she'd taken a few sips. 'Now then, is summat wrong?' She told him the events of the week. 'What Ned's brought you to, eh? What's the new room like?'

'Pretty squalid but you mustn't blame Ned. I couldn't have stayed in Albert Road.'

'Aye,' he said heavily, 'not once word got out about you and him.'

Rose smiled. 'I've been busy at my new lodging. I used half a bar of carbolic but at least my room is wholesome now. I even cleaned out the privy. I couldn't bear to use it until I did!'

'Ee, lass!'

'It'll be good practice for Australia.' Her lip trembled.

'Now, don't tek on. I shall tell Ned all about it. An' I shall tell him I was right – you are the lass for him. Brave as a lion. He'll be at the tea rooms tomorrow, to see you home. If you're living in Derby Street you need to show them you've a chap to look after you.'

Rose nodded; she'd be very thankful to let her landlord know that.

Hayden looked at her appreciatively, 'Ned's been a new man since he found you, full of hope. Cheerful? He doesn't even complain when that sour bi— woman whines about his

179

scrubbing. I hope you two'll be as happy as you deserve.'

'Thank you.' Hayden shied away from so much emotion and turned on the silent, adoring bitch. 'Stop arguing wi' me,' he growled. 'Nag, nag, nag all day long.'

From Monday onwards, events began to move rapidly. Ned had his answer from the company and waved the letter excitedly at Mu. 'They've confirmed their offer, they agreed we can leave in June with the second boatload.'

'What date in June?'

'Saturday the fourth. We have to be in Liverpool the night before.'

'Liverpool?'

He laughed, carefree at last. 'We catch the boat there. There's a list of what I shall need, clothes and such.'

'Better let me have that. I'll see what I can do.'

'Thanks, Mu.'

'So ... When am I going to meet your young lady?'

'I shall ask her round tonight. I do hope you two get on.'

'It'll scarcely matter,' Mu answered sadly, 'it's for such a short time. I shall miss you – I shall keep on at Lionel to change his mind. Once he knows you're really going, maybe he'll think again.'

Ned re-read the company letter. 'They must have some vacancies ... "We have had one or two cancellations." I expect, when it comes to it, some people can't face the parting.'

Mu's gaze was steady. 'Lionel won't budge yet, it's not in his nature. Maybe when he sees how well you do. I know how I shall feel the day you go though, pet. It'll be the second worst day of my life. The other was when the telegram came for Mum and Dad about George. Come on, you'll be late. Don't want to give the old bat another excuse to sack you.' She followed him to the door. 'If she starts to rile you, think of Rose and count to ten.'

'I always do,' Ned grinned, 'otherwise I'd have shoved her head in my bucket before now!'

180

*

Harold wanted to assert himself. If he supervised the replacement order for Hunters, if they were pleased, past mistakes would be forgotten.

Mardell, the new deputy head clerk, disagreed, 'Your place is at your desk, Brigg. Dealing with that basket of correspondence—'

'*Mr* Brigg, if you please. Some of us have standards when it comes to the courtesies, Mardell.'

'And some of those letters have been there for over a week...'

'I am perfectly capable of supervising Wilson as well as replying to our customers.'

'Before you leave tonight, I want that basket emptied.' Mardell caught the muttered 'impertinence'.

Simmonds appeared. 'Can I have a word, Mr Mardell?'

'Sir.'

Inside his office Simmonds said, 'The list of those who'll have to take a drop in wages, I'd like your comments.'

Mardell glanced through the names and nodded. 'I agree.'

Simmons pointed to another name. 'He'll have to go.'

'Yes,' Mardell's face was expressionless.

'He's given me a good enough reason this time.'

'Perhaps,' Miss Lawson suggested, 'you might like a few moments with your young man. You may use my office.' It was a grandiose description for the cramped space beyond the bead curtain but Rose was grateful. 'Not too long. I rely on your discretion.'

'There's so much to tell,' Ned said later. 'You wouldn't believe. Forms ... You must take them and read them at home, Rose. I've marked where you'll need to sign. And I've found out about a marriage licence. Provided you've not changed your mind, that is?'

'Oh, Ned!'

Moments later, he asked, 'Now you've moved, which church will it be?'

181

'There's St Cuthbert's in Newport. I doubt if anyone we know would hear the banns read there.'

'Best keep it a secret as long as we can. Now, this is a copy of what you'll need to take to Australia. Mu's seeing to my things, bless her.'

She scanned through it. 'There doesn't seem much I shall have to buy. I can manage.'

'If we get married on the twenty-eighth, we can spend the two nights up on the moors before we leave for Liverpool. I've got the loan of a cottage.'

Roses eyes sparkled. 'Oh, Ned – where? Tell me?'

'Not on your life. That's my secret!'

His brown eyes were so full of love, so kind and understanding. She put her hand in his. He murmured, 'The twenty-eighth then?' Rose nodded timorously. 'May I kiss you?' He was so gentle, her arms went out, her body clung to his. Finally, he broke from her and smoothed back her hair tenderly.

'Right, Miss Bossom, fetch your hat and let's be off. I want to see this drunken monster you told Hayden about. Will I need my sword?'

'Judging by last night, your bucket might be more appropriate. He was – unwell– several times.'

'Dear me!'

'According to his wife, it's another of his little weaknesses.' Rose looked at Ned speculatively, 'Have you any little weaknesses I should know about?'

'Why, yes, I fall in love with girls who rick their ankles and drop on the pavement in front of me, It's a well-known fact.'

Their laughter was so happy, people turned to watch them go past. Older ones shook their heads. No sense of propriety, these days. The war had a lot to answer for.

Chapter Eight

Averting a Catastrophe

'Is Mrs Porteous at home?'

Hoskins recognized Harold Brigg and was doubtful. 'I shall have to enquire.'

No proper respect; Harold swallowed a tut-tut and produced his card. 'It is in connection with my sister-in-law, Miss Rose Bossom.'

When Hoskins returned he was a shade more welcoming. 'Mrs Porteous will receive you.'

Harold bestowed his hat, gloves and scarf: he'd no intention of leaving without being offered a glass of sherry. Mrs Porteous was sitting at her tapestry frame in the window embrasure.

'Mr Brigg, madam.'

Harold savoured the details greedily. Such beautiful rose-wood furniture – what a silly girl Rose had been to leave all this. According to Gertrude her new address was in a most unfortunate area. He bowed over the outstretched hand.

'Thank you for allowing me to pay my respects, madam.'

'Is Rose . . . Is she well?'

'Well, but still very obstinate, I fear. Which is why I come to beg indulgence on her behalf, as does my wife.'

Mrs Porteous withdrew into her shell. 'I have no favours to offer, Mr Brigg. Rose chose to leave despite my most generous offer.'

'Madam, Gertrude and I were dumbfounded.' Harold was utterly sincere. 'That such an offer be turned down without even a word of thanks. It pained us to learn how she had behaved. We marvel at your generosity, I assure you.' Mrs

183

Porteous unbent as far as to incline her head. 'Which is why I am here today. Rose, a delightful girl in so many ways, has this streak of wilfulness that can be curbed, have no fear of that. Given time. I myself propose to cure her of it. And once she begins to appreciate all that she has tossed away she will return, humble and penitent, to your service.'

Mrs Porteous didn't recognize in this picture of submissiveness the girl whose company she now missed so badly.

'I would much rather that Rose returned of her own accord, without any undue pressure from you, Mr Brigg.'

Harold concealed his chagrin. 'It will be so skilfully applied she will not be aware of it, madam.' Mrs Porteous remained unconvinced. 'As for Gertrude, she will also speak to her sister. They are very close.'

'And the purpose of this visit ...?'

He was miffed. 'To assure you of our endeavours, on your behalf, so to speak.' She stiffened and Harold added hurriedly, 'And to ask that the vacancy of companion be kept open a little longer. Until Rose has had time to – to come to her senses.'

Mrs Porteous had had enough. Harold was astonished to see her ring the bell.

'There is no vacancy, as you describe it, Mr Brigg. However, if Rose chooses to call, I shall be glad to see her again, provided ...' she stared expressively, 'she comes of her own volition and not for any other reason. Mr Brigg is leaving, Hoskins.'

The damn fellow was already standing there with his hat and gloves. Harold was peeved. He had timed this visit extremely carefully, with an eye to the tantalus. Now, *sans* refreshment, he would be late home and, as it was Thursday, have to eat whatever boring dish Gertrude had contrived from the last of the joint. No doubt it would be dry as well as tasteless.

He walked along Albert Road, trying to decide which fine house might have been his, had he married more wisely. Despite the lack of sherry, the day had been reasonably satisfactory. At the rolling mill he had finally contrived to put Jack Wilson on the spot. Tomorrow, he would have his revenge. The idea had elated him to such an extent, it was the reason he'd called at Albert Road.

He'd thought of a way of demonstrating Jack Wilson's unfitness for the post of works manager and had requested a meeting with Mr Simmonds. Slightly to his surprise, he'd had a prompt response. Mr Simmonds would see Harold at 10.00 a.m. tomorrow. No matter how Wilson might plead, he would insist on Wilson being dismissed. Thinking about that almost banished his annoyance with Mrs Porteous. Dash it, he was entitled to a libation. Or a cocktail. Harold knew these were now being served in smarter houses before luncheon or dinner. Perhaps he and Gertrude could invest in a shaker to stand on the sideboard? But then again, they had no sideboard.

Mrs Porteous had a very fine one, he'd glimpsed it through the dining room door. Six feet long, of finest mahogany, with a silver epergne displayed on top. Quality, rich and solid, the sort Harold appreciated.

In the rolling mill, gossip travelled. Simmonds now knew why Brigg left five minutes early on Friday nights. He was anticipating their interview tomorrow with a great deal of relish.

Derby Street looked neither better nor worse in the spring evening. The weather was mild, the doors stood slightly ajar but the warm soft air couldn't compete with the gasometer. If you lived here, you had to learn to put up with the smell.

Ned tapped on the front door and waited. He could hear Rose's step, she was hurrying down the stairs but her expression startled him. She had obviously been crying.

'Ned, thank goodness you're here!' He stifled the urge to take her in his arms.

'Wait till we get round the corner.' There were too many eyes and ears in Derby Street.

Once they were out of sight he asked, 'What's happened?'

'The landlord arrived home completely drunk. He smashed his fist into his wife's face – she should have gone to hospital but she refused. Her nose is so swollen, I wonder she can still breathe.' Rose's voice began to shake and Ned took her arm, urgently.

'Don't take on, pet. Don't be upset.'

'But I'd no idea people could treat one another like that. There was blood everywhere. Her nose is probably broken and all she would say was, "No hospital ... those busybodies ask questions." I begged her to let me call the police.'

Ned understood the domestic niceties. 'We'd best not interfere. She'd might be treated worse by him if we did. Did you ask the neighbours to help?'

Rose nodded. 'They refused because he attacks them if they do.'

'If only I could afford to take you somewhere safe!'

'It's my own fault, I should have stuck it out with Mrs Porteous. Ned, I shall have to tell Gertie about us. She's the only refuge I have. If that man starts hitting his wife again ... I don't think I could stand it.'

'Come and meet Mu,' he urged. 'We'll have a quiet evening and when you're feeling better, we'll see what can be done.'

Gertie tired of waiting for Harold to return. The supper was ruined, he'd have to make do with bread and cheese. She was bored with being cooped up, she wanted to be out and about. She had Rose's address, it was in an area she hadn't visited before; it would be an adventure!

Only slightly apprehensive, she wrote Harold a defiant note, donned her newly trimmed felt hat and set off. Crossing Newport Road and Cannon Street she reflected that Rose had a much longer walk to the tea rooms nowadays. The surroundings increased her apprehension. As she turned into Derby Street, her first impression was that Rose must have lost her senses: leave Albert Road for this?

Gertie willed herself to continue until she found the right house. She was aware of people staring. They were watching her because she was knocking at this particular door. Suddenly, Gertie was afraid. She was even more anxious about Rose. She pounded on the door and, as it opened, recoiled in horror at the sight.

The woman's face was pulp. Her nose stretched above her cheeks in a bloody weal of battered flesh. Her eyes were so swollen, they were slits. Thick sore lips had difficulty forming the words. 'What d'you want?'

Gertie swallowed. 'Miss Rose Bossom? Does she live here?'

Behind the woman, came a roar. A man, crashing against the wall in a rage. 'Is that her?' he bawled. 'Where's her rent? She can give it me, not you.' He thrust the woman aside, grabbing at Gertie's bag. 'Give it me!'

She'd never seen anyone so horrifying! Behind her glasses, Gertie's eyes were round with terror. She gave one tiny scream and fled. Down the street, past jeering children, forcing herself to go faster than she'd ever run before.

Gulping for breath, she sped across the two main roads and turned into Fleetham Street. She didn't pause in the shop but rushed up the stairs in search of Harold.

'You must come, you must do something,' she babbled. 'Rose ... it's the most dreadful place ... the woman – Rose could be killed! There's a madman living there.' The felt hat, so jaunty before, dangled off the back of her head. Her clothes were awry, her face wet with tears.

Harold looked at her coolly. 'Gertrude, I have had a trying day. A visit to Mrs Porteous on your sister's behalf ended without the courtesy of refreshment or thanks, and what do I find on my return? No supper on the table.'

'Harold, you don't understand!'

'Allow me to finish, Gertrude. As the bread-winner I trust I am entitled to some consideration?'

'Harold, Rose is in the greatest danger imaginable—'

'Then she is an extremely ungrateful female,' he said irritably. 'There she was, living in absolute luxury ...'

'I agree but we must do something *now*! She may be in the greatest possible danger—'

'There is a time for everything, Gertrude. Do I have to impress upon you I am faint from lack of nourishment? I shall wash my hands and when I return, I expect to find food, served with care and courtesy, upon the table. After supper, we can consider your sister's predicament.'

Muriel had done her best to welcome her prospective sister-in-law. The parlour fire had been lit, the children banished to play in the street and a supper of ham and salad was on the table. Rose realized this was a choice feast. And she thinks I'm better than she is – which is awful!

Exerting herself, Rose described her life. She made it plain she earned her living because she'd no choice. Gradually Mu began to relax. Afterwards, as Rose helped her wash up, talk drifted to Australia.

'Ned wants us to come but I can't persuade Lionel,' she sighed. 'I'm thinking of the children. I worry about bringing them up here where there's so few prospects.'

'Once we're established, you could come and join us? We'll have our own place eventually, Ned has set his heart on it.'

Muriel looked at her curiously. 'Wouldn't you mind sharing your home? We're not what you're used to.' It was baldly spoken but it wasn't meant to offend.

'In Australia that sort of thing doesn't matter according to Ned. I admit I was brought up to think otherwise but everything's changed now.'

'It must be hard for you. For people like us it's the same as it always was.'

Rose looked at her levelly. 'That's rotten, especially if you were hoping for something better.'

'A land fit for heroes? Ha'way! Whoever believed that kind of rubbish – it had to come from a man, didn't it? Women wouldn't go making such rash promises.'

'She's so much more cynical, thought Rose, yet she can't be much older than I. I don't suppose she would have turned a hair in Derby Street. Memory of that returned and Mu noticed.

'Are you still worried about going back?'

Rose tried to laugh it off. 'I was wondering if I've the courage.'

'You have to, your things are there,' Mu said practically. 'Don't worry; Lionel and Ned will make sure he understands not to lay a finger on you. I can't suggest you stay here, there isn't a spare inch.'

'I shall manage,' Rose said quickly.

'I'll ask among my neighbours if you like, there's bound to be someone who could squeeze you in.'

Somehow, it became imperative that Rose should prove herself independent and worthy of this kind family.

'Provided Ned gives the man a good scolding, that should settle the matter. I have a key to my room. I shall scream very loudly if he tries to break down the door.'

Muriel nodded. 'Keep a hat-pin handy,' she advised. 'Don't be squeamish. Stick it in hard if he tries anything.' Which valuable piece of advice had never been heard in Clairville Road.

'I'll remember,' Rose promised humbly.

'Have you settled on the twenty-ninth for your wedding?' And with this much more welcome topic, the rest of the evening passed off happily.

Flanked by Ned and Lionel, Rose turned the corner into Derby Street and stopped. 'There's Gertie . . . and Harold. Oh my goodness, I think he's arguing with – Oh, no!'

Harold was, indeed, haranguing. Even as they watched, a fist, round and solid as a shiny cobble thrust forward from inside the house and made contact with one protuberant eye. Harold staggered, recovered slightly and, regaining his grip on his umbrella, charged at his unseen assailant. Gertie began to scream.

'He could get hurt,' Ned shouted. He and Lionel began to run.

Behind them, Rose called out, 'Gertie, come away, the man is dangerous.'

As if by magic, doors opened up and down the street. Neighbours stood with arms folded prepared to enjoy themselves.

Harold Brigg had height and bulk but not much else. He was already in retreat by the time Ned and Lionel arrived. They rushed forward landing blows where they could until, finally, they brought the man to the ground.

On the doorstep, his wife's screams changed to indignation. 'Don't hit him too hard, he's got to go to work tomorrow!'

'Don't worry, missus, he will be able to,' Ned panted.

Rose comforted the terrified Gertie. 'They'll see to him, dear. Let us move a little further off.'

'Look at Harold! Did you ever see such a sight?'

Her husband sat in the gutter, his clothes dishevelled, nursing his battered eye.

Gertie moaned, 'I warned him how it would be. He wouldn't listen to me, he never does! It's your fault, Rose. How could you possibly live in this place? And what is Ned Harrison doing here?' She trembled and Rose put her arm round her.

'I've been visiting Ned at his home, dearest. He and Lionel came to help me deal with the landlord. Now shall we take Harold to the chemists and ask them to bathe his eye?'

'Visited Ned Harrison – at his home?' In the midst of all the mayhem. Gertie was shocked. 'Rose, he's not at all the sort of person you should be meeting socially ...'

Suddenly, it seemed pointless to keep everything a secret; Rose wanted to share her joy. 'I'm going to *marry* Ned, Gertie. He asked me and last Sunday I accepted him. Wish me happiness, dearest.' Rose's eyes were shining but there was real horror on Gertie's face. Seeing it, Rose added quickly, 'You don't know him as I do. Ned is a dear, good man, the truest friend I've ever known—'

'Oh, no.' Gertie shook her head violently, 'No, I won't hear of it. It's just not possible, Rose. If Mother and Father were alive ...'

'If they were, things would be different, I agree,' she said

190

evenly. 'The world's changed, Gertie. I believe Ned and I will be very happy together.'

Her sister was staring back at him as though Ned were some kind of lesser species.

Despite her intention not to provoke, Rose said pointedly, 'If we could put back the clock, I doubt whether you would be married to Harold so consider your words carefully for I wouldn't want us to quarrel.'

Gertie's disdain changed to indignation. 'Of course I should be married to him! If Father had been alive, if I'd had a proper dowry, then Harold and I would be in a nicer house with servants of course, but I'd still be his wife.' Rose's eyebrows went up at this sudden shift of attitude. Gertie said heatedly, 'You should be grateful to Harold. Only this evening he visited Mrs Porteous on your behalf, to beg her to keep her offer open.'

Rose said angrily, 'He had no business to, I shall not return to that house.'

'You certainly can't stay here!' Gertie gazed where various bodies were extricating themselves from the tangle. 'These people behave like animals!'

'That's a dreadful thing to say. And kindly remind Harold for the umpteenth time not to interfere in my affairs.'

'He'll certainly forbid any such marriage—'

'He hasn't the right! How many times do I have to tell you? Gertie, please, don't let us quarrel.'

But these days Gertie could be as pompous as Harold when she chose. 'I refuse to let you throw your life away. How can you be so stupid as to lower yourself?'

'As you did, you mean?'

'How dare you!' They'd never quarrelled so bitterly before yet neither seemed able to stop. 'At least Harold has *standards*. When I think of what he has done for you . . .'

'He visited Albert Road because he wanted to see inside that fine house,' snapped Rose. 'Don't pretend, Gertie. You sound like a sanctimonious prig.'

'Oh!' Gertie went to grab her husband's arm and yank him

upright. She gazed contemptuously at Ned. 'If you marry that person, Harold and I will never speak to you again.'

Her husband clutched his handkershief to his face. 'Gertrude, I think I may be going blind!'

'Harold, stop making a fuss and listen to me.' She pointed at Ned. 'Rose intends marrying that labourer.'

'She can marry the devil for all I care. Gertrude, I require medical attention *immediately*.'

'Of course you do, let me help you, dearest.'

In harmony for once, husband and wife stumbled away down Derby Street.

Ned had heard the exchange. The tears on Rose's face hurt him far more than his bruises. His darling, impulsive love was already regretting her quarrel. He said gently, 'I doubt you'll have any more trouble here. We've threatened the chap with the constable if he lays a finger on you or his wife.'

Rose dashed away the tears. 'I must apologize for my sister.'

'Don't worry, pet. It was bound to happen. Far better she find about us while there's still time for it to blow over. She might see things quite differently by our wedding day.' He sounded more optimistic than he felt and Rose was blunt.

'Neither of them will be in church. Oh, Ned, why did they have to come here tonight!'

He grinned as he brushed the dirt off his clothes. 'Brigg'll have a corker of a black eye tomorrow. Pity he never learned to use his fists.'

'He's a fool,' said Rose shortly.

'At least your sister knows about us now. She'll decide to make the best of it, families do. You'll see.'

'But what happens when I tell her we're off to Australia?'

Harold allowed the women of Fleetham Street to minister unto him. Queenie scurried off to purchase salves, Mrs Porter applied antiseptic and Gertie, more disturbed by Rose's news than she cared to admit, assured her spouse fiercely he should never trouble himself on her sister's behalf again.

'She doesn't deserve our help either now or in the future.'

But Harold intended to keep one foot in the door at Albert Road. 'We must forgive,' he announced magnanimously. '"Forgive them their trespasses," remember that, Gertrude.'

'But Harold . . . didn't you hear what she said? She intends to marry that dreadful workman. I will make it plain we cannot receive them here, it would be too shaming.'

And to think he had once considered Rose for himself. Harold pursed sore lips. 'It is now up to me to act in Rose's best interests. I shall do as I think best.'

What that was, he refused to divulge. Indeed, he said it merely to impress Gertrude for he hadn't the foggiest notion what to do. Later it occurred to him his sister-in-law could no longer be offended by the suggestion of a married man as a dancing partner.

If the coarse, rough behaviour of the working class attracted her – Simmonds need not hesitate. Harold had not the slightest qualm in offering up his sister-in-law now. He would mention it during his interview with Simmonds tomorrow morning.

Curled under his blanket, Ned gazed at the moon. So much had happened this evening but he was thankful for one thing: Mu and Rose had taken to each other. He knew how apprehensive Mu had been. 'It was silly of her, Rose is such a grand girl.' His precious love had been brave too, returning to those digs. He'd made her promise to jam a chair under the handle besides turning the key.

'Only a few more weeks,' Ned whispered to the moon, 'then, please God, we'll never be parted. I can take care of her for ever.'

The following morning, Gertie had changed her mind: Harold must bestir himself over Rose's concerns after all, but her husband was preoccupied. 'Harold, please listen,' she insisted, 'you have to convince Rose the very idea of becoming that man's drab is intolerable, otherwise I couldn't bear it.'

'Later, Gertrude. I shall attend to your sister's affairs in due course. First things first: give this sausage another minute under the grill, would you.' A man needed fortifying before such an important interview: how else could he destroy Jack Wilson? He set forth finally, with a confident step despite his multi-coloured eye. He had worked out a grand tale of derring-do to account for *that*.

He would joke of a drunken rascal who dared to insult Gertrude, of the drubbing he'd given the fellow and of the crowds who had beset them, during which one man had actually managed to land a blow. After Simmonds had expressed admiration, Harold would hint at Rose's predisposition for such rough-mannered men. Once Jack Wilson had been disposed of, naturally. First things first.

And tonight ... Harold's grasp tightened on his umbrella, he felt his throat constrict. Tonight, he would see his son at last! The great day had finally dawned.

At 10.00 a.m. he strode into Simmonds' office, eager to ruin Wilson, ready if necessary to offer up Rose on a platter, full of a self-righteous glow.

Simmonds' preamble passed over his head. Harold, slow to grasp that his opinion was not being sought, did not pay attention at first. Minutes later, it dawned on him it was he, not Wilson, who was under attack. Simmonds was listing systematically Harold's various sins of omission – twenty-three enquiries allowed to lapse for more than five days in his in-tray, plus the theft of stamps.

'Stamps?' Harold jerked upright. 'You're accusing *me* of stealing?'

'You ordered the post-boy to bring you half a dozen.'

Damn! Harold suddenly remembered the wretched things were still in his wallet. His hand went instinctively to his pocket and hovered. To produce them now would be to confess his guilt.

'A trifling matter of postage ...' His voice trailed away. The face opposite was implacable. 'It wasn't *stealing*.' There was all the difference in the world between the accidental pocketing of stamps and the *taking* of something which didn't belong to

194

one. 'I must protest ... I requested this meeting to discuss Jack Wilson's attitude.'

'An excellent works manager.'

Harold rushed in, 'Not in my judgement.'

Simmonds eyed him narrowly; was the man a complete idiot? 'Your opinion, like the wire for Hunters, isn't of a sufficiently high standard, Brigg.'

It dawned on him slowly that Simmonds had used his own choice of word.

'I must protest—'

'No. No more protests. We've had enough of your pretentious ideas. You're fired, Brigg. You can have fifteen minutes to clear your desk. If you're not out by ten thirty, I shall let it be known you've been dismissed for the theft of those stamps.'

It was the ultimate humiliation and Harold finally realized it.

'I – I ... But you were my best man!'

Simmonds was icy. 'Why bring that up?'

'Rose is available to be your dancing partner,' he plunged on incoherently. 'She's chosen to live among the riff-raff in Derby Street. I'm confident, if you wish to possess her, you have only to apply yourself ...'

Furious though he was at this bald suggestion, Simmonds' lip curled. 'What fine *standards* now, eh? And I hear you have offspring, born outside your marriage. What a veritable pillar of society you turn out to be, Brigg!'

Harold could not believe his ears. 'I – I ...' He would strangle those Winnots!

'Is that how you came by that eye? Silken dalliance in Haverton Hill?' Simmonds pretended to examine his watch. 'Twelve minutes left. Empty your desk and leave the premises or you'll be branded a thief. Here ...' A manila envelope was pushed across the desk. 'Your benevolent society contributions and a reference – which is more than you deserve but times are hard. You'll need it to find work elsewhere.'

Harold didn't want to look elsewhere, he was desperate to

remain here. 'I've been at Hills since leaving school—'

'And been a pain in the neck for most of that time. We're sick to death of your self-important blustering. It's over, finished. I want you out of this mill for good. Why are you standing like that?'

In vain did Harold summon support of a member of the Brotherhood. He shifted his feet, took the manila envelope and shambled to the door. 'What shall I tell my wife?'

'You'll think of something. Close the door behind you.'

As he emerged Harold realized everyone knew. Conversations died mid-syllable. People froze, then immediately pretended to be busy.

His desk was full of the detritus of years. He began to stuff his pockets with cards, business addresses, old diaries, then realized none of them mattered. He would never deal with these customers again. He emptied everything into the waste basket. Through the back of his neck he could feel eyes staring. He wanted to scream unrestrainedly but there were six stamps in his wallet which meant he couldn't speak.

A thief! He'd never work again if that got out. It wasn't his fault – he'd *intended* using them on office business. Never had a man been so unfairly treated! At twenty-nine minutes past the hour, Harold Brigg reached for his umbrella. In silence he walked to the door, his coat over his arm, trailing the ferule. He looked neither to right nor left and none bade him farewell.

Throbbing through his head was the constant refrain: 'What shall I tell Gertrude?'

He was on his third whisky when he remembered he was due to meet his son. He looked beyond the bar at his reflection: something had to be done about that eye. He stood up. The flyblown mirror wasn't flattering but seeing himself properly for the first time in months, Harold began to understand why Mrs Porteous's butler had been so dismissive.

I look – threadbare, he thought bitterly.

The suit, which dated back to his first marriage, was worn

and shiny despite Gertie's care. His collar was frayed, there were marks on the front of his old overcoat.

In his pocket was the manila envelope with those precious contributions towards old age. Harold banished the idea of decrepitude, he scorned the notion of providing for Gertrude – why should he? Hadn't she deceived him? He was obsessed with a feverish need to impress his infant son.

Leaving the pub, Harold headed toward Corporation Road. First there was the matter of his injury. A black leather patch was the chemist's suggestion. Examining himself for the second time that day, Harold agreed it looked, 'Quite – distinguished.'

There was no time for bespoke tailoring. In Linthorpe Road Harold searched for a suit from the rail. The assistant's servility was balm.

'Good quality? Of course, sir. These are the best, a light-weight summer suiting. How fortunate sir has a *presence*. It needs a gentlemanly figure to carry a check . . .

'May I suggest a cream shirt, sir, with a softer collar. Points are not what the *younger* gentlemen are wearing nowadays . . .

'Brown shoes are perfectly acceptable since the war. So many changes, yes, sir. But at least Germany has been brought to her knees. Would sir require socks? And a tie? Watered silk, I imagine?

'Macintoshes have a much sportier cut. This scarf might have been made to match, don't you think?

'I'm glad you've decided to replace that old bowler, sir. It had seen better days . . .

'Brown leather gloves. Self-stitching is much more *prevalent* since the Prince of Wales took up golf . . .

'Cash or account, sir?'

Back on the pavement, Harold stood tall, his confidence restored. He walked slowly past plate glass windows. People he'd never seen before nodded automatically. A fine figure of a man! That's what they were thinking. What on earth had possessed him to throw himself away on Gertrude Bossom when in clothes like these he could have won a widow with a fine house, like Mrs Porteous?

Shopping had left him peckish. Harold sauntered into Hintons where the fashionable congregated. He ordered a light collation of scrambled eggs and spinach with a pot of best Ceylon and began to rearrange the facts of his dismissal into a more acceptable version.

It was high time he left the mill. He'd been there too long. These days, young men moved around and sampled various businesses before committing themselves. In his new clothes, Harold felt as young as the next man.

He was vague as to which new venue would benefit from his talents but that was a mere detail. The thrust of his argument as far as Gertie was concerned, was 'New Horizons'. He was half-convinced he'd coined the phrase himself. It pleased him so much he left the waitress the change from his half-crown.

There was time to fill before he could present himself in that dark alleyway for his meeting with George Winnot. He took a tram to Albert Park. He couldn't think why he and Gertrude hadn't visited here more often, really the flowers were positively enchanting. He raised his new bowler to the prettiest nursemaid pushing a perambulator and was extremely annoyed to see her summon a park attendant. Nothing but a silly chit of a girl after all.

All the same ... rain was threatening, he might as well return; it wouldn't do to sully his new mackintosh.

Harold spent the rest of the afternoon in the public library, pretending to read the news but in reality searching the columns of the Situations Vacant. His new-found confidence began to waver when he saw how few there were. The qualifications were not those he possessed, either. He had a pencil to note down likely box numbers but put it away unused. How extraordinary; not a single position to suit a man of his experience.

'New horizons ...' There was a slight note of panic that hadn't been there before, then he caught sight of the clock and cast doom aside. Time to go at last! After weeks of waiting he was about to meet his own posterity.

*

George Winnot was uneasy at the sight of him, which gratified Harold but as if to redress the balance the man immediately demanded fifteen shillings.

'Fifteen . . .!'

'Five shillin' as per usual plus the ten bob extra for seeing the bairn, as agreed.'

'Afterwards.'

'Now.'

'Oh, very well.' It was amazing how much money seemed to have vanished since this morning. There had been enough in that envelope to make him feel rich. Once again, Harold felt fear tighten the muscles of his stomach.

'There you are, damn it. Let's go. I haven't got all night.'

'You're to behave towards Ruby, like. And not frighten the kiddie.'

'For goodness sake, what d'you take me for! All right, I give you my word.'

They used the Transporter rather than go the long way round. To his annoyance, Harold found he was expected to pay both fares. Increasing panic meant even pennies had to be guarded from now on. Side by side, in dirty workclothes and strutting elegance, they made their way to the turning off Clarence Street.

It was darker here. Harold gripped his umbrella. What unfriendly spirits lurked in these dark entries between the houses? How many curs with dirty feet who might brush past his new trousers? The door opened. Outlined by the gaslight was the remembered shape. Ruby's throaty voice called softly, 'Keep your voices down, the pair of you. He's asleep.'

Gertie had had a simply awful day. Her head throbbed, she couldn't seem to concentrate, not even the gentle action of crochet helped. How could her sister allow herself to be degraded by that rough man? To have his calloused hands touching her – urgh! It made Gertie sick to think of it. She was so distraught, she invited Mrs Potter to take tea but before both cups were poured, yet another problem arose. Her landlady fiddled with her apron frill.

'I've been meaning to speak before ... I decided to wait until you came with the rent this evening – I'm afraid I'm going to have to ask you to find somewhere else, Mrs Brigg. It's not been the same since Miss Rose left. It's been so *crowded.*'

'You mean, leave here?'

Mrs Potter became embarrassed. 'It was only a *temporary* arrangement, me living in the room behind the shop with you and Miss Rose up here. It was never intended for a *man* to come. There's been so much upheaval – he's too big for this place, Mrs Brigg. He breaks things. I'm not blaming him but he can't seem to help hisself.'

Gertie remembered the handle twisted off the bedroom door, the row of hooks which had collapsed under the weight of Harold's clothes. Her husband complained of the flimsy nature of the fixtures and fittings.

'If I arranged for those items to be repaired ...?'

'I'm sorry but my mind's made up. It's not as though the rent recompensed me. It was low as a favour to you and Miss Rose. When she first called, I was that sorry for the pair of you – proper young ladies on your own. Well, that's all changed. You're a married lady now. Mr Brigg can afford a proper place, surely? I thought, from the way you talked, you were keen to move?'

So, the matter had finally been settled despite Harold. They would have to rent one of those furnished houses after all.

'How soon ...?'

'No rush.' Mrs Potter was relieved to find her so amenable. 'If Queenie and I could move back upstairs in a fortnight or so. Queenie does so hate living out, and I'd prefer her back on the premises, the way we used to be. I only agreed, because of you and Miss Rose, you see.'

'Yes.' Gertie's head was beginning to throb once more. One blessed thing after another. The doorbell rang. They heard Queenie panting up the stairs. She put the heavy box on the nearest chair.

'Addressed to Mr Brigg,' she told them.

Mrs Potter saw the name on the label. 'Has he been buying hisself some new clothes?' she asked innocently.

Remembering Harold's strictures against herself, Gertie was piqued. 'Oh no. Not without consulting me.'

'You'll soon be able to go shopping for your new home,' Mrs Potter reminded her. 'Queenie, you can move back in the week after next. Mrs Brigg's agreed to go.'

'I shall have to discuss it with Harold first.'

'He'll agree.' The end of her problem was in sight and Mrs Potter was firm. 'The arrangement was only with you and Miss Rose. It was never intended for a married couple.'

The doorbell tinkled once more. Queenie toiled down and up again. 'It was your sister but she didn't stop. She said to give you this,' and handed Gertie the envelope.

An oil lamp smoked in one corner. That and a candle made deep shadows in the small, smelly room. Harold grasped the candlestick and held it above the crib.

'Don't spill the wax,' Ruby spoke automatically, her eyes taking in every detail of his appearance. 'Done well for yourself, I see.'

'Tolerably well.' It dawned too late he'd been foolish to come dressed like this but after the events of the morning, it had been essential to bolster his self-esteem.

He examined every feature of the tiny sleeping face. Emotions were stirring that Harold had never experienced before. For the first time he began to understand Man's primitive need for a child. His voice was thick as he said, 'Let me hold him.'

'It took ages to get him to settle.'

'For a few moments, that's all.'

Still grumbling, she bent to lift the baby.

Through the half-open door, her brother called, 'You all right, Ruby?'

'Yes.'

Harold's senses had never been more acute: he held his

201

breath as he stretched out stiff, tense arms.

Ruby placed the swaddled form upon them. 'Support his head,' she instructed, 'they've no strength in their necks at this age.' His hand cupped the down-covered skull: flesh of his flesh. There was a feeling in his breast so strong, he wanted to shout. This tiny human being was a part of him!

'He's like you, so people say,' Ruby was deliberately off-hand, 'poor little bugger, it's not much of a compliment.'

Which meant other eyes must have gazed on this miracle. Affront nearly choked him. That *his* child should be exposed to such a coarse scrutiny! Ruby moved closer, he could smell her scent. Once such a thing would have excited him but not now.

'Got one of your own on the way?' she asked.

'No.'

She sniggered. 'Doesn't rich little wifey let big bear have fun and games any more?'

He reddened. 'Hold your tongue.'

She shrugged. 'Didn't take you long to put me in the club. You've paid Alf?'

'Yes.' If only she'd leave him alone with the child but she was already reaching out, impatiently. 'A moment longer. Please!' Harold stared down, willing the infant to open the minute veined lids, desiring above all things for a sign of recognition. Instead, the tiny mouth opened in a yawn. He glimpsed empty crimson gums, the minature cavern of a throat and that was all.

'Come to Mummy, then,' crooned Ruby. 'Mummy'll settle you in your cot. She's got to go out soon and earn some more money.'

It was a cold douche.

'Out?' he queried sharply. 'Out, for what reason?'

Ruby mocked him. 'Hold your tongue. That's no business of yours.'

He watched impotently as she tucked in the blankets and trimmed the smoking wick.

'Anyway, it's not as bad as you think. I've got two regular fellas now. Proper businessmen, not like you. They treat me right but they don't want to know about Val. That's why you'll have to keep paying.'

As she snuffed out the candle flame he asked, 'Who cares for him while you are gone?'

She shrugged, 'Whoever's about. If he starts yelling, there's a bit of rag to dip in milk and put in his mouth. There's usually someone to do that.'

All Harold's instincts were to seize the child and demand that he be allowed to become its protector.

'You'll see he comes to no harm?'

'What's it to you?' Ruby's eyes glittered. 'You and me could have wed only you were too much of a snob. I'd not had many when I met you, we could have made a go of it.' His distaste showed and she spat at him. 'Get out! If you think five bob a week entitles you to *sneer*, think again! I've been good to that kid. I knew it would cost me but I went through with it. Some don't. They get rid of 'em.'

'I never intended to criticize—'

'Get back to your rich wife! Much good may it do you. And next time you want to see your bastard, it won't be an extra ten bob, it'll be a quid.'

Harold walked home. In trams there were children holding tightly to parents' hands and he couldn't bear the sight. Neither Ruby nor her brothers would accept that he could no longer afford to pay. They refused to believe he'd lost his job. He could get another, they jeered, with his rich wife's connections.

If he failed to turn up next Friday with five shillings, they promised to visit Fleetham Street and show the baby to Gertrude. By the time he reached his own front door, Harold wanted to howl. But who would be sympathetic if he did? Certainly not his wife.

Let her not utter one word of reproach tonight, he thought savagely. In the space of a day he'd lost his situation and his posterity. Gertrude was nothing but a millstone; she didn't love him, she was forever carping at him.

His wife didn't come to the head of the stairs. She stayed where she was, huddled in the small armchair. He could see her tears. For a terrifying moment he wondered if she'd discovered everything. He noticed the empty table. She hadn't even bothered to prepare supper. Instead, she held out Rose's note, sobbing, 'They're leaving for Australia as soon as they're married. I shall never see her again – I can't bear it!'

Australia! Australia! For once, Harold's slow brain moved at extraordinary speed.

He read the brief details, the name and address of the company office in Newcastle, he printed them into his memory. Suddenly misery slipped away. All thought of the child vanished. Harold felt his spirits soar; optimism reasserted itself because fate obviously had heard his cry and was offering a helping hand.

Chapter Nine

Comrades

Only one representative remained in the Newcastle office, the other having departed with the first batch of emigrants. The remaining one, Captain Hislop, gazed at Harold doubtfully.

'I'm not sure I fully understand, Mr Brigg? You say you wish to apply for a position – I don't believe we've received a form and the interviews are at an end.'

Harold had been rehearsing his plea throughout the night while Gertrude slumbered. He hadn't told her of his dismissal. If all went well, there'd be no need and why humiliate oneself unnecessarily? He'd even managed to divert her indignation at his new clothes. She'd been too worn down with sorrow to care.

He'd left the house before she was awake and caught the first train. Now it all depended on whether he could convince this interviewer. He exerted himself to appear eager, open and honest.

'My future brother-in-law, Edward Harrison, made the suggestion, sir. I took the liberty of applying to you directly as time is so short . . .'

For a moment the interviewer looked blank. 'Oh, Ned Harrison. He said nothing to us.'

'That is because I asked him not to,' Harold lied glibly. 'I do not believe in nepotism, sir. By my own efforts shall I rise—'

'But, Mr Brigg . . .' Hislop cut across the protestations. 'Why exactly *are* you here? We came to England in search of men with brawn and mechanical aptitude.' He indicated Harold's

205

pristine suit. 'It is a life of toil out there in Australia. The future may offer unlimited opportunity certainly, but everyone must spend the first three years on an outstation. Wives would be required to work as well.'

'My wife and Ed— Ned's fiancée are sisters, sir. As close as two women could be. Gertrude is as accustomed to toil as Rose.'

The interviewer looked him up and down coolly. 'And you, Mr Brigg? What has been your employment to date?'

'For the past fifteen years, I have worked in Hill's rolling mills of Middlesbrough, manufacturers of high quality wire.'

The man's eyebrows rose. 'In a mill?' With great prudence, Harold did not enlighten him further. 'From your appearance, I assumed yours to be an office background.'

'It's my own fault,' Harold was deprecating. 'If I may explain? My mind was made up about Australia some time ago. In my opinion, it is the true land of opportunity. Yesterday I took the plunge and handed in my notice but my wife insisted it was necessary to create a favourable impression here,' Harold shrugged, 'Hence these clothes.'

Hislop remained unconvinced. 'You're saying that had you come today in your normal working garments ...'

'In my overalls, as much a man of "brawn" as ever Ed— Ned was.' Harold stretched out clumsy fists in what he hoped was a workmanlike gesture.

'Harrison has a trade, Brigg. During your time at the mill, as well as handling machinery, did you drive any vehicles? Or during the war, perhaps? I assume you volunteered?'

Harold picked his way through the minefield. 'To my infinite regret I was not allowed to serve, my work being deemed of national importance.' He'd impressed him this time but the awkward question followed.

'What exactly did you do at the mill, Brigg?'

Harold described a job that combined both manufacture and inspection of wire. He overdid it: Captain Hislop was incredulous.

'You want to give that up for *labouring* work? With those

206

qualifications, you'd find a much better position here than in Australia.'

Harold shut his ears to the word 'labouring'. He'd wriggle out of that once he got there; the essential thing was to ensure his passage.

'New horizons,' he said earnestly, 'that is my sole desire, sir. A land where a man can stand tall. As for Gertrude, she and Rose are inseparable.'

'We can't promise they'd be near one another. Australia's a huge country, Brigg.' Hislop steepled his fingers. Eventually he said, 'We've had a couple of cancellations. In each case the wife decided that she couldn't bear to be parted from her relatives.'

'Rose and Gertrude have no other family. They are all in all to one another.'

'Uh-huh. And you, Brigg ...?' There was still doubt. 'Do you give me your solemn word you would stay three years? You will be required to sign a binding contract.'

Harold was dignified, 'I stayed fifteen years with my last employers.'

'You continue to give the impression of a man unused to manual work.'

Harold sighed. 'I shall impress upon Gertrude how wrong she was. Far better throw these garments into the Tyne than lose the opportunity of a lifetime.'

'Far better not,' the other said pointedly, 'they must have cost a packet.'

'Out of my savings.' At least Harold could be sincere about that. 'I assumed she knew best.'

Hislop made up his mind; at least the fellow looked strong and healthy. 'All right. Fill in this form, ask your wife to complete her portion. Provided the answers are satisfactory and your employer gives a proper reference, the position is yours. Now, to whom do I write at the mill? To the works manager?'

The idea of Jack Wilson receiving the enquiry nearly made Harold stumble but he had his answer pat: 'I persuaded my employer to write a reference before I left. As he was loath to

207

see me go, the tone is not inspiring. However, such as it is ...'
He proffered Simmonds' letter. Captain Hislop glanced at the
signature.

'Signed by the Sales Manager?'

'It is the custom at Hill's. All references are composed by
him whether for office or rolling mill employees.'

'Odd custom ... And as you say, not very enthusiastic. In
fact, I can't find a smidgen of enthusiasm anywhere.'

'It was a final attempt to discourage me from leaving.'

'Hmm.'

Doubt redoubled; wisely, Harold held his tongue.

'And Ned Harrison definitely suggested you apply to us?'

'He knew of my desire for new horizons.'

'As you said before.'

'And for the sake of Rose and Gertrude.'

'Frankly, Brigg, I'm not interested in domestic issues.
Provided the wives agree to do their share of the work, that's
all I'm concerned about. You have no children, I take it?'

For one brief instant Harold remembered the miracle of his
son. He was about to put the entire world between himself
and the boy – he must be mad!

'I – we have no children.'

'Very well. Harrison's recommendation counts more with
me than this ...' Hislop waved the reference. 'We were both
very impressed with him and glad he found himself a wife.
You must be pleased he's marrying your sister-in-law.'

Harold forced himself to sound eager. 'Gertrude is particularly delighted.'

'Let me have the forms back by return of post and provided
there are no snags, consider yourself one of the party.
Welcome aboard, Brigg.'

As Harold shook hands, the same question that troubled
him yesterday returned with a vengeance: how on earth am I
going to tell Gertrude? A thought plopped into his mind; at
least he'd shaken off the Winnots. He wouldn't rush back
home. He would take his time, spend the rest of the day here
preparing a careful tale to take back to Middlesbrough.

Hayden was waiting for Ned outside the school gates. 'She kept you late tonight then?'

'The bitch? Of course she did, always does.'

'Bitches are God's creatures, don't you go maligning 'em.'

'Why not train Boadicea to bite? A juicy piece of head-mistress's calf – we'd all be grateful.'

Hayden gave an exaggerated sigh. 'I come to do you a favour. D'you want to hear about it?'

'You can tell me while we walk. I've got summat to tell Rose. If yours is good news, I'll stand you a cup of tea.'

'Tea?' Hayden was disgusted. 'It's beer, I deserve. I've found you a better job.'

Ned stopped. 'But I'll be sailing in a few weeks.'

'It's only *for* a few weeks and it's three times the rate you're earning now.'

'Doing what?'

'Handyman-chauffeur at a house in Phillips Avenue. I sell me vegs there. It was the love-apples made me so popular. The cook thinks they're marvellous.' Hayden puffed out his chest. 'I grew 'em from seed, an' all. Anyhow, their regular handyman is having an operation and needs time to con-valesce so they're looking for a temporary replacement. I told 'em about you. The appointment is for ten o'clock tomorrow.'

'I've never driven a car!'

'Time you learned then. The regular lad, Charlie, will show you what's what. He's not going into hospital till the day after tomorrow.'

'What about the school?'

'Ha'way! Send her a note wrapped in your wash leather. Now, is there anything else or does your lordship think the situation will suit?' His hand was seized.

'Thanks, Hayden. You're a real pal!'

'Think nothing of it. You'll buy me a decent drink after we've visited Rose.' They set off in a mood of contentment.

'My news'll please her. Mu's found her a decent room to rent in the next street. Oh, that reminds me, I heard on the grapevine Harold Brigg got the sack. I don't know whether Rose knows. She'll be upset on account of Gertie.'

'He'll find it difficult to find a new position,' Hayden observed. 'By the sound of him, he's more gob than owt else.'

Ned grinned. 'Rose says he's got two left feet and they're both size twelve.'

When Hayden saw the girl's face light up at the sight of Ned, he felt easier in his mind. The boy's affections were deep. Despite Rose's present humble status, the gap between them was still very great. He sensed she didn't yet know the same great yearning as Ned did for her but judging by appearances, there was hope.

'This lad'll have a toasted bun. I need summat stronger.'

'Did you hear? Muriel's found me a room!'

'Aye, great news. Will you move in tonight?'

'Certainly not! In Derby Street, I have to pay in advance. I shall go on Friday evening, not a moment before. Mind you,' Rose laughed light heartedly, 'I shall start packing the minute I get back.'

'We've had another piece of luck,' and Ned told her about the temporary job.

Hayden watched contentedly. They would make a go of it, these two. They weren't rushing their fences, they were getting to know one another gradually. He'd warned Ned to give Rose time. So many changed circumstances for her – yet she'd managed to cope, even with the drunken landlord. Rose'll do, he thought. Whatever Australia might turn out to be like, she'd manage.

He listened as they discussed solemnly all that Ned might learn in the brief weeks of chauffeuring. Ned asked what sort of car it was and Hayden was baffled.

'I dunno. It's got a lot of brass but I told them you were expert at polishing, you've had so much practice.'

Rose said softly, 'Thank you for thinking of us. You're a dear, kind man.' Leaning forward, she kissed him on the cheek.

'Ee ...' Hayden was shocked as well as pleased. 'You don't

want to be doing that in front of customers. What will Miss Lawson say?'

'I don't think she noticed.'

'There's one other thing,' Ned said carefully. 'Harold Brigg. Did you know he was given his cards yesterday?'

'No!' Startled, Rose asked, 'Are you sure? Poor Gertie – what will they do? D'you think he'll find another situation?'

'It might be difficult, the way things are.'

'I must go to her. I wrote to her about Australia which was cowardly. I must go round – she'll be distraught with this happening as well.'

'I'll go with you.' Ned saw Hayden's face. 'After I've bought this chap his pint. We'll be back by the time you close.'

'You will,' Hayden rose. 'I've got to see to Boadicea. Come on, I've got a real thirst.'

Gertie woke late with a throbbing headache, the result of yesterday's tears. Then to discover Harold had disappeared without even having breakfast. His note claimed he was visiting Newcastle. What did it mean, why wasn't he going to work?

She noticed the parcel. She dimly recollected astonishment at her husband's elegant appearance last night and his garbled explanation which she hadn't understood. This package must contain his old clothes; she began to unpack them. A white paper protruded from the jacket pocket. More fluttered out. Receipts; she spread them on the bed.

Behind the glasses her eyes wouldn't focus properly because the total was impossible: £48.5s.0d? Harold couldn't have spent that much! On clothes, all for himself? Apart from her fur, even on her mother's wildest forays, they would never have dreamed of such extravagance – it was *obscene*.

She recalled the deprivations since her marriage. On the chair were the darned stockings – her only remaining pair. Harold's new socks were a cashmere mix, it said so on the bill. The tie was woven silk foulard. He'd even bought new shoes.

In a cold, clear-eyed state, she made herself breakfast.

211

Where had Harold found such a large amount of money? She would have it out with him when he came home – those fine clothes must be an indication he'd had a rise. In a couple of weeks they would be leaving for their new home, she would need money for furnishings, she would make a list of what she needed. Yesterday's sorrow hit her like a blow.

Rose mustn't desert her! She couldn't be left alone with Harold! It wasn't possible that her sister actually *cared* for Ned Harrison, she couldn't be so unladylike as to permit a working man to touch any part of her person. Gertie turned her mind resolutely away from the thought of physical contact; it was not to be contemplated and that was that.

She gazed at the shabby little flat. There was much to be done before the move: a thorough overhaul of all their possessions, washing, ironing and the like. There was nothing like exhaustion to dissipate nervous irritability. When Harold returned she would demonstrate she'd made a start.

The weather was fine and Gertie set to with a will. By the time Rose and Ned were nervously enquiring below if Harold were home, damp garments were hanging on the landing and the flat was bare of ornaments, now packed in boxes.

In the shop, Mrs Potter kept her voice low. 'She was that upset when she got your note. Mr Brigg came home very late, which didn't help. When she found out you two were off to Australia ...' The shopkeeper shook her head sadly. 'She was inconsolable. I shall be sad, too, Miss Rose. I'm sure it's for the best, and I hope you and Mr Harrison will both be very happy but I dread to think how it'll be for Mrs Brigg. Perhaps the move will help take her mind off it.'

'The move?'

'I had to ask them to leave. Queenie wants to come back and to tell you the truth, I'd like to sleep in my old bed again. I only let upstairs as a favour to you. Mr Brigg – he's too big for this place. He breaks things.'

Ned asked cautiously, 'Have Mr and Mrs Brigg decided yet where their new home is to be?'

'They've made no mention. I expect they'll be looking at

houses this weekend. Shall I send Queenie to tell Mrs Brigg you're here?'

'There's no need.'

Rose glanced at Ned who said firmly, 'I'm coming with you.' Halfway up they conversed in whispers.

'It sounds as if he hasn't told her of his dismissal.'

'Poor Gertie! Why do I always have to be the bearer of bad news?'

'Better you than someone else. We'd best tell her before he gets back, then she's time to come to terms with it.'

Rose called gently, 'Gertie, are you in? It's me, dear.'

Gertie peered down. 'Are you alone?' Seeing Ned revived all the hostility. 'I don't want that man in here. You can't marry him, Rose, you simply can't!'

'Gertie, listen.' Rose concealed her feelings and took Gertie's hand. 'Ned and I are betrothed as you and Harold once were. One reason we came tonight is to ask if you and he will be at the church to share our joy.'

'Of course we shan't.' Gertie flounced back into the parlour. 'What joy can there be in marrying a man like that? And you can't possibly go to Australia.' She collapsed in a chair staring balefully at Ned. 'That's your fault. Rose would never have dreamed of such a thing had you not suggested it.'

'Mrs Brigg, I'm deeply honoured Rose has accepted my proposal. I want to give her all that she deserves but that's not possible if we stay here in Middlesbrough.'

'You're not going to pretend it will be any different in Australia? I suppose you've told her lots of lies to make her believe you? All men do that.' Gertie was nervously pleating her skirt. 'It's the opposite side of the world, full of criminals. You simply can't go!'

She was so near tears, Rose was on her knees, stroking the agitated fingers. 'Gertie, Ned has a position. We shall be working hard for the first three years, there'll be privations of course but I truly believe we shall be able to make a decent life for ourselves eventually.'

'You must stay here and learn type-writing.' Gertie ignored

213

Ned as if by doing so he might disappear. 'Once you're in an office, you'll meet a nice boy. Someone like Cecil. I'm only thinking of your happiness, Rose!'

It was such a wail, Rose was torn between laughter and tears. She waited for Gertie to subside.

'Shall I fetch a glass of water?'

'If you would, Ned.' She gave him a grateful glance. 'Now, Gertie—'

'Rose, listen.' Gertie's eyes were feverish, 'Marriage is simply dreadful. That man will beat you and do dreadful things. You'll end up like that poor woman in Derby Street—'

'Gertie, that is stupid.'

'It's not, it's not! In bed – it's degrading. And you have to put up with it if you want children. I thought we'd only have to do it once or twice – the prayer book doesn't help – Harold is forever pestering, it sickens me every time he does it!'

The high-pitched cry reached Ned in the kitchen.

'Harold's too big for the tub so he has to go to the slipper baths in Cannon Street – he puts it off. He says only the hoipolloi go there, he's often quite *unpleasant* to be with. Please, Rose, wait for a nice boy.' Dainty, fastidious Gertie! Rose was appalled.

'Ned and I are to be married because I *care* for him. Truly I do. He loves me. If there were the slightest chance of succeeding here, we'd stay. And things have changed, you know. The old taboos about class – they're being observed less and less.'

'Not by *me.*'

Rose tried to make her see things differently. 'In Australia it'll be a new beginning. There we'll be treated for *who* we are not whether we were born in a house or a slum.'

'People always want to know,' Gertie said coldly. 'Breeding will out, you know.'

At that Rose lost her temper. 'Harold's not particularly well bred or truthful. Has he told you yet he's been fired?'

Gertie's cheeks went white then flamed red. Rose shouted to Ned for the water but the sight of him made Gertie struggle out of her chair.

214

'Get away from me! Leave me alone!'

'She'll do herself a mischief,' he muttered.' We've got to calm her down.'

'Aah! He's started, Rose. He wants to attack me already.'

Rose took the glass and aimed its contents deliberately. Gertie choked then burst into tears.

As steadily as she could, Rose said, 'Bring me a towel, Ned. And then would you mind waiting outside. I've told her of Harold's dismissal.' It had been one disaster too many for Gertie Brigg and Ned understood.

'I'll be in the kitchen, I'll make us all a pot of tea.'

It was a dull brown brew by the time Rose poured it. 'I'll take her a cup and then we'll leave. It's useless. She refuses to come to our wedding. She's adamant Harold can't have been sacked – she claims his new clothes prove it.'

'Whatever she says it's the talk of our street.'

Rose sighed. 'I'm sure Gertie knows the truth in her heart. She claims if we leave Middlesbrough, she'll never have anything to do with me again. Wait for me here.' Rose carried the cup through to the parlour. Ned heard her say, 'I'm sorry to leave you like this. I refuse to believe you and I cannot be the friends we always were. Please ...'

The appeal was ignored, Silently, Ned guided her down the stair. They began to walk towards Derby Street. He waited for the tears to begin and when they did, led her into a corner until the storm had subsided.

'Dear love! What you have to endure for my sake.'

'Oh, don't be silly!' Rose blew her nose impatiently. 'It's Gertie I'm worried about. She obviously loathes being married to Harold, yet at the same time feels compelled to defend him. I find it incomprehensible.'

Ned gazed at her with sad, serious eyes. 'That's because she knows her marriage was a mistake. It's a terrible fate to be faced with that for the rest of your life. There's still time to withdraw. I shall not utter one word against it if you do—'

'Oh, for heavens' sake!' Despite her indignation, Rose was

quavery, 'Don't start being *noble*. Be true and honest – I depend on you for that.' She looked at him, startled. 'Ned – *you* haven't changed your mind, have you?'

His laughter bounced from the grimy walls on either side. 'Oh, Rose ... the very idea! I love you to eternity, don't you understand?' Outside her digs, he reminded her, 'You won't forget to warn them you're leaving on Friday?'

'As if I could!' She kissed him of her own accord and disappeared indoors. Ned went home on wings, she'd never done that before. Maybe the incredible had finally happened and Rose Bossom loved him as much as he did her.

'We're comrades, that's what we are,' he whispered. 'From two sides. We've come together and accepted one another, plain and simple. No secrets, just plain honest trust.' Overwhelmed by his good fortune, he gazed at dirty clouds darkening the pure blue of the sky. 'It's a miracle, a ruddy great miracle!'

Harold had wandered Newcastle seeking inspiration for an acceptable tale to convince Gertrude, but to no avail. Finally, when he could delay no longer, he boarded a train. It was during the journey a solution occurred.

'I shall tell her it was for her sake. To prevent her separation from Rose, all done because of that. Her peace of mind was my sole concern.'

It was unanswerable; if it had all been for her, how could Gertrude complain?

Gertie listened impassively. He failed to note the hollow eyes, the new despair. When he uttered the phrase, '... so yesterday, for your sake, Gertrude, I took the decisive, irrevocable step—' she interrupted.

'You were dismissed.'

Harold stumbled. 'What?'

'You were dismissed from Hill's. Everyone's talking about it. What you did afterwards, I still can't understand. I've seen

216

the receipts, I know you spent forty-eight pounds on clothes. I want to know why.'

Harold amended his tale quickly. 'I had to equip myself for the visit to Newcastle. I went there to enlist my services, and to book us a passage. Knowing how devoted you are to Rose—'

'Book a *what?*' Gertie was shrill, wide-eyed.

He hastened to his conclusion. 'We are going to Australia so that you may be with your sister. I did it for your sake, Gertrude.'

'Rubbish!' She faced him, small, frail, almost demented. 'You did it because you cannot bear to admit what happened. You will go to any lengths, subject me to whatever humiliation is necessary to avoid the truth. I've had enough, Harold. I don't want to speak to you or see you any more than is necessary. For the rest of our time in these rooms, you can sleep in here. During the day you will absent yourself – is that understood? The way I feel just now – I wish to be *separate.*'

'But I have given my word.'

'Your word?'

'Gertrude, we *have* to go to Australia, I've signed the forms for both of us.' She was bound to him, she'd have to follow wherever he led.

'I'll never forgive you – never!'

Chapter Ten

A Second Wedding, May 1921

The move away from Derby Street to the warm, rough friendliness of an area where she was already known as 'Ned's girl', was, when Rose looked back on it, the last period of calm for some considerable time.

It didn't feel like it. To begin with there was a bustling camaraderie, a constant coming and going in the terrace. No one like Rose had ever rented a room here before. She found the inquisitiveness unnerving.

'Ignore it if you can,' Mu advised. 'People don't mean to be unkind.'

'Oh, they're not. It's just . . . they ask the most extraordinary questions. Whether I've ever had "a maid to run my bath".'

'And have you?'

Rose blushed. 'Nurse used to do it but only when Gertie and I were little.'

'There you are then. Kids round here get dunked under the pump or share the tub in front of the fire. Can you find a place for these on the clothes-horse?'

Rose handled the newly ironed garments carefully. 'I'd like your advice,' she said shyly. 'Would you help me choose what to wear for the wedding?'

'Of course I will!' Mu dumped the iron back on the hob. 'We'll do it now, before I have to get supper ready. In return, you can do me a favour, if you would.'

'Of course.'

'Teach my kids to eat properly. I've seen how Ned holds his knife since he met you. I want my lot to do the same.'

*

It required, Rose soon discovered, the collective opinion of the entire street before the final choice could be made. Women crowded into the small upstairs room eager to examine Rose's wardrobe. Muriel was fashion's arbiter.

'Now that's very smart ...' It was the first of the two blouses Gertie had made. 'I can just see you in that, Rose. It's a bit severe, though. You need something softer for a wedding.'

'It was intended for office wear.'

Mu nodded approvingly. 'She's a lovely seamstress, your sister.'

There was a sigh from one young mother who detached an arm from her infant to point at a dress.

'Is that real silk, miss?'

'The panels are silk georgette. It's my old tea-gown. I last wore it when Gertie was married.'

The mother pointed to the second blouse. 'Is that silk as well?'

'Poplin. Gertie made both for my twenty-first birthday.' Rose felt half-apologetic as she watched the roughened hand stroke a sleeve.

'I hope someone makes me something nice when I'm twenty-one.'

'The tea-gown is a bit worn out and this red dress is a bit formal,' Mu said critically. 'You'd be better in one of the blouses. If we press your black skirt, that'll set it off nicely.'

Collective opinion finally settled on the Edwardian shirt-waist.

'Even though it's an old-fashioned pattern, it's very *stylish* but you'll have to do sommat frivolous with your hair.'

'Tuberoses,' the young mother announced. 'I saw it in the paper: "the Prince of Wales danced till midnight with a girl wearing tuberoses in her hair."'

'Ha'way,' Mu was impatient. 'Where's Rose going to find those in Middlesbrough?'

It was Hayden who solved the problem of flowers. He arrived the night before the wedding, very pleased with himself. 'I've

219

raided every single allotment. There's one or two prize blooms. With luck the owners won't find out till the ceremony's over. There was no point in *asking* any of 'em – they're too mean to give you a weed.' As they cooed over his basket, he added sentimentally, 'A bonny choice for Ned's bonny girl.'

'There's enough for buttonholes and posies,' Mu was enthusiastic, 'and we'll use the rest to decorate the parlour – the place'll look a treat! Lionel, nip next door – tell her I need to borrow her big jug.'

Rose drew him aside. 'Hayden ...'

'Yes, lass?'

'Will you give me away? There's no one I would rather choose.'

'Eee ...' He gazed anxiously at muddy moleskins, 'I doubt I can still get into me suit. It was bought when I were a young man. I was planning to stand at the back of the church, you see.'

Mu was practical. 'Have you got a clean shirt?'

'A'course I have,' he retorted, 'a nice white one for to be laid out in.'

'Well, put that on and come round early. I'll see what I can do with those trousers.'

Suddenly, he was overcome with delight. 'I might manage it. Do I have to say owt?'

'Not a word,' Rose reassured. 'You take me down the aisle and stand beside me during the ceremony, that's all.'

'I can do that.' Hayden swelled with pleasure as the idea took hold. 'Boadicea'll have to wait in the porch but she's a good dog, she'll be no bother.'

'Be really early,' Mu warned. 'Them knees'll need a scrub.'

Later that night the two lovers were left alone by a tactful Mu and Lionel. To be in a silent house confused them at first. Ned took her hand, tentatively.

'I bought the train tickets this morning. Two singles to Liverpool. We leave Middlesbrough a week today, Thursday, at five past nine.'

Rose's face was suddenly frozen. He guessed the reason.

'You have two whole days after we return from Osmotherly. It should give you plenty of time to make your peace with Gertie.'

'If only she'd come to the church.'

'There's been no word?'

'She didn't even reply to my note.'

'She might still come.' It was a forlorn hope. 'I'm afraid it's him. Your sister wouldn't hold out if it weren't for Harold Brigg.'

'Do you know if he's found a new position?'

Ned shook his head. 'There's been no word in the street if he has. It's early days.'

'Not if they have to leave Fleetham Street on Saturday,' Rose reminded him. 'Mrs Potter was determined that they should. It'll mean extra expense, moving house. Poor Gertie, she must be so worried ...'

'Yes, well ...' The evening before his wedding, Ned had other things on his mind. 'Would you like to see the ring?'

It was his pride and joy that thanks to the chauffeuring work he'd been able to buy Rose the band of her choice. They sat side by side while she slid it onto her finger.

'It's so beautiful, Ned.'

'And tomorrow it stays on for good. I wish I could've given you an engagement token.'

'Ssh!' She put her finger to his lips. 'This is the most beautiful ring in all the world, why should I need another?'

'One day, maybe.'

'We'll see.'

'Did you look inside, where they've put our names and the date?'

The ring was examined more closely and, given such proximity, the two merged into an embrace which tightened until Rose could no longer breathe. As they broke apart, an image of Gertie's face flashed into her mind. The words which had disturbed her so dreadfully resurfaced and Rose cried out, 'Ned, you will be gentle tomorrow? I'm so unsure about it all!'

221

It was like the cry of a trapped animal.

He touched her cheek. 'Please don't be afraid. Put your trust in my love, Rose. It'll be a new experience for both of us but I shall do my utmost not to hurt you.'

Her face was burning, she hid against his shoulder. 'Gertie made it sound horrid. I've been lying awake, wondering how it would be.'

Ned squeezed her hand. 'It won't be like that for us,' he murmured. 'I couldn't bear it if you dreaded our love-making.'

He meant every word but Rose had spent too many nights fearful not only of love-making but of the marriage itself.

Honesty compelled her to admit that had her parents been alive she wouldn't have been about to marry Ned. After that first rescue, he would have been allowed to call once, to enquire after her health, then discouraged. It would have been an amusing incident for her mother to describe over the tea-cups, then forgotten.

Those days were gone. Ned might not be the lover of her childhood imaginings – a vague colourless figure drawn from books – instead his passion for her shone out, a constant loving flame.

'Dear Ned ...' Had Gertie guessed what intimacy with Harold might be like, was that why she'd wanted to withdraw at the last minute? If only I hadn't dissuaded her, Rose thought sadly. She realized it would be better if her sister didn't come tomorrow. Gertie might see it as her duty to try to prevent her marriage but Rose had made her choice just as Gertie had done and wasn't about to change her mind. Please God it would turn out for the best.

'I'm yours,' she whispered to Ned, 'for ever and ever, my dearest.' His eyes were so full of love. Here was the tenderest plant, she must treat it with the utmost gentleness and maybe one day her own affection would match it. 'I shall do my best to be the wife you deserve.'

Gertie Brigg had had a dreadful time. Following Harold's

return from Newcastle and his outrageous suggestion concerning Australia, nothing more had been said. Nothing more *could* be said. The whole idea was preposterous.

Nevertheless, it hung like a black cloud over her every waking moment. How could Harold have committed them to such an enterprise without even consulting her!? What did he mean by it? She didn't know whether to laugh or cry – she certainly didn't intend to speak to him until he apologized: silence at least brought relief.

Harold obeyed her edict, disappearing each morning with pained stoicism. Gertie continued to sit at the breakfast table, pretending to read the newspaper as he donned his new mackintosh, shook his head over the barometer and picked up his umbrella.

Where he went, how he spent the days, she didn't know or care. It was enough that she needn't set eyes on him again till nightfall. As for herself, she couldn't sit still. She washed and cleaned, packing their possessions ready, as she still hoped and believed, for the impending move to a furnished house.

Once or twice she wondered whether she should begin viewing properties but by evening, when yet another day had gone by, she let the subject pass. They sat mute over their meagre supper, disinclined to speak. Fleetham Street, for all its faults, was now a sanctuary: what would happen on Saturday?

Harold's thoughts were of how he might persuade Gertrude to make the down-payment towards their passage. Each time he tried to introduce the topic, his courage failed. The deadline was Friday, the day Rose and Ned were due to be united, the final day before Mrs Potter regained possession of her upstairs rooms.

It was imperative he drop a hint to Harrison as to what he'd done. Ned was in touch with the office in Newcastle. A wrong word and all might be revealed; Harold might lose his only chance of escape. He had to act, he and Gertie had to be on board that boat, yet inertia continued to paralyse him as it did his wife. Nights spent on the sofa left Harold sleepless and humiliated. A man of his disposition had to start from a position of strength. Tired, sapped of bombast, he lacked the energy to be decisive.

Thus the days passed without the impasse being resolved. Husband and wife stuck to trivialities such as the necessity for refilling the coal scuttle rather than risk any serious discussion.

The night before the wedding, summoning up a morsel of courage, he asked casually, 'Shall you go tomorrow?'

'Of course. So will you.' Astonished, he remained silent. Gertie's needle flashed in and out for several minutes before she explained, 'You will have to give the bride away. Rose is not being married in St Hilda's, there's certainly no one she can ask in Newport so there's nothing else for it. According to Mrs Potter, the ceremony is due to begin at ten thirty. We ought to leave here by ten to allow plenty of time.'

She waited for a response. Harold cleared his throat.

'You'll wear your new suit, Harold. Let me have the trousers and I'll press them under the mattress.'

In his shirt tails, he tried to insist on a decent night's sleep in the bed. Gertie was implacable. He handed over his garment and retreated to the parlour.

He cursed as he thumped the sofa cushions. Tomorrow, not only was the rent due plus five shillings for the Winnots, it was the deadline for the passage money, yet he still hadn't spoken to Gertrude. His only other choice was to withdraw from his own savings. All those years accumulating largesse to impress the Brethren – Harold was close to tears.

'I have reached my lowest ebb, I might as well kill myself.' He recoiled from using the foulard tie as a noose, it had cost too much. He had another, much better idea. Not death, but a visit to Mrs Porteous. She had money, why hadn't he thought of that before? Immediately he felt more cheerful, his imagination began to bubble. 'I shall throw myself on her mercy and ask for a loan. I shall explain it is for Rose's sake. We journey to Australia in order to exert a beneficial influence over the headstrong girl.'

The story rolled along unchecked. Harold saw himself reinstated as guardian and protector of innocent womanhood. He pictured the sisters by the rail of the ship, sheltering from the storm under his manly arms. If they went to Australia together, he would explain to Mrs Porteous, it was for one simple reason: that Rose might see the folly of her ways. Afterwards, once the scales had dropped from her eyes? Why then, they could all return!

He alone would reinstate Mrs Porteous's desired companion. Rose, dutiful and humble at last, would finally take up her position and all would be well. Even better, the widow would feel financially obligated to Harold Brigg.

For the first time in days, he was almost happy. Tomorrow, as he led Rose up the aisle, he would cast on her a look of such reproach she would immediately comprehend how she was demeaning herself. At the same time, he would squeeze her arm, press a kiss on her forehead, to indicate his loving forgiveness. Yes, he rather looked forward to kissing Rose again. As for Harrison, Harold would hold himself aloof ... Damn!

The dream shattered into fragments as he recalled how he depended on Ned's co-operation to ensure their passage. He had to insinuate himself into Harrison's good graces. Harold threw himself onto the unyielding broken springs; he'd never been so uncomfortable in his life. Damn, blast and hell! That he should be in a position where he depended on Harrison's goodwill. It was monstrous.

He must persuade Gertrude to part with forty pounds – he hadn't enough *time* to work on Mrs Porteous. He would tell his wife at breakfast to visit the bank. As for the Winnots ... Harold sat up and counted his remaining small change: 3/11½d. It had been an extremely expensive week, as his wife had refused to provide luncheon. The Winnots would have to forgo their blood money, that was all there was to it. The child wouldn't suffer. What mother would deny her babe food? Besides, Ruby had found a new protector. Harold tugged angrily at the blankets. Whoever he was, the stranger could pay for the privilege.

225

'Why should I provide? What the hell do I get out of it?'

He tossed and turned. Tomorrow he would have to reveal to Harrison he and Gertrude were to accompany them. No doubt there would be a tiresome scene.

'I shall have to endure it,' he groaned. He had to prevent Harrison revealing his former occupation at Hill's. 'I shall explain discreetly, that once Gertrude and I arrive in Australia, we shall not trouble him further; we shall make our own arrangements. As soon as I find a situation more suited to my talents, we shall disappear.' Surely Harrison would understand?

'Gertrude is unsuited to the primitive life,' Harold declared, rehearsing his argument. 'I cannot expose her to it. All Harrison has to do is remain silent.' Having thus found a justification for breaking his word, Harold saw no reason why others should not agree.

But would Ned be so understanding? Suppose the man turned out to be another sneak? 'With his background he is unlikely to behave like a gentleman.' And suppose Gertrude refused to hand over that vital forty pounds?

All in all, tomorrow looked like being an extremely difficult day.

It dawned bright and cool enough for Gertie to wear her fur. Breakfast at Fleetham Street was silent. Having practised several possible openings, Harold ended up using none. Time enough after the ceremony, he told himself feebly.

'Once Gertrude has enjoyed the consolation of a glass or two of wine, we shall go to the bank,' he promised. It was to be hoped whoever was providing refreshments would not stint on the beverages and, with this pious thought uppermost, Harold followed his wife downstairs.

As he shut the street door, Gertrude asked, 'Did you give Mrs Potter the rent?'

'Of course I didn't.'

'No "of course" about it, Harold. We owe her a final week and today is the day it's due. Kindly pay her immediately we return. I don't want there to be any bad feeling.'

As if we've anywhere else to go, he raged inwardly. We can scarcely move our possessions out onto the pavement. Gertrude was being as obtuse as only she knew how. Still mute, afraid to say one word about the catastrophe facing them, Harold Brigg took his wife's arm and proceeded down Newport Road to the church.

Despite Gertie's prediction that few would be there, a small crowd had gathered. She recognized Miss Lawson with another of the waitresses from the café. One young woman was, she felt sure, Mrs Porteous's maid. In the porch Ned was very pale. Beside him, also sporting a buttonhole, was a dark-haired man whom he introduced as his brother-in-law and best man.

Gertie nodded stiffly. 'We've come so that Harold may give away the bride,' she told the groom. 'As you know neither of us is in favour of the match; we're simply here to support my sister.'

Ned and Lionel looked at one another. They murmured something which Gertie didn't catch. She stood apart, making no further attempt to converse. Harold was aware of furtive glances in their direction.

'Why not go inside?' he urged.

'Not until I've spoken to Rose.'

'You don't intend ...?' he coughed, awkwardly, 'That is to say, you won't attempt to *interfere*?'

Behind her spectacles, Gertie's eyes were implacable. 'I shall explain that if she insists on going through with the ceremony, you will act in Father's place.'

'I think perhaps it would be better not to *alienate* either party.' Particularly in view of Harold's dependence on Harrison's cooperation.

Knowing nothing of this, Gertie replied, 'I shall act as I think best, Harold.'

There was a small cheer. Rose and Muriel were approaching, surrounded by well-wishers. Lionel hustled the groom inside while the rest moved forward to greet the bride. As she caught sight of Rose, Gertie was extremely shocked; what a disgraceful outfit! No veil, no gloves, no attempt at a gown!

At the neck of her blouse was the old-fashioned cameo that had belonged to their grandmother. With Mu's help, Rose had fashioned a coronet of white flowers and was carrying a matching bouquet. In Gertie's opinion, she looked like a gypsy.

Happy, smiling, Rose cried out, 'Gertie! You've come!' and rushed to kiss her. 'Thank you, thank you. This is the happiest day of my life – having you here has made it perfect,' which was ridiculous considering her sister was about to give up her status and become a drab.

'I came to ask if you still intended to marry that person?' Gertie said woodenly.

Rose flared, 'Of course I'm marrying Ned!'

'Then Harold will give you away. That is the only reason we came this morning.'

Joy evaporated; Rose kept her voice steady. 'In that case, there was no need. Hayden has kindly agreed to support me. He has been a good friend to both of us.' She indicated the sturdy, elderly figure beside her.

Gertie couldn't believe her eyes: a labourer in an ill-fitting jacket and moleskins!

'I cannot permit it.'

Rose was very angry. 'Go inside, Gertie. Take Harold with you. Either that or go away. I won't let you spoil my day.' She went to take Hayden's arm.

'Hadn't you better do as she says,' he muttered. 'He is your brother-in-law. Family, so to speak.'

'And you are my friend. Please ...' Tears sparkled in Rose's eyes.

He gripped her hand tightly. 'A'course I will, pet, an' gladly. Ready, then?'

'I'm ready.'

'Sit, Boadicea. Good girl.'

228

Muriel and the rest had already entered the church. The distant notes of an organ began to swell. Arm in arm, Rose and Hayden began the walk up the aisle and, much to her chagrin, Gertie Brigg found that she, Harold and a nondescript mongrel were the only ones remaining in the porch.

Deprived of his role, Harold suggested, 'Gertrude, allow me to escort you home.'

'Oh, don't be such a fool! Come along. If we stand here much longer, we'll catch fleas from that creature.' Head high, clutching her fur, she swept inside. Harold followed.

Rose was behaving with a shameful lack of decorum, smiling at everyone, responding to greetings on every side. A bride should comport herself modestly. Fancy being married in a blouse and skirt like some common girl! As for those people crowded into the pews, singing with gusto, they'd no sense of propriety either. Some of them weren't even wearing hats!

Gertie watched in disbelief as a small child ran forward to stand between Rose and Ned at the altar rail. They made no attempt to push her away. Instead each took a hand as the vicar bent to whisper, 'Stay still while I marry your Uncle Ned to your new aunty.'

Where was the dignity? Why not slap the child and return it to the mother! Harold tut-tutted as he caught sight of Gertie's expression. The need to ply his wife with alcohol was even greater now. After this travesty, she might need brandy before she could be persuaded to part with forty pounds. Hearing the bride and groom exchange vows made him morose; I should have married Rose, to save her from all this, he thought. Or better still, Mrs Porteous.

The ceremony over, they followed the congregation through streets where people stood in doorways to wish the newly-weds good fortune. As for the mongrel, Harold was astonished to find it included in the wedding party.

In Muriel's shabby front parlour, there were flowers everywhere. Gertie found herself crushed into a corner while children rushed about, thrusting plates of sandwiches at everyone. The noise was intolerable and her head began to throb.

'I don't think I can stand much more of this!'

Harold couldn't believe it: wherever he looked, there were only cups of tea to drink. 'Good God!' The cur had been given a saucerful of milk. A tray arrived in front of him. 'Sherry, whisky, whatever else you've got,' he demanded.

The young housewife shook her head. 'There's elderberry wine but we're keeping that to have with the cake.'

He was doomed. What if he couldn't force Gertrude to go to the bank? Even his plan for a private word with Harrison was frustrated because of the crush. Harold hadn't enough in his pocket for the rent. If Mrs Potter chose to put them out on the street tomorrow, what would become of them? He had a horrifying vision of two lonely figures, heading for the work-house.

A suicide pact, he thought feverishly; he would put the idea to Gertrude tonight. And if he suddenly found *he* lacked the courage to go through with it, at least he would inherit what was left in her bank account.

'Thanks for coming. It's made all the difference to Rose.' Ned Harrison had appeared in front of him. 'She's been worried for both of you ever since she heard you'd lost your situation.'

The cheek of the fellow! Forgetting the need for tact, Harold drew himself upright. 'There was no need, no need at all.'

'That's good. It'll make her very happy if you've found something else?' Ned waited but Harold declined to elucidate. 'I understand you and Mrs Brigg will be moving from Fleetham Street,' he said eventually. 'Rose is very anxious to keep in touch. She'll be visiting before we leave for Liverpool – you will let us have your new address?'

'Ah, yes ... Liverpool.' Harold remembered belatedly. 'Harrison, I've been meaning to have a word ...' He broke off to glare at a small girl.

Ned picked her up, saying, 'There's a lot to do before we leave but Rose won't forget to call.'

'Concerning Australia—' Harold began.

'We'll be living in a hostel until they decide where we're to be sent. Once we're settled, Rose will write with the particulars. Excuse me, I must take my niece back to her mother.' Before Harold could say another word Ned had gone. Gertie reappeared.

'We must go. There are too many people and my head's simply bursting!' but from the opposite side of the room Rose had seen her.

'Gertie!' She pushed her way across. 'I'm sorry I was cross outside the church – I couldn't bear you to hurt Hayden's feelings – he's been so kind. Wish me joy, Gertie, I'm so very, very happy.'

Head swimming, Gertie gazed at the flushed, happy face. Rose couldn't really be enjoying all this? Her sister's hair was in disarray. One of the children had hold of the bridal posy. Distracted by it, Gertie said jealously, 'Those are lilies – and white roses!'

'I know!' Rose laughed guiltily. 'Hayden took some from a prize bush but we're sending the poor man an apology plus a slice of wedding cake!' She leaned across and kissed the pale cheek. 'It meant so much to see you there. I'll come round before we leave.'

Suddenly, Gertie felt as if she and Rose were the only two in the whole world. The crowd fell away leaving them in an oasis of quietness. 'Harold says we're going with you to Australia.'

'What!'

'I don't know what he means by it.' Gertie rubbed her throbbing forehead; too much had happened for her to believe one single word. 'It's probably one of his fibs. He can be so aggravating at times.'

'But – Gertie, is it *true*?' Rose's face was so eager Gertie could take no more.

'Don't build your hopes because I really don't know. Perhaps by the time you return from your honeymoon, I shall. Are you going to Redcar?'

'Osmotherly.'

Gertie struggled to find words but none came. 'Good luck,' she said finally, and hurried to the door.

Outside, eyes closed, she waited until she felt Harold beside her. 'Is it true?'

'Is what true, Gertrude?'

'Do you really intend that we go to Australia with Ned and Rose?'

He seized the opportunity. 'I do. I have sacrificed myself for your sake but it depends on sending forty pounds towards the cost of our fares. *I* have obtained the situation, Gertrude. It is up to you to do the rest.'

Her pale eyes looked at him. 'The truth is you're in a pickle and you think you've found a way out. It's not for my sake at all. *I* don't want to go. If you insist on it, you can pay the damn fare yourself. You've eighty-seven pounds saved. I found your bank book while I was clearing out the chest of drawers. You've been keeping me short while you saved thirty shillings a week ever since we married. Don't you even *think* of cadging money from me ever again!'

And with that she stalked off down the street.

He was too stunned to follow. 'She *swore* at me ... Gertrude used a blasphemy!' Good God! And she'd searched his belongings – how dare she ... But he needed to telegraph the money to Newcastle and there wasn't a moment to lose.

Walking briskly, Harold arrived back from the bank before his wife.

Mrs Potter was waiting. 'Had you forgotten the rent, Mr Brigg?'

He bit back sarcasm. 'Not at all, Mrs Potter. Er, I'm glad to see you ... there's been a slight change of plan. Mrs Brigg and I will be departing next Thursday morning rather than tomorrow.'

'In that case, you can pay double,' the landlady said promptly, 'for the inconvenience. And no further delays, Mr Brigg, I want those rooms back.'

He forced his smile to remain in place, 'And so you shall. thank you for being so – accommodating.'

Mrs Potter was on the lookout when Gertie finally appeared.

'You never told me you were staying on? It's a dratted nuisance, it means Queenie can't move straight back in. I must say I'm surprised *you* gave me no warning, Mrs Brigg.'

Gertie forced herself to say, 'I wasn't entirely sure what our plans were.'

'Mr Brigg told me Thursday morning and that's final as far as I'm concerned.' She modified her tone. 'Wasn't it a happy wedding? I've never seen Miss Rose look so pretty.'

Recovering, Gertie answered, 'She did look quite – attractive.'

'Radiant, I'd say.'

As soon as she could, Gertie made her escape. She finally had her answer. Next Thursday was the day Rose and Ned were due to leave for Liverpool. If she and Harold, with no new home to go to, were also leaving here, it must be as part of the exodus.

'Harold doesn't want to go to Australia any more than I do!' Indignation choked her again. 'He never even asked me!' Separation from Rose was preferable to that fate.

If only he hadn't lost his situation ... Perhaps Hill's would take him back? Hope revived. If *she* begged Mr Simmonds to reconsider? 'I'll go to the mill myself!' It was a bold enterprise; she quaked at the thought. 'I'll have to do it now before I lose my nerve!' Harold consistently refused to explain why he'd been dismissed. It was probably a silly little upset, Gertie decided optimistically, something easily put right.

The motor-cycle and sidecar were heavily laden as Rose and Ned headed south. She groaned as they bounced over a rut.

'Are you all right?'

'It's the eggs! We shall have an omelette if that happens too often.'

'I don't want to stop until we reach Swainby. It's a much longer journey than Roseberry.'

'Don't worry.' Rose gripped the basket of provisions. Mu and her neighbours had been generous. If the eggs were cracked, there was still plenty of bread and cheese. She smiled at his anxious face. 'We shall have a feast!'

And what would happen afterwards? She shivered slightly; and what on earth did Gertie mean about Australia? She would ask Ned as soon as they arrived.

The streets near the rolling mill were full of men heading home at the end of their shift. Gertie shrank against dingy brickwork to let them pass. The receptionist was reluctant to let her enter. Now, sitting opposite Mr Simmonds, Gertie tried to control her trembling.

'I came to ask if there was a possibility ... any chance that my husband ... if his position remains open?'

'Definitely not.' Seeing the vivid blush, he asked curiously, 'Brigg didn't put you up to this?'

'Harold doesn't know I'm here.'

'I see ...' He was sorry for her. 'Didn't he tell you the reason?'

She shook her head. 'My sister and her husband – they heard he'd lost his situation. Harold refuses to speak of it.'

Simmonds was diverted. 'Rose – is *married*?'

'Yes.'

'Well, well, well ... I fear there's no possibility of reinstatement, Mrs Brigg.' He was intrigued. 'I didn't realize your sister was engaged.'

'It was a short betrothal.' Seeing the sly grin develop Gertie was suddenly furious; she'd come on a fool's errand and now the man was being insulting. 'My sister and her husband are emigrating next week. I'm very pleased she is no longer in a position to endure pestering from married men. Good afternoon.'

Equally furious, Simmonds said, 'You can find your own way out?'

'Of course.'

He waited until she'd reached the door. 'The reason for the dismissal was dishonesty. Brigg stole six postage stamps.'

'Stole ...?'

'Good afternoon, Mrs Brigg.'

Outside, in the shadow of a wall, Gertie cried her heart out.

*

It was dusk when Ned and Rose drove down the long winding road from Swainby. Ahead they could see the glow from lamps in the windows of the Queen Catherine public house but Ned had slowed down and was examining the low stone houses on the left.

'It's near the pump ... blue curtains at the window. Ah, this could be it.' Moving stiffly after the ride, he found the heavy key under the specified plant pot. 'Right first time. We've arrived, Rose, this is the cottage. Let me help you out.'

He felt her cold hands as she handed him the precious basket. 'We'll have the fire going in no time. Just you go inside, I'll see to our things.'

There was a single downstairs room, low-beamed with a vast stone fireplace half filling one wall. In a narrow cupboard was a winding stairway. Beyond this, a lean-to scullery. Rose picked up the heavy kettle. Tea first, then she would look upstairs.

Ned left her alone while he unloaded the bags and coaxed the kindling alight. Dry logs had been laid on a bed of ash, country fashion. When they were ablaze he set the kettle to boil and went through to the scullery. 'How are the eggs?'

'Two are cracked, we can use those for breakfast. We've cold ham tonight and some of Hayden's love-apples.'

Ned chuckled. 'I know they're really tomatoes but I prefer his version. Shall I make up the bed?'

'Yes, please.' Rose tried not to be embarrassed.

It was cold under the eaves but the feather mattress was inviting. Ned decided it wouldn't do for them to be chilly, not tonight. After supper, he'd make one or two changes. He went outside and helped himself to plenty of wood from the stack.

Candles danced and flickered as they sat on the rug in front of the fire. The blue curtains were tightly shut, they were alone in a private world.

Ned raised a glass of Mu's wine: 'To the wife of my dreams, to you, Rose, my love. My word, it's a bit cosier here than it was up on Roseberry. You were so cold that day, your lips were frozen, d'you remember? You could hardly say yes when I asked you to marry me.'

Slowly, gently, he chattered until she had relaxed enough to slip into his arms. Together they finished the wine, staring at pictures in the heart of the flames. Eventually Rose stirred. 'We'd better clear the dishes.'

'I'll put more water on for a wash, then I've things to attend to.' From the scullery she heard the bumping and saw with amazement he was lugging the feather bed downstairs.

'What are you doing with that?'

'Just for tonight. Give me a hand to move the settle.'

He made an island in the centre of the small room, surrounding it with furniture then, pouring her a bowlful of hot water, Ned went outside so that Rose might undress in private.

The stars were bright and cold. In the village, the windows were dark. Folk rose early here; their days followed the sun. Ned could hear sheep on the hills, the constant chuckle of water in the beck; he wondered if there was any comparison with Australia. It wouldn't be so blessed cold, that was certain. He rubbed his arms to warm them and tapped on the scullery door.

'Are you in bed?'

'Yes.' It was a timid sound. He undressed and sluiced himself. Towelling vigorously he contemplated his shirt but decided against putting it back on. Naked, he returned to the room and began building up the fire. He could sense Rose watching him. Her voice quivered as she said, 'I've never seen anyone – undressed.'

He sat back on his heels. 'Not even Gertie?'

'Goodness, no! Mother was very strict.'

He set fresh logs where they could easily be tossed onto the blaze. 'We always bathed in front of the fire – you've seen how Mu does it with her kids. And my father, when it was his turn, I used to help scrub his back.' Still kneeling, he said, 'Come and join me by the fire.'

Rose crept out from beneath the soft eiderdown. He

reached out to touch her thick, dark-gold hair. 'You're trembling. You're not cold?'

'No.' Forcing herself to be honest, 'I'm frightened.'

'I know, pet, but there's no need. I'll not hurt you – I couldn't. I love you too much. Take off your nightgown, I want to see how beautiful you are.'

Nervously she undid the buttons and, after an effort, lifted it over her head. He gazed in delight and wonder. 'You really are lovely, Rose ... Your body ... your white skin ... I'm the luckiest man in the whole wide world!' As she made as if to cover herself, he murmured, 'Please ... let me feast my eyes.' He touched the soft, pearly texture of her body and, leaning forward, kissed her breasts. She shivered suddenly. 'Come closer if you're cold.'

This time she said flatly, 'It's your hair. It's soaking wet!' and Ned laughed.

'And the water was freezing!'

'Here ...' Using her nightgown, Rose began to mop it dry. Ned drew her into his arms and together they stretched out together in the firelight.

Ned led her hand along his body just as he had, when touching hers. 'It's not wrong, I know it isn't. We were made to enjoy each other, Rose.' She wished she didn't feel so apprehensive; what they were doing, she'd always been taught it was wrong! She almost shied away when he put her hand in one particular place. 'It's love for you that makes me grow like that.' His accent was so different from Cecil's, his skin hadn't the downy gold hairs – she was finding it difficult to swallow!

'Please, Ned, you won't ...'

'Hurt you? I shall try not to. If I'm clumsy, you must forgive me. It may be difficult the first time.' Suddenly, urgently, he knelt over her, his hands reaching and parting her thighs. 'Let me come inside you, my love.'

Blood pounded, leaving her breathless. Ned pressed her down into the feather bed. He whispered his love as he entered her body then his mouth was so tight against hers, she couldn't cry out. She felt the sudden push deep inside as a

237

flood of warmth pervaded her. There was a last thrust and Ned gave a shuddering groan. His heart thudded, she could feel it racing breathlessly. He was joined to her. That's what it must mean: one flesh, complete and indivisible.

Was love-making always like this? It wasn't as bad as Gertie made out. Rose said aloud, 'I can't think why she made a fuss.' To her astonishment, Ned groaned. 'What's the matter?'

'Didn't you *feel* anything?'

She considered. 'A bit embarrassed but that's because we have no clothes on.'

'Oh ... no ... oh, Rose!'

The rooms in Fleetham Street were dark when Gertie returned. She was thankful. She made herself a hot drink and sat in the gloaming. At the end of this terrible day, she knew there was no alternative: they had to leave Middlesbrough and Australia was as good a place as any to begin anew.

She would tell Harold about the visit to Simmonds. He would be angry but what did that matter? There was so much she needed to know. Would the four of them be together on the voyage? What was to happen once they arrived?

Rose and Ned would be working on a farm but that wouldn't suit her husband. Even ducks made him nervous. Walking in the park, he'd once chosen a different path rather then encounter a belligerent drake. Gertie yawned. She might as well go to bed as sit up and wait. There was a heavy tattoo on the street door. Reluctantly she went downstairs. One of those two strange men was on the doorstep. 'Yes?'

'Is he in?'

'If you mean my husband, no, he's not.' She spoke loudly to hide her nervousness, 'It's far too late for you to come calling.'

'I'll be back tomorrow – and he'd better not bilk me this time.'

'I don't understand?'

'*He* does.' Alf Winnot's aggression made her reach to check the door-chain. 'Just see that you tell him.'

238

*

Ned had the consolation that Rose didn't object to their love-making.

'It's an odd sensation but quite pleasant,' she told him. Such honesty was disheartening but he scolded himself; he must give her time. 'Gertie said Harold "bothers" her far too often.'

'Aye, well . . . Maybe if she doesn't enjoy it.'

'But it's not at all disagreeable,' Rose said primly.

He hid his disappointment and pulled the eiderdown round them. 'That's good enough to start with for me, pet. I reckon we're lucky to suit one another so well. Now, go to sleep. It's been a long, long day.'

She shifted under the bedclothes. 'It feels very odd to be beside a naked man.'

'Put your nightgown on, you'll feel more comfortable.' Give it time! They had the rest of their lives in front of them. As her arms reached up, firelight glinted on her ring. Ned took her hand and kissed it. 'Sweet dreams, my beautiful, wonderful love.' Despite his disappointment he was asleep within minutes.

When Harold returned, Gertie said, 'That man was here . . . he said he'd be back tomorrow.'

Damn and blast those Winnots!

In bed, without her spectacles she stared at the blur that was her husband. 'I visited Hill's to ask Mr Simmonds if he would reconsider—'

'You did *what?*'

'Don't shout. He told me why you'd been dismissed.'

Harold recoiled. 'Have you bought those tickets?'

'Yes,' She was pitiless. 'As your wife, I shall have to endure the shame for the rest of my life. Thank God my parents did not live to see this day. Goodnight.' She turned her back and Harold Brigg returned to the sofa.

Chapter Eleven

Port Outward ...

On the final morning of their honeymoon, Rose and Ned climbed the moor up above Sheepwash. The gorse was in wild yellow bloom, lambs staggered and bleated anxiously, the whole world was displaying the miracle of renewal, yet they were about to leave it behind.

The last two days had been spent learning about one another; they'd had so little time together before, it startled Rose to realize it. 'I committed myself to him for life without knowing the first thing about Ned as a person.' After a pause, she murmured, 'I've been quite lucky ... All things considered.' Which meant their love-making. She refused to delude herself. 'You're being a snob, my girl, but it's got to be faced: he's no gentleman.' Ned's voice in the heat of passion had a thick Middlesbrough accent. Because she couldn't be swept along Rose found herself becoming too much aware of it. 'You prefer it when it's dark, too,' she scolded, 'you're embarrassed when he wants to stare at your body ... or worse still, touch certain parts of it.'

Would it have been different had Ned been a gentleman? She'd no idea; it was certainly too late to wonder about it. 'If only mother hadn't drummed into us that nice girls have to "put up with it". I can't let myself go the way he wants me to, I'll never be able to do that.'

Nothing but the fates would prevent Ned giving her the sun, moon and stars if sheer hard work could achieve it. If only he could be satisfied with a bit less ... Less? Rose sighed as she acknowledged, 'Well, less fondling, I suppose.'

But considering how little she had known, he seemed the kindest, most gentle of lovers, especially compared to her perception of Harold Brigg. What Gertie must have to endure! Now the forbidden subject had been partially revealed – imagine being in bed with *him* ... Urgh!

Did Rose have any regrets? She'd always been too impulsive, Cecil and Father had warned her against it. 'If I hadn't married Ned,' she thought, watching a bird soar away over the moor, 'I'd probably have ended up a spinster, scrimping, saving, terrified of old age.' And if Australia lived up to expectation maybe things would be different and the social difference between them would cease to matter?

Ned was quiet, she guessed his mind was full of what was to come. He was a thoughtful, generous man. 'I've been lucky,' she told herself very firmly indeed, 'it's up to me to make him a good wife.'

They walked in companionable silence, savouring every view, trying to print them in memory. On the highest point, Ned called a halt, spreading the rug and anchoring it with stones. 'We can see the whole world from here – it'll do for our picnic, unless you want to press on.'

'No, this is splendid.' She settled down beside him, the springy heather acting as a cushion. For a few minutes they let themselves be dazzled by sunlight and bewitched by skylarks.

He was the first to break the spell. 'That remark Gertie made, about going to Australia. Do you think she really meant it?'

'She said afterwards it might be one of Harold's fibs. He tells them all the time, to impress people. It's an automatic habit. I don't think he notices he isn't telling the truth any more. He used to exaggerate dreadfully when he and Gertie were courting. It could be the same thing this time.'

'On the other hand ...'

Rose began to share his concern. 'You don't think ... He surely can't have seen the same article Hayden found?'

'If he did, what use would it be to *him*? You've seen the

company leaflet, they want people with practical experience, prepared to do manual work.' Ned indicated the sheep. 'They're going to teach us how to deal with animals, maintain vehicles and machinery – that's not a life to suit Harold Brigg.'

'Poor Gertie. Perhaps he was trying to soften the blow of our departure by promising her a future visit. Even if there isn't the least possibility, Harold wouldn't care about that.' She tried to explain. 'He would make the gesture without worrying how it might be achieved. That's the sort of man he is. We'll never become like that, will we?'

'Definitely not. Come here.' She reached out obediently, to be encompassed by his arms. 'When I tell you I love you,' Ned murmured into her hair, 'you might as well know I mean every word.'

He was kind, this man. His arms were strong. I do love him, I do, I do!

'You can say that as often as you like,' she replied politely but she'd triggered his laughter again. 'Now what have I said?'

'It's not what you say – it's *how*. I know women are supposed to be modest about love-making but you make it sound like a substitute for afternoon tea.' He was so bright-eyed, waiting for her response, Rose's heart quailed.

'I quite like making love. I'm sure I shall come to enjoy it in time.'

The slightest encouragement made him happy. 'You're almost behaving like a hussy!'

'Oh, I don't think I'll ever manage that, at least only with you,' she added mischievously. 'I certainly didn't want to kiss and cuddle Mr Simmonds.'

Ned was outraged, 'I should think not! Goodness gracious – what happened to all that careful upbringing with nurses and governesses and the like?'

'Only one governess and she left after a few weeks because Father couldn't really afford it. Gertie and I went to school after that ... Until Mother went to that wretched fortune-teller, of course. It was all a long time ago.' She yawned and stretched cat-like on the rug. 'Isn't this weather heavenly? I

242

hope it lasts and lasts all the way to Australia.'

For once Ned wasn't interested in meteorology.

'D'you feel like . . .?'

'You mean here? Out in the open?'

'Mmm.'

'What if somebody comes?'

'Rose – there's a clear twenty-five-mile view in every direction.'

'Those little lambs . . .'

'Those little lambs know what's what.' His kisses grew fiercer. 'So did their mothers, that's how they come to be here.' But Rose was stiff and tense. After a few minutes, he gave up and rolled onto his back, staring at the sky.

'I'm sorry.'

'It's quite all right.'

But she knew it wasn't. 'It's just . . . I'm not very used to it yet. Give me time, Ned. Please.'

'We'll try again once we get to Australia.'

She thought about their impending return to Middlesbrough. 'It'll feel strange going back to my room.'

'We can't be together on Mu's parlour floor.'

'Certainly not! What about the voyage?'

'According to the company letter, it's four to a cabin and as all the couples will be strangers, men and women will be segregated.'

He sounded so glum she forced herself to say cheerily, 'I shall find us a secret hideaway, where you and I can at least be private.'

Ned grinned. 'There'll be twenty other couples doing exactly the same thing.'

That idea made her chuckle. 'Bet I find the best, most private place of all. Ned . . .?'

'Mmm?'

'Does Mu know how to avoid having babies?'

'Eh?' He stared and she blushed.

'I thought . . . as we'll both be so busy to begin with . . .' She looked at him helplessly, 'I don't know who else to ask. Our

243

old doctor believed women should never stop having them, to make up for those who were killed in the war.'

'Mu knows something about it. She and Lionel were desperate not to have another. She wrote off to this lady doctor who has a clinic in London.'

'She won't mind if I ask her?'

'Of course not.' He caressed her hair. 'You do want to have one eventually, though?'

'Oh, yes.' She and Gertie had often talked about that. 'Two. One of each.'

'Not sisters?'

'There were three of us to begin with,' she reminded him quietly. 'We had a brother just as you and Mu did. It was much more fun when Cecil was alive.'

'Aye ... I can imagine. I still miss mine. Not having him there at our wedding, that hurt.'

'Two children will be sufficient and as you're obviously the sort of chap who needs a *harem* to satisfy his needs I'd better find out how to avoid having thousands.'

He forced himself to play along, 'You're the insatiable one! But you're right. I should have thought of it before. I'll talk to Mu if you like?'

'No, thanks.' It would be embarrassing enough without him joining in.

She'd discovered a weakness in this stocky, sturdy lover of hers; he couldn't bear to be tickled. To distract him, she seized a fern frond and tickled the back of his neck until he could stand it no longer.

If only Rose could let herself go in other ways, Ned thought longingly, as he rolled away in the grass.

Coming down from the moor they stopped to drink at the spring.

'This water tastes of primroses and violets.'

'As long as it doesn't taste of sheep.'

'I wonder if there are any becks in Australia.'

'Artesian wells and bore-holes, if we're lucky. And water everywhere after the "wet".'

244

The sun had gone down; Rose pulled her cardigan closer. 'At least there won't be chilly north-east breezes.'

'It might be cold at night. We'll see.'

People in front gardens nodded as they strolled back along the lane to the cottage.

Their neighbour called out, 'You're leaving this evening then? Here's half a dozen eggs and a jar of honey to take back with you, m'dear.'

Rose was embarrassed. 'Can I pay you for them?'

'A 'course not!' The elderly gardener winked. 'Been a tonic, seeing a pair of bright eyes go past. Any chance you'll be visiting us again?'

'We're off to Australia on Thursday.'

He leaned on his fork. 'My word, that's far enough. Going to make your fortune?'

'Just a decent living,' Ned said evenly.

'Aye, well ... it's not easy nowadays. Good luck to you.' The old man watched them go. All that sacrifice and still the young ones hadn't got 'owt. 'Meks you wonder what it was all for,' he grumbled to a robin.

They tidied the cottage, setting out kindling beside the bed of ash in the grate. Outside, the motor-cycle and sidecar were once more laden with their possessions. Ned tucked her in and fastened the door. 'Shall you go round to see Gertie tonight?'

'It'll be too late. Tomorrow will be soon enough.'

'I have to start cleaning the cycle tonight. I promised I'd hand it over good as new.'

Rose understood. 'I'll spend half an hour with Mu and then go back to my room.'

'I've a chance to do more chauffeuring, tomorrow and Wednesday. I'll cancel it if you'd rather but it gives me a chance to earn a bit extra before we go.'

'Don't worry about me. There's the washing, ironing, Gertie to visit, then the packing. Two days is scarcely enough.' It was the best way; keep on working until they were too tired to think.

245

The drive home was quiet and dreamlike under a rising moon. On the outskirts of Middlesbrough, Ned reached across and kissed her gently. 'Honeymoon's over, Mrs Harrison.' The enormity of what she'd done swept over Rose.

She choked back nervous fears and said calmly, 'It's the beginning of the rest of our lives.'

Gertie plucked at the frayed edges of a cushion. 'I was expecting you all day yesterday, Rose.'

'I'm sorry. We got back late on Monday and then there was so much to do. We still haven't finished packing and we leave early tomorrow.'

'So do we.'

'Goodness!' Rose snatched a glance at Ned. 'It is true then? Not one of Harold's—' She picked her words more carefully. 'He's definitely booked a passage?'

'We're travelling on the same boat, all four of us.'

'Gertie, how marvellous! What an extraordinary coincidence.'

Ned asked cautiously, 'What's Mr Brigg planning to do? He's surely not applied to the same company?'

Gertrie shrugged. 'I've no idea. As usual he refuses to explain. All I know is we leave on the same train and travel to Australia on the same boat.' To Rose she added, 'He claims it's so that you and I can be together but that's one of his fibs, of course.'

Rose was bewildered. 'Do you want to go with us? You've never said so before. Did you ask Harold to arrange it?'

'Oh, no. Harold's in a pickle so he's decided to cut and run – you knew why he'd been dismissed, didn't you?'

'I ...' Rose looked nervously at Ned; he obviously knew more than she did. She reached across and took Gertie's hand. 'Not the whole story but I'm so sorry, you've obviously had a dreadful time. Perhaps with a new start, everything will improve.'

Gertie's cry was heartfelt. 'But I want to *stay* in Middlesbrough, Rose. Harold could have used the money to rent a little house where I could have invited my friends – it's cost us forty pounds for those two tickets, you know.'

Rose knew Ned was thinking the same: was it possible that Harold *had* been taken on by the same company?

'It's no use,' Gertie blew her nose. 'What's done is done and Mrs Potter will be glad to see the back of us. It's been very difficult, she wanted us out last Saturday. She keeps saying she'll be glad to have her old bedroom back. I can't think why, it's a beastly uncomfortable mattress. Would you like some tea? We've just about enough milk left.'

Rose followed her through to the kitchen, skirting the various suitcases at the top of the stairs. Once they were out of earshot, Gertie looked at her curiously. 'How does marriage suit you?'

'I've been lucky, Gertie. I know you think I've married beneath me but Ned and Muriel are good decent people. Whatever happens, I know I can trust Ned.' In view of the way Harold had treated his wife, this sounded perilously close to sarcasm and Gertie was immediately tearful.

'Please, Rose, don't! It's been dreadful, especially since I discovered Harold is a thief. I went to see Mr Simmonds and he told me.'

'Oh, Gertie, no! He can't be that, surely? Here, take my hanky, yours is soaked. Where is Harold, anyway?'

'Goodness knows. Probably with those dreadful men. One of them came round demanding money.' Incoherently, the tale emerged.

When Rose returned to the parlour, she murmured to Ned, 'I think Harold is in a worse mess than we thought. According to Gertie, he's being blackmailed.' She saw Ned's face. 'What do you know about it?'

'Nothing for certain but there was a tale going about—' He broke off as Gertie appeared with the tea. 'I'll tell you later.'

They made desultory conversation, glancing at the clock, aware of what remained to be done. They arranged where they would meet on the platform the following morning and

247

Ned said finally, 'We're due to see Hayden. I don't want to keep the old chap waiting.'

'I'll fetch my hat.' Rose kissed Gertie. 'It's very odd. I thought tonight you and I would be crying on one another's shoulders because we might never see each other again.'

'I know.' Gertie laughed shakily. 'I shan't believe it's true until we're all on that boat.'

Ned held out his hand, 'Until tomorrow then.'

Gertie was still reserved; she nodded distantly. 'Yes. Good-night.' Rose pretended not to notice her coolness.

As they walked along, she shook her head. 'It's amazing. What d'you imagine Harold will do on an Australian out-station?'

'Nothing *useful*, that's for sure. What I want to know is how he wangled a passage?'

She halted, 'D'you think Gertie knows that the *women* are also expected to work?'

'I doubt it. She's obviously not seen any of the company leaflets.' Rose was silent. 'Let's not worry about it, pet. Try and be cheerful for Hayden's sake.' She took his arm: this would be the worst parting of all. Mercifully, Boadicea provided a diversion.

Hayden greeted them in a furious temper, 'She's drunk! The silly, stupid bitch ... I poured out a glass of me home-made brew, to try it, like. It weren't ready so I tipped it in a saucer, to use for catching wasps and the daft bitch drank the lot. Now look at her.'

It was a sorry sight. The mongrel's legs were splayed, she gazed up bleary-eyed from a pile of newspapers.

'She's lost control of her ruddy bladder. I dursn't let her near her bed, she'd mucky it up.'

Ned bent down to tickle an ear. 'Poor old girl ... you'll have a terrible hangover tomorrow.' Boadicea broke wind.

'Ha'way!' Hayden was disgusted, 'Behave, can't you. Let's go outside, I can't breathe in here.'

He led the way through the blue gate and shut it behind them. 'So she knows she's on guard. Not that a burglar'd feel

248

tempted with that stink. I'll show you me vegs, shall I?'

It was to put off the inevitable that made him lead them along each of the rows, naming the varieties, predicting their chances of surviving a late frost. Finally, when they came to the last of the seedlings, Hayden ran out of things to say.

'That's it then. You two'd better be off.' Suddenly there was an unbearable tension.

'Hayden . . .'

'Don't waste your breath, lad. It was my idea so I shall have to put up wi' it. See you two mek a go of things, that's all I ask.'

Rose pleaded, 'Will you come and join us once we have a home?'

He stared unseeing at his neighbour's patch. 'Thanks for asking, lass, but I'm too old. Besides, who'd look after the old gels? No, I shall end up where I began, right here in Middlesbrough.' He thrust a small package at Rose. 'Pop this in your suitcase, you can open it once you get there. I'll have to stay with Boadicea, I can't leave her while she's poorly.' He strode blindly past the gate, back inside the shed.

Ned's heart was overflowing. Rose, knowing it, threaded her arm through his and led him gently away.

'We'll walk a bit.'

His voice trembled, 'There's the packing to finish.'

'It can wait. Let's walk.'

It was midnight before the two modest trunks and the box were corded. Each was labelled: NOT WANTED ON VOYAGE. All they had was one small bag of necessities each, nothing more was permitted. 'I don't suppose the cabins will be luxurious,' Ned warned, 'it said in the leaflet we'd only have one small locker per person.'

'How fortunate I don't have much,' she teased. 'I even gave my old tea-gown to Mu's friend.'

'Not the blue one? I liked you in that.'

'Ned, when is there likely to be an opportunity to wear that on a sheep farm? No, I've been sensible. Everything in that

249

trunk is *serviceable*.' She was anxious about the cardboard box. 'I wish the tea service could have fitted in as well. I hope there's sufficient padding.'

'We used every newspaper we could find.' Ned recalled the collection of luggage at Fleetham Street. 'You don't think Gertie and Harold were planning to bring all that lot?'

Rose sighed, 'I think I counted five suitcases – plus the enormous trunk belonging to Harold. There was even a label on the mahogany table, he can't be intending to take that?'

Ned snorted. 'As long as he doesn't expect us to help carry it.'

They were to discover soon enough. At the station Ned stowed their luggage without difficulty while Rose kissed Mu and the children.

'Remember what I've told you,' Mu mumured. 'It's worked for Lionel and me so far. Tell Ned to be patient. You can't afford any little ones just yet.'

'I will. Thanks for everything. We'll send word as soon as we're settled.'

Mu grinned. 'Make it sound really attractive, it'll help me give Lionel that extra push.'

'Look, Mammy, look ...' her toddler pointed to where chaos had broken out further down the platform.

Rose groaned. 'It has to be Harold.' Ned saw it too and cursed.

But Harold had spotted them. In his elegant clothes, he strode towards their group. 'Ah, Harrison, the very man!' The loud voice echoed under the vast glass roof. 'I don't seem to be able to make these porters understand. A simple matter of transferring bag and baggage from A to B as it were ...' he flourished his umbrella. 'Perhaps you could explain.'

'You've got too much stuff and they won't shift it unless you pay them. Get a move on, there's the guard!'

'I don't suppose you could—'

'No, I couldn't.' Ned pushed Rose into the carriage ordering, 'Don't become involved, let him sort it out.' She hung out of the window. Harold was now hurrying back to

250

where Gertie was stranded amid their possessions.

'Gertrude, kindly pay those men.'

'I've only half a crown, Harold!'

'That will be ample.' Immediately another heated argument broke out.

Rose cried in agony, 'Gertie! She'll be left behind!'

'She won't,' Mu called. 'Look, the old skinflint's found his purse.'

The guard shouted a warning. Porters flung suitcases pell-mell on top of those already in the van. The whistle blew. Harold shoved his wife inside and fell in behind. The porter slammed the door, the train began to move. There was a wild cry as Gertie Brigg looked back at the platform.

'Harold – grandmother's table – it's still there! Do something!'

Trying not to laugh, Ned called to his sister, 'Looks like you've won a decent bit of furniture, Mu. Don't let the kids ruin it!'

From further down the train, Harold's bellow could still be heard, 'That valuable item is my property, I demand it be sent on. Porter, put that on the very next train, d'you hear!'

Ned yanked at the window's leather strap to shut out the sound. He and Rose collapsed into corner seats facing one another.

'You know, I can just about tolerate Gertie with her stuck-up attitude, but as for that buffoon ... If he tries to patronize me once more—'

'Ned, I'm sorry. I love Gertie dearly but I feel exactly the same.'

'All the way to Australia! He may not get there,' Ned told her darkly. 'One dark night, his body may accidentally disappear over the rail of the ship ...'

'Ssh!' She tried not to giggle, 'Here they come.'

Gertie wept while Harold continued to fume until Rose told him to be quiet.

'It was Gertie's table anyway, not yours.'

251

'Even so, a valuable piece ...'

'You should have sold it, not tried to bring it.' Rose was tart. 'You saw the leaflet – "limited space in the hold" – and why didn't you let Gertie read it? She's brought far too much as well.'

Harold turned on his weeping spouse. 'Matrimony has not improved your sister's temper, Gertrude.'

Ned, worn out by the past few days, having feigned sleep at first was now deeply unconscious. Rose half resented it as she searched her bag for sal volatile. Harold disappeared to check that his various suitcases hadn't been damaged and she persuaded Gertie to close her eyes.

'We shall need to be alert in Liverpool. Don't over-excite yourself, it isn't worth it for the sake of that old table.'

'No doubt you have the tea service safely packed away?'

Oh dear, oh dear, thought Rose. 'Yes,' she said briskly, 'it's with my clothes and I expect you have the silver dressing-table set. Fortunately Ned and I didn't have much to start with and we've pruned it down to all but the absolute essentials, as instructed by the company. Didn't Harold tell you *anything*? We're only permitted three items in the hold plus one small cabin bag apiece.'

'Well, I didn't know,' Gertie declared petulantly. 'He didn't return till midnight, he'd been seeing someone in Haverton Hill. All he said then was that Mrs Potter must refund us two days' rent because we'd overpaid. She refused of course, she and Harold had words and that's what made us late.'

'Never mind. It's behind you now. Try and rest.'

Rose leaned back in her seat. Other people's back gardens flashed past, bursting with the sharp yellows and blues of June. It still seemed incredible to have Gertie beside her. Up to the very last minute, Rose had fully expected Harold's plan to fail. But what on earth did her sister expect from this adventure? Thanks to Ned, she at least was prepared but Gertie appeared to know nothing. 'Is it up to me to tell her she'll be cooking and cleaning on a sheep station? I sincerely hope not!'

252

Damn Harold! Gertie's tired, pale face was relaxed in sleep against the headrest. Her frail, dainty sister – how would she cope with the dust and heat?

'Harold must explain. This time he must do his duty and be made to tell her the truth.' Which was easier said than done.

Liverpool was dark and wet. In the station there were other couples, together with the interviewer from Newcastle. He introduced himself as he shook Rose's hand: 'Captain Hislop. Glad to make your acquaintance, Mrs Harrison.'

They clambered onto the bus which was to take them to the boat. Rain blotted out the city. Inside the dock gates, swaying overhead lights showed patches of greasy tarmac between tram lines. On either side were storage sheds; cranes loomed over them, creaking menacingly.

Their vessel was nothing but a shape at the end of the quay with glowing portholes on the upper decks. To their left was a walkway for superior second-class passengers. Those who were even more privileged were borne in cars to the entrance to a carpeted, well-lit gantry. Beside it were uniformed stewards with umbrellas to welcome the elite aboard. Rose clung to Ned's arm as their crocodile stumbled along in the wet.

'Captain Hislop has asked all the men to give a hand with the baggage,' Ned told her. 'Can you and Gertie find your cabin? I expect you'll be together.'

The sisters mounted the slippery gangway. Oily water swirled beneath as they stepped onto the vessel. Perhaps Rose had a premonition of what lay ahead; it dawned on her then that she would be at the mercy of the elements for the next eight weeks.

She was prepared for the spartan, cramped conditions; Gertie was not. One aspect was an unwelcome surprise to both, however; their inside cabin had only a small ventilation grille high on the wall. Down below, the two bottom bunks would be extremely stuffy.

Gertie discovered to her horror she was expected to share with strangers. Ignoring the sensibilities of the two former maids who were nervously waiting to introduce themselves, she cried, 'I can't possibly stay here!'

'Hush, Gertie.'

'Find Harold, tell him to speak to the officer in charge. We must have a cabin to ourselves, or at the very least, share with you and – Harrison.'

'Gertie, the company have arranged matters like this. We're all to be segregated, four to a cabin. These ladies will be our companions for the voyage.' Gertie snorted at the word. 'Stop making a fuss.' Rose could be sharp when she chose. She apologized to the other two, now staring poker-faced. 'My sister, Mrs Brigg, was unaware of the arrangements. I'm Rose Harrison. Have you any preference over the bunks?'

'A top one for me,' the first said promptly. 'I'm Maisie, by the way. I like a bit of breeze.'

'I'm Doris, miss. It'll be shocking in here once we reach the Tropics.'

'Then you must have the other top bunk and Gertie and I will sleep below.' It would be claustrophobic but that couldn't be helped.

There was a shout from outside. 'Passenger name of Brigg, open the door please, madam.'

Rose called, 'One moment.' The door opened into the corridor. A steward immediately pushed three of Gertie's suitcases inside.

'You'll have to keep these in here, madam. You've too much baggage for the hold.' Their two fellow travellers began to complain.

Half an hour later, Rose sank back against her pillow. Maisie and Doris had gone in search of their husbands.

Gertie's voice grated in her ears. 'What shall we do with them, Rose? There isn't enough room. D'you think they'll give us a bigger cabin?'

'Throw the wretched things overboard. One small cabin bag, that's all you're supposed to have.'

'Don't be silly. All my embroidered sheets and pillowcases are in this case. Harold said there wasn't room in his trunk. And this has traycloths and the dressing-table set as well as my winter coat. I couldn't leave my trousseau behind, Rose!'

'Don't cry, I couldn't stand it.'

'You're so hard! It's marriage to that beastly man that's made you so callous – What's that!'

The rumbling grew until the cabin vibrated. Rose felt her bunk shake and her skull was filled with noise.

'I think it's the engines,' she said faintly. 'They must be on the other side of that panelling.'

Gertie's eyes were round. 'It's not going to be like this all the way to Australia? I shall die!'

And so shall I, thought Rose in a panic. Sorry, Ned, I don't think I can stand it.

Captain Hislop was extremely angry. Most of his party, particularly Harrison, worked with a will alongside the stevedores. Loading had gone smoothly until the advent of Harold Brigg.

For reasons best known to himself, he had begun issuing orders, uttering strange nautical terms, until told curtly to stop.

'Stop telling others what to do and take hold of that handle, Brigg. You, there, take the other end. Lift it into the net. One, two, three – lift!' Harold's end didn't budge.

'Too heavy for me,' he bawled. 'Harrison, give this fellow a hand, would you.'

'Brigg!' Captain Hislop had once commanded a fine body of engineers against the Bosch. 'Brigg, on the count of three, *lift that trunk*!' This time it rose six inches before crashing down. Harold clutched his chest and coughed.

'Get on board,' roared Hislop. 'Report to my cabin after supper.'

Unabashed, Harold retrieved his umbrella and strode up the gangplank, nodding to members of the crew as he attempted to mount the stairs to the second-class deck. From the quayside, Ned paused long enough to see him ordered below, before he seized the next piece of luggage.

The ship was under way by the time Ned had located his cabin. He stowed his few possessions and went in search of Rose.

'What's all this clutter?'

'Gertie's trousseau. There were too many bags for the hold.'

'Let's see what we can do about it.' Weary though he was, he found a steward to cajole and succeeded in finding alternative stowage. When he returned, Rose was still on her bunk. 'Are you not feeling well?'

'Just a little tired. It's been a long day.'

'It's a pity it's so noisy. Will it bother you?' She saw his concern, the sweaty lines of fatigue.

'No, of course not,' she lied. 'What's your cabin like?

'Fine. Quieter than this. Where's Gertie?'

'She's gone to complain to Harold. The other two women have gone to find their husbands to complain about Gertie.'

'Hey-ho ... What about you?'

Rose managed a smile. 'I've no complaints at all.'

He bent down to kiss her. 'Tomorrow we'll find that hidey-hole where we can be private.'

'Before the others do, you mean? Ned, I don't think I'll bother with supper tonight.'

He realized she was exhausted. 'Sleep well. I'll fetch you bright and early for breakfast.' He stretched tired muscles. 'I must tidy myself, I'm due to report to Captain Hislop in half an hour. He's seeing each of the men tonight. Tomorrow, it'll be your turn.'

And Gertie's, Rose realized. 'If she and I see him together, that might be best.' Ned pursed his lips, he thought it was time the Briggs stood on their own feet. Rose guessed. To divert him, she asked, 'Perhaps you'll discover what Harold's position is to be?'

'He must have made a tremendous impression to be taken on at all. Sleep well, pet.'

*

256

Ned's interview began on a sour note. 'I must say I'm disappointed, Harrison. What on earth possessed you to recommend Brigg?'

'I never recommended anyone, sir,' Ned said hotly, 'least of all him.'

Hislop's eyebrows went up. 'Did you tell him about the company?'

'No, nothing. I never speak to him if I can avoid it. I believe Rose wrote to her sister about my interview, that's all.'

'So you didn't contact him in any way?'

'The first we knew they were coming was at our wedding. Gertie mentioned Australia – we never realized she meant they would be on the same boat. We only discovered yesterday they were with the same company as well. I was astonished.'

Hislop steepled his fingers and gazed at him intently. 'What exactly was Brigg's position in the rolling mill?'

Ned grew cautious. 'I couldn't really say ... he used to talk of quality control.'

The captain was brusque. 'I'm asking for the truth, Harrison.'

Ned took a deep breath. 'I believe he worked in the Sales Office, as one of the clerks there. He must have had a lot of seniority, he'd been at Hill's a long time.'

'Why did he leave?'

Ned reddened. 'I'd rather you asked him that.'

'I intend to.' Ned remained silent. 'Did Brigg leave of his own accord?' No answer. 'Very well. If you were in my shoes, what position would you consider him for? Anything to do with machinery?'

'I don't think so, sir.' Ned considered. 'In an office maybe. He'd know his way round, he'd probably be quite useful there.'

'There are no offices in the outback.' Ned stared at an empty shelf above Hislop's head. 'It's a pity the pilot boat has gone, we could have been rid of the problem. As it is ...' The captain's mouth tightened. 'We've a few weeks to turn Brigg

257

into a useful human being. Let's hope it's not an impossible proposition. All right, cut along. Lifeboat drill in the morning. First lecture tomorrow afternoon, two o'clock. Don't be late. Oh, how's your wife settling in?'

Ned responded quickly, 'Settling in fine, sir.'

'Good man.'

Harold's bravado collapsed under the hail of Hislop's accusations. When invited to respond, he was sullen.

'I did not exaggerate in Newcastle – I need new horizons as much as Harrison does.'

'Obviously.' The sarcasm was heavy. 'I'd say your need was even greater.'

'I can contribute much ... Years of experience in the wire industry.'

Hislop choked back his fury. 'Brigg, you made a fool of me. What makes me particularly angry – you've filled the place of another, more capable man. God knows there are enough desperate souls in England nowadays. Unless you buckle down and learn what is required ...' His fury increased as he recalled how Harold was being subsidized. 'You signed an agreement, remember: for the next three years you will work wherever the company chooses to send you. Is that perfectly clear?'

'Certainly.'

'During the voyage there will be lectures illustrating every aspect of our work. You will attend, Brigg. You will learn about machinery, sheep and stock-rearing, how to survive; how to be useful, in fact.' Harold's expression was pained; Hislop glowered. 'If I could off-load you, I would. It's too late for that, unfortunately. From now on, I expect *total* co-oper-ation. You, more than anyone else, have a lot to learn.'

This was too much for Harold. 'I must protest. My education has been far superior—'

'Get out!'

'I beg your pardon?' But he rose, quickly enough, and disappeared. Only after he'd gone did Hislop remember he hadn't asked what, if anything, Brigg had told his wife.

The following morning Gertie and Rose were the last to be interviewed. Captain Hislop recalled his surprise at the sight of them in Liverpool station. These two were more like the women his mother used to invite to tea. Company wives were usually from a different social background.

They weren't alike but, side by side, there were similarities as well as differences. Mrs Brigg obviously considered it unnecessary to make the best of herself; Harrison's wife took pains. Despite her obvious queasiness, Rose looked intelligent; Gertie Brigg refused to meet his eyes. Perhaps she was nervous? And perhaps he was being old-fashioned in relegating her to the role of flower arranger? The world had changed so much, Hislop reminded himself, he must not prejudge. Women such as these had worked in factories and hospitals during the war and made a damn fine job of it.

He'd heard about the upset in the cabin. His expression grew stern. Couldn't be doing with that sort of nonsense. Gertie's apparent fragility disturbed him. Life would be tough; the sooner she knew that, the better. He began to summarize what the next three years would be like.

Rose listened, nodding when he repeated what she already knew. As for Gertie, she stared uncomprehendingly. He paused to ask if she'd understood? Uncertain, she looked at Rose.

'Captain Hislop has explained what is expected of us, Gertie. He wants to know if you have any questions?'

'That is the kind of work you and Ned are to do.'

'We've all been engaged on the same terms. We'll be sent to the company sheep-stations and cattle ranches where the men will become part of the team and we will look after them, doing the cooking and cleaning.'

Gertie stared: clean, like some drudge?

'Initially your engagement is for a period of three years, Mrs Brigg. Those are the terms, agreed by your husband as well as yourself.' Hislop flicked through the file in front of him. 'I have the contract with both your signatures.'

'Harold said nothing to me. He signed on my behalf as well as his own.' Her glance at Rose was desperate.

'Perhaps I can explain more fully to my sister.' It really was too bad of Harold!

'My husband told me he would be taking up a managerial post,' Gertie announced. 'He hopes to be in contact with the Brethren once we reach Sydney. There was never any suggestion I should do domestic work. Those with whom we've been forced to share – they were in service – one of them can take my place.'

Rose resisted the urge to shake her. 'Gertie, we are all being treated exactly the same, don't you understand?'

'But we're *not* the same.' Her sister's face was mulish. 'It's perfectly obvious they are working class and we are not.'

'I'll explain.' Rose caught her breath at the sight of Hislop's thunderous face. 'I'll make sure Gertie understands.'

'Pray do, Mrs Harrison,' he barked. Then to Gertie, 'Take it from me, madam, the company will not put up with any nonsense, either from you or your husband. As for "class", everyone works in Australia. There's no disgrace in it. The sooner you grasp that fact, the better.'

Unfortunately Rose didn't hustle Gertie outside fast enough. 'Harold said he wasn't a gentleman,' she muttered.

Ned had found a sheltered corner on the patch of lower deck permitted to steerage passengers. 'Hislop thought I was to blame. Now I think he's sympathetic.'

'Gertie didn't help,' Rose sighed. 'It's Harold's fault but she really had no idea.'

'And now that she has?'

'She refuses to accept it. She says if Harold had explained, she would have refused to come.'

Ned was thankful it wasn't his problem. 'These lectures are partly to see how well we work together. We've been sorted into groups. I know how fond you are of Gertie, pet, but I refuse to work with Brigg. I'd have his share to do as well as my own.'

She was curious. 'Who is his partner?'

'So far, no one. Captain Hislop's given him all sorts of basic information, charts to do with machinery, that kind of thing. We were invited to visit the engine room. He was the only one to refuse. I think he was afraid to get his hands dirty.'

'What about you?'

'I've been – it's really interesting, Rose. As soon as you're feeling better, I'll arrange another visit. The second lecture was good, too. Sheep-rearing is mainly on the stations further south, it's too hot for them up north. We shan't be short of mutton, that's for sure. They serve it at every meal.' He caught sight of her face. 'Are you still feeling sea-sick?'

'Could you ... a glass of water?' She was huddled in the companionway when he returned.

'Won't the diesel fumes bother you in here?'

'I'm sorry, Ned. The sight of all that water ... with no horizon in sight. I never realized what a rotten sailor I'd be.'

'Take my arm and close your eyes. We'll walk up and down outside. It could be our last fresh air for some time. They say tomorrow it could be rough.'

The conversation between Mr and Mrs Brigg was acidic.

'Harold, have you committed me to any form of domestic work?'

'Kindly don't use that accusatory tone, Gertrude. It is not fitting for a wife to address her husband—'

'Captain Hislop insists I shall have to do cooking and cleaning for working men on one of those farms.'

As usual Harold backed away from confrontation and made a vague conciliatory gesture. 'A little light housework perhaps, the kind of thing you did in Fleetham Street.'

'Cooking for up to a dozen "hands",' Gertie persisted fiercely, 'cleaning a bunk-house, washing sheets? Would you describe *that* as "light work".'

'Gertrude, pray don't exaggerate. You are describing a *large* property, such as the one to which Harrison and Rose will be allocated. I intend seeking a modest enterprise on the outskirts of one of the principal cities, Sydney or Melbourne for choice. I do not intend that we shall be *cut off* from Antipodean culture. The occasional concert or theatre ... I doubt whether the standard will be as high as Middlesbrough but we shall learn to make do.' He assumed a grave expression. 'We must make sacrifices if you and Rose are to be together.'

'If they are on an outstation and we shall be close to a city, I doubt if we shall even see one another.'

'There are trains, Gertrude! Heavens above, civilization has spread its benefits further than Stockton and Darlington. There may even be telephones.'

She peered at him through her spectacles. 'What about you? Will you be capable of working with animals? You never liked the ducks in Albert Park.'

'Sheep, Gertrude,' he informed her haughtily, 'do not have the same aggressive instincts as game birds. I see no problem there. However, I intend to apply for a less *arduous* task, such as running the order books. That is work for which I am already highly qualified. Someone has to do it; why not I?'

She was suspicious. 'Captain Hislop didn't mention a choice. He was adamant we would all be treated alike for the first three years.' Her voice rose with indignation. 'Harold, I cannot cook and clean for working men, I absolutely refuse!'

'Moderate your tone, Gertrude, otherwise we may be ordered below.'

'Why bring me up here if we're not entitled?'

'As my wife you shall have the best that is available. This may only be second-class but I consider it superior to steerage.' Gertrude stared moodily at the grey, heaving ocean.

'Rose insisted I should have to work. She said that's what signing the forms meant but you never explained, not a single word on what you had committed me to. She tried to per-suade me it wouldn't be so bad once I got used to it. She said the sunshine would more than make up for the rest.'

He managed to ignore the main issue by suggesting, 'I fear your sister is under Harrison's influence.'

Gertie was easily diverted. 'She seems fond of him.'

Harold shook his head. 'When I remember the benefits of Albert Road ...'

'She said she was proud to be his wife.'

'Deluding herself to make life tolerable, no doubt.' He saw a uniformed figure bearing down. 'Let us descend, Gertrude. I believe we've had the best of the day up here.' Being caught in the wrong part of the ship didn't leave him abashed. 'I believe those are storm clouds ahead, my man?'

The steward was curt. 'All passengers to leave the decks immediately, Captain's orders.'

During their passage through the Bay of Biscay, Gertie made a surprising discovery: she was a good sailor whereas most of the others were not and Rose suffered worst of all. Daily Gertie sallied forth to the dining salon and usually found herself eating alone. When she knocked on his door, Harold refused to leave his bunk. Back in her cabin she tried to tempt Rose with a bowl of bread and milk.

'I'm sorry ... I couldn't possibly. Perhaps Maisie or Doris ...?' But the two from the upper bunks struggled outside, away from the stench of sickness.

The ship gave a fearful lurch. Rose began to retch once more. When the attack was over, Gertie suggested, 'Let's go outside? If we hold onto the rail we can't come to any harm.'

'I couldn't, I'm terrified of the ocean – I feel so ill! Gertie ...'

'Yes?'

'Is my handbag still under my pillow?'

'I can't think why you don't put it in your locker. It must be so uncomfortable.'

'It contains the bank draft. All our savings. We'll deposit it as soon as we arrive but I'm responsible until we do. Didn't you and Harold do the same? The leaflet suggested it?'

'Harold complains he has no savings,' Gertie said flatly.

'Maybe an Australian bank can transfer yours for you. Have you seen Ned today?'

'He's probably at one of those lectures. I really don't know why Harold continues to go, it's not as if he'll be working on the land.'

Although she registered this, Rose was too ill to care what it might mean.

It was several weeks before she began to recover. Worried by Ned's concern, Captain Hislop arranged for a visit by the ship's doctor. The consultation was brief, the conclusions vague. '*Mal de mer* ... newly married ... only to be expected. Fresh air, light meals once she feels up to it.'

'How long before she's fit?' demanded Hislop.

'Month. Month and a half. These things vary.'

To Rose's grateful relief, the other women in their cabin insisted on taking turns with Gertie to sit beside her bunk. This was despite the further animosity generated when Gertie scoffed at their habit of wearing maid's uniforms.

It was Maisie who explained: 'We've no other clothes, me and Doris. Our mothers put us into service at fourteen. Print wrapper and cap every morning. Black and best apron for afternoons. We've never worn anything else.'

Rose gave a feeble smile. 'You both look very trim.'

'D'you think we'll wear uniform in the bush?' She ran her finger inside her collar. 'It's very hot now we're this far south.'

'I believe Australia is less formal.'

'It'll be nice to leave off stockings. They stick to your legs this weather. Are you feeling any better today?'

'A little.' Rose always said that. After emptying the slop bucket Maisie wrung out the flannel in lavender water and replaced it on her forehead.

'How's that?'

'Wonderful. I'm so grateful.'

'Your husband's nice. Been married long?'

'Four weeks.'

'My word,' she laughed. 'Oswald and I have been wed ten years. Kept it secret, of course. He was the coachman, I was upper parlourmaid but the mistress didn't permit married servants so we couldn't afford to let anyone know.'

Rose was astounded. 'How on earth did you manage?'

'It was difficult,' Maisie said frankly. 'Whenever we had the

264

same days off, we stayed with my aunt – not that she often left us in peace. We're really looking forward to Australia. Did you know your husband has organized deck quoits, like they have in first-class?'

'No?'

'He's a card! Cadged bits of wood and rope and chalked out the squares.'

'I wish I could see it.'

'You will, when you're better.'

'It's all that water ... it makes me so afraid.' But this was beyond Maisie's imaginings.

'Your sister organized a Sewing Bee.'

'Did she?' Was Gertie learning to join in at last?

'To teach fine embroidery. I think she was hoping people from second-class would come but they didn't, of course.'

'She means well.'

Maisie didn't comment.

Ned spent the evenings with his wife.

'We're off the coast of Egypt, that's why it's so humid,' he explained. 'You wouldn't believe the strange boats they have, big white sails and a high rudder. Little children sailing them, too.' She was so gaunt, this dear love of his. 'Have you managed to keep any food down today?'

'A little. Ned, is there any fruit? My mouth is so dry.'

He was popular enough among the stewards for a portion to be smuggled down from the first-class dining room.

'They call it water melon. Try it, Rose. It's very juicy.'

Slowly she managed to chew and swallow. 'It's good ... very good.' She smiled faintly. 'Thank you. That's really freshened me. I don't think I shall be sick tonight.'

Ned went in search of the chief steward.

'What's a chap got to do to earn more fruit?'

If Captain Hislop knew of the daily stints of washing up he turned a blind eye. He understood the reason and respected Ned; if it helped his wife regain her strength that was all that mattered.

265

*

The subjects covered by the lectures broadened. They began studying the characteristics of the land. Ned repeated the strange aboriginal names, trying to memorize them. He asked which particular area he should concentrate on but the Captain wouldn't be drawn.

'Until we find where the vacancies are, we can't be sure. Each time I return, there are changes and gaps to be filled. You won't be kept waiting long. A few days in the hostel, to acclimatize, then off to your posting. I want your wives to be involved in that discussion. It means a great deal to a woman to know about her future home.

'Right, gentlemen. Today, we'll consider the land to the north of New South Wales ...'

Rose was well enough to walk. Clinging tightly to Ned, she ventured on deck, although the sight of the ocean renewed her fears. They had left behind familiar skies and sunsets, now there were tropical shapes to the clouds. Thanks to Ned's efforts, there was also the occasional dish to tempt her.

'These fish were caught off Colombo, Rose. They've had them in the ice chamber since we left – see how fresh they are. Try a mouthful.' The two of them were crouched in a quiet corner among coils of rope and stores. He willed her to finish the small plateful. She was so thin! He remembered her plump, beautiful shape first seen in the firelight. Now, the waistband of her skirt was held in place with safety pins and the jumper drooped.

'If only I can fatten you up! Captain Hislop says there'll be no stinting on grub once we arrive. You will try and put on weight, Rose?'

'This is high fashion nowadays,' she joked. 'Haven't you seen the pictures of flappers? They use bust bodices to flatten their chests.'

'I prefer you *rounded*.'

'I'll do my best. This really is delicious.'

266

'It's called mullet. They serve it with an egg sauce in first class.'

'Oh, Ned! I hope you don't get into any trouble.' She handed him the empty plate. 'My compliments to the chef. I haven't seen much of Harold lately. Is he still attending the lectures?'

'For all the good it does, yes. He and Gertie tend to disappear – to avoid mixing with the rest of our group. I think they've found a hidey-hole on the second-class deck.'

'Poor Ned.' She stroked his cheek. 'I promised I'd find us the best on the ship ... Ned.'

'Yes, pet?'

'Will you give me your word we never, never go to sea again?'

He laughed. 'There's not much chance of it,' but she was deadly serious.

'I have this nightmare; I'm drowning and so are you. We're being ship-wrecked, choking ... the waters are crashing over us – then I wake up and have to bite the sheet to stop myself screaming.'

'Dear love! I'd no idea it was that bad. Of course we won't go to sea again, we've no reason to anyway.'

'Thank you. I should give up wanting to live if I had to face this voyage again.'

He calmed and kissed her, murmuring, 'Try not to be frightened. They say it'll be fine weather from now on, all the way to Perth.'

There was a sense of frustration, watching others disembark. Having come so far, able to see the land that was to be their new home, the steerage passengers weren't encouraged to go ashore. This wasn't their official port of entry.

'Just for a few minutes,' Rose begged. 'If I could feel land under my feet – it might help me feel better.'

'I'll ask Captain Hislop.'

'Provided I neither see you disembark, nor return, and provided you do not upset anyone in authority – go ahead.

267

Not more than fifteen minutes, Harrison.' And with that, Hislop deliberately walked to the opposite rail.

In the shelter of a wharf, Rose stood, feet apart, swaying slightly. 'Land ... it doesn't move, it's so solid. And the sun is shining!' She held up her emaciated face, 'Kiss me, Ned. We're almost there.'

For Harold and Gertie Brigg the sight of Perth brought them closer to reality. For Harold the sea voyage had become an interlude where he could indulge his fantasy and Gertie had allowed herself to be swept along. Anything was better than thinking about work on an outstation. She avoided the lectures too whenever she could. Daily visits to the second-class deck they began to regard as their right; dodging the stewards was part of the game. And in their smart clothes they told themselves they were the equal of other passengers.

Now they watched the bustle of disembarkation knowing that, within a few days, they would be called on to make good their joint promise. Even so Harold had tried to avoid the inevitable, putting to Captain Hislop his suggestion that he run the company books. He'd been given short shrift. Very short indeed.

'The fellow was positively rude.'

'What did he actually say?'

The words had been forceful; Harold softened them. 'That there was very little likelihood ... no possibility at all in fact.'

'You knew what their terms were before we left even if I didn't. There was no suggestion it would be other than farm work. Have you asked if we can go to one near Sydney?'

Harold had; his face darkened. 'That simple request too, was vehemently denied.' Hislop's reply had been that if Harold had paid attention he would have realized there were no company farms within a hundred miles of Sydney or Melbourne.

An obstinate look spread across his wife's face. 'Whatever happens, I refuse to become a labourer's drudge, Harold. You can't force me, no one can. You brought me all this way under false pretences. It's up to you to get us out of this pickle.'

'How?' Metaphorically, Harold wrung his hands. 'How am I to achieve that?'

For Gertie, the solution was obvious. 'Take me back to England, of course.' She looked down at the bustling scene on the quayside, the sun shining on clapboard sheds, not a brick building to be seen anywhere. 'I don't like it out here. It's far too foreign.'

'Gertrude, I have no resources left. In my pocket is a five-pound note, that is all I have in the world.'

She remembered her bank book. 'How much do tickets cost?'

'Double what we paid, possibly even more than that.'

It didn't take her long to do the sum. 'I haven't sufficient?'

'No. And we should arrive, penniless. It would mean – the workhouse – or penal servitude! I could be forced to break rocks – with my bare hands!'

But Gertie wasn't listening; far more crucial as far as she was concerned was avoiding the degradation of domestic service, three whole years of it.

'I think I know where we might borrow the money. As a loan.'

Chapter Twelve

Starboard Home

Steerage passengers were frustrated to hear the comments from those above who could wander and glimpse the coast off the port bow, their own view being so much more restricted. Ned, nipping in and out of the steward's quarters, tried to give Rose a taste of what he'd seen.

'We passed Adelaide today – just a river mouth and Kangaroo Island was all I could see, the town itself was in the haze. Not long before we arrive in Melbourne. They say that's got fine buildings and it's a pity we shan't be there long enough to go ashore. Never mind, maybe we can have a holiday there one day.'

'Maybe.' She was abstracted.

'You're not feeling ill again.'

'No!' Rose roused herself. 'Thanks to all those *exclusive* treats from the first-class galley ...'

Ned grinned. 'Yes, well ... I've made a few friends. I'll introduce you if you like.'

'Captain Hislop might prefer that we didn't. It could make for jealousy.'

'With Harold, you mean.'

'Gertie's been behaving very strangely. She refuses to talk. I tried to interest her in Australia but she's taken to doing embroidery which was always her way of retreating from anything unpleasant.'

'Harold's quieter. It could be they've both accepted they'll be working for a living.'

She sighed. 'As long as Captain Hislop understands it wasn't our fault.'

'He's a wise old bird,' Ned said firmly. 'He's been watching everyone. I'm sure he'll do his best for us.'

'I hope I shan't let you down.' Rose bit her lip. 'Once or twice I wondered if I'd have the strength.'

He kissed her cheek. 'There's still another week. You'll be fully recovered by then.'

After they passed Melbourne, anticipation grew. There was a flurry of mending, washing and repacking. The slackness of the voyage was past, they were eager to be ready. All of them were up at dawn to see the glorious curve of Sydney habour as their ship nosed its way towards a berth on Circular Quay. The hawsers were passed ashore for the final time. Rose held Ned tightly. The nightmare was over.

He voiced her thoughts. 'We'll never need to go to sea again, pet.'

Her soft sigh was heartfelt. 'Thank God!'

Further along the deck Gertie and Harold were silhouetted against the rail, silently watching the shoreline. Bells were rung. Voices called over the loudspeaker.

Ned squeezed Rose's arm. 'That's it then. Best collect our bags.'

Another long, long wait. A shuffling forward two by two. Questions. Their papers had been examined at the first port of entry, now they were stamped again. More questions. Finally, nothing but a gangplank between them and the quay. Noise. Bustle. Sunlight so brilliant Rose was dazzled.

'Over here,' Ned guided her, 'there's the bus waiting to take us to the hostel.'

'It's so bright ... there's no smoke anywhere.' She laughed from sheer surprise and delight. 'There's land beneath my feet – for ever and ever. Dry land, Ned!' She looked back over her shoulder at her tormentor, the ocean. A stiff breeze had whipped up waves out in the bay. 'White horses – it's choppy enough out there to be Redcar!'

'But warmer?'

271

'My word, yes!'

She heard friendly voices with such a strange accent. 'Watch your step, miss. In you get. Not much further.'

Still unsteady, she reached out to lean against the vehicle. 'I need to find my feet, Ned.'

'Close your eyes, take a deep breath.'

She heard Gertie's voice. 'Do you want my smelling salts?'

'No, thank you.'

She and Ned were the last to climb aboard. Rose looked down the bus at the row of familiar faces; everyone was smiling except Gertie and Harold, which gave her a pang. She knew she was grinning like an idiot. 'Isn't it marvellous to be here at last!'

It was the cue to let go. Maisie, boisterous, wanted them all to sing. Rose heard Harold's tut-tut, Gertie's contemptuous sneer. A spurt of anger made her clench her fists. It was harmless – why spoil it?

She slid into her seat beside Ned. 'I could slap my sister sometimes!'

He put an arm round her. 'I could do even worse to Brigg.'

The hostel deflated them. Two large wooden huts with a smaller cluster beyond, in a compound surrounded by a wire fence. Inside the one labelled WOMEN, Rose gazed at the double line of metal beds. She heard one disbelieving voice, 'It's worse than the boat – it's a ruddy dormitory.' Others joined in.

When Gertie's shrill, 'I can't stay here, I absolutely refuse!' topped the rest, Rose pushed her way back outside.

The smaller huts, described as 'The ablutions blocks and the Mess. Women to do the cooking, men the washing up', resembled Cecil's description of the army training camps at Aldershot. Apart from the sunshine, there didn't appear to be much difference.

Rose was thirsty. There was a tap in front of FEMALE ABLUTIONS. She began splashing her face and arms. The water was warm, not cold.

'Bagged yourself a decent bed?' Ned had come to find her.

She shook the droplets off her face. 'I haven't bagged anything. There was a fuss ... Gertie, of course. I left them to it.'

'Osmotherly was luxury compared to this,' Ned sighed. 'It's only for a few days. D'you think you can stick it?'

'Oh, Ned ...' To let disappointment show would be unfair, his eyes were so vulnerable. 'Of course I can. Perhaps if there was some way Gertie and I could give ourselves some privacy? For when we undress?'

He brightened up. 'We could rig something, I expect. Shall I take a look?'

Other husbands had already been pressed into service. Bodies were perched on stools, passing ropes to one another, draping blankets. Rose found Gertie alone on the furthest bed. She sat beside her. 'Ned will make us a screen, dear. It won't seem so bad, you'll see.'

Gertie looked at her with loathing. 'This is the most *squalid* arrangement I've ever been forced to endure. How *could* you bring me to this!'

'What?'

'If you hadn't been besotted with that man, Harold would never have been so stupid as to follow you here. It's your fault, Rose, no one else is to blame and I shan't forgive you for it, ever.'

Rose gaped, bereft, for once, of words.

'I sincerely hope ...' Gertie began again then stopped. 'Never mind,' she finished lamely but Rose had found her voice.

'How dare you blame us! Harold lied to trick his way on board. You know he did, using Ned's name to escape from the shame of his dismissal.'

'That's as may be—'

'That's the truth.' Rose was unforgiving. 'Unless you apologize – and behave decently from now on – I shall move to that empty bed beside Maisie.'

Gertie reacted quickly. 'No, stay here. Please. It's the shock,

273

that's all. It's like being in prison.'

It wasn't much, not sufficient to placate her. Rose turned her back and began unpacking her bag.

When Ned had finished, she asked, loud enough for Gertie to hear, 'Will you be helping Captain Hislop make up the rosters?'

'Probably.'

'Could you put Gertie and me down for Mess duty tomorrow morning? We did nothing to help on the boat and everyone was very kind when I was ill.'

Good girl, he thought. 'You're sure you can manage?'

'Quite sure,' Rose was firm. 'Now, Gertie, shall we investigate? I believe the ablution hut has showers.'

'I shall ask Harold to take me to an hotel.'

'Don't be so silly, you can't afford it.' Grabbing her sponge bag Rose marched off.

Disappointment was put aside when the food turned out to be as the Captain had promised, fresh and plentiful. After the grudging, stodgy fare on the boat, it was a feast. When stomachs were full, Hislop rose to explain that there would be an outing for those eager 'to see the sights' and, by suppertime, he would already have a list of postings to offer.

'Today's Monday. The first batch of you will leave on Wednesday, the rest by the end of the week. Everyone will be out of here by Saturday. I hope you can tolerate that, ladies and gentlemen. It's not the best of accommodation but it's clean and adequate. A transit camp if you like, but a transit to a better life. We keep the gates locked to protect your baggage. You're at liberty to explore but please be back for supper. The gates will be closed each evening at eight thirty precisely.'

Gertie and Harold did not go sight-seeing. Only as the charabanc wound its way back during the late afternoon did it occur to Rose to ask where they'd gone.

'To an hotel, of course,' Ned joked.

'They haven't any money. Harold only has a five-pound note and Gertie hasn't transferred *her* savings.'

274

'Perhaps I'd better warn them. It'll be easier to sort things out in Sydney than the outback.'

Rose gave his hand a tender squeeze. 'Maisie's right, you are a kind man. Gertie treats you rudely yet you still want to help.'

'I aim to put half of Australia between me and Brigg,' he warned.

Harold, however, had not been idle. After enquiring at several shipping offices on Circular Quay, he returned triumphantly to Gertie.

'We're in luck. There's a passenger vessel leaving for England tomorrow midnight. They have a double cabin in second class.'

'Have we enough money?'

'That depends on how much we can expect to borrow.'

Gertie told him. Incredulous, his optimism began to bubble: release was at hand. 'We shall have a sufficient margin to travel in comfort. And once we reach England—'

'Harold, let us extricate ourselves from this wretched country first. There will be time to make plans once we're at sea.'

Nervousness returned. 'You're right, it will need discretion. I don't know how we stand in law, having given certain undertakings ...'

'You have.' She was complacent. 'My conscience is clear.'

'Nevertheless, we must proceed with caution.' The thought of an arrest, of being frog-marched into a foreign gaol, was enough to concentrate Harold's wits. 'Gertrude, what I suggest we do – and I beg you will comply for the sake of our future – is this ...'

There was a convivial spirit that evening. More good food had been washed down with jugs of beer. Hislop waited until the plates had been cleared away before indicating the large wall map.

'If I could have your attention ...' Silence was immediate. 'These flags indicate where there are vacancies, ladies and gentlemen. I shall describe the properties, then call each couple in for a discussion. In alphabetical order. Half tonight, the remainder during tomorrow. Afterwards, I shall put up a list. If anyone objects, they're welcome to make a case but unless it's valid, postings won't be changed. The company's decision is final.

'And talking of lists, tomorrow morning, Mrs Harrison and Mrs Brigg have kindly volunteered to cook breakfast.' Laughter rippled at the sight of Gertie's face. Hislop added maliciously, 'I understood you had volunteered, Mrs Brigg . . .?'

Rose kicked her under the table. 'Everyone has to take a turn, Gertie.' She turned to the captain. 'What time, Captain Hislop?'

'Six o'clock. The men eat at five in the outback but we keep lazy hours in town. Now, the first vacancy is here, in South Australia . . .'

Hislop was flanked by two company colleagues. Harold and Gertie faced them. They were doing their best to act naturally but with Harold, this meant too much joviality.

'We are here to learn our fate,' he boomed cheerfully.

Hislop was cool. 'With your lack of skills, Brigg, we've very little choice. We're putting you with an experienced team where we hope you'll learn on the job. It's the homestead up near Thargomindah, mainly sheep and dry as a bone much of the year. You'll do what's asked and I expect you to co-operate, to make up for past deceptions. I'd like your word that you'll do your best?'

Harold cleared his throat.

One of the other men asked, 'Was that a yes, or a no, Brigg?'

'Yes, naturally.'

'And you, Mrs Brigg, I trust it's clear what is expected of you? You'll be working under the supervision of the station manager's wife. There are aborigines on the property, their women give a hand from time to time – you've no objection to working alongside, I trust?'

276

Determined to be calm, Gertie had difficulty nevertheless. 'You mean – black people?'

'I mean the native population, Mrs Brigg. They come and go but mostly the women with children stay close by the homestead.' There flashed through Gertie's mind all those embroidered donations to the London Missionary Society.

'I could take the Sunday School classes perhaps.' The company officials glanced at one another.

Hislop addressed her earnestly, 'Mrs Brigg, you will assist with the cooking and cleaning. Whether your help is needed in other spheres is up to the station manager and his wife.'

Gertrude caught Harold's eye and pulled herself together. 'Yes, of course.'

'I don't want there to be any misunderstanding?' They were silent. 'Very well. You'll be issued with travel warrants and tomorrow morning we'll see your baggage goes over to the station. Your train leaves early on Wednesday. It's a long journey. Rest as much as you can beforehand.'

Despite the tension, the following day had a dreamlike quality for Gertie. She woke early and listened to the small sounds of others sleeping. Beyond the barred window, the sky was already bright. She knew what she had to do; she had convinced herself it wasn't wrong; fate had provided a way out and it was up to her to take advantage.

She turned on her side, willing Rose to wake up. Ought she to apologize for yesterday's outburst? Better not; it might make her sister suspicious.

She needn't have worried: as soon as she opened her eyes Rose broke into her usual friendly smile, 'Morning, dear . . . is it time?'

'Yes.' Gertie pulled on her wrap.

Rose yawned and whispered, 'At least, this early, we shall have the ablution block to ourselves.'

'Yes.'

They made their way across.

'Would you look after my things while I have a shower?'

'Of course. I think I'll have a good wash, as there's no one about.'

Rose smiled. ' "A good wash", Nanny used to say, "means top half first," and when that was done and clad, "the bottom half", and "Don't forget to do the in-between bits." '

It was bliss to feel hot water gush over her. In the cabin there had been one small basin. Struggling to wash while avoiding indecent exposure in front of Maisie and Doris had been part of the nightmare. Now she let her waisted body revel in the luxury. Ned had warned her there might be shortages ahead.

'I think I'll wash my hair. I'll be very quick!'

'All right.'

For Gertie, brushing her teeth, came the realization she'd be unable to bid Rose goodbye. Her blurred reflection stared back. They might never see one another again; her determination faltered. She heard Rose singing as she ducked in and out of the spray. Shutting her heart to it, Gertie did what she had to do and dressed quickly.

There would be a letter of explanation, Harold had given his word, once they were safely back in England. After that, they must wait and see. Procrastination, 'putting off the evil day', another of his ways of wriggling out of unpleasantness. Gertie tried to convince herself it would be all right, this time. But what if they didn't repay? Would she and Rose be separated for life?

It was too late to turn back, she couldn't face the thought of those three years of servitude. Leaden-footed she made her way to the mess hut.

Rose, wet hair neatly tucked in a turban, was surprised to find her sister already at work. 'You've put me to shame. Shall I fry the bacon and eggs?' Instructions as to how the cooker worked, where everything might be found, occupied them until the rest of the party began straggling in.

Eventually, the inevitable happened: the smell of fried food made Rose feel faint. To Ned's surprise, Gertie took charge.

'I can manage. You take her outside until she's feeling better.'

They walked round the compound, inhaling the clean air and marvelling again at the bright clarity of Sydney sunshine.

'How are you feeling now?'

'Much, much better. I must go and see how Gertie—'

'Leave her to it. It'll do her good. Now, how about tea and toast? Could you eat that if I bring it out here?'

They were due to be told their posting after lunch.

Balancing his plate on his knee, Ned asked curiously, 'Did Gertie have anything to say? I gather Brigg's been offered that place in Queensland?'

'No, not a word. I don't think she cares where they go but she is resigned, at least I hope so. Yesterday she said she wished they'd never come.'

Ned and Rose were offered employment on a homestead north of the Darling river in New South Wales. 'The nearest town is Wilcannia, about fifty miles away but the telegraph is nearer. It's good territory, Malinga; rarely dries out like some. Rich, lush country near the river. It's a big property. You'll be out in the bush much of the time, away from base,' Hislop explained. With Rose he was more hesitant, 'I'm afraid the station manager's wife has a bit of a reputation.'

His colleague chimed in, 'She's a tartar.'

Rose's valiant smile fell away. 'I wish I wasn't feeling so limp.' The men looked at one another. 'I shall be all right,' she said quickly. 'I'm sure I shall manage. I haven't much energy at present, that's all.'

'You should pick up now you're off that boat,' said Hislop. 'Baines is a good boss, easy to work for, the rest of the men respect him. It's just that his wife ...'

Again his colleague came to his rescue, 'Children were the problem before so you'll be all right, Mrs Harrison.'

Rose looked nervously at Ned. 'I can only offer to do my best.'

Hislop nodded, 'We appreciate that. It may not be for long. Mrs Baines has expressed a preference to be nearer her sister in the Northern Territories and we're trying to arrange a

279

transfer. Anyway, good luck. You've earned our gratitude already, Harrison. All that work keeping the others occupied on board, quoits, exercises and the like. Nothing worse than boredom – don't think I didn't notice.' He shook hands with the tanned, healthy-looking Ned. 'The voyage has certainly transformed you. We must hope Australia can do the same for you, Mrs Harrison. We decided yours was the partnership strong enough to withstand Mrs Baines.'

I hope you're right, thought Ned. He touched Rose's hand.

'I'm a lucky man.'

That afternoon, no one remarked when Mr and Mrs Brigg went for a gentle stroll but then no one knew their ultimate destination: the luggage office at Circular Quay. How fortunate, Gertie and Harold told one another, the railway station was so near to the shipping lines; it was an easy matter to arrange the transfer of their baggage.

It rankled with Gertie that she'd had to leave some possessions behind.

Harold was impatient, 'Had we not, suspicions would have been aroused immediately. As it is, I pray our absence goes unnoticed long enough for us to be safely on board that boat.' He stared at it, only two berths down from their inbound vessel. 'I flatter myself they will not come searching for us here but supposing I'm wrong?'

'That nightdress had six inches of smocking on the front.'

'You will have plenty of time to embroider another. You left a few items in your locker as well?'

'My navy shoes,' she said and laughed. 'They were always too narrow. I left a note suggesting they might fit Maisie. They won't, of course; she has enormous feet.'

Harold's rage was barely under control, 'A note!'

'Inside the locker, Harold, tucked under the shoes—'

'Where any busybody can find it! The first place Rose is bound to look – how could you be such a fool? Come on.' They had planned a leisurely afternoon, well away from any chance encounter with the rest of the party.

Now Gertie hurried after him, panic stricken. 'Where are we going?'

'I shall have to persuade them to let us on board immediately. For goodness sake, woman, if that note is found, Hislop and his minions may come after us. They could issue a warrant for our arrest. And this time, Gertrude, the blame would be entirely yours.'

She was mute as he negotiated, slipping coins into the steward's hand. In the privacy of their cabin, she whispered, 'Are we safe now?'

'God knows. It could mean prison if we're caught.'

She clenched her nails into her palms in terror. They daren't be seen. They stayed in the cabin for the rest of the day, listening to the familiar noises of a ship taking on passengers. When night came, Gertie lay awake waiting for the first rumbling from the engines.

'Now we're safe!'

'We can't count on it. If they telegraph ahead, we could still be picked up at Brisbane.' This was their only scheduled call before leaving Australia. Harold hissed melodramatically, 'We could find the police waiting for us, like Crippen and Ethel le Neve,' but Gertie had recovered her resilience.

'I know I took the draft but it was you who cashed it. Anyway, Rose won't give us away.'

That same afternoon, directed by Hislop, Ned and Rose went to a bank.

'If you use the company one, we can give you a reference.' Ned nodded appreciatively. 'Could be you'll need a loan for your own schemes eventually.' Hislop was genial. 'I can't see you labouring longer than your three years, eh? Then who knows what you might decide to do.'

Light-heartedly they walked up Macquarie towards Hunter Street, deciding to spend two pounds of their savings on necessities.

'There won't be any shops in the bush and I really need a new hairbrush. There's scarcely more than a tuft left on the old one.'

'Such extravagance,' Ned grinned. 'It might be managed, though. D'you think I can afford a shirt?'

'It'll be cheaper if I make it. We'll buy enough material for two.' They entered the tall, cool building. 'Here, you do it.' Rose unzipped the inner pocket of her bag. 'I shall be so thankful to be rid of it at last ...'

He saw her face and guessed immediately. Even so he had to ask the question. 'What's happened?'

'It's not here – it's gone.' She couldn't, wouldn't believe it. 'Ned, it was here this morning. I took it out as I always do, unfolded and looked at it!' She held out her bag, willing him to work a miracle, 'Please, help me find it?'

'*When* this morning?'

'As soon as I was up. Last thing at night, first thing in the morning ever since we first put it there – what's that?'

Ned had run his finger round the suede pocket and found the scrap of paper. Smoothing it, he read, '"Harold and I will repay the loan as soon as he is established again." It's signed "Gertie".' Rose went so pale he thought she would collapse.

'Gertie ...?' Her voice begged him to deny it.

'I'm afraid so. Here.' He held out the paper but she pushed it away.

'No!' Customers in the bank turned to stare. 'Not Gertie!' Ned hustled her into a quiet corner. 'Don't take on, pet, please.' He was alarmed. Great sobbing breaths racked her.

'How dare she! How dare she steal our savings. We'll go back and demand she hand it over immediately. How could she do such a thing – to me?'

She tried to break free, determined to return with all speed. Ned held on grimly, trying to think things out.

'Rose, wait for a minute: it's pointless going back to the hostel, they won't be there, that's for sure. They'll be keeping cavey somewhere, perhaps in a hotel.'

Faintness and sorrow had been transformed into rage. 'On our money? It makes me boil!'

'They must be planning to stay out of sight until their train is due, otherwise the game would be up. The trouble is, they could have already cashed that draft with no difficulty at all.'

'But that's wicked!' The enormity of it was reaching her in stages. 'We must find them. I shall complain to Captain Hislop. They shan't get away with it. We can't let them, Ned, it's all we have.'

It never occurred to either of them that Gertie and Harold had already made their escape. Instead, they waited at the compound gates, becoming increasingly anxious. They were still there when Hislop came to lock up for the night.

'You should have told me immediately. Have they taken their things?'

'Gertie's left her nightdress and toilet bag which is odd if she's gone to a hotel.'

Hislop looked at Rose pityingly. 'The shipping offices are closed but that's where you should have gone first. My assistant will begin checking as soon as they open tomorrow.'

'Shipping offices?'

'Don't you think it's more likely, Mrs Harrison?'

Rose refused to accept that Gertie could have acted so treacherously but Ned was realistic. 'They've done a bunk, you mean? They could certainly travel in style.' He was bitter. 'That draft was for just on two hundred pounds.'

Rose said slowly, 'Used our money – for boat tickets?'

'When you think about it, they weren't likely to stay here, were they?' Hislop demanded. 'They'd already realized coming here was a mistake. Brigg couldn't have coped – your sister refused even to try. It's not likely they'd have gone somewhere else in Australia. God knows where they *are* headed but I reckon they've disappeared for good. With your savings.'

'To think that Gertie could have done such a thing – to me!'

'It might have been Harold's idea,' Ned suggested.

'No,' her voice was tight, 'he didn't know that draft was in my bag. Only Gertie knew that. Apart from you, she was the only person who did. She left the note, she is responsible.'

'There may still be time to have them arrested,' Hislop hesitated. 'It would mean bringing charges. I fear you would become involved, Mrs Harrison.'

Despair swept over her. 'I couldn't prosecute my own sister. I just couldn't.'

'Don't fret. I understand.' Ned took her hand. 'I couldn't have done it to Mu.'

Tears spilled down Rose's cheeks, 'Mu would never have done anything so dishonourable. It breaks my heart to know that Gertie could.'

Word spread as it was bound to do. The rest of the group learned that Captain Hislop had decided against pursuit. There was general agreement with that. As for the wrong done to Ned and Rose, Maisie approached her in the dormitory.

'Everyone put in what they could. It's not much but it'll tide you and Ned over.'

'Oh, no, I couldn't.' Rose was red with shame.

Maisie hugged her roughly, 'We want you to have a few bob in your pocket. You'll need it for odds and ends.'

'You've been very kind.' Rose seized her hand. 'Maisie, can I write to you? I've no family now. I'd like to feel I had one friend in Australia.'

'Why, bless you, of course you can. Don't expect a reply. I didn't have much schooling.'

'Just a line, perhaps? To tell me all is well.'

'At Christmas, you mean? I can manage that.'

There were too many leaving in the morning for those remaining to get much sleep. Addresses were exchanged, promises made and possessions repacked. Finally there was silence as each lay in bed, wrapped both in fear and hope for the future.

The dull ache of betrayal meant Rose couldn't enjoy the journey at first. Ned made her comfortable and, as the last suburbs of Sydney slipped past, went to the viewing platform at the rear of the train. From time to time he hurried back.

'We're headed for the mountains, Rose. See how thick the trees are, blue gums they're called. It's the sap sucked up by the heat that makes the haze. Isn't it magnificent country!'

Compared to the moors of North Yorkshire, it was vast. 'Do look. I'd hate you to miss it. We go over the top then down the other side. It'll be hot again on the plains.'

With the constant stops to take on more water, the sheer friendliness of everyone in the carriage, Rose began to respond. It was cooler and fresher up here. As for the money, it had meant as much to Ned as to her; his life savings had been taken yet he had shrugged off despondency.

Should she have agreed to prosecute? She couldn't have gone through with it. Far better ignore it, they could consider what to do later. She looked at the view. Nearing the peak, the windows had been shut to keep out the mist. It was cold enough to make her unpack her cardigan. Ned appeared again; their destination was further than he'd first thought. 'A day and a half altogether. Would you like a cup of tea?' Mindful of limited resources they decided to defer the treat and Rose dozed.

Another twenty-four hours; she'd better make the most of it, it might be the last chance to be lazy. The next time Ned roused her it was to show her the first settlement since descending to the plain. Rose gazed sleepily at scattered homesteads with tidy paddocks and grazing horses.

'This is Dubbo. We can stretch our legs, maybe buy some food.' He patted her hand. 'You're looking better. Shall we see if there's any fruit?'

He couldn't be still; she watched him stride the length of the platform. Eager, absorbing every detail, he came back to report. 'There's a woman selling *damper* bread from a basket, plus some apples and pears. Shall I buy some? That restaurant car's expensive.' He returned triumphant. 'She had strawberries as well!'

In the comparative luxury of their second-class cabin, Mr and Mrs Brigg were beginning to enjoy themselves. They were beyond the reach of Australian law and would not, Harold was now confident, discover the police awaiting them at Southampton.

285

'Why should Hislop persist? It wouldn't be worth his while. He would have to pay the same amount to ship us out again.'

Although happy to be at sea, Gertie didn't fancy any more voyages. 'I don't think I could face a third passage.'

'Make the most of this one. Enjoy the breezes, let the ozone improve your health.' Harold believed nature's bounty was his to dispense. 'Who knows what may lie ahead?' The spare cash made him buoyant. 'Let us meet people, *revel* in the fun of being afloat.' Officially second-class, he now saw nothing wrong in visiting the deck above. 'We may safely assume our fellow travellers are like-minded people, Gertrude. We can *risk* human contact.'

'Harold, we will pay back the money?'

He brushed this aside as he always did. 'Of course we will.'

'You see, I gave Rose my word.'

He paused, tie in hand. 'When was that?'

'I left a note in her handbag promising we would repay.'

'Did you sign it?'

'Naturally.'

'In both our names?'

'Harold, it was for both our sakes. You as much as I have benefited. It was Harrison's savings as well as Rose's inheritance that have enabled us—'

'Yes, yes.' It was distasteful to be reminded of that.

'I want your solemn promise that we will repay every penny as soon as we are able.'

'Quite. As soon as we *are* able, though God knows when that will be.'

'So I don't think you should be throwing money away on excessive tips,' she said tartly. And with a shrewd dig, 'It makes you appear unsophisticated.'

Day merged into uncomfortable night on the train. There were so many request stops. Each time Rose peered out she could see nothing but an empty, dusty plain dotted with pallid trees and scrub. In the middle of this vastness the occasional car or buggy waited beside the track for passengers.

286

Ned hoped their transport would prove substantial. 'We don't want to leave our trunks behind. There won't be a station with a left-luggage office.'

They were travelling alongside a river. Rose heard astonished murmurs at the level of water. She found it difficult to believe it could ever dry out, it seemed wide and deep enough. She and their fellow travellers were old friends by now. When they realized the Harrison's small stock of food was exhausted, her neighbours offered to share their own.

'I'll never be able to repay them,' Rose thought wretchedly. 'First Maisie, now these strangers' generosity ... All because of Gertie.'

Would she ever see her sister again? Ned believed Gertie and Harold might be heading for America. Would Gertie ever write and let her know? There was no way Rose could contact her.

'If only she'd repay Ned's money I wouldn't mind so much.' He had worked so hard for those few pounds. Harold Brigg mustn't be allowed to benefit. But how could she prevent it?

She hadn't realized how much she had been depending on Gertie's presence: somewhere in this vast emptiness, her sister would be there, to comfort and console if only by letter as the distances were so great. Now her only consolation would be Ned. Would this be enough?

She prayed Ned was unaware of her lack of desire for him. At present he was too absorbed to worry about their personal life. On the boat, love-making had been impractical. And once she had to resume? 'I shall co-operate and try and do what he wants,' Rose thought bravely. It's not so bad and he's such a kind man, I can't let him down.' The door to the corridor slid open and she smiled. He'd returned once more from the viewing platform.

'Rose, isn't this a marvellous country? So much space! If I can't make a go of it here, I don't deserve to be born. Look at that sky – isn't it magnificent?' He was off but again she didn't follow; lethargy and misery over Gertie sapped her. She

287

glanced up at her small cabin bag. She'd torn up Gertie's note and offered the navy shoes to Doris instead of Maisie. As for the nightdress, she'd kept it. Gertie's hairbrush too; waste not want not in this wilderness.

At a telegraph junction, people had gathered by the track to exchange news and gossip. Food was for sale, water to drink. Another bucketful for rinsing faces and hands. Rose emptied the small scoop over her face and neck.

'I think I was dehydrated,' she exclaimed, 'that's why I've been so tired.'

'That's a danger we'll have to watch,' Ned agreed. 'They never move without waterbottles here. Not much further.'

It looked the same as every other halt; a place with nothing particular to distinguish it, the flattest landscape she'd ever seen. A group of poincianas with a few galahs wheeling and screeching above and the endless, silvery brown scrub stretching to the horizon in every direction. Brown dust dotted with dead thorn bushes and dry tufts of grass, not a scrap of green anywhere. Even the sky, sombre and overcast, merged with the land.

If she'd been in Middlesbrough, Rose would have expected a thunderstorm followed by rain to clear the air. Here it hadn't rained for the last four years.

A horse and cart waited, the driver leaning somnambulantly, hat tipped over his eyes. As Ned hesitated, he called, 'Two for Malinga Creek?'

'That's right.'

Ned jumped Rose down and hurried to collect their baggage from the van. When all was unloaded, the train slowly shuffled away. The cart driver watched until it was a distant dot on the horizon. Admiration loosened his tongue.

'My word, she moves like lightning, don't she? Guess we ought to get started. Sorry about the cart. The missus took the truck.' He lowered the tailboard. First their trunks were heaved aboard, then the precious box of china; finally Rose was invited to climb in. 'You'll be more comfortable in the back. You need to keep a hold on the rail up front.'

'Is it far?

'We won't reach Malinga till tomorrow. We'll do three, four hours and then make camp.'

Rose braced herself, feet against the duckboard, her cabin bag acting a cushion.

'You all right, pet?'

'Perfectly, thanks.' The cart lurched forward. She gritted her teeth. For Ned's sake, she would stick it out. What a pity Harold's wasn't here. An image of him perched up front in his fine clothes instead of Ned made her giggle. As for Gertie, faced with camping in the outback – what on earth would she have done? Rose began to laugh aloud. Ned stared over his shoulder.

'Don't worry, just an idiotic idea.'

'Cover your head. There's still a lot of heat in the sun.' Not to mention the flies. After half an hour, Rose gave up trying to brush them away. Captain Hislop had mentioned them but not how many! The cart half tilted as it hit a rut.

Trying to keep her voice light, Rose called, 'When do we reach the road?'

'Ain't no road. Don't worry, missus. I know the way.' In this featureless land? If she hadn't been so uncomfortable, Rose might have been impressed.

Making camp meant stopping when Joe the stockman considered they'd reached a suitable spot. Rose looked about. They were near a copse of dead trees but the ground was as dusty, the scrub as prickly as elsewhere.

Ned immediately began helping. She sat on one of their trunks as the two men kindled a fire then watched as Joe quickly mixed up a dough before putting it beneath the ashes to cook. 'Damper'll soon be ready, missus, then we can have supper.' She went to help Ned collect more wood, trying not to shudder at the insects they disturbed.

The meal was cold mutton, carved into chunks, with hot greyish bread covered in bits of ash. There were no plates. Rose spread a hanky on her lap.

'Eat up before the flies do,' Joe invited, 'and don't worry about table manners. We don't bother with knives and forks.' He took a swig at the water-bottle and passed it across. Rose hesitated because he hadn't wiped the neck then did the same before handing on to Ned. 'Just enough to wet your whistle,' Joe warned. 'We'll need the rest tomorrow.'

'Is there anywhere you can refill it?'

She hoped the question wasn't foolish but he answered seriously enough. 'When we come to the telegraph, there's a well. Should reach that by midday. We can water the horse there.'

Ashamed, Rose took more notice of the animal.

'What about feeding her?'

'Just a mouthful tonight. The old girl knows the routine. Stops her oversleeping, dreaming about what's to come. Now, d'you happen to know the purpose of the dunny shovel, Ned?'

It was winter and bitterly cold as soon as the sun had gone down. For Rose the contrast was unbelievable. Shivering, she crouched nearer the fire while the men, apparently oblivious to the cold, gazed at brilliant constellations in the black velvet universe. 'Look, Rose ... the Southern Cross! Remember reading about it in the library?'

'I'm dreadfully cold.' Ned abandoned star-gazing and unpacked his old greatcoat. Fully dressed, Rose huddled beneath it. Joe's spare blanket was spread on the ground and she tried to ignore the thorns poking through and scratching her skin.

When camping had first been mentioned, she'd remembered a smart row of tents in Albert Park. Those had been pitched on a grassy knoll; here there wasn't a blade of grass nor even a shred of canvas for protection.

It had been in late spring in the park, with tulips and vivid wallflowers. She couldn't remember seeing any flowers since leaving Dubbo, all those hours ago.

Ned crawled in beside her and Rose tried to close her ears to the strange, wild noises of the night. Soon he was breathing regularly; she could even hear Joe snoring from his chosen place, beneath the cart. Trying not to disturb Ned, she rubbed her frozen arms across her chest.

They hadn't been this close since Osmotherly. He'd become a stranger on the boat, brown and muscular and now covered in dust. Cecil's friends used to smell of soap, their starched shirts reeked of cleanliness, but this was her husband. Wherever he led, she was bound to follow. She realized in this alien land she was utterly dependent on him. Fear brought tears dangerously close until the hobbled mare gave a sudden looming cough and Rose fairly leapt out of her skin.

The two men woke refreshed. Ned's years in the army meant he could sleep anywhere except in a soft bed. One look at Rose and he knew she was better left to herself for a while. He kept busy helping Joe with the food then wetted the corner of a towel and told her to use it for her face and hands. 'I expect we can wash when we reach the well.'

'What about the homestead? Are there hot showers there?' Tiredness, the itchy feeling from sleeping fully dressed, made her sharper than she intended.

'I expect so.'

She was trying, unsuccessfully, to adjust twisted stockings and garters without the men being aware when she saw the spider. It was three times as big as any she'd ever seen in her life, mottled red and black and within an inch of her foot; Rose screamed hysterically. Joe got there first, his knife in his hand.

One glance and he shrugged. 'That can't do you much harm. It's the smaller red ones you've got to look out for, they're dangerous. And the little brown ones – they can really do damage.' He'd failed to reassure her.

'Ned, Ned! Kill it!!' Without knowing how she got there, Rose found herself perched up on the cart. The spider had scuttled off but one lacy garter lay in the dust.

Chuckling, Joe picked it up. 'You lost something, missus?' Furious, Rose stuffed it into her pocket. It made her even more angry to see Ned laughing as well.

'Worse things happen at sea, pet. Kettle's boiling, soon have a hot cuppa.'

There was no milk or sugar; Rose slowly realized she hadn't yet seen a cow in Australia. Were those commodities a thing of the past?

It was Sunday morning and Harold had an important reason for wanting to impress his new friend from first-class. 'Walter is conducting his own private service in the smoking lounge. I may be called upon to Say A Few Words.' He gazed complacently at the mirror. 'One cannot predict whether the spirit will bring the gift of tongues ... one can but hope.'

'You'll speak whether it does or not; you always do.'

He was piqued. 'I *may*, Gertrude, that is all I can promise. Walter has urged me, if I feel so moved.'

'It's been Walter this, Walter that, ever since you met him.'

'I shall introduce you to him before the service begins. Afterwards, we may be invited to visit their *suite*.'

Church services were the only occasions when second-class passengers were officially permitted to mingle with first-class. Religious observance was, in consequence, a high point of the week. Gertie, mindful of her appearance, rejected one elegant hanky for another and asked, 'What's his wife like?'

'Mrs Paige is charming. She was, I understand, a considerable heiress.'

Walter Paige, tall, thin, heron-stooped in pin-stripe and high winged collar, gazed admiringly at Harold. He had watery blue eyes. Throughout his life stronger men had drawn him like a magnet. Once on board, he was attracted to Harold immediately and his relief at seeing him this morning was obvious.

'Harold, you've come! We have attracted quite a handsome congregation, as you see. I feel positively overwhelmed!' He shook his head in wonder. Looking about, Gertie thought there must be twenty-four or so, not more. 'I have done as you suggested and taken as my text, "The Sinner that Repenteth".'

Closing her ears Gertie took her seat and gazed covertly at the other women's hats. Did she repent? She told herself constantly that she wasn't really a thief even if in her heart she

292

knew it was true. A year ago nothing would have induced her to rob Rose but a year ago, she hadn't been married to Harold Brigg.

At a nod from Walter, Harold stood. He begged forgiveness from the Almighty in such resolute tones, one or two began to feel uncomfortable. He fixed his eye on those who failed to react, predicting only the contrite would find true peace. He drew their attention to their situation, a frail craft resting on the bosom of the deep and, from personal experience, described the terrors of a storm.

Nerves, dormant since lifeboat drill, began to twitch. Sins, long forgotten, resurfaced to trouble hitherto steadfast minds. When, during the final hymn, the collection was taken, many added far more to the coins already tucked inside their gloves; there was even a pound note.

Walter Paige shook each departing hand. When all had gone, he clasped Harold fervently. 'My friend, thank you. Thank you from the bottom of my heart. What an inspiration! I saw their faces, Harold. You touched those sinners' hearts. My goodness, yes!' He realized Gertrude was waiting patiently. 'Mrs Brigg, forgive me. May I introduce you to Ethel.'

Ethel Paige might have been an heiress but as the ugly, ungainly woman rose, Gertie was prepared to be gracious. Mrs Paige was gauche. She moved clumsily, dropping her open handbag and gloves.

As Walter and Gertie crawled about retrieving the trail of objects, Harold called encouragingly, 'May I congratulate you, Mrs Paige. You lead the hymns in such a musical manner, the tempi were perfect.' Her possessions restored, the lady murmured something. Walter beamed.

'My wife asks if you will join us for a spot of luncheon?' Harold inclined his head in gratification: it was the answer to his prayer. 'Gertrude and I will be delighted.'

In the first-class dining room, his grace was so loud, that unblessed food hovered on guilty forks. His reaction to any witticism from Walter was equally generous. By the time he and Gertie were back in their cabin, Harold was supremely confident.

'You must understand what this could mean, Gertrude.' His voice was muffled as he bent to unfasten his spats. 'Walter is a very wealthy man. He has done me the honour of confiding the purpose of his visit to England. He intends building a tabernacle ... in the Stockton or Middlesbrough area.'

'Middlesbrough!'

'The north-east is the land of his forebears. That is to say, some great-grandfather or other was born in the area. Because he has been so fortunate, Walter feels it only right to give thanks to God in the form of a church, suitably endowed. The precise location has yet to be chosen but there will be a vacancy once it is built, for a superintendent to minister to the flock.'

'You couldn't do that! Preach the word of God?!'

Harold remained surprisingly confident. 'Walter's church will not be *affiliated* to either Canterbury or Rome, no indeed. It will be evangelical, a lone voice crying in the wilderness of sin.'

'Your sins could become public knowledge if we return to Middlesbrough. I never dreamed you were even considering it.'

He looked at her pityingly. 'Have you forgotten my sermon already, Gertrude? What of *forgiveness*?' In shirt-tails and suspendered socks, he challenged, ' "Let he that is without sin cast the first stone, for I am ready." '

'Where do you intend we shall live? Is there to be a house as well as a church?'

'All in good time,' he promised vaguely, 'all in good time.'

The journey was, Ned considered, unnecessarily slow. When questioned Joe answered readily enough. Yes, there were motor vehicles but only two at the homestead at present. One was crook and the missus had taken the other without telling her husband.

294

'He told me to meet you, then he had to leave. Won't be back for three, four days. That's when Mrs Baines decides she needs the car to visit a friend and told me to use the cart instead.'

'Will she be there tonight?'

Joe shrugged. 'Dunno. She gave me instructions 'bout you and the missus.' He sounded slightly embarrassed. 'Mrs Baines says to put you in the bunk-house.'

This sounded odd, Ned wasn't sure why. He'd sort it out when they got there.

Jolted black and blue, the hot sun beating down on her head, Rose set herself goals to help her through the day. Only so many more miles and she'd enjoy cool, fresh water. But the well bucket was lined with green slime, unfit for drinking. After they'd watered the horse, she rinsed her hands and wetted the corner of the towel once more. Her whole body was covered with grit, the result of a dust willy that had swept over them, scooped up by a sudden gust of wind.

She combed her hair and more dust clogged the teeth. Lines of it congealed where she'd frowned, a dusty brown network which showed how she'd look as an old woman. Rose tucked the mirror back in her bag. What did it matter? By nightfall she'd be standing under a really hot spray.

There was a post marking the boundary. Joe pointed it out. 'The company want Mr Baines to fence the property 'cause of the 'roos and rabbits. So far he never had enough spare cash.'

'How much further?' asked Rose.

'Ten mile.' He looked at the sky and clucked. 'Come on, old girl ... before it gets dark.' The tired mare responded, knowing it was her best chance of a feed.

The homestead was dark when they arrived. At the back, kerosene lamps spilled soft light into the yard. On four sides, stretching out from the house, wooden outbuildings formed the sides of a square.

There was a long, low shape of the bunk-house. Ned could hear cheerful male voices, some of them cussing, as stockmen assembled for their supper. Beyond it, in the corner, was the woodpile. Behind that, more shouts came from the blacks' quarters. Facing the house were shearing sheds and stables, with storage barns making up the final ramshackle row.

As the cart drew up in the yard, Joe gave a yell. Doors opened, men emerged, calling out as they helped them to unload. The mare was unharnessed and led away. Joe began the introductions but stopped to ask, 'Missus back yet?'

'Nah.' His fellow stockman, Andy, showed white teeth in a mahogany-red face. 'Reckon she left it to you to break the bad news, Joe.'

Ned was alert. 'What bad news?'

'She says you and your wife got to live in here, with us.' Andy led the way. The bunk-house had slatted sections separating the length into cubicles. Clothes and gear were thrown over the slats or dumped in piles on the floor; there was an all-pervading smell of male sweat. At the far end, within sight and sound of the other occupants, was a slightly larger cubicle. In this were two narrow beds, a small cupboard, a row of wooden pegs on the wall; nothing else.

Ned could feel Rose standing behind him. 'Surely this is intended for blokes like yourselves?'

Embarrassed, Joe nodded. 'Visiting hands, sure. Sometimes a couple of swaggies if they're people we know. But before she left the missus said it was good enough for a couple of Poms.'

From one of the cubicles, came a snigger.

'It most certainly is not.' Up to now Rose hadn't spoken but her tone was sufficient to straighten their spines. 'Show me where the other couple stayed, the one with children who had to leave.'

That warned them how much she already knew. Silently, Joe led the way outside, further down the yard to a small, wooden building on stilts, sandwiched between two large sheds. 'This is it. She says it's to be kept for guests from now on. Somewhere for them to stay. Don't know who she has in mind.'

Rose mounted the steps and pushed open the door. A

296

column of ants scuttled away as light fell across the floor. There was a squeaking and a bat skimmed overhead to freedom in the night sky. She stopped herself flinching and walked round, examining the rusty stove, the plain table and chairs. She picked up a dingy, shabby teddy-bear.

'They must have left in a hurry ... this looks well loved.' No one contradicted her. Beyond the kitchen-cum-living-room was a door leading to two bedrooms. The first had a cupboard and a metal-framed bedstead. The further smaller room was unfurnished. She and Ned returned to where the two stockman waited.

'It'll do. It's not up to the standard promised by Captain Hislop but we'll manage. Who can help me clean it? Tonight, I mean. We cannot go to bed until we've dealt with these ants.'

Joe and Andy glanced at one another. 'The blackfellows could give a hand – but I guess we better wait till Mrs Baines gets back. She might not want—'

'Mrs Baines obviously made a mistake,' Rose's voice was steely. 'Of course we won't move into the bunk-house. It wouldn't be fitting, nor would any of you want it.' She paused until there were nods of agreement. 'I shall take full responsibility when Mrs Baines returns. Now, could you send those black people with their brooms, mops and buckets.'

Ned waited until the men were out of earshot. 'D'you think this is wise, pet? To start by antagonizing the woman?'

Rose's eyes blazed. 'Start as we mean to go on, Ned, otherwise she'll trample all over us. To put us with the men was a deliberate insult. Now, can you please find out what the bathing arrangements are here? I shall be filthy by the time I've finished.'

She'd piled the chairs on top of the table when she heard the tap on the door. 'Come in.' The door creaked open. Two aborigines, the first natives Rose had ever met, stood there.

She tried to stop her hand trembling. 'How d'you do. I'm Mrs Harrison.' Silence. Wide-apart eyes continued to stare. The boy was blue-black, he was so dark. Beside him the girl, obviously his sister, had a disconcerting mop of fair curls. Flat, squashed noses, flaring nostrils, thick lips and such an impenetrable expression, Rose despaired of making contact.

'Have you brought buckets? Good. Now I want us to sweep every cranny to get rid of the ants, then we'll sluice the floors and walls. That should do for tonight. Tomorrow I'll give the place a thorough turn-out. May I borrow that?'

Seizing a broom she marched through to the back and began pushing the dirt before her, out through the steps into the yard. After a moment or two, the girl did the same. Satisfied, Rose handed a bucket to the boy. 'D'you think you could fill this?'

An hour later when Ned returned, arms full of logs, the little house was already transformed.

'I say ... doesn't look bad, does it?'

Arms akimbo, Rose surveyed it. Her hair was lank, her body was running with sweat despite the breeze gusting through the plank walls. 'It'll do. I shall white-wash it eventually.'

'Hang on, hang on.' Dumping the logs, he opened up the stove. 'It's only temporary accommodation. Keep your energy for when we have a place of our – good grief! I don't think anyone's cleaned this out for years. Let's hope it'll heat the water until I've enough spare time to dismantle it.'

She waited until the paper spills were alight and he'd adjusted the intake of air.

'Did you say – heat the water?'

'This is how they do it, in pans on top of the stove. No showers, I'm afraid, nor baths, because of the drought.' Ned sat back on his heels. 'Honestly, Rose, the place could be much more comfortable than it is. There's a generator but that's not working. I had a look at the truck – the sump was bone-dry! Andy says the shearing machinery is held together with string – no wonder they needed a mechanic. The last English bloke was a farm worker, good with sheep but not much else.'

There was a shuffling and the two aborigines reappeared. Rose smiled tiredly. 'Have you finished both bedrooms? Shall I take a look?'

Ned followed. Divested of cobwebs, bats and ants, the floors had been roughly scrubbed and dust removed from the old bedsprings.

'That's fine,' Rose was satisfied. 'At least we can sleep without fear of being bitten.' She asked anxiously, 'Ought I to give them something? I've a sixpence in my bag.'

'I don't think so. They work here, same as us.'

'Thank you very much, both of you.' She held out her hand. The boy shrank back but the girl grinned this time and made a noise.

'What did she say?'

'I think it was her name. Sounded like – Ida.'

It took an hour to heat enough water for Rose to sponge herself, kneeling in the galvanized tub Ned had found on a hook in the yard. Outside, the rest of the homestead was in darkness. Ned's coat hung over the window. By the light of the stove, she soaped and rinsed herself from head to toe. Ned came in as she was fastening the buttons on her nightdress.

'Better?'

'At least I feel decent again.'

'I brought the single mattresses over from the bunk house. If we push them together and snuggle under my coat, it should be comfortable enough. Tomorrow we'll ask about bedding.'

It was the first time they had been properly alone since Osmotherly. Rose was tense as he took her in his arms.

'No, pet. You're out on your feet. There'll be time for loving when we're feeling more like it. You hop into bed. I'll have a wash and put the tub back where I found it.'

She was asleep when he climbed in beside her. Deep lines of exhaustion showed where the illness had left her weak. Ned gazed for a minute before extinguishing the lamp. 'Poor, dear love. It wasn't much of a start. I hope the old besom behaves herself tomorrow.'

They'd been up a few hours and Ned was lying beneath the truck when the noise of an over-revved engine told him Mrs

Baines had returned. He hadn't time to wriggle out before she had slammed the car door and disappeared inside the homestead. Rose appeared at the entrance to the cook-house, hands covered in flour. 'Do we knock and introduce ourselves?'

'I think we wait.' After a moment or two, he murmured, 'Don't look but she's staring at us from behind a shutter. I think we just carry on.'

'How very odd.' But she went obediently, and Ned returned to the truck. Joe had been forthcoming about 'the boss'; he hadn't responded to a single enquiry about Mrs Baines.

'Let's hope it was just having children about that upset her.' Ned was optimistic. This was such a wonderful land, surely nothing could mar it.

Joe had told Rose how many she could expect for the midday meal. The hands were working in the paddocks near the house, they would all be back. Ida had shown her the side of lamb in the meat safe, the dry stores and vegetables dug from the patch behind the blacks' quarters. They would have a casserole, Rose decided, with treacle tart to follow.

She worked alone, keeping one eye on the clock, waiting for a summons from the house. None came. At noon, she went outside to tug at the bell-rope. Mrs Baines was standing on the verandah.

Catching sight of her, Rose smiled eagerly. 'How d'you do, Mrs Baines.'

'Who the hell are you?'

It was, thought Rose, the most stupid question the woman could have asked. Her ready smile tightened slightly as she continued to hold out her hand.

'I'm Rose Harrison, Mrs Baines.'

'Oh, no. Your name can't be Harrison, it must be Baines.'

'I'm sorry?'

'The only person who gives the orders at Malinga is Josephine Baines.' She was tall, much taller than Rose, in her early fifties, with a face leathery from too much exposure to the sun. She swayed slightly, dark eyes glittering as Rose looked up at her. Was the woman entirely sane? 'Did you hear what I said?'

'Yes, Mrs Baines.'

'What were you about to do?'

'Ring the bell. Joe told me—'

'I give permission for that!' It was a screech. Rose knew the stockmen were watching. She wondered where Ned was. Mrs Baines lurched down the steps. Her hands were clenched, she looked as if she would snap. 'I said – I give permission for everything at Malinga. Is that understood?'

'Perfectly, thank you.'

She hates me, thought Rose astonished. She's only just set eyes on me, so why? But it was more important to stand her ground than worry about it. Keeping her voice steady, she asked, 'As lunch is ready, may I have your permission to ring the bell?'

'Lunch? Lunch!'

Oh, Lord! She remembered too late. 'I meant dinner.'

But Mrs Baines had her excuse. Vituperation poured out. Rose was nothing but a stuck-up bloody Pom. How dare she countermand an order and take over the guest house. She could bloody well shift her stuff to where she'd been told, she and her useless Pom of a husband. As for work, Mrs Baines would teach her: Rose would be on her knees before the day was through.

Rose held herself taut. Ned had appeared from one of the sheds but she gave an imperceptible shake of the head: she would deal with this herself.

'Mrs Baines, may I give the signal so that the men may eat before the food goes cold? As for our living arrangements, I would prefer to discuss that matter privately.' The mouth opened to scream at her again. 'In private, Mrs Baines. It is not *my* custom to behave like a fishwife.' Grabbing the rope, Rose drowned any possible reply with the clapper.

On the long table with its parallel benches she had placed two jugs filled with twigs and dried grasses she'd found growing behind the small house. Two feminine touches to enliven a drab room.

301

Mrs Baines stood in the doorway for a moment, apparently watching the men eat. They did so in silence, hunched over their plates. She launched herself into the room, sweeping both jugs onto the floors and scattering their contents.

'Filthy, dirty ... just the sort of thing to attract flies. Don't you know anything about hygiene?' There were sycophantic sniggers as the hands waited for Rose to respond but she said not a word.

Afterwards, as she washed the stack of dishes, Ned came up and squeezed her shoulder. 'Want me to tackle her?'

'No.'

'Maybe we should wait till Mr Baines gets back.'

'Ned, leave this to me.'

'According to Joe, she gives up once the tears start.'

'Does she indeed! Well, she's in for a disappointment.'

The sight of Rose's face made Ned anxious. 'If you're sure you don't want me to ...?'

'Quite sure.'

'I'll be under the truck if you need me.'

Rose had finished cleaning the cook-house when the summons came. She faced Mrs Baines in the homestead kitchen, aware of unseen listeners. The mad eyes didn't appear to glitter as fiercely – or was that imagination? She waited, determined not to be provoked.

'I meant it, about you and your husband moving into the bunk-house.' This time it sounded defiant rather than an order.

Rose answered firmly. 'It isn't suitable accommodation. Ned and I are in the proper quarters and there we shall stay while we're at Malinga.'

Mrs Baines' tension increased. She stared out of the window, gripping the sill tightly.

Rose sensed she'd won the battle. Barely concealing her satisfaction, she asked pleasantly, 'Would you like to give me the menu for this evening? Joe only told me what to do for – dinner.'

Mrs Baines transferred her gaze back inside the room. Even

her voice had lost its edge. 'Think you're a lady, don't you?'

'Mrs Baines, I'm a working man's wife. I shall do my best while I'm here. You'll never have cause to complain of laziness but if there's one more insult or senseless order, I shall write to Captain Hislop and complain. Now, would you like to explain what you want done or do I apply to Joe?'

There were a couple more accusations, of appropriating kitchen staff to do her own housework, of using the tin bath without permission, which Rose chose to ignore. Finally, Mrs Baines announced, 'I want to see the state of the cook-house.'

'Certainly.' Rose held open the door and flyscreen, forcing her to come and inspect.

She watched as Mrs Baines checked every surface for grease. Finally the woman scraped her foot deliberately across the spotless floor. 'Dear me, this'll have to have another scrub.'

Rose swallowed her temper. 'Do I do that or does Ida?'

'You get down on your hands and knees—'

'I know how to scrub a floor, Mrs Baines. Captain Hislop assured us we wouldn't have to do *all* the work. I'm asking whether I shall have any assistance?'

'Captain Hislop ... I suppose you're going to whine to him every time you're asked to dirty your hands.'

'I don't whine but neither do I put up with bullying. As a result of your action, I now have to do unnecessary scrubbing, therefore I shall not be doing the cooking this evening. By my calculations, my quota of work will be complete by then.'

The two of them faced one another; Mrs Baines was the first to give way. She turned abruptly and left.

Gripping the scrubbing brush with both hands and bringing it down hard on the floor helped cure the shakes but Rose had scoured the area twice over before she was calm enough to find Joe. She explained there might not be a hot supper for the hands.

'The men won't starve, however, there's plenty of cold meat.'

He pursed his mouth. 'They expect hot tucker. They put up with cold on Sundays but not during the week.'

'In that case, they must apply to Mrs Baines.' Seeing his expression, Rose said contemptuously, 'Unless they're too scared?' and left him.

Ned found her unpacking her trunk, hanging up her clothes in the wardrobe.

'I've brought us some grub. The men are upset but I think they understand. No one has stood up to her before, you see.'

'So none of them tackled her about supper? What cowards they all are. So much for brave Australians.'

Seeing her fraught state, Ned began to set out the tin plates and battered cutlery. He tried to help her understand. 'Mrs Baines loses her rag regularly, according to Andy. Every month there's a build-up of tension. She screams and shouts at any female within range, or worse still, any kiddie, then it's over for another spell. Apparently the Baineses once had a child but he died. He's buried beneath that tree in the small paddock.'

Rose was past being sympathetic. 'She'll have to learn new habits. I can't cope with that behaviour for the next three years.'

'Eat up then. You'll need to keep up your strength.'

'Ned, when Mr Baines gets back—'

'When he does, I'll have a word. You've done what you had to, in your own way. It's important that I make a favourable impression – Mr Baines has a good reputation as a boss.'

Rose stared at him. 'Are you suggesting—'

'I'm not suggesting anything *or* accusing you. I doubt if anyone could please that woman but you haven't made life easier for yourself.'

The gulf between them was suddenly wide.

'Ned, the woman is mad and a bully and very, very common.'

'Is she?' That made her pause.

'Of course she is, you've seen her. She condemns herself every time she opens her mouth.'

'Maybe she doesn't like being reminded of it.'

Guessing what he meant she scoffed, 'I've always referred to the midday meal as lunch.'

'Pet, it's their country. It's up to us to fit in. It seems to me ...' his gaze was sad, 'Gertie stole more than money, she took away your sweet nature. Surely Mrs Baines is to be pitied, even if she is a pain in the neck?'

Rose was silent. They hadn't quarrelled before. Despite his plea, after the day's turmoil, she was furious. As her husband, Ned should have supported her, at least in private. Without discussing it further, they cleared away the dishes; he fetched wood from the pile and set one pan of water to boil.

'Joe warned me to use it sparingly. This'll be enough for a wash. Part of it will do the dishes. We may have to fill buckets from the billabong when it comes to the clothes.'

'I can't use that! It's mostly churned-up mud because of the animals.'

'I know. But it hasn't rained for over four years, that's why the dust is so bad. The men only wash their clothes when it's necessary.'

Rose's self control snapped; she burst into angry, frustrated tears. 'This is a terrible place! Now I know why the bunk-house stinks like a midden – I can't bear to be dirty even if you and the other men can. I was brought up to be decent. Why should I sink to the level of a slut? It'll drive me insane to be sweaty and filthy; I shall die in this wilderness! I'll never see England again.'

'Hush, pet. It's not that bad. You'll get used to it.'

'And don't try and coax me!'

'All right, I won't. Now, get undressed. I'll borrow the tub again. It'll make it easier to sponge yourself, standing in that.'

As usual, he gave her privacy to undress and stayed in the bedroom until she'd put on her nightgown.

When he joined her in bed, he demanded gently, 'Give us a kiss, pet. It's not good to sleep on a quarrel.' She responded grudgingly. Ned kept his voice bright. 'When you're a bit more rested, we'll work out when we can be more loving. Remember what Mu told you?'

Rose moved as far from him as she could, convinced she

305

never wanted him to touch her again. In the dark, she visualized his dirt-stained hands and shuddered. 'It won't be easy to calculate,' she answered coldly, 'I haven't re-started my times of the month since I was ill.' Turning her back, she promptly fell asleep but it was a considerable time before Ned closed his eyes.

Chapter Thirteen

An Offer of Employment

As their vessel made its stately way back to England, Gertie Brigg was left alone to reflect while her husband spent his days cultivating Walter Paige's friendship.

It was an unhappy period; gradually, with increasing shame, Gertie acknowledged that supposedly harmless white lies, once told to ensnare a husband, had led to her losing the affection of the only person she cared for.

None of it was her fault, of course. Gertie found it easier these days to adopt Harold's habit of avoiding culpability. She had been swept along by circumstance, she declared. Her life had begun to go wrong from the day her husband had been dismissed. But then, hadn't he behaved in precisely the same manner over the stamps as she had over the money draft? And how much worse to steal from one's own flesh and blood. Struggle as she might, Gertie couldn't reconcile disparate facts and her conscience began to trouble her worse than toothache.

Even embroidery failed to soothe. It didn't matter how often she repeated, 'It wasn't my fault!' the empty air seemed to mock her words. And what of the future? Here they were, heading back to England without the least idea of what they would do once they arrived. Harold was useless. If asked, he would simply shrug and say vaguely, 'Who can tell?'

It was also unpleasant to discover how much more expensive life was in second-class. One reason was Harold's determination to continue dispensing largesse to impress people.

As a result their stack of money was dwindling far too quickly.

To distract herself from worrying, Gertie tried to join in the free social activities but these were geared to couples and Harold was always with Walter. Instead she drifted into the writing room but realized she had no one with whom she could correspond. As for the second-class lounge, it was prudent to avoid the inquisitive ladies there. Reluctantly, she returned to their cabin, constrained from seeking out Mrs Paige because of Harold's assiduous attention towards Walter.

Composure, a calm analytical mind, were not traits she possessed. On her own, she brooded and became increasingly desperate. She would *never* have stolen that money if it hadn't been for Harold. How could she have treated Rose so shabbily? And what was to happen to them? But just as Harold had refused to answer her questions during those dreadful days immediately prior to Rose's wedding, so he remained stubbornly silent now. The colder the weather, the nearer to Europe, the more frightened Gertie became.

Walter Paige's dependence, however, increased daily. Son of a powerful father, he had been denied access to family wealth until his fiftieth birthday, his parent being too well aware of his son's weak nature.

But Mr Paige senior had died and the fiftieth birthday had arrived. The trustees could find no valid reasons for withholding the fortune. For the first time in his life, Walter had real money in the bank. He also had a mission: God had instructed him how to spend it.

As he repeated again to his new friend, 'Everyone advises against building a church but I am determined, Harold. God spoke to me in a dream, you see.'

Harold had been told too many times; he responded automatically, 'A sacred obligation indeed.'

It was difficult to prise money out of the fellow even for a round of drinks because every penny was to be dedicated to the Great Work. Harold was bored as well as thirsty. It was sheer drudgery, dancing attendance like this. If only he had some other prospect, another wealthy passenger to woo. He begged his Redeemer privately to pay attention to his predicament.

'At home in Wynyard they didn't understand,' Walter's reedy voice meandered on. 'The minister there wanted me to endow his church but it wouldn't have been fitting. My tabernacle will be built in my great-grandfather's birth place. Had he not left the town for Australia, we would never have become rich. It will bear his name, in appreciation.'

'Very appropriate,' Harold commented promptly, 'extremely commendable.'

Walter's face shone. 'How it encourages me to hear you say so, Harold. I shall see the building rise. I may even see a congregation in the pews before we depart for Europe. Ethel has a great desire to visit Italy, you know.' A trifle wistfully, he added, 'If only I can persuade sinners to come and repent, then I shall have done my Master's bidding.'

'In a fine modern building, you can be assured of people's interest,' Harold replied with as much warmth as he could muster. 'Folk grow tired of old churches and repetitious services. You, if I understand, are offering direct communication with Almighty God. Repentence, followed by forgiveness, which will give a man the right to speak to his Maker. How glorious to converse with Him who maketh all things plain!'

He glanced expectantly at the overhead panel but the only voice was that of the deck steward summoning finalists to the shuttlecock championship.

Walter's eyes brimmed over with hero-worship. 'Oh, Harold, to hear you express it comforts me greatly. When you speak, people will understand. You can remind them of their great sinfulness, I've heard you do it. Once they have begged forgiveness, naturally they will be in that state of grace which passeth all understanding.'

'Of course.' Harold was confident.

Walter twisted his hands, afraid he might be denied. 'Harold, would you consider a permanent position in our tabernacle?'

Harold could scarcely keep his expression impassive; at last! He'd no idea prayer could be so speedily answered; had he a divine mission after all? He prompted, gently, 'I don't think I quite understand?'

'As superintendent. It would give Ethel and me much peace of mind if we knew you were in charge.'

'Walter, I—'

'Don't refuse, I beg of you! Think it over. Discuss it with your wife. Say a prayer together.'

Harold didn't need to consult either his wife or divine providence; he had his answer ready.

'Walter, I have prayed. I have fallen on my knees and confessed my unworthiness to be your friend. An all-seeing God heard those prayers, knew of my plight and has seen fit to pass judgment upon me. I, too, need to confess: I am the greatest sinner of all. I cast myself before you, touch the hem of your garment with my lips.'

'Oh, dear.' Walter's knuckles were nearly disjointed.

'Our redeemer has ordered me to bare my soul,' Harold declared with gusto. 'Only then can you judge whether I am worthy to be the custodian of your holy portal.'

'Goodness.'

Harold had rehearsed his version of the facts in anticipation of this moment; now confession came easily. 'You remember I explained the reason why Gertrude and I travelled to Australia in search of new horizons?'

'You found a lack of opportunity in Middlesbrough?'

'That was part of it, certainly. The rest shames me even to remember: I was guilty, inadvertently guilty, of the theft of postage stamps.'

'Pardon?'

'A busy office, a dozen clerks demanding my attention; I slipped a couple of those stamps into my pocket intending to post the envelopes on my way home. But Walter, I forgot to do so.' Walter Paige looked bemused, as well he might. Harold leaned forward. 'There was an additional factor; jealousy. It is a canker, Walter. In a position of authority was a man jealous of my *popularity*.' Harold shrugged magnificently. 'It is not boastfulness, there is no other word.'

'Oh, quite. I do understand.'

'Neither was there any possible defence against this jealous colleague once he saw the opportunity to rid himself of a rival.'

'And did he, did this person ... what did he do?'

'He threatened me with exposure.'

'Over two postage stamps?'

'You may well look amazed. I felt the same. It may have been more than two, I cannot remember. But in the heat of the moment, I was also guilty of the wretched sin of pride. I poured scorn on my jealous accuser: "Tell the world for I am not ashamed. Tell them I slipped those stamps into my pocket without thinking. But tell them this also: I am no thief".'

'No indeed.'

'Then without thinking of the consequences, I declared, "Unless you accept I am speaking the truth – I resign! Walter, at the end of that interview, I walked out of that building and I have never, never returned. I refused to abase myself to that miserable cur!'

'Nor should you have done. Good heavens, over a few tuppenny stamps.'

'Gertrude understood. She gave me strength. "We will leave for Australia immediately," she declared. Alas, she can be as impetuous as I on occasion. And what did we find, when we arrived?'

Walter assumed they had found Sydney.

Harold looked grave.

'We found we had made a mistake. Our *bodies* had arrived on foreign soil but our *hearts* were forever in Middlesbrough.'

'Ah, yes.' The difficulty was obvious.

'Once again, Gertrude took charge. "We must go back," she cried. "You will not be content until we set foot once more on our native soil." She insisted I book the last available second-class cabin on this vessel.'

It was, he flattered himself, as satisfactory an explanation as anyone could wish for; there was no need to elaborate on the

311

duration of their stay in Australia.

'From what you'd told me before,' Walter ventured, 'I understood Mrs Brigg couldn't bear to be parted from her sister and that was the original reason for leaving England.'

'That is what I give out, my dear fellow. Even now I cannot bring myself to confess that inadvertent, stupid, miserable theft. You are the only recipient of that secret. I beg you will honour it with your confidence.'

'Not a word,' Walter assured him breathlessly, 'not even to Ethel.'

'And so, the final judgment rests with you. I have obeyed my conscience, I have told you – all. It is up to you to decide whether I am worthy to lead your flock.'

Walter's wrists twisted in their sockets. He wasn't normally called on to exercise moral judgment. He cleared his throat. 'Did you post the letters?' Harold frowned. 'The ones you kept the stamps for, did you send them?'

'Ah, I see. Yes, they were despatched a day or so later.'

'Well then, the fellow was being far too precipitate.'

'It takes a perspicacious mind to understand, Walter.'

'Why should that prevent your acceptance of my offer? Have you not confessed? A contrite heart deserves its reward. Besides,' Walter added vaguely, 'theft amounts to more than a few pence.'

'Thank you, thank you. I shall remember you and Ethel in my prayers.' He was bursting to tell Gertrude. Having shaken Walter's hand to seal the bargain, Harold hurried downstairs to the lower deck.

Unlike steerage, their cabin had a double-sized bunk. They had now been at sea for over four weeks and had not availed themselves; now the moment had arrived, he would not be denied. Without explaining why, Harold embraced his spouse and demanded that she disrobe.

'No, thank you.'

'But Gertrude, you are my wife. Besides, I bring glad tidings – we have reason to celebrate.'

'Let us order tea then, that would be much more enjoy-

312

able.' His brow was thunderous but she hurried on before she lost her nerve. 'I've been meaning to tell you for some time. I find The Act extremely distasteful. I always have, ever since you first explained it to me.'

This, as far as Gertie was concerned, should have been sufficient. Not so. Jubilation vanished, Harold was full of anger and demanded a proper explanation. Exasperated, thoroughly embarrassed, she burst out, 'If you must know, I dislike it intensely when you touch me. I simply cannot stand your hands grabbing at me. You're too large and rough – your body is covered in hair – it's simply horrid. And when you – do what you have to – I feel *violated.*'

'It is what Mother Nature devised,' he shouted furiously, 'there is no other way human beings can procreate. It is sanctified by the church, ordained in the book of Common Prayer—'

'That's as may be, but I still don't like it! As for children, I don't believe we shall have any. We have tried often enough. Far too often. You never listened when I said I didn't want to. Some couples can't, so we might as well accept we're like that and give up now.'

The fault wasn't his. It made him wild to think so and when her tears began, Gertie added fuel to the flames.

'It was my dearest wish to have a baby, the only reason I married you if you really want to know,' she sobbed. 'On the morning of our wedding, I wanted to call it off. Rose scolded me. Then I realized if I had a child, it would be someone to love. That's why I went through with it.'

Through gritted teeth her husband urged, 'Then why not let big bear make his little playmate happy one more time? And once I have *explained* why I want to nuzzle your little pink—'

'Didn't you hear a word I said? I *hate* it when you start romping about. My insides freeze up, I come out in goose-pimples. It's all so beastly!'

'It is your duty! A man has his needs, Gertrude!'

But she was adamant. 'Not if it makes me ill. When you

313

start that silly bear nonsense, I feel positively sick.'

It is difficult to hear one's love-making thus described and remain sanguine. Thoroughly enraged, Harold slammed the cabin door and sought solice in the first-class bar.

On her own, Gertie shivered. Had she succeeded in discouraging him for good? She gazed at her tear-stained reflection. If only they could have had a child before this, it would have been some consolation. She'd submitted without protest so why hadn't it come about? Before her marriage, she'd imagined it would take only one performance of The Act and nine months later, she would be nursing a child.

She wondered briefly if Rose were pregnant. Working men beat their wives, as she knew from her visit to Derby Street. She'd even read articles in the newspapers: they kicked the foetus in the womb causing dreadful malformations. Was Rose being subjected to such abuse as well as having to endure The Act? She'd never know, she couldn't even write and ask. 'Oh, Rose!'

In the first-class saloon, a slightly embarrassed Walter Paige sought out his prospective superintendent.

'I thought I might find you here.'

'Walter, my dear fellow, may I order you a libation? Waiter, another whisky soda and whatever Mr Paige so desires.'

'A glass of water.' When the waiter had disappeared, Walter said tentatively, 'The thing is, Harold ... I went to tell Ethel that you'd accepted my offer and we had shaken hands ... that's when she reminded me what we'd previously agreed.'

'Which was?' Harold was curt. Denied his oats, was he also about to lose his new situation? After less than an hour?

Walter's hands resumed their washing motion. 'I should have remembered. Ethel and I were to have spoken to you together so that she could enumerate the various conditions attached to the position.'

'Conditions?' If he was required to be celibate, that wouldn't be a problem.

314

'When we first discussed the matter, we decided the superintendent should lead by example. There is no other way, I absolutely agree with Ethel on that. You will therefore be required to sign the Pledge.'

'The Pledge?'

'Eschewing alcohol.'

'I'm aware of what it implies.' Indignation churned in Harold's breast: first celibacy, now this? But after a brief pause, common-sense plus the need to survive prevailed: to be superintendent would mean a job for life, delivery from all his difficulties – why jeopardize the situation? He gave a noble smile and emptied his tumbler into the cuspidor. What did it signify? He'd order a bottle to be sent to his cabin later. 'My dear fellow, of course. Waiter – make that *two* glasses of water. Walter, you and Ethel have led me back to the true way. If the superintendent of the tabernacle cannot show himself chaste in word, thought and deed – how can he persuade others?'

Overwhelmed by such swift compliance, Walter stammered his thanks and hastened back to report his success to his spouse. Harold ordered his bottle and took himself off to the second-class smoking room where he would be safe. What a fate, he thought gloomily. But then, what possibilities for a change of behaviour?

If Gertrude persisted in denying him his rights, he was surely entitled to seek gratification elsewhere? He'd never enjoyed possessing her, he found her whining protests tiresome. More important was his posterity. Committed to Australia, he'd banished all hope of seeing Valentine again. Now the little chap was seldom out of his mind. Had the boy taken his first step? Was he asking for his papa? Harold was uncertain as to the attainments of a six-month-old infant.

'Gertrude has brought it on herself,' he thought, lighting a cigar. 'I would have gladly given her a son but she has denied me the possibility ...'

How satisfying that all things conspired to suit his own desires. He might even look up Ruby Winnot: one would have to be discreet, of course, it wouldn't do for the new superintendent ...

On second thoughts, perhaps Ruby wasn't a suitable proposition. A widow with her own backdoor, perhaps. Even one living in Albert Road! Fanciful erotic images began to play in Harold Brigg's mind.

Her husband's new appointment gave Gertie an excuse to call on Mrs Paige. Her welcome was, however, less than effusive. Gertie drew off her gloves. 'I came to add my thanks to those of Harold. What a wonderful opportunity, superintendant of the tabernacle.'

'Ye-es,' Mrs Paige said doubtfully. 'Walter was extremely hasty. He forgot we had agreed to discuss the matter before deciding.'

Gertie asked cautiously, 'the offer has not been withdrawn?'

'Walter forgot to make it plain that, as superintendent, Harold would be required to sign the Pledge.'

Gertie saw no difficulty; she could endorse the decision with enthusiasm. 'How very right and proper.' Any move to curtail unnecessary expenditure was welcome. 'Harold will be glad to comply, I can promise you of that. We never keep spirits at home.'

But Mrs Paige continued to gaze at her hands rather than her guest. 'I had intended ... as did Walter originally, that the post be offered to a *family* man. Forgive me if that sounds impertinent, Mrs Brigg.'

'Not at all.' Gertie was poker-faced. 'Perhaps ... who knows ... if God sees fit.' She offered an excuse. 'We have led such a peripatetic life in the months since we were married.'

'My dear Mrs Brigg, how thoughtless of me, of course you have. Neither you nor your husband would have welcomed a child under the circumstances. We must hope that once you are settled—'

'Indeed, yes.' Gertie slid away from the subject. 'Which raises the question of where we shall live and what salary Harold can expect. In the excitement, my husband forgot the practical aspects.'

'Of course.' Was it imagination or did Ethel Paige sound

more authoritative? 'As it's so hot today, shall we order iced tea?'

'How kind.' She gave her hostess a charming smile. It wavered during the conversation that followed. When discussing money, Mrs Paige lost all traces of shyness. She was far more able than her husband over matters of finance and proceeded to prove it.

A chastened Gertie emerged an hour later having secured an income of three hundred and fifty pounds per annum. It was more than he'd earned before but she knew Harold would consider it inadequate. He'd developed very grandiose ideas about the status of a tabernacle superintendent.

It could have been worse. Mrs Paige's first offer had been three hundred. Gertie had stuck to her guns. The cost of living was excessive nowadays, a rented house in a suitable area required a parlourmaid plus a woman to do the rough, how else could one maintain standards?

To her dismay, Mrs Paige had been able to calculate wages without the need of pencil and paper and was equally well versed in the price of groceries. All things considered, Gertie felt she'd managed quite well whatever Harold might think.

Stretched out in their cabin, he was enjoying his first whisky from the forbidden bottle. A peppermint lay beside it, ready to freshen his breath. He watched lazily as his wife removed her hat. He was no longer angry; in his mind's eye he was already the established companion of some delightful little widow. He had a candidate in mind. 'Been benefiting from the ozone?'

'I've been visiting Ethel.'

'A suitable companion,' he opined. 'Though an Australian, she remains a lady.'

'Your income will be three hundred and fifty pounds a year.'

The tumbler came down with a bang. 'You and Ethel Paige have been discussing my private affairs?'

'It is Ethel who will be responsible for your salary. Walter may be building the temple but she will be funding it. Just be thankful I've pushed it up from three hundred.'

'Three . . . !'

'They assumed we would use the collections for any little extras.'

'Extras? A man could not *live* on three hundred pounds per annum.'

'Not a man with expensive habits, certainly.' Gertie looked pointedly at the whisky bottle. 'I persuaded Ethel we would need the collections for the upkeep of the building. I also convinced her we required an adequate income to maintain our status in Middlesbrough. I doubt if you could have done any better, she's a very astute person.'

Harold felt as if he were being steamrollered. 'Gertrude, I scarcely think you and Mrs Paige are the right and proper people, however astute—'

'*She* holds the purse-strings, Harold. Her husband has been allowed enough trust money for the building, that's all. We shall be entirely dependent on Ethel for a salary, please remember that.' He was reaching over to top up his glass. 'I don't think you should. We're joining them for dinner and she has an excellent sense of smell.'

Gertie lay on the bed, a sachet of lavender on each temple. Doing business had been extremely wearing. Eyes closed, she admitted, 'They wanted to offer the post to a family man.'

'Ah . . .' She stiffened. Was he about to suggest his wretched love-making? To her relief, he said, 'Don't upset yourself. I shall always respect your wishes in that department.'

A wife who continued to refuse him her favours had given him all the licence he needed.

Chapter Fourteen

Margaret, 1922

With the return of Mr Baines, life at Malinga changed for the better. He proved, as Captain Hislop had promised, fair and capable. The atmosphere improved and tension faded. Hands went about their tasks without sniggering at Rose's gaffes: Mr Baines' presence discouraged that. Quarrels which had been loud before were conducted discreetly or dismissed as too trivial.

The boss ruled his kingdom in a quiet, determined fashion. A tall man with a sad, contemplative face, he'd never been known to raise his voice. The day following his return, Rose saw him walk out to the mound under the pepper tree at the edge of the small paddock. He stood with bowed head for several minutes. Curious, she saw Mrs Baines in her usual shadowy place at the window: why had she not accompanied her husband? Rose shrugged; her dislike of the woman was too great to let her wonder over it. It was part of the madness, she decided, and left it at that. The fact that Mr Baines had taken over the reins again was enough, especially if it meant his wife would no longer interfere.

Ned, as arranged, had the first interview. He reported back enthusiastically. The boss had put him in charge of maintaining machinery and vehicles. Ned would help with other tasks when necessary but this was to be his main responsibility. 'Which is what I'd hoped,' he told Rose mysteriously. 'If all goes well, in three years' time I shall have gained all the experience I need.'

319

In the days that followed, during the brief periods when she wasn't preparing food, Rose began to explore the property, always returning via the billabong where the black women did the homestead washing. She still couldn't understand their pidgin talk, nor they her northern accent, but they smiled and nodded to one another and she gradually lost her fear of them.

'It was all that nonsense when I was small,' she told Ned. 'If I was naughty it was always the bogeyman who would come for me – he was black, like the devil. These people may be black but they seem perfectly harmless.'

To be at Malinga was like living in a small village in the middle of nowhere. There was no church, shop or pub; the hub of the universe was Mr Baines' office. Everyone, even a travelling salesman with seed samples, had to check there first before showing his wares to Joe. Such travellers were commonplace except during the wet. Rose began to accept there would be the occasional new face at meal times, cheerfully regaling everyone with the latest gossip from Wilcannia.

Four days after Ned had met the boss, she was summoned for her interview. Mr Baines bade her be seated in the small neat office built into a corner of a barn and began to assess what difficulties might lie ahead.

His wife's attitude was the problem. Josie resented every new female. This time, he wasn't worried about Mrs Harrison's capabilities: Joe had described her as willing and adaptable; he'd heard enthusiastic reports of her cooking. Ned had warned him she wasn't yet fully fit, which was a worry, but what concerned Baines was that his dear Josie had screamed hysterically that Rose was stuck-up and a trouble-maker. She demanded the Harrisons be dismissed as soon as it could be arranged. Alas, he'd been faced with this before. The company knew a little of his wife's condition, they were sympathetic, but unless there was a valid reason, they would expect him to cope.

Mrs Harrison's youth and vivacity were obvious. Her dainty cleanliness struck him, too. She looked fresh despite having cooked twelve hearty breakfasts – the hands preferred mixed grill topped with fried eggs before they started work. Remembering Ned's warning, he looked and found signs of strain.

'Very sorry to hear about the voyage, Mrs Harrison. Hope you're not overdoing things. Don't work too hard 'til you're really fit. Is Ida helping you like she should?'

'I'm not altogether certain what her duties are, sir. I'd be grateful if you could explain.' Baines sighed. Josie should've dealt with that. No wonder the well-spoken voice and cool demeanour had upset her. Born on the wrong side of the tracks herself; desperately, touchily aware of it and with bouts of depression since Martin's death, Josie would be upset by this confident young woman simply being there. For the next three years the two of them had best be kept apart. It wouldn't be easy but he would do his best.

'Reckon you needn't concern yourself with cleaning the homestead, Mrs Harrison. There's plenty of help available for my wife. We'll put Ida to assist you permanently in the cook-house, as it seems to suit you best. You're in charge there from now on; Mrs Baines and I will leave all the planning to you. When it comes to ordering, you keep a weekly list and let me have it on Fridays, I'll telephone it through. Next one to visit Wilcannia can collect. By the bye, you know the men don't expect hot food on Sundays?'

Rose thanked him warmly. 'Joe explained. I realize I'm not fully recovered, but I soon will be,' she added quickly, 'and I'm fit enough to do my share of other work as well as the cooking. Captain Hislop said we should be prepared to help with the cleaning.'

But Mr Baines insisted on easing her burden still further. 'Ida's brother Jim-Jim can scrub the cook-house floor. We'll make that his task as well as keeping the stove fired up.'

'Ned was helping me with that.' She looked at him seriously, 'Shouldn't the floor be my responsibility also?'

'When you're fully fit. We're not slave drivers on Malinga, Mrs Harrison. And your husband's far more valuable to me tending the machines. Did my heart good to hear the truck start up yesterday, sweet as a nut.'

'And the generator,' Rose said proudly. 'Ned worked half the night on that.'

'You quite comfortable in your quarters?' Joe had told him about the bunk-house. God alone knew why Josie had suggested that, or why she'd made Joe use the horse and cart to collect them. Was her condition getting worse? Baines wondered gloomily.

Rose was asking, 'May I have your permission to whitewash the main room? In my spare time, of course.'

'Surely. I think there's tins of whitening powder in the store.' He looked at her quizzically and saw the beginning of a blush.

'It would help make me feel clean when there's so little water to spare.'

This he understood. 'Must've come as a shock after England. I remember one worker telling me he just used to turn on a tap as often as he liked over there.' Mr Baines shook his head in amazement. 'One of these days maybe it'll rain enough here. Now, one more thing. You have any problems, I want you to tell me or Joe. Understand?'

Rose did. 'Yes, sir, thank you.' What a relief! She never need approach Mrs Baines again. She heard herself add, 'I think Ned and I have been very lucky in being sent to Malinga.'

Mr Baines allowed himself a shy smile of pleasure. He watched her walk back across the yard. If only Josie could accept this woman wasn't a threat and might even become a friend. It was all too late. Nothing had helped since Martin's death.

Various small additions for their comfort appeared. Rose never knew who was responsible but Ned made it his business to find out. 'That old tub we can have to ourselves instead of using the one in the yard. Ida knew about it and cleaned off the rust.' On another occasion, 'That's a rug Mrs Baines had spare. I think the boss suggested it to her.'

'Do I have to thank Mrs Baines personally?'

322

'Write a note and I'll deliver it.'

That night, admiring the way Rose was gradually transforming the small house into a home, he teased, 'Ready to unpack your beautiful china yet? And what about Hayden's present, we still haven't looked at it.'

'When this room is finished, not before. I'm saving them both as a treat. Once the walls are white, those cups and saucers will look so pretty on the shelves. It'll help make me feel we belong.'

He watched her clean the inevitable dust off the table top, and risked mentioning a much more personal matter. 'Rose ... I don't want to embarrass you, but ...' He stopped because she had already gone scarlet.

Head down, she rubbed at an imaginary mark. 'I expect they'll start again soon.'

'You don't feel ill?'

'I feel better every day. When I'm completely back to normal, that's when it will happen.'

'If they don't ... Have you ever thought – you could be expecting a baby.'

'No!' Stricken, she looked at him.

He took her in his arms. 'There's no need to be frightened. It might be earlier than we planned but if you are pregnant—'

'I'm not, I'm not. I can't be. We haven't made love for ages.'

'Not since Osmotherly,' he agreed. 'I told you I'd never force myself on you, nor will I.'

Half-ashamed, she hid her face in his shirt; she'd taken advantage of that. 'I'm sorry I haven't been more loving. So much has happened. I still don't feel completely well but I *can't* be pregnant, I simply can't.'

'Think back. Not since before Osmotherly, right?'

Face still hidden, she whispered, 'I thought it must be the sea-sickness.'

'I was watching you today, the way you were easing your back. Mu used to do that.'

Now her eyes were big with fear; she was remembering that small mound in the paddock.

'Ned, I couldn't have a baby. Not out here, without enough water.'

'Of course you can! Aborigine woman have them all the time.'

'That's different,' she said stiffly. 'How could I possibly manage when there isn't a doctor for miles?'

He sat her down at the table, 'Rose, if you think there's any possibility at all, we must ask Mr Baines if we can visit the doctor in Wilcannia. But first we need to try and work it out.'

She already knew the answer; it had been her first thought every morning but she'd been too embarrassed to discuss it. 'It was before we were married,' she mumbled. 'Now it's over three months since ... since I ...'

Despite his anxiety, Ned felt elated. 'That's a long time. Have you ever missed as long before?'

'No.

'We'll wait a little longer, just in case. If you feel any different, you would let me know?'

She nodded, thankful to share the burden.

'Once we're sure, I'll tell Mr Baines.'

'Ned, I can't have a baby. Mrs Baines is mad, she might want to kill it! Remember what Andy said?'

'Forget the tittle-tattle,' Ned said firmly. 'You concentrate on getting fit. And let Ida carry the heavy things from now on.'

Rose hadn't had a period for over four months before he finally approached the boss. It was the time of year when sheep were being driven nearer the homestead for shearing. Mr Baines and the rest were away from dawn to dusk. Every paddock was full and itinerant shearers appeared daily, impatient for the clip to begin. It was the busiest time of the year and any interruption was unwelcome.

'Are you sure?'

'Not entirely, but I think so, sir. Yesterday there was even a movement – that's when we decided we must tell you.'

Baines cursed silently. The previous couple had arrived with a toddler. Josie had been warned, had promised to co-operate but had finally become impossible. In the end she'd

324

succeeded in having the family transferred. The very idea of a helpless infant on the property filled him with dread. 'This is a blessed nuisance, Harrison.'

'Yes, sir.'

At the sight of Ned's face, Baines immediately resumed his normal, courteous manner. 'I'm sorry. You both must be very happy and we must do all we can for your wife. I'm concerned for *my* wife, however, as I expect you realize.'

'Yes.' Beyond the lamp, Ned's eyes were full of sympathy.

Baines said abruptly, 'Our son's death from meningitis at the age of three nearly deranged her. There can never be another child. I fear my wife . . .' His voice trailed away.

'I'm very sorry.'

'But you understand why I can't afford to have her upset?'

'Ought I to write to Captain Hislop?' If they had to break their contract, Ned's hopes and plans might come to nothing. He tried not to let the worry show.

'Leave it to me. Is your wife able to continue in the cook-house?'

'Oh yes. She's feeling fit these days.'

'Take her on a picnic next Sunday to celebrate. You deserve a day off.'

They borrowed the cart and set out for a water-hole about ten miles distant. Away from the homestead, sparse grassland petered out into bare ochre-coloured dirt thick with stones and tufts of silver-grey scrub. In the last few weeks the sky had changed from leaden winter grey to metallic spring blue and the temperature had rocketed. Gradually, the shimmering deceptive horizon gave a positive silhouette of a clump of trees.

Rose said with relief, 'This must be the flattest place on earth. I thought we were headed into the middle of nowhere.'

'Trust me. Andy showed me the landmarks. We came out this way once when I helped with a spot of boundary fencing.'

'This landscape is the same wherever I look.'

'But it's not, it's really wooded near the river. See those trees, they're quite different from the big palms nearer the house. The trunks might remind you and me of silver birches but they're called ghost gums. By moonlight it's easy to see the reason, they gleam like white skeletons.'

'Urgh! What a lot of birds though,' Rose was surprised, 'like the ones in the pet shop at home.'

Ned stopped himself saying this was now home. 'Parakeets. There'll be more nearer the water.'

They carried their belongings down the steep, cracked mud bank to the lip of the pool. Prickly scrub grew dense, backed by massive trees whose roots dug deep.

The water level was almost comic. At the bottom, where the mud shelved steeply with concave precision, was a small circle of turgid green liquid. It had an occupant. In the centre a heron dipped his head in search of food.

Ned froze. 'Rose, isn't he beautiful? Blue as a kingfisher.'

Sunlight glistened on the deeper colour of the neck and pinion feathers. The bird spotted them. Paler wings unfolded and extended in an effortless sweep; tip to tip, they measured nearly five feet across. It stood poised before lifting out of the water, lazy wings beating slowly, up into the sun. Blue against blue and beneath, the dark thickness of leaves as it skimmed the tree-tops.

Ned sighed. 'So beautiful. Beats Albert Park,' he challenged.

Here was no municipal privet, laurel or rhododendron and not a single flower, only wild savagery and the beautiful, wonderful bird. If only *I* didn't feel such an alien, Rose thought sadly; Ned absorbs the place through his skin, he loves it so much. Aloud she said, 'if we sit very still d'you think it'll come back?' She wondered if she could ever lose her fear of the wilderness. Ned was quickly in tune with the life here so why couldn't she be the same?

They lay quietly, gazing up at tiny multicoloured chattering birds in the branches overhead. 'Perhaps they have those instead of flowers,' Rose said absently.

'What, pet?'

'Birds. And butterflies. Some of them are enormous. I miss

the gardens, though. It's nearly autumn at home and I keep remembering the chrysanthemums will be out.'

'Our child will call this place home, not England,' Ned said gently.

'I suppose it will. How very odd.' She touched the place where the foetus lay. 'It really is true, Ned. I felt it move again today.'

'May I touch it?' He'd never asked before. She took his hand and held it against her stomach. Beneath was the throb of a pulse. Ned could scarcely breathe. 'It's alive!'

'Of course it is! And growing,' she laughed. 'When we get to Wilcannia, I'll have to buy hooks and eyes. My skirt doesn't fit any more.'

For the outing today, Ida had woven her a straw sun-hat. This was tilted against the glare. Beneath it, her skin had the dusky glow of renewed health. Her arms and legs were brown – she'd long ago shed stockings. Her blouse had been altered, the sleeves had gone plus the high-buttoned collar. Instead a vee shape showed the pink freckled base of her neck. Ned kissed it hungrily.

He didn't beg, he said simply, 'Rose, I do love you so.'

There was guilt because she'd denied him so long but there was also wonder as Ned finally awakened her own desires. She had a momentary concern for the child in her womb but dismissed it; such a marvellous sensation couldn't possibly hurt! Rose opened her arms eagerly; he came into them, naked love shining in his eyes: this is my home and my reward.

They set out in the truck before dawn for the long journey to Wilcannia. The town was busy. A boat had docked at this, the furthest port up the Darling river. From outlying districts people had congregated. Rose and Ned made their way through the crowds, keeping beneath the awnings the width of the pavements.

The surgery was busy. When her turn came, the doctor was brisk. 'Ah, yes ... from Malinga. We had a call from Mr

Baines. Right, young lady. Onto the couch, let's have a look at you.'

The cheerful young man disappeared with Rose and the nurse behind the screens. Ned waited, watching the dappled shade of a eucalyptus make patterns against the flyscreen. He was half anxious, half full of hope: what would it cost? Would he and Rose end up like Mu and Lionel, scared of ever-present debt? But when she re-emerged, her obvious happiness made him forget his fears.

'Right, Mr Harrison.' The doctor picked up the calendar from his desk, 'Let's calculate when you'll become a father.' Euphoria swept away his senses. Ned was still in a daze when the voice brought him back to earth. 'I take it you agree with Mr Baines' suggestion, that the confinement should take place here rather than at the homestead?'

From their nods the doctor saw the three of them understood one another and was thankful; he didn't need the added complication of Josie Baines. Long ago he had warned her husband she should be admitted to the sanatorium but the man couldn't bear to be parted from her.

'We've lost our son, we need to hang on to each other, doctor. I can look after Josie myself.' But her mental state hadn't improved and this baby might well exacerbate matters. Thank heavens it wasn't his problem.

Rose had turned to Ned in dismay, 'I've just realized – a stay in a hospital – can we afford it?'

The doctor interrupted cautiously. 'According to my notes, Mr Baines has notified the company. They'll arrange to defray the cost until you can afford to repay.'

Rose felt hot with shame. Damn Gertie for leaving them little better than paupers!

Outside again, she and Ned found a bench beside a bare patch of earth that declared itself a municipal garden. Ned began to read the list he'd been given, 'Basic layette ... Rose, this lot will cost a fortune!'

'No, it won't. If we can find a shop that sells material, I'll buy cambric, flannel and some wool for a shawl. I can still sew. The results may not be marvellous but a baby won't mind. Oh, and we shall need netting to protect him from the flies?'

'Him?'

'It,' Rose said firmly, 'but there definitely is an it. I listened to the heartbeat through the stethoscope.'

'Did you indeed.' He was jealous but it didn't last. Rose had been so loving last Sunday. All those months of being patient, it had been worth it. Was her attitude toward him changing as well? He was sensitive enough to know he didn't measure up to her ideas of a gentlemanly lover.

She was grinning as if she'd partially guessed at his thoughts. 'I asked if it was all right for us to ... you know. I felt very daring – our old doctor at home would have had a fit! This one said it was normal and natural to want to behave like that.'

'Oh, Rose!'

'But not out here,' she pretended to be scandalized, 'keep your hands to yourself, my man.'

'We ought to thank Captain Hislop for the hospital loan. We shall have to repay eventually of course, but it's taken a weight off my mind.'

'I'll write to him,' Rose promised. 'If I knew where Gertie was, I'd write to her as well and *demand* she return our money. I feel so angry. Being penniless when we need the cash is too embarrassing!'

As Rose wouldn't have had the energy to feel angry a few weeks ago, she was obviously on the mend. Ned was supremely happy. The doctor had assured him all was well and, as a healthy young woman, Rose could have 'dozens of babies'. One would be sufficient at present, he decided; please God it didn't end up under the pepper tree.

'We must make sure you're in Wilcannia when the time comes.'

'Absolutely,' she agreed light-heartedly. 'To be stuck out at Malinga doesn't bear thinking about.'

*

The news spread on their return. To her surprise, Rose found her hand being wrung by several of the stockmen. It would be good to have a kiddie about the place, they assured her. They would teach the boy to ride, to survive in the bush. Andy gave her the baby's first gift: a hunting knife with a carved bone handle.

'Used to belong to my old dad. The blade's still good. Slice of a chookie's head in the blink of an eye.' Rose swallowed and thanked him: it was the thought that counted, she told herself.

Only later did one or two remember Mrs Baines and the awkward murmurs began. 'Anyone mentioned it to the missus?'

'The boss knows,' replied Ned tactfully. Mrs Baines was bound to notice soon anyway. These days Rose had a much more stately gait, adjusting the rhythm of her life to her changing girth.

Summer was bad, hotter than anyone remembered and late summer was even worse. Sweltering out on the boundaries of the property, men cursed as they struggled to install rabbit wire. They worked in pairs, the first two hammering in mile after mile of wooden posts, two behind, digging the wire a foot deep below the surface before fastening it to the posts. Four days out on the boundary then back for half a day to load up with supplies and recover from the heat.

Despite her good intentions, Rose watched lethargically as Ida and Jim-Jim took over most of the cooking. The boss's instructions had been strict: Mrs Harrison was not to overtire herself. Instead, she sat in the shade peeling the endless daily buckets of potatoes.

By the beginning of March, the land was so dry, cracks ran deep and wide across the pasture. There was no grass, just tinder-dry stubble. No sign of life anywhere, thought Rose, except her kicking child. She'd recently had one of those whims known only to pregnant women: the white-washing had to be finished before the baby's arrival. Their little home had to be perfect.

Ned was taking his turn with installing the boundary wire. Most of the men were out in the bush at present, there weren't many needing to be fed. She and Ida finished their tasks early. Rose would rest until the sun had gone down when it was marginally cooler, then begin in earnest.

After three days, it was almost finished. Tonight she could finally unpack her china and discover what Hayden had given them. How pretty the room would be when Ned came home! It was the final task before she set off in a fortnight's time, for Wilcannia.

It was also the night the rains began. For days the sky had been bursting with heat and thunder. Emptying the rubbish into the pit that evening, Rose felt heat beat against her skin, reflected by the stones in the yard. Distant objects were illuminated by enormous blasts of lightning. Her head ached fearfully.

Never mind, the room was finished; she'd even cleaned the second bedroom. It was awaiting the cradle the blackfellows were making. All that remained was to arrange those white and gold cups with their pattern of poppies and cornflowers.

She used Andy's knife to cut through cord and battered cardboard. Outside, the pattering became a torrent as water fell from the skies, hammering on the tin roof. Inside, the humidity was intense. Rose wiped sweat from her eyes and lifted the first layer of carefully crumpled newspaper. Beneath it were splinters, gold and blue, white and scarlet, nothing but fragments. It was impossible to tell whether these had been cups or plates. Weeping, Rose searched frantically. This china was her one remaining link with home, it was a symbol of all the happy times. Cecil and his friends had drunk from these cups after their tennis parties.

She reached the final layer and found one delicate coffee cup, perfect and unblemished, and set it on the table. Tears were mingling with the sweat, she didn't bother to wipe them away. She struggled to her feet, crunching through broken porcelain. The room stifled her. After all the happy anticipation, disappointment was too great. Where was Ned? She

331

needed him as she never had before. Outside, on the top step, she called his name, reaching instinctively for the rail. Rain and tears blotted it out and Rose fell the three remaining steps into the mud.

Pain. It bit into her unconscious mind forcing her back to the present. It had been going on for hours but now it was so sharp, Rose screamed. Ida's face was close to hers. She couldn't make out what the girl was saying because of the pain. Shadowy figures stood beyond the lamp but she couldn't see Ned among them. Rain was pounding on the roof. Noise, pain, she was smothered by everything, sinking under the agony. She screamed Ned's name. Why were they all ignoring her?

Joe muttered, 'We can't leave her on the floor.' There was a soaking wet blanket beneath her, the one they'd slid under her to carry her in from the yard. Rose's outstretched clenched hand drummed against broken china and newspaper. Her palms were bleeding. Ida was touching her cheek, murmuring, trying to soothe her but the pain was coming in waves, forcing out deep shuddering groans that drowned every other sound.

The two stockmen braced themselves to lift her when the door burst open. Mr Baines, water streaming from him, shouted, 'What's been happening? They said an accident.' He caught sight of Rose. 'God Almighty! Has the doctor been sent for?'

'Mrs Baines couldn't get through, boss. Lines must be down. Mac's gone down to the telegraph but it's bad out there. By the time he sends the message, I reckon the roads will be flooded.'

'Andy, take the truck – it's higher off the ground – and take Bill with you. Do everything you can to get the man here. Where's Ned?'

'He and Chris should be at the far end of the five-mile. We've sent Jim-Jim to find them.'

'Let's get Mrs Harrison into the bedroom.' Taking Andy's

place he and Joe lifted the blanket, trying to ignore Rose's screams as they eased her onto the bed.

'Ida, come here, girl.' He gave quick instructions and she disappeared. Stripping off his soaked coat, he knelt beside Rose, noting the convulsions before saying, 'Mrs Harrison, can you hear me?'

Through pain-clenched teeth, Rose muttered, 'Yes.'

'You've had an accident and it looks as if the baby may have started—'

'*Ned!*'

'He's been sent for. Ida's mother knows about babies. She'll stay with you 'til the doctor gets here.' He saw the twisted, ugly mask of her face. 'Shout all you want, girl,' he urged, 'shout the roof down if it helps.'

He jerked his head at Joe and shut the door behind them. 'Looks like she's well into labour. Those pains were regular. Josie was like that before the doctor got here but thank God he did. This time we may not be so lucky. Why the devil did the lines have to go down?'

'Maybe Mac got through.'

'Not if the break's on this side. Did Josie manage to make *anyone* hear?'

Joe shook his head.

'Must be serious.'

Ida returned and they waited helplessly as three aborigine women began laying warm cloths on Rose's belly. They cleaned her ragged bleeding hands and one of them reached gingerly inside her vagina. Ida came to report. 'Baby not right, boss. Have to move before can come out.'

'Dear God! Tell your mother I want to speak to her.' When she appeared he said, 'It could take the rest of the night before the doctor gets here.' From the look on the woman's face, Baines knew there wasn't that much time. There was a consultation between mother and daughter.

'My mother not want,' Ida explained, 'baby not wait but she not want.' Baines didn't blame her. To meddle with the sick white woman was dangerous and she didn't want the responsibility. It was equally obvious that Rose's labour couldn't be halted.

He said to Joe, 'We'll have to do something. I can't have her husband come back and find her ...' He couldn't bring himself to say it.

The stockman suggested, 'I've turned 'em often enough inside a ewe. Reckon it's the same sorta thing?'

'I've no idea but we'll give it a try. You'll need to clean up. There's some chloroform in the house from when Mac broke his leg. Maybe that'll ease her.'

They were soaked by the time they'd crossed the yard. In the homestead, there was no sight of Mrs Baines. Her husband yelled until she reappeared. 'Josie, why aren't you by this phone? Have you got through yet? Have you spoken to Wilcannia?'

She put out a hand as if to prevent him getting closer. 'The lines are down.'

Trying to be less harsh, he chided, 'I know, they told me, but we have to keep trying, Josie. We have to get through to someone. Mrs Harrison is bad.'

From where he stood, Joe didn't like the expression in Mrs Baines's eyes.

'Reckon we'll need that chloroform pretty soon, boss.'

'We'll need disinfectant too. Josie, I don't want you to move from this phone, understand?' Baines went off to the store cupboard. Being alone with the woman made Joe feel uncomfortable. She sat beside the bamboo table, dabbing at her mouth.

'I can't help it. There's nothing I can do. The lines are down.'

'Just keep trying, missus,' he pleaded. 'If there's someone – anyone who knows about babies ...' She did, all women knew a little, but this one was crazy.

He went through to the kitchen and began scrubbing his hands and arms. Suppose he accidentally killed one of them? It happened sometimes with the ewes. Joe could feel the cold sweat break out down his spine.

Ned and his partner were crouched together out in a clearing away from trees. Jim-Jim and his brumby appeared out of the rain like a spirit. He shouted at Ned. There was a sudden blinding crack and the horse jerked wildly.

'Why's he here? What's he saying?'

'Sounded like your missus has started.'

'She can't have, not for another three weeks!'

'Maybe the doctor got it wrong. We'd better get back. Give us a hand with the stuff?'

Ned grabbed tools and back-pack frantically. 'You get in and I'll give it a turn.' They raced back to the vehicle, Ned gripped the starting handle. After several turns he knew it was a waste of time. He had to strip and dry the plugs before the spark would ignite.

When he finally climbed into the driver's seat he asked. 'Do the roads round here flood in the wet?'

'Not half, mate!'

'So the doctor's not likely to get through?'

The other man squirmed. 'He's a goer. He'll have a damn' good try.'

The wiper motor burned out with the force of the rain. Ned drove with his head out of the window. Led by Jim-Jim, they began the dangerous journey back.

Baines explained what he intended to do but the elderly black women shook their heads over the chloroform. 'Too big medicine,' Ida said softly.

'Could be,' Joe agreed.

Baines said, 'She's got to have *something*. You're bound to hurt her.'

'We got medicine,' Ida pointed to a bowl, 'make missus sleepy.'

Joe shrugged. 'Let's give it a try. It'll be stuff they take themselves.'

Baines nodded reluctantly. They watched as Rose was

335

persuaded to swallow a spoonful. Above the noise of the rain, they caught another sound.

'The doctor! He must've got through.'

'Praise be!' But it was Andy, exhausted and barely able to speak.

'Couldn't make it, boss. Road's so bad, the truck got stuck. Had to leave it. Don't know if Mac got through.'

'Go to the house. Help yourself to a whisky. Stay with my wife. Any response at all, let us know.' Andy stumbled away. Baines was haggard. 'Even if someone does respond, they couldn't get here in time. Not now.'

'No, boss.'

'Let's see if that stuff's taken effect.'

There was a red-hot knife tearing at Rose's belly. Although she felt it, she couldn't cry out. It was a grunt instead of a scream.

Joe paused. 'She all right?'

'She's alive. Try not to ...' What was the point? Joe was doing all he could. Sitting in a huddle, the black women stared expressionlessly.

It seemed to Baines a lifetime before Joe leaned back on his haunches.

'I think it's shifted so's the head's pointing down ... don't know why she's bleeding so much, though.'

Baines's knuckles were white. He spoke urgently to the women. 'Can you help the baby be born now? Can you stop the blood?'

Dark hands moved across Rose's belly. One woman was spooning more of the liquid into her mouth. Baines had a sudden panic: suppose they accidentally poisoned her?

He heard the outer door again and hurried through, praying for a miracle. Instead of the doctor, it was Andy once more. This time, he was dumb.

'What's happened? Have they repaired the line?'

He said reluctantly, 'Line wasn't down, boss.'

'What!'

'Your missus went to the kitchen for something, I picked up

336

the phone, cranked it a couple of times, the operator answered immediately. Claimed there hadn't been any trouble. I talked to the surgery but Mac had already got through. He'd talked to plenty of other people as well. Everyone's flooded out but there hasn't been a breakdown. Mac told 'em to let *you* know he'd be a while getting back because the water's over five foot deep in places. Guess that call must've come through when none of us was in the house.'

Baines' mind was reeling. Fear for Rose's life, for the child, simmered on top of a mixture of anger and pity. It shook him so that he wanted to howl. He threw back his head but no sound came. With all the control he had left, he said calmly, 'So you spoke to the surgery?'

'The doc had left a message. He said to do what we could and if it was humanly possible he'd get through. He said if the baby came, to watch out for the cord.'

'Oh, Christ!' Was that the reason for the blood? Putting aside his own agony, Baines slipped back into the bedroom. The women were crouched over Rose. Ida was holding one of her hands, Joe the other. Both were urging her to push.

Baines cried out, 'The cord, Joe, it could be the cause of the bleeding.'

'They've worked that out. Hang on, boss, I think it's about to be born.'

A bruised purple head protruded as fingers eased the choking umbilical noose up and over. 'Baby come, baby come,' crooned Ida into Rose's ear, 'you've got to try a little bit more, missus.'

Baines heard Andy's whisper, 'There's neighbours on their way, boss. The Cullens have a relative who's a nurse. They're bringing her over. I'll ride out to meet them if that's all right?'

'Thanks.' But Andy had moved closer, drawn by the miracle of new life.

'Is that the baby? Is it alive?'

'God knows ...' If it died, Josie could be to blame. This time, he wouldn't argue with the doctor. He'd arrange for her

337

to enter the sanitorium before she could do any further damage.

The child was so still, if only it would move! Rose was crying out, a thin wail of anguish. Surely she hadn't guessed it was dead?

One of the women had scooped up the baby and was blowing into its mouth and nose. She massaged, slapped it and continued to blow. Baines and Andy were staring at Rose. With a final effort the pulpy afterbirth had been expelled and, with it, lots more blood.

'Lord, boss, I hope that doctor gets here soon.'

Until he did, they were helpless. There was another faint sound. They stared at the woman holding the baby. She was squeezing it now, urging it to cry once more. The tiny mouth sucked in air with a shudder. Baines and Andy let go theirs simultaneously. One, at least, had survived.

It was midday before Jim-Jim led the truck into the yard. The two men climbed out and collapsed. They'd had nearly ten hours of negotiating flood-waters. On hands and knees Ned hauled himself up the steps.

Baines met him in the doorway. 'Thank God you're back. She's been asking for you.'

That meant Rose was alive. Half Ned's tension evaporated. 'Is it . . . is it over?'

'Last night. Joe and I did our best.'

'Alive?' croaked Ned.

'Yes, yes,' Baines cursed himself; Harrison's eyes were black with desperation. 'Both of them are. The doctor got through, he's with them.'

Ned clung to the table. The room was swaying. He saw Joe staring at him. Beyond him, in the corner, Ida was folding bits of blanket to line the wooden cradle. She stared too. Ned tried to raise a hand in greeting.

'Is the doctor . . .?'

'Hang on, mate. Take a seat, you're all in,' Joe pushed him into a chair. 'He's tending to your wife. Ida, go and ask if Ned can see her.' The girl slipped away. Joe poured a measure of whisky into a tin cup. 'The boss brought this over. Get it down.'

Ned was gazing at the delicate tiny cup with its gold handle and patterns of poppies and cornflowers.

Joe noticed. 'Your wife must have been unpacking. We found a whole heap of broken china on the floor. This was all there was, on the table.'

With trembling hands Ned placed the cup in the middle of the empty shelves. 'That's where she intended it should go. Poor Rose. Only one survivor.' Tears fell, he could do nothing to prevent them.

Joe said hesitantly, 'You got two survivors, mate. The doctor reckons we had to do what we did, otherwise they both could've died. Rose lost a lot of blood. There's a nurse come over, she's seeing to the kid. One of the blacks got her breathing all right. They knew what to do once the baby was born, see. Trouble was, they couldn't do much about the bleeding.'

Ned let the words trickle in with the whisky. 'They're both alive, you're sure of that?' It was all that mattered.

'The baby had a mauling but the doctor says she'll pull through. Her hair's dark, darker than your wife's.'

She. It was a she after all.

Joe caught sight of the horn-handled knife. 'Don't know what she's going to make of Andy's present! Didn't look much like a tomboy to me.'

'Rose ...?'

Joe stopped chuckling. 'Don't fret. She'll survive. She never stopped asking for you. She was bloody brave, I'll tell you that. When I think ...' But it was far better not to describe what had happened. The door to the bedroom opened. The young doctor gazed at them tiredly.

'Morning, Mr Harrison. Your wife's asleep because I gave her an injection. Come and meet your new daughter.'

He stood aside. Ned walked straight past him and went to the bed, laying his head beside the unconscious face. Trying

339

not to sob, he brushed his lips against Rose's cheek.

'She won't wake for another four or five hours, far better she doesn't, so try not to disturb her. This young woman is asleep as well. Don't worry about her appearance, those marks will soon disappear.'

Getting to his feet wasn't easy this time. Filtered light through the shutters showed his gaunt, shattered state. Nurse and doctor exchanged glances; this man was too exhausted to be entrusted with a baby. He stumbled across to stare at it in the nurse's arms. A blotched purple face and a fuzz of brown-gold hair. The tiny eyes were shut.

'Is she . . .?'

'Babies are tougher than you think. They come into this world prepared to survive. She's black and blue now but she'll be right as ninepence in a few weeks.' Ned couldn't take it all in, he looked back at Rose.

'Your wife will need plenty of rest and care. We've managed to repair most of the damage.'

The doctor recalled his earlier assurance about 'hundreds of babies'. Once Rose was over the worst he might not see the couple again for several months. 'I must warn you now, there can't be any more children. I'm sorry, Harrison. Your wife's had too rough a passage, another pregnancy would be too much of a risk. Just be thankful this baby is fit and healthy.'

Joe half carried Ned to the bunk-house. With the sedative insisted on by the doctor, Ned slept for twenty-four hours. He missed the departure of Mr and Mrs Baines for Wilcannia, the efforts of both neighbours and the hands to rescue stock and sheep and move them to higher ground, the care with which the nurse encouraged his daughter through her first tentative hours of life.

When he awoke the rain had eased, the normal daily pattern had been resumed and he could smell hot food. He was ravenous, but as memory returned, his heart lurched. He was across the yard and up the steps in an instant.

'Ssh.' Ida was rocking the cradle, 'Baby sleeping.' This

340

time, examining her more closely Ned could see the huge area of bruising. 'Pretty,' Ida crooned, 'pretty baby.' She wasn't pretty, she was disfigured, he thought wildly. Rose mustn't be allowed to see, it could destroy her.

'Rose?'

'Ssh!' The voice in the bedroom was much more authoritative. The nurse paused in her knitting. 'Mr Harrison, we mustn't disturb our patient. She needs to sleep.' She took in his dishevelled state. 'Why not have a shave? Tomorrow, if she's well enough, you can have five minutes together.'

But Ned's eyes were still on Rose's face. 'Does she know how bad the baby is?'

The nurse was stern. 'If you mean that beautiful little girl, there's no reason to tell her that. Those bruises will fade and I won't have her upset. Do you understand? It could affect the milk.' He nodded. 'When the time comes to put the baby to the breast, I'll make sure your wife understands. That fall was a great shock to her system, remember.'

'Fall?'

'Down the steps into the yard. That's what started her off.' Comprehension reached him. 'So that's why ...'

'It wasn't a normal birth, no. Given time, she'll recover. You go and have your tea, Mr Harrison. Come and see your wife tomorrow. I'll try and answer any questions then. Just accept that both of them will recover given time.'

She joined him at the cradle. 'Have you decided what to call her?'

'Margaret.'

Hayden's package lay on the table. Ned picked it up. They'd been intending to open it once the room was finished – perhaps it was something he could put on the shelves, in place of the missing china.

It was a small, framed photograph of the Transporter bridge. On the back, Hayden had written, 'To remind you of home.'

No, thought Ned, not any more. This was home, this was where he belonged. In the bedroom was a new Australian;

341

already the very idea of her tugged at his heart-strings. He would honour Middlesbrough in a different way.

'We'll add another name. Margaret Muriel, after my sister.'

It was June before Rose resumed her work. As she began to learn what had happened, she felt hot with shame – that a stockman had reached inside her body, had touched her *there*! And for black women to have been the ones to ease her baby into the world ... What on earth would Gertie have said!

Gradually, the nurse helped her see things in perspective; without that help she and the baby would probably have died. Suppose Joe had done nothing? Gradually, Rose shed her false modesty. What greater service could anyone have rendered?

The hands welcomed her back enthusiastically. Ida's cooking repertoire was small and a muted cheer greeted the first tasty casserole for months. Enthusiasm changed to embarrassment when Rose insisted on making the rounds of the table to thank them. Ned watched proudly; what a long way his dear love had come from the social niceties of Clairville Road.

'Joe, I want to thank you most of all. She's the best ewe lamb you ever helped into this world. As for the rest of you, I know how well you've been caring for her while I've been ill. It's been such a comfort.'

'Aw, I wouldn't say that! Except for Andy, of course.' Andy was puce.

'I hear you're the best at Malinga for changing a nappy, is that right, Andy?' A ragged cheer went up.

'Aw, Lord, Mrs Harrison, give a bloke a chance.'

'And Mac was responsible for the perambulator. It has the most incredible wheels, Mac.'

'I found 'em in Wilcannia. Makes it easier to rock, though, having those really big ones on the back.'

'Thank you for all the toys. I think she's a little young for the gun, Bill.'

'She'll grow into it,' he told her comfortably. 'Have her

shooting bunnies in no time.'

'Maybe she'd better learn to walk first. Now how about syrup sponge for afters, gentlemen?' There was general agreement that life was definitely looking up.

Out of the chatter, one remark caused the rest to prick up their ears.

'Did you know Captain Hislop is planning a visit?'

'When d'you hear that?'

'Yesterday in Wilcannia. They'd had a message to book a room. Guess he's come to see the boss about Mrs Baines, seeing she's not ready to come home yet.'

'Maybe they'll offer the property to someone else?'

'I hope not,' Ned said, 'Mr Baines is a good boss. Why shouldn't he carry on on his own?'

''Cause it's too much for one bloke,' Andy replied, 'that's why the company always has a married couple in charge. Which makes it difficult, under the circumstances.'

In the end, the compromise suggested involved Rose.

Captain Hislop and Baines had spent several days riding the perimeter of the property. They were tired but satisfied. The wire was proving effective and the heavy rains had revived the land. With a healthy profit from the wool plus adequate water, they could afford to be complacent about the coming summer. The one remaining problem was an assistant for the boss. Ned and Rose were summoned to a meeting.

The Captain summed up the situation. 'While Mrs Baines is in the sanatorium, we want Mr Baines to continue the good work here. But it needs a woman to oversee the kitchens and deal with the day-to-day running of the place. So ... We wondered if Mrs Harrison would care to take it on instead of continuing in the cook-house.'

'Me?' Rose was startled.

'Your wife would work here in the house, Harrison. She would supervise the staff, run the homestead as well as take charge of ordering the stores. All the work normally done by Mrs Baines, in fact.' This was said tactfully as Hislop now knew just how much Baines had previously taken on his own shoulders.

343

'Who would cook if I'm to do the other work?'

'We've discussed various possibilities. Is there anyone here you think suitable?'

Rose said slowly, 'Ida's young. She enjoys *assisting* but that's all.'

Hislop nodded. 'We agree. We think it better to hire someone locally.'

'How long would this arrangement continue?' asked Ned.

'We want Mrs Baines to have plenty of time to recover,' Hislop said diplomatically.

'I was wondering about our contract?' He reddened. Remembering the loan for Rose's medical care, he wished he'd phrased it less baldly.

Hislop glanced at Baines. 'We can promise you would not be asked to continue after the three years were up. I take it you have already made plans?'

Ned reddened even more. 'I haven't discussed them with Rose but yes, I've had an idea or two.'

Rose said quickly, 'D'you want to discuss it in private?'

'No. It involves you as well, pet.'

She smiled. 'Then I had better stay.'

'I was hoping to open a repair depot for farm machinery and vehicles. One that offered refreshments as well, on one of the main highways. If we could find somewhere not too far from the railway too, we could maybe supply the trains with food. Rose has the catering experience. I'd run the mechanical side. It's just an idea at present, mind.'

Hislop considered it. 'It would need capital.'

'Aye. And we've none.' Rose was crimson.

Hislop said briskly, 'If Mrs Harrison consents to run the homestead, if we can fill her vacancy, then Malinga can continue as it is for the next two and a half years. That's when we can review the situation and decide what to do next.'

Ned realized shrewdly that Baines would be nearing retirement age by then. Whether or not Mrs Baines had recovered, the company could make any necessary transition far more harmoniously.

344

Hislop was speaking to Rose. 'I had intended to offer additional remuneration, Mrs Harrison. It occurs to me that a loan on beneficial terms for your future enterprise might be a more suitable reward? Talk it over and give me your reply in the morning. I shall be leaving for Wilcannia in the afternoon.' He slid an envelope across. 'A small gift.' His eyes twinkled. 'I'm glad the sea-sickness had a tangible result. Congratulations, I hear she's thriving.'

They talked as they bathed the child that evening. Rose soaped and sponged while Ned held the towel ready to dry her, delighting in her healthy pinkness.

'What do you think, pet?'

'You certainly surprised me. I knew you were making plans but not for such a big enterprise. Can we manage, just the two of us?'

'I was thinking of dropping a line to Oswald and Maisie – he's mechanically minded and we worked well together. You quite liked her. They'll be finishing the same time as us.'

'It's a big responsibility. What would happen if we failed?'

'We'd all sink together.' Ned sounded cheerful. 'I doubt we will if we try hard enough. Come on, young lady. Let's be having you.' He wrapped the slithery bundle tenderly and took her onto his lap. 'Miss Margaret Muriel Harrison, what pink toes you have. What a pink nose. Yes ... and a pretty little face. I remember when you were nothing but a squashed Victoria plum.'

Rose watched contentedly. The child was now healthy and normal. She wished her own recovery had been as good. The doctor assured her the birth injuries had healed well but she knew she wasn't as strong as before.

'You're looking sad. Are you worried? Would the work here be too much?'

'No,' she reassured, 'if anything, I shall find it easier, not being on my feet all day. I used to help run the tea rooms, the paperwork here might not be that different. Provided they find the right person for the cook-house, of course. I shall enjoy this challenge. And it'll be good practice for helping you run your "depot".'

Ned chuckled but one irritation remained for her. It was a matter of honour to Rose not to be in debt and she felt she'd let her husband down.

'If only Gertie—'

'Hush, pet. I doubt we'll ever see a penny of that money. Let's save what we earn here and make do with that.' He lifted the baby high and she laughed down at both of them. 'Let the past be – this is our future. You two are all I care about.'

Chapter Fifteen

Valentine, 1922

It never ceased to amaze Harold Brigg that a simple matter of building a tabernacle could be the cause of so much delay and disappointment. He and Walter had, after all, done most of the work; they'd spent the remainder of the voyage planning every detail of the design.

Four pillars supporting the ceiling were to be carved with symbols of forgiveness and love, the ceiling itself would have a sublime portrait of the Almighty, reaching out His loving arms. The cloth covering the superintendent's table would be embroidered with a suitable quotation from the psalms. The collection plate would be a simple platter of oak. A tasteful adjoining wing would be for various activities plus a handsome study for the superintendent – every single item had been considered, discussed and decided upon: all the builder had to do was carry out the work. First, however, came estimates, which were a tremendous shock.

'Five times the amount we originally planned!' Walter Paige stared in disbelief. 'Five times? Harold, the sum I have at my disposal is finite. It cannot stretch and multiply itself five times over.'

'My dear fellow ... would your trustees, perhaps ...?'

Walter shook his head. His trustees were of his father's choosing; they had agreed to hand over his fortune but only in modest portions and at intervals, to ensure extravagance was kept within bounds. From experience he knew what their answer to a request for extra funds would be.

347

It was Harold's turn to frown at the incredible total. Those damn pillars were costing more than the rest of the building put together. As for joinery!

Ethel took Walter's copy from his nerveless fingers. 'May I...?' She ran her eye down it, 'All the inessentials must go, that's obvious. There's far too much ostentation here, Mr Brigg. People can worship in a simpler setting.'

Dipping pen in ink she began to score through items. 'An upstairs gallery for the overflow ... A private room for the superintendent – you won't need that, will you? Separate ditto for Sunday school – they can meet in the tabernacle. Four hand-carved pillars, goodness me!' In less than five minutes, she'd halved both the cost and size of the project. Harold scarcely had time to protest, then remembered he couldn't anyway. This woman was, as Gertrude constantly reminded him, the source of their future income.

Gertrude herself, although not entirely happy, was now installed in a modest, rented house in Jamieson Street. It was on the wrong side of the Newport Road but that couldn't be helped, she'd had enough upheavals in the last six months to dampen any social ambitions. She heard the roar as her enraged spouse returned to their new abode that evening.

'Ethel Paige is utterly mean-spirited! She lacks vision, imagination – if she has her way, I shall end up preaching forgiveness in a shed! The architect is a rogue, we should never have employed him. His fee, Gertrude, is out of all proportion to the cost. There was nothing for him to do, Walter and I have *designed* the building yet he insists on redrawing our plans.' He returned to his main grievance, 'If Ethel deprives me of those pillars, I shall insist Walter pay the architect off and we deal with the builder directly. That way we could save ourselves the fee.'

'When can building work begin?'

'That's another piece of tomfoolery! Once we have a site, plans have to be submitted to some authority or other for approval.'

'Do they really?' Gertie's attention was centred on the guest

348

list for her first At Home since their return. Former friends were being invited, both to renew acquaintance and to meet Mr and Mrs Paige. Invitations had been written in her best handwriting:

Mrs Harold Brigg
At Home
between 2 and 4 p.m.
on Saturday, 5th December.

'Harold, would it be politic to invite Mrs Porteous?'
'Pardon?'
'As you and Walter are still looking for benefactors.'
'Indeed we are. Thank you, my dear, an excellent notion. Even if we cut costs to the bone we shall still be over our limit. Why Walter can't summon up the courage to apply to those trustees, I cannot understand. The money has been left by his father and grandfather, it should be available whenever Walter requires it – dammit, a man oughtn't to have to beg!'

But Gertie was beginning to have doubts. Had it really been a wise suggestion to invite Mrs Porteous? She didn't want to be drawn into discussion of Rose and the widow was bound to ask questions. Friends' curiosity could easily be dealt with; Gertie would give an expressive sigh and shake her head. Rose's marriage had been unsuitable, they would assume the worst; politeness would prevent them delving further, but could Mrs Porteous be relied upon?

Gertie discovered she'd run out of pink writing paper. What a relief, the widow could be ignored. Next time, perhaps. Harold had impressed on her how important it was, to hold as many "At Homes" as possible. As superintendent-elect, it was up to him to drum up support.

Calling on Ethel at her hotel the following morning, Gertie discovered the design of the tabernacle had been further modified. As well as the pillars and upper gallery, the side pews had now disappeared, also the entire wing containing the ancillary rooms. All that now remained was a small oblong hall reminiscent of one of the humbler Wesleyan chapels.

'Is that how it will be?' Gertie asked, astonished. In her eyes, such a reduction brought with it an inevitable diminution of social status.

'I hope we can afford to retain the porch,' Ethel mused. 'The weather in Middlesbrough is so horrible at this time of year, isn't it? Without these nonsensical stained-glass windows, of course. Otherwise, yes. This is all Walter can afford.' Was it Gertie's imagination or did Mrs Paige look smug.

'What about additional money from benefactors?'

'Who are they and how much will they donate? Harold has not produced anyone so far.'

'We've only been back four weeks.'

'Quite.' Four weeks, it was implied, was sufficient time to dig for gold. 'Nearly a month and nothing settled,' Ethel emphasized. 'You do realize Walter and I are determined to depart for Europe by the spring? It is essential the foundations be laid and the finite cost agreed by then.'

Gertie recognized authority when she heard it. 'I'll explain to Harold.'

'If you would. I'm afraid Walter's ideas have constantly exceeded his resources which is why his late dear father insisted on those trustees. In their wisdom they have allocated a sufficient sum; my contribution, as you already know, will be the continued support of its superintendent.'

Mrs Paige could, if she chose, increase the sum allocated for the building from her own considerable fortune, but plainly this was not to be. Gertie wondered warily if there was to be any cheese-paring in the level of support?

'I trust the reduction in the building will not affect the income Harold and I can expect.'

'I was coming to that ...' Gertie's heart sank. 'After further deliberation, Walter and I have decided that a percentage of the Sunday collections *must* be used to supplement the superintendent's income. The rest can, as previously planned, be set aside to maintain the fabric. Mr Brigg needs encouragement to build up a regular congregation. Relying on part of their subscriptions will provide such a stimulus.'

Gertie cast refinement aside. 'How much can he depend on?'

'Three hundred pounds per annum. My original proposal, if you remember? Walter and I are confident that given his talents, Harold will increase this to a handsome sum. Even more so with the help of those many benefactors.'

These had been conjured up out of a too-vivid imagination. Ethel probably guessed as much. Gertie's mouth tightened. She'd feared this would happen, ever since disputes began to erupt over the building work. Now they would have to make sacrifices. Mentally, she substituted cucumber sandwiches for salmon on her tea-party menu but she kept her smile in place and continued to exchange pleasantries.

When Harold returned home that evening, she broke the bad news. He was appalled: the remainder of Rose and Ned's money had been spent weeks ago; he was already overdrawn.

'Gertrude, we cannot maintain proper standards on three hundred pounds a year! Costs have risen nowadays.'

'We shall have to. Ethel was adamant. She is impatient because so little progress has been made.'

'I have exerted myself to the utmost ...'

'If you'll take my advice, you'll find a site before she persuades Walter to abandon the whole idea.'

'She wouldn't dare!'

'Harold, once Walter's money runs out that could be the finish. She is determined to leave for Europe. Why not choose a site tomorrow, that way he's committed.'

'One cannot rush the work of the Lord.'

But his wife had acquired a new steeliness of character. She had a modest home at last, she was determined to hang on to it.

'There's a vacant plot at the end of Duncombe Street, I noticed when I walked in the recreation ground.'

They might be living on the wrong side of Newport Road but this was even worse.

351

'Gertrude, our tabernacle must be in a *salubrious* area.'

'I should have thought there were as many sinners there as there are anywhere else.' He didn't deign to respond.

'Have you remembered to invite Mrs Porteous?'

'No, I ...' A lack of pink paper seemed a feeble excuse. 'I thought I would include her some other time.'

'Gertrude, it behoves us *both* to think of the future. Mrs Porteous could be the one on whom we are forced to depend, to supplement our income.'

A note on inferior-quality writing paper was despatched that evening.

By Saturday, the small house had been dusted and polished within an inch of its life. A fire was burning in each of the downstairs rooms. Upstairs, the silver dressing-table set was placed where any lady was bound to notice, should she require to powder her nose. The new parlourmaid was wearing one of Gertie's specially embroidered aprons, and at two-fifteen precisely the first visitors began to arrive.

Gertie had given considerable thought to the various pitfalls. Old friends would undoubtedly want to know about the Australian adventure and Harold's version was the only one which would withstand scrutiny. They had gone to be with Rose, in search of new horizons which failed to materialize – 'we were labouring under a misapprehension', was his interpretation. Gertie intended to avoid the difficult subject as much as possible and concentrate instead on recruiting a congregation.

'We must spread the word,' Harold decreed, 'fill the pews. Walter and Ethel need proof that we shall be successful.'

Ethel in particular needed convincing she wasn't wasting her money.

The trickle which began at two-fifteen had become a modest flood by twenty past and included Mrs Paige. Gertie, flushed and happy, shook hands, kissed cheeks and introduced her special guest. Everyone was ready to admire the little house – 'So convenient! Everything so close to hand, my dear,' – and tell Gertie how well she looked.

Carefree for the first time in weeks, when the first query about Australia came, Gertie answered blithely, 'It took very little time for Harold and I to be certain we had made a mistake. We knew our rightful place was back here in Middlesbrough. Sugar, Mrs Eccles?'

'But your sister ...?'

'Ah, well ... her husband *was* satisfied which meant, of course, poor, dear Rose had to agree to stay.'

Another, bolder than the rest, trilled, 'By "husband", you mean that workman!'

Gertie sighed affectedly. 'I'm afraid I do, yes.'

Ethel Paige was puzzled, 'What workman?'

Gertie hastened to elaborate. 'When I mentioned that my sister had married beneath her, I perhaps didn't make it clear that her husband is little more than a manual labourer.'

'Then he should do well in Australia.'

In the silence, teaspoons scraped against the sides of cups. Gertie's hand shook as she added hot water to the pot, she must be more careful! The doorbell provided a welcome diversion.

'At last. I feared she hadn't received my note – this must be Mrs Porteous.'

This time the chill *frisson* was followed by a stillness. Ladies froze like so many statues.

'Mrs Brigg, you *surely* cannot mean, not the widowed Mrs Porteous, from Albert Road?'

Gertie's nerves, finely tuned, twitched violently. 'I do, yes. She was once kind enough to offer Rose the position of companion which is how Harold and I ...' What on earth was wrong?

'In that case,' the questioner put down her cup and began to ease on her gloves, 'your sister was fortunate to marry Mr Harrison after all. Had she stayed in Albert Road, she might have become similarly tainted.'

'Tainted!'

Gloves in place, the lady adjusted her veil. 'I fear I have

remembered a previous engagement—'

The door opened, the parlourmaid announced, 'Mrs Porteous, madam.'

The widow advanced, then stepped aside to permit the other lady to pass. 'Good afternoon, Mrs Brigg.' Utterly confused, Gertie greeted her new guest and ordered the maid to serve the sandwiches. But several other former friends were also suddenly surprised by the lateness of the hour and hastened to depart. Mrs Eccles remained long enough to consume a buttered scone but when she too declared she must go, Gertie followed her into the narrow hall.

'Mrs Eccles ...?'

The older woman patted her hand. 'You weren't to know, dear. Such a pity but I fear Mrs Porteous has lost her reputation.' She kissed Gertie and whispered, 'If I were you I'd get rid of her as soon as possible.'

Back in the living room, unaware of English social nuances, Ethel Paige continued to converse with a subdued Mrs Porteous while her ruffled hostess looked on.

When Harold arrived with Walter at three-thirty precisely, although surprised at the lack of guests, he was at his most charming with the two remaining. Mrs Porteous heard the tabernacle described in glowing terms. Ethel was enthused over as the sublime organizer and by the time the maid cleared away, he was extremely pleased with himself. He waved until the last visitor had disappeared and returned to the living room, rubbing his hands.

'We can congratulate ourselves, Gertrude, a most happy renewal of our social life here in Middlesbrough.'

'At least you've recruited your first sinner.'

'I beg your pardon? And what happened to all your other friends?'

Gertrude told him. To her surprise, he wasn't indignant, merely thoughtful, which added to her temper. 'I only invited Mrs Porteous because you insisted.'

'Oh, quite ... but then, how was I to know? Lost her reputation, has she? Well, well, well ... No one explained why, I suppose?'

354

'Harold!'

'No, naturally ... Not a suitable subject for ladies ... Too indelicate.' He wasn't dismayed, far from it. If Mrs Porteous was now without friends, it could suit his plans exceedingly well.

Harold saw the wisdom of Gertie's advice; the site on Duncombe Street was acquired, footings were dug and the foundation stone engraved. On a bitterly cold January day, Walter Paige, eyes streaming from the north-east wind, tapped a gavel on each of the corners and declared the stone to be well and truly laid.

The reporter from the *Gazette* copied the inscription:

> To the sacred memory of Jeremiah Paige
> who left this town to make his fortune.
> Honoured by his grandson,
> Walter Jeremiah Paige,
> 22 January 1922.

There was a celebratory supper in the Temperance Hotel which had been the Paiges' home since November. The following morning, clad in her full-length sables, Ethel bid farewell to a shivering Gertie in her silver fox.

'We shall make a brief visit on our way back to Australia. We shall hope to hear Mr Brigg conduct a service.'

'The pleasure will be mine, dear Mrs Paige.'

Ethel gazed at Harold gravely. 'The bank has been instructed to make staged payments to the builder, Mr Brigg. Those arrangements are not to be exceeded, as I'm sure you understand. Your remuneration will be credited on the first of each month. I trust the building will proceed on schedule and be completed by Easter.'

'I shall endeavour to see that it is.'

She nodded as if she expected no less, dropped her gloves and scarf but finally succeeded in boarding the train.

Near to tears, Walter reached out to clasp Harold.

355

'Goodbye, old chap. Thank you for making my dreams come true.'

'Thank *you*, my dear fellow.'

Clasping Gertrude until the train was out of sight, Harold decided the time had arrived when he could safely implement the second stage of his plan. Sleet had begun to fall; they quickened their pace. On the tram he showed concern that his wife should be wearing damp clothes. Once home, he ordered the maid to replenish the coal scuttle.

Finally, when Gertie was warm and comfortable and they were alone, he began, 'Whilst I shall always respect your wishes in respect of The Act, my dear, it seems to me there is a resultant gap in our lives ...' Behind her glasses, Gertie stared at him cautiously. 'Here I am about to enter into a new and most satisfying phase of my career. You, on the other hand, remain in the most lonely of all situations—'

She misunderstood. 'I shan't invite Mrs Porteous again, Harold. I shall speak to Mrs Eccles before my next At Home, to check the names. I don't lack friends, there are plenty of others to invite.'

'I wasn't referring to that, Gertrude, necessary though it is to ensure a full congregation. I was referring to your position. By now, in the opinion of society, you should have that most precious possession, a child.' She straightened in her chair. 'Please, let me finish. I have been pondering the problem, ever since you made your feelings plain.' Gertie found her heart thumping uncomfortably. What unpleasantness was he about to suggest this time? 'You are, I take it, still desirous of acquiring an infant?'

'Yes.' It was more of a squeak than a reply.

'I also. A son who would bear the name of Brigg.'

'Not if it means—'

He held up his hand. 'Gertrude, have I not already given my most solemn word?'

'How then?'

'By adoption.'

She was shocked. 'Oh, no!'

'What better way, what more charitable Christian act, than clasping to our bosom one who has already been rejected?'

'Yes, but ...' Gertie had never met anyone who had done such a thing.

'Remember during the war, those whose fathers were killed were taken in by their relatives? It is not such a strange procedure nowadays.'

She said stupidly, 'But Cecil didn't have any children, he wasn't married.'

'Of course not, but there are many, many other unwanted infants whose dreary existence is without hope until a loving couple arrives to claim them. Could not you and I consider – an orphan?'

'Oh, no, I don't think so,' Gertie was shaking her head. 'Not unless we knew who his parents were. Even then ...'

'An infant, Gertrude, helpless, holding out his little arms for someone to cherish and nurture him.'

She looked at him narrowly, 'Had you a particular child in mind?'

'No, no,' he answered hastily, 'I was speaking metaphorically, seeing in my mind's eye ...'

But Gertie distrusted that particular organ. 'I don't think so, thank you, Harold. It doesn't sound at all satisfactory to me.'

He didn't press her. He let the idea take root, and grow.

The tabernacle rose, stark and unadorned as the staged payments were handed over and various additional cuts were made. Elm was rejected in favour of pine, coloured tiles replaced by clay. Even the superintendent's table was bought second-hand in Sussex Street and Gertie had to agree to embroider the cloth. Harold protested at each new compromise but he had no choice. Tiring of his lamentations, Gertie suggested he begin practising for his new profession.

'How can I minister to sinners when the building is not yet complete?'

'You could say a few words in the chapel at the end of

Linthorpe Road. They never have much of a congregation, I should think the minister there might welcome a helping hand.'

'If you will attend the service to give me your support, Gertrude.'

Never one to waste an opportunity, Harold took as his text: 'Suffer the little children to come unto me.'

The plasterers had finished before he raised the subject again. Gertie didn't argue, she agreed to think about it. Finally she introduced it herself. 'I've always wanted a baby.'

He tried to keep the triumph out of his voice. 'I know, Gertrude. How can I forget the passion with which you expressed yourself – that you only proceeded with marriage in order to beget a child. Those words are imprinted on my memory.'

'Yes, well ... I didn't know anything about the begetting part in those days.'

'We can still achieve the desired result,' he urged. 'We can have our own babe to love, if you so desire.'

'Provided we know everything possible about his parents and he comes from a good home. I don't want some unwanted by-blow from a Dock Street slum, Harold.'

'Trust me, dearest. I shall make enquiries. Until I have found a suitable infant, I shall not raise your hopes.'

That evening, he set off for Haverton Hill.

Ruby Winnot had not let the grass grow. Her one lapse had made her cautious. She needed a permanent protector, instead she had found two: brothers, well-placed professional men with wives, families and respected positions in society. Jointly they had leased for her a house in Tennyson Street and instructed Ruby to rid herself of Valentine.

The older solicitor called on Mondays and Tuesday evenings, the younger on Thursday and Fridays. Wednesday, being market day in nearby Stockton, Ruby was at liberty to do her weekly shopping.

By a stroke of good fortune, Harold, directed by a former

neighbour, found his way to the house on a Wednesday evening.

'You can't come in, I've got my reputation to consider.'

'Don't be silly, Ruby.'

'You know why you're not welcome.'

'It's the child I want to see, not you. My son.'

'He's not here.'

Harold loomed large. 'Where is he?'

She debated briefly. 'Oh, get inside. We'll stay downstairs and you're not to sit near the window, understand?'

'Perfectly.' The superintendent-elect also preferred not to advertise his presence.

She shocked him by lighting a cigarette. He was even more affronted by the solid furniture, her elegant dress and long silver earrings. Ruby had done well for herself, she'd also had her hair shingled and it suited her.

'You seem very nicely placed. Where is Valentine? Have you farmed him out with one of your family?'

'No.' She inhaled, releasing the smoke slowly, 'My mother didn't want him, nobody did. Not as a permanent fixture.'

'I assume he wasn't wanted here either.'

'Children cost money, Harold. I get a decent allowance but I've got to think of the future. You left me high and dry.'

'I was penniless.'

'Your wife's still got a few bob, hasn't she?'

'Ruby, I haven't come to waste time, I want to see the boy.'

'A quid.'

'Ten shillings. Not a penny more.'

'You always were mean.' It was half-hearted, she wanted him gone. Tucking the note away, she said, 'He's in the Union Children's Home, in Linthorpe Road. Annie Smith's looking after him. Tell her I sent you and she'll let you have a peep.' After a pause, 'Well? That's what you wanted to know. You'll get nothing else from me.'

'I want to adopt him.'

'Oh, do you!'

'On condition my wife never learns the truth about his

parentage. I shall keep the birth certificate myself. As far as she's concerned, he'll be an unwanted orphan. If you've any consideration for the boy, you won't object.'

'He may have been unwanted but I was a good mother,' Ruby said heatedly. 'He'd be with me now if I'd had my way.'

Harold understood. For once he dropped his pretentions and spoke from the heart. 'Ruby, as there's no likelihood of him coming here why not let me give him a home? My wife is unable to have children but she wants one as much as I do. I believe she will care for him as a mother should.'

'What if I want to see him? Where he is now, I can watch them out walking. I like to see Val in his pram.'

'It might be arranged,' Harold said cautiously, 'provided you are discreet.'

She gave a brief hard laugh. 'What chance have I got to be otherwise, thanks to you.'

'I want to make amends, Ruby.'

'You want a son, you mean, and your wife can't provide one.'

'I've been honest,' he said with dignity.

Ruby stubbed out one cigarette and reached for another. Silver bangles clashed on her bare arm. 'Where d'you live?' She had acquired sophistication, a harder edge. She wasn't the old flirtatious Ruby. He gave her his address, nervous she might take advantage in some way but that wasn't in her mind. She was only interested in the location. 'From there, it's a long way to the park. Could your wife be persuaded to go that far sometimes? I couldn't bear it if I never saw him again.'

'Very probably.'

Ruby thought quickly. It was a way out of her difficulties. 'All right,' she said. 'I'll tell them he can go for adoption. They've been urging me to sign the papers.'

'Thank you, Ruby.'

She didn't look at him. 'Close the door behind you. Don't come here again.'

He went twice to the Home before revealing anything to

Gertrude; he needed to prepare the ground carefully. He told her the boy was the result of a liaison between two students at Durham University; young people who couldn't marry, whose parents would have been horrified at the news. The girl had handed over the baby within days of its birth and wanted nothing more to do with him.

'I tell you this in confidence, Gertrude. I was permitted, unofficially, to glance through the boy's history but they do not want it discussed at the Home.'

Gertie was far more concerned with her own feelings. Was she prepared to accept another woman's child? Could she freely give all the love in her heart? The only alternative, months and months of wretched love-making with no guarantee of a result, was a sickening prospect. She made up her mind.

'I agree to see the boy, that is all. If I find I don't like him, there will be no compulsion to go any further.'

'No.' Harold realized with a shock that she might turn him down. 'I have to warn you, Gertrude, boys with his exceptional background are not born every day,' but she had that obstinate look, there was no point in arguing.

'The final decision is to be mine.'

'Very well, Gertrude. I will abide by it.'

He need not have worried. When the day arrived, her emotions in a whirl, Gertie watched the door open and the nurse carry the boy into the bleak reception room. Valentine was put on the floor and encouraged to crawl the short distance. Gertie fell to her knees, all reservations gone, love welling up inside, and begged him to come. The child didn't move. Bright, dark eyes inherited from Ruby stared at her impassively.

'Come to Mummy then, come to me,' cried Gertie but the child knew this wasn't his mother, he wasn't prepared to take a stranger on trust. He continued to contemplate her.

Beside her a tall man boomed, 'Valentine! Show us what you can do. Come along, my boy.' Father and son stared at one another. The nurse gave a quick prod. It was difficult enough finding homes in these impoverished days. The boy still didn't move so she whisked him up and placed him in Gertie's arms.

Trembling, Gertie cuddled him and cried his name softly, planting kisses on his cheeks and neck. She had found him at last, the one whom she could adore for the rest of her life: 'Dearest little Valentine, I shall care for you now,' but the boy continued to stare over her shoulder at the tall man with the loud voice.

Chapter Sixteen

The Tabernacle, 1923

To everyone's incredulity and dissatisfaction it was late summer before the tabernacle was finally completed. A blustery day which held the promise of autumn and made Ethel Paige even more determined to be gone. Once the dedication date was decided, she had immediately booked their tickets for Australia. They were to catch the London train on Monday morning. Tomorrow, Sunday, they would perform the opening ceremony and hear Harold preach on the subject dearest to Walter's heart: repentance and forgiveness. In her opinion, they had done more than enough to pander to the memory of one rather disagreeable old man.

Harold and Gertie had striven to ensure a full congregation. Leaflets had been delivered to all the houses in the vicinity. Gertie had secured promises from every acquaintance she could think of, except Mrs Porteous, naturally; forgiveness could only stretch so far. Finally, the *Gazette* had promised to send a photographer and reporter.

Four brass bandsmen were to lead the small procession, which included two insignificant civic dignitaries, the only ones Harold had been able to muster. Outside the porch he would say a few words which, Gertie urged in view of the weather, should be as few as possible. He would then hand Mrs Paige a pair of ceremonial scissors and invite her to cut the ribbon and declare the building open.

The first idea, to use a ceremonial key, was abandoned when the lock proved troublesome. A brightly coloured ribbon would be just as effective. Alas, in the last minute rush, ceremonial scissors had been forgotten. On her best tapestry cushion therefore, Gertie carried her pinking shears.

The band struck up, the wind blew the sound raggedly away. Several small boys danced alongside excitedly. Harold threatened them with his stick. Marching behind, accompanied by the maid holding on to an unwilling Valentine, Gertie remembered another windy occasion when Harold's hat blew away. Would the same thing happen today and would one of those urchins race to retrieve it?

They arrived at the tabernacle porch without mishap. Harold struck a pose in front of the noticeboard which carried the times of the services, the superintendent's name and address plus the warning: THOU GOD, SEEST ME.

He began to speak, the crowd began to shuffle. After ten minutes or so, Ethel whispered in her spouse's ear. Walter shifted uncomfortably. Another minute and she jabbed him with her elbow. With the utmost reluctance her husband moved forward and tapped Harold on the arm. There was a muttered exchange. Harold's eyebrows were reproachful. He caught sight of Gertie's face: remember, her expression conveyed forcefully, that Ethel is our only source of income. The peroration ended. He beckoned Gertie forward. Feeling extremely silly, she proffered the cushion to Ethel who, for once in her life, managed to pick up a pair of scissors without dropping them.

The promised photographer appeared and took charge. The lady must stand on the other side because the light was better, she must lift the ribbon unnaturally high so that it could be seen. When he gave the word, not before, she should cut it. 'Right, madam, face towards me and cut the ribbon if you please.' Ethel did as instructed and managed to slice through the end of her finger.

In the mêlée that followed, many people shouted instructions at other people, who took no notice. In their midst, an agitated Walter succeeded in finding a handkerchief and binding his wife's digit. Ethel said irritably, she didn't know why there was so much fuss and surely it was time to go inside?

Solicitously, Harold escorted her into the front pew. Carrying Valentine, Gertie slipped in beside her. Walter Paige followed. Once again, the photographer appeared. The previous photo 'might not come out' so could he take one more?

The group posed stiffly round the superintendent's table. Head high, Harold held an open bible. The others gazed outwards with unfocused stares: Ethel and Walter on one side, Gertie with Valentine balanced against her hip on the other. There was a flash, the photographer declared himself satisfied, the congregation settled in the pews and the first service began.

Within a quarter of an hour Gertie found herself swallowing a yawn. Harold had such an unfortunate tendency to wander off the point. After exaggerated thanks to the minor dignitaries for gracing the occasion with their presence, prayers of dedication began; these were followed by more prayers, for the soul of far away Jeremiah Paige, for his grandson Walter, for present members of the congregation and for those who were yet to come. Prayers for the rest of the inhabitants of Middlesbrough, in fact. When the congregation finally raised their heads, Harold gave them an extremely long and obscure passage from Leviticus before launching into the sermon. The subject, naturally, was sin.

The more impassioned Harold became, the more those treacherous strands of hair bounced above his ears. One of Gertie's friends whispered to her neighbour, who giggled. Harold kept going. He pleaded, he *demanded* the Almighty pardon those present. He paused, eyes fixed in a heavenly direction as if expecting a reply. In the silence, someone coughed. There was smothered laughter from the back. Gertie closed her eyes. This wasn't the stuff to impress Ethel Paige.

Harold was well into his stride. He waggled a finger, he leaned over his table and called on them to examine the contents of their hearts and not to be afraid of what they might find. He might have gone on forever had not Valentine begun to wail.

Gertie shushed him. She pushed rusks into his mouth, a sweet, she bounced him up and down but the boy wouldn't be silenced. Eventually Harold stopped preaching and sternly ordered her to take the child home. She slunk down the aisle, followed by an eager parlourmaid. In the porch, the girl said loudly, 'I do hope the lunch isn't burnt to a cinder, madam. It's gone one o'clock.'

The door was ajar, her voice penetrating. Throughout the congregation, other ladies began to murmur anxiously. Ethel raised her wrist and tapped her watch. Harold could not afford to ignore the signal. With the utmost reluctance he announced the collection would be taken during the final hymn.

Over lunch, Walter was ecstatic. He had fulfilled a sacred trust. 'My mission is accomplished. I can return to Sydney with a thankful heart, Harold.'

'If I were you,' Ethel said coolly, 'I would have a travelling clock behind that table. An hour is sufficient for the morning service. An hour and a quarter, ample. People were becoming extremely *restive* by the time you finished, Mr Brigg.'

Harold thought of several cutting ripostes but couldn't afford to indulge in any of them.

Mrs Paige had not done her worst, however; on reaching for the mustard, she knocked over the gravy boat. 'Oh, dear me, I am so sorry, Mrs Brigg. On your nice embroidered cloth, too.'

'It's quite all right.' Gertie, helped by the parlourmaid, dabbed at the dark brown stain. Ethel's clumsiness was a perpetual anxiety; how fortunate she would be gone tomorrow. As if in agreement, there came a fractious wail from upstairs.

'Have you chastised that boy, Gertrude?'

'Yes, Harold.'

To Ethel, he said complacently, 'Valentine must learn discipline. "Spare the rod and spoil the child" etc. etc.'

Walter said fatuously, 'Such a dear little chap. I said to Ethel, how wonderful that you are now a family man, as we always hoped you would be.'

Harold cleared his throat. 'A family is an additional expense, of course. Not that Gertrude or I would have it otherwise, not for an instant—'

Mrs Paige demanded, 'How much was the collection this morning?'

'Two pounds, four and threepence.'

Walter was impressed, 'I say!'

'Provided you don't bore them with over-long sermons, Mr Brigg, the congregation should provide that necessary supplement.'

'If they come in sufficient numbers, certainly.'

'That is up to you to bring others into the fold,' Ethel countered serenely.

'Spotted dick?' offered Gertie. 'With custard sauce?'

'Thank you, no. Who is taking the Sunday School this afternoon?'

'I am,' Harold told her. 'Until such time as we can engage other teachers.'

'As it begins at two-thirty,' Mrs Paige consulted her invaluable watch, 'I fear you will have to forgo dessert.'

After Harold had gone, Gertie took her guest upstairs for a final glimpse of Valentine. The boy was asleep. Ethel Paige watched curiously as Gertie tucked in the covers.

'Was it a sudden decision, to adopt the child?'

Such brusqueness was disconcerting; Gertie gazed at the sleeping face rather than her guest. 'Harold had been considering it. He suggested it when it became obvious we were ... unlikely to have children.' She'd begun to think of Valentine as entirely her own and resented such questions.

'When will you tell the boy he's adopted?'

'Oh, I don't think we'll ever ...' She saw Ethel's expression and conceded, 'When it becomes necessary.'

'I believe it is in the boy's interests to be told. How interesting that he should resemble Mr Brigg.'

'Oh, no, not at all.' Gertie knew this was impossible for when Valentine was awake he looked far too intelligent.

*

367

The photograph plus a short article appeared on page three of Monday night's *Gazette*. Muriel and Lionel were astonished.

'Rose never wrote that her sister was coming back, did she? Or that her hubby was working for the church?'

'I wonder why they didn't stay in Australia?' Something about the photograph disturbed Mu. She frowned. 'D'you remember when it was the Briggs got married?'

Lionel pondered. 'As far as I can remember, three or four months before Ned and Rose. Not long before, anyway.'

'There wasn't a baby on the way, was there?'

Lionel laughed scornfully. 'Miss Bossom wasn't that kind of girl.'

'Hmph!'

'Well, she wasn't. You remember at Ned's wedding, a real toffee-nose. And that tale Rose told Ned, about her sister believing in a "Mr Right"? She was the sort that always keeps herself pure. Anyway, when we saw her there was no sign of a baby.'

'Something doesn't add up. It's September now, right? They were married about February a year ago?'

'About then, yes.'

'Lionel, this kiddie is at least seventeen or eighteen months old. Which means he was born two or three months *after* their wedding.'

Lionel examined the photograph for himself. 'You could be right.'

'So where did he come from? When Rose wrote that she and Ned were expecting, she never mentioned her sister already had a baby. I'm sure she would if she'd known.'

'She might not. She's never referred to Gertie since they landed in Sydney, you've often remarked on that.'

'I thought maybe they'd had a tiff but babies are different. Woman always write about them.' Mu was confident.

'Well, you'd better ask. It's your turn to send a letter, isn't it?'

'When I've got the time. I'll send her this an' all.'

She cut out the photograph and tucked it behind the clock as was the way, Mu didn't tackle her correspondence for several more weeks.

'Post! Letter for you and the missus, Ned.' He was high on the beam in the shearing shed, adjusting a cable.

'Isn't Rose about?'

'Andy's taken her and Margaret into Wilcannia to do the Christmas shopping.'

'Of course.' The boss trusted Rose to order the stores herself nowadays. She'd learned to drive and sometimes went on her own, the trip making a pleasant break. Ned climbed down, saw the envelope was from Mu and tucked it into his pocket.

Later that evening, they bathed the baby together as they always did, chatting over Wilcannia gossip. The letter was on the shelf, beside Hayden's view of the Transporter. Finally, with Margaret tucked in her cradle, Rose slit open the envelope. The newspaper cutting fluttered onto the table. She smoothed it, saw the photograph and gasped.

Ned came to stare at it. 'Well, I'll be – blowed.'

'I don't believe it!'

'It's definitely Harold Brigg, pet. Nobody else could look like him. And your sister. With a ... a boy?' They stared at one another. 'He's bigger than Margaret.'

'It can't be ... it's just not possible.' Voice shaking, Rose read the line of type beneath the photograph. ' "With the new superintendent are Mr and Mrs Walter Paige, and Mrs Harold Brigg, with Master Valentine Brigg." ' Completely bewildered she said, 'Gertie wasn't even pregnant. She grumbled often enough about trying for a baby. I don't think she liked having to, you know ... with Harold.'

Ned gave a brief chuckle, 'I often wondered how they got on.'

'They didn't, according to Gertie. She loathed being in bed with him. And if she wasn't pregnant *then*, how could she possibly have a child this age?'

'What does Mu have to say?'

Rose hurried through sentences dealing with the weather and Lionel's bad back before she reached the relevant paragraph.

' "The enclosed was in the *Gazette* last September. We did not know your sister was back in Middlesbrough, Rose, or that her hubby had taken up religion. The baby was a surprise, too. He must be very big for his age ..." '

She broke off. Ned was gazing into space. 'What is it?'

'D'you remember a conversation we once had in Fleetham Street? Before we were married. We were discussing Brigg, about why he'd been sacked and everything. I'd just heard another rumour, I was about to tell you but Gertie interrupted. As I remember it, Brigg had been seen with a couple of pitmen from Haverton Hill and the talk was, they had a sister and that he'd been seen with her as well.' For the sake of her feelings, Ned added, 'It must've been before he met up with Gertie, of course.' Rose sat very still, her thoughts in a whirl. He waited.

'Gertie said she thought Harold was having to pay those two men. She believed it was to do with the Brethren but I remember saying to you that night ...' She stared at him.

'Aye. You thought it could be blackmail. Looks like it might have been, especially if there was a bairn.'

Rose stabbed at the cutting with her finger. 'But he surely wouldn't expect Gertie to take another woman's child in order to avoid paying for it? Ned, that's horrible!'

'Hang on a bit.' He examined the cutting closely. 'See how she's cuddling him? Doesn't look particularly upset about it to me. Perhaps we've made two and two add up to five. She looks really – proud. Yes, that's it. Your sister looks pleased with herself.'

Rose took the cutting again reluctantly. It was as he described, Gertie's chin was up and, despite the effect of the flash, Rose recognized the smug expression. Her sister used to look like that when she'd succeeded in attracting a tennis partner.

'Does Mu have any more to say?'

She continued reading the letter. ' "... must be very big for his age," ' she repeated. ' "According to the tabernacle notice-board, Harold is superintendent as well as being in charge of the Sunday School. Elsie from next door went to morning

370

service but she didn't think much to it. There wasn't a proper choir and the sermon was very long. Your sister plays the harmonium occasionally. We wondered what made them decide to come back."'

Rose flung the letter down. 'I'll read the rest later. I feel so – so angry.' She walked about in her agitation. 'Harold Brigg, take up religion? What humbug!' Ned waited patiently for her temper to run its course. 'How could they steal our money and use it to open a church!'

'I don't think they did, pet. The article mentions this Mr Paige being responsible for the building. Finish reading that, at least.'

She looked at the few brief sentences and eventually resumed the letter but Mu could tell her nothing more. The rest concerned the progress of their children and ended with loving enquiries as to Margaret.

'"I am sending a little parcel, not much. Just a woolly for her to wear on her birthday. I thought red might suit her if she has your colouring. We'd love a photo one day. Lionel joins me in wishing you all the best. Yours fondly, Mu."'

Ned tried to make a joke: 'A woolly for her birthday? D'you think Margaret'll come out in a rash, bless her.'

'She can wear it next winter if Mu's made it big enough. Ned, what shall we do about . . .?'

He stared briefly at the cutting. 'Goodness knows. What do *you* want to do?'

'I shall write to Gertie. Mu says the tabernacle's in Duncombe Street, that should be sufficient to find her.'

'Will it do any good? What d'you intend saying to her?'

'I doubt I shall wish her a happy Christmas.'

'Don't be too hard. It could have been because of him.'

'Gertie stole our money,' Rose said implacably, 'until she returns your savings, I shall never forgive her.'

'Leave it a day or two,' he urged, 'when you've had time to consider.' He began heating the water for their nightly wash. 'What about the boy? Will you tell her you've seen the article?'

'Of course.'

It wasn't a long letter. She didn't show it to Ned but despatched it quickly so that it arrived in Middlesbrough six weeks later. Harold handed it to Gertie to open.

She gave a small shriek. 'Rose's handwriting! How did she know where to send it?' Opening it, she read greedily. Happiness disappeared and her colour faded. 'Oh, Harold, it's brutal! Not like Rose at all!'

He read:

Dear Gertie,

Ned's sister forwarded the cutting from the *Gazette*. We read of Harold's new profession with interest. I'm sure you realize why I am writing, to ask you to refund the money you stole in Sydney. That draft included Ned's life savings, as you were aware. We shall need every penny once we leave Malinga.

We now have a daughter, Margaret, born last March. We noticed that you and Harold have a son.

I hope you are well. Ned and I look forward to hearing from you.

Rose.

Seeing the accusation in black and white jerked Harold to his feet.

'How dare she write to you like that. To my wife.'

Gertie paused in her sobbing. 'What d'you mean, how *dare* she? It's true, we did steal it.'

'You may have done—'

Gertie screamed at him, 'Stop it, stop it! Don't you ever blame me again! It was because of you I had to do it.'

'For God's sake, moderate your voice. Do you intend the rest of the street to hear?'

'I don't care. I don't care about anything any more – if only I could see Rose and explain. It's such a dreadful letter, so unkind, not the way she used to be with me.' She turned on him. 'You promised we should repay. You gave me your solemn word!'

372

'When we are able, Gertrude. I have never deviated from that.'

'You've never made any attempt—'

'How could I? How could *we*? You're always complaining, saying how much things cost. Look at the ridiculous price you paid for Valentine's shoes. I'm sure you could have found a cheaper pair in the market.'

She sat up straight and said coldly, 'As wife of the super-intendent, do you really expect me to shop there? And what about your expenditure? Is it necessary for you to be out every evening?'

'Gertrude – I'm warning you—'

'Trying to worm your way into the Brethren? If they'd wanted you as a member, they would have invited you by now.' She'd goaded him too far.

'I have never criticized the way you spend your time. I have never complained when you refused to honour your wedding vows. I've even provided you with a son to keep you happy,' he declared recklessly, 'but a man has his needs, Gertrude. If I choose to absent myself occasionally, you have only yourself to blame.' He rose and strode through to the hall to collect his coat and muffler.

'During my prayers today, I shall offer up a silent plea for an improvement in your temper and that your sister shall become less discontented with her lot.'

'I'm sure if we repaid them, she'd be her old sweet self in no time.'

'That is your concern, Gertrude. Despite your protests, it was you who first told me of that draft. You undertook to remove it, it is up to you to make what reparation you choose.'

Having shrugged off all guilt, Harold left the house. He had come perilously close to boasting where he spent his evenings; within a hairsbreadth of telling her, in fact. That would never do. Outside, he inhaled the smoky winter air. That had to remain a secret, between him and Mrs Porteous.

On her own, Gertrude consoled herself in her usual way. She gave the parlourmaid her orders for the day and went to

Valentine's room. The boy was already rattling the side of his cot. He'd nearly outgrown it. In a month or two, they would have to think about buying him a proper bed, from Dickson & Benson naturally. Fancy suggesting she buy the dear boy clothes from the market – the very idea! Gertie lowered the side.

'Come to Mummy then? How's Mummy's boy this morning?' Valentine gazed at her without smiling, which disconcerted her. Gertie ran a group at the tabernacle for Mothers and Babies on Tuesday afternoons; those babies gurgled happily. Why couldn't Valentine behave like that, just once?

She lifted him onto her lap and began to undress him. 'We can't call you Mummy's boy for much longer, can we,' she cried, idolizing him. 'You're far, far too big.' She swooped down, her glasses cold against his skin as she snuggled into his neck. 'Mummy's little man, eh, Valentine? That's what you've become.'

She recalled Rose's letter: a daughter called Margaret. 'You've got a cousin,' she told him and in saying so, her long-dormant conscience began to prick. As she washed and dressed the boy, delighting in each new sign of progress, she began to wonder if Rose were doing the same with her little baby. Did she have to buy clothes in the market – could she even afford that? Ned's wages were undoubtedly lower than Harold's.

When Valentine was ready for his walk, she removed her bank book from its hiding place beneath the fox fur. There was very little left. Despite her New Year resolutions it was amazing how often the housekeeping money ran short. As Harold always lost his temper if she mentioned it, Gertie usually withdrew a small amount privately, promising herself she would repay the following month but somehow she never did.

How much could she afford to send Rose? Only this morning Harold was lamenting that Ethel and Walter had not been generous at Christmas. 'Perhaps they intend to send a gift at Easter. In acknowledgement of my efforts to garner a larger flock.'

Gertie hoped they wouldn't query the actual numbers. Despite Harold's efforts, the flock remained small: it no longer contained many former acquaintances or civic dignitaries. People living nearby still came, poorer people. The collection plate had copper rather than silver nowadays.

Today the wind was icy. After giving Valentine the briefest possible airing, Gertie left him with the parlourmaid and hurried to the bank. The clerk felt bound to point out that if she withdrew five pounds, less than four remained. Gertie agreed but it was the smallest amount she dare send. The thin white banknote was also easier to post. If Ethel and Walter were generous at Easter, if Harold agreed to divide the gift, maybe she could send a cheque to Rose. How wonderful to be able to pay back the balance with a kind, reproachful note, accusing her sister of a lack of faith.

On the tram, Gertie composed a chatty letter listing the events of the past twelve months that Rose would be sorry to have missed: the harvest festival at the tabernacle, the arrival of Valentine's two front teeth – Valentine! She'd grown so accustomed to thinking of him as her own. Gertie sighed; the truth was so often unpleasant but thanks to Harold's influence, she'd learned to ignore it most of the time. She would fudge an explanation for Rose.

It proved more difficult than she had anticipated. After spoiling several sheets of paper, Gertie gave up and resorted to formality. She couldn't express what she truly felt, the truth was repugnant. Instead, stilted phrases suggested by the *Ladies' Companion* would have to suffice.

At Easter, a modest package arrived from the Paiges. 'As is the custom in the church we attend here,' Ethel had written, 'we wish to show our appreciation with our gifts.'

Inside, inscribed by Walter, was the book of Common Prayer for Valentine; silks plus a tapestry pattern for Gertie and a sealed envelope for Harold. She watched anxiously as he opened it. From where she sat, she couldn't see anything resembling a cheque. Had Ethel paid money directly into the bank instead?

'How much have they sent?' she asked. Harold tossed the letter across. Walter sent his very best wishes and enclosed a list of texts for sermons during the forthcoming twelve months. The tabernacle was, he assured them, uppermost in his mind every day of his life, and Ethel joined him in wishing them all prosperity. When she saw Harold's face, Gertie knew their thoughts were the same: 'How *can* they wish us prosperity if Ethel does so little to ensure it?'

Rose received her letter with its enclosure. She unfolded the banknote. As he saw it, without letting his feelings show, Ned asked, 'What does Gertie have to say?'

'About the money? That the "enclosed" is "on account".'

He gave a brief, sad smile. 'To be honest, pet, I never expected to get that much. Let's forget about the rest.'

'Never!' She blazed at him, 'I won't *allow* Gertie to ignore what she did.'

Ah, well, he thought, give it a bit longer and maybe she won't feel so strongly. Aloud he asked, 'What about the lad? Does she write about him?'

'Almost ...' Rose's temper had already switched to contempt, 'Listen to this florid piece of camouflage: "Please accept our sincere congratulations, dear Rose, upon the arrival of Margaret. It is the one essential touch to make any union ideal. However perfect the bond between wife and husband there is something lacking in childless homes, which is why Harold and I rejoice to have a little stranger named Valentine. He's such a dear, sweet boy, all a mother could wish." *Mother*, indeed!'

Ned waited. 'That's it? No explanation?'

'No, none. I know Gertie. She was hoping to bamboozle us with all that flummery. The rest concerns her social calendar since their return; apparently we missed a wonderful harvest festival celebration at the tabernacle.'

He grinned, 'You better tell them the wool clip here was pretty good. Any explanation regarding the tabernacle?'

'She says ...' Rose found the place, 'that "Harold had a

376

stroke of good fortune in meeting Walter Paige and has found his true *métier* in bringing forgiveness to sinners." '

This time, Ned's incredulous laughter stopped her. Despite her feelings, Rose had to join in.

'My word,' Ned was wiping his eyes, 'I hope the good Lord has a sense of humour. Talk about setting a poacher to catch a thief...'

'All the same, I shan't be sending any more letters until Gertie repays the rest.'

'Rose, suppose she can't? What if this five-pound note is all she can afford? I don't suppose Brigg earns much of a screw. She's not like you, she'll be staying at home with the boy, not out somewhere earning her living.'

'If I owed a debt, I wouldn't rest until I'd repaid every penny.'

'I know, pet. By the time we leave here, our savings account will have in it more than Gertie stole. You even paid in your annual bonus from the boss – don't think I hadn't noticed. You never spend an unnecessary penny but I wish you'd treat yourself occasionally.'

Rose gave a brief shrug. The sun had long ago bleached the colour out of her blouses and skirts but what did it matter? There were only the hands to notice if she was shabby. As for Margaret, she played with the black babies, all of them naked except for knickers and a vest, in the shade by the billabong. The child only put on clothes for the outings to Wilcannia. The thought of it made Rose smile.

'A penny for them?'

'I was thinking of all the clothes I had to wear before I was allowed out when I was a child. Petticoats, stockings – a liberty bodice, coat, gloves, hat – look at our little monkey.'

'Aye.' Ned stood in the doorway and shaded his eyes. 'She's happy and healthy, that's what matters.'

'When we're ready to leave, Margaret and I could have a few new things then. You'll need a smart wife to run the office of your new depot.'

Always a joke, but Ned didn't mind. It was closer to

becoming reality with every month that passed. The company would notify him of any likely property when the time came to leave. At Christmas, Maisie and Oswald had responded enthusiastically to the suggestion they might join the enterprise.

He kissed Rose before setting off the drive to the well-head near the telegraph junction. With the boss's permission, Ned was cleaning and refurnishing it, having devised a cover that would allow rain water to pass through but prevent dirt silting it up after the wet.

As always, he felt at peace while driving the endless miles across the plain. As usual, he thought about Rose. She worked very hard, she'd taken over additional paperwork leaving Baines free to visit the sanatorium more often. She was expiating her former dislike of his wife, Ned knew. Not that they ever discussed it, for Rose had a need for privacy in certain areas of her life.

The boss demonstrated his appreciation with extra amounts credited to their savings account, always with the same brief comment, 'With thanks, M. Baines.'

Ned sometimes wondered if Rose had the same attitude towards their love-making. Once the morbid thought occurred, did Rose force herself to be kind because of the injury done him by Gertie? He quickly dismissed it. The magic had been there once, that day beside the water-hole. Rose had enjoyed their love-making then just as much as he had. If only the doctor's warning weren't uppermost in their minds. After Margaret's birth, it was inevitable and made it difficult to recapture the magic. Rose tried to relax but he could feel her stiffening when she asked, 'Are you sure it's all right?'

'Yes, pet, quite sure. There's no risk at all.'

And then there were all those ghosts that came between them, those long-dead friends of her brother. 'She'll have to learn to take me as I am,' Ned whispered to the empty lonely landscape. He never troubled her more than he had to but how he ached with love sometimes, as his beautiful wife lay asleep beside him.

378

Chapter Seventeen

The Shack in the Wilderness, 1927

Ned and Rose eventually stayed on at Malinga far longer than
their original contracts had stipulated. It was Ned who, after
discussing his future ambitions with Captain Hislop, finally
realized they had no other option. He chose his words carefully when explaining to Rose but she understood immediately.

'You made plans for the depot *before* our savings were
stolen?'

'It was while we were on the boat when the idea first came,'
he admitted. 'By the time we arrived in Sydney I'd worked out
roughly what we could expect to save, how much capital we'd
have by the end of our time here. That changed of course, but
we've managed far better than I could have hoped, thanks to
your wages,' he added loyally.

'We still haven't sufficient capital?'

'No. The company are willing to advance a loan but we
need more before we can start.' Yet again, Rose silently cursed
Gertie.

'So what do you suggest?'

'If you're agreeable, I want to ask if we can stay on here.
Although we might be able to earn more in a town, we're
living rent free. Nor do I want to leave the company's employ.'

'Of course not.'

'About another two years should do it. Mr Baines has
promised a rise come the new year. I'd like you to check my
figures before I write to Captain Hislop but I don't think I'm
being over optimistic.' He produced the small notebook

containing the calculations. Rose ran through them before asking, 'What about Oswald and Maisie?'

'I dropped them a note,' Ned confessed. 'I thought it best to be completely honest. I explained how we were placed, how much we'd managed to save and what the Captain suggested was the minimum amount. This came from Oswald today.' Rose smoothed out the sheet of paper.

My dear Ned,
    Hoping this finds you In The Pink, us being in similar gd health. Yr letter received & contents duly noted.
    Maisie also ests 2 more years to reach total sum, assuming our share to be one half.
    A new boss here. Conditions are good so what is 2 more years? Weather continues fine. Sincere gd wishes to Rose & baby,
        Yrs faithfully,
    O. Robson

'Bless them,' Rose whispered, heart-felt. 'I must write and thank Maisie.' How will I ever make it up to them? she wondered.

There was no new boss at Malinga yet. It was obvious to everyone that Mrs Baines wasn't responding to treatment but the company were content to let her husband have sufficient time to accept the fact. Meanwhile the seasons came and went, the cycle of life continued and the rhythm of work never faltered.

Correspondence went on between the four as to their eventual plans. Maisie and Rose wrote with ideas of the café they might run but until the precise location was known, nothing more could be done. Gertie remained silent but at regular intervals, at Christmas and on birthdays, Mu kept them abreast of the Middlesbrough news.

She had seen Gertie walking with her little boy in Albert Park. 'She goes there regularly,' Mu had written. 'The lad is always dressed very smartly, quite the little toff.'

380

Ned had chuckled but Rose felt uneasy. She remembered Gertie's passionate desire for 'someone to love'. It was dangerous to concentrate all one's emotion on a child. Hadn't their mother been guilty of that same sin, demanding too much from Gertie? Surely her sister hadn't forgotten.

No risk of our daughter behaving as dutifully as we did, Rose thought ruefully. Margaret was definitely 'Daddy's girl' but she also had a mind of her own. She was the friend of everyone on the property, totally without fear of either black or white.

'Which is as it should be,' Rose reminded herself. 'Let her keep her innocence and not feel inhibited as Gertie and I did. She can accept life on her own terms. I shall have to warn her of the pitfalls soon enough.' Rose was standing at the window of her 'office', the former living-room of the homestead, where Mrs Baines used to keep watch. Since his wife's departure, the boss found the kitchen sufficient to sit in during the evenings. He'd given up his small office in the corner of the barn as well. This had been fitted out for the cook from Wilcannia. She had made good use of her time. It was an open secret that she and Mac planned to marry and move into the small wooden house as soon as Rose and Ned had moved on.

'We're all in limbo,' Rose thought lazily. 'Waiting for the next stage in our lives to begin. It's not unpleasant but I shan't be sorry to leave here,' and despite her resolve not to think about Gertie she began to wonder what her sister might be doing today. 'A little toff'? Gertie has always dressed her dolls in the latest fashion, was she doing the same to the adopted Valentine? 'He'll have the stuffing knocked out of him once he goes to school if she does.'

As usual her thoughts came full circle: was Harold Brigg the real father? If so, had Gertie truly not minded? 'I would,' Rose said aloud. 'If I were married to that man I couldn't have given the boy a home.' But she knew it was the very idea of Harold which filled her with repugnance. Gertie obviously saw him in a different light. Or did she? 'Hey ho ... poor silly Gertie ...' After checking that Margaret was not playing too close to the shearing sheds, Rose returned to her desk to begin the day's work.

It was 1927 before Baines finally made his decision and offered his resignation. After that events moved quickly. There was a quick exchange of letters: Maisie and Oswald were ready to take the plunge. Ned accompanied the boss to Wilcannia and had a separate interview with the captain. He came back with details of three possible locations for the depot. There were no photographs. Rose persevered with the agent's descriptions and tried to use her imagination.

'I've sent copies to Maisie and Oswald and asked them to telegraph their opinion,' he told her. 'We need to be ready to leave in about two months.'

'Mr Baines has definitely decided to retire?'

'Yes. He's over age but I reckon the company turned a blind eye because of his wife. He's decided to move closer to the sanatorium – he's got himself a job there, part time, helping run the grounds.'

Rose was shocked. 'Surely he doesn't need to do that?'

'Try and see it from his point of view. Nothing to do all day except worry about Mrs Baines. At least he'll be kept busy. He'll have neighbours at his new home, he won't be so lonely. Besides, I don't think he could bear to move too far from Malinga.'

Rose knew he was thinking of the grave. 'Oh, Ned, I should have done more,' she said, ashamed. 'All the time we've been here, I made no real attempt to befriend the poor man.'

'You couldn't. We're the same as the rest of the hands. The boss has to be in charge on a property like this, he can't afford to treat anyone differently.'

In other words, Rose thought wryly, I'm not the young lady from Clairville Road who can behave graciously if she remembers to, I'm simply a labourer worthy of her hire. She asked curiously, 'Have you decided how you'll run the depot when you're the boss?'

'I've wondered about it. As there'll only be Oswald and me

to begin with, discipline won't be a problem. I doubt either of us will need to wear ties.'

She realized he was poking fun. 'You don't want Maisie and me to act as bosses' wives with the natives?'

'God forbid! I want you to do one thing though, to please me.'

'What's that?'

'Treat yourself next time you're in Wilcannia. I'm sick and tired of that old blouse. Why not use it for rags?'

When he'd gone, Rose ran her finger over the contrasting braid, now faded to an indeterminate grey. It had been so pretty when Gertie gave it to her on the evening of her twenty-first birthday.

Each day now brought changes and decisions. The homestead was to have a thorough overhaul. The Baineses' possessions were moved out and a firm came to instal electric light. Decorators removed all the traces of serviceable brown and green. These days, lighter colours were fashionable and it was rumoured the new boss and his wife were comparatively young.

Rose concentrated on their plans. Ned, advised by Captain Hislop, had finally chosen a run-down garage in the Northern Territories. She and Maisie would be starting their café from scratch. She selected pottery and cutlery, chairs and tables from catalogues. Pound for pound the company would match their savings as well as arranging a loan on favourable terms. When Ned discussed it, Rose was amazed how he'd thought out every single detail. She'd been so immersed in the business side at Malinga, the very idea of the depot had become a far-off pipe dream. Being honest, she admitted these thoughts to him.

Ned hid any hurt behind a smile. 'I've been planning our future all the time. If you consider the scheme's workable then I'm satisfied.'

'The risks are enormous – suppose we have one of those dreadful freak storms they're always talking about? Isn't it an area renowned for its peculiar weather?'

Instantly he looked so anxious she could have bitten out her tongue.

'There are risks – I lie awake sometimes.'

'Why did you never tell me?'

'You need your sleep. Your work here is very responsible.'

'Oh, pooh!' She was angry at his selflessness. 'Ned, from now on, we have to be a proper partnership. We share everything, especially the worries, promise me?' His expression made her humble, she'd forgotten how much he loved her.

'Rose, can you run Mr Baines over to the sanatorium today? I need to change the chain on the tractor.'

Rose nodded, reluctantly. She wasn't really busy, the packing was almost finished but the boss couldn't drive because of an injury to his wrist; all the same ... It might mean another encounter with Josie Baines.

Ned murmured, 'Thanks, pet. He'd rather it was you. He doesn't want any of the hands to see her.' Telling herself not to be squeamish, Rose consigned Margaret to Ida's care and fetched her hat.

After an initial apology, the boss made no further effort at conversation. Rose struggled but with only taciturn replies to her bright enquiries, relapsed into silence. There was no point in being sympathetic if he wouldn't co-operate. She concentrated on driving instead.

As they drew near and Mr Baines roused himself to give directions, she found herself uncharacteristically nervous. Would she have to converse with Mrs Baines? Could she bring herself to be kind?

They were admitted through the high solid gates and drove towards the single-storey building. Rose glimpsed hunched figures among the trees, accompanied by the nuns who ran the hospital.

'I daresay you'd like a cup of tea, Mrs Harrison. If you go inside, someone will look after you.' They had parked by the main entrance. Without looking to right or left, Rose walked swiftly through the door, scolding herself for being a coward. She was alone. Mr Baines had left her.

'Yes? Ah, yes ...' The sister obviously knew of the arrangement. 'You'll have come over from Malinga. Would you like to follow me, please.' Rose was shown into a small shuttered office with an adjoining washroom. 'Make yourself at home. I'll bring tea directly.'

Waiting, Rose opened the blinds a crack. She felt braver now with the protection of the building around her. The door opened again and the sister set down her tray. Joining Rose, she too stared outside. 'There they are, d'you see. It does the heart good to see them, doesn't it?' Slightly apprehensive, Rose stared at the distant flower bed where Josie Baines knelt with her trowel. The boss crouched beside her and Mrs Baines appeared to be listening to him.

'Sugar?'

'No thank you.' Rose took the cup. Outside, the boss seemed to be asking a question.

'Ah, that's good ...' the sister nodded approvingly. 'She's recognized him today.'

As Rose watched, Mrs Baines leaned forward suddenly to touch her husband's face.

'There! He's learned not to flinch.' Seeing Rose's lack of understanding the nun explained, 'In her condition, Mrs Baines' hands are always icy cold, d'you see. Takes a bit of getting used to.'

Rose cleared her throat. 'Is there ... will she ever get better?'

'Oh, no.' Below the wimple the eyebrows rose, 'She can only get worse. We haven't yet discovered a cure. But we mustn't give up hope. Dear me, no.' She resumed her vigil at the window. 'All we can do is offer them love ... and he surely does that, poor man.'

Rose found herself saying defensively, 'She once put my life and that of my child in danger.'

The nun sighed. 'Yes, she would. Her dead child – that was

385

the cause, in my opinion. She cannot bear the sight of the crib at Christmas. Will you be all right in here?'

'Yes, thank you, sister.'

'That's good.' The nun gave one of her beaming smiles. 'Have a rest, now. It's a long drive back. Close your eyes, you'll be perfectly safe.'

Rose listened to the swish of her skirts fading away. She returned a final time to watch. The boss had an arm round his wife and Josie Baines stared up at him as though she'd never seen him before.

In sickness and in health . . .? Dear Lord, don't let Ned go mad, Rose thought, I don't know whether I could love him enough for that. And her cheeks flamed as the shaming truth reached her.

On the way back, to her surprise, Mr Baines was cheerful. 'She was so much better today, Mrs Harrison. The nuns agreed. They said we mustn't hope for too much, of course. Still a long way to go but Josie actually smiled when I said goodbye.' He stared contentedly through the windscreen. 'I'm sorry you won't be here to see her full recovery but I mustn't be selfish. You've served far longer at Malinga than the company required.'

With an effort, Rose managed to say, 'Ned and I have been very lucky. We shall miss you – and Mrs Baines.'

Echoing the sister, he said quietly, 'That's good. When you think about Josie, there won't be any bad feelings?'

'None at all.'

He gave Ned and Rose the old truck as a farewell gift. Heavily laden, surrounded by well-wishers, with Margaret wedged between them, they set off at first light on a pearly morning that would turn into heat before noon. They had one last task before departing on the road for South Australia. In the small shop on the side street in Wilcannia, they posed for a photograph. Ned paid extra for the postage. One copy would be sent to Mu, the other two to their new address. Rose hadn't asked why there had to be two but she guessed: if ever she made her peace with Gertie, Ned intended the second to go to her.

Heading west, they stuck to the main road that ran parallel to the railway line rather than risk travelling cross-country. There would be hotels in some of the small towns, as far as Port Augusta. After that, going north on the highway, it would be nothing but desert until they broke free of it at Alice Springs. Camping, resting when the heat was too much, it would be a long, long trip with a young child. Whenever possible, Ned intended to top up the two large water barrels he carried. He'd stocked up with every conceivable spare part for the truck. He'd also tried to persuade Rose to go by train. She brushed talk of danger aside.

'I'm not travelling in comfort simply to wait for you in Alice Springs. Why should you drive the truck all that way on your own? Heavens above, Ned, that's no way for partners to behave.'

He suggested it was what most women would prefer. 'Maisie and Oswald will be travelling that way.'

'Only because they haven't got transport. Besides,' she said primly, 'it'll be nice for Margaret to see something of the countryside.'

'Rose, it won't be like the run out to Osmotherly.'

It was as different as anything could be. At first, Rose enjoyed glimpses of small isolated houses with red corrugated roofs and white verandahs. Heading west, passing mile after mile of grassland and sheep station, the air was cool enough to make them perky. After three days, when the last of the small hotels was behind them, they turned onto the highway.

Less than fifty miles further on, it had dwindled to a dirt track, littered with sharp stones. Ned began to worry about spare tyres. He'd brought only four and prayed they would last through the desert. He shouted to Rose above the noise and jolting, 'We must remember to keep plenty in stock at the depot.'

She nodded, trying not to open her mouth because of the dust.

387

They stayed one night in a small silver-mine encampment; the next, in bare empty desert on the edge of a dried salt lake. The flatness of the south had given way to low ranges of hills, some of them with patches of trees. But after the Pimba plains, even trees disappeared. It was incredibly hot, the same burning heat that had killed the first explorers in their search for an inland sea.

The third time they broke down, when Ned had to repair a leaking hose, Rose knew what it was to be afraid. They were the only living things on a barren empty earth that stretched from one horizon to the other. The sun burned through the soles of her shoes, it beat down so fiercely she cowered with Margaret in the only patch of shade beneath the truck. If she'd once considered Malinga barren, she realized it was an oasis compared to this.

Ned groaned as the spanner slipped out of his dizzy grasp.

Before she could stop herself, Rose said, 'We're not in any danger? You will be able to mend it?'

He was dust-covered, caked in dirt from head to foot, his eyes bloodshot. 'Trust me.' It was nothing but a croak.

To spare him further effort Rose crouched silently beside the child. Why had she not realized, or Ned not told her, that they might die? It happened, she had read about it in the newspapers; bodies discovered by other travellers, their skin burned black from exposure to the sun. Now they too were in mortal danger. She'd never feel cool English rain on her face again – the sun was boring a hole in her skull, Ned was a blur, she'd die without ever seeing Gertie ...

There was a movement beside her. Margaret was holding out her hand. A tiny beetle crawled across her palm.

'Where on earth did you find that?' The child smiled as she offered it to her mother and Rose tried to conquer her fears. She mustn't infect her daughter with them. So far, Margaret didn't appear scared, she was enjoying the journey. She told her mother the insect's aboriginal name. 'If we get through,' Rose promised her through parched lips, 'one day I'll tell you all about Albert Park. It's a really beautiful place when the flowers are out.'

By the time they arrived in Alice Springs, there had been a subtle change in their roles. The desert had tested them to the utmost. Without Ned's foresight they wouldn't have got through. Those meticulous preparations Rose had been inclined to scoff at, all had been needed eventually. They were down to the final six inches of water, the last of their tyres was so torn Ned had bound it round with a rope and on that they'd limped forward for the last twenty miles.

They'd left the worst of the arid desert behind when they crossed into the Northern Territories. There were trees at the border behind the roughly painted boundary sign. Now, much further north, the landscape undulated. Gone was the terrifying flat nothingness of the centre of Australia. Ahead, she could glimpse outlying houses. The earth was lighter in colour. There was no blood-red dirt, here large boulders emerged from a pale pink dust. Trees had leaves and gave shade. The land was higher, it was a welcoming, cooler place altogether.

Ned slowed to a stop. 'Well, pet, looks like we've finally got here.'

Rose couldn't keep her relief hidden. '*You* did, you mean.' She was suddenly brimming over with gratitude. 'Bless you, Ned. There were so many times when I didn't think we'd make it. Here, give Margaret a hug.' The child clung to him. 'Your father is a very brave man, not to mention far-sighted. Your silly mother hadn't the first idea what to expect.'

He kissed Margaret tenderly, 'Had to make sure Daddy's girl got through safely, didn't I?'

For a fleeting instant, Rose felt jealous then scolded herself: she'd never been as open and loving as Margaret, even though Ned asked for so little.

'Thank you for looking after us both.'

He reached out to include her in his embrace. 'It's only the beginning, pet. From now on, we can reach for the moon and

389

the stars. There's nothing to stop us, all it needs is hard work.'

Maisie and Oswald had left the address of their lodgings at the telegraph office: Rose and Ned pulled up outside a small, low roofed building with a verandah.

'Hello ... is that you, Rose?' Shading her eyes, Maisie stood at the top of the steps. 'Eee, you haven't changed!' She hurried to fold Rose in her arms. 'Don't you look bonny – and so well! And was this the cause of all the trouble?' She bent to kiss Margaret. 'Hello, baby. Fancy the rest of us thinking you were nothing but sea-sickness!'

The familiar comforting sight of Maisie in her cotton wrapper, with her solid legs and commonsense sandals, brought a lump to Rose's throat. She'd lacked proper female companionship for over six years. 'You haven't changed either, Maisie. Oh, but it's good to see you!'

'I have, love. I've stopped wearing corsets because of the heat – look how I've spread. But I'll tell you something, I like it out here now I'm used to it. All this sunshine – it's quite a tonic, isn't it? Oswald, Oswald they've arrived.' In an aside, she muttered, 'He's mending the woman's wheelbarrow. He's turned out to be ever so handy, you'd never think he used to be a butler.'

They talked late into the night. First they told each other what had happened since Sydney, then they discussed details of their partnership. Ned was full of what he'd learned on the journey. Each time they'd passed another vehicle, they'd stopped to exchange news.

'It's part of survival in Australia. You check the other fellow's all right, he does the same for you and tells you of any problems ahead. You never pass anyone,' he explained, 'and that's the way the drivers will learn about us. I told everyone where they could find us and that we'd be open for business in a month or two.'

'Hope you're right.' Oswald had already hired a vehicle and investigated the proposed depot. He was guarded. 'It'll take a bit of fettling, nothing we can't tackle, mind, but might take longer than a couple of months.' Even more reserved was the description of their living quarters; 'Not in the luxury class but there's room to expand once we can afford it.'

He and Maisie had a list of essential purchases. Tomorrow they would stock up and, the following day, the party would set forth.

'Maisie and I will see to everything. We know our way round Alice Springs. You take it easy, Ned. You can leave Margaret here if you want to explore. It takes all of ten minutes to walk the length of the main street. They say it's growing all the time but at present this town's not much bigger than Cowpen Bewley.'

The landlady offered the newcomers the use of her verandah for sleeping quarters. There being no shortage of water, Rose washed every single garment and then herself. To be clean lifted her spirits, she felt ready to tackle anything. That evening, she went to tuck in Margaret's mosquito net. As usual, the child was sleeping peacefully, totally unruffled by strange new surroundings. Rose felt a surge of affection for her.

'One day, if we can afford it, I hope she'll go back and see Cowpen Bewley for herself.'

In the darkness, Ned's voice was firm, 'Only if she wants to, pet. She might prefer to stay in Australia, where she belongs.'

Even though Oswald had exaggerated, it didn't take long to see the sights. Ned stopped beside the new hospital building, solid red stone set into thick walls with inset windows. Above was the inevitable corrugated roof and an airy room rising to a small second storey. 'I'm glad to see this. I wasn't sure how far we'd have to travel if ever we needed help.'

Rose had automatically moved into the shade. 'Oswald was very cautious last night. Did he say anything more about the depot? All Maisie would admit to was that he was depressed when he returned.'

'He repeated it would take more work than we had anticipated. We've discussed the extra cost – he and Maisie have saved nearly as much as we have, bless them. They're willing to plough in every penny.'

'Did you explain that Gertie still hasn't repaid us?'

'Just the bare bones,' Ned said easily, 'I left you to tell Maisie if you felt like it.'

'I shall remind Gertie about the balance when I send her our new address.'

'Don't build up your hopes,' he warned. 'Oswald's heard that things are very bad in England just now. Your sister may not be able to afford to pay.'

'Hmph!'

A little further on, he asked hesitantly, 'Last night, when you said you wanted Margaret to go back, were you hoping she'd settle over there?'

'Goodness, no.' Rose looked at him with concern, 'I don't want to lose her any more than you do, I meant a *visit*, that's all. To meet Mu and Lionel – they are her uncle and aunt.' Ned waited. Rose stressed, 'They're her *only* family as far as I'm concerned.' She added optimistically, 'Maybe Margaret will be the one to persuade them to come out here and join us.'

One thing at a time.

'Let's see what kind of home we can offer them before we suggest that, pet.'

They drove slowly out of Alice, laden to the gunnels, past the railway station that marked the end of the line.

'They say they'll extend it eventually, as far as Darwin,' Oswald told them.

'When they do, we'll be ready. If possible, we'll try and link our business to the railway, it'll be easier for spares to be delivered. I'm keen to see how far we are from the highway.' Slightly perturbed, Ned added, 'I suppose the traffic's lighter on this side of Alice Springs, I hadn't thought of that.'

'It is at present but there's Barrow Creek, Tennant Creek, Daly Waters and several places in the outback. They all rely on transport. We'll be the only maintenance depot for miles.'

Ned brightened up. 'Then the sooner we're established, the better.' He negotiated a pile of stones. 'Is this still the main road?'

'Afraid so, old chap.'

'As I was saying, once we're settled in, I thought I'd offer to do repairs on the spot in the local homesteads, while you run the main workshop.'

'Sounds a good idea. Might take a year or two.'

To Ned this was far too slow but he didn't argue, he needed all his concentration on this stretch. Squashed beside him, with Margaret on her knee, Rose pointed to kangaroos leaping away through the bush.

Maisie asked, 'Have you ever tried cooking them? They're dreadfully tough but better than nothing if the pantry's bare.'

'Urgh!'

The trees were plentiful here despite the dried-up river beds. It was early, still only pleasantly warm. Instructed by Oswald they turned off the highway with Ned wrenching at the wheel to avoid thick scrub and rock.

'We shall have to re-do this track.' Oswald clung to the dashboard as they bounced up and down. 'I thought we might put up a sign to the depot.'

'Very necessary, I'd say.'

'Slow down, we're at the boundary – where you can see that red-painted stone, that's the marker.'

They were thirty miles or so north of Alice, in a shallow bowl of land inside a curve of low hills. A mixture of trees and thorn bushes was the only vegetation in the grassy plain beyond. Far more numerous were the dark, reddish-brown termites' nests, some of them nearly four feet high.

Rose gasped, 'Oh, Lord ...' Ants had been a pest at Malinga, furniture legs had to be wrapped in greaseproof paper and stood in shallow saucers of water to deter them, but what would *these* monsters be like?

The truck jolted past the last clump of grey scrub and there in front of them was the depot.

393

Ned found his voice, 'That's surely not it?'

What had once been a carefully levelled piece of ground was now choked with thorns. Beyond it, bordering a concreted area, parallel wooden posts supported sagging wire mesh laden with overgrown creepers.

Oswald said evenly, 'I was disappointed at first. Then I got to thinking about it. There are plenty of possibilities, Ned. I decided the first job would be clearing that area and cutting back the creeper. That mesh is intended to provide a shady parking for customers, d'you see.'

Ned was still too shocked by the dilapidation to commit himself.

'Let's show you the rest.' Oswald led the way to the corrugated sheds behind, pointing out distant landmarks that formed the boundary of the property. Ned wandered through them followed by Rose leading Margaret by the hand. The workshops were on solid concrete bases but full of rubbish and wornout machinery, apart from the final one.

Oswald slapped the old Ford car affectionately. 'What about this then? I don't think there's anything wrong with her, or that lorry over there. I queried that with the agents when I got back to Alice, they said both vehicles were included in the sale. It means you and I will have a truck each and Rose and Maisie can share the car. She's in working order, I tried the starting handle. She fired after a bit but the tank was empty.' He pointed to a generator. 'I had a look at that. All it needs is a thorough overhaul.'

'Aye, I can tell.' But Ned was recovering; this at least had once been a properly organized workshop. There were rows of rusting tools on hooks, a foot pump, some welding equipment. He asked, 'Did you discover how it got into such a state?'

'I chatted to one or two blokes in Alice. The previous owner and his son were drowned. They got washed away in a sudden flood trying to cross what had been a dry river bed. The widow decamped soon after. You can't blame her, living out here on her own. I reckon other people came by and helped themselves to odds and ends. Otherwise ...'

'Otherwise, sheer neglect. Where's the house?'

'This way.' They emerged into a hotter world and Margaret shouted with delight; near their old truck was an emu. Oswald immediately chucked a stone and the bird ran off. 'Pesky thing. It still thinks it's a pet but it could have a go at our tyres. Better see baby doesn't chase after it, Rose.'

Holding back the struggling child, she and Maisie followed round the back of the sheds where there was a solid-looking water tower and wind pump.

'I shinned up,' said Oswald. 'The pump's in working order as the agents promised and there's plenty of water.'

'Thank heaven for small mercies.'

'There's also a well. The water tasted sweet and clean. There you are, that's the house.'

About fifty feet away, behind a low wooden railing that had once been painted white, backed by glowing red poincianas and silvery gums, was a log cabin under an inverted vee-shaped, shingle roof. One side of the vee came down low, supported on poles and providing a shady area which was furnished with sagging cane chairs. Behind these was the door, masked by a flyscreen which creaked to and fro. Rose moved forward, pushed it aside and peered into the gloom.

The internal area, nearly forty feet long and twelve wide, was divided into four rooms, each opening onto the passage in which she stood. The rooms were paired, two and two, linked by an opening. The walls were the rough underside of the logs, the raised floors were of planking except where insects had eaten their way through. The windows had flyscreens, not glass, and were shuttered against the sun. The two rooms at either end had wide wooden-slatted platforms attached to the walls. Rose realized these were intended as bedsteads. A thought flashed into her mind – we haven't any mattresses – but what was one additional misery among so many?

Maisie had walked the length of the passage and called, 'The kitchen's down here – and a sort of bathroom.'

They trooped along to gaze at the iron stove and rickety

395

table standing on a piece of stained linoleum, protected by a corrugated-iron roof. Beyond, wooden screens fenced off a galvanized pipe which ended in a shower head. Ned examined it. The pipe was fed by a tank on stilts.

'That fills from the water tower,' Oswald told him. 'It's a long run and the pipe's perforated. I reckon we should change the system and have it fill via the underground supply instead.'

'How does the water heat up?' asked Rose. It was a stupid question but she wanted distraction from the horrible disappointment.

Both men managed to smile; Ned wiped away the sweat.

'It stands all day in the sun, pet. By night time, it's well-nigh boiling, shouldn't wonder. Where's the whatsit?'

'Over there. Maybe that should be our first job instead.' With a grim face, Oswald indicated the small wooden hut buzzing with flies. 'It's overflowing. The tank needs emptying and the soakaway will have to be re-dug.'

'Only to be expected, I suppose.' Ned's voice was carefully neutral. Neither man had expressed their feelings, they daren't. For one to give way would betray the other. 'What we'd better do is move the truck nearer the workshops. If we clean out the first one, we can store stuff in there temporarily. I didn't see too many ants. Provided we keep everything off the floor, it should be safe.'

'Before we do anything,' Maisie asked, 'can we taste that well water? I'm dying for a drink.'

'Good idea. It's over here.' Oswald led the way. 'It had a sort of thatched cover once but the supports must have given way.' He lifted up the metal disc. 'The bloke who made this knew what he was doing. Look what a tight fit this is – and see inside. The sides are clean, the footholds are secure. I climbed down to within sight of the bottom.'

'You daft ha'porth,' Maisie was horrified. 'On your own? You could've been drowned!'

'Well, I wasn't. But we'll have to watch out for baby. I reckon you'll have to fasten her to something solid when she starts wandering outside, Rose. Until she learns not to go too close. Take hold of the rope, Ned, we have to haul by hand because the handle needs fixing.'

Everything needed fixing, thought Rose in despair. All their wonderful dreams had vanished. They had marvelled at the bargain price, the amount of land that was included, the reliable water supply; they should have known better. Neither she nor Ned had thought to query the precise condition of the property.

The bucket appeared. She scooped a handful over her face and the coldness made her catch her breath.

'What absolute bliss!' She tilted back her head to let it trickle into her mouth, 'It tastes like champagne!' The relief at finding something to match their hopes made them laugh like children. Ned splashed Margaret as she held out chubby fingers to catch the drops.

'Here.' Maisie grabbed the bucket, 'We ought to drink a toast. Give us your hands.' She sloshed water into their palms. 'It's a bit more of a challenge than we expected but I expect we'll manage. Come on, Rose, say something appropriate.'

Slowly, Rose lifted cupped hands; I must have faith, she thought. Here's Oswald calmly planning what to do first – he knew what it was like but he didn't suggest to Maisie they pull out. She hadn't complained, either. They've invested their life savings, they trust us. Ned won't let them down and neither must I. She took a deep breath.

'To the shack in the wilderness and those who dwell therein. May we all prosper.'

'To the shack!'

Hard work, Ned had said. They had never worked so hard in their lives. It was decided the track to the highway was the first priority and this meant digging out flints, stones and thorny scrub before levelling the rock-hard dirt. Sometimes Rose and Maisie could barely drag themselves back to the shack at the end of the day. Ned felt guilty that women should do such heavy work but Rose reminded him wearily that partners should share the bad as well as the good.

Originally, they'd promised themselves a month, maybe two, to 'knock it into shape'. It took a further six before the track was finished and drainage ditches dug to prevent it being washed away in the first flood. Next they began to tackle the forecourt.

Hot weather arrived; they began work at dawn, stopped at midday and resumed again in the evening. Often they continued till midnight. One day a week, Rose and Maisie washed and baked, cursing the insects that were the ever-present enemy.

'Once we've got all the scrub cleared from round the shack,' Maisie panted, 'a few sweet-smelling climbers round the little hut should improve matters.'

Rose leaned on her fork. 'How long will that take?'

'Honeysuckle grew quickly enough at home. Given plenty of rain, of course.'

Rose flapped at the flies. 'What d'you mean, rain? I can't even remember what that looks like.'

Maisie managed a dutiful snort. 'Out here, it's wet, warm and there's not much of it, but when it comes, I shall strip off and stand there til I'm soaked – it'll be heavenly!'

One day, when it was too hot to do anything physical, Ned took Oswald aside. 'There's a hell of a lot still to be done but if we don't open for business soon, we could end up broke.' Perhaps it was his training as a butler but Oswald's placid expression didn't change.

'I was thinking the same thing myself. D'you mind if I make a suggestion?'

'Go ahead.'

'We should concentrate on setting up the workshops instead of worrying about our quarters. Increase stocks of spares and fuel and so on – then advertise. I've talked it over with Maisie. She doesn't mind if we all go on living in the shack. A place of our own isn't important at this stage.'

'It's very good of you both. I still think we need more help. At Malinga, we had the blacks,' Ned said slowly. 'We relied on them to do plenty of jobs during shearing. I know some people don't trust 'em but we never had any bother, probably because the boss treated 'em fairly. Let's put the word out in Alice. See if any turn up.'

That evening, when it was cool enough to sit outside, there was a discussion between the four of them.

'We ought to ask Captain Hislop if we can extend the loan,' Rose suggested. 'We need to fit the workshop out properly. You said there were several items you still needed to buy.'

'I'd hoped to spend a bit of money on making us all more comfortable,' Ned sighed. They were still sleeping on his old greatcoat stretched over the wooden slats. In their room at the opposite end, Maisie and Oswald managed with a couple of blankets.

Rose pushed back the hair that was plastered to her forehead. 'Luxuries come later. Right, Maisie?'

'Right.'

'Besides, I've had a look at the packing cases. Some of the crockery we ordered is packed in straw. If we buy calico, Maisie and I can make temporary mattresses using that.'

Ned looked at her gratefully. 'More work for you two, I'm afraid.'

Rose shrugged it off. 'It's important we open for business as soon as possible. You go into Alice and arrange the advertisements. Tomorrow I'll write to the captain about the loan. Shall I tell him when we expect to have the depot sign up?'

Ned glanced at Oswald. 'By the end of the week?'

'Why not.'

'I want to line the track with those old lorry tyres,' announced Maisie.

Ned frowned. 'Whatever for? Drivers might bump into them in the dark.'

'Not once I've painted 'em white,' she told him. 'I'm going to fill them with flowers. They'll lead the way into the depot.'

He stared. 'Maisie, even if we could get hold of seeds, flowers wouldn't survive; they'd die in this heat.'

'Not daffs and hollyhocks,' she said patiently. '*Australian* flowers. Cactuses, things like that. They look ever so bright when they're out. I want to pretty the place up.'

'Pretty it?' Rose was incredulous. That was the sort of remark women made when making their nests. For her the depot would never be anything but a savage wilderness, to be beaten back and tamed. Yet despite the privations, Maisie and Oswald obviously looked on it as home.

Why can't I see it in the same way, she wondered? Why was she the odd one out of the four? 'Must try harder!' Rose gave herself a mental shake.

'I think I should set up a proper office area, Ned. It'll be more businesslike having everything in one place.'

'You don't mean – build a room with a desk?'

She grinned. 'All I meant was, use one of the packing cases as a table. Out here on the verandah, where Margaret can play and I can keep an eye on her. And if we keep all our papers in biscuit tins on a shelf, maybe the ants won't get at them.'

From then on, with their own preferred tasks, work became less arduous. Instead of fretting over unanswered letters, Rose tackled these every morning. She gave a wry smile when Ned pointed out how much easier it would have been had she had those type-writing lessons. She began a routine monthly report to Captain Hislop, too; it might make future borrowings easier if he knew precisely how the company money was being spent.

She also took over the housework and cooking. Maisie's surprisingly heavy touch with pastry caused Ned to murmur to Oswald that perhaps his wife would prefer to stick to gardening full-time. Fortunately, Maisie was delighted and, while Rose rearranged the 'kitchen' to suit herself, sang happily and tunelessly as she laid out vegetable beds.

It was another few weeks before the first truck limped in for a major repair but, by then, Ned's reputation, as the right man to call on in an emergency had been established. The first oblique request had come via the postie.

'The generator needs fixing at the Cavanagh place.'

'What about Mr Cavanagh, why can't he mend it?'

'He's locked up in Alice. Went on a bender. Ain't likely to be let out before next week, he did so much damage.' Ned was still dubious. The postie dropped a casual hint. 'Mizz Cavanagh is a great talker. She's got friends in Daly Waters, Tennant Creek, all over the place. If she likes you, she'd spread the word quicker 'n lightning.'

Apart from the generator, a rear axle needed straightening and a warped door planed and rehung before Mrs Cavanagh declared herself satisfied.

'I'm really most grateful, Mr Harrison. Let me know what I owe, won't you. Even if Cav were here, that lot would've taken him a year to fix.'

'Would you like me to take a look at that old refrigerator while I'm here?' Ned offered tiredly.

'I've got myself a new one. You can have that if you like. Warn your wife it needs a good clean out.'

He returned home in triumph. Rose's eyes glowed when she saw it. 'A refrigerator, oh, Ned! Cool drinks ... maybe we could even risk buying butter again!' She almost salivated as she imagined the taste.

'Hang on, hang on. It doesn't work and we may not be able to mend it. Have you any idea how they work, Oswald?'

The former butler searched his memory. 'At my former establishment, there was a cool room, a dairy, a larder, a game larder, several cellars and an ice house at the bottom of the garden. I don't recollect a refrigerator.'

'Well, I can't quite see us building an ice house or a cellar,' said Maisie, 'so you two get your heads together, then when it's working I can make us ginger beer. It's the one thing I am good at.'

'With fresh food, we can think of offering refreshments to customers.' Oswald was optimistic. 'We should begin planning those overnight cabins, Ned. We'll need another water-tower fairly soon, to be on the safe side. We don't want to miss the chance of filling up during the wet.'

Ned felt overwhelmed, 'We definitely need more help.' He stared anxiously at Rose, 'Can we afford to pay a decent rate if I find someone in Alice?'

'I'm sure we can.' Later, as she examined their account books with fingers crossed, she thought, 'It's the best way I can help, by taking care of our finances. Just as I used to for Gertie.'

Two years later, in 1929, the depot was scarcely recognizable. The poincianas now reached out protective lower branches over the roof of the shack. The sign, DEPOT – REPAIRS, ACCOMMODATION, was in place on the highway, and down either side of the track, Maisie's tyres now spilled brilliant colours, leading the eye towards the parking area. To one side of it, tables and chairs were protected by bamboo screens. Customers who came in for a simple repair were offered light refreshments. Those who had to wait longer could have a hot meal and for travellers who needed an overnight stay, there were the two brand-new brightly painted wooden cabins. Most of all there was a thriving atmosphere about the place.

Meat was now delivered twice a week by a firm that kept Darwin supplied. Vegetables grew in the shadier patches of land behind the cabins where Maisie viewed the depredations of wild life tolerantly.

'If I get half a crop, I'm lucky but I do wish Oswald could bring himself to shoot that wretched emu.'

'Oswald did kill the snake,' Rose reminded her. 'You and I couldn't have tackled it.' The memory of it still gave her goosepimples.

'Good job Margaret spotted it before I stuck my fork in among the lettuces, that's all I can say.' Maisie giggled; for two north-east housewives, their conversation must sound distinctly odd.

Today for the twice-weekly wash, there were two galvanized tubs on a new concrete base close to the well. Rose went to wind up the bucket, ready for rinsing. From the sheds came the distant noise of welding and sawing. As well as repairing tractors and trucks, the men were constructing another three-roomed shack, destined this time for Oswald and Maisie. It would stand a short distance from the original one. Linking the two homes, Maisie had already planted a double row of saplings, now guarded by a small black boy with a stick, whose duty it was to keep the emu at bay.

The blacks had arrived unannounced one morning and were now installed in humpies beyond the second water tower. Their women had been recruited to help with weeding and housework; the men, wherever they could be useful. Today, as well as those working under Oswald's supervision in the sheds, two more youths were renewing the white-painted squares that divided up the parking lot. Tomorrow there would be plenty of work for everyone, when excavations began for the installation of new petrol tanks.

Another extended loan from the company, Rose remembered with a qualm. The suggestion for the tanks had come from Captain Hislop but the decision to go ahead had been hers. The four of them had discussed it, of course, but had finally accepted her advice. Very rarely did Ned or Oswald query her judgement.

Their money was paid into one bank account. After bills and a portion of the loan was repaid, a solemn ceremony took place on the first day of every month when Rose reported to the other three how things stood and whether they could withdraw their modest allowances. It was a matter of honour not to spend these unnecessarily. The new cabins were properly furnished but the shack was still the same and if either Oswald or Ned urged their wives to spend, the women convinced one another luxuries were unnecessary.

'Have you thought any more about schooling for Margaret?'

'Ned's already made enquiries. They can take her from the start of next term. She'll have to stay in Alice from Monday to Friday and come home for weekends. I thought of asking that

403

woman where we first lodged if she'd board her.'

'She'll miss her freedom, little minx.'

Rose began folding dry clothes while Maisie emptied the rinsing water into cans ready for watering. After nearly fourteen months of drought, not a drop would be wasted. At the sound of a familiar engine, both women looked up.

'Post!'

When they'd first arrived, the man refused to risk his van over the track. Now he pulled up smoothly on the forecourt. Maisie fetched a jug out of the fridge and took the glass across to where he sat at one of the tables.

'Beer?'

'Ta, Maisie. Where's my beaut, where's little Maggie?' He gave his special whistle and the child came tearing across from among the trees, brown-gold hair flying, dust spurting under her bare heels. Both arms went round the old man's neck.

'You're early!'

'No, I'm not. You were playing and you forgot the time. Here you are, some bills – and a letter for your Ma.' Margaret rushed away with them. The postie watched for a moment. 'Saw her dad out at the Williamses,' he told Maisie.

'He went over there the day before yesterday.'

'Ned said to tell Miz Harrison he'd serviced the tractor and hoped to be back tonight.' He downed the last of his drink and picked up the wide brimmed hat. 'Any messages?'

'Just let everyone know we're fine.' The usual reassurance passed from neighbour to neighbour along the line. When he'd gone, Maisie sought shelter on the shack verandah, it was so blisteringly hot.

Rose was seated in one of the old cane chairs, staring at her letter.

'Anything wrong?'

'This is from Mu. Bad news. I don't know how I'm going to break it to Ned.'

'Oh?' Maisie sat beside her.

'Hayden, his friend, has died.' Rose swallowed. 'He gave

me away at our wedding . . . he even brought his dog. She had to wait in the porch . . .'

After a moment or two, Maisie asked sympathetically, 'When did it happen?'

Rose checked the date and was distracted, 'Three – no, four months ago? Goodness, Mu must've forgotten to post this.'

'Was he an old man?'

'Not really. Ned was always hoping he'd come and join us but he had responsibilities of his own. Poor Hayden. He couldn't get a job, that's all he ever really wanted. Just an ordinary job, so that he could hold his head up. Life's too cruel for some people . . .'

'It is.' Maisie wiped away the sweat, 'We've been very lucky.' It was obvious Rose needed time to recover. 'Like a glass of water?'

'Yes, please.'

'Stay there. I'll fetch it.' She went in search of Margaret first. 'Mummy's got a headache, pet. Let's you and me leave her quiet for a bit, eh?' When she returned, Rose had finished the rest of the letter.

'According to Mu, things are very bad. Firms are closing early for Christmas and several aren't expected to re-open. I do wish Lionel would agree to come here. We could certainly use an extra pair of hands and their children would have a much better life.'

Maisie flicked at the flies. 'If things are that bad, they might. Why don't you and I decide where their cabin will be, then if I plant a few trees now, it'll be nice and shady by the time they come.'

Rose laughed. 'That's what I like about you, Maisie. Always the optimist.'

Maisie smiled. 'I had to be. Look how long it took before Oswald and I could be together. Any other news?'

Rose's mood switched. 'Just the usual remark from Mu about seeing Gertie and the boy in the town. Valentine was wearing school uniform this time. Oh, and a reference to the tabernacle looking shabby. According to Mu it needs a coat of paint.'

'I nearly forgot. The postie saw Ned. He expects to be back tonight.'

'Not too late, I hope. Margaret won't go to sleep until she's seen him and I shall have to – to break this news. It won't be easy.'

'No.' Maisie eased her sticky limbs out of the chair once more. 'When will you tell him?'

'After supper.'

'Take him for a bit of a walk. We'll look after Margaret.'

'Thanks.'

But after Rose had told him, the pain was deep and she could do little to comfort him. She nursed Ned as she would a child, trying to soothe away the agony.

'I owed him so much, Rose.'

'I know, dearest.'

'He gave me all he had so that I could win you. That half-sovereign was the only coin in his box.'

'Oh, Ned ...' She was shaken by that. 'I do so wish he could have come out here.'

Ned broke away from her and rubbed his eyes. 'How could he, with his mam and aunt depending on him.'

'We did send money that first Christmas,' she reminded him, gently. Over the years they must have sent five times the original loan.

When Ned replied, his voice was so low she barely caught the words. 'Aye ... but there's some debts you can never repay.'

Margaret returned from school one Friday afternoon to discover that Uncle Lionel had finally made his decision not to emigrate to Australia. As usual, her mother gave her the letter to read.

Lionel says he's too old to dig up his roots. I'm sorry but this time it's final and he won't change his mind. His friends are here, his mum and dad. He still manages to get work. He's worried he might not be able to settle in a

406

new country, same as Rose's sister Gertie and her hubby.

Maybe you could come here for a holiday? You know you're always welcome, especially Margaret. I talk to her photo whenever I dust it, ask her when she's coming to visit her Auntie.

Thanks for the money. We are buying new winter coats for the bairns.

Yours fondly, Mu.

Margaret waited until her mother had finished answering the phone to a customer.

'Winter coats – phew!' She pulled a face. 'That money was intended for auntie's birthday, wasn't it?'

Rose said severely, 'It was. Just be thankful we can afford to buy you a present as well as your clothes.'

'Why bother buying coats? When will they ever wear them?' Her daughter was already sloughing off shoes, socks and school uniform, padding off barefoot and half naked.

'In your bedroom with those things, please, Margaret, don't drop everything on the floor. You don't know how lucky you are, always feeling warm. And do your homework before you go out to play for once . . .' She was talking to the empty air.

If I'd behaved like that, Nanny would have complained to Mother, Rose thought, amazed. Such disobedience meant the cane, that thin flexible instrument which raised such painful weals.

She'd slapped Margaret once. It had upset Ned so much she'd never done so again. I'm a bad mother, far too easy-going, she thought. Maisie's right when she called Margaret a little minx. I wonder if Gertie ever has to chastize her boy?

'Oh, Gertie!'

Chapter Eighteen

Crisis at the Tabernacle, 1929

It was February, the coldest recorded month for thirty-four years. Not that Gertie Brigg had seen the reports. On the moors the drifts were over five feet deep. In the town, despite frantic efforts, the roads were treacherous with snow covering the thickest ice imaginable. No paper boy dare venture forth.

Other deliveries had failed to arrive. If Gertie didn't reach the shops today, they would dine on bread and butter, and not much butter either, she realized, checking supplies. No milk, scarcely an ounce of tea or sugar. It was essential she make the effort and go out. Schools were closed, Valentine was restless, he could help carry her basket. She opened the door a crack to test the wind.

'It's a blizzard!'

'Oh, mother! You always make such a fuss.' He'd ceased to be a little chap she could fuss over, he was now an impatient schoolboy. What was worse, he seldom obeyed her. Whenever Gertie raised her voice, he simply stared with those intelligent, unnerving eyes, waiting for her to finish.

'Is that it, Mother?' It was so *rude*.

Gertie would fling up her hands in protest. 'Don't you dare speak to me like that, I'm your mother.' Was there disbelief in those eyes? She could never be sure nowadays, not since that dreadful encounter in Albert Park. She'd never gone there since.

It was the day they'd purchased Valentine's first school uniform. Always eager to see him look smart, Gertie had insisted he put on his new clothes. He'd showed signs of rebellion even then. 'Do I *have* to, Mother? I'll only have to change out of them when we get back.'

'Of course. And naturally you'll take them off afterwards, new clothes cost money, Valentine. You must make those last as long as possible.' Her mouth was tight as she echoed Harold, 'Ethel Paige is a mean-spirited woman.'

Valentine hadn't understood at the beginning. Now, it was the refrain he disliked most. Once he'd asked, 'If Mrs Paige won't give Father enough money, why doesn't he find another church? A big one with more people?'

At this, Gertie had been vehement if not entirely coherent. 'The tabernacle is a sacred trust, Valentine. Besides, it's not affiliated, there can be no transfer. And it has given your father professional status. He's never had to demean himself since he met Walter Paige. It has enabled him to join the Brethren which was always his ambition.'

Alas, Harold had not even begun the ascent of that particular ladder. He remained on the bottom rung, another source of disappointment. Because of this, he failed to include Gertie in any of the social events which wives were permitted to attend.

'You wouldn't enjoy yourself, Gertrude. So many other women will take precedence. Far better wait until I have been given advancement.' So Gertie waited. She sighed more to herself than Valentine, over these various disappointments.

'Your Father will have to remain at the tabernacle until he reaches pensionable age.'

A pension was money given to poor old men, Valentine knew. How old was Father? He looked frightfully ancient because of his silly hair. Those insecure strands which bounced like greasy black string when he got in a lather. As soon as he uttered the word 'sin' it brought them tumbling round his ears.

Valentine was bored with sin. He'd once asked what everyone had done that they needed to apologize to God quite so often. That had brought forth condemnation: Middlesbrough was a sink of iniquity whose inhabitants were unable

409

to control their depravity. When he'd asked what that word meant, he'd been sent to bed without his supper.

Punishment could be shrugged off. He was a tall, gangling boy. His feet were large, his face, apart from his eyes, solemn. He was also far more intelligent than his parents realized. He too remembered that encounter in the park, not that he dwelt on it nowadays.

On that occasion, the new leather shoes squeaking and stiff, he and his mother had walked along familiar paths, gravitating towards the lake. His mother held back, it was always so *damp* down there, but Valentine had rushed ahead. If he'd got to be paraded he was jolly well going to go where he wanted.

A woman was sitting on one of the benches watching the ducks. She was very smart with short dark hair and her eyes seemed to sum him up at a glance. As he drew alongside she spoke his name: 'Val?'

He stopped. Only friends called him that; at home his parents were strict. Out of sight, he could hear his mother's voice, faint, plaintive: 'Wait for me, Valentine.'

He had stared at the strange woman. Something about her was familiar. She was smiling.

'You've grown,' she said. 'You're very like your father.'

'Yes.' He knew that from the mirror when he brushed his hair.

There was another, more urgent call from his mother and the stranger said quickly, 'Do you know who I am?'

'No, madam.' He hoped he hadn't made a mistake but he couldn't remember her from the congregation. There weren't many strangers unless it was holiday time and none were ever as pretty as this. He made polite conversation. 'I'm five and a quarter and I start at junior school next term.'

'Do you? I think I can guess the date of your birthday.'

'Can you really?' When she did, he was impressed. His mother arrived, panting. She saw the woman and instinctively clutched at her fur. As she'd fallen silent, Valentine assumed his mother was out of breath.

'Mother, this lady knows who I am.'

410

'Come away!'

'She even knows when I was born.'

'Come *away*!' Behind the glasses, his mother looked terrified, he'd no idea why. She said peremptorily, 'Did you hear what I said, Valentine? Come with me at once.'

But he didn't want to offend the strange lady. 'I'm sorry, I don't remember you at all.'

'We met a long time ago.'

'Did we—'

His mother's screech drowned his reply. She was dragging at his sleeve, almost tearing the precious new blazer. 'Valentine, you must never disobey me again, do you hear? I shall ask Father to beat you if you do.'

He had managed to snatch one last look: the strange lady was being naughty. She had her head hunched over her bag and was lighting a cigarette. Father said women who did that in public were 'handmaids of the devil'.

Gertie had trembled all the way home. She had insulated herself from reality for all these years. To have her delusions blown apart in an instant, and by such a smart, attractive, self-possessed woman, was bitter indeed. She didn't tell Harold of the encounter; she forbade Valentine to speak of it. As far as she was concerned, it had never occurred. She blotted it out of her mind, she had to: the very idea of confessing the truth was impossible.

Today in the bitter arctic weather with Valentine stumbling beside her, Gertie slithered her way to the corner shop. There were no buses or trams, not another person to be seen. Even the milk-woman with her pony and trap had stayed at home.

The fierce cold frightened her: if only Harold hadn't had to go to the tabernacle, but Ferguson, the handy man, had arrived with a gloomy face to announce that snow had brought down a section of roof. 'I warned you the wind had got under those tiles, Mr Brigg. Must've loosened them altogether. I was passing this morning and I saw this ruddy great hole—'

411

'Yes, yes.' Harold had never put aside the regular sum for maintenance demanded by Ethel Paige. As he saw it, such a thing wasn't possible when his salary couldn't support the standard of living he judged essential to his own well-being. As a result there was a list of jobs waiting to be done but this disaster couldn't be ignored. He'd donned coat, hat, scarf, gloves and galoshes and disappeared into the storm. Gertie had no idea when he would return. Ferguson had been doubtful whether any workmen would agree to come out, either.

'Why should they if it means a ladder, Mr Brigg? A man couldn't risk it in this weather – he might fall and break his neck.'

Did that mean Harold would have to climb up himself? Was it wise for her clumsy husband to attempt such a feat? Next minute, sleet making her glasses opaque, Gertie had lost her footing and tumbled heavily. 'Valentine!'

'Oh, Mother!' He was on his knees, pulling at her arm, 'Get up, please get up!' She could hear the fright in his voice, he wasn't a troublesome schoolboy any more, he was her little man again, dependent on her. 'Please, Mother!'

'I'm all right ... I think. I can't see, that's the trouble.'

'Here.' He rubbed the sleet off the lenses. The world came back into focus. Gertie's hands were numb as she struggled on to all fours. She felt her knees poke through torn stockings.

'Goodness, suppose someone sees me like this?'

'Oh, Mother!' She could see the tears on his face, he was shivering with fear and cold. 'No one's anywhere *near*. Let's go home.'

'We have to buy food. Give me your arm.'

It was the shop she most wanted to avoid but the weather prevented them going further. The shop-keeper emerged from the back, astonished to hear the bell but this particular customer wasn't even welcome.

Gertie steeled herself. 'Good morning, Mr Palin. What terrible weather.'

'Mrs Brigg.' He reached beneath the counter and produced a red ledger. Thumbing through, he found the relevant page.

412

'Seven pounds, ten shillings and fourpence outstanding.'

Gertie straightened her shoulders. 'It hasn't been possible for my husband to visit the bank, Mr Palin.'

'Nothing to stop him giving me a cheque. Always assuming it would be honoured.'

Her head was throbbing, her knees were stiffening from the fall but they had to eat, she couldn't afford to be offended. 'Mr Palin, I assure you my husband will settle our account in full as soon as it's safe to walk abroad. Meanwhile—'

'Meanwhile, Mrs Brigg, if you want to buy from my shop, you pays cash. No more credit.'

'Very well.' Her mother would have scorned to be treated so. How the world had changed! Gertie couldn't afford either anger or shame. Her thoughts raced, she had about two shillings and some coppers in her purse, that was all. Say, two and threepence at the most. She began to calculate as simultaneously she reduced her order to the bare essentials, 'A quarter of tea, a pint of milk . . .'

'No milk. We haven't had a delivery for five days.' He put a small tin of evaporated milk on the counter and Gertie tried to remember the price.

'Mother—'

'Hush, dear!' She daren't lose track. 'Six penn'orth of mixed root vegetables – have you any marrow bones?'

The shopkeeper sneered, 'Didn't know you kept a dog.'

'We don't,' Valentine said promptly.

'Half a stone of flour. And yeast.'

'No yeast. We've sold out.'

'Any eggs?'

'I can let you have half a dozen.'

'How much is that?' Harold's next salary wasn't due until the first of March, there were still two weeks to go!

'Two and fourpence three farthing.'

Her hands were stiff and shaky, she couldn't manage the clasp.

Valentine took the purse. 'I can do it, Mother.' He looked up in surprise. 'There's only one and tenpence halfpenny.'

Damn! She must have forgotten paying someone? Oh, of course, the coalman last Saturday. She had to brazen it out, they couldn't exist with less.

'Kindly add the balance to my account, Mr Palin. My husband will settle as soon as humanly possible.'

The man was surly. These days far too many tried to press for credit.

'This is the very last time. Not another penny, Mrs Brigg.'

Red-faced, Gertie handed over her basket and the pathetic purchases were put inside. Nothing but soup and dumplings – had she any suet? She couldn't remember but she daren't ask for some. Valentine took the basket and held open the door. Snow blinded them as they made their way home.

In the tabernacle, Harold was deeply depressed. Ferguson had not exaggerated the size of the hole. From inside they could gaze up through an opening roughly four feet square. The cause was obvious. Tiles, loosened in earlier gales, had let in rain-water which had frozen and expanded. With increasingly heavy snow, the ceiling below had finally given way. Lumps of ice and powdered plaster covered the pews and floor. Snow continued to fall. Harold brushed flakes aside impatiently; he needed a scapegoat.

'I blame Mrs Paige. If she had not been so parsimonious—'

'Nay, let's get the furniture shifted and the hymn books stacked out of the wet. We can sort out who's responsible later. Come on, Mr Brigg. It'll take the two of us to lift this ...'

Reluctantly, Harold allowed himself to be coerced into manual labour, even taking a turn with the mop and bucket. He felt like Canute trying to stem the tide.

'If we sets the ladder on the table, we might just get enough height.'

'You don't mean – the superintendent's table?'

'There's nowt else will take our weight, Mr Brigg. We need to sling the tarpaulin under the beams so that it'll catch the worst of it. You can't risk more snow falling inside, look how much damage has been done already. As soon as we can, we

414

must find a proper firm to see to the roof.' Ferguson shook his head, 'It won't come cheap, especially during this spell. I hope the tabernacle's well insured.' But that was something else Harold had never managed to afford.

Ferguson disappeared in search of tarpaulin and ropes and Harold mopped desultorily in the soft, freezing silence, the snow falling down the back of his neck if he ventured too close to the hole.

'This is pointless ... This is absolute nonsense. I shall complain to Mrs Paige in the strongest possible ...' but he paused, recollecting the reply to his Christmas letter which had obviously contained too much protest.

'Walter and I were disturbed and annoyed by the tone of your many requests,' Ethel had written. 'Also the lack of information when we had specifically asked certain questions concerning the tabernacle. These I list again.'

Harold had tossed that page aside, they were the same every year: by how many had the size of the congregation increased, what maintenance had been done, had the outside been painted as required in the terms of the lease? Etc. etc. There had also been a figure suggested for insurance purposes.

He'd made the mistake, the first year, of exaggerating the membership. Ethel had congratulated him, pointing out how the larger collections must have enhanced his salary. She had recommended setting aside various sums to pay for a pension and Valentine's education but she hadn't said a word about an increase to the £300 per annum.

It would have been possible for he and Gertie to live within their means but Harold had never been convinced of the necessity. He sallied forth in elegant clothes, living testimony to the power of prayer. At the beginning of his ministry he suggested that Gertrude and Valentine might like to accompany him on his promenades but when his wife explained she would need a smart new hat, he realized it wasn't necessary: he alone was sufficient advertisement.

He quickly became recognized as the tabernacle superintendent. He convinced himself the very sight of his tall manly figure would remind sinners of their guilt. Waiters at the King's Head, seeing their regular luncheon customer, would remember they had to repent. At Hintons, the pretty waitress serving his tea would find her thoughts turning to sin. The fact that none of these back-sliders had so far appeared at the tabernacle was a mere trifle. If Christianity had been struggling for nearly two thousand years then Harold Brigg could afford to be patient.

If only Ethel Paige would co-operate! Had he been in any other employment, Harold was convinced that by now his salary would have risen. The cost of living had increased dreadfully and the value of money had slumped. In Germany, men needed wheelbarrows when visiting the bank yet Ethel remained impervious to any appeal, preferring instead to carp. As for Easter gifts, these had dwindled. Only a book-token for Valentine last year, nothing for Gertrude or himself except Walter's confounded best wishes, of course; those were as abundant as ever.

Harold quickly tired of his present task and, finding a dry spot, sat to consider his circumstances. He had tried so hard. Over the years, he had given Gertrude permission to conduct Bible classes for mothers and children, as well as prayer meetings for older women. He himself conducted an hourly meeting every Monday evening for young men on the threshold of manhood, an hour of contemplation to increase their awareness of sin. Afterwards it was his custom to call on Mrs Porteous. She who had once spurned his efforts on Rose's behalf was now grateful for his company.

Friendship had, to his great satisfaction, finally been consummated by love. At least that was how Harold thought of it. His initial overtures had been indignantly repulsed. On that first occasion, Harold had been made aware the lady's welcome extended to two glasses of sherry, nothing more. But time had increased her loneliness. Mrs Porteous discovered that a woman's reputation, once lost, can never be regained. Female friends had disappeared entirely. Gentlemen, she discovered, regarded her in a different light and, on being

416

informed their desires were not to be gratified, failed to return.

Harold Brigg had more determination than most, he had continued to call. It was true he'd considered seeking consolation elsewhere but had finally rejected the notion. He was known in the town, among the Brethren also; in his role as a guardian of morals he couldn't afford to be seen with any of Ruby Winnot's successors.

He appeared on Monday nights as though nothing had happened. After six months he tried his luck again. Mrs Porteous wearily agreed, not because his charms were any more enticing but because she feared losing the only friend she had. Alone in the great empty house, she sometimes wondered if she would go mad. Harold was, at least, presentable. He kept her amused with gossip from meetings and events to which she was no longer invited. There was another reason. That brief affair, the cause of all her misery, had awakened dormant appetites which none but a lover could satisfy. As no lover was available, Harold Brigg would have to suffice.

There was no butler to admit him nowadays. Eloise had left. The only domestic was a bad-tempered crone who rarely heard the bell. Mrs Porteous opened the door and led the way to the small sitting-room. She invited him to fill his glass – he helped himself to brandy not sherry nowadays – and when pressed to Harold's tempestuous breast, indicated the sofa.

She declined to climb the stairs and risk being seen by her attendant. She wasn't prepared to have passers-by notice the electric light in her bedroom so early in the evening. Whatever her need, or that of Harold Brigg, these days Mrs Porteous had a keenly developed sense of self-preservation: they would remain here in this room.

Harold put down his glass and began to fumble with the fastenings on her lace gown. She had closed her eyes but almost immediately opened them again. 'A moment, Harold.'

God! He couldn't stop now. 'What is it?' He hadn't meant to sound so tetchy.

'The door. Turn the key so that we cannot be interrupted.'

He raced across the room and back again, braces undone,

417

trousers sagging. Her gown, already loose across her shoulders, sank to the floor. Taking care, Mrs Porteous stepped out of it. Harold leapt upon her and the sofa rocked ominously.

'Perhaps we'd better ... on the rug,' she whispered faintly. Her crêpe-de-Chine underslip was above her knees, she moaned a little, not from ecstasy but in dispirited acknowledgement that she had crossed the Rubicon: this was how it would be every Monday evening from now on. Harold entered her enthusiastically. He crowed with delight as her slip fell from her shoulders revealing a perfect bosom, much more enticingly rounded than Gertrude's.

'Let Big Bear have a taste!'

'Not so loud!'

Although he now arrived home much later on Monday evenings, Gertie noticed her husband was in a far better temper. The brandy fumes were equally apparent. Apart from instructing the young on sin, he had obviously enjoyed a further assignation. She stifled curiosity. He had stuck to his word and left her in peace. Like Valentine's birth, some mysteries were better left unresolved. She was thankful she had never followed Ethel Paige's advice and told the boy about his adoption. That might have led to awkward questions, delving into a past she preferred to leave undisturbed.

Gertie had resolutely closed her eyes on the incident in the park, convinced any explanation would only upset Valentine. That the sharp-eyed woman who knew *her* son's name was connected in any way ... Gertie drew back from acknowledging who she must be. When he was older, perhaps. But the longer Gertie delayed, the more difficult it became. Finally she decided that Valentine might be *harmed* by the knowledge. She also guessed she might be, too, if she enquired too closely into Harold's affairs.

After the unpleasantness at the corner shop, Gertie sent the boy to bed and huddled over a fire, small and damped down to conserve supplies; it was doubtful if the coalman's horse and cart could venture forth at present. There was little

418

comfort in her home these days. There had been once, when they'd first returned from Australia and Harold's needs had been less extravagant. What fun she'd had arranging and re-arranging her possessions in her new, if modest home. After-noons spent deciding how she would lay the dinner table, which pretty tablecloth, which napkins. She and the maid spent hours displaying flowers and candles to best advantage. Not that Harold ever commented on their efforts.

As soon as she realized their income was disappearing too quickly, she had tried to implement a budget, the way Rose had shown her. Harold refused to be governed by it. In the end, Gertie gave up. It was easier; it meant her husband lost his temper less frequently.

Tonight she crouched close to the fire. The heat burned her legs but the cold lapping at the back of her ankles made her chilblains itch. When the front door opened, the force of the wind lifted the carpet and caused smoke to pour down the chimney.

She greeted her husband with the latest dismal news from the wireless. 'The Danube is frozen for a distance of over twelve hundred miles. They say conditions could get worse.' Harold didn't give a fig for Europe, his problems were closer to home.

'We have a crisis on our hands, Gertrude. Thanks to Ethel Paige's parsimony, we now face a bill for close on a hundred pounds.'

'What!'

'That is the estimate for repairing the roof. But first, let us have supper?' He stretched his hands to the fire. 'I am chilled to the bone and exceedingly hungry.'

'Valentine and I have already eaten.' Hugging her cardigan round herself, Gertie hurried through to the kitchen. Annie, the maid, had gone to stay with her elderly parents when the first bad weather had threatened. Gertie was thankful; it was one less mouth to feed. The shock of Harold's remark made her feel sick: a hundred pounds? They couldn't possibly . . .? He must be saying it to frighten her. She stirred the contents of the pan.

Standing in the doorway Harold observed the various changes. 'What's all this?'

'Nightlights to stop the pipes freezing rather than use up paraffin. I can't afford another delivery at present. Harold, next time you go out, would you please give Mr Palin a cheque. We owe him over seven pounds.'

'Housekeeping is your responsibility, Gertrude, not mine.'

'I haven't any money left.'

'Use your bank book.'

She was scornful. 'That account was closed because it was empty, you know perfectly well.'

He brushed an agitated hand across his thin locks. 'Gertrude, I cannot conjure up extra funds.'

'You keep me so short, how can I manage? It's not fair!'

'I pay the rent,' he thundered, 'I also pay the rates, what more do you expect?'

'Harold, after Annie's wages, I am left with fewer than thirty shillings for food and clothes. Valentine has grown these last few months – I simply cannot manage.'

The soup boiled over, the disaster compounded by Gertie's tears. 'You go out every evening,' she wailed, 'you spend money on drinks for the Brethren and goodness knows what else. Don't deny it, because I can smell your breath.'

'Not a drop of alcohol has passed my lips today,' he was genuinely irritated, 'would to God it had, for I am *perished*. What's this?'

'Soup. With bread and a cup of tea. Don't complain. Valentine and I had the same.'

'Gertrude, in this weather a man needs sustenance.'

'So do we but that's all there is.' She picked up the tray. 'I'm not using the dining-room, to save on the gas fire. You can have this on your knee in the living-room, as we did.'

'*Standards*, Gertrude—'

'They cannot be maintained on thin air!'

His meagre collation consumed, Harold waited until his wife had washed up. 'Gertrude, I was not exaggerating when I used the word crisis. The tabernacle has been badly damaged by the elements. It is unusable until the roof is repaired.'

'Shouldn't you claim on the insurance?'

'We have no insurance! Dammit, woman, you know as well as I—'

'Don't swear at me, Harold!'

'There was never enough spare cash.'

'Ethel intended you to use the collection money. She's reminded you every Christmas.'

He sulked. 'The collections were never as large as she imagined.'

'That's because you told fibs.' It was said without rancour, who was she to criticize? 'So what do we do? You can't *put off* having it mended and you'll have to pay Mr Palin or we'll starve.'

'I am beset from every side!' Harold ran his hands through the thin strands. 'Can you not spare me from domestic harassment at least?'

'You must have *some* savings, you can't have spent all of your salary? Mrs Beamish across the road, her husband runs a little car and they don't have more than six pounds a week.'

'Gertrude, Beamish is a commercial traveller. I cannot take luncheon at some low café. When I am seen abroad by members of our congregation, they need to have confidence in their superintendent.'

'As if any of them would venture into The Star and Garter! Valentine and I have had nothing but bread and butter for lunch for days!' she cried.

'This is getting us nowhere. We shall have to sell some item to raise sufficient money—'

'What, for instance? We don't own the furniture.'

'Your silver dressing-table set – a useless bauble—'

'Oh, no.' She was adamant. 'The only treasure I have left. You shan't have that. You threw away that valuable mahogany table . . .'

'I did not throw it away! Those relatives of Harrison's stole it.' He forced himself to be calm. 'Gertrude, we cannot afford domestic help. When Annie returns, you will have to give her notice.'

421

'No!'

'Valentine isn't an infant, the housework here is trivial.'

Gertie quivered with rage. 'We don't pay her that much.'

'Her wage will contribute towards Palin's account at least. As for the roof ...'

'Well?' She stood over him like a virago. 'Are you going to admit to Ethel you have no insurance?'

'Of course not.' But with Harold, hope sprang eternal even in the worst quandary. 'You don't think however ... an approach to Rose ... A request to her and Harrison to extend their existing loan?'

Hysterical laughter threatened to choke Gertie. In his bedroom, Valentine woke with a start. He looked at the heavily frosted window pane. Were there banshees outside? Gradually he realized it was his mother. He also heard his father's rumble. Finally, when it was quiet, he hunched back into a ball to try and keep warm.

Downstairs Harold attempted dignity. 'It was merely a suggestion, Gertrude.'

She blew her nose and adjusted her glasses. 'The most stupid one you've ever made. Now, if you really have no money you'll have to borrow enough to mend the roof. As the only security you can offer is the tabernacle you'll have to repay as quickly as possible, before Ethel discovers what's happened.'

'If we took out a loan, the most I can afford to repay – if I cut my life to the bone – would be ten shillings a week. Gertrude, it would take years!'

'Then we must do as other churches, organize sewing bees, sales of work, jumble sales and so on.' She nearly added, 'You'll have to work for your living for a change.'

'That would degrade the house of the Lord.'

'Nonsense.' Gertie never thought of the tabernacle as a consecrated place; to her it was simply a building. 'And we'll do it together or not at all. I'll organize the sewing but you must certainly play your part.' She rose. 'I'm off to bed. If you want a wash tonight, you'll need to boil a kettle.'

'Why? What's wrong with the geyser?'

'It isn't working. I think the hot-water tank may be frozen.'

She added as he uttered his first groan, 'Let us pray our landlord has had the foresight to pay his insurance,' and went upstairs.

The Brethren were unsympathetic, their conditions for lending money were stringent. Harold applied to Mrs Porteous instead. Her terms were even more usurious; he could have the sum at two and a half per cent per annum but all sexual favours were denied until he had repaid every penny. He did his wretched calculations again; the most he could put aside, if he gave up lunching in style, would be one pound a week. Nearly two years before he could again taste those delightfully rounded ... it was monstrously unfair! Defeated, dejected, Harold accepted her offer but, within a month, fate smiled on him.

The terrible winter was followed by a lean spring. A shaky north-east economy could not withstand the ravages as the Depression increased. More businesses closed. Those out of work could not afford to put money in the collection plate. The congregation dwindled to the old who were conscious of life's shortening span or children whose parents wanted rid of them for an hour on Sunday afternoons. Valentine was an additional cause of pain: he'd begun to question why he was forced to attend morning and evening services when his friends were permitted to play.

He was level with Gertie's shoulder now, too big to spank, not yet amenable to reason. What would happen when he was taller still? Gertie trembled. Why couldn't he have remained sweet-natured? There was a row of photographs on the mantelpiece: Valentine on each birthday morning. He looked so charming in that velvet Fauntleroy jacket she'd made for him. Today in jersey and shorts he positively glowered.

'Mother, I asked you a question.'

'Don't you use that tone to me!'

'Why won't you answer?'

423

She tried to coax. 'You know your father relies on you to carry the collection plate, that's why we need you at both services.'

'Anyone could do that.'

'You're so reliable. Besides, there's the Carnival procession at Easter – our Sunday school has been allocated half a float this year – we'll need a reliable person to be in charge of that.'

'Not me, thanks.' He scuffed a chair leg but Gertie restrained herself.

'Why ever not?'

'If you must know, Mother . . . I'm sick of being laughed at. Chaps at school make rude remarks about Father, you know.' Red-faced, he lunged for the door.

'Where are you off to now?'

'I'm going to play with Raymond.'

'No, Valentine, you mustn't.' She hurried after him down the passage, 'He's not a nice boy at all.'

'Oh, Mother! Of course he is, he's my best pal.'

'But his father . . .' It was no use, he was beyond the gate. How difficult to make him understand that a boy whose father was only a postman was not a suitable companion for a superintendent's son. Gertie found herself wondering whether Rose had similar problems, then she remembered that Margaret's father was Ned Harrison. The Raymonds of this world would be perfectly adequate companions for *her*.

The following Monday evening, Harold returned home in an irritable frame of mind. 'Gertrude, it has become a matter of urgency to repay the loan more quickly. Apart from our tabernacle activities – and certainly the whist drives are proving popular, we gained a profit of eight shillings and fourpence last week – it is imperative we reassess our position.' He placed on the table a pad of paper and pencil. 'I want us to make a careful examination of our spending as I'm sure additional economies can be made.'

Gertie thought quickly. 'Very well, Harold.' Deceptively docile, she sat, wrote, and pushed the pad across. 'I shall be glad to demonstrate it can't be done. See . . . these are the bills

I pay every week. Every item is essential.'

'Yes, but—'

'At the end of the week, if I'm lucky, I have a few pence left over.'

'Almost a shilling to spend on yourself, you mean.'

Gertie gave him a long, cold stare. 'You are not suggesting that I should contribute *that* to your repayments ...?' His mouth opened but nothing emerged. 'I'm saving to repay Rose. I don't care how long it takes,' Gertie declared passionately, 'my conscience won't leave me in peace. I wake up remembering that debt. Before I die, Rose must have the entire sum.'

On a bob a week there wasn't much chance of that. The only economy left to them was to move into rooms but Harold hadn't the courage to tell his wife directly. He was wondering how to fudge an explanation when the door bell rang.

'Mr Clayton to see you, Harold.' Gertie withdrew and Harold reluctantly offered his guest the chair nearest the fire. Clarence Clayton was hovering between youth and manhood, impeded by acne and a lack of judgement. He needed an idol to worship and believed he'd found one in Harold. He attended every service and joined in social activities but so far Harold hadn't singled him out; Clarence Clayton needed praise as much as a plant needs water. He clasped his hands in supplication.

'Mr Brigg ...'

'Yes, Mr Clayton.'

'Please, call me Clarence.'

'Very well.' Harold assumed a benign expression and hoped this wouldn't take long.

'I come to bear witness of sin, Mr Brigg.'

'In what way?'

'I know I am a poor, unworthy creature—'

'We are all unworthy creatures, Clarence.'

'But I am willing to confess in order to receive redemption.'

'Of course.' Every member of the tabernacle was willing to do that.

425

'But there are those who are *unwilling* to confess, Mr Brigg. They are even more miserable sinners than I am.' Clarence's eager shining face made Harold uneasy.

'I don't think I quite follow?'

'My next-door neighbour, Mr Brigg. He's a sinner. I know because I saw him do it.'

'Do what?'

'Her on the other side, she'd been washing her best sheets. She'd only put them on the bed because they'd laid out her aunty that used to live with them. She wanted to do her best because of people coming to pay their respects. The line goes across the alley, Mr Brigg.' He paused to make sure Harold was still with him. 'Anyway, I was up in my room. I hadn't gone to work because of my asthma. I saw him on the other side come from the outhouse, look round to see if anyone was watching, then nip into the alley and take those sheets. He was back indoors, quick as a flash.'

Harold frowned, 'Why should he bother to steal bedding?'

Clarence was astonished. '*Linen* ones, Mr Brigg. Uncle's willing to lend anyone seven and six on linen sheets, no questions asked.'

The rates offered by pawnbrokers were one of life's mysteries.

Harold pursed his lips. 'What did you do?'

'I prayed for guidance, Mr Brigg.'

'I should have thought prayer was unnecessary. Surely if the police were informed ...?'

Clarence said sadly, 'He's a very big man, Mr Brigg. He'd still be there, and so would I, long after the police had gone. That's why I prayed. And the Lord heard my prayer. He knew I was frightened. He told me what to do. I heard his voice as clear as I hear yours.'

Harold was interested: hitherto, none of his parishioners had claimed a direct communication.

'What did He say?'

'He said I should bear witness in front of the full congregation, Mr Brigg. I must pray that my neighbour will see the error of his ways and confess his sin. That would mean he'd

426

have to give Mrs Ives back her sheets. There's a lot of the congregation know him, you see. They'd be on my side.'

Harold saw the logic; Clarence needed the protection of the entire membership of the tabernacle. But there was still the risk of slander. 'I think we must pray in more general terms. Be less specific. We need not mention the sheets were linen, for instance.'

His supplicant's face fell. 'The Lord was quite specific, Mr Brigg. I heard Him.'

Harold assumed his most authoritative aspect. 'When I, as superintendent, rise from my place and invite you to bear witness – you must pray for the sinner to repent. You can name him if you wish but do not describe the stolen items in any particular detail. Do you think you can manage that, Clarence?'

'Oh, yes, Mr Brigg.'

'And you are quite certain it happened just as you described? You were not mistaken?'

'No, Mr Brigg. Shall I do it at both services?'

'The evening one will be sufficient.' It was more sparsely attended, there would be less risk. On the following Sunday Harold invited Clarence to say his piece.

It was a passionate denunciation, well rehearsed. People awoke from their torpor. Whispers spread among the dozen or so who were present. Rumour spread like wildfire throughout the neighbourhood. Clarence kept well away from the thief but the shame that the sin was now public knowledge reached the man and had its effect. The linen sheets were retrieved from the pawnbrokers. Late one night they were stuffed inside their owner's backdoor.

The following Sunday a radiant Clarence stood beside Harold as together they gave thanks for redemption of both sin and bedlinen. Among the congregation – much larger this week – arms were raised as others remembered wrong-doers and queued up to 'bear witness'. At the finish, the collection plate contained at least thirty pieces of silver: Harold Brigg had struck gold.

427

Chapter Nineteen

A Visit to Sydney, 1932

'Ned, are you there?' Rose thought she recognized the legs protruding from beneath the road grader but she couldn't be sure. It was encouraging to see another of these machines in for servicing. With the company's backing, she had tendered for and won the contract. Maintaining machinery used to resurface the highways meant a regular income which was highly satisfactory.

Ned slid out from beneath the digger. 'Got a problem?'

'No, an invitation, for all four of us. Captain Hislop has a proposition to make. He suggests you and I visit Sydney to hear what he has to say.'

'Sydney? You mean he's not coming here?'

'He thinks it's time we had a break instead.'

'That's decent of him.'

'He suggests we take a fortnight off. Once we've heard about it, we come back and discuss it with Oswald and Maisie, then they can go down for their two weeks and give him our answer. He also suggests we take Margaret.'

That made Ned very happy. 'A proper family holiday! Does he drop any hints as to what it's about?'

'Not a word.' Rose held out the letter but he indicated his filthy hands.

'Give me the gist.'

'All he says ...' Rose found the place, '"a proposition which the company hopes might interest you." There's a bit about how pleased they are with our continued progress ... etc, etc.

Oh, and he asks if you and Oswald could estimate the size of the remaining land from behind the building line of the cabins to the edge of the boundary.'

Ned frowned. 'All the empty scrub?'

'Sounds like it.'

'There was a sort of estimate with the original paperwork but it wasn't very accurate.'

'If you and Oswald drive round the boundary and measure it that way, it would probably do. A few more photographs might help.'

Ned nodded. 'Those you sent at Christmas were certainly appreciated. Does he suggest a date?'

' "As soon as possible." Once we let him know, he'll book us in at a hotel – at company expense.'

'My word!' he grinned. 'It must be some proposition.' Taking care not to dirty her blouse, he gave her a hug. 'All due to your clever management, my pet.'

'And your hard work, and Oswald's. Not to mention Maisie's gardening.' Rose found excitement bubbling up as the prospect took hold. 'What shall I tell him? How soon can we be ready?'

'You and Oswald work it out, he'll be the one left to cope.'

Fortunately Oswald's curiosity was as great as their own.

'The end of next week would suit me. Maisie's dying to know what it's about.'

She was also ready with advice. 'You'll need a decent outfit, Rose. Women are smart in Sydney, I remember remarking on it at the time. Nearly as posh as in Darlington.'

'I shall go shopping once we get there,' Rose promised.

'Bring back plenty of magazines,' she pleaded, 'I want time to plan my wardrobe.'

'Women!' Oswald pretended to be disgusted. 'An important proposition and all they can think of is clothes.'

'Oh, I haven't forgotten you,' Maisie assured him, 'when it's our turn, I'm going to buy you a new shirt.'

*

At ten years old, Margaret couldn't decide whether she wanted to go or not. Some classmates were jealous, others tried to frighten her.

'There are thousands of motor-cars, you'll probably get run over.'

'No, I won't.'

'What will you do if you get lost?'

Margaret Muriel Harrison knew the answer to this one. 'Find a policeman,' she said firmly, 'ask him the time and then tell him who my mummy and daddy are. He'll know where to look.'

The prospect of a train journey conquered her fears but various strictures, concerning hotels, revived them.

'You will not drop your clothes all over the place,' her mother instructed. 'You will keep your shoes on *at all times* and you will wear your hat and gloves when we go out. D'you hear?'

'Yes, Mummy.'

'And you are not to wander off alone. Sydney's a city, not like the depot.'

'Will there be lots of people to talk to?'

Should I warn her of the dangers? Rose sighed. Ned wants to preserve her innocence – but I am *worried*. In the end, as usual, she said nothing.

Margaret was ecstatic over the train. Her own little cabin with a bunk, hooks for her clothes and a wash-basin! Most magical of all, attached to the end carriage was a viewing platform where she and Daddy could stand and marvel at the vast starlit sky.

'It's long past her bedtime,' Rose reproached when they finally returned.

'It's an adventure, let her enjoy herself.' Ned had sloughed off his everyday working self and was carefree. 'Besides, Margaret was so excited, I had to tire her out. She's darned heavy now she's half asleep. Give me a hand.' Rose undressed her daughter and tucked the sheets in firmly. Watching, Ned asked quietly, 'A penny for them, pet?'

430

'I was remembering the last time you and I were on a train.'

'I thought so ... so was I. Remember those kind people who shared their food because you and I had no money.'

Even after this distance of time, Rose flushed. 'I felt so ashamed.'

'You needn't have been.' He sought her hand. 'It's the way folk are out here, friendly and keen to help. If we found a young couple in the same straits, we'd do the same.'

'I expect so.'

'Of course we would. Thank God we can offer help these days.' He laughed softly. 'Looking back, I really enjoyed that journey. I felt life was beginning for both of us at last.'

'And I sat brooding over Gertie's wickedness.'

'Aye ...' Ned sobered up. 'Not still bitter, are you, pet?'

'I wonder about her. How she is, whether she and Harold are happy together, that sort of thing.'

It was on the tip of his tongue to suggest she could write and ask, then he reflected that if she wanted to, Rose would anyway. She'd tell him the result but she wasn't the meek type who would seek her husband's permission first.

They shut the communicating door and settled to read for a while. Rose rechecked the latest set of figures. He waited until she'd finished.

'Shall I order a pot of tea?' On the train, it came with milk, which was a treat.

She smiled gratefully. 'Fancy being waited on ... makes me feel like a lady all of a sudden.'

'You are a lady,' he told her seriously, 'you always will be. That's why I'm such a lucky chap.'

She watched him give their order without a trace of his former nervous hesitancy. When the steward had gone she quoted, 'When Adam delved and Eve span, who was then the gentleman?'

He smiled in recognition. 'That was one of Hayden's favourite sayings.'

'Well, it's come true, the way he promised. Ever since we began at the depot we've been accepted for who we are. No

431

questions about our background, we're simply Rose and Ned, which is how it should be.'

Ned stared down at his hands before saying, 'Another of Hayden's remarks was that all you and I needed was time to get acquainted. I know I'm not the sort you dreamed of when you and Gertie were at Clairville Road – but its not been too bad, has it, pet? Life for me ... Well, it's pretty well bloomin' marvellous, when I think about it.'

'Oh, Ned. Come here ...' After a moment or two she murmured, 'Don't forget that steward is about to come bursting in with our tea.'

He released her and said with studied nonchalance, 'They do say that when you make love on a train, it's something really special.'

'Do they indeed! And where did you hear that?'

'Ah, well, that would be telling. It'd be fun to try though, wouldn't it?'

'I can't think why you never suggested it before,' she teased.

'What – on that first journey? In a crowded carriage? Have a heart! Besides, we weren't so easy with one another in those days.'

'No.' As he kissed her again Rose tried to convince herself everything *had* changed, but as usual she was honest. Ned's was such an open ardent nature, she never quite succeeded in matching it. If only she could give of herself in the same generous fashion. However much she tried, that reserve instilled by her mother interposed. Maybe on this holiday she could rid herself of stupid inhibitions? This dear man deserved so much more.

Their hotel, solid and old-fashioned, was in a quiet cul-de-sac behind Elizabeth Street. 'Near enough to those fashionable shops for me to run back to and lock myself in my room if I feel too tempted,' Rose laughed.

'You will allow yourself to be tempted though, won't you?'

'Oh, yes!'

A note from Captain Hislop suggested tactfully that they

might prefer a few days exploring Sydney before he called on them. He could imagine the excitement after the constant grind of the depot; he wanted the two of them to be beyond that stage when discussions began.

Meeting them at the hotel was deliberate. The proposition his board of directors was considering would involve massive investment and he wanted to reacquaint himself with the Harrisons before either side committed itself.

On the appointed day they were waiting for him in the writing room, chosen by Rose because it was usually empty at that time in the morning. As on the first occasion, Captain Hislop was struck by her air of quiet self-possession. This was a woman who had not been brought up to be subservient. Today, elegant clothes enhanced that authority. Was she fully recovered? There had been a question mark over her health since Margaret's birth. From her reports, Hislop knew of the heavy labouring work all of them had been forced to do at the depot.

Rose moved easily as she rose to greet him, her skin glowing, her eyes bright. The captain found himself thinking, not for the first time, that Harrison was indeed fortunate. Ned himself had filled out. No longer the skinny pale applicant of Newcastle days, he was now tanned and stocky. His manner was more assured, too; the security of the depot had done that. Hislop listened as coffee was poured and the two chattered about their holiday to date. As far as he was concerned, his first impressions were definitely favourable.

Sitting quietly with her crayons, Margaret studied him. Auntie Maisie had told her about this man. 'He helped us all find a new life here. He was in the Australian Army so he knew what your dad and uncle had gone through.'

Margaret thought the newcomer looked friendly. He was tall with crinkly greyish hair and a little moustache. He was very polite and held a chair for Mummy to sit down. As Daddy and he talked both of them removed their jackets and loosened their ties. Unconsciously, Margaret eased off her new shoes. This hotel with its huge rooms had carpet

433

everywhere. Socks came off next and her toes contentedly buried themselves in the pile. Even the *bathroom* had a carpet. This was Margaret's favourite spot – with a shining porcelain lavatory and taps you could turn on and off as often as you liked. Those and the miracle of the sea surrounding Sydney were the first two things she had described in her letter to Maisie and Oswald.

Today she gazed critically at the picture she'd drawn for them of Sydney Harbour Bridge. She'd made it go from one side of the paper to the other because it was so big. Now she added the most important detail.

'This was built by Dorman Longs of MIDDLESBROUGH!' she wrote. 'Daddy says the best riveters in the world worked on it. His friend who died used to work there. We went on a ferry to Manly yesterday but Mummy was sick so we came straight back. This morning it RAINED! We have bacon and egg for breakfast. We have been in five shops. Mummy has a hat with a veil which Daddy says is saucy.'

She gazed at her mother's new pale blue costume and crisp white blouse. These were the smartest clothes Margaret had ever seen but she remembered the argument before her mother agreed to buy them.

'A costume isn't practical, Ned. When will I have occasion to wear it?'

'You might,' he insisted, 'when it comes to discussing that important business proposition, you have to look capable. You're the business manager at the depot, remember.'

'Oh, what nonsense!' Secretly flattered, Rose had capitulated and treated herself to three frocks as well. Margaret's favourite was the one of soft material with a floaty skirt, a bow at the neck and wide sleeves. It reminded Daddy of the dress Mummy had worn when Auntie Gertie was married.

Gertie and Harold Brigg; that mysterious aunt and uncle who had adopted the boy in the newspaper photograph. Margaret had been allowed to keep the cutting when her mother was clearing out old papers. She rolled the name on her tongue, silently: Valentine Brigg. It was much more romantic than Margaret Muriel Harrison. Returning to her letter, she wrote:

'I have two new frocks and four pairs of knickers and patent-leather shoes with a bar across the top like Princess Elizabeth.' She paused again, sucking her pencil in search of inspiration. Sydney had been astonishing but she wasn't prepared to admit to being dazzled, not at ten and a quarter.

As well as buying clothes, she and Mummy had been to the hairdresser's. As a result, Margaret's plaits had disappeared and she now had shorter, curlier hair with a side parting and a slide. Everyone knew you were half-way to being an adult once you had a hair-slide.

And if Sydney was exciting what must Middlesbrough be like with all those wonderful relatives? One day, when she was properly grown-up, she would travel to the opposite side of the world and meet every single one, including Valentine Brigg. Meanwhile, she must think of something else to fill the rest of her letter.

The others had forgotten about her. Coffee things had been pushed aside and the table was covered in papers. They were talking seriously as Mummy explained what the columns of figures meant. Daddy produced the packet of photos. Unnoticed, Margaret sidled up to explain about the one taken especially for her.

'That's our emu,' she announced delightedly when it appeared. 'Uncle Oswald says he's a dratted nuisance and one day he's going to break its neck and stuff him down the well.'

Captain Hislop's mouth twitched. 'Dear me, what a dreadful fate.'

Her mother looked pained. 'Margaret – shoes.'

'Yes, I know.' She'd been warned not to interrupt. As she retrieved her socks, Margaret wondered if one social lapse meant she wouldn't be included with the lunch party but Daddy gave a wink so she knew it would be all right.

She and Rose went to 'wash their hands' before leaving for the

435

restaurant. Margaret turned on the taps and let water stream into the basin. This was on top of a porcelain pillar, not perched on a table with a bucket beneath to collect dirty water for the vegetable bed. The soap was nice and smelled of lavender.

'Ready?'

'Yes, Mummy.' Margaret dabbled her fingers in the water and wiped the rest off on the towel. Daddy was in the bedroom, watching her mother adjust her eye-veil.

'So far so good?'

'I hope so, Ned. I wonder why nothing's been said?'

He smiled. 'There hasn't been time. You've been talking non-stop, or hadn't you noticed? The captain gave you a good grilling over those contract figures.'

'He hadn't seen them before. They weren't included in the last return.'

'He was obviously surprised at how good they were. I was proud of you, pet.'

Rose picked up her gloves and turned to face him. "How do I look?"

He examined her, mock-critically. 'You'll do.'

'Will I do as well?'

'Let me see,' he stared down, 'are they clean?' Margaret held out both palms. 'And the backs?' These were grubby.

'Shall I spit on them?'

'Come through here.' He rubbed the dampened flannel over her face as well. 'It may be boring but try not to chatter in the restaurant. Captain Hislop has important things to tell us. Mummy and I need to pay attention.'

But over lunch, the captain began to question them about life in Middlesbrough. Rose described her early days at the tea rooms.

'It took so long to save for that secretarial course but if only I'd managed it! It included double-entry book-keeping, just think how useful it would have been to us now.' Margaret listened with rapt attention; the best riveters came from Middlesbrough, maybe the best typists did as well?

436

'Would you have been the best secretary in all the world, Mummy?'

'Hardly! I might have made a better job of the paperwork if I had been trained though.'

Captain Hislop said thoughtfully, 'Perhaps you could spend a day with our company accountant while you're here? He has no complaints, I assure you, but he might have one or two suggestions.'

'Well, I ... I don't know.' A little surprised, Rose looked at Ned.

'It's a grand idea,' he urged promptly. 'Margaret and I can look after ourselves for a day.' Margaret held her breath. Did that mean they could go swimming! Daddy had promised to take her if there was time.

Captain Hislop was speaking again. 'As for the proposition mentioned in my letter, we'd like you both to attend the company offices at ten tomorrow, if that's convenient. Our board members will have had time to examine the plan of the depot by then. Thank you for the comprehensive details, by the way. They will enable our surveyor to begin work.'

What type of work? Ned was dying to ask.

'Tell me, when the petrol tanks were installed, was there any problem over siting them?'

Slightly thrown, Ned replied slowly, 'I don't remember any, do you, Rose?'

'No. The ground was rock-hard, everyone had to use pick-axes.'

'And beneath? It wasn't soft, sandy soil?'

'It wasn't,' Ned said fervently. 'It was back-breaking work every inch of the way.'

'Good.' Hislop smiled at the two baffled faces. 'We shan't know until we've had a full geological survey, of course, but if we go do ahead and build an aerodrome, we don't want the runway to start sinking.'

'An aerodrome ...!'

'That's what we'd like to propose for that empty land behind the cabins. The company have been in touch with the government about a grant. We think the depot could prove an ideal site. Provided there is sufficient space for hangars and an office, plus a separate area for the fuel pumps. It's a big project.'

'My stars!' Ned was staring at him wildly. 'Oswald and me ... we could never build all that.'

Captain Hislop's laughter brought the restaurant to a standstill. When he'd recovered he said, 'Thanks for the offer, Ned, but we intend using a contractor and a team this time. Now, Mrs Harrison, if we do, we shall need to think in terms of catering for those hungry men for at least eight months, probably longer.'

Rose was dismayed, remembering the bunk house and the drudgery of hot meals every day. 'Not like Malinga.'

'No, not like that at all. Those days are past as far as you're concerned. All we'd want you and Mrs Robson to do would be to supervise any local staff hired for the period of construction. We would be responsible for fitting up a temporary kitchen and storerooms. It would be up to you to decide where those should be sited, by the way. They'd be for your own use once the 'drome was finished. We would arrange for extra cabins to be built, for housing the team. Again these would become your property afterwards. It is our intention to enlarge the depot without cost to yourselves in return for using the extra land to expand the company's interests. Your responsibility would include the recruiting of additional local staff for cooking and cleaning.'

Despite her whirling thoughts, Rose managed to consider the question calmly. 'I don't think that would be a problem. Many of our neighbours would be glad of a chance to earn a little extra. We might have to offer them transport.'

'That's easily arranged.'

'But what about an additional water supply?' The size of the operation was beginning to worry Ned.

'Don't concern yourself over that,' Hislop said firmly. 'If necessary we can arrange bowsers on a daily basis, possibly down from the north. As for the idea in general, you both need to consider it long and hard. Don't get your hopes up, not yet. Much has to be done before we know whether it's feasible.' He smiled at Margaret. 'We might have to consider penning up that emu. We couldn't have a dratted nuisance holding up progress, could we?'

She shook her head solemnly. 'You mustn't put him in a pen. Uncle Oswald built one once and he tore it to pieces with his claws.'

'Sounds ferocious.'

'Leave it to me,' Ned said quickly. 'If I explain to Oswald, I'm sure he'd stuff that bird and present him to you as a company mascot. Now, Margaret, are you going to finish that ice-cream before it melts?'

Lunch over, the captain left and the three of them wandered away from the bustling city centre, down toward the harbour. There was a stiff breeze, waves danced towards them across the bay. Margaret leaned over the railing, absorbed by the squawking, soaring sea-birds. Ned found a bench nearby.

'Well,' he demanded, drawing Rose's arm under his, 'what d'you think?'

'I'm still trying to take it in. It might never happen, of course.'

'No, but supposing it did?'

She peeled back the fluttering veil that threatened her eyelashes. 'I hope it won't become a nightmare.'

'What!'

'I don't want you to lose control, Ned. It's your depot. Yours and Oswald's. What Captain Hislop described, we'd be overrun for at least a year. And when it's finished, suppose no one wants to use the aerodrome or those extra cabins? We don't fill the ones we've got half the time. We could end up owning a white elephant that would ruin us.'

He squeezed her hand. 'I'm sure the company have been into all that but we'll find out tomorrow. We'll make a list of questions tonight. Whatever happens, the depot must always belong to us.' He gazed at where Margaret stood. 'It's her inheritance, one day.'

This sounded fatuous to Rose. 'Good grief, Ned. Our child doesn't need an aerodrome! And aren't you forgetting Maisie and Oswald?'

'Calm down, pet. Half of everything belongs to them, it always will, but Margaret will benefit from whatever we leave her. I wonder if Oswald and Maisie would object if we renew the invitation to Mu and Lionel? We're definitely going to need extra staff to run an aerodrome.'

'Ned, listen. We have to be sure the project will go ahead. We can't even begin to recruit cleaners until we know that. As for Mu, until we have a clear idea of what we can offer ...'

'Aye, I know. I'm getting carried away, as usual.'

First things first indeed, thought Rose. Recruiting, supervising, organizing the paying of wages ... She needed to keep her head.

'If I do accept the captain's suggestion and spend a day at the company offices, what will you do?'

'Hire a car and take Margaret along the coast. I thought we could go for a swim. The captain said there's a good place to teach kids at Rose Bay.'

Rose's expression had changed. "Ned, you will take care.'

'Listen, pet, I know how you feel but we don't want her to be afraid of water, do we. I'll take it in easy stages.'

'I'm being silly.'

'No, you're not, you couldn't be. Both feet on the ground, that's you. It makes me thankful every time I remember it. But there's always a danger we might molly-coddle Margaret because she's our one and only, we must remember that.' He watched for a moment as a liner nosed its way up the harbour towards a berth. 'It doesn't seem that long ago since we were on board one of those and you made me swear we'd never go to sea again. We'll never need to, thanks to the depot. I understand enough about the figures today to see how well placed we are.' He sighed happily. 'And next time we visit Sydney, we might even own an aerodrome.'

'It'll be a tiny place in the middle of nowhere,' Rose said severely, 'and we don't own anything, not outright. Thanks to

440

the company we've a *share* in the depot, that's all.' She couldn't dampen his enthusiasm, not today.

'I realize that, pet. But the business is building up and the captain assured us we'd probably own most of it, one day. Listen, suppose we invite Amy Johnson or Jean Batten to fly in and declare our 'drome open. That would put it on the map. We could end up famous!' And we could end up bankrupt, she thought. She was anxious not to hurt his feelings but mindful of her role.

'Before we agree to anything, we have to consider every blessed snag. We also need Oswald's and Maisie's consent. I want to know exactly how much the company estimate it will cost and what our outlay will be. I don't mind more hard work but I have to be able to see our future clearly. And now, if you don't mind, I'd like to go back to the hotel before I lose my hat.'

He grinned and called to Margaret. 'Come on, you.' He wondered how much his daughter had understood and had his answer immediately. She ran towards him, eyes shining.

'Daddy, can I learn to fly like those sea-gulls?'

The day of the swimming expedition, the breeze was fresh. Urged on by Ned, after the first plunge Margaret raced up and down the beach to get warm.

'Is this what Mummy means by cold? My teeth are *chattering*!'

Ned recalled icy north-east winds. 'Not quite. Here, let me give you another rub.'

Snug inside the towel, Margaret sighed, 'I wish she could have come.'

'She's busy, pet.'

'She's always busy.'

'No, she's not,' he protested loyally. 'Besides, your uncle and I need her to look after the depot for us.'

Margaret turned the idea over in her mind.

'Couldn't Auntie Maisie help? Or somebody else? Other mummies don't work all the time.' Ned half wished Rose

441

didn't but would never dream of saying so.

'Your auntie works very hard growing the flowers and vegetables. Besides, your mam enjoys using her brain. So will you, one day.'

Margaret registered first incredulity then doubt. 'I don't think I'll bother thanks, Dad. I'll stay at the depot with you.'

He shook his finger at her. 'That's no easy option. Don't start imagining you can sit around at home eating strawberries with a silver spoon because you're the boss's daughter.'

'What's strawberries?'

'One day, if you're very good, I'll order us some. Ready for another go?'

'Yes, please!' She shot off towards the curling edge of the surf. Ned followed with a slower, loping stride, secretly admiring her fearlessness.

'When I was a kid, Mu had to drag me in. Frightened of paddling, I was – Hey – Margaret! Don't go in too deep – wait for me!' He struck out wildly as the small head bobbed ahead amid the waves.

'I'm on tip-toe!' she screamed, wildly excited, 'the sea's lifting me up!'

He grabbed her arm, dragging her back to a safer depth. 'It's too deep, the currents could knock your feet from under you.' She was sober now, seeing his fear and feeling the undertow against her body.

'The Tasman is very big, Dad. Is it as big as the sea at Redcar?'

'Bigger. Where it joins the Pacific, it's the biggest ocean in the world. Now, rest your chin in my hand. Try kicking your legs the way I showed you.'

Margaret splashed and coughed and finally gave up.

'I've swallowed ever such a lot!'

Ned was unsympathetic. 'I told you to breathe *out* through your mouth, not in.' She was sulky; swimming wasn't such fun after all.

'I'd like to go back.'

'Not until you've managed one stroke – with both feet off the bottom.'

'Oh, Dad! I'm shivering!'

'Don't be a baby.' Only when all four limbs were flailing in the water did he relent. 'That's better! Now we've something to tell Mummy.'

'Race you back!' She was enveloped in the towel once more by the time he arrived. 'Dad ...'

'Yes?'

'The depot isn't all that big really.'

'Yes, it is, it's enormous!' Large enough for an aerodrome anyway.

'I meant compared to Sydney. Is it as big as Middlesbrough?'

'Not quite but it's big enough for your uncle and me, and for you one day.'

Margaret appeared not to hear, she didn't want him to see her disappointment; her portion of the world, hitherto the most important spot in the universe, was in danger of being diminished. She gazed at the crashing, surging waves that filled the horizon. If that was only a sea, what must an ocean be like?

'Australia's quite big, isn't it?'

Ned guessed the direction of her thoughts. 'Huge. It needs four oceans to go all the way round: there's the Pacific on this side, the Indian on the other, the Timor sea to the north and the Southern Ocean down below Tasmania.'

She felt reassured. 'You will tell her I managed one whole stroke all by myself?'

'I promise.'

One of the depot's young trainee mechanics met them off the train. In their new shack, Maisie and Oswald had prepared a celebratory supper. All four waited until Margaret had been despatched to bed.

'Well?' Oswald demanded.

'We've had a wonderful holiday.' Ned tried to keep his expression impassive.

'And? Come on, put us out of our misery.'

'And – Margaret wants to take flying lessons. I reckon I might as well. How about you?'

As realization came, Oswald's face lit up. 'Bloody hell!'

'Oswald!'

'Sorry, Maisie. But – heck! Bloody hell anyway. So that's what it was about. An aerodrome. Well, well, well ... Of course I'm going to learn to fly. Bet I beat you to it. I always used to envy them during the war, flying above the trenches, their feet nice and dry.'

And how many of them failed to return, wondered Rose? And why do I always have to be the one to apply the brakes?

'It might not happen,' she warned. 'It's too soon to be certain. There has to be a thorough survey of the land first.'

Maisie looked at her shrewdly. 'You don't like the idea, Rose?'

'It's not that ... I'm not altogether convinced we can cope.' She fiddled with a salt cellar rather than see their excitement fade. 'The company are being very fair but there are dangers and you need to know all about them before you make any decision. My view is that I don't want us to lose what we have. We've worked too hard for it.'

Ned reached across and took her hand. 'I was really proud of you in Sydney. You spoke to those company directors, and they listened. They made several changes because of you. But remember, they're on our side, pet. They don't want us to go under and I don't believe they're trying to make us commit ourselves too far. Now, let Maisie and Oswald have a look at that list of questions and answers.'

In her room, Margaret watched a gecko dart about the wall above her head in search of food. The air was absolutely still, she could hear the distant voices even if she couldn't catch the words. Mummy was talking a lot, Daddy a bit, Uncle Oswald every now and then. Margaret yawned. Auntie Maisie was having her turn now and the comforting sensible sound sent her to sleep.

'It seems to me,' Maisie was saying, 'the company are taking all the financial risk. We aren't responsible for repaying

444

that government loan, they are. If the worst comes to the worst, we'll end up with extra buildings and cabins. If it goes according to plan, we'll have an aerodrome as well?'

'As far as I can see, yes,' Rose agreed.

'Well, I can't see any reason not to let the survey go ahead. If the land is suitable, fine. If it isn't, it'll make for easier digging and I can use the excavations to plant a few more trees.' She waited until their laughter subsided. 'Would anyone like another beer?'

'Yes, please.' Rose sighed contentedly. 'I knew I'd feel better once I'd discussed it with you, Maisie.'

'You and I usually see things the same way. One step at a time, eh?'

'Exactly. You know, I was thinking today ... how we've changed. I don't suppose you ever saw yourself making decisions as big as this?'

Maisie considered this seriously. 'I wouldn't say we're any different. It's just that possibilities exist over here which could never happen at home. Back in England, I was expected to know my place and stay there. That was what I hated the most. I used to feel like screaming sometimes. Fortunately, I managed to keep my opinions to myself. "Yes, madam, no madam" – I kept that up right to the day I handed in my notice – but it was an effort sometimes. Thank goodness we've left all that behind.'

'Here, here,' Oswald said fervently. 'Hey, did you remember to tell Rose about her parcel!'

'Sorry, I didn't. It came while you were away, Rose. We put it in your office.'

They trooped across the short distance between their two homes. The pathway was edged with white-washed stones and swept twice daily to rid it of Maisie's abhorred 'creepie-crawlies'. Tonight dingoes barked in the distant scrub. Closer to came the rustle of night creatures and the occasional croak of a frog. Rose could smell heavy frangipani as well as the dusty lavender they'd planted. Being away, even for so short a time, made her sharply aware of what they had achieved.

445

'Office' was too lavish a description for this particular corner, though. Her temporary packing-case desk still had one of the old cane chairs drawn up beside it and the overhead shelf was now loaded with tins of paperwork. The large package was tucked against the plank wall.

'I wondered about trying to improve things.' Rose searched for a pair of scissors. 'When the company people arrive, we should at least try to look efficient.'

Oswald and Maisie glanced at one another. 'Perhaps you and Ned should consider building yourselves a new home altogether,' Oswald suggested. 'This old shack looks so shabby compared to our place. Maisie and I feel guilty about it. We were discussing it while you were away.'

Rose was startled. 'You don't mean – pull this one down?'

'Why not? It would make sense because it's in the best situation with the shade from those trees. We've had a bit of practice with the cabins, I reckon we could build you a really decent home.'

'I don't think I want one, thanks.' The more she thought about it, the more the idea upset Rose. She remembered the first desperate days, patching shingles, fitting new plank flooring; they'd worked night and day to prove to themselves they could succeed. To her, the old building was a part of their lives and she couldn't bear to see it go. She said defensively, 'It's not as though it isn't comfortable now the fans are installed.' The flyscreens fitted properly too and last year they'd finally replaced the home-made mattresses. She might not have thought about it before but now that she did, Rose knew the answer.

'The shack stays. We might need to be reminded of what it meant to us one day.' Slightly guiltily, she realized she hadn't consulted Ned.

He said reassuringly, 'It suits me, always has.'

'It's no use building me an elegant home, Oswald, you know how I feel about housework. Besides, mightn't it be a good idea for the company to see these living quarters? They'd realize we weren't wasting money unnecessarily.'

446

'A very good idea,' Maisie said approvingly. 'Come on, open the box. According to the label it's from Captain Hislop, I want to see what sort of present he's sent.'

Ned stripped away the final layers and lifted the object onto the table.

'A typewriter.' Maisie's voice was flat. 'Why on earth send you a huge great thing like that?'

Rose smiled ruefully. 'Because I'm not a fluffy little creature worthy of chocolates or scent.'

Ned had discovered other items in the box.

'A Pitman's instruction manual ... spare ribbons. An eraser. Three packets of carbon paper ... bond foolscap. The lot.'

Rose ran her hand over the sleek, cold grey metal and remembered Gertie's wail of protest long ago. 'I think it's a splendid gift and very, very suitable. Now I can go ahead and demean myself.'

Maisie was mystified.

Rose explained light-heartedly, 'I'm about to become a career woman at last.

Chapter Twenty

Rebellious Thoughts, 1935

Valentine and his friend Raymond were engaged in the apparently aimless pastime of chucking stones across the surface of the Tees to see who could skim the furthest. Inwardly, following the end of their penultimate school year, they were contemplating the future with mixed feelings.

'I'm jolly lucky,' Raymond announced. 'Dad was so pleased when he read my report, he told me I shan't end up working for the post office.' He narrowed his eyes, took aim and hurled his pebble.

Valentine counted six plops before commenting, 'There are worse things. It would be a regular job.'

'Yes, but Dad explained that's all it is, a job. He says it pays the rent but there's no fun delivering letters in the winter. He doesn't want me to end up with a weak chest.' Raymond tried to sum up the heart-to-heart discussion of yesterday evening without sounding a sissy. 'When Dad became a postman it was a step up in the eyes of *his* father. At the time Dad didn't realize it could be a dead-end job. Grandad was ever so pleased but *he* used to deliver coal, you know.'

'Did he really?' Valentine was diverted. 'Where did he keep his horse?'

'In a shed down by the railway sidings. Dad said he cried when the cat-meat man came to take it away.'

'I expect you could get fond of a horse.'

Raymond was less sentimental. 'It's pretty awful cleaning up after them. I had to help on Saturday nights when I was

448

little. They slobber horrid green slimy stuff sometimes. Anyway, Dad doesn't want me to do any of that, he wants me to better myself.'

'How?'

'If my matric is good enough next summer, he's going to help me apply for an apprenticeship at I.C.I. I won't be bringing in a wage for ages but Dad says it's not important because I'll have a proper trade at the finish. He's willing to sub me and I think that's jolly decent of him.'

'So do I.' Valentine was envious. When he'd handed over his report, Harold had picked on his one weak subject, Scripture, and made a fuss. Valentine's cheeks burned at the memory.

Seeing his friend so glum Raymond asked tactfully, 'Have you decided what you're going to do?'

'I refuse to follow in Father's footsteps, whatever else.' Valentine threw his stone with more force than skill. 'The trouble is, he never listens to what I want. He still thinks he can tell me what to do.'

'What does he suggest?'

'Well ...' Harold's ideas were so nebulous, Valentine found them difficult to capture in words.

'He wants me to stay in Middlesbrough, find a job that pays a big wage so I can give them a lot of money for my keep – he has no idea what sort and he doesn't particularly care – and be available whenever he needs me at the tabernacle.'

To Raymond, this latter idea sounded pretty dismal. 'How does he expect you to earn plenty of money? It's hard enough trying to find a job that pays even a measly wage these days.'

'That,' Valentine said succinctly, 'is something my father prefers not to think about.' Which was all very well but not much help.

Raymond was thankful his parent had a practical turn of mind. He said sympathetically, 'What about your mother, can't she help?'

Valentine remembered the tears last night. 'She's on my side but it's no use pretending she wouldn't be pleased if I did

449

all those things, Ray. She'd be damn thankful if I could contribute. I feel guilty about having a big appetite, it means she only has small helpings. They both behave as if we're rich but we really haven't much boodle.'

'No.'

The entire street knew how often Gertie Brigg had difficulty in paying her bills.

'The trouble is, it's always pretence in our house.' Valentine dropped his guard. 'From morning to night, neither of them behaves normally. Whenever Father sets off it's as if he were going on some great mission instead of the silly old tabernacle. He talks of "business appointments" when what he really means is discussing repairs with old Ferguson.' Valentine threw several stones in quick succession before saying defiantly, 'When he went out last night, I had a quick look inside his attaché case.'

'What? The one your father uses ...? When he goes to the ...'

Valentine nodded: the solemn container of his father's masonic apparel. Again, the street knew of the weekly ritual and watched with amusement as whichever small boy Harold could persuade carried this object to the Freemason's hall in Marton Road, Harold walking behind as if having no cognizance of it before surreptitiously rewarding the bearer with twopence. Valentine, unrewarded, had successfully rebelled against performing this task several years previously.

'What did you find?' Raymond asked curiously.

'Various bits and pieces.' Guilt and a certain loyalty to his father made Valentine hold back from a full description. 'It's all part of the same thing, Ray. There were clothes for dressing up, embroidered pinnys, things like that. Those men are pretending to be what they're not. Fancy calling yourself a "mason" if you can't even hold a chisel.'

'But isn't it a bit different,' Raymond floundered. 'Isn't it a secret society where they try and help one another?'

'If that's all it is, why can't they do it openly?' Valentine demanded. 'Why keep it secret if there's nothing to hide?

450

And why be so po-faced about who can join and who has to be kept out. You should hear Father carrying on when the "wrong sort" has been nominated.'

This was too deep; Raymond didn't have an answer. Valentine regained control over his feelings. In a calmer voice, he added, 'What makes it worse is that Father can't really *afford* to take part. Whenever the masons want to raise cash for charity, he puts his name down for a subscription, then there's a row because we can't pay some bill. I used to think Mother made too much fuss. Now I don't because I've seen how carefully she works things out. She really hasn't any spare cash and it always ends up with shouting and Father banging out of the house. I think he should stay at home and save his money. He's out nearly every evening, you know.'

Again, the collective opinion of Jamieson Street was that Harold Brigg was out far too often but that his wife probably preferred it that way.

'That's why I feel guilty because I'm not earning a few bob.'

'If you left school now, that's the sort of wage you could expect for the rest of your life – a few bob.' Raymond echoed the wisdom of his parents. 'Menial work isn't well paid.'

'Anything would be welcome as far as my mother's concerned. She's got some money saved, a few pounds, that's all, but she told me once that was for her sister, Rose. I think she'd like to help me, but then again, it's probably so she could boast about it to her friends.' He mimicked Gertie's refined tones with cruel accuracy: "My son at the university."'

'What?'

Valentine had reached the point of confession and stumbled on, his long face reddening. 'That's what I'd really like, Ray. I don't want to leave school next summer, I want to move up to the lower sixth and try for Newcastle in a couple of years. I made the mistake of telling Mother a few weeks back. She told Father and last night there was an almighty fuss. You'd think he'd be pleased. All he said was, he hadn't gone to university, so why should I?'

Nevertheless, such an ambition cost real money. Raymond

451

asked cautiously, 'Is there any chance you might get there?'

'Not unless there's a miracle and that sort of thing doesn't happen. Unless you go down to the tabernacle and confess to being a sinner, of course. Then you're promised "the miracle of forgiveness".' Valentine chucked another stone savagely. A frightened moorhen sped away. 'If it came to it, Mother doesn't really want me to leave home because of Father. Whenever there's a shouting match, I end up piggy in the middle. She hopes I'll stay in Middlesbrough for the rest of my life because of him. I won't, of course. As for Father, it doesn't matter how good my exam results are. Last night, when I showed him my report, he just ranted about Scripture and said he wasn't interested in the rest.'

Raymond was astounded; no wonder his friend looked so bitter. 'But you were top of the class, what more does he want?'

'I pointed that out. Mother was flapping about the way she does. 'At least say you're pleased, Harold.' He couldn't even bring himself to do that.'

'How beastly!'

'I have been trying to find a way. I even wrote to Mrs Paige. She pays Father's salary, you know.'

'Yes.'

It was breaking the code to talk about it but Valentine had gone too far to pull back. 'The trouble is she's never given Father a rise. And things cost much more nowadays which is why there isn't enough.' Raymond nodded sagely; this was real man-to-man stuff. 'Anyway,' Valentine admitted bravely, 'I wrote and asked if she could give any help with my plan to stay on at school.'

'Gosh! Any luck?'

'No. In her reply she said she had urged my father to put aside money for my education and now was the time to apply to him for it.'

Raymond giggled. 'She doesn't know your father very well!'

'I'll say.' Valentine summed up his father's character with cold detachment. 'If he has sixpence he spends a shilling and expects to end up with change. I damn well know he hasn't saved any money for me.'

His friend screwed up his face in an effort to think of a solution. 'Supposing you managed to get an evening job. Delivery boy, something like that. Would that help?'

Valentine looked at him cynically. 'Ray, what chance have I got when there are queues four deep all the way down the street from the labour exchange? No, Mother can't help, Father *won't*, Mrs Paige has refused. I shall probably have to run away and try my luck in London.'

At this, Raymond was goggle-eyed. 'Would you really, Val?'

At fifteen, Valentine wasn't entirely brave. 'I might.'

The earlier mention of Rose had given Raymond an idea. 'What about that aunt of yours in Australia? Why not write to her instead? They say there are chances for a chap out there.'

Valentine was despondent. 'There was a family row when I was a kid. No one writes to anyone any more. Besides, I don't want to spend the rest of my life shepherding sheep, I want to use my brains.' Frustrated at every turn, he thrust his hands in his pockets and began to walk along the tow path. Raymond followed. There was no doubt his pal was clever enough to try for university. In some ways Raymond envied him but when it came down to it, to be the son of a tabernacle superintendent was no great cheese.

The Briggs were always a target for speculation. Despite his fine clothes and arrogant manner there were those who claimed Mr Brigg had had to flee to Australia once because of some catastrophe. A man of straw was the received wisdom. As for Gertie, she might be a lady but it was a pity she thought so highly of herself; snubbing those she considered inferior didn't endear her to anyone.

The tabernacle no longer drew crowds. Those who had once been avid to see others denounced were now preoccupied with the basic struggle to keep body and soul together. Unemployment had bitten deep in this area of Middlesbrough.

453

Harold's Monday meetings had also failed to attract new blood. The rise in his fortunes which had begun with Clarence Clayton's denunciation had lasted only a brief period. Harold had attempted to recruit new material from among Valentine's school friends. This had brought the worst confrontation of all: Valentine refused point blank.

'If you must know, Father, I haven't asked them because I feel too embarrassed.'

'What on earth do you mean?'

'Why should they come simply because you want to lecture them about sin? They know the difference between right and wrong. It doesn't need you ranting on about it—'

'Hold your tongue!' Harold was furious. 'I do not rant. And if your friends consider themselves free of the devil's contamination . . .'

'Whether they are or not, it's their business, Father. They don't want to babble in front of warts like Clarence. He's a pretty disgusting specimen, you know.'

'How dare you criticize!'

'Look, I'll put up with it, if I must.' Having gone too far, Valentine was fast losing his courage. 'If you think it does me good, I'll come, but please don't ask me to bully my friends into it because I refuse.'

With that he'd slammed out of the dining-room, up the stairs to his room. His mother was in the kitchen doorway, wringing her hands. She did that a lot but he couldn't help it, Father was so provoking. All the same, the argument hadn't done his prospects much good.

'Damn, damn, damn!' Valentine whispered. His father was already outside, hammering on the door.

'Valentine, I demand you let me in.'

They'd been through this rigmarole so many times. Valentine kept the key in his pocket because his father had once tried to take it from him. A chap had to have some privacy. He'd pulled the pillow over his head to blot out the shouting.

'I shall have to run away . . . it's my only chance.' But where could he go, and what would he do when he got there? As

454

usual his thoughts went full circle without reaching any conclusion.

This afternoon, Raymond suggested, 'Why don't you come and talk things over with my dad? He might have a few ideas. He sounded jolly sensible last night.'

Years of imbibing Gertie's strictures made Valentine recoil instinctively. 'Goodness, I couldn't do that.' And just as quickly he tried to cover up his rudeness. 'You know what my mother's like if she thinks I've even been to your house to tea.'

'Yes, she thinks we're not good enough. Well, my dad doesn't carry on the way yours does. He doesn't shout. And he never pretends, he's honest.' It was all true. Raymond was hurt and Valentine apologized.

'I know he is. He's a jolly good sport. But I don't think he can help me, Ray. No one can. I haven't a bean and everything costs money. Until I've found some way of earning a bit ... saving, you know.' But that prospect was so unlikely he turned the conversation to happier topics. 'What sort of apprenticeship will you try for?'

'Chemical engineering.'

'If I could, I'd like to study maths.'

'To teach it, you mean?'

Valentine stared at the horizon, wondering if he dare speak openly of his dreams. 'I might. At university they would suggest other things I might do. I think research would be interesting.'

'Why maths? I know you're good at it but you're better at French.'

'I like it because it's clean,' Valentine flared. 'When you work out the solution to a problem, that's it and there's no arguing.'

Finite, thought Raymond, not like the fudging Val had to put up with at home. Golly, being grown-up wasn't much fun for some people. Perhaps he could help.

'Val, you remember last Christmas when Dad got me that temporary job at the post office? Would you like me to ask if he

455

can fit you in this year? It's pretty boring but you do get paid on a daily basis ...'

'Would you?' Val was full of gratitude. 'I really envied you that chance.'

'I'll ask him tonight. You won't save much, I'm afraid. The pay's not that good.'

'It would mean I could give Mother a decent Christmas present. She's had that old felt hat so long it looks like a tea-cosy. She's set her heart on a new one but they cost seven and six, she told me so herself.'

Raymond was astonished. Clothes for his mother? What on earth had come over Val? 'Doesn't your father pay for her hats?' Valentine blushed scarlet. His father was too mean and he must've sounded an absolute fool. Ray was saying, 'Your father always looks smart. He must spend a lot on himself.'

'Yes, he does.' Too much, Valentine knew. 'The trouble is, *I've* grown such a lot, Mother's had to buy extra for me.' Which meant no money left for Gertie to spend on herself but this was too shaming to admit.

His friend sighed. 'I wish I knew how you did it.'

'Father's tall. I suppose I take after him. Come on. It must be nearly time for tea.'

'I say ...' An awkward thought had occurred to Raymond. 'Won't there be a fuss when your parents find out about the post office? There is a form to sign, you see. They have to give their consent.'

'Oh ...' Val's dark eyes were sombre. 'No doubt there'll be the usual rant and Mother will say it's not *suitable*. I shall tell them how jolly lucky I am.'

It sounded brave but he wasn't looking forward to it. They walked back briskly and Raymond pondered his friend's various problems.

'I'm glad I don't have to put up with what you have to,' he offered finally. 'I think you manage jolly well.'

Valentine tried not to show how much Ray's tribute affected him. 'I'll tell you something, Ray. There isn't much I don't know about keeping up appearances and telling fibs

456

about your neighbours. It's pretty ghastly on Sunday some-times, especially if one of the beastlier specimens points the finger. One chap actually dribbles he gets so excited.'

'How disgusting!'

'I've half a mind to go to Africa when I leave home,' he said recklessly. 'Live among the natives where no one gives a fig about sin.'

'There are missionaries,' Raymond pointed out. 'I don't suppose you could avoid them.'

'The arctic then. You don't hear of missionaries preaching to Eskimos in their igloos. Because it's so cold, I expect. I don't mind where I go so long as there isn't a church full of people pretending to love God while they're being spiteful behind one another's backs.'

Bored though he was with Methodism, Raymond decided his parents' choice of religion had been more satisfactory.

Valentine made his way to the back of the house. His father did not permit him to have a front-door key. 'When you have demonstrated a sufficient sense of responsibility, my boy.'

I'm not a boy, Valentine tugged angrily at a straggling buddleia twig which dripped over the pathway, I'm nearly a man and if it wasn't for Mother, I'd leave home tomorrow. He wouldn't, of course. That would mean an end to schooling; he couldn't risk that. Half-resentful, Valentine peered through the steamy kitchen window.

His mother had become thinner. Quite apart from the small helpings at supper, she only nibbled at midday. His father lunched out, naturally. Valentine was served tasty savoury dishes while his mother pretended she lacked an appetite. They usually sat conspiratorially at the kitchen table rather than in the chilly dining-room. Once Valentine had mocked their 'lack of standards' and his mother had actually giggled.

Today, Gertie was happy. The time was approaching when Valentine would be home. She lit the gas under the kettle in anticipation. Always a hot cup of tea and a few minutes of chat before he went upstairs to begin his homework. Then she would be left alone once more, to prepare their tea and Harold's supper. Talking to Valentine was the high spot of her day.

At five o'clock she would go upstairs to wash and change. Her mother had done so at three o'clock, in anticipation of callers but no one called on Gertie Brigg and At Homes were a thing of the past. Besides, without Annie, there was plenty of housework to fill her time.

She checked the stockpan simmering on the stove. She and Valentine would have soup and bread and dripping. It was amazing how he could demolish half a loaf with no trouble at all. No longer her 'little man', he was as tall as Harold. When the two of them shouted at one another, Gertie felt like a leaf buffeted in a storm with no way of escape.

She shivered and rubbed her forehead. Pray heaven there wouldn't be another argument like last night. Her head still ached because of the sleepless night. Poor, dear Valentine, so proud of his report and Harold too jealous to look at it. After the boy had rushed upstairs, she'd accused her husband to his face of being envious. Memory of Harold's incandescent rage made her feel sick. He'd called her such vile names, berated her for failing to do 'her duty', of being nothing but skin and bone.

'If I am, it is you who are responsible.' She shivered.

A small retaliatory notion began to swell and take shape inside Gertie's imagination: why not 'bear witness' of his cruelty towards her and Valentine at next Sunday's evening service? The audacity of it made her laugh aloud. Goodness, that would give the neighbours plenty to talk about! The idea of their gaping astonishment fuelled her sense of humour. She took off her spectacles to wipe away hysterical tears – and caught sight of the blur outside the window.

'Valentine? Is that you?' She pulled open the back door. 'What are you doing waiting outside?'

'Nothing.' He slouched in, disturbed by her mood. Gertie offered no explanation but busied herself with the tea-pot.

458

'Where did you and Raymond get to today? Anywhere exciting?'

'Just the river.'

'Oh, Valentine, I hope you didn't—'

'Of course we took care, Mother, we always do. Please try and remember I'm not a kid any more.'

Gertie retorted brightly, 'Don't use slang, dear, you know I don't like it.'

He maintained a sullen silence, knowing she wanted him to talk and hating himself for denying her even that small pleasure.

'Would you like a piece of bread and jam?'

'Yes, please.'

She gave one of her secret, silly smiles, 'It's not going to spoil your appetite for tea, is it?'

He groaned silently then saw her lip begin to tremble. 'No, of course not,' and in similar vein, 'I could eat a horse.' He watched her move across to the dresser. From the back she looked stoopy as if cowering from Father's booming. He wished she wouldn't hunch her shoulders. It didn't help that her clothes were so shabby, her cardigan had shrunk from being washed so often.

'Mother . . .'

'Yes, dear?'

'Ray thinks his father might be able to get me part-time work in the post office at Christmas.'

'Oh, Valentine . . .'

'If he does, I hope you will give your consent.'

Gertie retreated behind the inevitable obstacle. 'I don't think your father will agree to it.'

'Leave him to me,' Valentine interrupted roughly. 'I've had enough of his nonsense.'

'Valentine!'

'Mother, we're desperate for money. At least let me try and earn some. I shall ask Ray's father if there's any work available for the rest of this holiday and for next Easter. And another thing – when I go back to school in September I shall tell them I'm going to stay on and try for university.'

Gertie stood open-mouthed, still clutching the bread-knife. 'Have you told your father?'

'No, of course I haven't. But he's not going to spoil my life so you'd better get used to the idea. I shall ask at school if there's any chance of a scholarship and save every penny I can.'

Except for buying you a new felt hat, he thought miserably, even that anticipated pleasure was diminished at the sight of her unspoken terror over battles yet to come. 'You will back me, won't you, Mother?'

'Oh, Valentine ...' Abandoning the loaf, she came and hugged him tightly. Her birdlike frame reawakened his guilt. Recalling his earlier frank discussions with Ray, he decided to rid himself of one horrid secret. Let there be nothing but openness between the two of them at least.

He muttered huskily, 'I wish you hadn't married Father. I realize you had to because I was on the way.' He felt her go rigid. 'Don't worry, I worked it out for myself. Father once mentioned the date of your marriage and I knew when I was born, of course. At least you and I can be honest about it but if you don't want to discuss it, it's not important.'

She was staring at him with such terror and her face was so ashen, he was convinced she was about to faint.

'Mother, it doesn't matter one little bit. Here, come and sit down.' He rushed to pour her a glass of water, spilling it because his hand was shaking. 'I won't ever mention it again but I wanted to tell you I appreciate what you did.' He waited until she'd taken a few sips and tried to make a joke of it. 'Think what a dreadful fate might have overtaken me if you hadn't married Father!'

There was no response, she wouldn't even look at him. Valentine burst out, 'I just wish Father didn't bully you so often, it makes me so angry I want to hit him. I won't, though. I'll stick it out for your sake. But you must help me convince him about staying on at school. Promise me?' Even in her stupor, Gertie managed to nod. Valentine gave her a quick, hard squeeze. 'Thanks, Mother. Thanks a lot. I'll go to my room, if you don't mind. I'd like to do a bit of work before tea.'

After he'd gone, she moved automatically to replace the loaf in the breadbin and sat for a long time with limbs too leaden to support her, trapped in the web of her own deceit. Why had she not told Valentine the secret years ago? If she did so now, it might drive him from home altogether; she'd certainly lose his affection.

'He's all I have,' she whimpered to the empty air, 'I daren't tell him the truth.' There was no comfort anywhere, only trepidation over the future.

Chapter Twenty-one

Growing Pains, 1938

It had taken far longer than Mum and Dad or even Captain Hislop had anticipated before the aerodrome was finished. The day before her sixteenth birthday, Margaret Muriel Harrison felt very sophisticated as she realized she and the 'drome had grown up alongside one another. But whereas everybody noticed how the runway was developing, no one gave a thought to how much she had changed. Except Dad, of course.

That original optimistic company estimate of eight months had come and gone without a sign of activity. At the end of ten months, when the captain visited the depot to boost their morale, Uncle Oswald shrugged off the delay. 'Don't worry about us, sir, we take the long view. Besides, the machinery side is doing nicely.' Even so, Dad had become extremely depressed and Mum had had to chivvy him about it.

But that visit had done them all the world of good, according to Auntie Maisie, and Margaret had been allowed to tag along as Dad and Uncle had shown the captain over the property. It was his first visit and he was impressed. She'd heard him say, 'A most attractive place for any traveller to stop, whether for a repair or simply to break a journey. I congratulate you. It was to be expected that you'd put your backs into it but this time you've surpassed yourselves.'

There had been serious talking at mealtimes. It wasn't a lack of enthusiasm that had halted progress, Hislop assured them, but a lack of willing investors. Recession and storm clouds over Europe meant bankers were unwilling to part with their money.

Margaret didn't understand. Mum had explained privately, 'It's the reason your Auntie Mu is always worried and why Uncle Lionel is never sure of his job. We can thank our lucky stars the recession at home hasn't reached us.'

Today Margaret hugged herself as she remembered how she was about to bring changes to that far-off family. The one thing Dad desired in all the world was for Auntie Mu to come out here – and Margaret had thought of a way to entice her!

As to what the trouble in Europe might be, Margaret remembered Dad and Uncle Oswald had been unusually quiet when the captain left. Unknown to Rose or Maisie, they'd had a serious chat before he had boarded his train. Afterwards, Oswald suggested a quiet beer before the two of them returned to the depot.

They sat brooding in a bar. Eventually, Ned stirred. 'I never thought we'd have to go through that lot again.'

'I doubt we will,' Oswald said stoutly. 'You heard the captain. This time there's people talking peace and appeasement. Maybe that'll do the trick. Anyhow it's helped the government make up its mind about our loan.' Like Ned, he saw the development of the aerodrome in personal terms. 'Now they've stopped being woolly-minded about money, seems to me it won't be long before the whole thing gets started. Same again?'

'Please.' Ned was preoccupied with another of Hislop's suggestions. When Oswald returned he said, 'If we do apply for that vehicle franchise, we ought to take on another mechanic. One that can be specially trained.'

'Agreed. Tell you what, Ned ... I don't think we ought to worry Maisie and Rose with that gossip about war. It might never happen.'

'No.' Ned certainly didn't want to revive memories of Cecil for Rose. 'We'll forget about it.'

'Fine.'

*

As far as Margaret was concerned, the next excitement was the new garage area. Motor cars began to arrive, supplied under the franchise agreement. Salesmen and mechanics followed, accommodation had to be provided quickly. The bunkhouse and kitchen promised by the company were erected ahead of schedule. Once agreement was reached over the aerodrome and the construction gang appeared, more accommodation went up and the daily shuttle began for the women who came in to cook and clean.

A proper servicing department for the cars came next. Extra cabins were needed for potential customers who'd travelled long distances. Each one had a picnic table and chairs in front, a small parking area to the side. At Auntie Maisie's suggestion an additional ablutions block was built. Mum said wryly it was merely an excuse for more sweet-smelling shrubs but Auntie Maisie had been really busy, putting in whole clumps of eucalyptus between the cabins, so everyone could enjoy a patch of shade.

More and more people were journeying between Darwin, Alice Springs or the Kimberley Plateau these days and the cabins were seldom empty. As Dad constantly remarked, the whole continent was opening up. As for Margaret there was never a dull moment.

She was encouraged to help. At weekends she served visitors with ginger beer and ice-cream; she helped her mother with stapling and filing. She listened as Rose discussed problems with the construction foreman. It was costing a 'helluva lot more money' than the original estimate, according to him. Mercifully these costs were being borne by the company, otherwise, Margaret overheard Mum confide to Dad, what with the extended loan for the franchise, her hair would have turned white by now.

Back in her room, Margaret rolled the forbidden word on her tongue, helluva, helluva, helluva ... The Abo boys laughed when she used it. She rolled over on her bed to stare out at the awning and marquee, erected for her birthday celebrations tomorrow. What a party it would be! Everyone had been invited. Mum tried to argue but Margaret had pointed out how unfair it would be to exclude anyone. 'They're all my friends, Mum!'

Rose had gone in search of Maisie. 'How on earth will we feed forty of them?'

'Nearer seventy, I'd say.' She wiped the sweat from her forehead. 'We'll manage. The girls in the cook-house have promised to give a hand. What'll we offer the emu, birdseed?' Rose's face made her chuckle 'Didn't you know she'd included him? She nailed up a proper invitation card: "Miss Margaret Muriel Harrison requests the pleasure of the company of The Dratted Emu, Esquire, etc. RSVP to The Shack." Made Oswald laugh.'

'Did you know she'd also been round the humpies.'

'Yes ...' Maisie added carefully, 'She regards the blacks the same as she does everyone else.'

'Half the population of Australia are Margaret's friends,' said her mother acidly.

'Why, what's wrong with the other half?' Maisie demanded.

'It's not funny, Maisie. If we have to cater for an army, what I want to know is – how?'

'Well ... I've tripled the orders to our suppliers this week – Charlie's got a pit dug and the blacks are roasting a pig. Friends and neighbours are bringing contributions. We'll offer beer and soft drinks and I've asked Mrs Tyler if she'd make a cake. She said she'd be delighted. Let's face it, Rose, it's not every day your only daughter's sixteen. We want to have a proper "do". Did you know she'd borrowed a gramophone and all her school friends are bringing records?'

Rose stared in horror, 'You mean for dancing? We can't possibly ...'

'Yes, we can, on the garage forecourt. The boys are putting up coloured lights. Oswald is really looking forward to it. He's scrubbed the mildew off his old togs and he's going to act as master of ceremonies and propose a toast.'

'Maisie, this was intended as a straightforward simple birthday party ...'

465

'Better find your dancing shoes. When Oswald announces the first waltz, he's going to invite Ned and Margaret to start the proceedings. After that, we can all take a turn.'

Rose felt as though she were losing her grip. 'Why wasn't I told any of this?'

Maisie said kindly, 'You're always so busy, love, what with running the business side and everything. We thought we'd take the weight off your shoulders for once. We think of baby as our daughter as well, you know.'

In her room, Margaret was half exultant, half nervous. She knew her mother was in for a few surprises. More than that, Margaret intended making one very important announcement. Her parents were giving her five hundred pounds. This colossal sum was intended for university fees but Margaret planned to use it for a different purpose. The trouble was, would Dad agree?

She opened one of her bamboo boxes. She'd had a chest of drawers once but it had rotted during the wet. These were better. Two were for clothes, one for newspaper cuttings and old letters.

Over the years, the paper had yellowed but here were all the souvenirs of Middlesbrough – which had given her the idea.

First the picture of the Transporter, a wedding present from Dad's friend Hayden. It used to stand on the shelf in the living-room but when the glass was accidentally chipped, Margaret had begged to have it.

There were snapshots of Auntie Mu and Uncle Lionel at this wonderful place called Redcar where the sea crashed against the rocks and the cold winds blew. She remembered the magical sea at Sydney. If she closed her eyes she could still feel the waves at Rose Bay.

She examined the tiny figures, their clothes pinned against their bodies, hair streaming in the wind. What was it like to be really cold? Her mother had described it but Margaret couldn't imagine it.

There was a postcard from a place called Osmotherly. The

grass was bright green and the sheep were so fat! On the back was written; 'Happy memories! Yours fondly, Mu.' Mum had blushed but refused to explain. 'Later,' she'd said to Margaret, 'when you're older.' She always said that.

Letters from Auntie Mu, one written on the back of an old receipt. How difficult it was to find work, how Lionel's back was troubling him. Mu had seen the mysterious Auntie Gertie with Valentine at the Coronation Celebrations. 'The boy is very like his father nowadays.'

This was one bit of family history Dad had revealed, which Margaret had never forgotten. Valentine had been adopted by this aunt and uncle who owed Mum money and worked in a tabernacle. It was rumoured the boy was Uncle Harold Brigg's love-child, only nobody said so, out of politeness. Margaret thought it the most romantic story she'd ever heard.

There was one more photo, of dead Uncle Cecil and his friends. Margaret considered the white-flannelled figures looked stuck-up, they stared so disdainfully, but Dad had whispered how fond Mum had been of him and the confidence made Margaret feel important.

Finally, she took out the precious letter and unfolded it. Her application had been redirected because the secretarial school had moved to Borough Road East, Middlesbrough, but the principal was in receipt of her application. Provided Miss Harrison's academic qualifications proved equal to those of an English student, she would be given due consideration. In view of her age, if she could confirm she would be staying with a relative or guardian, a provisional place could be offered from the beginning of the September term. Margaret kissed the sheet of paper and slid it back inside the envelope. This was the bombshell she intended to explode tomorrow. There was a tap on the door, 'Margaret, are you there?'

'Yes, Mum.' She shoved the envelope under her pillow.

Entering, Rose said automatically, 'Don't call me Mum, it's sloppy.'

'No, Mummy.'

Faced with Margaret's happy excitement, Rose wished she

467

didn't have to act so severely but *someone* had to make her daughter realize what she'd done. 'This party of yours. You had no business to make so much extra work for Maisie.'

Happiness was instantly replaced by tragedy. 'Auntie said she didn't *mind*, Mummy. And Uncle Oswald's really looking forward to wearing his butler's suit.' In this heat, he was risking a heart attack, thought Rose sourly. 'Please wear your floaty dress, Mummy. It's still a secret but there might be some *dancing* afterwards!' Shining bright once more, Margaret waited for her mother to be pleased. Rose thought of Ned, and capitulated. If I scold, she'll only be upset and so will he. It's my own fault, we've spoiled her too much already.

If only the Wilcannia doctor hadn't been so positive all those years ago. Rose sighed inwardly. She would have risked another pregnancy, she had wanted to urgently at times but Ned had been unwilling. Was it that spectre which interposed itself when she tried to give herself to him whole-heartedly? These days she was constantly preoccupied with all the problems the aerodrome had created and bone-weary by the time they went to bed. I'm not much of a flirt at the best of times, she acknowledged dryly, and nowadays, permanently tired. Guilt irritated her; she tried to shrug it off and transferred her attention to Margaret who was flinging clothes on the bed in a frenzy as to what she should wear.

Rose pretended to frown. 'Not shorts, I think.'

'Of course not!'

'And – with shoes, perhaps?'

Always bare with splayed toes, Margaret's feet were as leathery as a black child's. She hadn't Rose's womanly figure, she was lithe and slim, constantly on the move. As for that hair ... Rose sighed again. It was long, straight and thick. She had tried to curl it but heat and damp defeated her. She'd even suggested Margaret have it cut short once more but Ned had protested, 'Leave it, it's her best feature.'

These days it was brushed smooth and tied at the back of her neck with a flat bow. 'Old-fashioned', had been Rose's reaction but Maisie had murmured, 'Look, she's trying to copy you,' and Rose remembered the photo Cecil had taken when she was seventeen.

She hadn't seen it lately; Margaret must have squirrelled it away. It was all part of a pattern. When her daughter wanted to twist her round her little finger, she would sidle up, put her arms round her waist and wheedle, 'Tell me a story, tell me about that day in Albert Park when Cecil tried to row you across to the island.' It rarely failed. Once or twice, Ned had demurred, 'Do you have to keep telling tales about Middlesbrough?' But these were the ones Margaret preferred: memories of nieces, nephews, aunts and uncles – Gertie and Harold didn't feature often, naturally – and she wanted real people in her stories, not fictional heroines. Today Rose allowed herself to wonder if Gertie was similarly manipulated by Valentine and what sort of father Harold Brigg had turned out to be?

'I doubt if he spoils Valentine as much as we do Margaret.' Five hundred pounds – Maisie had been shocked; she was probably right.

Rose concentrated on the selection on the bed.

'I know the tussore silk is your best but the blue suits you better . . . it'll need washing and ironing. Have you a matching hair ribbon?'

'Somewhere,' Margaret rummaged, 'and white stockings.'

'Good heavens. Without a hole in them? Wonders will never cease.' Rose caught sight of them. 'Filthy, naturally.' She pulled herself up: I'm being too hard, she chided, I mustn't criticize so often. 'Would you like me to deal with them?' but Margaret had already gathered everything into a bundle.

'It's all right, Mummy, you're too busy. I can do them myself. I might even starch my dress.'

As she raced off, Rose called after her, 'Never mind starch, what about a petticoat to go underneath?' She wondered if she should try and find one but stopped herself; it would mean searching through Margaret's possessions and that was forbidden. For Ned it was a matter of pride that they were able to give their child absolute privacy.

469

'It's something I never had,' he'd explained. 'Not once, from the day I was born.'

So no petticoat, unless Margaret chose to find one herself. Rose returned reluctantly to her type-writer. The office work never seemed to slacken. She shrugged off feelings of inadequacy over her daughter and, straightening the paper and carbon in the platen, began a reply to a customer. 'Dear Mr Burrows, . . .'

She would be firm about the cheque, however. That five hundred pounds would go directly into Margaret's savings account.

The weather surprised Maisie as usual. 'Turned out nice for your birthday.'

Margaret chuckled, 'Why d'you always say that?'

'Because I was born in England. Weather like this – they'd never stop talking about it. Many happy returns, from your uncle and me.'

Margaret was overjoyed. 'A handbag – a real one!' She ran her finger over the beading. 'Thanks so much, Auntie. It'll be just the thing for—' Stopping herself, she kissed and hugged Maisie again. 'Wherever did you find it?'

'Remember Jim who drives the truck up from Sydney? I told him what I wanted and his wife found it for me.'

'How amazing!' Margaret bounced outside, the bag on her arm. 'Hey, dad, look – all the way from Sydney!'

She'd kept up her bright appearance but inside the collywobbles had begun. Should she produce her bombshell at midday? Maybe there wouldn't be too many people around? But friends continued to call with their gifts. Finally, when her parents, Maisie and Oswald had gathered for a quick cup of tea before changing for the party, Margaret announced, 'Dad, about that five hundred pounds . . .'

'It's going into the bank,' Rose said quickly. 'Next time one of us goes into Alice, we'll pay it in for you.'

Margaret concentrated on her father. 'I've decided how I want to spend it, Dad.'

Ned tipped back his wide-brimmed hat. 'Which university are you aiming for? Sydney or Melbourne?'

'I'm going to do what Mum planned, before she married you.'

Rose frowned. 'What's that supposed to mean?'

Margaret handed her the letter from Middlesbrough; Rose read it and passed it to Ned. When he'd finished, his face was impassive.

'This isn't your doing, then?'

'Certainly not. I'd no idea what she'd been up to.' Rose took it, handed it Maisie and stared at her daughter. 'It's utterly ridiculous, you realize that? You can't possibly go to England—'

'Listen! You're always saying there's too much office work for one person. You swear sometimes because you never had a chance to learn properly and your fingers keep making mistakes. I *want* to learn shorthand and typing *and* book-keeping. I shall become the best secretary in the world and then I'm coming back here to the depot, to work for you!' Margaret was tense with the effort of trying to make them understand.

Rose simply shook her head and repeated, 'It's just not possible.'

'I can pay Auntie Mu rent while I do the course – she never has enough money – then I can persuade her and Uncle Lionel to come back with me to Australia.'

'What?' Ned asked, startled.

'Don't you see, Dad? We'll all be together the way you and Mum always wanted.' She tried to wind her arms round him but for once her father didn't respond. 'I'll only be away for a year but I'll bring them back with me, you see if I don't.'

'She's got it all worked out,' marvelled Maisie.

Margaret turned to her eagerly, 'Don't you think it's the best use of my five hundred pounds?'

Maisie wasn't caught so easily. 'That's up to your mam and dad, love. Come on, Oswald, we need to get ready.'

Seeing Ned's pain made Rose furious. His expression told

her he'd already resigned himself to losing his darling daughter but couldn't bear the thought. She promptly attacked Margaret, 'You can't go all that way, you're far too young. No arguments. Tomorrow, you can write and let the college know you won't be taking up their offer. Now, go and change. Your guests will be arriving in less than an hour and I don't want the evening spoiled. This party is costing us all a great deal of money.'

The sparkle fizzled out. White-faced, Margaret walked away.

When she'd gone, Ned said quietly, 'We can't stop her, pet. She's ready to fly the nest.'

'She's only sixteen!'

'She's entitled to leave school this summer if she wants. I know we had hoped she would go to university but it's obvious she's set on seeing all those places you've told her about.'

Rose felt the accusation as keen as a blade. 'Ned, it's not my fault!'

'I'm not blaming you. I've told her about Mu and Lionel often enough, and Hayden. It's a world Margaret's been wanting to explore since she was a child. It's become a part of her life. We're both responsible.'

'You're not suggesting ... You don't intend to let her go?'

'Providing Mu's agreeable, yes. You write, you'll do it better then I would. Ask if Margaret can stay with them. If the shipping company can provide a reliable guardian – we must agree. You heard what she said. She wants to persuade Mu and Lionel to come, and she wants to come back here herself to help you.' He kissed Rose on the cheek. 'We could do with the best secretary in the world, especially one who can type. We'd only be losing her for a twelve-month, let's not be selfish about it.'

Rose dashed away her angry tears. 'Don't joke. It's you who'll suffer, that's why I'm so cross.'

'Yes, pet, I know. But she's doing it because she loves us. Thanks to you she has such a sweet nature. Listening to her

472

tonight, I was remembering the day I first met you. Our daughter can behave in the same impetuous fashion occasionally. Now, go and find a pair of boots because I'm going to ask for a dance later on. I'll break the glad tidings to Margaret.'

He walked along to the end room and tapped on the door. From inside came the suspicion of a sob. 'It's me, Margaret.'

'You can come in.' She was sitting in front of the wall mirror that doubled as her dressing table. On the bed were the newly starched dress and clean white stockings, plus the new handbag.

Ned avoided her tear-stained face and kept his voice matter of fact. 'Your mam and I have had a chat. Have you really thought out what your idea will mean? You've never been away on your own before. England's too far to do anything about it if you're homesick.'

'That's why I want to stay with Auntie Mu, dad. She's been inviting me for so long. It'll be family − I shan't feel lonely living with them.'

Ned acknowledged the truth of that. 'She's been a good sister; she looked after me really well when I was at rock bottom.'

'I shall be repaying her with a proper rent, don't you see? You and Mum needn't feel embarrassed while I'm doing that.'

'And what about secretarial work? Do you want to end up a business woman like your mam?'

'I'm not as clever as she is,' Margaret declared frankly. 'She's always making important decisions. All I want to do is help with the letters and filing and keep the customers happy. I shall be good at that. I know so many of them already.'

'If you went to university, you might find you're cleverer than you think.' His daughter's obstinate expression reminded him so much of Rose.

'Then you'd want me to have a proper career and leave here for good. I'd only see you and Mum at holiday time. That's not what I want, Dad. I want to go on living here, among my friends.'

473

Which reminded him of another worry.

'Your mam says you've invited the blacks tonight.'

'Yes?'

He tried to be tactful. 'I don't want to interfere but now that you are growing up ... There is a difference in the way some of the boys think of you nowadays.'

He was miffed when Margaret giggled, 'I know, Dad. "An ordinary friend isn't the same as a *special* friend." Mum lectured me about it last birthday.'

Did she so? I wish she'd told me, he thought.

Margaret went on, 'You needn't worry. The Abo boys don't bother inviting me the way they used to. They're growing up too, Dad. Some of them are planning to leave the depot. I can't take part in their ceremonies and they don't want to join in mine. After supper tonight they won't be dancing, they'll be going back to the humpies. Uncle Oswald has given them some beer.'

Not too much, Ned hoped. The once easy-going relationship with the blacks had degenerated since the arrival of the harder working, heavy drinking construction gangs. The problems he and Oswald had to contend with sometimes turned ugly. Reluctantly, he'd had to warn Margaret against too much intimacy with former companions. Rose had been equally stern about giving the bunk-house a wide berth.

Margaret was looking at him seriously. He could see she had forgotten the Abos and was totally preoccupied with her own plans. She didn't understand his pain when she demanded, 'Can I go to Middlesbrough, Dad?'

He forced himself to sound light-hearted. 'If you must. We shan't stand in your way.'

'Oh, Dad!' The arms went round him, she buried her face on his shoulder. Ned wanted to shout aloud from a sense of betrayal that she should be so eager to leave. Instead, he kissed and hugged and convinced her he was delighted.

After that the party was a complete success with Margaret in a haze of delight. Rose collected the motley gifts as her daughter

474

hugged and kissed each newcomer and told them the news.

'Look, Mum, a mongoose – isn't she sweet! She's just what I'll need when I get back, I expect my room will be full of snakes by then ... Yes, isn't it wonderful? I'm going to stay with Dad's sister in Middlesbrough.'

A *fait accompli*, Rose noted wryly. Margaret never expected a refusal: if she loved you, why would you want to turn her down? And tonight her innocent, vital daughter loved the whole, wide wonderful world.

Ned's expression made Rose's heart turn over; pain had been replaced by sad resignation. She dreaded the thought of waving Margaret off on her journey. What would Ned do then? How could he bear the days until she returned? If only the girl would wait a little longer.

'One of Ned's pennies for them?' It was Oswald and Rose forced a smile.

'I was worrying about Ned when the time comes to say goodbye to Margaret.'

'Aye, it'll be worse for him.' He cleared his throat. 'Rose ... about this scheme of baby's. Maisie and I were wondering ... Have you and Ned considered what's going on over there?' Rose frowned. 'You know, in Europe. It might be better if baby waited.' Politics didn't interest Rose but she agreed whole-heartedly with the suggestion.

'She is too young but Ned pointed out most of the girls on the course will be the same age. And if she went to a typing school in Sydney, we'd only see her in the holidays so the result would be almost the same.' Oswald realized she hadn't understood. He was silent. Rose wondered if she'd offended him in some way. 'Your handbag is a popular gift, look at her showing it to everyone.'

They watched Margaret laughing and skipping from table to table. Rose's voice tightened. 'She's behaving like a six year old, never mind being old and sensible enough to leave home.'

Oswald said awkwardly, 'She'll be well looked after, you'll have no worries there, Ned's sister will see to that. Baby will be a proper young lady when she comes back – a real help to you. As Maisie said, what a novelty that will be, eh?' Rose managed a smile. 'The 'drome is nearly finished, she might fly home in an aeroplane.'

If she feels the way I do about sea travel, she'll have every reason to, thought her mother. They waited as the last of the trestle tables was cleared away and on the garage forecourt the coloured lights were switched on to oohs and ahs from the guests.

'Time for me to do my stuff.' Oswald snatched a glance at Rose and was satisfied to see she looked calmer. He rose, extremely dignified in his ancient dress suit. 'I trust that you will reserve one dance for me, madam.' Rose inclined her head at his gallantry.

'I shall be delighted.'

He bowed, the stiff shirt front creaking slightly. 'Thank you.' Marching into the centre, he clapped white-gloved hands, calling, 'Ladies and gentlemen, if I could have your attention ... Our anniversary girl, Miss Margaret Muriel Harrison, will be partnered in the first dance by her father, your host, Mr Edward Harrison.'

With majestic tread, Oswald offered his arm to Margaret and led her onto the forecourt. She waited, pink-faced, as he did the same to a stunned Ned. Rose watched her daughter, the blue, full-skirted dress and old-fashioned ribbon jogging a childhood memory. It was Alice standing there in her own personal Wonderland, not her daughter at all. Then Ned arrived, holding out stiff arms. They were whispering but Rose was too far away to hear.

'The last time I danced a waltz was with Aunty Mu – when I was seven!' Ned hissed frantically. Margaret wasn't the eager schoolgirl ready to throw her arms around him, she was an elegant young woman and he was suddenly nervous of letting her down.

She said coolly, 'It's all right, Dad, it's only one-two-three-and.'

'And – *what*?'

'Ssh – I'll show you!' They began giggling helplessly. The

476

illusion of Alice vanished for Rose. They're in their own private world, she thought; the rest of us are not permitted to glimpse inside.

Applause faded as the scratchy selection from *Careless Rapture* began. How her mother would have ridiculed all this, and Gertie. Despite her resolve Rose had to find her handkerchief. Here we are, under a tropical moon, dancing in front of petrol pumps with moths as big as ping-pong balls, but I don't find it silly. And there's Ned gazing at Margaret, full of love and pride although his heart must be almost breaking. Don't you dare let him down, my girl, she whispered silently.

Seeing the semicircle of wide-eyed black children, Rose thought suddenly: how Cecil would have sneered. The idea shocked her. Why should I imagine such a thing? Because it's true, I suppose. What a narrow-minded group we were in those Clairville Road days.

If only she hadn't told Margaret so much about Middlesbrough ... She sighed; it was too late to worry about that.

Maisie interrupted her introspection. 'Oswald's enjoying himself.'

'He's doing splendidly. His appearance has frightened everyone into their best behaviour.'

They watched as, slightly abashed, guests joined the couple on the dance floor. Ned's face was alight, he had both hands round Margaret's waist. It wasn't much of a waltz but Rose had never seen him look so happy. She sounded flat despite the effort to be grateful.

'Thanks for everything, Maisie. The meal, organizing all the helpers – it should have been my responsibility but I couldn't have coped nearly so well ...' Her voice quivered. 'It's been – quite a day.'

Maisie's arm tightened round her shoulders. 'Cheer up. She'll be back at the depot before you know it.'

Dawn was nearly breaking before they finished clearing away the last of the debris. Rose announced she needed a shower.

'You cut along,' Ned told her. 'I'll just check the marquee's ready to dismantle.'

477

She stood a long time, letting the water soothe her tired skin, feeling the muscles relax one by one. It had been a wonderful birthday party, one Margaret would remember all her life. Quietly she made her way back to their bedroom. Ned was waiting for her. He took off her wrap and tenderly folded her nude body in his arms.

'I've been waiting to do this all day ... Thank you, my darling girl.'

Between kisses Rose murmured, 'Thank me for what?'

'For giving me a perfect pearl to cherish.' She stifled the tiny, jealous flame that was always there, ready to spring into life and devour her pleasure. In moments of great affection, Ned always referred to Margaret as his pearl of great price. Now he lifted Rose onto the bed, running his fingers over the dappled pattern the early sunlight marbled over her skin.

'A rose-red ruby ... as well as a pearl. Was ever a man so blessed?' Then, as never before, Rose experienced such an ecstacy of loving passion, the whole world span on its axis. How could she have doubted Ned's love? They came together in one final exhausting overpowering climax. Through it, she heard him mutter, 'My dearest, darling girl. You won't ever leave me?' Had she been able to, Rose would have laughed: What a question to ask!

'Never, never, never.'

'That's good.' He wrapped her fingers round a kiss and was immediately asleep.

The letter despatched to Mu the following week was businesslike:

Dear Muriel,

Your present arrived two days before Margaret's birthday. She hasn't had an opportunity to wear the beret and scarf yet, the temperature here is still in the nineties, but hopes to thank you in person.

She has applied to Wades (now in Borough Road East) for the twelve-month secretarial course beginning

478

next September. Ned and I were let into the secret on her birthday. It sounded a madcap idea at first but she has always been eager to meet the rest of her family as well as see Middlesbrough. She is also determined to become a secretary rather than try for university as we had hoped.

Would you and Lionel agree to let her stay? She would pay £3.0.0d per week for her keep, as well as help with the housework. If you have any worries at all, please say no. Margaret is very young and I realize it would be a responsibility. She can easily wait another year.

Ned had a photographer take the three of us at the birthday party. Margaret is holding a mongoose, now christened Hermione, a present from a black friend.

We send our love and hope Lionel's back is improving. If only we could bottle some of this sunshine, it would do him the world of good and we certainly have plenty to spare. Thank you for the customary news of Gertie. As usual, we haven't heard from her or Harold.

With best wishes,

Your loving sister-in-law,

Rose.

Mu's initial reaction was delight. By return she posted her consent. A month or so later, when events in Europe resulted in a protest from the British prime minister to Herr Hitler, Lionel persuaded her to write again deferring the visit, but by the time that letter arrived, Margaret was already en route for Southampton. Ned, increasingly anxious, cabled them, begging Lionel to be at the quayside to meet her.

The dragon guardian provided by the Cunard company didn't believe in being lax even in the arrival hall. She compared Lionel's prematurely ageing features with the photograph supplied by Margaret. 'This must have been taken several years ago?'

'Aye, it was.'

'Have you any other proof of identity?' Fumbling through pockets produced a library ticket. The dragon scrutinized it.

479

Peeping out from behind her, Margaret whispered, 'Uncle Lionel – it's me!' He grinned: my word, she was bonny! Such vivid colouring compared to an English child and obviously bursting with health. As for that hair ... Mu was going to have her hands full with this one.

'I can tell it's you. Like your mam and your dad, you are.'

'Am I really!' Margaret had been confined too long, now she began to jog with excitement. 'No one's ever said that to me before.'

The dragon relinquished her responsibility with something approaching relief.

'This looks satisfactory, thank you. I shall write and tell your parents you've arrived safely, Miss Harrison. Kindly remember to do likewise. Your father will be on tenterhooks until you do.' Her tone to Lionel was significant. 'I found her quite a handful, Mr Maynard. I wish you joy.'

Margaret was bubbling over, she was in England at last! Lionel waited till they were on the train before he asked, 'She seemed a bit upset. What did you get up to on the boat?'

'Oh, *that*. Boats are splendid places for enjoying yourself, Uncle, but the dragon kept interfering. She wouldn't let me dance with the officers, she insisted I go to bed ridiculously early. Really, she was an absolute *nuisance*.'

'Aye, well ... I hope you're going to listen to your Auntie Mu and not be a trouble.'

Her eyes widened. 'Me – trouble?! Oh, how can you say such a thing? I love you so!' She flung her arms round him, much to Lionel's embarrassment. 'I'm so *pleased* to be here!' Realizing she'd ignored the rest of the carriage, she turned to the other passengers. 'Hello. I'm Margaret Harrison.' To her amazement, they all pretended to be deaf.

Lionel was worn out by the time they reached Middlesbrough. The taxi pulled up outside the small terraced house. Margaret's eyes were popping out of her head. 'All these properties ... so close together! And tarmac roads everywhere!'

'Yes, well, it's like that in England,' he said tiredly. 'You go

480

inside, find your aunt. I'll see to this luggage. Now then, driver, how much do we owe?'

The front door opened. Aunt and niece stared at one another. Margaret was momentarily speechless. Then, 'You look just like my dad!'

'So do you, pet. And you remind me of Rose as well.' Mu held wide her arms. 'Welcome to England, Margaret.' It was so familiar, so reminiscent of Ned. Sobbing, Margaret rushed to be hugged.

Mu was firm. Everything could wait till tomorrow. They had a cup of tea, Margaret was taken up to the room she was to share with her cousin June and ordered to say her prayers and go to bed. Exhaustion overtook her mid-sentence and Mu finished tucking in the blankets. Downstairs, Lionel was re-reading the letter she'd brought from Ned.

'It is very good of you to give our daughter a home. Rose and I would like to thank you by offering you and Mu a holiday. When Margaret finishes her course next summer, perhaps the three of you would like to visit Paris? Mu was always saying she'd like to go there when we were young. Rose and I would also like Margaret to see something of Europe. The enclosed is a contribution towards the fares.' Two twenty-pound bank notes lay on the table; Neither Mu nor Lionel had handled one before.

'Margaret's already given me five pound for the train fare and taxi ride,' Lionel grumbled. 'Put the money in my hand straightaway – "There you are, Uncle. This is from Dad. I'm not to be any expense." They must be rolling in it.'

Mu shook her head over the letter. 'I don't think so but Ned wants to be generous. Paris? Fancy him remembering.' She glanced at her husband. 'I'm surprised Ned suggested it now, though. I saw today they've started digging trenches in the recreation ground – I doubt whether anyone will go on holiday this year, least of all abroad. It said on the wireless there's bound to be a war sooner rather than later.'

'Living so far away, maybe they don't understand.'

The following Sunday, Margaret began her first proper letter home. The dragon had supervised the postcards from every port, this time she could say what she pleased.

'Dearest Dad and Mother,

It has rained every day since I arrived. Sometimes it doesn't stop even for a minute. June says this is normal. I told her we have a drought nearly every year. She says everybody in Middlesbrough can use as much water as they like.

Uncle Lionel met me. He is a very nice old man and has grey hair and a curvy back. Auntie Mu is a little bit fat. She talks like Dad and is very kind. When I am home-sick I listen to her and think about the depot. How is Hermione? I am sharing a room with June. She is nineteen and works in the grocery department of the Co-operative stores. She earns 22/6d a week which is a very good wage and has a permanent wave. She gives Auntie Mu ten shillings and saves 7/6d for her bottom drawer. She is hoping to become a film star like Norma Shearer. We went to the cinema with her friend Edwin on Friday to see Mickey Rooney. Edwin did not believe we had no cinema.

I know what being cold means. My bed is under the window. When the wind blows it rattles a lot. Auntie Mu said I could have a paraffin stove whenever I liked because three pounds is too much. I think they must be poor because the food is always the same. We have damper all the time and roast pork on Sundays. The milk comes every morning in bottles to every property in the street.

June has pictures of the little princesses and thinks they are sweet. Yesterday we went to Redcar but the waves were so rough we could not walk on the beach. Uncle Lionel says this is an Indian summer.'

Margaret chewed her pen, reluctant to mention one particular adventure. To her surprise she had discovered June knew very little about Valentine. Revealing the secret gave Margaret a chance to show off. Both agreed a visit to the tabernacle was absolutely necessary, if only to glimpse a love child.

'I shall tell mother we're visiting Peggy in Thornaby,' June decided, 'we will go and see her afterwards so it won't be a real fib.'

They were nervous as they slipped inside the shabby building, trying to mingle with the worshippers. There was a fanatical air about some of them. They accepted hymn books from a young man with rabbity teeth who guided them into a pew. All about talk of repentence was loud. June recovered first and began to look round. 'Do you know what Valentine looks like?'

'Auntie Mu sent us a newspaper cutting when he was a baby. He's about a year older then me.'

'Not that one over there with red hair?'

Margaret smothered a giggle. 'I hope not! Look at his Adam's apple!' There was a murmur as Harold took his place behind the superintendent's table and she whispered excitedly, 'That must be my uncle.'

June was surprised. 'He's quite old then? Can you see your aunt?'

A thin woman with a mangy fur at her neck, accompanied by a tall, dark-haired, handsome youth hurried past.

Margaret shook her head. 'Perhaps they haven't come.'

June was dismayed. They might be stuck here for over an hour, could they slip out now without being conspicuous? It was too late; Harold was on his feet, bidding them all welcome and announcing the first hymn.

Gertie was flustered. Valentine had been so *difficult* this evening. Raymond had acquired a new bicycle and had offered Valentine a ride. She had refused to let him accept, tomorrow would be soon enough; as a result he stood sullen and silent beside her, making no attempt to join in the singing.

483

She often wondered whether it had been worth the battle to keep him on at school. And when Valentine left for the university, would she ever see him again? Depression, heavy and thick as a fog, settled on Gertie and threatened to choke her.

She went through the service mechanically, not hearing Harold's commands to the Almighty, staring ahead at nothing as passionate voices 'bore witness' of sin. The final hymn was announced. The harmonium came to life, people rose and Valentine set off with the collection plate.

He reached the pew where June and Margaret stood. A nut-brown girl with eyes full of laughter and marvellously thick hair gazed at him with open curiosity. Valentine stared back. Margaret grew nervous. She wondered if she hadn't offered sufficient but her shilling glittered among the pennies. June nudged her, 'Is this ... is he the one ...?'

Margaret suddenly realized it probably was. She muttered, 'Are you Valentine Brigg? I'm your cousin, Margaret.'

Valentine jerked to attention. Cousin? Then he saw his fellow collector on the opposite side had nearly finished and hurried to catch up. A female cousin? He dimly remembered Mother talking to him once – Aunt Rose in Australia had had a baby daughter.

Was this the girl? She wasn't exactly pretty but she looked jolly good fun. When he got home, he would ask Mother about her. A cousin? A chance of claiming kinship with that vivid-looking, charming girl? What a piece of luck!

Harold gave the benediction, people shuffled into the aisles. Following them, Gertie and Valentine began to move towards the door.

June said conspiratorially, 'We'll let the sinners go first. We don't want to get mixed up with them.'

'Goodness, no!' The service had been horrid and the tabernacle was simply awful. Imagine coming here week after week!

Margaret looked round and found Valentine – if indeed it was him – advancing towards them. He stared, his serious face with the dark intelligent eyes examining her. She blushed. The thin woman beside him hadn't noticed. He murmured to her and the woman's head jerked up. She too stared at Margaret. Behind her glasses, the pale eyes grew fixed, colour drained from her face. She gasped one word: 'Rose!' and fainted. In the mêlée, June and Margaret scurried away. They didn't say a word on the journey home except to swear one another to secrecy.

'I don't think Ma would like it if she knew where we'd been.'

'No.' Margaret felt sure Rose wouldn't either; all the same if that good-looking young man was her cousin, Valentine Brigg – what absolute bliss!

Chapter Twenty-Two

Consequences, 1939

Mu knew that Rose depended on her for news. Margaret wrote every week, Mu far less frequently but she filled in the gaps, including, eventually, mention of the outing to the tabernacle.

Guilt made June uncomfortable and after few weeks she confessed. Mu waited in vain for her niece to do the same; Margaret remained silent.

Mu looked for excuses; Margaret was finding the strict discipline at the college very different to anything she'd known previously and the attitude of the other girls unsettled her. They mocked her accent and her innocent friendliness, particularly towards the school caretaker. When she had defended herself by explaining, 'My dad had to do that job once,' they had rejected her completely and sent her to Coventry.

Furious, tearful, Margaret had marched in front of the class the following morning and demanded to know the reason. Girls sniggered at one another. As for the teacher, she said coldly that Margaret should go back to her seat and stop making a fuss.

Mu hadn't the heart to scold. She could understand how reality was failing to live up to expectation: Margaret's longed-for romantic dream was fast disappearing. On this occasion her aunt tried to explain. 'It's snobbery, pet. Over here, people see those sort of jobs, cleaning, caretaking and suchlike, very differently.'

'Dad only did the work because he couldn't find anything else.'

'I know. Don't take on. We were proud of him, very proud. Those were bad times but Ned never gave up. And now he's made something of himself. He's determined you shall do the same so stick at those lessons and don't worry about the silly lasses.'

Privately, she warned June there were to be no more visits to the tabernacle. 'If he knew the pair of you had visited the place, Ned would be very angry – as for Rose, she'd be livid. Gertie Brigg still owes her all that money, remember.'

June had no intention of going again; the experience had been dreary. However, Margaret was a delightful newfound relative, always eager to be impressed by June's worldly experience as well as being an extremely useful companion for outings to the cinema. Her mother couldn't object to Edwin's presence if Margaret was there as chaperone.

But Margaret wasn't interested in make-believe, she had come to England to meet real people. That first encounter with Valentine had increased her desire to know him better – her new cousin looked so sophisticated and handsome compared to boys at the depot.

By chance, or so it seemed, Valentine was outside the cinema when she and June emerged one night. There was a brief exchange of courtesies. June waited impatiently, catching fragments borne on the wind.

'. . . wondered if we could go for a walk?'

'. . . absolutely super!'

'. . . after school?'

'. . . so many places I want to see. Do you know Clairville Road?'

When Margaret finally rejoined her, her cheeks were pink and June was once again sworn to secrecy.

'Mother won't like it, neither would Aunt Rose.'

'Neither of them will find out.'

But Mu did find out a few weeks later when June said carelessly, 'Peggy came with Edwin and me last night.'

'What about Margaret, wasn't she with you?'

June said lamely, 'She didn't want to see Shirley Temple.'

'Where did she go?'

'I think she met Valentine Brigg. They go for walks some-times.'

'What! How long has this been going on?' June was corn-ered.

'Since Christmas. He was outside the cinema one night and spoke to her.' It was now February and Mu was distraught.

'What on earth will I tell her dad?'

'If you don't say anything then he won't need to worry,' June suggested.

'Oh, you're a great help! Apple of his eye she is and we're *responsible*. Next time, miss, you don't let Margaret out of your sight, is that understood? And take that gas-mask upstairs, I'm forever tripping over the wretched thing.'

'Mum, it's her birthday next week, Margaret's nearly seven-teen.'

'I know. And she's the friendliest girl for her age I've ever met, which makes it worse. Listen, June, neither her father nor Rose would want that girl to go for walks with young Brigg, so from now on, she doesn't.'

Mu's next letter to Rose was composed with care:

I found out from June that the girls visited the tabernacle when Margaret first arrived. On that occasion they happened to see Valentine Brigg. According to June, Margaret introduced herself. The two of them met again recently and went for a walk but I've told Margaret how unhappy you and Ned would be to know about it. I suggested when she wants to, she goes out with June or one of our boys. We're all very fond of her, Rose. She's working hard and passed the test for 100 words per minute last week.

Mu discussed with Lionel the need to be more vigilant. 'I've told June she's to warn me if young Brigg comes skulking round again.'

Lionel sighed, 'We don't want to punish Margaret too much, she's finding life tough enough at the college.'

'We'll leave it at that, then?'

'Aye.'

At the depot, Rose consulted Maisie. 'Ned wanted Margaret to catch the very next boat but I persuaded him to let her finish the course.'

'If Muriel is keeping an eye on her, that should be sufficient. You want Margaret to be properly qualified.'

'I do. I hope I'm doing the right thing.' Rose shrugged, 'It's our own fault because we spoiled her but I wouldn't describe Margaret as the most obedient girl in the world.'

Maisie hid a smile. 'Not always, no.'

'I don't envy Mu and Lionel.'

'No. Ned's counting the days till her course has finished.'

It was obvious to everyone now that any visit to Paris would have to be postponed and Margaret would come straight home. 'Oswald says first thing every morning Ned crosses off the dates on the garage calendar, he's never done that before. What will you do when she arrives, will you have a holiday together?'

Rose said slowly, 'That's an idea. We haven't had a proper one since the fortnight in Sydney.'

'Which is why Oswald and I think you should have another before Margaret has to buckle down to office work. Why not go to Queensland? Ned once said he wouldn't mind fishing off the reef. Plenty of young people go there, it's the sort of place Margaret might enjoy.'

Worries banished, Rose squeezed Maisie's hand. 'Why didn't I think of that? You're a good friend, Maisie. I don't know what I'd do without you.'

'Oh, give over!'

But despite Mu's vigilance, Margaret continued to meet Valentine. Having to be secretive about it added to the spice.

For her dad's sake she worked hard but her days at college were miserable. Her aunt and uncle looked after her well enough but they had children of their own and Margaret was no longer the centre of anyone's world. Rose's letters provided ten glorious minutes of comfort whenever they arrived but Margaret's friendly, sunny nature needed the warmth of another human being. Valentine, drawn irresistibly to seek her out, was becoming the one person on whom she could depend. With June's reluctant connivance, they continued to meet and walked through the quieter streets of Middlesbrough.

It was innocent enough at first; Margaret poured out her confusion and Valentine listened. He felt extremely protective towards this exotic, vivid creature, not embarrassed as he did with his mother.

When Gertie wept, Valentine longed to escape. If his cousin's eyed brimmed over, she brushed tears away, smiled and apologized, making him feel extremely adult. Her tales of adversity were designed to make him laugh whereas his mother's weighed him down with guilt. Even during maths, Valentine found his thoughts drifting, inevitably, to Margaret.

As for Gertie, following the encounter in the tabernacle, she flatly refused to attend any more evening services. She refused to discuss the reason for her faint to Harold, hinting at female problems, saying simply, 'Sunday morning is quite sufficient. My sins can be atoned for perfectly adequately and I don't think we should force Valentine to go so often. Sunday mornings and Sunday school are enough. We should encourage him to go out with his friends instead.' This was such a shift from her former stance, Harold became suspicious.

'You were against that previously.'

'Raymond has turned out so much better than I expected, such a polite boy. He cannot help being the son of a postman. I'm quite satisfied he's a suitable friend for Valentine.'

Suitable he might be but Gertie could not demean herself by social contact with Raymond's parents. She never discovered therefore, whether Valentine went out with his friend or not. Since meeting Margaret, he rarely did.

Gertie had confirmed tersely that he and Margaret were

490

related. On that dramatic Sunday evening when Valentine whispered in her ear, 'Look over there, Mother,' she'd refused to believe the evidence of her eyes, and collapsed. When she regained consciousness, common-sense returned: she realized who the girl must be. Rose must have sent her daughter to demand the stolen money.

Gertie had pulled herself together. She couldn't possibly tell Harold, he would make a tremendous fuss. Presumably Margaret was staying with her father's relatives and would return to Australia at the end of her holiday. Until she did, Gertie would stay away from evening services and ensure that Valentine did the same.

'You won't speak to that young woman, Valentine. She may be your cousin but it was impertinent of her to come to the tabernacle, she certainly wasn't there to worship. If you see her about the town, you can ignore her. We won't tell your father. She will be leaving Middlesbrough shortly so there's no reason any of us should become involved.' Encouraging him to see Raymond as often as he liked was intended to be a distraction but images of the now forbidden fruit fuelled Valentine's imagination.

The meeting outside the cinema was the result of careful planning. Equally so, the casual suggestion of a walk. Margaret happily agreed. Valentine could show her all those places in Middlesbrough she'd only heard about and which June declared too boring to visit.

Together they stood in Fleetham Street and gazed up at the first-floor windows. They wandered along Clairville Road until they'd found the right house. She had never known anyone so serious, tall and pale – and handsome! She told him her woes, she teased him to the point of exasperation. They quarrelled, Valentine disappeared, but the desire to see her was stronger than ever. He'd never known a girl like her, so vivacious and lively, so different from Raymond's giggly sister.

After June's indiscretion over their first meeting, the need to beware of watchful eyes sent them further afield where they

491

wouldn't be recognized. Because of the constant talk of war, their conversation nowadays was less of the past, more of the uncertain future.

'What will you do if it happens? Will you enlist?' Margaret asked curiously.

'I don't know.' Valentine assessed the possibilities with that part of his character inherited from his mother. 'The authorities may order it and then I'd have to go. If there is a choice, I'd rather find a way of avoiding it. Killing or being killed is absolutely pointless. Father managed to wriggle out of it last time because of his age.'

'People might say that was cowardly.'

'Let them.' He was cool. 'What do *they* matter? Now if you had an opinion . . .'

'Well?'

'That would be different.'

She felt breathless to be offered such power over another human being. 'Would it really? You mean if I thought you should go, you would?'

'I might.' Valentine wouldn't commit himself more than was necessary, his sights were still firmly set on university. It amazed him to know that Margaret had turned down the opportunity. He probed cautiously, 'I suppose you'll go back to Australia if anything happens?'

'I couldn't leave Dad on his own, heavens! Or Mother.'

'What's your mother like?' he asked curiously. 'Is she anything like mine?'

There was a certain hesitancy before Margaret replied, 'I don't think they look alike, exactly. I've only seen your mum once but my mine's taller. Her hair's sort of goldy-brown. She told me it used to be darker but the sunshine bleaches everything in Australia. Except your skin of course, that goes brown. Mum's eyes are dark blue. What colour are your mother's?'

Valentine didn't answer. Instead, he reached out and touched Margaret's cheek with his finger.

'You used to have brown skin. The first time I saw you, I

492

thought how different you were. You've faded a bit.'

'It's the rain,' she teased, 'it's washed it all away.' She stretched long legs out in front of her. 'Even my feet are pink these days. Mum used to grumble they were the same colour as the dirt and she couldn't tell if I'd washed them. Oh, I do miss all the sunshine, Val.'

He was indignant. 'We've had quite a lot so far this year. It's nearly summer, it doesn't usually get hot till then.'

'It's winter at home and it's miles hotter than this. And the wet has already begun, it's early this year.'

'There you are then.' Honour was restored. 'It hasn't rained here for nearly a week. Shall we walk a bit further?'

Margaret looked at her watch. 'We can't. I have to get back. We've got book-keeping tomorrow. I must revise, it's my worst subject.'

'When can I see you again?'

Her heart began to thump erratically. 'Do you want to?'

'Of course. You know I do.'

In a prim manner inherited from Rose, she said, 'A girl likes to be sure of her facts, you know.'

Valentine grinned. 'Miss Harrison, may I request a further assignation, at a time and place to suit your convenience?'

'You sound just like Uncle Harold!' They both found this so comical they roared with laughter.

He cried out, 'D'you know what makes that even funnier – Father is at an assignation right this minute.'

'What do you mean?'

'On Monday nights he takes a scripture class for young men. Afterwards ...' laughter interrupted. 'Afterwards he goes round to Mrs Porteous in Albert Road!'

Margaret waited until the paroxysm was past. 'Who's Mrs Porteous?'

'A little – *widow*.'

'I don't see why that makes it amusing.' She was cross at not understanding and he was embarrassed.

'Father's married ... she hasn't got a husband, that's why it's naughty.'

493

'But – why?'

'I don't *know*.' She'd pierced his *amour-propre*; he wished he did understand but, having given him the bald facts, Raymond had withheld further information. 'Come on, I'll see you to your bus. I shouldn't have told you anyway, you're such a sweet girl.'

'Don't be so patronizing! How did you find out about it?'

'I followed Father one Monday night. Raymond's dad is a postman, he knew who lived at that address.'

'I still don't understand why your dad shouldn't visit a widow lady.'

'No, well ... it doesn't matter. Come on or you'll be late.' As they walked along, he asked, 'I wonder why your mother and mine don't correspond. Mine keeps photos of your mother in her dressing-table drawer but it's a forbidden subject for conversation.'

The bus was approaching. Margaret signalled to it.

'Because your mum stole my mum and dad's life savings, of course. Surely you knew *that*?' The vehicle was slowing down. She turned to wish him good night and saw his shock. 'Val? You must have known? It was so your parents could come back to England but they've never repaid except for one measly five-pound note.'

The conductor called impatiently, 'Come along, miss.'

Margaret jumped onto the step. 'Val ... Val, don't be upset, it doesn't matter. It was ages ago and Dad's quite rich now ...' But the bus had moved on and she couldn't catch his reply.

Events of a cataclysmic nature were happening in Europe. Off a Sydney shore, one small but equally disastrous catastrophe had occurred. A telegram conveying news of it arrived at breakfast time in Jamieson Street. Wrapped in his misery, Valentine sat over eggs and bacon while his father tut-tutted. 'I tipped the telegraph boy, Gertrude. One assumes a reply will be needed when one receives an urgent communication – why else would the sender incur the expense – but the wretch

494

refused to wait. I shouted but he took no notice whatsoever ...
So, what have we here? From Sydney, New South Wales ...
from – oh dear, oh Lord!'

'What is it, Harold?'

'Walter's dead. The fool has got himself drowned.'

'Harold!'

'Listen to this: "Regret to inform you Walter Paige lost
overboard Friday stop. Remains washed ashore Sunday stop.
Letter follows stop. Ethel Paige stop." Remains? How indelicate.' Harold obviously relished the idea but Gertie was
already gagging over her breakfast. 'Poor chap. What a way to
go ... obviously not even missed until his *remains* were washed
ashore.'

'Harold!'

'What? Oh, sorry, my dear, are you not feeling well?'
Valentine rose from the table. Walter's abrupt demise left
Harold positively cheerful. 'Off to school, my boy, that's the
ticket. Study hard, be a credit to us. Poor old Walter, imagine
him being so careless. If it had happened to Ethel, that I could
understand, being so prone to accidents ... Mind you, he
always had poor eyesight. I said so the first time we met ...'

Valentine shut the dining-room door, took up his books
and left the house. He scarcely remembered the Paiges. These
days his mind was full of Margaret's accusation: was it true?
Was his gentle, oppressed mother a thief? In his heart, Valentine knew it must be so: Margaret was honest, she wouldn't
tell him a lie.

How could his mother have sunk so low? If only she and
Father had made an effort to repay. Despite the various financial crises, Father's income had been adequate at the
beginning. Why hadn't they done so then?

The shame of it made him too embarrassed to seek
Margaret out even though he wanted to, desperately. He
would leave it for a while. Not too long. He needed to see her
before she left for Australia. That thought made him even
more unhappy.

*

When Harold left the house that morning, he hadn't the slightest inkling of what destiny had in store. All he intended was to enquire how to despatch a sum for the purchase of a small wreath. The assistant bank manager interrupted his request.

'Ah, yes. One moment, Mr Brigg. We also have had a telegraphic communication from Australia. It concerns your account, I believe.'

With Harold, optimism continued to triumph over experience. He began to speculate: had shock encouraged Ethel Paige to be generous? He waited until the assistant manager had despatched a clerk in search of the document before explaining.

'The wreath is for the benefactor and founder of our tabernacle, a truly sad demise ... Washed overboard. Not missed until his *remains* were found on a beach. Shark-infested waters, you know, off Sydney, N S W. Sad. Very, very sad. My wife and I wish to convey to his widow our deepest sympathy.'

'Indeed? Ah, thank you, Collins. Yes, here we are. It is, in fact, a communication from Mrs Paige's bank in New South Wales, from the manager there addressed to the manager here, notifying us that the next payment into your account, which will include an enhanced sum, will be in full and, er – *final* settlement of her responsibility towards the tabernacle and, er, yourself. This asks us to notify you of that fact. Which we would have done immediately, Mr Brigg, had you not called in here this morning. It would have been in the midday post. However, you are here and that is no longer necessary.'

Harold's mind refused to co-operate. 'Pardon?'

'It would seem ... as I interpret it ... that this is a notification ... an indication you might say ... asking us to warn you of the, er, forthcoming termination of, er, payments. Yes, that is how I see it. How very distressing to have two such sad communications from the, er, Antipodes within so short a time.'

Comprehension was returning. 'Is that woman trying to cut me off without a farthing?'

496

'She is notifying you in advance of her intention to terminate the existing arrangement as from the beginning of next month. As I understand it.'

'The bitch!'

'Mr Brigg!' The assistant manager was scandalized. 'It may be that the poor lady, in view of the extremely distressing accident to her husband—'

'That poor lady,' Harold's quivering finger pointed accusingly at the cable, 'is as rich as Croesus. For her, three hundred pounds per annum is a paltry sum. She never loved her husband! Now she cannot wait to obliterate the memory of Walter – and that of his grandfather – for without her support the tabernacle cannot continue. Poor, dear Walter, his lifeless body picked up by some passing fisherman – far better leave him to the sharks. It would have saved the cost of the funeral.'

'A most unfortunate set of, er, circumstances. However, if you wish to telegraph money for a wreath—'

'Will flowers benefit a dismembered corpse?'

'I er, really couldn't say.'

'An absolute waste. I shall not give that woman the satisfaction of seeing how much we care. We will write. My wife will compose a suitable letter. It is all that is necessary.'

Before leaving, however, Harold withdrew an additional three pounds. He needed a decent lunch to sustain him after the shock.

That evening, when she was told, Gertie was bewildered. 'But we cannot manage without Ethel's money!'

'Exactly.'

'We shall be – destitute.'

'Don't exaggerate, Gertrude. Valentine will leave school immediately, no question about that. He will become our crutch and support—'

'No!'

'Gertrude, I am not prepared to lower our standards because of one selfish woman. Valentine will find work. I shall protest to Ethel, of course, in the strongest possible terms. I shall tell you exactly what to say. Do you realize, I was probably Walter's only true friend. If only he had stayed on here as my assistant and helped me run the tabernacle – as I'm sure his grandfather would have preferred – his remains would not now be in a coffin.' Harold's flow ceased abruptly. 'Yes, Valentine?' Why did the boy never knock? How much had he overheard? Harold fully intended Gertrude should break the news that Valentine must leave school, preferably when he himself was out of the house.

Valentine hadn't heard a word. He'd been hovering in the hall, summoning up courage to make his accusation.

'Mother, I know about the money you stole from Aunt Rose. I think you and Father should pay it back.' It was the most ill-judged interruption he was ever likely to make. That night, Harold's temper reached its peak.

No one now doubted there would be a war; at the depot, Rose and Ned wrote ordering Margaret to book her passage.

'I've enclosed another letter to Mu and Lionel, would you like to read it?'

Ned shook his head. 'You've asked them to come out here?'

'Not asked, I've *begged* them this time,' Rose was emphatic, 'plus the family, plus June's friend Edwin if he wants. We've plenty of jobs to offer and all of them would be better off here.'

'Let me see again what I wrote to Margaret.' It was simple enough.

My dearest pet,
    Your mother and I think it best you should come home immediately. On the radio and in the papers it is all talk of war. We remember how bad it was the last time. The north-east suffered because of the ship yards. This time it could be even worse. As soon as you get this letter I want you to book your ticket. Your mother has written inviting Mu and Lionel. Please try and persuade them, Margaret. You can tell them what a good life they would have with us. I'm sorry to rush you but your

498

mother and I are very worried. We won't be happy until we see your bright, happy face. Hermione is keeping your room clear of snakes. Sad to say, the old emu died. Oswald was quite upset. We gave it a decent burial but I think the blacks would have liked it for supper. Come home soon. We miss you.

Much love,
Dad
XXX
PS There is extra money in the bank for the tickets.

He glanced at Rose. 'Can't think of anything else, can you? I'll drive into Alice, make sure it gets there fast.' Everything was far more urgent now.

'I'll ring the post office and warn them you're coming.'

'Thanks. If only there was some way of phoning Mu. You're sure we shouldn't send a telegram?' Evening sunlight shone on his anxious face and the grey hairs that had appeared since Margaret's departure.

'We don't want to frighten them. It's Europe that's in danger, it hasn't affected the shipping lines. Don't worry. We'll get her home, you'll see.'

Ned couldn't even raise a smile. 'I hope you're right.'

These days Margaret was permanently miserable. At college she was despised and held herself proudly aloof, which was against her nature. Homesickness made her cry into her pillow. It looked as if Mum was right, she'd been so sure Margaret wouldn't enjoy herself over here.

She would stick it out. She would pass all the tests and take the certificates home for Dad. She mustn't let him know she was unhappy. She blew her nose. For heaven's sake cheer up! At least the sun was peeping through the clouds today. Maybe she could leave off the layers of woollen jerseys at last. If only Valentine would remember her existence occasionally, that would help. Tying her ribbon bow, she ran downstairs for breakfast. Uncle Lionel was crouched beside the wireless. She

499

whispered to Mu. 'Is the news bad?'

'Morning, pet. As bad as it could be, I reckon. Eat up. Lionel and I have been discussing whether or not you shouldn't pack your bags immediately.'

'I haven't finished my tests!'

'It's not typing speeds that matter if there's a war.'

'There might not be one ...' She couldn't leave without seeing Valentine! 'The League of Nations might stop the fighting.' Margaret pictured them, dressed like boy scouts, walking in, banging on the table and saying, 'Now look here, Herr Hitler, this can't go on, you know.'

'Drink your tea. You can go to college today but when you get back we'll have a serious chat. Neither of us want to lose you but it's your dad and mam we're thinking about. They'd be worried sick if anything happened to prevent you getting back.' Lionel had turned off the radio. 'Anything new?'

'Same only worse.' He sighed. 'There's plenty of shouting about rearming and building more vessels. Takes a war to bring back employment these days.'

Margaret spent the day scheming. Her impulsive nature made her want to knock at Valentine's front door but she knew that would be unwise. Could she send a note? If she typed the envelope Aunt Gertie couldn't possibly guess who it was from. Satisfied, she spent the lunch break at her machine but when she left college that afternoon, Valentine was at the gate.

'I had to see you. Can we walk for a bit?' Margaret tried not to bounce with delight. He was in his school uniform but he'd stuffed the cap in his pocket and looked so dark and moody! Decorous, not attempting to hold hands, they walked along the busy road.

'Is anything wrong, Val?'

'My father may have to close the tabernacle.'

'Goodness.' She'd never heard of that happening to a church. 'Can't anyone help? A bishop or someone like that?'

It was too difficult, he couldn't begin to explain. 'Last night I told Mother I knew about her stealing that money. She was

500

terribly angry, so was Father. Mother guessed it was you who'd told me. She said it wasn't true.'

'Yes, it was,' Margaret replied hotly. 'My mother said she and Dad were left penniless. Your mother and father stole their life savings to pay for the fare back to England.'

'I believe you. I know when my parents are lying.'

She was amazed. 'Do they often?'

'Father's the worst, he doesn't seem to care. Mother does it to cover up for him most of the time. I think that's why he likes belonging to the Brethren, because they're so secretive. He's told me I've got to leave school, so I'm going to run away.'

'Golly!' Surely no row was that bad?

Valentine's voice trembled despite his anger. 'Some of the things Mother said, that I didn't really love her, things like that. Because I'd been seeing you. It was absolutely horrid, Mags. She keeps on as though I were a kid. Father refuses to support me any longer. He says I'm old enough to make my way in the world, which is true enough. It won't be possible to go to university anyway, I shall have to join up. All my generation will.'

Margaret looked at him with stricken eyes. 'Not yet, Val. Please don't go yet.'

'I'm not going to stay with Father and Mother nagging all the time. I'm going to make a break for it.'

'Where will you go?'

'There's a farm near Seamer. I worked there once, convalescing after measles. I shall ask the farmer if he can take me on until I have to enlist.'

'Will I ever see you again?' She looked at him piteously. 'Auntie Mu wants to send me back to Australia but I don't want to go, Val, not if it means leaving you.'

His voice was suddenly very choked. 'Tell you what, there's a cottage at the farm. We stayed in it for my convalescence. It's empty most of the time. If you like, you can come with me. You could do the cooking and things while I work in the fields. Would you like that?'

'Oh, yes, please!'

'Right. I'll see the farmer this weekend. Once I know how things stand, I'll meet you outside the college, like today. Just make sure they don't ship you off in the meantime.'

'Rather!' Margaret's eyes were shining. 'But I'm only there three more weeks then it's the end of term.'

'I'll be as quick as I can. Bye, Margaret.'

'Au revoir,' she said solemnly. She floated home on wings. At seventeen, finding herself in love for the very first time obliterated every other thought.

She begged to be allowed to finish her tests; reluctantly, Mu agreed. A passage was booked for the day following the end of the course, then Margaret's affairs were forgotten. So many events were happening all of a sudden. June and Peggy were full of the developments at Thornaby now that the aerodrome was expanding. Rumours of the impending arrival of daredevil airmen made Edwin red-faced. Lionel became a warden. Mu, cursing like every other housewife, began stocking up in earnest. Each member of the household became engrossed in their own concerns and on Friday afternoon, Margaret disappeared.

When June arrived back from the cinema that night, she was wondering whether or not Edwin should grow a Ronald Coleman moustache. Her mother called from the kitchen. 'Is Margaret with you, June? Did you got to the pictures together?'

'Mmm?' Her daughter stood in the doorway, 'No, why?'

Mu lost her temper. 'I shall give that girl a piece of my mind this time. She never even asked, just slipped out without me seeing her. I assumed she was with you.'

'Edwin and I were with Peggy. I haven't seen Margaret since this morning.'

Mu stared. 'Didn't she come home for her tea? I left it set.'

'I put a plate over it and put it in the pantry.'

'Oh, Lord – what's she up to this time? Didn't she say anything?'

'No. Maybe Father knows.' But Lionel didn't return until late and, when he did, knew nothing. There was an anxious discussion. Finally, the police were informed.

In Jamieson Street where Valentine had failed to return after school, Harold coldly informed his wife she should have exercised better control. He locked the front door, mounted the stars, went to bed and slept. In the kitchen, Gertie began her solitary vigil.

Valentine had been astonished by Margaret's resourcefulness. When they met at the appointed spot, she had a suitcase and a large basket of food. 'How are we going to take all that? We'll be conspicuous on the bus.'

'We're going to buy a car.'

'What!'

'I've drawn some money from the bank. Here.' It was fifteen pounds. 'I've looked in the *Gazette*. There's one for sale at sixteen pounds in Hartington Road. We'll haggle.'

'I don't know how.'

'Oh, honestly, Val! People do it all the time at the depot. Dad's very clever. He pretends to let them think they've beaten him down. Come on, I'll show you how to do it. You carry the case.' Seizing the basket she strode off.

Panting to catch up, he asked nervously, 'Can you drive?'

'Of course.'

'You're too young anyway, in this country.'

'Valentine, you just said we couldn't travel on a bus.'

'I thought I'd better mention it, that's all.'

He marvelled at the efficient, speedy transaction and helped her load their luggage. Attempting nonchalance, he asked, 'Would you prefer me to take the wheel?'

'If you like. D'you want me to turn the starting handle?'

'Yes, please.'

Their course was unsteady but Margaret was unperturbed, everyone at the depot knew how to drive a car. After five miles, when Val suggested they stop for a rest, she told him, 'I checked the dipstick, we're all right for oil.'

'Oh, good.' Was that what she'd been doing? 'I say, would you like to have a go?'

503

'Yes, please, Val. My, what a lovely big steering wheel! I've never driven a Lanchester before.' Neither had he.

The farm cottage was half a mile from the house down a track.

'It's a real hideaway. No one will find us here.' But Margaret had begun to sound less assured.

Valentine swallowed and cleared his throat. 'It's rather a jolly little house. I hope you like it.'

It was cold and smelled musty. There were two rooms, one was the bedroom. He said uncertainly, 'I was much younger when we were here last. I slept downstairs, Mother and Father were up in the bedroom.'

Margaret said quickly, 'I'll sleep downstairs this time. Shall we light a fire?'

'Rather. I remember where they kept the coal, through here.' He led the way out of the dingy scullery.

Margaret promptly took on the role of housewife. 'My word, I shall have to give this place a thorough clean. What a good thing I remembered to buy Gumption. I thought we could have sausages and chocolate biscuits tonight.'

'Marvellous. I'm frightfully hungry.'

'So am I!' They were both conspirators but already consciences were at work. It was after they'd eaten and cleared away, when the blankets had been divided between the two of them, that anxiety began to show.

'Will your aunt be worried?'

'Terribly!'

'Did you leave a note?'

'You told me not to.' The reproach in her voice made him defensive.

'I'm sorry. I thought she and your uncle would try and interfere. We'll tell them, if you like.'

'Yes, I'd rather we did.'

'Maybe we should leave it a day or two, so they get used to the idea.'

'And Dad and Mum. Dad will be fearfully worried if he finds out.'

Valentine tried to hide his shock. 'Your aunt's not likely to tell him, is she?'

'I've no idea. I hope not.' So did Valentine. The idea of an irate Ned Harrison chasing him wasn't amusing. Side by side, increasingly preoccupied with their own private worries, they stared into the flames.

Eventually Margaret asked, 'What time is it?'

'Twenty past eight.' She'd imagined it to be closer to midnight. 'I'm supposed to start work at seven thirty tomorrow. The farmer told me to be at the back door at twenty-five past.'

'Have you an alarm clock?'

'No. I shall keep waking up during the night, to check my watch.'

'I'll do the same if you like.'

'Thanks.' He tried to lessen the strain. 'It's quite a jolly little cottage, isn't it?'

'Yes, very.' Equally valiant, Margaret enthused, 'Quite dry and ... homey. Especially with the great fire blazing away.'

'I'm glad you think so. There's plenty of coal and logs, we shall be quite snug.'

But for how long, she was desperate to know. She daren't ask for fear of appearing disloyal. Valentine poked the fire unnecessarily. He wished he hadn't suddenly remembered tomorrow's French exam; he stood a good chance of an excellent mark but it was too late to think of that now. 'Unless you want to stay up for a bit, I suppose we ought to go to bed. With such an early start.'

'Yes.' It was little more than a whisper.

He was over-hearty, 'Are you sure you'll be all right down here? We could swop if you prefer?'

The reply was swift. 'No, thank you.' It felt more *suitable* for her to be downstairs. Margaret gazed at her blankets spread over the wooden settle; it didn't look particularly comfortable. She said brightly, 'It's so cosy, I shall sleep like a log. Would you like bacon and egg for breakfast?'

505

'Yes, please.' He cleared his throat again. 'Can I kiss you goodnight, Margaret?'

'Better not. They might not like it.'

'No.' He was certain they wouldn't. Guilt resurfaced and wouldn't be quietened. 'Well, then ... I'll say goodnight.'

''Night, Val.'

She was hollow-eyed from lack of sleep when she roused him. The fire was out. She struggled with the unaccustomed task of lighting it but it defeated her and Val went to work on an empty stomach.

Throughout the day each worked hard to try and quiet inner misgivings. Margaret was amazed to find they'd used up all the kindling and set about splitting more logs. By the end of an hour she was filthy and tired with very little to show for it. That evening, supper was a quiet meal. Afterwards, they sat in silence watching the blaze. When it was time to go to bed, Margaret asked, 'Can we tell them tomorrow?'

'If you like.'

'It's just ... Auntie Mu will be so worried.'

So would his mother, thought Val. He admitted, 'We ought to act responsibly,' and this cheered her immensely.

'Of course we must. So what shall we do, write them a letter? D'you know where there's a post box?'

'I'll ask at the house. Goodnight.' It didn't occur to him to ask again whether he could kiss her. The day had been one of heavy physical labour and for both sleep was profound. An irate farmer had difficulty waking them when he banged on the door the following morning.

Mu and Lionel came to collect Margaret from the police station. It was many hours before they arrived. She hadn't seen or spoken to Val since they were driven away from the farmhouse in separate cars. Her stony-faced jailor hustled her into a small chilly room and refused to let her stir. Even when Margaret went to rise from her stool to ease her frozen limbs, the woman shouted at her to ask permission first. To see Mu's homely face at the barred window, brought a rush of thankful tears.

506

Neither her aunt nor uncle uttered a word of reproach. All Mu said was, 'I've brought your coat, I thought you might be cold.' On the bus back to Middlesbrough, she added, 'We sent a telegram to your Father, we had to. We didn't know what had happened, you see. We'd better stop at the post office and send another.'

'Leave it till tomorrow,' Lionel said gruffly, 'we might have worked out what to do for the best by then.'

'I'll need to go to college on Monday, to sit my final speed test.'

Despite her feelings, Mu looked at her niece compassionately, 'Ee, pet ... you can't do that. You've been expelled.'

Margaret bit her lip and tried not to think what Dad's reaction would be; she made one last plea for toleration.

'Nothing happened, Auntie Mu, we didn't do anything wrong.'

'That's neither here nor there.' The verdict, full of sadness, was final; Margaret knew there could be no appeal.

For the first time since the adventure began she felt thoroughly frightened. In complete disgrace, she waited in her bedroom to learn her fate. Downstairs, Lionel and Mu conferred.

'What'll I tell Ned!? God, Lionel, I feel dreadful. He must be out of his mind with worry by now.'

'Just tell him plain and simple and let him decide. It wasn't your fault. Seems to me the girl just didn't think. She may be seventeen but she acts like a kiddie sometimes. I don't think she realizes how serious it was or how desperate we were. We'll have to try and book an earlier passage.'

'I shall feel so ashamed ... handing in that message at the post office tomorrow.'

'Shall we try and find a way to telephone?'

'No! That would be even worse. I wouldn't know what to say in a phone box. Ee, poor Rose ... the disgrace!'

'This isn't getting us anywhere. We'll work out what to put in the telegram and first thing in the morning we'll send it. Margaret stays in this house till we get a reply. I'll find out about sailing times.'

'Ye-es.' From Mu's point of view, this was no real solution.
'Lionel—'

'Well?'

'Margaret is old enough. And June says she's very fond of the lad. I was thinking, it might be better if they ... you know. If they got married. I'm only thinking of Margaret's reputation, Lionel. Ned might not like it, of course.'

'Like it! He'd come for the lad with a shotgun. Have a bit of sense! Now, have you got pen and paper?'

But at her insistence they added a final, fatal sentence: 'Regret Margaret and Valentine Brigg spent two nights in cottage at Guisborough. Police had to be told. Margaret expelled from college. She is very fond of the boy. Mu and Lionel'

At the depot, Rose's tears ran unchecked. It wasn't the contents that upset her so much as the sight of Ned's face: their daughter had broken his heart.

'Will you give your permission?' she asked at last.

'If I must ...' She'd never heard him so full of despair. 'Is that what Mu means by it? That Margaret has to marry him?'

'I think so. It wouldn't simply be to save her reputation, would it? There must be more to it than that.'

Ned winced. 'Margaret must've been – going with him – for some time?'

'She's never mentioned him in any of her letters.'

'No.'

Rose tried to put a brave face on it. 'We don't know what he's like, Ned. He might be a decent enough lad.'

His shout hurt her ears. 'No decent lad behaves like that with an innocent girl!'

Rose strove to keep her voice steady. 'Will you let them come out here after they're married?'

The chair fell back with a crash. 'You do it. Send word to Mu. Fix it between you. I don't want to know anything about it ...' He fought back tears. 'If it's the only way for us to see

508

Margaret again, we shall have to agree. Now for Christ's sake, leave me alone!'

It was Maisie who came to the shack several hours later; by then Rose was beside herself with worry. 'We've found him at last, dear. He's sitting in the old truck at the end of the runway. The blacks are keeping watch for us. You go to bed. We can't have you both worn out.'

'I'll never forgive her for what's she's done!'

'No, well ...' Maisie had experienced Rose's passionate temper before. 'Maybe we'll all see things differently when we've got used to the idea.'

Rose pushed the sheet of paper across to her. 'What d'you think? Is that plain enough?'

'Is it what you're going to send to Mu?' Fumbling in the pocket of her wrapper, Maisie found her glasses.

'"To Muriel and Lionel Maynard stop Ned and Rose Harrison give permission for their daughter Margaret Muriel Harrison to marry Valentine Brigg stop."' Maisie looked up. 'Is that all?'

'What else d'you suggest? Love and kisses?'

'I thought you were going to invite them both to come here?'

'Eventually,' Rose answered listlessly. 'Not now. I couldn't find the words tonight. I'll send a letter in a day or two.'

'Don't leave it too long. The news on the wireless is nasty.' She came over and gave Rose a fierce hug. 'Don't go broody on me, lovie. He might turn out to be a nice young man, you never know. He could turn out to be handy with machinery and that would be useful.'

'With Harold Brigg for a father?' asked Rose sarcastically.

'Now you don't know whether or not that's true,' Maisie reproved. 'Let's hope it isn't. He and Margaret might want to have children one day. If they aren't cousins, there won't be anything against it.'

In Jamieson Street, Harold couldn't contain himself.

'Clarence Clayton, that spineless whining toad, has threat-

509

ened to "bear witness" next Sunday concerning "persons taken in adultery". No doubt there will be a full congregation and you and I will be pilloried! I blame you, Gertrude, I do indeed. If you had exercised even a modicum of control over that boy—'

'He's your son.'

Harold jerked to a standstill. 'What?'

'Yours as well as mine.' Harold breathed again. 'You should have exercised a father's control. But if anyone is to blame, it's that girl, Ned Harrison's daughter. She has seduced Valentine. Rose sent her over deliberately.'

'For heaven's sake, why didn't you tell me she was over here and that Valentine was seeing her?'

'You're never at home.' Her brief spurt of anger over, Gertie tried to control her sobs. 'Whenever I try to interest you, you always say it's my responsibility. School, homework, it doesn't matter what it is. Well, this time we're both involved. If they're all going to point the finger next Sunday, what I want to know is – what do you intend to do?'

'I ... I ... I haven't decided. Valentine must leave this house immediately.'

'That won't solve anything. He'll need money and neither of us has any.'

Harold began to shout. 'I cannot tolerate an adulterer living under my roof—'

'Do you know that he is?' He was stunned that she should ask such a question, even more when she said, 'Valentine told me nothing had happened between them.'

'Liar! I shall get to the bottom of it!' Gertie was apathetic. What did it matter? Whatever happened, she had lost the only person she cared about.

In the back bedroom, Valentine was silhouetted against the window. He'd had to hand over the room key and stood there defenceless as Harold stormed in.

'I want the truth about what happened, I demand to know what you did to that girl.'

'Nothing.'

510

'Don't you try and fool me. Did you fornicate with the slut?'

'Father!' Close to tears, Valentine yelled, 'I don't know what you mean!'

Savagely Harold described the sexual act as crudely as he knew how. Valentine felt sick.

'That's filthy and beastly. I love Margaret, I wouldn't do those things.' Suddenly, despite his misery, certain events in his father's life began to make sense. 'That's what you do though, isn't it? When you visit Mrs Porteous in Albert Road?'

For a split second nothing happened then Harold threw himself at him. Valentine side-stepped and his father crashed to the floor. From below they heard Gertie's terrified, 'What's happening? What are you doing to him, Harold?'

'It's all right, Mother. Father missed his footing.' Valentine came to the head of the stairs and stared down at her, white-faced. His mother and father did those awful things, all married people did. He said huskily, 'His lip's bleeding.'

'I'll fetch the Germolene.'

In the back bedroom, Harold snarled at him from his hands and knees. 'You'll damn well marry the slut. Your mother will arrange it and I shall announce it in the tabernacle next Sunday before Clarence Clayton can draw breath. Nobody's going to bear witness against the name of Brigg.' He was distracted by a ghastly wailing sound outside. 'What the hell is that?'

'It's an air-raid warning. They said they'd be testing them today.'

Chapter Twenty-three

An Outbreak of Hostilities, 1939

Margaret and Valentine were allowed to meet before their wedding provided a chaperone was present. The last of these stilted occasions took place in Mu's parlour with Gertie and Mu in attendance. Tea was offered and went cold in the cups. Margaret sat hunched and silent on her side of the table. Val could scarcely reconcile her with the sparkling brown maiden he'd first known. His mother didn't help; her open hostility unnerved them.

With some courage, Margaret broke the silence. 'Ten o'clock tomorrow, Val.'

'Yes.' He mouthed so that Gertie couldn't hear, 'I love you!' but she only stared, too downcast to respond. Aloud he asked, 'Will any of your friends be coming?'

'Friends?' She pronounced the word slowly as though she didn't quite understand. 'They're at the depot with Mum and Dad.' A tear oozed out. 'Mum's written ... she said Dad was still too upset. They want us to go out there after we're married. Mum said you could learn the business from Dad and Uncle Oswald. It would be a wonderful opportunity, Val.'

'In Australia?' He was acutely conscious of Gertie; this was enough to send her into hysterics.

'Yes.'

'We'll have to see.'

Margaret's voice wobbled, 'I have to go back, Val. I've promised Dad.'

'I know, but there's no point in rushing. If there is a war, I

512

shall have to enlist. It would be the same if we were over there. Australians will be called up as well.' This made sense.

Margaret nodded reluctantly. If only she could make him understand how eager she was to be home. 'After the war then? As soon as we can book our passage.'

This gave him a breathing space. 'Of course.'

'Auntie Mu's found us some nice rooms. We went to see them last night. They're very homey.'

Gertie spoke in a loud, cracked voice, 'After the ceremony Valentine's coming back with me.'

Margaret stared. 'Of course he isn't. Married people live together. Otherwise there's no point in going to the registry office tomorrow.'

'It's what you planned from the beginning, isn't it, you and Rose?' Her face was mottled as she twisted threadbare gloves. 'You came here deliberately to seduce my boy. You shan't have him. Harold has forced me to give consent to avoid any more scandal but that's as far as it goes. Tomorrow Valentine is coming home with me.'

Mu looked on with pity as the boy struggled with a situation he couldn't control. 'Mother, please! It wouldn't be a good idea for me to do that. You know Father wouldn't like it, he wants me out of the house.'

This sounded like equivocation to Margaret. She spoke out clearly in her own defence. 'I didn't plan anything, Mrs Brigg. Mum didn't want me to come to England, neither did Dad, it was entirely my idea. I wanted to meet the family – I'd heard all about you since I was little. As for what happened between Val and me – it just happened.' She leaned forward, trying to make Gertie understand. 'I do wish you'd stop being beastly. We haven't done anything wrong, truly we haven't.'

It was futile. Gertie had made up her mind and was determined to hang on to Valentine. 'Come along,' she ordered him, 'we've been here long enough.'

'Val ...' Margaret stared, pleading, 'Val, swear we shall be together otherwise I can't go through with it. Don't you love me enough?'

513

The strain of the past weeks showed in the tightness of her mouth, the dark shadows under her eyes. Seeing it, Gertie had a sudden flash of memory: Rose, holding the tray on her wedding morning, demanding to know if she still intended to marry Harold Brigg.

'Val?' Margaret repeated.

He glanced at his mother but she refused to look at him. 'The thing is, I can't afford to pay any rent.' He reddened. 'And I need to go to night school to finish my matric. They threw me out of high school, you know.'

Margaret was relieved. 'Don't worry, I have enough. We can be together, don't you see? You can study and if you have to enlist, I'll find secretarial work. I know we've been rushed into this but we can make a go of it, Val. If we're apart, if you go home with your mother tomorrow ... We don't stand a chance.' Vulnerable, helpless, her eyes never left his.

Gertie announced harshly, 'As this ceremony is for appearance's sake, it should be a marriage in name only. That's all that is required. She seduced you, Valentine. None of it was your fault. You must come home with me and start again.'

She'd gone too far this time. Valentine grabbed Margaret's hand. 'I won't let you down. Take those rooms. I'll have to rely on you for cash but please, Margaret, be there tomorrow.'

She was almost haggard as she searched his face for any further trace of doubt.

'Very well. Ten o'clock. Good afternoon, Mrs Brigg.' She walked out of the room, leaving them standing there.

Mu told Lionel later, 'I was proud of her. She's got enough backbone for the pair of them.'

'I do wish we hadn't insisted, though. It was Brigg coming round here, with all his loud talk of fornication. I believe the pair of them, you know. Margaret's a truthful girl and I don't think they did do anything wrong.'

He'd made her uncomfortable. 'How could Margaret hold her head up? She'd been expelled and everyone knew why.'

Lionel said sadly, 'No, they didn't. None of us knew for certain except the two of them. We've condemned them without good reason. As for what other people think ...?'

Mu said defensively, 'It's too late now.'

'It's not. I'm going to have a word with the lass and don't you try and stop me. I don't want to push her into making the biggest mistake of her life.'

Mu listened to him climb the stair. She'd done what she thought right, acted in Margaret's best interests. How could she send her home like second-hand goods, without a wedding ring?

Lionel tapped on the door. 'Come in.' Margaret was curled up on the bed, surrounded by letters from home.

'Can we have a chat?' He saw the shutters come down. 'I don't see eye to eye with Mu on this business, Margaret. I'm not sure your father would, either.' At the mention of him, her eyes grew dark. Lionel spoke matter of factly. 'If you want to marry young Brigg, well and good, but if you don't, and I can't see the necessity, just you tell me and I'll deal with any hoo-hah. I'll even send Harold Brigg packing and you and me can creep off to Southampton. I'll put you on a boat for Australia without anyone being the wiser.' It was the first real kindness since the scandal broke. Lionel waited for the floods of tears to subside as he stroked the cloak of hair. 'Well, lass, what's it to be? You decide this time. Don't worry about what anyone thinks. It's your life, no one else's.'

Margaret blew her nose. 'I've made such a lot of trouble, I never meant to.'

'Forget about that. It's not important.'

'The thing is ... I like Val a lot ... Very much indeed.'

'Enough to marry him, though? Auntie Mu's talked about what that means?'

'Yes.' Margaret had gone pink. 'I knew some of it from Mum, of course, but auntie explained everything else. All about how to be careful not to have babies. She told me it would be ups and downs for the rest of my life but the ups made up for it if the chap was right.' Lionel was a little taken aback; he hadn't analysed his marriage in such detail. Margaret went on, 'I hadn't planned to get married despite

515

what Mrs Brigg says but if I have to marry anyone, I'd want it to be Val. I do love him. And now he's agreed to go to Australia, that makes it perfect.'

'Aye.' Young Brigg had fallen on his feet, thought Lionel, jealous for his own sons. He'd seen Margaret's collection of photographs of the depot. The size and extent of it had stunned him. 'It'll be a grand opportunity for the lad.'

She was beginning to recover. 'Won't it, though? With Dad showing Val the ropes and me working with Mum in the office, we shall be so happy. You and Auntie Mu will come too, won't you? And June and the boys. That's what would please Dad most of all.'

The Briggs weren't included, he noticed.

'So you do want to go through with it tomorrow?'

'Yes. When Val and I ... when we can be together, on our own, we'll learn to be a proper married couple, you'll see.'

'Well, then.' He got to his feet. 'Best break the good news to your auntie. She was worried we'd pushed you into it. Now I can tell her it's what you want.'

Margaret tried to keep the sob from her voice.

'I wish you could convince Dad as well. His letters are really sad.'

But on her wedding morning a telegram arrived which had her bright-eyed and skipping about for the first time in weeks. Sent by Rose, it read: 'Father and I send you and Valentine heartfelt good wishes for your future happiness stop Come home soon stop All our love stop Mother'

'You see – Dad's come round, I know he would! He doesn't mind, he's pleased!'

'That's grand,' said Mu. 'That's the icing on the cake.' She wondered whether Ned knew anything about it.

Following the disclosure of Ethel Paige's perfidy, Harold had used part of her enhanced severance cheque to refurbish his wardrobe. He had described the necessity to Gertrude. 'In view of the forthcoming hostilities, who knows when we shall be able to obtain decent clothes again.'

'My sentiments precisely, Harold. I intend buying a new winter coat and a costume.'

'Ah ... As the bread-winner, it is essential that *I* make a favourable impression at interviews, etc, etc. However, we must not be *extravagant.*' But Gertie wasn't to be denied her share, it might be her last opportunity. Ethel's final cheque had been for one hundred guineas.

'If we have to close the tabernacle, we may both have to find work,' she said defiantly. 'I need new shoes. Suppose you let me have twenty-five pounds and I'll make the costume myself. Have you sent off any applications today?'

Harold had certainly discussed applying for various posts. He had stressed the importance of a properly written letter but as far as Gertie knew, pen had not yet been applied to paper. Until the last penny had been spent, she doubted whether he would stir himself.

Clutching at straws, Harold had made several passionate appeals from the superintendent's table but the collections had diminished rather than increased. Fewer people wanted to 'bear witness' against neighbours when sons and husbands suddenly appeared in uniform. Sins were forgotten as the threat of war increased.

Gertie passed sleepless nights, wondering how they would manage. Finally, she put it out of her mind; she was too exhausted to worry any more. They had coped in the past, no doubt they would again. Something would turn up.

But when that 'something' turned out to be Ned Harrison's daughter who then seduced Valentine, Gertie became obsessed. She began to scheme how the marriage might be prevented. If only she could stop them living together, it would give her time to arrange for an annulment.

On the morning of the wedding therefore, she dressed with care in her new costume and the hat Valentine had given her. She wanted him to be proud. She wouldn't scold, she would remind him persuasively of all those things he would miss if he didn't return to Jamieson Street. She tried to keep up the pretence that he would be back for lunch. After breakfast she

517

began setting the table with a pretty cloth and napkins. Valentine didn't notice as he stared out of the window but when Harold came in he saw the preparations.

'For God's sake, you're not suggesting they come back for some form of celebration?'

Gertie's dream began to dissolve. 'I just thought ... there's no need for Valentine to go away at all ... a marriage in name only ...'

'Don't be ridiculous. It's far too late. The boy has sinned, he refuses to repent, on his own head be it. After today, he and that girl can go where they please but they are not welcome under my roof.' Harold's pride in being a father had vanished as soon as his son had begun to exhibit signs of Ruby Winnot's intelligence.

They spoke in front of Valentine as though he were deaf. The boy clenched his fists. Father was so mean! Strutting about in his smart new clothes while Valentine had only his school blazer and flannels. In his pocket was the last of his pocket money and that was all. Knowing he'd be utterly dependent on Margaret was shaming.

As if reading his thoughts, Harold added spitefully, 'As ye have sown, so shall ye reap, Valentine. You may end up destitute − it may well bring you to repentance but do not come begging at the tabernacle. All I ask is that you keep your mother informed as to your whereabouts.'

Valentine shouted back, 'At least she needn't come looking for *me* in Albert Road!' In the silence, Gertie was baffled that Valentine should even think of such an expensive address.

In Australia it was night time and the moon was full. Rose knew where she might find her husband. He didn't speak as she got out of the battered old car, and came to join him, putting her arm round his shoulders.

'Try not to grieve, Ned. It may be what Margaret wants.'

'I wish I could think so. If I thought she was only marrying to avoid talk of "disgrace" ... That kind of gossip is nonsense. I wish I knew if that's what Mu had in mind.' Rose shared his frustration. If only there had been time to discover the facts but they'd had to rely on her judgement.

'The important thing is to get them both out here. I've reminded Margaret to book a passage. I wrote again today. If they catch a boat in a week or two, they should be here well before Christmas.' She risked a suggestion she knew would hurt. 'What it really needs is an invitation from you, Ned. Margaret would drag the boy onto the boat, provided you asked her.'

He sighed. 'I suppose so. I don't feel all that friendly towards Valentine Brigg.'

'Let's go back. Maisie and Oswald have a bottle of champagne. It's a celebration as far as they're concerned.'

'She's not their daughter.'

'She's as good as,' Rose replied firmly. 'Now act cheerful even if you're not feeling like it, for their sake.'

'You're a bossy devil sometimes.'

'I have to be, married to you.' Her tone softened. 'We can't aways control events, Ned. We just have to make the best of them.' Back at the car they paused for a moment, contemplating the property in the moonlight. Several of the cabins were occupied tonight and distant windows made patches of yellow in the darkness. Two small bi-planes were silhouetted against the hangar. Further off they could hear a party in progress in the bunk-house.

'The mechanics are celebrating,' Rose said cheerfully.

Ned was quiet. 'This'll all belong to Margaret one day. I want her to be in charge, not him.'

'Perhaps Val is the sort who'll work hard.'

He snorted. 'Me and Oswald will have something to say if he's not.' His change of mood made her glad and she hugged him.

'Come on. We don't want that champagne to warm up. I wonder where Margaret and Val are having their wedding breakfast. In the King's Head, d'you think?'

It was sufficient distraction to stop Ned brooding for a while.

Mu said as she brushed the thick, straight brown hair, 'To think I once helped your mam do this on *her* wedding morning. It *feels* like yesterday even if it's not.'

June had been to the hairdresser's. Her waves were tight and her scalp was red and blotchy. She perched on the bed, fiddling with the pearly white coronet Margaret had rejected.

'I don't know whether I should wear this as you're only going to have a ribbon. People might mistake me for the bride.'

Margaret didn't mind. 'Please, June, it suits you far better and it might be all the encouragement Edwin needs.' Her cousin went scarlet.

'No more weddings this year,' Mu said firmly, 'I couldn't stand the strain and I don't know where we'd find more dried fruit. I want plenty of warning from now on, June, so no surprises.'

'No, Mam.'

'There.' Mu surveyed her handiwork; Margaret looked so young, she felt tearful. 'I do hope we're doing the right thing.'

'Of course we are!' Margaret waved her precious telegram, 'Even Dad thinks so now. There's only one thing frightens me,' the smile began to slip. 'D'you think you can keep Mrs Brigg from kidnapping Val afterwards?'

'Of course we can, pet! We'll tie her up and lock her in the cellar if we have to.' But when Margaret had disappeared downstairs. Mu murmured, 'Keep your fingers crossed, June. Gertie Brigg could still think of a way to stop the ceremony happening at all.'

To Mu's relief, both parties assembled at the Registry office at the appointed time. While the documents were being perused, Margaret held herself aloof. I won't let anything spoil today, she thought, keeping her eyes tightly focused on the opposite wall. I'll pretend Dad and Mum are here beside me. I'll speak up clearly for their benefit and I'll do my best to ignore Mrs Brigg altogether.

This was difficult: Gertie sat in the opposite corner, her hand clamped to Valentine's wrist, radiating hostility.

'Will the bride and groom come this way.' As Gertie tried to follow, the assistant registrar intercepted, 'If you would kindly wait here, madam.'

'But I'm his mother!'

'We will summon everyone in due course. Only the bride and groom are required at present.'

In the inner sanctum, Margaret realized she and Val were holding hands for the first time since leaving the farmhouse. She smiled tremulously and he squeezed her fingers. There were more questions before they could finally take their places. Behind them, the door opened and the rest of the party shuffled in. There were a few stifled coughs. Margaret didn't look round; she sensed Val might.

'We're together now,' she whispered, 'no one else matters.' To her relief, he nodded and kept his eyes on her. He had transferred his allegiance and her heart was thankful.

'I, Valentine Brigg ...'

Side by side, smiling, excited now, they exchanged vows in strong, young voices while Gertie sobbed.

Outside, Edwin took a few brief snapshots. As they moved away, Mu said tentatively, 'We've arranged a little party, Mrs Brigg. We'd be very pleased if you and Mr Brigg—'

'No!' Gertie was vehement, 'I couldn't possibly—'

'We'd be delighted,' boomed Harold. Pray heaven there would be a selection of decent beverages.

He couldn't believe it – it was the same as last time! The same house, the same front parlour milling with complete strangers, the same sandwiches with tea, and finally a cake served with home-made wine. All that was missing was the smelly mongrel bitch. Harold felt aggrieved.

Standing beside him, Gertie felt as if her life had come full circle and she had lost everything. Some faces were vaguely familiar, they had probably attended Rose's wedding breakfast. Valentine avoided her, staying close to Margaret for protection. She couldn't bear it, her heart was breaking, her

521

life over. She clutched Harold. 'Please, we must go. I can't stand any more.'

'A moment, Gertrude. I feel it incumbent upon me to say a few words.' Gertie's mood changed in an instant; despair was banished, sheer rage took its place.

With a passion that he could hear, she whispered furiously, 'No!'

'I beg your pardon?' He'd never known her use such a tone.

'Have done.' It was a command, there was no arguing against it.

Harold said grudgingly, 'If you insist. 'My boy ...' but he was denied the satisfaction of patronizing Valentine also.

'Goodbye, Father.' He turned his back, whispering to Margaret, 'Where can we go to escape?'

'The kitchen.' They slipped away and a disgruntled Harold followed his wife outside.

'A shabby affair. What we have learned to expect from Harrison's people, I fear. Look out!' A newspaper boy nearly collided with him.

'Ultimatum! Latest!'

The opportunity to be dramatic had come at last: Harold threw wide his arms, 'If war is declared, what is to become of you and me, Gertrude?'

'Who cares? I don't.' She set off at a fierce trot leaving him to catch up if he could.

No honeymoon had been planned. Bride and groom took their belongings to the rooms Mu had found, together with a few hastily assembled provisions.

'It'll be like the farm,' Margaret said nervously, 'only this time we won't have to worry.'

'Not about what people think, certainly,' Val acknowledged. There were plenty of other problems instead.

First, though, there was the novelty of exploring their new quarters and unpacking. Margaret attempted to cook chops on the spluttering gas stove. Crouched together over the small card-table, they toasted one another with lemonade.

'To us.'

'To us, and to our future in Australia. Val, would you like to see more photographs? I brought them all with me.'

'Yes, please.' He was still hungry, the potatoes had been almost raw, his mother always mashed them. 'Is there any pudding?'

'Not tonight, no. There's what's left of the wedding cake, or an apple?'

'No, thanks.' Idly, he picked up the first photograph. A couple stared into the lens, shielding their eyes. The man wore a wide-brimmed hat and shorts. His shirt sleeves were rolled up like a labourer's. The woman was shapely in a loose cotton dress and a sunhat. 'Who are these people?'

'Dad and Mum. This is Hermione. And this is all of us on my sixteenth birthday.'

Val's eyes widened. 'In a marquee?'

'There were nearly a hundred people, everyone at the depot was invited, even the holiday markers and truck drivers. There's the old emu.'

Val's ideas were undergoing a rapid adjustment. 'Who's the manager at the depot?'

'I've told you before. Dad and Uncle Oswald. It was Dad's idea but they don't call themselves managers, they're partners. This is Uncle and Auntie Maisie.' The man was dressed like a butler and the plain-faced woman wore an old-fashioned floral wrapper.

Val was astonished. 'They look like servants. Why isn't your father wearing a suit?'

Margaret was open-mouthed. 'Val, the temperature that day was over a hundred degrees.' She'd made him feel foolish.

He said defensively, 'My father always wears a suit, whatever the weather. I thought he looked particularly smart today.'

'Yes, he did,' she wanted to placate him, 'and so did Auntie Gertie. She looked very nice.'

'You must try and like her, Mags. She doesn't mean to be unkind.'

Margaret offered more photographs: 'This is a view when

523

they were building the aerodrome ... you can see the runway in the background. These are the garages with the machinery and vehicle showrooms ... the cabins. This is our shack, and this is Uncle and Auntie's. Dad refuses to rebuild. He says the design is just right for the climate.'

Val tried to understand. 'If your family own all this, why live in a hut?'

Margaret chuckled. 'God, you're a snob, Val. I know Mum christened it The Shack but it's got fans, electric light, proper flyscreens, two shower rooms, everything to make it comfortable. There's no point in having upholstered furniture because of the ants but the bamboo stuff is fine.'

'But they're rich, so why go on living like that?'

She explained more plainly. 'There's money in the bank, certainly, but they still work, we all do. You and I will when we get there. The cash is ploughed back into projects. It's there when it's needed, of course. Like the five hundred pounds for my trip.'

'Five hundred ...!'

'Dad intended it for university. If you wanted to try for that, Val, I'm sure he'd be willing to pay. He's a great believer in education.'

Val had less than five shillings. In all the turmoil, he hadn't considered Margaret other than as his future wife – the responsibility, the knowledge that she was, still stunned him. Now, suddenly, there was the incredible prospect of an interesting, probably wealthy, future.

'What I can't understand ...' he needed to put everything in perspective.

'Yes?'

'The estrangement between your mother and mine, you said it was over a draft for two hundred pounds. They were close once so why does your mother keep up the quarrel? Your parents wouldn't even notice such a small sum.'

'Don't be *silly*,' Margaret was impatient. 'That two hundred pounds was all they had and your mum never even offered to repay.'

'It's haunted her ever since. She managed to save a bit towards it.' Not since Ethel Paige's cheques had ceased, of course. Again Val felt defensive but Margaret was remembering all Rose had had to endure from Gertie, the despair her dad had described when trying to start up the depot with insufficient capital. Love for him made her careless of Val's feelings.

'If she suffered, serve her right. I don't know why you find it necessary to stick up for her, Val, it's not as though she were your *real* mother.'

The world turned over and kept on spinning. Valentine stared. Margaret's lips were still moving but he couldn't make out a word, his head was so full of noise.

'What did you say?' His expression frightened her.

'I know about your adoption. Dad told me. Look,' she had fished out the yellowing newspaper cutting from among her treasures, 'I've always kept it. It's the photograph taken when the tabernacle opened.'

Val could barely contain himself; he shouted, 'So what? I've seen it thousands of times, Father has a copy. What does that prove? Mother had to marry him because I was on the way – that happens to thousands of people but she's my mother right enough.' His fists were clenched, his face red; Margaret was extremely frightened but stood her ground.

'No, Val. I'm sorry but Auntie Gertie can't be your mother. This was taken not long after they came back. She wasn't even pregnant when she left. And here you are, not a baby but a toddler. They adopted you. Mum, Dad, everyone knew about it.'

The sweat stood out on Valentine's forehead. 'Not true. It's bloody well not true!' His mother might be tiresome but he loved her dearly. How could he feel like that towards a stranger?

Margaret spoke softly to cushion the pain. 'I expect that's why your father insisted on filling in the details of your birth certificate this morning. Has he ever shown it to you?'

'No! I've never needed to see it ...' Valentine actually hated

525

her at that instant. Mother, adoring, worshipping him, begging him to come back home. 'Of course they're my real parents, you're telling me lies!'

Margaret went white as though she'd been slapped. 'Harold Brigg is your real father. At least, that's what everyone assumes because you're quite like him. But he must have had a lady friend before he met Auntie Gertie. Please Val, it doesn't matter.'

The little widow in Albert Road? The one Raymond told dirty jokes about?

'No!'

Yet so many details fell into place. Those obscure references when he was a child – the woman in the park! Valentine gave a sudden great cry and thumped the furniture. 'No, no, no!'

Margaret tried to stay calm. 'I'm so sorry, Val. I thought you knew. I meant it when I said it didn't matter—'

'Of course it matters! It changes everything. She's lied to me all my life, don't you understand? Father lies, he can't stop himself but Mother, never. Now you tell me my whole life is a lie. There was a woman once, she knew my birthday. We never went to the park again. She was very pretty. Nearly as pretty as you.' Margaret was weeping at the bitterness in his voice. 'Older, of course. Mother was very angry because I stopped to speak to her.'

'Auntie Gertie loves you as much as anyone can.'

'I keep telling you – she lied! Father praying at the tabernacle, telling people to confess their sins – those two were the biggest sinners of all. Because of them my life's a sham!' He leaned over her threateningly. 'Who am I? Can you tell me that? As it's common knowledge on your side of the family, do you happen to know my real mother's name?'

'No!' She rocked to and fro in her distress. 'Please, Val ... don't be hurt. It doesn't matter ... I love you!'

He straightened up, saying dully, 'That's not enough. Not any more.'

'What?' She watched in terror as he picked up his coat. 'Where are you going?'

'Out.' There was a thudding inside his head, the room stifled him.

She followed, gasping between her sobs, 'When will you be back?'

'I don't know.'

'You will *be* back?'

Valentine forced himself to answer. 'I expect so ... yes. Later.' He saw her fists pressed tightly to her face to stop the tears and loved her enough to pity her. 'Try not to worry.' He slammed the door.

Gertie's delight couldn't be hidden. 'You've come back!'

He pushed past her into the hall. 'Is Father in?'

'Upstairs. In his study.' This was the spare bedroom which contained a desk and chair. Valentine's silence, his cold expression, made her nervous. 'Do you want to go up?'

There was no need. Hearing the noise, Harold had come onto the landing. 'Who is it? Who's there?' He peered over the banister. Valentine's upturned face stared back. 'What in hell are you doing here?'

'Harold!'

Valentine's voice was icy. 'Who is my *real* mother?'

As if she'd been kicked, Gertie suddenly had no breath in her body. She clutched at the hallstand, imploring him. 'Valentine!' He refused to look at her. Upstairs, Harold began to bluster.

Valentine shouted, 'I asked you a question!'

'Don't you dare take that tone with me.'

Valentine turned his attack on Gertie. 'Even if he told me a name, I wouldn't know if it was the truth. Can you tell me? Do you know who she is? Was it that woman in the park?'

Gertie put out a hand to fend off the one person she loved, who now stared at her with such venom.

'I – don't know.'

'Liar!' He practically spat the word. 'It was her, wasn't it? She was dark, like me. And elegant.' Gertie was back in her dull, dreary everyday garments, his contempt encompassed

527

them. 'She knew my birthday, it had to be her.' He turned on Harold, now halfway down the stair. 'I know you're my real father – was it the little widow, is that who my mother is?'

'Get out of my house!'

Gertie grabbed at his sleeve. 'I should have told you before—'

'It's too late. Margaret told me. My wife. All her family knew. Why didn't you tell me first?'

'I didn't want to lose you!'

'You lied to me!' It was the cry of absolute betrayal. Fighting to keep his voice steady, Valentine said to Harold, 'Don't worry, you'll never see me again,' and, flinging open the door, he shouted, 'You bloody pair of hypocrites!'

He used such force, the letter box continued to reverberate long after his departure.

When it stopped, Gertie's tired voice filled the silence. 'If you really are Valentine's father, is that why you were in such a hurry to marry me? You weren't in love with me. You've never cared for anyone except yourself. Presumably you weren't prepared to marry the other poor woman. Did you imagine I was a better prospect, Harold? That I had money and might protect you from her?'

'I – I ...' he managed a feeble protest. 'You deceived me over your inheritance, Gertrude.'

Her tone was withering. 'As you deceived me. From now on you will sleep in Valentine's room. You are not welcome in mine.'

Rose and Ned learned of the consequences six weeks later when Margaret's letter finally arrived.

Darling Dad and Mum,

I hope this reaches you soon. Val has enlisted in the Navy. He didn't wait for war to be official last week, he did it the day after we were married.

On our wedding night I accidentally told him he was adopted. Mr and Mrs Brigg had never explained. He was

528

terribly upset. He said it would be better if we lived apart for a while and I agreed. I do love him so.

He is somewhere in Scotland. We gave up the rooms. As you can see, I'm back with Auntie Mu. When Val gets a pass, we'll probably meet in Glasgow and stay in a hotel. I've found an office job in Wilson Street. Not very exciting but it stops me worrying. We were all issued with identity cards today. The tabernacle is up for sale. Val went back to see his parents before he left, to try and patch things up. There was another terrible row. He says it was the last time he'll try. I expect he'll change his mind but it will take time. None of this alters our plans to come to the depot but that can't be until Val is discharged. Pray that this war ends soon.

Love to Auntie Maisie and Uncle Oswald. Tell Hermione to keep eating the snakes. I miss you all so much.

Love and lots of kisses,
Margaret.

Through her weeping, Rose heard Ned's bleak voice. 'She's had to grow up too fast, my little pet.'

The telegram arrived on Wednesday: '48-hour pass Friday stop Can we meet stop Somewhere near you stop love Val' It had been despatched from a Glasgow post office. Margaret's hands shook so much, she dropped it. Mu stooped to pick it up and heard the sad whisper, 'At least he wants to see me.'

'Of course he does. It only needed a bit of time. Where will you suggest?'

'It has to be somewhere special. To make up for last time.'

Mu pretended not to notice the despair. 'How about York? There's a smart hotel next door to the station. It's a nice town. Val might enjoy the change.'

'Thanks, you're a genius.' There was a flurry as Margaret realized the time and grabbed her coat. 'I may be late home – I need to do some shopping.'

'Take your time ...' The front door slammed. 'Take all the time in the world,' her aunt finished quietly.

Thanks to Margaret's energy and persistence over the phone, the hotel room was large, centrally heated, with a comfortable four-poster bed. Its disadvantages became obvious as the rumble went through below.

'That sounds a bit close.'

'It's a train, not a Messerschmitt, madam. Quite friendly, trains are.' The porter fastened the blackout, drew the curtains and switched on the lamps including those in the small alcove of a sitting-room. Margaret saw the table and two chairs.

'Is there anything to eat? My husband's coming down from Scotland, I don't suppose he'll have had a meal. He's on subs.'

Poor bastard, thought the man. Without her hat, the girl looked about fifteen. He doubted if she was married, not many were these days. They snatched what happiness they could and good luck to them. She'd got money, though. He eyed the pound note respectfully.

'Sandwiches, madam? I'm afraid the chef's gone home.'

'Sandwiches, a bottle of whisky, ice, two glasses and ginger beer, if you have any. Oh, and soup when my husband arrives. It's fearfully cold today. Will this be enough?'

The porter pocketed his tip and told her to put the fiver away. 'We'll add it to the bill, madam.' Which reminded her.

'I'm paying. Would you make sure they understand in reception?'

'Certainly, madam. And I'll do what I can about the soup.' For such a well-heeled customer, he'd make it himself if necessary.

She was on the platform when the train arrived; Val wasn't expecting that. He almost strode past her then he heard someone call his name. They stared, like strangers, slowly recognizing one another through the changes.

'Goodness – that duffle – I hardly knew you, Val.' He saw the smart coat with padded shoulders, the jaunty hat with a feather. There was a new self-assurance in his wife's appearance but the quivering mouth betrayed her.

'Hallo, Mags.' He kissed her on the cheek taking care not to disturb her hat. 'Did the emu donate that adornment?'

'I hope not!' She laughed shakily. 'Val, was the journey beastly? I'm awfully afraid I may have made a mistake about the hotel. Our room is practically on top of the platform. When the trains go through, it actually *shakes*.'

Grinning, he slung his kit bag over his shoulder. 'How far is it from the bathroom, that's all I'm worried about? The train was filthy.'

She was surprised. 'We have our own, of course. I booked the best they had.' Slightly disturbed, Valentine wondered if he could afford it.

The bed had been turned down, the lighting was low, there was warmth and luxury everywhere; it was the most splendid room Valentine had ever seen. Daunted, he listened as his wife told room service when to send up their food, and then led him through to the tiled room beyond. She turned the hot tap on full. They were still being cautiously polite with one another but he ventured a criticism.

'I thought we were supposed to economise?'

'Not us, not this weekend.' She produced a bottle of bath-salts. 'Look, June coaxed these out of the Co-op. They were the last they had.' Without asking, she emptied half of them into his bath. 'There. Supper in half an hour – is that all right?'

Pine-scented steam filled the room. 'It's awfully decent of you to arrange everything, Mags ... As usual, I haven't much cash on me.'

'I've plenty.' She said it quickly, breathlessly. Attempting to be casual, she added, 'I hope you approve of the four-poster. They didn't have a twin-bedded room.'

Twin-bedded? He was alarmed. 'Approve? Of course I do, I think the whole place is wonderful, the four-poster is a marvellous idea.'

She turned away, pretending to tidy her hair. 'That's good.'

Val pulled up his sweater to hide his red face. 'I won't kiss

531

you properly till I'm clean. I need a shave, my beard is scratchy.'

'I've ordered whisky – is that all right or would you prefer beer?'

'Whisky's perfect.'

Scalding water unknotted the cramping, debilitating fear in his stomach. Val lay motionless, aware of each particle of his body as the dread he'd lived with for weeks slowly oozed away. When his posting to submarines had been confirmed, he'd been too tormented with desire for Margaret and confusion over his birth to worry. Now, he knew he was a coward. There had been no escaping it the moment he climbed down into the sub; fear, real fear dominated his every waking moment.

As for his parentage, Gertie continued to keep up the pretence in a ludicrous note.

Your parents were university students, of excellent background but unable to marry and give you a home. That is what Harold was told before we decided to adopt you. I hope you will not make any more fuss.

Let me know when you are coming home. I look forward to hearing from you.

Your loving mother.

Gertrude Brigg.

Valentine recognized his father's fabrication just as easily as his mother's frail device: *Let me know when you are coming home.* Would she ever feel confident enough to rely on the truth? 'I must make it up with her, through.' It was ironic that he felt no affection for his father, only for Gertie.

As for *coming home*, that meant Margaret, if she would have him. 'I've treated her so badly,' he thought in a panic, 'does she still love me?'

He heard a trolley being wheeled into the other room, the sound of cutlery and glasses. He began to lather himself vigorously. When he'd sent the telegram, he'd been so full of fear, his only thought had been that Margaret might understand.

532

Now he wondered if he dare tell her. After the débâcle of their wedding night, he'd no right to inflict more pain. How to explain that as he lay in a bunk, with the ocean only a thin metal skin away, it was only her image that kept him sane.

The idiocy of his present situation diverted him. Here he was, basking in gallons of scented water while most of the time he lived in cold bloody fear of it.

Outside, quiet voices were followed by the chink of coins. Margaret must be using her Australian money to pay for all this. Her generosity humbled him. 'I've no right to tell her my problems. She'll only worry herself sick.'

And why do that when they'd come here for another reason entirely? He reached for a towel. The rail was heated. Valentine wrapped himself in thick soft warmth and tried to order his thoughts.

When he rejoined her there were cigarettes beside the whisky bottle. 'You think of everything.'

'I tried to. I expect I've forgotten something obvious.' She was so nervous he had to steady the match for her.

'Shall we have a drink?'

'Yes, please. Ginger beer for me. It reminds me of home.'

As well as the laden trolley there was now an electric fire and they settled in front of it with their glasses.

'The porter thought we might be cold,' she explained, 'the central heating is switched off early because of the coal shortage.'

'Our quarters are freezing most of the time.'

'You poor thing! Being cold makes me feel quite sick.' Margaret shuddered, 'Gosh, I can't wait to get back to the sun. Oh, you'll love it out there, Val, I know you will.'

Through the sitting-room arch, they faced the bedroom. He was aware of the imposing bed and knew she was too. They scarcely knew each other and had such a short time left. A clock ticked beside the bed. He could see the shape of the hands; already several precious hours had passed.

Margaret guessed his thoughts. 'Hungry?'

'Starving!'

'So am I.'

533

They fell to like ravenous children. When the soup had disappeared, the pile of sandwiches half demolished, she patted her stomach. 'This was almost empty. No wonder I felt so shivery.'

Val thought there might be another reason. 'I think I've had enough. Shall we push this trolley outside?'

They poured themselves more drinks and sat, side by side.

'Do you like being on submarines?'

'I hate it,' Val said simply. 'Every minute – every single second. I've discovered I'm a coward, Mags.' He tried to laugh. 'What a thing to have to tell your wife.'

Margaret's eyes brimmed over. 'Val, I'm so sorry. I've prayed every night. Is it very cold on the bottom of the sea?'

This made him laugh spontaneously.

'Cold? I'm sweating most of the time.'

For an instant she was puzzled, then said with relief, 'Oh, I see. Central heating. I'm glad they've thought of creature comforts for the crew. Dad always says the men at the depot deserve the best because they work so hard.'

I can't explain, he thought; I simply can't. It wouldn't be fair. All he said was, 'It's not quite like that. It's the equipment. And my hammock is squashed between the torpedo tubes, I spend half my life trying to avoid concussion.'

'That's because you're so tall. Are you bruised?' She took his head in her hands to peer beneath the dark fringe. 'You don't appear to have any scars.'

Those are all inside, he thought. Her large eyes were so close. She slid her arms round him.

'Please, Val. I love you so much.' Inside him, the pent-up dam burst. He hugged, kissed and when it grew too much, sobbed and clutched her to him, burying his face in her shoulder. She soothed, urging him to let go each terrifying aspect of his fear. When he'd told her the last of it, the horror fading slightly, he managed a watery grin.

'Fancy burdening you with that lot when this is a second attempt at a honeymoon. It was a rotten wedding night, Mags, I treated you so badly.'

And Margaret, who hadn't understood half of what she'd been told and only knew she must be strong, kissed the wet cheeks. 'It doesn't matter ... that's all in the past. I hurt you too, blurting it out about your mother; I'd no idea you hadn't been told.'

In her arms, the bitterness ebbed. Valentine gave a long quiet sigh. 'Mother must have guessed ... Over the years I've grown more like Father.'

'You're much more handsome!'

'Thanks.'

'Maybe she couldn't bear it,' Margaret said seriously. 'If she hadn't known at the beginning and then it gradually became obvious?'

Valentine remembered Gertie's reaction to the woman in the park. 'She came face to face with it once ... she knew then, she must have done. I think she's loathed Father ever since.'

'How dreadful to be shackled to someone and feel like that! She must have been so grateful to have you to love.' Margaret leaned back to see his face. 'You will see her again?'

'I'll – think about it.'

Satisfied, she slipped inside his embrace once more.

'I'm sure your real mother wouldn't want you or Auntie Gertie to be so wretched.'

He kissed the top of her head. 'You're a wise child, Mrs Brigg.' For several minutes they sat, marvelling that it had been so simple to reach this far.

'Do you still feel shivery?' Val muttered abruptly.

'Yes, but it's nothing to do with being hungry this time.'

'I know. I feel the same.'

'Shall we take our clothes off?'

'What?' He was startled but Margaret was already on her feet, unbuttoning her dress.

'It would stop us feeling awkward,' she assured him. 'I hate wearing so many layers, don't you? At home at the depot, I never have to bother with stockings, for instance.' He stared in fascination as she unfastened her suspenders, totally without coquetry. 'It's so lovely to feel fresh air on your skin – I don't

535

suppose you know what that feels like?'

Valentine remembered freezing breezes on Saltburn beach. 'Not really.'

The two wisps of silk were carefully deposited on a chair. 'My best pair,' she explained. 'They're in such short supply I must make them last.' Her dress dropped to the floor, cami-knickers came off in a trice, then her suspender belt. She turned to face him, lithe and unembarrassed, her voice only a shade husky as she saw his face. 'See how easy it is? Now take yours off.'

Electrified, Valentine kicked off his shoes and tore at his garments. 'My mother ...' he began, trying not to let his eagerness show.

'Yes?'

'She used to warn me about women like you.'

'Oh?'

'Using their wiles to entice innocent chaps like me.'

'I wouldn't know a wile if I saw one,' Margaret retorted cheerfully. 'Come on, it's lovely and cosy inside these curtains. And I've got us a treat.'

'What d'you mean?' As he pulled off vest and pants he saw she'd leapt onto the bed and was sitting cross-legged against the pillows, nursing a hot water bottle. Valentine's eyebrows rose. 'You never ordered that!'

Despite her provocative pose, Margaret reverted to her prim voice. 'I told the porter my husband felt the cold dreadfully because of his constant exposure to the elements.' Valentine strode over, took the hot-water bottle and dropped it onto the floor.

'Mrs Brigg ...'

'Yes, Mr Brigg?'

'I love you. ...' For the first time he kissed her full on the mouth. As she broke free gasping for air, Margaret slid flat beneath him, hugging him to her.

'It'll be all right, Val. You'll see. I've been wanting you for so long ... Don't be nervous.' Her arms clung as he eased himself onto the bed beside her, stroking her skin and thighs, kissing her breasts. She cried with delight at each new sensation as he tried to wipe lewd submariner banter and his father's crudeness from his memory. This magic had nothing to do with obscenity.

Margaret's lashes brushed his face. His dark hair was soft against her skin, her kisses fluttered across his neck and cheek. She arched her back and spread herself for him. 'Love me, Val.'

The desire he'd dreamed of overcame him. Margaret didn't pull away, she gave herself up to him, clinging tightly and crying his name, urging him to love her more. When the climax came, he felt her first stiffen and then, with a deep, glad moan, her body softened to accept him completely. Arms bound round one another, they rolled over, half conscious and unable to speak.

When they finally broke apart, Margaret turned onto her side and curled into a ball. Valentine called her name then realized she was asleep. Astonished, he shook her gently without a response. Eventually, he pulled up the bedcovers, closed his eyes and fell into the most contented, dreamless sleep he'd ever known.

She roused him at dawn. He found the blackout curtains had been drawn back. Trains were whistling and shunting below and his wife was looking particularly bright-eyed. 'You snuffle when you're asleep, did you know?'

Thank God he hadn't cried out and terrified her. 'You're like a kitten, you curl up and tuck your nose under your paw. I was hoping you'd purr.'

'Sorry to disappoint you ...'

'Disappoint!! My dear, good girl ...'

'I like being called that.' She ran a finger across his chest. 'And as we have had a nice rest and we *are* awake ...'

This time, he felt such a sweet tenderness he still ached with love for her when they finally broke apart.

Margaret stretched in supreme contentment. 'That was – purrfect!'

'I shouldn't have blurted out all that nonsense last night.'

'Of course you should.' She was on one elbow, mock scolding. 'Good heavens, what are wives for? I want to hear everything that's bothering you, my dear. *I* don't want *you* finding yourself a little widow!' Despite his shock, Val laughed. 'That's better!' Margaret's ebullient happiness increased. 'You see, I told you it didn't matter. Aunt Gertie loves you, so do I, that's the important thing. You are my dear, darling, handsome most beloved husband—'

'Come here, wife.' He pulled her down under the eider-down and held her close. Arms, legs entwined, utterly relaxed, they once more fell asleep.

He awoke in full daylight to hear her singing in the bath. When she emerged, brushing her hair, he said admiringly, 'How very smart.'

'This dressing gown was bought in your honour. I've a nightdress to match somewhere.'

'Don't bother to find it.'

'All right. Are you thirsty? It's a bit early to send for tea.'

'Is there any ginger beer left?'

She filled two glasses. 'This isn't as good as Auntie Maisie's. She's a whizz at ginger beer.' She let him undo her sash. The gown fell open and he ran his hand over her body. 'I like it when you do that, Val. It makes me all tingly inside.'

'Your lack of modesty is amazing.'

'Can I do the same to you or would you prefer to be coy?' When he laughed again, she said softly, 'That's better,' and touched his forehead. 'You looked so tense when you got off that train. I'm glad it's all gone.'

He caught her hand and planted a kiss. 'Thanks to you. And no, I wouldn't mind if you wanted to – explore.'

A little later she asked, 'When do you have to be back?'

'Oh-eight-hundred hours on Monday.'

She summoned up her courage. 'Val, I've checked the time-table, it would be possible.'

'What would?'

'If we left Sunday afternoon, you could break your journey

538

in Middlesbrough and spend half an hour with your mother.' She felt him draw away. 'Please!'

'Mags, I wanted this to be our special time together.'

'It is! But we're so happy and we've got the rest of our lives for loving. Your mother must be missing you dreadfully.'

'She smothered me sometimes, that's why I was always longing to get away.' And now I'm on submarines, I'm smothered all the time! The panic began to build up until Margaret leaned against him, her small breasts pushing every other thought out of his mind.

'Please, dearest Val. I want her to come to Australia with us. It's time she and Mum stopped quarrelling. Dad wants them to be friends again.'

Valentine kissed the tip of her nose. 'You won't be content until you've gathered us all up and whisked us off to that depot of yours, will you?'

'No, I don't suppose I will,' Margaret admitted candidly. 'But there's plenty of space. You and I can be absolutely private whenever we want.'

'And – my father?' He'd silenced her and chuckled, 'It's all right, he wouldn't fit in. He wouldn't emigrate anyway, I've heard his views on "the Antipodes". Mother certainly won't miss him.'

'We could tell her it's just a holiday,' Margaret suggested cautiously, 'then if she wanted to come back, she could.'

'Perhaps.'

'So you will visit her?'

'It means less time for us.' He saw how much this affected her; Margaret was fighting back the tears.

'I'd worked that out. It is important though, otherwise I would never have suggested it.'

Valentine didn't waste any more time. The hands of the clock were moving faster than before and his need to love his wonderful wife was overwhelming. As the trains carried the rest of the world to their destinations, he and Margaret came together with passionate intensity, clinging and exploring one another one last time.

'Never, never leave me, Margaret.'

She was lying back against the pillows, all passion spent. 'I couldn't,' she said simply, 'it wouldn't be possible.'

'Thank you.' He kissed her breasts, and reluctantly dragged himself away to dress. Downstairs, he slipped the remains of the whisky to the porter. The man gave a salute and wished him luck.

On the train they sat facing one another. We're like strangers now we're dressed, thought Val. She's hidden behind that smart coat and that ridiculous hat – I can feel her moving further and further away. The damn sub gets closer and closer ... He fought the fear, his face expressionless.

The next time he had a pass he would ask Margaret to meet him at the dock gates, they would stay at the first hotel they found, he wouldn't waste one precious moment of their time together.

She wasn't looking at him but staring out of the window. He saw the reflected tears in the glass.

In Middlesbrough, Margaret waited in the taxi round the corner from Jamieson Street. Gertie opened the door.

'Valentine! What a lovely surprise.'

It must be after five o'clock, he thought, automatically registering her 'afternoon dress'.

'Is Father in?'

'He's at the Lodge, I'm not expecting him back until this evening.'

Valentine hid his relief and walked inside. 'I wouldn't mind a cup of tea.' She almost tripped in her eagerness to reach the kitchen and found his hand under her elbow. 'Easy does it, Mother.'

'Oh, Valentine – I've missed you so much. How long can you stay?'

'Not long.' He let her fill the kettle and light the gas. 'I had forty-eight hours. Margaret and I have been together since Friday.' The words sank in slowly. 'She's a wonderful wife, mother. I didn't know it was possible to be so happy.' He saw her face and with a flash of insight knew that Gertie had never experienced the same joy.

'You don't know what you're saying, Valentine!'

He was filled with compassion for her. 'We haven't much time Mother. Please listen. Margaret and I love one another and when this bloody mess is over, we're going to Australia—'

'No!'

'Yes. Margaret wants you to come and live with us, bless her. She doesn't bear grudges. But you must start treating her decently.'

'Valentine!' The stream of invective began and this time he took her by the arms and shook her.

'Stop it, for God's sake. You've wasted so much of your life hating. Margaret isn't evil, she's the most honest, wonderful creature in the world. The wedding was forced on us but I thank God for it. I couldn't ask for a better wife.' He added more calmly. 'As for your silly letter – I'm Father's bastard, we both know that. You're not my mother but you've loved and cared for me and now I want to repay you. Come with us and we'll look after you, provided you're kind to Margaret.'

'I couldn't possibly – Ned Harrison's daughter?'

'Mother!' Seeing her rigid expression, he sighed, 'It's no good, is it? It was a waste of time coming here. But please, think over what I've said. If you give the word, Margaret will be round here like a shot.'

'I shall refuse to see her.' She watched him pick up the duffle coat. 'You're not leaving just because I cannot bring myself to ...'

'There's no more to be said.'

'You mustn't rush me, Val.'

He could no longer be coaxed. 'Margaret and I will be leaving on the first available boat after the war ends. Either you come or you stay here with Father. If you do that, I doubt whether you and I will ever see one another again. Think about it. And no more pretence.' He bent to kiss the pale cheek. 'Margaret wants you to be happy, and so do I.'

He walked away, closing the gate behind him.

*

541

On their way to the station, Margaret stared at him sorrowfully.

'Was it very bad?'

'She understands you and I will never be parted.'

'Oh, my darling!'

'I explained she would be welcome.'

'Did she agree?'

'It's difficult for her to change.'

'I'll write to her. I'll keep on explaining how much it would mean to Mum until she does.'

His face relaxed into a smile. 'I should have realized, before I married you.'

'What?'

'How persistent you can be. I bet you twist your parents round your little finger.'

'Dad, yes,' Margaret admitted. 'Not Mum. She can always see through me.'

'I look forward to meeting her. I could do with a few tips. Here we are. Shall we find a quiet corner for a cup of tea?'

They were unlucky. Beneath the vast curve of Middlesbrough station's roof, crowds shouted to one another. Children, parents, soldiers, sailors and airmen bidding one another farewell or forcing their way through to the buses waiting outside. The cacophany was deafening. Valentine was dazed. Margaret strained to read his lips.

'I can't face this. Say goodbye to me now, Mags.'

'Oh, Val, please!' The calm had disappeared, he was agitated.

'Go, quickly. Don't look back, I couldn't stand seeing you cry.' He was gone. She tried to glimpse his tall figure but the crowds enveloped him, making it impossible.

Later that evening, back at Mu's quiet terrace, Margaret wrote to Rose:

We were really happy for the very first time, Mum. A proper honeymoon at last. You and Dad don't have to worry about me, honestly. Val's the one I used to dream about, he's the kindest, most loving person in the world. My one and only. When you meet him, you'll understand.

He visited Auntie Gertie. Uncle Harold was out, thank goodness. Val suggested she might like to come with us when we come home. She hasn't agreed yet but I'm sure she will. She's so fond of Val. We didn't include Uncle Harold in the invitation. Val realizes he might not fit in.

'Not fit in? I'll not have that patronizing fool anywhere near my depot,' Ned declared passionately. Rose giggled, 'I think even Harold Brigg might guess he wouldn't be welcome. Poor Gertie. I wonder what they're doing for an income? Margaret doesn't say. I hope she gives us more news next time. At least, you and I can stop worrying,' she challenged him. 'Margaret is obviously in love.'

'Aye.' Ned shook his head: with Valentine Brigg? It didn't seem possible.

But the letters became infrequent and less cheerful. Leave for submarine crews had been cancelled. In Middlesbrough, Mussolini's entry into the war had brought angry people onto the streets to smash the harmless local Italian-owned ice-cream parlours. To Margaret it seemed crazy and cruel; she couldn't bring herself to describe it to her mother.

By the time she next wrote, in October 1940, the tentacles of war had reached as far as the depot itself. Captain Hislop had arrived with a group of officials to discuss the compulsory purchase of the property for use by the Royal Australian Airforce. Rose, Maisie and Oswald listened as Ned railed against it.

'I *know* everyone's worried about the Japs but what about us? We've built this place up from nothing – can't we lease it to the government for the duration?'

'That's not how they do things, Harrison. You'll be well compensated.'

'That's not the point!'

543

Rose couldn't bear it; the argument was lost before it had begun, she could see that. All their back-breaking work ... yet hadn't it been obvious this might happen? It was their fault for ignoring events in the world outside. Now the threat from Japan was too strong for them to fight.

Unable to watch Ned's despair, she went outside. Last night she had argued, 'Whatever happens, we must try and lease it so that Margaret and Val will have a home and a business to come back to.' Listening to the officials today, she realized how futile that hope had been.

She gazed at the gums surrounding the tidy forecourt, the gulahs wheeling overhead and remembered how she and Maisie had once used pickaxes to level the rock-hard earth. As she thrust a hand into her pocket she felt the shape of the envelope. Margaret's latest letter had arrived and she hadn't yet had a chance to read it.

Dearest Mum and Dad,

I'm very worried that somehow you may have seen the news before this reaches you. The bombing has been terrible in the north-east and we caught it in Middlesbrough last Sunday. A lot of property was destroyed including Val's parents' house in Jamieson Street. His mother had gone to church but his father was at home. Uncle Oswald came off duty to tell us. He was dreadfully shaken. It must have been quick, which is a mercy. It's so sad that Val and his father weren't reconciled but, as I told you in my last letter, Val's leave has been cancelled indefinitely.

There was an article in the *Gazette* about the work of the tabernacle (that was destroyed two months ago, did I mention it?). The obituary described Mr Harold Brigg as a 'brother in a masonic lodge'. I've cut out the references for Val to keep. His mother has been billeted in Cannon Street. Auntie Mu wondered if we ought to offer her a home here but she wouldn't be the easiest person to live with and we are tightly packed.

544

June is hoping to marry Edwin as soon as he can wangle leave. If they move in with his parents that will ease things here.

Don't worry about me. There's talk of directing women to essential war work. I hope they don't make me a land girl – you know how I feel about the cold! Whatever it is, it'll help me believe Val and I will be together that much sooner.

Rose was stunned; Harold Brigg wiped out in a matter of seconds. How did Gertie feel? She didn't believe her sister ever really loved him but what a dreadful way to lose a husband. Full of sympathy, ignoring her own problems, Rose went to her desk and wrote a quick, brief letter of condolence. Gertie did not reply.

When Margaret's next letter arrived a few months later, in 1941, the four of them were already assembling their belongings, ready for departure the following day. The postie shook his head over the activity in the aerodrome. 'Never seen so many uniforms. This place is buzzing all right. Here y'are. From my darlin' little Maggie, I reckon. Mind if I wait to hear how she is?'

There were two sheets of paper. Rose unfolded the first which was from Mu and had not escaped the censor's pen.

Dearest Rose and Ned,

Margaret has written to you separately about Val. I was with her when the telegram arrived. You've never seen a braver girl. Her first thought was for Gertie but your sister wouldn't open the door. When Margaret came back, she was very quiet. Then she said she'd made up her mind. As Val had gone, her place was with you. Lionel's pal knew of a ship due to leave from Sunderland ‹BLANKED OUT›. Margaret has signed on as a member of the catering crew which made us laugh even though we cried. Your daughter's a treasure, Ned, but she is a rotten cook.

The convoy is headed in your direction and Margaret says it won't be difficult once she gets to Singapore ‹BLANKED OUT›. She has guts and we are confident she knows what she's doing. She's a different girl from the one who arrived here but we're proud of her.

She will telephone before she sets out on the final leg. She wrote to Gertie before she left. That letter had me in tears. She and Val really did love one another, Rose, despite everything.

June and Edwin are married. She's working at Dorman Long's ‹BLANKED OUT› in Bowesfield Lane ‹BLANKED OUT›. I never thought my daughter would end up as a furnace worker ‹BLANKED OUT› but thank God she did because the Co-op where she worked was burned down last week. You wouldn't recognise Wilson Street ‹BLANKED OUT›.

Lionel has agreed we can leave as soon as this lot's over. It took Hitler to persuade him. I hope the Japs don't mess things up your end. Food rationing gets me down, especially the tiddly 2 oz of tea. I'm looking forward to a decent cuppa otherwise we're not too bad. We've got a cast-iron shelter in the yard so I feel safe when the sirens start.

We miss Margaret. She's a lovely brave girl and I look forward to hearing she's arrived safe and sound.

Your loving sister,
Mu.

Lionel lowered Margaret's haversack onto the Sunderland quayside. Tied up alongside, the filthy squat vessel didn't inspire confidence. He half regretted making the arrangement but it was too late to pull back. Margaret was taking the place of his pal's daughter, who, for a consideration of one hundred pounds, which would enable her to escape to America, was willing to lie low for a week or two. Margaret's worldly possessions had been reduced to this one small bag which was all any crew member was allowed. She had handed over to June all her heavy winter clothes. 'I shan't need them, honestly. You've no idea what the heat is like back home.'

'But what about the journey?' Mu had been anxious, 'The winds can be dreadfully cold at sea.'

Margaret had managed the ghost of a smile. 'I doubt whether I shall know whether it's blowing a gale or not.'

'She'll be down below in the galley,' Lionel had growled, 'working hard.' Now, seeing her shiver on the quayside, he wondered if they weren't both being stupid. 'You can always change your mind,' he offered lamely, wondering what would happen to his pal's daughter if she did.

Margaret shook her head. 'The sooner I'm on my way, the better, Uncle. I shan't be at peace until I'm back home with Dad and Mum.'

'Aye ...' He compared in his mind's eye the eager school-girl he'd met at Southampton with the hopeless, hollow-eyed woman in front of him today. Maybe Australia could heal her, he was damn sure she'd go to pieces if she stayed here, she was being far too brave. He was even more worried that she might find the passage too much, she looked so frail from lack of sleep.

'Have you got your story ready for when they start asking questions? And your papers?'

She patted the pocket of her navy serge trousers. 'Safe and sound. I'm to tell the chief steward I've been seconded at the last minute because Stewardess Millet was taken ill.'

'Don't volunteer to try to do too much,' Lionel warned. 'According to Jim there should be six of you. Let the others do their share, don't knock yourself up. And what about ...?'

She knew he meant the gold coins in the heavy body belt next to her skin. 'Safe and sound.'

The lined face creased with worry. 'I hope there's enough to buy you that ticket in Singapore.'

'There's plenty. I shan't need to work my passage from there, I shall travel in style.' They both heard the shrill whistle. Her voice trembled, 'That's it. I must go, Uncle.'

'Aye. Here.' It wasn't much of a gift; he shoved the bag of

547

ginger biscuits into her hand. 'Good for sea-sickness, I'm told.'

'Thanks.' They hugged one another, scarcely daring to speak.

'Goodbye, Margaret. I hope you find happiness again in your own surroundings.'

It's the only chance I have left, she thought.

'Don't forget your promise to come out. Dad's counting on it.'

'Mu wouldn't let me, not this time,' he replied. 'She's set her heart on it. See you in Australia. God go with you, pet.'

Margaret had scribbled her letter while she and Lionel waited for the taxi; Mu had tucked it inside her own. At the depot, Rose unfolded the enclosure with shaking fingers.

> Darling Dad and Mum,
>
> Val's gone. The telegram says, 'missing in action'. I don't suppose I'll ever know what actually happened. I'm on my way but it may take time. Don't worry. I'll get there. I miss you both so much.
>
> All my love.
> Margaret.

'Ned, Ned!' The postie dashed up to the verandah. 'Come quick, Ned, the missus is in a bad way.'

Through the haze, Rose felt Ned's arms go round her and his comforting steady voice.

'What's wrong, pet? What's been happening?'

'It's all right, Margaret's coming home. But Val's been killed. Oh, Ned ... our girl's a widow and she's only nineteen.'

They had been sailing on a zig-zag route well away from regular shipping lanes. Squeezed in a cabin with five other women, Margaret had had plenty of time to reflect on Val's fears. She understood every aspect now. The claustrophobia, the lack of privacy to hide one's terror and the constant spectre of death hovering over them.

The convoy had already lost one ship; sick at heart they had watched it go down. Orders meant that all boats had to continue rather than remain to pick up possible survivors. Since then, commands from the tannoy occurred almost hourly. It was ironic that she should be in danger from prowling submarines. She wondered how many German submariners were stifling their terror as Val had had to do.

Tonight she'd been allowed a precious half-hour on deck. It was Val's birthday and she needed somewhere private to weep but the tears refused to come. Margaret stared at a birdless horizon – not another living creature in sight. How much longer before they glimpsed land? She'd no real idea where they were except for the change in temperature. Tired limbs responded and stretched languidly as humidity wrapped her in its embrace.

'Darling Val, the water must be so cold wherever you are . . .' She remembered how grateful he had been for the warmth and comfort of that bedroom in York. And the thought that she was safe from cold forever finally brought release. Margaret let the salt water course down her cheeks as she called his name aloud.

Alone in her shabby, small room in Middlesbrough, Gertie Brigg did the same.

549

Chapter Twenty-four

Wartime, 1942

Gertie Brigg knew without a doubt that God as well as Hitler was determined to punish her. On that dreadful night, when she and Harold had 'had words', she had gone to church to beg the Almighty to bring her husband to his senses. There was no one else she could ask and Harold had become impossible. He had confessed that Ethel Paige's money was exhausted. Now that they were penniless, Gertrude must apply to Rose and Ned for sustenance.

'We are doubly related to them. Valentine is their son-in-law, they are bound to respond to your plea.' Gertie had refused, unequivocally. Harold had tried everything from booming to violence. When he'd finally accused her of lacking all femininity, of being the skinniest, most revolting-looking woman in the world, she had put on her fox fur and hat. Ignoring the sirens, she'd braved the blackout, gone to church and prayed for assistance.

Her request had been answered with such immediate annihilating efficiency, she'd gone half out of her mind. The Brethren had done what they could. For several weeks Gertie was incapable of making any decision. Not enough remains could be found for a funeral and this distressed her most of all. Harold had been so large, surely there was something? Her mind floated off into fantasy: a foot, perhaps? Shoes had always been a problem because his feet had been so big.

She had no possessions other than the clothes she stood up in. Fortunately her ration book was in her handbag which made it easier for a brother mason's family to welcome her. It was an uncomfortable arrangement, however, and when Margaret's letter arrived, this tilted Gertie close to madness.

It had been delivered by hand. The mason's wife watched Gertie open the envelope. Inside, the letter was folded round a telegram. The woman waited apprehensively as she fumbled for her reading-glasses and scanned the signature.

'Margaret – Brigg! How dare she use that name, she has no right.'

'Now, now, Mrs Brigg. If it is your son's wife, she has every right.' Yesterday the woman had answered the door to Margaret; the girl's desolate, haunted expression had troubled her dreams, yet Gertie continued to prattle as if the enclosed telegram had no significance.

'An arranged marriage, that's all it was. Arranged by Harold. I saw no reason for it to take place. That's why I refused to see her.'

Her hostess had heard all this before. 'What does she have to say?'

Gertie began to read in a dismissive tone. 'Dear Mrs Brigg, I am sorry you were unable to see me yesterday. I came to tell you the worst news of all. Our darling Valentine is dead ... I enclose the official telegram ... which was sent to me ... next of kin.'

The other woman avoided Gertie's face and looked at the enclosure. 'I'm afraid it's quite true, Mrs Brigg. "Missing in action."'

'NO!' It was a shout to wake the dead, the utter, most final cry of despair from the one left behind.

'Here, sit down ... have a cup of tea—'

Gertie hurled the cup at the wall. When the woman, with great restraint, didn't protest but insisted on reading her the rest of Margaret's letter with its generous, loving offer to care for Gertie, her guest became a raging termagant.

Margaret was responsible for all her woes. If she hadn't seduced Valentine, he would never have enlisted and never, never risked his life. The house rang with Gertie's demented

551

cries and by nightfall the mason's wife had visited the billeting officer.

Gertie was shifted from one household to the next, babbling, hysterical, exhausting everyone's patience. Her few possessions were mislaid, she became indifferent to her appearance. One embarrassed landlady admitted in confidence that she'd had to demand that Mrs Brigg take a bath. Eventually, the harassed official decided the only remedy was to take a firm line; Gertie was moved into a small box-room, fenced in by restrictions issued by a new landlady who saw herself as a custodian and would not tolerate any nonsense.

By now the wildness had run its course. Most of the time, Gertie sat in her room and stared at the wall. There were days when she wanted to scream aloud but she knew she had to stay there, a handkerchief stuffed in her mouth until she regained control.

Reality returned; a realization of her desperate plight. She began to be afraid, not of the war, she was indifferent to what was happening, but of her own penury. Harold had left her nothing. The masonic Brethren, their resources fully stretched, suggested she should enquire about her 'rights'.

It took all Gertie's courage to visit the Public Assistance department. How she'd scorned those who went there in the old days! Now she became one of the desperate, shuffling, displaced poor, facing stern men behind a grill. There was no privacy; she was ordered to speak up and found herself describing her circumstances to an audience. It was total humiliation.

When she discovered how little they could offer, she returned to her box-room to weep. All those tears which she hadn't been able to shed for Harold now poured down her face. The great well of sorrow for Valentine spilled over and joined them. Then, the following day, came a letter from Rose.

It was brief but Gertie puzzled over it for a long time. Rose and Ned had heard the terrible news. Margaret had written before she left for Australia. They were planning to build a new life and invited Gertie to join them. If she agreed, they would send the money for her fare. She could book her passage as soon as circumstances permitted.

Where was the mention of the two hundred pounds?

'It's a trap,' Gertie whispered. 'Rose wants me out there, then she'll spring it on me.' Memories of Harold's dramatic pronouncement returned. 'Suppose she tells the police what I did – they could be waiting for me on the quayside. I could end up in prison!'

There was a knock at her door. Her jailor, Mrs Vaughan, was on the landing pretending to dust.

'Pardon me, Mrs Brigg. I couldn't help noticing you'd had a letter from Australia – good news, I hope?'

Gertie became distant. 'A private matter, Mrs Vaughan.' She saw the woman's expression and quickly became placatory. 'It contains an offer which I fear I am unable to accept.'

Mrs Vaughan knew her history and had a shrewd idea what the offer might be. 'If your family want you to join them, I should go if I were you, once this lot's over.' She wanted rid of her impoverished lodger, preferring someone with cash who could make her laugh: if possible, a man.

Unfortunately, possession of the letter emboldened Gertie. 'Mrs Vaughan, I wonder if it would be possible to have a change of menu occasionally. We have tomatoes on toast nearly every tea-time and I would prefer a little more variety.'

The feather-duster became an object of menace as Mrs Vaughan brandished it. 'You get what you pay for in this life, Mrs Brigg. What the Public Assistance give me for your keep is criminal. I took you in because I was ordered to and you needn't start complaining about my generosity. I grow those tomatoes myself otherwise you'd have toast and margarine, and lump it. If you want variety, find yourself a job and pay me a decent rent.'

'Work?' Gertie thought she must have misheard.

'Why not? You're not that old. They're crying out for women to fill men's jobs.'

'But I have never worked.'

553

'Then it's time you started,' the woman replied tartly, 'and if you don't intend to emigrate, take my advice and start looking for somewhere else to live. I can't stand people who whine.'

There was nowhere else, the billeting officer had told Gertie plainly. In his words this was 'the end of the line'. She shut the door. The grubby walls of her small prison closed in on her and she wept, calling on Valentine as softly as she could for fear of giving displeasure, to ease her broken spirit.

On the morning of their departure, Rose found she couldn't look back. Far more than Malinga, the depot represented so much effort, such a happy, satisfying part of her life, that to gaze at it one more time would sap all self-control. Besides, they had a goal now: she must concentrate on the fact that Margaret was coming home. Yesterday had been spent leaving messages everywhere they could think of, to stop her journeying back here. All the shipping lines had been given her name and the company address in Sydney. They had rented a flat there while they decided what to do next but by the time Margaret arrived, that decision might well have been taken.

Look to the future, Rose told herself firmly; it was the only thing that mattered. But now, at the very last minute, their own departure had to be delayed. She hurried across to the other shack.

'You two get started,' she told Maisie, 'Ned's not feeling too good. He didn't get much sleep last night.'

'I'm not surprised.'

'He's resting for a while. We'll set off when he wakes.'

'We'll see you in Alice.' Maisie lowered her voice. 'I want to get Oswald away. The silly old fool went and put flowers on the emu's grave this morning. He said baby would have done it if she'd been here.'

Rose was touched. 'Please thank him for me.'

Ned was in their empty living-room in one of the old bamboo chairs. Rose adjusted the blinds to cut out more light.

'Is that better?'

'Thanks, pet. Sorry about this. I feel as if my head's splitting.' She went out to find the medical kit in their car. Maisie and Oswald were already driving off as yet another air-force truck turned in off the highway.

The sooner we're away the better. Rose shook out a couple of aspirins; all this noise will only make Ned feel worse. She wrung a towel out under the tap and returned to wrap it round his head.

'That's better!' Eyes closed, he reached for her hand. 'Just a bit longer.'

'No rush.' They had all the time in the world. Listening idly to the hubbub, Rose wished for the umpteenth time she'd written earlier to tell Margaret about the depot and that the blacks were caring for Hermione. Now there was nowhere to send the letter.

'You're not still worried, are you?' Ned had read her thoughts as he so often did.

'About not letting her know? Yes, I am.'

'She'll understand.'

'It's just ... she's lost so much.' Rose sniffed hard, determined not to lose control. 'Now she hasn't even a home to come back to.'

'She will have. Not this place maybe, but somewhere. When we've decided what to do. And Margaret's sensible. I don't think we've spoiled her too much, she'll understand we had no choice.'

'I wish we'd had another child,' Rose said suddenly.

'Why?' He was looking at her now. She hadn't mentioned the subject for years.

It's too dangerous only having the one, she thought. Aloud she said, 'A son. You would have liked a son.'

Ned chuckled. 'You can still surprise me. Real north-east thinking, that is. A son – to carry on his father's business. Well, pet, this father's just lost his business. And *I* think it's time we left this place and let those noisy RAAF beggars get on with it. Are you ready?'

'If you're fit enough?' His head throbbed but he managed to nod. 'Very well. But I'm driving.'

'I won't fight you over it.' In the car he pretended to be critical, 'You're not a bad driver, once you stop talking and concentrate on the road.'

It was sufficient to annoy and distract her as they drove past the flower-filled tyres for the final time.

The journey south had been planned in easy stages. Oswald suggested they take even longer. He wanted Ned to have time to recover. Apart from his headaches, there was now a new-found guilt over Val.

'If I'd been more welcoming at the start, the two of them might have got out in time. The lad might not have enlisted.'

It was useless for any of them to point out that Valentine Brigg would have had to to join up once he landed in Australia; Ned needed to take the blame. He had deprived his precious daughter of her 'one and only'. 'Will Margaret ever forgive me, d'you think?'

'Of course she will! She'll never blame you, Ned.'

Maisie and Oswald conferred privately. 'It's all part of losing the depot,' she said. 'We know he'd set his heart on handing it on to baby. When will you tell him our idea?'

'When the time seems right,' Oswald promised.

He had been cherishing a dream and wondered if Ned would agree to share it. The sequestration meant they had plenty of money. Oswald had Ned's same lack of enthusiasm to tackle another big project. In his view, they'd earned the right to please themselves instead. He introduced the topic when they were out of the desert region and staying overnight at Woomera.

The velvety black sky was a million miles above, dotted with glittering, multi-faceted diamonds. Rose felt like a speck in the vastness. Yet out in that same universe, heading this way, Margaret was on her way home. Flesh of my flesh. Tonight only the two of them existed, all in all to one another; even Ned no longer came first. 'If I reach out my hand, I could

556

encircle the earth and touch her … my daughter. Only the two of us.'

Out of the darkness, Oswald's voice came as a quiet, gentle intrusion into her private world.

'Do you two remember how marvellous we felt that day we landed in Sydney? It wasn't simply that we'd arrived, more the way the place struck us. I've always had it in mind to build myself a nice little home down there, one with a proper view. Why don't we do it together?'

'Two more shacks?' Ned joked.

'You and I can afford to splash out this time. If we could find the right bay, like the ones we saw from the ship, you and I could keep a boat.'

'What about building materials? There's a war on, you know.'

Oswald snorted. 'We'll manage. We'll lean on the company if we have to. They owe us a favour or two.'

'I don't want to spend too much capital. We need to set Margaret up in whatever she wants to do.'

'Now listen,' Oswald waggled a finger at him. 'There's enough for us to build ourselves a nice home with a bit of a garden and still have plenty left over for baby. If we had a boat, you could go fishing, you've always wanted to try that. Once she gets here, Margaret will need somewhere to stay. She'll need peace and quiet. She wouldn't find that in a flat in Sydney.'

'Provided the Japs don't come marching in and ruin everything.'

'Bugger the Japs,' said Oswald shortly. 'First that emu pestering the life out of me, now the war. If it's not one damn thing, it's another. You and I have done our share, Ned. I'm going to look for a steep-sided bay where no bloody airforce can barge in and take over. Are you with me, or not?' He hadn't meant to be so blunt but Ned immediately saw the appeal.

'Whatever we decide to do, we'll need somewhere to live. We might as well make sure it's what we want.'

'Exactly.'

'What about you, pet?'

It's what we all need, she thought; the warmth and strength of being together. Without hesitating she said, 'It's the perfect solution. Thank you, Oswald. When we drove away from the depot, I wondered if Ned and I would ever feel really happy again. Now I know that we will. All it needed was a new idea, the right one, of course.'

'And a bit of gumption,' Maisie said comfortably, 'Oswald's always been one for that.'

They didn't shake hands, they were still too British, but they smiled more frequently and the chatter during the remainder of the journey became lively and optimistic.

It was Rose who suggested that instead of two, they should perhaps consider building three small homes. 'Margaret won't want to move in with us, she's become independent.' It occurred to her later that Margaret might want to move out of the parental orbit altogether. Could she therefore offer a refuge to Gertie? That night, she asked Ned.

He gave a satisfied smile. 'My word, pet, you've come a long way. I'm glad you've got there at last.'

Slightly piqued, Rose replied, 'I have written to Gertie more than once. She's never replied.'

'Try her again,' he urged, 'tell her we'd be very glad to see her. Poor soul, she must be the loneliest woman in Middlesbrough nowadays.'

Oswald had done more than dream, he now showed them architects' house plans as well as advertisements for boats and fishing rods. They welcomed every distraction. In the small flat they now occupied, they listened to the radio more frequently. At the depot, they had been isolated. Here in a town with constant reminders of men in uniform they began to realize just how bad the situation had become.

Oswald refused to be morbid. 'I'm not being selfish but it's no use worrying and it's not up to us. What we should do is concentrate on finding the perfect site before baby gets here.

558

I've been given details of a few more today.' And they would ignore the news and settle to discussing the various inlets on the map.

The bay, when they found it, was steep enough to deter even a seagull, with advantages Ned and Oswald were quick to spot: these were the natural rock formations which could be levelled and made wide enough to take three single-storied homes.

Oswald couldn't curb his enthusiasm. 'Each can be angled to have a different view of the sea ... we can link them with wide stone steps. Maisie says she's always wanted to try her hand at a terraced garden. At the bottom level, we can have a ladder down to a pontoon for the boat.' To find his dream about to become a reality overcame northern phlegm. 'Ee, Ned. What a marvellous spot, eh?'

Ned was squinting at the sky, irritated with himself. 'Perfect, I'd say. Sorry, Ossie, I've got one of my heads. I need to get out of the sun.' Oswald waited until he had settled in the car and closed his eyes. Rose and Maisie were right; leaving the depot, plus the constant worry over Margaret, had taken its toll. Being in a flat didn't help; they all chafed at being cooped up.

'So the sooner we all move out, the better.' It was a couple of hours before he completed his survey and returned. 'How are you feeling now, old chap?'

'Fine. Quite recovered thanks.' Ned stretched lazily.

'Good.' Oswald was bursting with it. 'Because we needn't bother with any of the other sites, this is the one. D'you mind if Maisie and I stake a claim to the top level for our nest?'

Ned chuckled. 'Eyrie, more like. Go ahead. I picked the depot. Your turn this time.'

'Thanks. We can bring the bosses out here in the morning. Provided they feel the same, we can settle with the agents tomorrow afternoon. With a bit of luck, you and I can start work in a couple of weeks.'

It took longer than that but at least Ned had regained his zest. They fell into their respective former roles without difficulty. Rose organized a corner of the flat as her office, spending her time on the phone chasing supplies. Maisie took herself off to the bay to plan her garden. Oswald and Ned, with the company's help, rallied a scratch workforce and set about blasting and levelling the rock.

Then, on 7th December, the Japanese invaded Pearl Harbour.

After the first shock, Maisie put the news in perspective. 'If it means the Yanks come into the war, it'll be over that much quicker.'

Ned burst out, 'What about Margaret? Shipping's not safe anywhere in the Pacific.'

'Ned, she won't be coming that way. She'll be travelling via Singapore.'

'Of course. Sorry.' He forced a smile for Rose's benefit. 'Stupid to get so worked up. So, Oswald: what's the plan for tomorrow?'

Work was his release. Ned needed to have something ready to show Margaret. He and Rose would live on the middle level – only the foundations had been completed there – but down below, with a pontoon already in place for Margaret to swim or sail from, the smallest bungalow had to be finished first.

He worked as he had done when they'd first gone to the depot, until exhaustion forced him to stop. Rose didn't interfere; fatigue meant that he slept, and sleep, blessed unconsciousness, gave Ned a respite. Surely they would hear from Margaret soon? It was her self-imposed task to check for messages at the company offices every morning. Afterwards, she would drive out and join Maisie in the half-finished top bungalow, where the two of them were already making curtains. Those for Margaret were nearly finished.

It was the day on which work on the three broad flights of concrete steps had begun. From the bottom level, Ned heard Oswald calling. Obviously an extra pair of hands would be welcome up top. He began the climb but had to pause. The blinding headache had returned with a vengeance.

The overhead sun seemed to pierce inside his skull, splitting it apart. Ned fell forward, clawing at the earth clenching his teeth, his whole body contorting in a spasm as the pain bit savagely. He lost his grip and, unable to save himself, slithered a few feet.

Oswald shouted uncertainly, 'Ned? You all right?' There was no answer.

One of the team mixing concrete leaned on his shovel. 'Is he crook? Shall I go down?'

'It's all right, I'll go. Give my wife a shout.'

'Okay, mate.'

Oswald's face loomed over Ned, blotting out the sun. He heard the sturdy, commonsense voice telling him to take it easy.

'Rose . . .'

'Yes, old chap. She's been sent for.' Oswald glanced up. Rose was already hurrying down the slope, careless of her safety, sending stones glissading past. 'She's on her way.' He waited until she was kneeling beside Ned before murmuring, 'This time I'm sending for an ambulance.' But when he reached the top again, Maisie had already done so. She handed him a blanket.

'Wrap Ned in this and take him a glass of water. Is it another of those headaches?'

'I've no idea, he couldn't speak. He looks bloody poorly! I wish he'd been sensible and seen a doctor.'

'Now Oswald, stay calm. Warn the men they'll need to give a hand. It's going to be an effort getting the stretcher back up.'

Rose continued to kneel beside Ned, stroking his forehead, talking tenderly, trying not to show fear at his contorted features. Voices urged her to stand aside, workmen helped her up the hillside into the ambulance. Maisie sat opposite, gripping her hands tightly. 'Let them see to him, Rose. They know what's best,' and through the nightmare, she could feel a tremor in the rough, familiar hands.

Maisie's afraid, Rose thought in surprise. Why? Ned's been overdoing it but he'll be all right. It's only reaction, losing the depot, worry over Margaret, we all know that. I should have made him ease up.

561

In the hospital, she was ushered into a waiting room and offered tea. She could hear Maisie answering questions through the open door.

'No, he hasn't seen a doctor ... quite some time, now I come to think about it ... Headaches, yes, then today when Oswald spoke to him, he didn't seem able to move.'

Rose was alert. That couldn't be right. Surely there had been some reaction when she spoke to Ned? Or in the ambulance? Try as she could, she couldn't remember any. Maisie was explaining, 'His daughter's on her way from England. Ned's very worried. We thought that was partly the reason.'

When she came back, Rose asked, 'Can I see him?'

'Not yet. They're doing some tests. They'll come and tell us.' Maisie's expression was so serious Rose wanted to see her relax.

'It's happened before, Maisie. Ned should have worn his hat, I keep reminding him.'

'Yes.' No palliative words this time.

When the doctor finally entered, Rose was ready for him. 'I want to know what's wrong.'

He hesitated. 'We've done a lumbar puncture, we're waiting for the result. It could be an aneurysm.' He might have been speaking Chinese.

Rose fought her panic. 'When I said – tell me, I meant what do you intend to do? Does Ned need medicine? He takes aspirin when it gets too bad. He has been overdoing things as Mrs Robson told you ...' She stopped because the doctor was shaking his head.

'I'm very sorry, Mrs Harrison ... very sorry. It may be too late. Would you like to sit with your husband?'

She was frozen, numb. She saw the shrug he gave to Maisie. Ned's going to die, thought Rose incredulously. He's going to die because no one's doing anything to help him. He can't die from a headache, that would be utterly stupid! Rigid with anger she walked stiffly down the corridor. She sat beside the high bed. Ned's eyes were closed. His face was pallid against the white pillow. Everything in the room was white, the walls, the blinds, the nurse's apron.

Suddenly Ned opened his eyes; the dark pupils were the only colour in the room. He stared in her direction, seeing, unseeing. It seemed to Rose that he smiled. She was hanging on to her emotions, clasping her hands so tightly she daren't let go even to reach out and touch him.

'Ned ...'

The eyes tried to focus on her voice. He sighed.

'Hallo, Margaret.'

The aneurysm, which had been leaking for so long, finally ruptured; a massive haemorrhage began. Within a few seconds, Ned was dead.

Captain Hislop was apprehensive when he answered Rose's formal request for an interview. He came to collect her from the ante-room, ushered her into his office and retreated behind the desk. She was composed. He reminded himself it was unlikely for Rose Harrison to appear otherwise. With some relief he cleared his throat.

'How are you, Mrs Harrison?'

'Very well, thank you. It's good of you to see me.'

'If there's anything, anything at all ...' Her face began to change and he said quickly, 'I drove out to see the new property last week. The work is progressing – I gather the third bungalow is nearing completion.'

'Oswald was determined to keep to schedule.' Rose took a deep breath. 'Captain Hislop, I came to ask – is there a vacancy here that I could fill?'

He frowned. 'Surely there's no need for you to work?'

'No, none. But this waiting, doing nothing, is very difficult. When Margaret finally arrives, the first thing I have to do is tell her ... about Ned.'

'Quite.'

'Mr and Mrs Robson are dear friends but I'm becoming a burden simply by being there all day. I've spent much of the last four weeks out walking. Sometimes I drive into Sydney, to watch the liners coming in. That doesn't help – I start imagining ...' Hislop nodded. 'If I had a routine,' Rose continued, 'some way in which I could be useful, it would give me a sense of purpose until Margaret returns. Now the building work is finished there's very little organizing and, consequently, nothing for me to do.'

'Yes, I understand.'

She smiled. 'It was you who turned me into a career woman, with that gift of a typewriter.' Hislop found his thoughts creeping back to his initial reaction that day in Liverpool: Rose Harrison was still a fine-looking woman.

'We've several vacancies with so many men called up. What did you have in mind, Mrs Harrison?'

She immediately became business-like. 'Temporary work. So that I can leave without causing too much disruption. And although I can type, I'm much better at being persuasive on the phone.'

'As I know to my cost,' he acknowledged gracefully. 'Leave it with me. I'll send you details of what I think might suit and you can make the final choice.' He glanced at his watch. 'Had you any plans for lunch?' A little surprised, Rose admitted she had none. 'Then perhaps you will permit me? There are few in the office these days with whom I can reminisce about Malinga.'

After exhausting the topic of Malinga they turned to personal matters. Rose was encouraged to describe how Ned's affairs had been settled. She found it a relief to talk.

'The solicitor suggested that instead of one account and one set of investments, we split the capital equally, between Mr and Mrs Robson and myself. Oswald insists their share will be left to Margaret eventually but I think it's best not to look too far ahead. Whatever happens, my daughter will be extremely well provided for. In a material sense, she's a lucky young woman. My worry, of course, is how the loss of her husband has affected her. There's no doubt they were deeply in love ... but when I remember how much longer Ned and I had together ...'

Hislop waited for a moment before offering, 'More coffee?'

'Thank you.'

'If she, like you, needs time to recover,' he said quietly, 'and if an office routine would dull the ache while she decides what to do, don't hesitate, Mrs Harrison. Ned was one of the best. His daughter deserves all the help we can offer.'

Rose replaced the cup in its saucer slowly, carefully. When she was able, she said, 'Thank you. Thank you very much indeed.'

It had been cathartic. Rose left the restaurant feeling buoyant for the first time in weeks. She and the captain shook hands and she made her way briskly to her car, past a news hoarding: Singapore had fallen.

Rose had been working for the company for three months before the official notification reached her. The tone was one of reproof as well as commiseration. Mrs Margaret Brigg's position on the crew list of that particular vessel had been irregular. However, it was with great sadness that, following the loss of the convoy with all hands, her death must now be assumed as fact. The illegible signatory tendered his deepest sympathy to Mr and Mrs Harrison who had been the two persons named on Mrs Brigg's documents.

Redirected from the depot, the letter reached Rose at the company office. She managed a brief word to her secretary, telling the girl she wouldn't be back, then rushed blindly out of the building, and through the streets. When she came to her senses, she was sitting on the bench overlooking the harbour, where once a little girl had asked her father if she could learn to fly like the birds.

Overhead, seagulls still swooped and shrieked. Below, Rose was immobile, remembering her great fear of the ocean when Margaret was a warm foetus safe inside her body. Had the significance of those terrors been revealed at last?

She sat so long and looked so ill, a passer-by came to enquire if she was all right. Reluctantly, Rose got to her feet. She had to go back and break the news to Maisie and Oswald.

There were times when Maisie couldn't bear to see Rose's

sorrow. Tears could not provide relief this time. Like some doom-laden prophetess of old, she sought to blame herself for Margaret's loss.

'Those nightmares on the boat – I thought it was my own death – I made Ned swear we'd never go to sea again – but it was Margaret drowning, choking to death! If only I'd warned her.' And the agony would once more become too great. Maisie nursed her as tenderly as she could.

'This wicked, cruel war ... you couldn't have stopped her, Rose. Margaret was bound to try and come back. How else could she have done so? When this terrible time is past, you will see it differently.'

Rose had another deep need, to confess her shortcomings over Ned.

'If I'd loved him enough, but I didn't, not as much as he deserved. That's why he called out for Margaret before he died.'

Again, Maisie did her best. 'You made Ned very happy, you know you did.'

But not enough! Rose wanted to scream. I should have tried harder, been more generous. Maisie didn't understand. Perhaps Gertie might? Hadn't she found love-making a strain because both of them had been brought up to think of it as 'not nice'?

Maisie insisted Rose stay with them in the top bungalow. During the night, when her sobbing could clearly be heard, Oswald would toss and sigh, 'What's going to happen?'

'It's too soon to worry about that. Rose will decide in her own good time.'

'D'you think she'll marry again?'

Maisie was emphatic. 'She could never forget Ned and she's got nothing left for anyone else.' Her plain face creased in sorrow. 'As for baby ... I thought you and I had missed out, not having a kiddie, but I'm thankful we've been spared when I listen to that.'

Gradually, inevitably, when the tears had run dry, Rose recognized she could not remain idle. She sent her apologies to Captain Hislop, this time office work wasn't the remedy, and received a sympathetic reply. Instead she began finishing what Ned had begun, furnishing and decorating what was to have been their home. Maisie, though worried, didn't ask questions nor did she try to prevent it when Rose announced she was ready to move into the bungalow. Both of them knew the time had come for Rose to be on her own for a while.

Her need to do some kind of work was eventually fulfilled by the Red Cross. Maisie agreed to enrol as well, not without a grumble.

'They'd better not give me bandages to roll. I rolled miles of 'em in the first war. The mistress of the house considered it *suitable* work for servants.'

Rose smiled faintly. 'We could always volunteer for munitions.'

'Bullets? Not unless I can make one with Hitler's name on it.'

It was the beginning of another period in limbo, just as it had been at Malinga. I'm marking time, waiting to discover what it is I must do, Rose thought. By the time the war is over, I should have some idea. Life can't be over – I'm only forty-three.

Each evening, she joined them in the top bungalow, to listen to the bulletin. Slowly, the tide of the war began to turn, first at El Alamein, then in Stalingrad. The Russians pushed westward, the Allies prepared to invade Normandy and London endured the first rocket attacks yet hope continued to revive. With great caution, Rose began to consider the future.

Her decision didn't come suddenly but as a result of quiet contemplation. It filled her with relief. She shied away from it at first but finally saw it as the only possible solution.

The following morning she arrived at the top bungalow intending to explain but found Maisie in an unusually irritated state.

'Oswald's left me to do the dirty work ... he's pushed off. Claims he's gone to see a man about a boat. He hasn't, of course.'

'What's the problem?'

'Captain Hislop. He's written asking Oswald and me if he can rent or buy baby's bungalow. You know why, of course?'

'No.' Rose was genuinely mystified.

Maisie's irritability increased. 'You're probably the only female who worked for the company that didn't know the captain was a widower.'

'No, I didn't. That doesn't explain why he wants to move in here.'

'It's because of you, stupid.' Exasperated, Maisie demanded, 'Isn't it obvious – he's taken a shine to you.'

'He hasn't!' Rose's shocked disapproval made her laugh.

'Cheer up. He'd never do anything improper, he's too much of a gent. But if you want my opinion, the only reason he'd like to move in down below is so that he can be nearer to you.'

'Good heavens.'

'What answer do Oswald and I give?'

Rose gathered her wits. 'Tell Captain Hislop he's most welcome to rent Margaret's bungalow but that I shall no longer be here. I'm going back to Middlesbrough.'

'Oh, no! You're not, are you?' It was her turn to be shocked. Maisie looked so bereft, Rose hugged her tightly.

'Listen, dear. I've thought it through very carefully. I once promised Gertie I'd look after her. I think she probably needs me still. I must go and find out.'

'Oh Rose, we shall miss you!'

'I shall miss you, very, very much. And I shall come back to visit. I shall bring Mu because she'd bound to want to see Ned's grave. And I'm going to write to our old neighbours at the depot, telling them about my bungalow. When they visit Sydney, they can stay here so that you and Oswald won't be lonely. You can show off your garden, you'll enjoy that. Just make sure my place is empty when I want to come.'

'We will. Oh, Rose ...'

Oswald hadn't been spinning a yarn about the boat. The day

568

before Rose left for England, there was a quiet naming ceremony from the pontoon. She lifted the glass high.

'I name this beautiful yacht, the *Margaret Rose* ... God bless and keep safe all those who sail in her.' A stream of golden champagne splashed over her stern.

'It was Ned's idea,' Oswald told her, satisfied. 'He chose the name. It was to be a surprise when baby got back.' Rose stared across the bay, expressionless. 'Ned reckoned we'd never tire of this. Even if he didn't see it finished, he enjoyed being here, planning for the future. I think it made up a little for losing the depot.'

Rose said slowly, 'I've learned to be thankful he went when he did. It could have happened at any time but if Ned had lived a couple more months ...'

Maisie summed it up. 'He didn't have the sorrow of it, but he and Margaret must be together now, otherwise none of it makes sense.'

Rose had one last duty to perform and told Maisie she would be out for lunch.

'Any idea where she's off to?' Oswald watched the car drive away.

'I think so, yes. Better wait and see if she wants to tell us about it when she gets back.'

Rose had suggested the same Sydney restaurant and Captain Hislop was already there when she arrived. It saddened her to see how smart, how obviously new and elegant were his suit and tie. Maisie had told him of her plans. Surely he didn't imagine she would change her mind at this late hour?

They gave their order and Rose began to toy with her glass of sherry.

'Shall I make it easier for you, Mrs Harrison? I think you may have suggested this meeting so that I might wish you God speed, which I do with my most sincere good wishes.'

Rose felt ashamed that he should have been the one to speak first. 'After all your kindness, I couldn't leave without saying goodbye.'

569

He inclined his head. 'Ours has been a long acquaint-anceship. To my sorrow, I've had to stand by and watch you lose all you held dear.'

She took a quick sip and kept her emotions on a tight rein. Please, dear God, don't let him speak of it, not here, not now. Perhaps the Captain sensed her tension.

Without looking at her, he continued, 'I can understand your decision to leave Australia. Forgive me if this is imperti-nent but have you any clear idea of what you will do back in Britain?'

Rose hesitated. 'I want to see Ned's family . . . see that they are all right. Then, perhaps, join up with my sister—'

'Your – not the one who . . .?'

Rose tried to shrug it off. 'The same. That affair was over a long time ago.'

He was still concerned. 'Might I ask . . . have you been in touch with Mrs Brigg?'

'No.' Rose added flatly, 'Gertie has lost her husband and her child, we have that much in common. If she feels as desolate as I do occasionally, I think she might be glad of my company. We were very close at one time.' Before Harold and Ned came into our lives, she thought.

The head-waiter arrived to lead them to their table; it gave Rose time to compose herself. She changed the subject delib-erately, inviting the Captain to talk of company matters.

He did so, finishing, 'One of the reasons I was glad to accept your invitation today was to ask whether you would be inter-ested in representing our interests over there? It would mean living in London, of course.'

It was Rose's turn to be surprised but when he suggested she take time to consider, she found she could make her decision without delay.

'If I'm to look after Gertie that means staying in the north-east. Where her friends are . . .' For a brief moment she wondered if Gertie had any friends left. 'And Ned's family, of course. Besides . . .' She looked around the busy restaurant, full of prosperous businessmen. 'As Oswald says – I've done

570

my share – and gained my independence. We must let the young have their chance now, Captain Hislop. That was all Ned asked those many years ago when he came back.'

'I'm standing down myself, as a matter of fact.'

'Are you?' Opposite, the silvery head was bowed as he gazed into his glass. He was, as Maisie insisted, still a good-looking man. Rose examined the features dispassionately. Captain Hislop was precisely the sort of gentleman her mother intended she and Gertie should marry. She gave herself a mental shake. 'May I wish you a happy retirement, Captain.'

'Thank you.' He raised his wineglass. 'To our continuing friendship, Mrs Harrison. May I, when I take my planned holiday in England, call on you, perhaps?'

Why not, Rose thought defiantly? It would certainly make Gertie sit up.

'I should be delighted.'

After supper, when Rose had left them, Oswald said pensively, 'That trip to Sydney didn't change anything then?'

'Of course it didn't. How could it? We'll just have to learn to be patient and wait for her to come and visit.'

Rose descended alone to the pontoon to make her farewells. 'I'm leaving all that matters here,' she told the silvery waves, 'I can't think of you lost at sea, Margaret. You were a land creature, always basking in the sun. And Ned. This was your country, my darling. Me … I'm betwixt and between. Half of me wants to stay but what would I do? You two ghosts don't need me any more.'

She gazed once more at the graceful white shape on the water. The names were in the order he had chosen. Any guilt or chagrin had long since been washed away in tears.

'You loved us both, Ned. I did my best but Margaret gave you her whole heart.'

She climbed back up, calm and determined. 'You promised I need never go to sea again, my darling. Bless the clever man who invented the aeroplane.'

Chapter Twenty-five

Aftermath, 1945

'What happened to the roof?' Rose was on Middlesbrough station platform, gazing open-mouthed at the destruction.

The porter was sarcastic. 'Heavy rain, what d'you think? We was bombed, of course. Bank holiday Monday, 1942.' He began pushing the laden barrow.

Rose fell into step beside him. 'I've been away.' Mu's letters had certainly been short on detail. 'Was it bad in Middlesbrough?'

'Bad enough. Taxi rank's this way, madam.'

'Oh, good heavens ...' Rose was staring at the ravages in Zetland Road. 'Is the rest of the town like this?'

'You'd better take a look. Lady's been away, Fred. She'd like a tour of the sights.' He finished loading the suitcases and held open the taxi door. As he received his generous tip, politeness returned. 'Thank you, madam. Been away long?'

A lifetime, she thought. 'Since 1921. In Australia.'

'Ah.' The far side of the moon. 'You'll notice a few changes, courtesy of 'itler. Makes you wonder if it was worth while when you see what we've got to show for it.'

'We couldn't let them march in and walk all over us!'

'No. Quite right. Nasty 'abits, those Nazis. T.T.F.N. madam.' He slammed the door.

And what on earth does that mean? she wondered.

'Where to, lady?'

'The King's Head. I shall need you to wait while I register.'

Goodness knows where she'd find another cab in this alien town. 'Is this – Cannon Street?'

'What's left of it. The streets behind copped it far worse.'

She remembered Harold. 'My brother-in-law was in Jamieson Street the night it was bombed.'

'Uh-huh. I doubt you'll recognized Linthorpe Road.'

When they drove down it, Rose was stunned. 'What about the King's Head – it is still standing?'

'Oh, yes.' He grinned, 'Provided you've got your ration book, they'll even welcome you.'

When later she shivered in the chilly bedroom, Rose told herself her blood was thin after life in the tropics. 'I've grown soft. I must try to put on a layer of blubber!' How, was the problem. During her brief stay in London, she'd begun to learn what 'shortage' really meant.

As the taxi drew up, Mu's front door opened. 'Ee, pet. I've been on the lookout since breakfast time.' They hugged one another, broke apart and laughed out of nervous excitement, scanning each other's faces, trying to find the young women they once were.

'Just let me – sort things out.'

'Of course.'

She watched as Rose paid the driver, drinking in every detail. Rose adjusted her memories to the changes. Mu's hair was streaked with grey, she was thinner, her face deeply etched but the warmth of the voice was exactly the same. Why had *she* never noticed before how much it was an echo of Ned's!

'Come in, come in. There's just the two of us. Lionel won't be back till tea-time. I wanted you all to myself for a bit.'

'It *is* good to see you, Mu.'

'Come on through to the back. We don't light a fire in the front except on Sundays.'

The one in the kitchen burned brightly enough. The electric light was already on because the room was dark. Mu looked her up and down once more, then came back for another hug.

573

'Rose, I'd have known you anywhere even though you're so smart. Sit down. No, wait a bit.' She spread a clean tea-cloth over the seat. 'Lionel's overalls aren't always clean. Here, take a look at these while I brew up. I've been keeping them specially. I didn't know whether Margaret had ever sent you copies. I'll just fill the kettle.'

They were the snapshots of Margaret and Val on their wedding day. Rose stared at the tense, young faces and became very still. From the scullery, Mu called, 'They were very happy at the finish. I was ever so thankful.'

'Yes …' There was one of Valentine, standing defiantly apart from his parents. 'He really must have been Harold Brigg's son.'

'Oh, yes.' Mu stood in the scullery doorway. 'Looked more like him the older he got, except Val was quite handsome. He didn't take after his father for brains, thank goodness. Ever so intelligent. And really nice manners. He could thank your sister for that, I reckon.'

'How is Gertie? Have you seen her lately? I wrote from London but there was no reply for me at the hotel.'

Mu was reticent. 'It's difficult for her. You'll see a lot of difference there, I'm afraid. I hear from Edwin occasionally.' Rose looked blank. 'My son-in-law.'

'Oh, yes.'

'He and June are still with his family. Houses are like gold dust since all the bombing. But after his demob he found a job in the Public Assistance Department.' Again Rose didn't understand. 'Your sister goes there – he's forbidden to discuss details, naturally – he said she was having a struggle. He feels quite sorry for her.'

As Mu finished making the tea, Rose sat silently cursing herself. Why hadn't she used her common-sense? Of course Gertie must be short of money – but to have to come down to that! She said with an effort as Mu came back, 'I don't suppose Harold Brigg left much.'

'Not a penny. I believe there were a few debts too but the masons probably took care of them. The tabernacle was up for

574

sale when it was bombed. Milk and sugar?'

'Please.'

'Would you like a scone?'

'No, thanks.'

Mu looked at her critically, 'You ought to try and put on a bit of weight. A north-east wind could blow you away.' She broached the subject that had puzzled everyone. 'I was surprised when you said you were coming back.'

Rose took a sip of her tea. 'There was nothing to keep me in Australia.'

'I suppose not.' They stared at the flames.

Rose explained, 'I've kept the bungalow overlooking the bay. I shall take you and Lionel on holiday there one day, when you feel up to it. You'll be able to see the home Ned built for Margaret. He was so proud of it.'

Mu blew her nose. 'I'm glad you didn't have to sell it.'

'Oh, no. There was no need.'

Rose was obviously as flush as she looked, Mu thought. With something like regret she wished she'd used her best teacups.

'Have you decided what you'll do now you're here?'

'I once promised Gertie I'd look after her. I shall probably regret it if she proves difficult.'

'She's a ten-bob-a-week widow, pet. She may be proud but she needs all the help she can get.'

They sat and talked until the fire was low and memories had run their course. Lionel returned, like Mu thin and tired with a gauntness stamped on him by the war, which Rose found disturbing.

She learned much more about the destruction. Over 800,000 houses had been lost altogether and when he and Mu escorted her back to the hotel it seemed to Rose as though half of Middlesbrough was included in that total.

An idea had begun to coalesce in her mind. First it was necessary to write again to Gertie; Rose had no intention of taking her by surprise. The note was despatched: two brief sentences telling her she was now in Middlesbrough and would like to call.

*

During the few days she had spent in London before journeying north, Rose had not been idle. The car she had ordered was delivered to the hotel and June was invited to act as chauffeuse. The ex-furnace worker was delighted.

The following day, they toured Middlesbrough until Rose felt sure of her surroundings. Finally, June asked, 'Seen enough, auntie?'

Rose sighed. 'It's a great relief to think I might be able to find my way about once more. Show me where Gertie lives then we'll go back to the hotel.'

They drove past a row of identical drab front doors with raw gaps where bombs had struck. Rose shook her head. This area didn't look much better than Fleetham Street. Apart from the damage, she'd forgotten how dismal the town could be when smoke blew in from Billingham. When she remarked on it, June laughed.

'We were jolly glad of that smoke. In fact, they thickened it up during the war. They burned oil to add an extra black cloud round ICI when the Luftwaffe were on their way.'

'I'd no idea ...' Rose shook her head at the crumbling, boarded-up shops in Wilson Street. 'All this – terrible desolation. We had no cinema at the depot, we never saw the news until we lived in Sydney.'

'We were lucky,' June said simply. 'People like Mrs Brigg lost everything. And Mum always claims it was the war that killed Uncle Ned, as well as Margaret.'

'Perhaps.'

Did Gertie still grieve for Harold the way she did for Ned?

They had pulled up outside the hotel and Rose became practical. 'How much did you earn at Bowesfield Lane?'

'Two pounds a week. That included extra for shift work.'

'I'll pay you two pounds, ten shillings. Here's a week in advance. Tomorrow, if Gertie hasn't replied, I shall want to visit Saltburn and Redcar, to see if the wind is as cold as I remember.'

'It will be,' June promised firmly. 'Ten o'clock?'

576

'Fine.'

The following morning, it took less than a quarter of an hour driving past pill-boxes and tank-traps, sand-bags and barbed wire for Rose to be convinced. 'I shall look for somewhere in the country.'

'Do you think Mrs Brigg will want to join you?'

'I think so – I hope so. I doubt if Gertie really likes being on her own.'

June glanced sideways at the tall, elegant figure; it was a different aunt from the vivid young bride with flowers in her hair. 'Mam and Dad were wondering if you might marry again.'

'No, June. There'll never be another to equal Ned.'

'Mrs Brigg has been a widow even longer than you.'

Rose smiled sadly, 'I fear marriage was always a disappointment for Gertie.'

The reply from Gertie, when it came, was brief:

'I cannot repay the money. I have no savings, only my widow's pension. If you would like to call, I shall be pleased to see you on Wednesday afternoon between 2.00 and 3.00 pm when my landlady will be out.'

Rose parked the car a distance away. She arrived on foot and knocked. Would Gertie have arranged for the current Queenie to answer the door?

'Is it you, Rose ...?'

She was so frail! So old behind the familiar glasses. Rose's heart churned.

'Yes, dearest, it's me. How are you, Gertie?'

Her sister ducked away from her embrace and scuttled off down the passage, calling, 'Don't wait on the step. Through here.' Rose followed.

She doesn't want the neighbours to see me. Despite all the years, Rose's antennae were sharply tuned. Do I look too smart? Poor dear Gertie, she can't bear the contrast – why didn't I wear something plain?

Unlike Mu's welcoming kitchen, this one had dark brown lincrusta and heavy crimson curtains. Rose longed to pull these apart so that she and Gertie could see one another properly. Under the dim bulb her sister was shabby. The dress had darns at the elbows, a dingy, lacy collar did nothing to help. June was right, some people had lost everything; Gertie, her dignity and self respect. Her voice quivered with fright.

'I've no money, Rose. Nothing. I had saved a little but I needed it.'

'Gertie! That's not why I'm here!'

The table had been set. No dainty tablecloth but cups and saucers that didn't match.

'I can't offer you biscuits ...' Gertie attempted to act the hostess, adjusting a spoon as though it were silver. She caught sight of the clock and her mood changed, 'If we could have tea now, before Mrs Vaughan gets back.' She disappeared into the scullery. Rose heard the pop of the gas.

'She's terrified of me. She can hardly bear to be in the same room – it's simply dreadful to see her in this state. Very quietly, she waited for Gertie to return with the teapot.

'Mrs Vaughan lets me use this room when she is out.'

Without thinking, Rose asked, 'Not the parlour?'

After a split second, Gertie said quickly, 'That hasn't been properly aired today.'

'I – see.'

'I cannot afford a proper rent, merely what they allow me at the Assistance department. Harold spent every penny.'

'Gertie, about that draft ...'

'If Valentine had lived, I'm sure he would have provided, if he hadn't had to marry so young!' Behind the glasses Gertie's eyes overflowed with a mixture of anger and self-pity.

'We'll leave that for another time. Do you have a nice room?'

'The box-room. There's no view.'

Rose put down her cup. 'I'm thinking of buying a house.'

'You weren't depending on that two hundred pounds?'

'Try and forget about that money, Gertie. It doesn't matter, it was all a long time ago.'

'I've never been able to forget,' she burst out. 'It's been with me night and day. I took it while you were washing your hair. I put it in my locker until Harold and I went out then he cashed it. We went to the shipping office and he bought the tickets. I couldn't work like a skivvy, Rose, I just couldn't. I had to get away!'

'It doesn't matter.' How many times? Rose needed to escape from the gloom which was weighing her down. 'Shall we go up to your room?' Perhaps she could convince Gertie there.

'After we've washed up. Mrs Vaughan doesn't like to find unwashed dishes. She often leaves me hers to do as well.'

Dear Lord, thought Rose, you've been reduced to being a skivvy even though you don't realize it. Upstairs, Gertie opened the door reluctantly.

'There isn't room for a chair.' Rose saw a narrow bed, a single wardrobe, a bedside table, a strip of carpet. 'I lost everything. Clarence took a collection from the members of the tabernacle. He gave me that photo of Harold.'

Familiar features stared pompously. If that comes with us it'll have to go where I can't see it, Rose thought.

'I lost every single memento of Valentine, that was the worst! And the silver dressing-table set, of course.'

It was as vivid to Gertie as if it were yesterday. Rose remembered what she had seen of the destruction. Gertie had endured that bombing, night after night, no wonder she looked so careworn. She must let her take her time, talk it out of her system. Rose went to sit on the bed; there was a clatter, something rolled over.

'What on earth ...' It was an upturned plant pot. Under it a candle stood on a saucer.

Gertie explained. 'It's for heating the room. We learned to do it during the war. You light the candle and put the plant pot over it. It doesn't take long to warm up, otherwise I have to keep my coat on in here all the time.'

Rose said urgently, 'We'll start looking at houses first thing tomorrow. I thought we might drive out to Great Ayton.'

Gertie stared: Rose had said 'we'. Did that mean she was being included? Was it possible ...? Did Rose intend ...? Stupified, she said the first thing that came into her mind.

'Have you a car?'

'Yes, and thanks to Lionel and his friends, enough black market petrol coupons.' She saw Gertie's face and added cheerfully, 'Don't worry, I don't suppose I'll end up in prison.'

'Are you very rich?' Gertie asked suddenly. 'You look as if you are.' She had relaxed enough to examine the smart outfit more closely. That long red herringbone coat must be the New Look. Rose's hair was swept up, her hat had a small black veil. Altogether her sister looked extremely prosperous.

'Ned and I made a profit on our property. You and I can afford to buy a decent house.'

'In Clairville Road?'

'No, Gertie. No going back.' Hope faded.

'I suppose you're right.' She heard a sound below and whispered, 'Mrs Vaughan!'

Rose was puzzled. 'Are you going to introduce me?'

Gertie was high-pitched 'She doesn't approve of visitors. You're here as a special favour.'

To hell with that nonsense, Rose thought angrily; you and I have earned the right to exist without favours from anyone. She picked up her bag.

'I shall call for you tomorrow at half past nine. I've details of five or six houses. We could have lunch somewhere and make a day of it.'

'That would be lovely,' Gertie whispered.

From down below, a strident voice called, 'Is that you, Mrs Brigg? Is there someone with you?'

'Oh, dear!' To see her sister old, shabby and now cowering like some beaten creature made Rose furious.

'Gertie, pack your things. After tomorrow, you're not

coming back, you'll move in with me. I'll explain to your land-lady.' She sailed downstairs. On the landing her sister looked down anxiously, the way she had the night Rose twisted her ankle, when Ned . . . Not now!

'Mrs Vaughan? I'm Rose Harrison. My sister will be leaving tomorrow and joining me at my hotel. Kindly return her ration book.'

The woman bridled. 'I don't see why she should be in such a hurry.'

Rose was acerbic. 'She's doing it as a favour to *me*.'

The three-storied house was on the outskirts of Guisborough. Built of grey stone, flat-fronted, it had a Georgian elegance Rose found satisfying. She noticed the neglect among the beech trees in the garden, the peeling paint on the window frames. As they mounted the shallow steps and entered the front door, she told Gertie she would enjoy arguing over the price. Gertie stared nervously at the handsome wide hall.

'It's huge. Surely you can't afford . . .?'

'Yes, we can. Besides, we shall need a large house. I want to invite Mu and Lionel to join us, Gertie. They could have the whole of the top floor. Their married daughter needs a home. She and Edwin could move in to their terrace house and begin their family. It's high time there were a few children about.'

Gertie was bewildered; so much was happening so quickly. She followed Rose through the baize door.

'I don't think I know those people.'

'Of course you do. We went back to Mu's house for our wedding breakfast. So did Margaret and Val.'

Oh, *those* people! Gertie sniffed. 'All I remember of your wedding was the small girl who interrupted the marriage service.'

Rose laughed delightedly, 'That was June. You'll like Muriel, she's a good kind person, she'll enjoy helping me run this place – we shall have plenty of other help, of course. We'll need a couple of rooms for visitors. Maisie and Oswald are bound to come and stay.'

581

'What will I have to do?' Gertie was trembling, 'I'm not used to people, Rose.'

She took her hand. 'Yours will be the most beautiful room in the house, dearest; a refuge when you want it to be. But I hope you'll want to join in, Gertie.' I want to give you back your self-esteem! She said persuasively. 'Would you like a room overlooking the rose garden? Lionel will enjoy knocking that into shape.' One idea followed another, as she began to work out their requirements.

'Mu's boys, they'll need a room each. I think we had better add two more bathrooms. Let's see what's through here. Oh, thank goodness, a decent-sized boiler. Proper central heating, Gertie. No more candles!'

On the first floor, Rose found what she was hoping for and gazed with a full heart at the view of Roseberry Topping.

Behind her Gertie complained. 'Why come and live here, out in the country?'

'Memories. Special ones I don't want to forget.'

'All *my* memories are in Middlesbrough. There were articles in the paper after Harold died, you know. Some people thought well of him. Mrs Porteous came to the memorial service.'

All those dead animals and caged birds! Eloise, who gave her the silk underwear ... Rose shivered.

Gertie went on, 'I don't know why she came. I didn't speak to her afterwards. I nodded, of course. She'd lost her reputation by then, you know. Harold once visited on your behalf, perhaps that was the reason.'

Rose asked gently, 'Gertie, is there the slightest chance you might want to marry again?'

'Oh, no! Harold was my Mr Right.' Rose tried to hide her surprise and Gertie added defensively, 'I couldn't stand it when he wanted to perform The Act, of course.'

'The what?'

'In bed. I had to forbid him in the end.' She gazed at Rose with frank curiosity. 'Did you and Harrison ... Were you and he ...?'

582

But Rose couldn't bear any mention of Ned in the same breath as Harold Brigg.

'Here.' She took the photograph from her bag. 'You said you'd lost your mementoes of Valentine. This was taken at their wedding.'

Gertie held it between finger and thumb as though it might scald. The two young faces smiled at her.

'I'm glad they had a little happiness,' Rose said sadly.

'I thought you'd sent your daughter ...' she grew flustered, 'because of the money. And that was the reason she seduced Valentine.'

'Oh, Gertie!' That damn two hundred pounds! 'They were young, they were attracted to one another – can't you accept that? And why did you never tell Val he was adopted? It nearly ruined what little they had.'

'He was mine,' Gertie said pitifully. 'My sweet little boy. She took him from me.'

She wouldn't tell Rose about the dark-haired woman in the park, there was no need to do that. Perhaps one day, when her sister had become less – overpowering.

'Children fly the nest, Gertie. Ours would have been caught up in the war whatever happened; we couldn't have prevented that. Let us be thankful they found one another first. Here,' she took the photograph and set it in the centre of the mantelpiece. 'We'll leave it there ... to welcome us when we move in.'

'Rose, are *you* likely to remarry?'

'No, but neither do I intend to live like a recluse. We shall have a housefull of people, especially at Christmas, so you'd better get used to the idea.'

'Will we?' Normally, Gertie dreaded Christmas.

Rose was listing on her fingers. 'There's Muriel and Lionel, June and Edwin, the two boys, all their friends. Maisie and Oswald from Australia—'

'Oh, Rose, it'll be like the old days at Clairville Road!'

Not so. There would be ghosts: Ned, Margaret, Valentine, Hayden, Cecil ... no, not Cecil, he was too far away. And not

583

Harold Brigg. I shall have him exorcised if he turns up, she thought!

'Forget the old days, dearest. Think of the future.' She was forty-five, Gertie was forty-nine, surely it wasn't over yet?

'Where are we off to now?' Rose was steering her outside.

'After we've bought this house . . .' Rose reached over, tugged at the mangy piece of fur and chucked it into the hedge.

'What are you doing!'

'I'm treating you to a new coat.'

'Oh, Rose! With a fur collar?' Oh, dear!

'If that's what you'd like.' She curbed her feelings.

'Yes, please!' Gertie was remembering what it felt like to be sublimely happy. 'I forgot to ask — why did you come back?'

Rose obviously hadn't heard. She walked ahead, calling over her shoulder, 'Let's see if we can find lunch in a pub.'

The north-east wind had a cutting edge. I must be mad, Rose thought, giving up the sunshine, the easy-going, hard-working camaraderie for this. She stared back at the façade. The house had pretentious flat columns worked into the stonework. It represented so many things Ned had been eager to leave behind: was it a betrayal?

'I shall fill it with those who loved him and were kind to me. I shall take them to Australia eventually, introduce them to Oswald and Maisie who will talk of Ned and show them what we achieved. Gertie will regain her dignity here, although not too much! And I shall leave everything to Mu's children. They will inherit what Margaret and Val should have had: it's the best I can do.'

She shut the gate and made a mental note to mention the squeak to Lionel. It might restore his sense of purpose, being here. He need never worry about the next wage packet, she would pay him a decent wage and there was certainly plenty to do.

Gertie had shed years already at the prospect of new clothes. It wasn't going to be easy, listening to all that bitterness but Rose would have to be patient.

Her conscience was scornful: 'You'll not change your spots at your time of life, my girl. I must try. I will manage it somehow.'

She'd been dreading picking up this burden; now for some reason her spirits began to lift.

'I asked why you had decided to come back?' Gertie repeated.

Perhaps, when everything else had gone, duty brought a certain satisfaction? Rose turned the ignition key and pressed the starter button.

'Goodness knows.' That was too light-hearted. She wondered if she dare suggest it was because she had pushed Gertie into marrying Harold on that fateful wedding morning? Would Gertie have had the courage to withdraw if Rose had added her strength? There was no way of knowing, not now Gertie had reinstated him as her *Mr Right*. Instead Rose said simply, 'You are all I have left, Gertie. I need you now just as I used to in Clairville Road.'

Gertie's fingers went automatically to where the fur should have been. 'That's all right then. I expect we shall shake down together, as Harold used to say. I hope life in Australia hasn't coarsened you, Rose? He used to worry a great deal about that.'

Rose gritted her teeth; not only *Mr Right* but a fount of wisdom, spouting aphorisms from beyond the grave to try her new-found patience? Ah, well . . .

'Have you any idea where we might find you a coat?'

Her sister sighed happily. 'Drive me back to Middlesbrough and I'll show you.'